BOOKS BY HARRY TURTLEDOVE

The Guns of the South

THE WORLDWAR SAGA
Worldwar: In the Balance
Worldwar: Tilting the Balance
Worldwar: Upsetting the Balance
Worldwar: Striking the Balance

COLONIZATION
Colonization: Second Contact
Colonization: Down to Earth
Colonization: Aftershocks

THE TIME OF TROUBLES
    SERIES
The Stolen Throne
Hammer and Anvil
The Thousand Cities
Videssos Besieged

THE VIDESSOS CYCLE
The Misplaced Legion
An Emperor for the Legion
The Legion of Videssos
Sword of the Legion

THE TALE OF KRISPOS
Krispos Rising
Krispos of Videssos
Krispos the Emperor

Noninterference
Kaleidoscope
A World of Difference
Earthgrip
Departures

How Few Remain

THE GREAT WAR
The Great War: American Front
The Great War: Walk in Hell
The Great War: Breakthroughs

AMERICAN EMPIRE
American Empire: Blood and Iron
American Empire: The Center
    Cannot Hold

COLONIZATION: DOWN TO EARTH

Harry Turtledove

THE RANDOM HOUSE PUBLISHING GROUP • NEW YORK

A Del Rey® Book
Published by The Random House Publishing Group
Copyright © 2000 by Harry Turtledove

www.delreybooks.com

Library of Congress Catalog Card Number: 00-109770

ISBN 0-345-43023-9

Manufactured in the United States of America

First Hardcover Edition: February 2000
First Mass Market Edition: January 2001

OPM 12 11 10 9 8 7 6 5 4

☆ **1** ☆

Atvar, the fleetlord of the Race's conquest fleet, and Reffet, the fleetlord of the colonization fleet, were having a disagreement. They had agreed on very little since Reffet brought the colonization fleet to Tosev 3. Atvar was convinced Reffet still had no real understanding of the way things worked on this miserable planet. He didn't know what Reffet was convinced of—probably that things on Tosev 3 were in fact the way the Race had fondly imagined them to be before sending out the conquest fleet.

"I do not know what you wish me to do, Reffet," he said. They were equals; neither of them was *Exalted Fleetlord* to the other. They could be, and often were, equally impolite to each other. "No matter what you may believe, I cannot work miracles." He swiveled his eye turrets this way and that to show exasperation.

Reffet swiveled his eye turrets, too, and hissed for good measure. "I do not see that it is so difficult. The ship the Big Uglies have launched is under very low acceleration. You have plenty of time to send a reconnaissance probe after it and keep it under close, secret observation."

"And you brought starships across the light-years between Home and here!" Atvar exclaimed. "You must have had good officers and good computers, for you surely were not up to the job unaided." He paced across his office, which had been a suite in Shepheard's Hotel before the Race occupied Cairo. It gave him plenty of room to pace; Tosevites were larger than males and females of the Race, and, naturally, built in proportion to their own size.

"Leave off your insults," Reffet replied with another hiss, an angry one. His tailstump switched back and forth, back and forth. "I repeat, I do not see that what I have asked is so very

1

difficult. As I said, that ship, that *Clewis and Lark*, is under acceleration of no more than a hundredth of the force of gravity."

"Lewis and Clark." Atvar took no small relish in correcting his colleague and rival over even minute details that shouldn't have mattered to anyone save a Big Ugly. "That it is under tiny acceleration does not matter. That it is under continuous acceleration does. If we are to observe it closely and continually, our reconnaissance must be under acceleration, too. And how, I ask, do you propose to keep that secret? A spacecraft with a working engine is by the nature of things anything but secret."

"By the Emperor!" Reffet burst out. He lowered his eyes to the floor when naming his sovereign. So did Atvar, on hearing the title. From training since hatchlinghood, any member of the Race would have done the same. Still furious, Reffet went on, "These accursed Tosevites have no business flying in space." He used an emphatic cough to underline his words. "They have no business having instruments that let them detect what we do when we fly in space, either."

Atvar let his mouth fall open in amusement. "Come here, Reffet," he said, walking over to the window. "Come here—it is safe enough. I intend no tricks, and the riots seem to have quieted down again, so no Big Ugly is likely to be aiming a sniper's rifle in this direction at the moment. I want to show you something."

Suspicion manifest in every line of his forward-sloping body, Reffet came. "What is it?" The suspicion filled his voice, too.

"There." Atvar pointed west across the great river that flowed past Cairo. "Do you see those three stone pyramids, there in the sand?"

Reffet deigned to turn one eye turret in that direction. "I see them. What of it? They look massive, but weathered and primitive."

"They *are* primitive—that is my point," Atvar said. "They are as old as any monuments on this world. They were built as memorials to local rulers eight thousand years ago, more or less: eight thousand of our years—half that many for the years of Tosev 3. Eight thousand years ago, we had already had a planetwide Empire for more than ninety thousand years. We had already conquered the Rabotevs. We had already conquered the Hallessi. We were beginning to wonder if the star Tosev—this world's star—had any interesting planets. Here, civilization was just hatching from its egg."

"And it should have taken much longer to hatch, too," Reffet said irritably. "The Big Uglies should still be building monuments much like these, as we were not long after we started gathering in cities."

"Truth." Atvar's voice was sad. "They should have. In fact, we thought they had. You will have seen this picture of a Tosevite warrior in full battle regalia before you set out from Home, of course."

He walked over to the hologram projector and called up an image. He had seen it countless times himself, both before reaching Tosev 3 and since. It showed a hairy Big Ugly in rusty chainmail, armed with sword and spear and iron-faced wooden shield and riding a four-legged beast with a long head, an unkempt mane, and a shaggy tail.

"Yes, of course I have seen that image," Reffet said. "It is one of those our probe took sixteen hundred years ago. From it, we assumed the conquest would be easy."

"So we did," Atvar agreed. "But the point is, in those intervening sixteen hundred years—eight hundred of this planet's revolutions—the Tosevites somehow developed industrial civilization. However much you and I and every other member of the Race may wish they had remained primitive, the sorry fact is that they did not. We have to deal with that fact now."

"It was not planned thus." Reffet made that an accusation. The Race moved by plans, by tiny incremental steps. Anything different came hard.

Atvar had been dealing with the Big Uglies for more than forty of his years. By painful necessity, he'd begun to adapt to the hectic pace of Tosev 3. "Whether it was planned or not, it is so. You cannot crawl back into your eggshell and deny it."

Reffet wanted to deny it. Again, every line of his body showed as much. So did the big breath of air he sucked deep into his lung. "I think I would rather deal with the Tosevites than with you," he snarled. "I know they are aliens. With you, I cannot tell whether you have become half alien or are simply addled like an egg gone bad."

That did it. Atvar drew in a deep, angry breath of his own. It brought the stinks of Cairo—the stinks of Big Uglies and of their food and their wastes, as well as the stinks from the hydrocarbon-burning engines they had developed themselves— across the scent receptors in his tongue. "Go away," he told Reffet, and added an emphatic cough of his own. "I have not the time to deal with your stupidity. Whatever the Big Uglies in that spacecraft do, they will not do it soon. I am facing a serious uprising in the subregion of the main continental mass called China. I have to deal with that now. I will deal with the American spacecraft as I find the chance, or when it becomes urgent. Meanwhile, good day."

"You *have* turned into a Big Ugly," Reffet said furiously. "All you care about is the immediate. Anything that requires forethought is beyond you."

"Tosev 3 will do that to a male—unless it kills him first," Atvar answered. Then he paused. Both his eye turrets swung thoughtfully toward Reffet. "Have you any notion how many casualties the Big Uglies' continual revolts have cost us?"

"No, I do not." Reffet sounded peevish. As far as Atvar was concerned, Reffet sounded peevish far too often. The fleetlord of the colonization fleet went on, "Had you done a proper job of conquering this planet, I would not have to concern myself with such things—and neither would you."

I will not bite him, Atvar thought. *I will not tear his belly open with my fingerclaws.* But he hadn't known such temptation to pure, cleansing violence since a ginger-induced mating frenzy in Australia. Fortunately, he had no ginger coursing through him now, nor could he smell any females' pheromones. That let him stay his usual rational self. "Deal with things here as they are, Reffet," he said, "not as you wish they would be. Our casualties have been heavy, far heavier than anyone could possibly have anticipated before we left Home. Like it or not, that is a truth."

"Very well. That is a truth." Reffet still sounded peevish. "I do not see how it is a truth to concern me, however. I am in charge of colonists, not soldiers."

"All you care about is the immediate," Atvar said, waggling his jaw as he dropped it to turn his laugh nasty. He took malicious pleasure in bouncing the other fleetlord's words off his snout. "Anything that requires forethought is beyond you."

"Very well." Now Reffet sounded condescending. "What fresh nonsense is this?"

"It is no nonsense at all, but something we would have had to face sooner or later during our occupation of Tosev 3," Atvar answered. "It might as well be now. Have you noticed that this is a world consumed by war and rebellion, that the Big Uglies in the regions we occupy continually try to overthrow our rule, and that the Tosevites' independent not-empires—the SSSR, the Greater German *Reich*, the United States, and also the weaker ones like Nippon and Britain—train large numbers of their inhabitants as soldiers year after year?"

"I have noticed it," Reffet admitted, "but you are the fleetlord of the conquest fleet. Soldiers are your responsibility."

"Truth," Atvar said. "They are. This is not Home, where, save in a Soldiers' Time of preparation for conquest, we have no soldiers, only police. Here, we will need soldiers continuously, for hundreds of years to come. Where shall we get them, if we do not begin the training of males, and possibly females as well, from among your precious colonists?"

"What?" Reffet cried. "This is madness! It is nothing but madness! My colonists are colonists. How can they become fighters?"

"The males I command managed," Atvar said. "I am certain I can recruit trainers from among them. Think, Reffet." He didn't bother being sardonic, not any more; the more he thought on this, the more important it looked. "How long can the Race endure here on Tosev 3 without soldiers to defend us?"

Reffet did think. Reluctantly, Atvar gave him credit for it. After a pause, the fleetlord of the colonization fleet said, "It could be that you are correct. I shall not commit myself further than that without analysis from my experts. If you would also convene a panel of your experts to examine the issue, I should be grateful."

With any other member of the Race on or near Tosev 3, Reffet could have given an order and heard *It shall be done* as reply. Having to make a polite request of Atvar surely grated on him. Atvar knew having to make a request of Reffet grated on *him*. Here, the request was nothing if not reasonable. "I will do that, and soon," Atvar promised. "It is something we need to examine, as I said."

"So it is." Like Atvar's, Reffet's temper seemed to be cooling. He said, "If it proves we must do this thing, it will make us different from the members of the Race back on Home and inhabiting Rabotev 2 and Halless 1."

"Males of the conquest fleet are already different from all other members of the Race," Atvar replied. "My hope is that, over the course of hundreds of years, we will gradually incorporate all the Big Uglies into the Empire and assimilate them to our way of doing things. If we succeed there, the differences between those of the Race here on Tosev 3 and those living on the other worlds of the Empire will gradually disappear."

"By the Emperor, may it be so," Reffet said. He and Atvar cast down their eyes again. Then, half talking to himself, Reffet went on, "But what if it is not so?"

"That is my nightmare," Atvar told him. "That has been my nightmare since we first discovered the Big Uglies' true nature. They change faster than we do. They grow faster than we do. They are still behind us, but not by so much as they were when we came to Tosev 3. If they, or some of them, remain hostile, if they look like they are passing us . . ." His voice trailed away.

"Yes?" Reffet prompted. "What then?"

"We may have to destroy this world, and our own colony on it," Atvar answered unhappily. "We may have to destroy ourselves, to save the Race."

Under an acceleration of .01g, Lieutenant Colonel Glen Johnson had to wear a seat belt to stay in his chair. His effective weight was just over a pound and a half—not enough for muscles used to Earth's robust gravity to notice. Any fidgeting at all would have sent him bouncing around the *Lewis and Clark*'s control room. Bouncing around in a room full of instruments wasn't recommended.

He turned to Colonel Walter Stone, the American spaceship's chief pilot. "This is the best seat in the house," he said.

"You'd best believe it, Johnson," Stone answered. The two of them might have been cousins: they were both lean, athletic men in their early middle years; both crew cut; both, by coincidence, from Ohio. Johnson had started in the Marines, Stone in the Army Air Corps. Each looked down his nose at the other because of that.

At the moment, though, Johnson wasn't interested in looking anywhere except out through the panoramic window. It was double-coated to reduce reflection; peering out through it was about as close as a man could come to looking out on bare space. He saw more stars than he had since another guy after the same girl sucker-punched him in high school.

The *Lewis and Clark* was aimed roughly in the direction of Antares, the bright red star at the heart of Scorpio. The Milky Way was near its thickest there, and all the more impressive for not being dimmed and blurred by the lights and air of Earth. But Johnson didn't pay much attention to the stars liberally sprinkled thereabouts. Instead, leaning forward in his seat, he peered farther south, toward a region that, even against the black sky of space, wasn't so heavily populated.

He suddenly pointed. "That's it! At least, I think that's it."

Walter Stone looked at him in bemusement. "Which one? And what's it supposed to be, anyhow?"

"That faint orange one there." Johnson pointed again. "I think that's Epsilon Indi, the star the Lizards call Halless. They rule a planet that goes around that star."

"Ah." Enlightenment filled Stone's craggy features. "You look farther west, and up closer to the equator, you can spot Tau Ceti, too. That's the place the little scaly bastards call Home." A moment later, he said "Home" again, this time in the language of the Race. Returning to English, he went on, "And Epsilon Eridani's farther west still. Rabotev is the Lizard name. Nothing to make either one of 'em stand out much. They're just stars like the sun, a little smaller, a little cooler. Epsilon Indi's quite a bit smaller and cooler."

"Yeah." Glen Johnson nodded. "What I wouldn't give to be able to pay a call on the Lizards one of these days, you know what I mean?"

"Oh, yes." Stone nodded, too. "I know exactly what you mean. I'd say the line for that particular craving forms on the left."

"But they can come here, so it's *important* that we figure out how to go there," Johnson said. "Look at history. The people who discovered other people usually came off pretty well. The ones who got discovered didn't have such a happy time of it. The Spaniards got rich. The Indians ended up slaving for them. No way in hell the Indians could have sailed to Spain, except in Spanish ships."

"Yeah. That's interesting, isn't it?" Stone didn't sound as if he liked the way it was interesting. Then he stabbed out a finger at Johnson. "But what about the Japs? What about the goddamn Japs, huh? They got discovered instead of the other way round, and they're still in business."

"Yes, sir, that's right, they are, damn them. But you know how come they're still in business?" Without giving Stone a chance to answer, Johnson continued, "They're still in business because they wised up in a hurry. They learned everything they could from us and England and Germany and France, and inside of nothing flat they had their own factories going and they were making their own steamships and then they could damn well sail wherever they pleased. They started playing the same game everybody else was."

"Yeah, and then the slant-eyed sons of bitches chose to sail for Pearl Harbor and give us one right in the nuts," Stone growled. Like most purely human conflicts, the one between the USA and Japan had gone by the boards when the Lizards attacked. It was gone, but not forgotten.

"Oh, hell, yes, sir," Johnson said. "But that's the point: they were able to sail across the Pacific and kick us when we weren't looking. If we're able to do that to the Lizards one of these days, we won't be so bad off. Even if we don't do it, we won't be so bad off, because we can."

"I see what you're saying," Stone told him. The chief pilot waved around the *Lewis and Clark*'s control room. "This isn't a bad first step, is it?"

"It's a lot better than what we would have had if the Lizards hadn't come, I'll tell you that," Johnson answered. "I wonder if we would even have been in space by now." He shrugged. "No way to tell, I guess." He didn't say so aloud, but he thought of the *Lewis and Clark* as the equivalent of the first Japanese-built coastal steamer, which had surely been a clumsy, makeshift vessel that barely dared sail out of sight of land. It was very fine in its way, but what he wanted were battleships and aircraft carriers out on the open sea.

Stone coughed. "You're not supposed to be here to start a bull session, you know. You're supposed to be here to learn how to fly this thing in case Mickey and I both wake up dead one morning."

"Sir, the only controls that are a whole lot different from ones

I've used before are the ones for the reactor—and if I have to mess with those, we're all in a lot of trouble," Johnson said. The motor sat at the end of a long boom to minimize the risk for the rest of the *Lewis and Clark* if anything went wrong with it.

"One of the reasons you're learning is that we're all liable to be in a lot of trouble," Stone pointed out. "Face it: you came aboard because you were curious about us, right?" Johnson could hardly argue with that; it was the Gospel truth. Stone waited to see if he'd say something anyhow, then nodded when he didn't. "Uh-*huh*. Okay, you aren't the only one. What if the Lizards send a present after us? What are we going to do about it?"

"Or the Germans," Johnson said.

Stone shook his head now. "They can't catch us, not any more. This may not sound like a hot ship—.01g? Wow!" He had a gift for the sardonic. "We tack on a whole four inches to our velocity every second. Doesn't sound like much, does it? It adds up, though. At the end of a day, we're going five miles a second faster than we were when that day started. Regular rockets kick a lot harder to start with, but once they're done kicking, it's free fall the rest of the way. The Nazis don't have any constant-boost ships, though I'll bet you dollars to doughnuts they're working on them now. The Lizards, damn them, do."

"All right," Glen Johnson said agreeably. "Suppose they come after us at, say, .1g? That's ten times our acceleration. We can run, we can't hide, and we can't even dodge—the *Lewis and Clark* is about as maneuverable as an elephant on roller skates. So what do we do then? Besides go down in flames, I mean?"

"If we have to, we fight," Stone answered. "That's what I was coming to. The fighting controls are right here." He pointed. "We've got machine guns and missiles for close-in defense. None of that stuff is much different than what you used on the *Peregrine*, so you know what it can do."

"Nuclear tips on the missiles and all?" Johnson asked.

"That's right," the senior pilot said, "except you carried two and we've got a couple dozen. And that doesn't say anything about the mines." He pointed to another rank of switches.

"Mines, sir?" Johnson raised an eyebrow. "Now you've got me: I don't have the faintest idea what you're talking about."

"There are five of them, one controlled by each switch here," Stone explained. "They're the strongest fusion bombs we can build . . . and they're equipped with the most sensitive timers we've got. If we know the Lizards are trying to come up our rear ends, we leave them behind, timed to explode right when the enemy ship is closest to them. Maybe we nail it, maybe we don't, but it's sure as hell worth a try."

"Even if we don't wreck it, we might fry its brains." Johnson grinned. "I like that. Whoever thought of it has a really sneaky mind."

"Thank you," Walter Stone said.

Johnson's eyebrows jumped. "Was it you?"

Stone grinned at him. "I didn't say that. I said, 'Thank you.' Here, let's fire up the simulator and see what you do if the Lizards decide to take a whack at us after all."

The simulator was a far cry from the Link machines on which Johnson had trained before the Lizards came. Like so much human technology, it borrowed—stole, really—wholesale from things the Race knew and people hadn't back in 1942. The end result was something like a game, something like a God's-eye view of the real thing, with the *Lewis and Clark* reduced to a glowing blip on a screen, the hypothetical Lizard pursuit ship another blip, and all the things they might launch at each other angry little sparks of light.

Johnson "lost" the *Lewis and Clark* six times in a row before finally managing to save the ship with a perfectly placed mine. By then, sweat soaked his coveralls and slid away from his forehead in large, lazy drops. "Whew!" he said. "Here's hoping the Lizards don't decide to come after us, because we're sure as hell in trouble if they do."

"Amen," Stone answered. "You will get better with practice, though—or you'd better get better, anyhow."

"I can see that," Johnson said. "First couple of missions I flew, the only thing that kept me from killing myself was fool luck." He paused, eyeing the man who was training him. "You practice on this thing a lot, don't you?"

"Every day, every chance I get," Stone said solemnly.

"I figured you would. It's as close as you can come to the real McCoy," Johnson said. The senior pilot nodded once more.

Johnson took a deep breath. "Okay. With all the practice you put in, how often do you win?"

"A little less than half the time," Stone replied. "The goddamn Lizards can do more things than we can. Nothing's going to change that. If you can't handle the notion—well, too bad."

"They shot me down," Johnson said.

"Me, too." Walter Stone reached over and slapped Johnson on the back. Without the safety strap, the blow would have knocked Johnson out of his chair. Stone went on, "We had to be crazy, going up against the Lizards in those prop jobs."

"They were what we had, and the job needed doing," Johnson said. The life expectancy of a pilot who'd flown against the Lizards during the fighting was most often measured in hours. If Johnson hadn't been wounded when the Lizards knocked his plane out of the sky, if he hadn't spent a lot of his time afterwards flat on his back, odds were he would have gone up again and bought himself the whole plot instead of just a piece of it. He didn't care to dwell on those odds.

Stone said, "I think we've put you through the wringer enough for one day. Why don't I turn you loose a couple minutes early so you can make it down to the mess hall before shift change?"

"Thank you, sir," Johnson said, and unbuckled his belt. "My next shift back here with you, I want another go at the simulator."

"You wouldn't be much use to me if you didn't," Stone told him. "Somehow or other, I think that can be arranged."

Catching one of the many handholds in the control room, Johnson swung toward the mess hall; at .01g, brachiating worked much better than walking. He almost approached eagerness. For good stretches—sometimes even for hours at a time—he could forget he was never going home again.

Lieutenant Colonel Sam Yeager was muttering at the Lizard-built computer on his desk. Sorviss, a male of the Race who lived in Los Angeles, had been doing his best to restore Yeager's full access to the Race's computer network. So far, his best hadn't been good enough. Sam had learned a great deal on the network pretending to be a male of the Race named Regeya. As Sam Yeager, human being, he was allowed to visit only a small part of the network.

"You son of a bitch," he told the screen, which said ACCESS DENIED in large red letters—Lizard characters, actually.

He was picking up the telephone to let Sorviss know his latest effort had failed when his son Jonathan burst into the study. Yeager frowned; he didn't like getting interrupted while he was working. But what Jonathan said made him forgive the kid: "Come quick, Dad—I think they're hatching!"

"Holy smoke!" Sam put the phone back on its hook and sprang to his feet. "They're three days early."

"When President Warren gave them to you, he *said* the best guess for when they'd hatch might be ten days off either way." Jonathan Yeager spoke with the usual impatience of youth for age. He'd turned twenty not too long before. Sam Yeager didn't like thinking of it in those terms; it reminded him he'd turned fifty-six not too long before. Jonathan was already on his way up the hall. "Are you coming or not?" he demanded.

"If you don't get out of the way, I'll trample you," Sam answered.

Jonathan laughed tolerantly. He was a couple of inches taller than his father, and wider through the shoulders. If he didn't feel like being trampled, Sam would have had a devil of a time doing it. The overhead light gleamed off Jonathan's shaved head and off the body paint adorning his chest and belly: by what it said, he was a landcruiser-engine mechanic. Young people all over the world imitated Lizard styles and thought their elders stodgy for clucking.

Sam's wife Barbara was standing in front of the incubator. The new gadget made the service porch even more crowded than it had been when it held just that washing machine and drier and water heater. "One of the eggshells already has a little hole in it," Barbara said excitedly.

"I want to see," Sam said, though getting close to the incubator in that cramped little space wasn't easy. He went on, "I grew up on a farm, remember. I ought to know something about how eggs work."

"Something, maybe," Barbara said with a distinct sniff, "but nobody—nobody on Earth, anyhow—has ever watched a Lizard egg hatch till now."

As she often did, she left him struggling for a comeback. While he was struggling, Jonathan gave him something else to think about: "Dad, may I call Karen to come over and watch them with us?"

His girlfriend was as fascinated by the Race as he was. She wore body paint, too, often with nothing but a tiny halter top to preserve the decencies. She didn't shave her head, though some girls did. But that wasn't what made Yeager hesitate. He said, "You know I didn't get these eggs to entertain you . . . or Karen."

"Of course I know that," his son said indignantly. "Do you think I'm addled or something?" That bit of slang had made it from the Lizards' language into English.

"No, of course not," Sam answered, doing his best to remember how touchy he'd been when he was twenty. "But it's liable to be important not to let anyone know we have Lizard eggs—or hatchlings, which is what we'll have pretty darn quick now." Eighteen years of minor-league ball and twenty in the Army had given him a vocabulary that could blister paint at forty paces. Around his wife and son, he did his best not to use too much of it.

Jonathan rolled his eyes. "What are you going to do, Dad, hide them in the garage whenever people or males of the Race come over?"

"When males of the Race come over, I just might," Sam said. But he sighed. His son had a point. His orders were to raise the baby Lizards as much like human beings as he could. How was he supposed to do that if they never met anybody but his family and him? With another sigh, he nodded. "Okay, go ahead. But when she gets here, I'm going to have to warn her she can't blab."

"Sure, Dad." Jonathan was all smiles now that he'd got his way. "This is *so* hot!" The Race liked heat. That made it a term of approval. He sprinted for the telephone.

Worry in her voice, Barbara said, "Sooner or later, the Race is going to find out that we have these hatchlings. There'll be trouble when that happens."

"I expect you're right," Yeager said. "But it'll be trouble for the government, not trouble for us. If we have to give them up, we have to give them up, that's all. No point to worrying too much ahead of time, right?"

"Right," Barbara said, but she didn't sound convinced.

Sam didn't know that he was convinced, either, but he forced whatever worries he had down to the bottom of his mind. "Let me have a look, will you?" he said, as he had a moment before. "I'm the only one in the house who hasn't seen the eggs this morning."

Now that Jonathan was gone, Barbara had a little more room to move on the service porch. As she stepped aside, Yeager lifted the lid on top of the incubator and peered down. The two eggs inside, both a good deal larger than hen's eggs, were yellow, speckled with brown and white; he would have bet they got laid in sand. Sure enough, one shell showed a small hole. "Will you take a look at that?" he said softly.

Barbara had already taken a look at that. Her question—typical of her questions—was very much to the point: "Do you really think we'll be able to take care of them, Sam?"

"Well, hon, we managed with Jonathan, and he turned out okay," Yeager said.

"I see three things wrong with that as an answer," she said crisply. She ticked them off on her fingers: "Number one, we're twenty years older than we were then. Number two, there are two of these eggs, and there was only one of him. And number three, not to belabor the obvious, they're Lizards. It won't be like raising babies."

"It's supposed to be as much like raising babies as we can make it," Sam replied. "That's why we've got the job, not a fancy lab somewhere. But yeah, you're right; from everything I've read, it won't be the same."

"From everything I've read, too." Barbara set a hand on his arm. "Are they really going to be like little wild animals till they're three or four years old?"

He did his best to make light of it, saying, "What, you don't think Jonathan was?" Instead of letting her hand rest quietly on his sleeve, she started drumming her fingers there. He coughed sheepishly, then sighed. "From everything I've been able to pick up, that's about right. They don't learn to talk as fast as babies do, and they're able to move around by themselves as soon as they hatch. If that doesn't make them little wild animals, I don't know what would. Except we're supposed to do our best to turn them into little tame animals instead."

"I wonder if we can," Barbara said. "How many stories does the Race tell about eggs back on Home that hatched in out-of-the-way places, and about Lizards that lived like hunting beasts till they were found and civilized?"

"Lots of them," Sam allowed. "Of course, we have stories like that, too."

"Wild children." Barbara nodded. "But even in those, something always helps the babies when they're small—the she-wolf suckling Romulus and Remus, for instance." She had her literary references all lined up; she'd done graduate work in medieval English. "And just about all of our stories are legends—myths, really. The ones from the Lizards sound like news items; they read as if they came off the United Press International wire."

Before Yeager could answer, Jonathan came running back onto the service porch. "Karen's on her way," he reported breathlessly. "She says not to let them hatch before she gets here."

"Fine with me," Sam said. "Did she tell you how we were supposed to manage that?" Jonathan glared at him. He'd been glared at by professionals, from managers and umpires all the way up to generals and a couple of presidents. He wasn't about to let his son faze him. He pointed down into the incubator. "Look—the Lizard inside the other egg's starting to poke his way out, too."

They jockeyed for position in front of the incubator; it wasn't easy for all of them to see at once. Sure enough, both eggshells had holes in them now. Jonathan said, "Those are more tears than cracks. The shells look kind of leathery, don't they, not hard, like hens' eggs are."

"*As* hens' eggs are," Barbara said, and then, under her breath, "Honestly, I don't know what they teach people these days."

Having watched a lot of chicks hatching, Sam knew it didn't happen instantly. Sure enough, the tears in the shells hadn't got much bigger before the front doorbell rang. Jonathan dashed off to the door, and returned a moment later with Karen. "I greet you, Senior Ordnance Specialist," Sam said in the language of the Race, eyeing her body paint. With both Barbara and Jonathan there, he conscientiously didn't eye the skin on which the body paint was displayed. That wasn't easy—she was a pretty redhead, and freckled all over—but he managed.

"I greet you, superior sir," she answered in the same language. Like Jonathan, like the rest of the younger generation, she couldn't remember a time when the Lizards hadn't been around. She and he studied their language at UCLA the same way they studied math or chemistry. Despite aping the Race, they took Lizards more for granted than Sam or Barbara ever would.

Four people crowding around the incubator made looking in harder than ever. Karen happened to have the best view when the first Lizard's snout poked out of the shell. "Look!" she said. "He's got a little horn on the end of his nose."

"It's not a horn, it's an egg tooth," Sam said. "Turtles and snakes and ordinary small-*l* lizards have 'em, too, to help them hatch. It'll drop off in a few days."

Little by little, the baby Lizards (*hatchlings* sounded reproachfully in his mind, in the language of the Race) fought their way free of the eggs that had confined them. They were a light greenish brown, lighter than they would be as adults. Their scaly hides glistened with the last fluids from the eggs, though the lightbulbs in the incubators swiftly dried them. "Their heads look too big," Jonathan said.

"So did yours, when you were first born," Sam said. Barbara nodded. Jonathan looked embarrassed, though Karen's head had undoubtedly looked too big for her body when she was a newborn, too.

Hearing voices above them, the Lizard hatchlings turned their tiny eye turrets toward the people. Sam wondered what he looked like to them. Nothing good, evidently; they skittered around the bottom of the incubator, looking for somewhere to hide. Jonathan hadn't done *that* when he was a baby. *And thank God, too,* Sam thought.

He reached in to grab one of the Lizards. It hissed and snapped at him. Also unlike Jonathan as a newborn, it had a mouthful of sharp little teeth. He jerked his hand back. "Where are those leather gloves?" he asked.

"Here." Barbara handed them to him. He slipped them on, then caught one of the Lizard hatchlings behind the head, as if it were a corn snake back on the Nebraska farm where he'd grown up. It couldn't get away and it couldn't bite, though it tried to do both. He carried it up the hall to the spare room that wasn't spare any more. When he set it down, it scurried into one of the many hiding places he'd set up in the room: an upside-down bucket with a doorway cut into the side. Carefully closing the door behind him, he went back and captured the other hatchling. "All right, we've got 'em," he said as he started up the hall with that wiggling little Lizard. "Now we get to make something of 'em."

Felless was doing her best to talk sense into an official from the Great German *Reich*'s Ministry of Justice: an inherently thankless task. "If you do not do more than you have to control ginger smuggling into lands ruled by the Race, it is only natural that we have retaliated as we have," she told the Big Ugly. "Is it not just that we should assist the passage of Tosevite drugs into the *Reich*?"

The official, a deputy minister named Freisler, listened as his secretary translated Felless' words into the guttural language of the Deutsche, which she had not bothered to learn. He spoke with what sounded like passion. The secretary's reply, however, was all but toneless: "Herr Freisler rejects this equivalence out of hand. He warns that drug smugglers seized inside the *Reich*, whether Tosevites or belonging to the Race, will be brought before People's Courts and will be subjected to the maximum punishment allowed by law."

"Will be killed, you mean," Felless said with distaste. The secretary wagged his head up and down, the equivalent of the Race's affirmative hand gesture. The Deutsche had a habit of killing anyone of whom they did not approve completely; even for Big Uglies, they were savage.

And to think I was fool enough to specialize in the Race's relations with newly conquered species. Felless let out a soft hiss of self-derision. When she'd wakened from cold sleep after the colonization fleet got to Tosev 3, she'd discovered that hundreds of millions of Tosevites remained unconquered, the Deutsche among them. She'd also discovered that the Big Uglies, independent and conquered both, were far more alien to the Race than either the Rabotevs or the Hallessi.

And she'd discovered ginger, which was an irony in its own right. Thanks to the Tosevite herb, her own mating behavior had acquired a frenzied urgency not far removed from that of the Big Uglies. The same was true of other females who tasted, which was the greatest reason the Race tried so hard to suppress the trade. Even as she argued against ginger to this Freisler creature, she craved a taste herself.

She took a breath to tear the Big Ugly limb from rhetorical limb, but her telephone hissed for attention before she could speak. "Excuse me," she told the secretary, who nodded. She took the phone from her belt. "Felless speaking."

"I greet you, Senior Researcher," a male said into her hearing diaphragm. "Slomikk speaking here."

"I greet you, Science Officer," Felless replied. "What news?"

"I am pleased to inform you that both hatchlings from your clutch have lost their egg teeth within a day of the normal period," Slomikk said.

"That is indeed good news," Felless replied. "I am glad to hear it. Out." She broke the connection and returned the phone to its belt pocket.

"What good news is this?" the Deutsch secretary inquired.

Perhaps he was politely interested—perhaps, but not probably. What he was probably doing was seeking intelligence information. Felless did not care to give him any. "Nothing of great importance," she said. "Now . . . your superior there was attempting to explain why circumstances that apply to the Race should not apply to the *Reich*. So far, his explanations have merely been laughable."

When that was translated, the Big Ugly named Freisler let out several loud, incoherent splutters, then said, "I am not accustomed to such rudeness."

"No doubt: you have made the Tosevites who came before you afraid," Felless said sweetly. "But I do not fall under your jurisdiction, and so cannot be expected to waste time on fear."

More of the Deutsch official's blood showed under his thin, scaleless skin, a sign of anger among the Big Uglies. Felless enjoyed angering the Deutsche. Their murderous style of government—and their irrationality—angered her. That they were misguided enough to reckon themselves— Tosevites!— the Master Race angered her even more. Getting a little of her own back felt sweet.

She did not think of her hatchlings again till she was leaving Freisler's office. He had not yielded in the matter of curbing ginger smugglers; angering him had also left him stubborn. Diplomacy—and the idea that she needed to be diplomatic toward Big Uglies—still came hard to Felless, as it did to many of the Race.

She hadn't been lying when she told the Deutsch secretary the news Slomikk gave her was of no great consequence. The only reason the hatchlings crossed her mind was an idle wish that she still had an egg tooth herself. Were it so, she might have torn the arrogant, noisy Freisler apart like an eggshell. The temptation to violence the Big Uglies raised in her was appalling.

So was their weather. They did not heat the interiors of their buildings to temperatures comfortable to civilized beings (by which, in her mind, she meant females and males of the Race). But leaving the grandiose Justice Ministry and going out onto the streets of Nuremberg was another savage jolt. Blaming the Tosevites for the cold made no logical sense. Trying not to freeze, Felless cared little for logic.

Fortunately, her heated motorcar waited nearby. "Back to the embassy, superior female?" asked the driver.

"Yes, back to the embassy," Felless answered. "I must report the Tosevites' obstinacy to Ambassador Veffani."

"It shall be done," the driver said, and set the motorcar in motion. It was of Deutsch manufacture, but ran reasonably well. The Big Uglies had been in the habit of fueling their motors with petroleum distillates; now many of them burned hydrogen, another technology stolen from the Race. Tosevites seemed to take such thefts, and the changes that sprang from them, for granted. They would have driven the Race mad. Felless more than half believed dealing with change on Tosev 3 had driven a good many males from the conquest fleet mad.

Nuremberg's main boulevards struck her as absurdly wide, even for the capital city of an independent not-empire. The Nazis, the faction ruling the Deutsche, had an ideology that assumed bigger was automatically better. A constable in one of their preposterously fancy uniforms—which also served an ideological function—halted traffic so a female Big Ugly leading an immature Tosevite by the hand and pushing another in a wheeled cart could cross. She took her time about it, not caring that she was inconveniencing Felless.

Felless tried to take advantage of the inconvenience by studying the way the female cared for her hatchlings. The one in the cart was as absurdly helpless as all newly hatched—no, the Big Ugly term was *born*—Tosevites were after emerging from their mothers' bodies. But even the one that walked by itself clung to the female who had presumably given it life. Of its own free will, it submitted itself to her authority.

Hatchlings of the Race, till reason truly sprouted in them, assumed that their elders were predators, and did their best to avoid them. Maybe that was why obedience and subordination were so thoroughly drilled into those hatchlings once they became educable. The lessons almost always sank deep. But Big Uglies, who began so compliant, ended up more individualistic than members of the Race.

Paradox. The changes came with sexual maturation, of course. That propelled Tosevites toward the autonomy to which they clung so fiercely from then on. The Race stayed on the quieter path, untouched by hormonal tides except during mating season—*or when stimulated by ginger,* Felless thought. Ginger disrupted patterns unshakable back on Home.

After what seemed like forever, the constable permitted traffic to move again. Now that her attention had been drawn to them, Felless kept noticing Big Uglies—mostly females, by their wrapping styles and the length of their hair—caring for Tosevite hatchlings of various sizes.

She tried to imagine leading her own pair of hatchlings down the street, holding each one by the hand. The absurdity of the notion made her mouth drop open into a wide laugh. The little creatures would do their best to bite her and escape. Civilizing hatchlings wasn't easy. It was, in fact, one of the first specializations the Race had developed, back at, or rather before, the dawn of its history. Systematically civilizing hatchlings had helped lead to civilizing the Race.

The motorcar pulled to a halt in front of the Race's embassy to the Greater German *Reich*. Felless sighed with relief, not only relief at escaping the absurd fantasy that had filled her mind but also at seeing a sensible, functional cube of a building. The newer Tosevite structures in Nuremberg partook of the Nazis' passion for immense pretentiousness. The older ones struck her as hideously overdecorated. Escaping to simplicity was a delight.

Felless hurried to Veffani's office. The ambassador said, "I greet you, Senior Researcher. I am glad to see you resuming your full range of duties after laying your eggs."

"I thank you, superior sir," Felless replied. Either Veffani or

Ttomalss, an experienced researcher in Tosevite psychology, had fertilized those eggs; they'd both mated with her when ginger made her seasonal pheromones spring to life. Had she been a Tosevite, she knew she would have cared which one was the father. Luckily, being a female of the Race, she didn't need to worry about that. Business came first. "Superior sir, I regret to report that the Deutsche appear unyielding on the matter of ginger smuggling."

"I am disappointed, but I am not surprised," the ambassador said. "Corrupting us appears to be part of their strategy."

"Truth," Felless said, though Veffani had been tactless. He could scarcely help knowing she was one of those ginger had corrupted, not when he'd been stimulated to mate with her. She feared he also knew she still craved the herb, though penalties for females who used it grew ever more severe.

"They do not fear our countersmuggling efforts, then?" Veffani said.

"If they do, they give little sign of it," Felless said, "though you have warned me they are adept at bluffing."

"They are better than adept. They are liars from the moment they leave their eggshells—uh, that is, the bodies of their mothers," Veffani corrected himself.

"What is our course to be, then?" Felless asked.

"I shall have to consult with my superiors," the ambassador replied. "My own inclination is to continue on our present course until its failure is manifest. That has certainly not been proved. The Deutsche *will* smuggle. We should do the same, to show them the game has its prices."

"Truth, superior sir," Felless said. "In fact, if you will recall, I was the first to warn the Deutsche that we were on the point of instituting such a policy." She wanted credit for it, too.

"I do recall, Senior Researcher. I was there, after all." Veffani sounded amused.

She didn't mind if he laughed, so long as he remembered it. But, having reminded him, she thought it wiser to change the subject: "Slomikk tells me my hatchlings have shed their egg teeth." As he might have sired them, that might be of some small interest to him, as it was to her.

"Yes, it would be about time for that," he agreed, with the

polite attention she'd expected. "Now, back to ways of dealing with the miserable Deutsche . . ."

Monique Dutourd angrily shook her head. "No, I don't want to go to the cinema with you," she told Dieter Kuhn. "I don't want to go to supper with you. I don't want to go anywhere with you. If you care anything at all about making me happy, go away and leave me alone."

Kuhn was slight and dark. He looked as much like a native of Marseille as Monique did. She'd assumed he was a Frenchman when he enrolled in her Roman history class at the university. He wrote French like a native. But he was no Frenchman. He was a *Sturmbannführer* in the SS, in Marseille to bring ginger smuggling through the port under the control of the *Reich*.

He folded his arms across his chest in the lecture hall, which was, to Monique's dismay, empty but for the two of them. "I do not ask this because of my duty," he said. His spoken French was good, but doubly alien in her ears: he used Parisian French, not the local dialect, and had a guttural accent that showed he was from the wrong side of the Rhine. "I ask for myself."

"How big a fool are you? How big a fool do you think I am?" Monique demanded hotly. "You've arrested my brother before. Now that Pierre's gone back on the arrangement he had with you, you want to kill him. The only reason you ever cared about me was to get at him."

"That was a reason, true," he agreed with a brisk nod not in the least French. "But it was not the only reason. I have always found you attractive."

He'd said that before. He'd done so little besides saying it every now and again that she'd put it down for just another ploy. She'd wondered if he preferred boys, in fact. If not, wouldn't he have tried harder to get her into bed? A woman in occupied France who told an SS man no ran all sorts of risks, but he'd never used his position to take advantage of her, either.

Never till now. Smiling not so pleasantly, he went on, "You should be friendlier to me. Would you really care to have the *Reichs* Security Service examine the political content of your lectures on the Germanic invasions of the Roman Empire? Believe me, I can arrange it."

Ice ran through her. When the Germans investigated you,

they locked you up, threw away the key, and decided later—sometimes much later—whether they wanted to find it again. But Dieter Kuhn had given her warnings like that once or twice before. He hadn't followed up on them. And so she shook her head again. "Go away," she said, and then added a localism that meant the same thing but was a good deal stronger.

She hadn't really thought he would understand it. By the way his face froze, he did. "I believe you will discover you have made a mistake," he said, and turned on his heel with a military precision altogether Teutonic. When he strode out of the hall, she discovered to her surprise that she felt worse alone in it than she had with him.

She looked down at her hands. They were shaking—a curious mixture of fury and fear. Her legs felt very light as she went downstairs to liberate her bicycle from its slot in the rack. She rode north up Rue Breteuil toward her flat, which was not far from the Old Port, the one that had attracted the ancient Greeks to what they'd called Massilia. The weather was crisp but not cold; even February in Marseille rarely had much bite.

As she pedaled along, Frenchmen whistled at her. She was used to that, and ignored it. A couple of *Wehrmacht* troopers in a field-gray Volkswagen utility vehicle also loudly approved of the way she looked. She ignored them, too. They didn't know who she was, just that she was a woman they found pretty. That made them harmless.

She wished something would make Dieter Kuhn harmless, too.

Along with the Frenchmen and -women and Germans on the streets of Marseille, she also saw a fair number of Lizards. They'd held the city, and much of the south of France, during the fighting, and still did a lot of business with the Greater German *Reich* here. Some of that business was legitimate, and craved by the occupiers. But the Nazis would have suppressed the rest if only they could. Ever since it was named Massilia, Marseille had been a smugglers' paradise.

And so, when Monique noticed a Lizard slowly walking past her block of flats, she didn't think much of it. She came to a stop and got ready to lug the bicycle upstairs. In this part of town, unlike the university, it would not be waiting for her in the morning if she left it in the street.

Before she could manhandle it into her building, the Lizard came up to her and spoke in hissing, not too grammatical French: *"Est-ce que vous êtes Monique Dutourd?"*

"Yes, I'm Monique Dutourd," she answered with some surprise. "What do you want with me?"

"You are the brother—no, I err, the sister—of the famous Pierre Dutourd, is it not so?" the Lizard asked. "I seek to reach the famous Dutourd on a matter of business for both of us, but I have the difficulties. You can, it could be, help?"

His business had to be ginger, ginger or drugs for people. "Go away," Monique said quietly. She wanted to scream it. Dieter Kuhn or some other Nazi was surely keeping an eye on her. The Germans wanted her brother, too.

"But why do you wish me to go?" the Lizard asked. His kind, she had heard, were naive, but she hadn't expected him to be so naive as to ask a question like that. Before she could say anything, he went on, "There could be much profit in the business I do with your famous brother. Some of that profit would go to you, as middleman."

Monique laughed in his face, which startled him into drawing back a step. "Go away," she repeated. "Don't you know the Germans spy on me? They are also looking for my brother, my famous brother." She laughed again, though doubting the Lizard understood the irony. "They are looking for him so they can kill him."

"But why is this?" The male seemed honestly bewildered. "He still smuggles ginger to the Race. It is only that now he smuggles also other things to you Tosevites. Could they care so much about this?"

Explaining things struck Monique as more trouble than it was worth. Without even bothering to tell him to go away again, she started taking the bicycle up the stairs. She had papers to grade and, with a little luck, a long-stalled project on the epigraphy of the cult of Isis in Gallia Narbonensis to work on.

Finally sensing he wasn't going to get anywhere, the Lizard called after her: "Tell him my name is Ssimachan. He will know of me. He will want to do business with me. We can make much profit together, he and I."

Monique had no intention of telling Pierre any such thing. This Ssimachan struck her as so inept, he was far more likely to bring danger with him than profit. He probably had swarms of *Gestapo* men following him, too. If they happened to run into the ones who were, or might be, shadowing her . . . That was as unpleasant a thought as she'd had in quite a while.

She sautéed squid in olive oil for supper, a meal the Romans would also have enjoyed. Then she went through the papers as fast as she could. As usual, Dieter Kuhn's—he went by the name of Laforce in her classes—was very good. She snarled something under her breath. He never gave her any excuse to fail him, or even to give him less than a superior mark.

After recording the grades, she got out her photographs and photostats and copies of drawings made and published by classicists over the previous three centuries. If she ever finished her monograph on Isis-worship in this part of the world during Roman times, she could publish it without too much fear. Unlike remarks on Romano-German relations, the cult of Isis held few modern political overtones.

At about eleven, her yawns made her realize she wouldn't get anything more done that night. She put away the inscriptions and her notes, got into a nightgown, and went to bed. She'd sometimes thought her life would be easier had Dieter Kuhn wanted nothing more than her body. Even so, she was delighted to sleep alone.

The peremptory knock on her door came, in the best cinematic style, a few minutes past midnight.

Too logy with sleep to be as frightened as she should, she staggered out of bed and went to the door. "Go away," she said, as she had to the Lizard. "You damned drunk, you're trying to get into the wrong apartment."

"You will open at once, in the name of the Security Service of the Greater German *Reich*," a cold voice from the hall replied. After that, she wasn't sleepy any more, and was as frightened as anyone could reasonably have expected her to be.

Numbly, she opened the door. One of the Germans standing in the hall aimed a pistol at her. Another one shone a bright flashlight in her face. Two more stepped forward and grabbed her by the arms. They hustled her down the stairs and into their waiting van. She hoped they'd closed the door after her, but didn't get the chance to look back and see. If they hadn't, her apartment would be picked clean by the time she got back.

Of course, that assumed she would be coming back. The glares the Nazis gave her made such an assumption look worse by the minute.

The Palais de Justice lay on the Rue Breteuil; she cycled past it every day. What the German occupiers meant by justice was liable to be different from what the builders of the Palais had in mind.

Her captors frogmarched her into the building, then shoved her at a trio of hard-faced blond women in field-gray. "Search her," one of the men said in German, and the women did, with a thoroughness none of her doctors, not even her gynecologist, had ever come close to matching. They enjoyed probing her at least as much as men would have, and didn't bother hiding it. She was smarting in more than one sensitive spot when they flung her into a cell.

Humiliated, terrified, she lay down on the hard, lumpy cot and dozed off. She was in the middle of a nightmare when another brilliant light pried her eyelids open. A couple of German troopers hauled her off the cot with effortless strength. "Time for questions now," an SS man said cheerfully.

They sat her down and started grilling her. The questions were what she might have expected: about her brother, about his dealings with the Lizards, about the Lizard who'd tried to use her to reach him. Her chief interrogator grinned at her. "Your precious Pierre won't be very happy when he hears we've nabbed you, will he?"

"I don't know. He might not even care," she answered. If the Germans were using her as a lever against her brother, they were liable to be disappointed. She hadn't even known he was alive till Dieter Kuhn told her, and the milk of human kindness ran thin in his veins.

But her answer wasn't what the German wanted to hear. "Lying bitch!" he snarled, and backhanded her across the face. Things rapidly went downhill from there.

She told the Germans everything they asked, everything she knew. It wasn't enough to satisfy them. Nothing, she thought, would have been enough to satisfy them. At one point, she moaned, "At least let me telephone the university and let them know I won't be in today." Whatever happened to her, she—and her administrators—reckoned classes sacred.

Her interrogator didn't. He slapped her again, and painfully squeezed her breast through the thin cotton of her nightgown. "I hope they fire you, whore," he said with a laugh. "Then you can turn tricks for a living, the way you did with that kike of a Goldfarb. Who put him on to you, anyhow?"

"I don't know," she answered. "He never told me." That got her another slap.

After some endless time—long enough for Monique to piss herself, for they made her go through that humiliation rather than pausing long enough for her to use a toilet—they took her back to the cell, without food, without water, without anything worth having. She didn't care. She was past caring. She lay down and fell asleep, or perhaps passed out.

And then, of course, someone shook her awake. Blearily, blurrily, she looked up (one eye was swollen nearly shut) and saw Dieter Kuhn standing over her. "*Bonsoir,* Monique," the SS-man said with a pleasant smile. "Would you care to take supper with me tomorrow night?"

She knew what she wanted to tell him. She almost did. But now she also knew what could happen to anyone who made the Germans unhappy. She'd thought she knew before, but now she understood the difference between academic knowledge and personal experience. Though she hated herself, what passed her bruised, dry lips was one croaked word: "Yes."

Group Captain Burton Paston, the commander of the RAF radar station on the outskirts of Belfast, looked from the papers on his desk to Flight Lieutenant David Goldfarb, who sat across the desk from him. "You truly wish to resign your commission in the Royal Air Force?" Paston sounded incredulous, as if Goldfarb were coming to him for permission to commit some particularly sordid crime.

"Yes, sir," Goldfarb said firmly.

Paston scratched at his salt-and-pepper mustache. "And why, might I ask, do you seek to do such a thing?"

"It's in the forms I filled out, sir," David Goldfarb answered. Group Captain Paston should have read them. That he hadn't was a bad sign. "My family and I have the opportunity to emigrate to Canada, but the Dominion won't accept any serving officers in Her Majesty's forces."

"A policy of which I heartily approve, I might add." Paston peered at Goldfarb through the top half of his bifocals. "Why would you want to emigrate, in any case?"

"Sir . . ." David stared at the station commander in dismay. Group Captain Paston hadn't come along yesterday. He was no fool; Goldfarb knew as much. If he was deliberately acting obtuse, that had to mean trouble ahead. Taking a deep breath, Goldfarb laid it on the line: "Sir, you know I'm a Jew. And you have to know that things have been getting harder and harder for Jews in Britain the past few years. . . ."

His voice trailed off again. His parents had fled to England from what was then Russian-held Poland to escape pogroms before the First World War. But now, with the United Kingdom shorn of its empire by the Lizards, with the Greater German *Reich* across the Channel, Britain was slowly accommodating herself to the masters of the Continent. That left little room for people like David Goldfarb and his family.

"And you want to get out while the getting is good, is that it?" Paston asked.

"Yes, sir, I'm afraid that is about it," David answered.

"Caring nothing whatever for the service that took you out of East End London and made you into someone worthy of respect," Group Captain Paston said.

Goldfarb's cheeks and ears heated. "I'll care for the RAF till my dying day. But I must say, sir, I haven't always got whatever respect I may be worth from some RAF officers—not you, sir, I hasten to add. But there are some in this service who think one of Her Majesty's officers has nothing better to do than help smuggle ginger, which is how I ended up in the Nazis' gaol in Marseille."

"If we can hurt the Lizards in no other way than with ginger for the time being, then ginger we must use," Paston said. "I do admit, the line between official and unofficial can grow blurry in those circumstances, but—"

"Not half!" Goldfarb broke in. "Some of those blokes"—he had Group Captain Basil Roundbush, a former colleague and current oppressor, in mind—"have got themselves rich off the smuggling trade."

"None of which has anything to do with you," the group captain told him, his voice suddenly distant and chilly. "Nor can I in good conscience accept a resignation based on petty personal

problems. Accordingly, your request is denied, and you will return to your normal duties at once."

"What?" David yelped. "You can't do that!"

"Not only can I, Flight Lieutenant, I just have," Paston
answered.

He was right—he could. Goldfarb hadn't expected that he
would, though. Paston had always been pretty decent, as far
as commanding officers went. But Goldfarb had point-blank
refused to do any more smuggling for Basil Roundbush, and
Roundbush had promised he'd regret it. "My God!" he burst out.
"They've told you to keep me stuck in the service so I can't leave
the country!" He didn't know exactly who *they* were, but he did
know Roundbush had friends in high places.

"I haven't the faintest notion of what you're talking about,"
Group Captain Paston said, but for the first time he spoke with
something less than perfect self-assurance. "And I have given
you quite enough of my time, too."

"You want to be rid of me," Goldfarb said. "Well, I want to be
rid of the RAF. I'll do that any way I have to, believe me."

"By a deliberate show of disobedience or incompetence, do
you mean?" Paston asked, and David nodded. The radar-station
commander gave him a thin, chilly smile. "If you try that, Flight
Lieutenant, you will indeed leave the RAF. You will leave it with
a bad-conduct discharge, I promise you. And you are welcome
to see how well you do emigrating with that on your record."

Goldfarb stared at him in dismay. He could have said several
different things. Any one of them might have brought him the
sort of discharge Group Captain Paston had mentioned. At last,
after some effort, he managed, "I believe that's most unjust, sir."

"I'm sorry you think so," Paston said. "But I have already told
you I have no more time to listen to your complaints. You are
dismissed."

"Why, you—" Again, David Goldfarb bit back a response that
would have landed him in trouble. Shaking, he got to his feet. As
he turned to leave the group captain's office, though, he couldn't
help adding, "They *have* got to you."

Paston busied himself with the papers in his in basket. Goldfarb didn't think he was going to answer, but he did: "We all
have to do certain things for the sake of the service as a whole,
Flight Lieutenant."

"And I'm the pawn to be sacrificed, is that it?" Goldfarb said. This time, Group Captain Paston didn't reply, but he didn't really need to, either.

Still shaking his head in disgust, Goldfarb strode out of his office. He didn't slam the door behind him, however much he wanted to. That would have been a petty revenge, and the revenge he wanted was anything but petty. How to get it without ending up in trouble much worse than a bad-conduct discharge was, unfortunately, another question altogether.

A couple of enlisted men saluted him as he walked out into the watery February sunshine that was the best Belfast had to offer. To them, his officer's uniform spoke more loudly than his sallow skin, his beak of a nose, and his curly hair of a brown (now graying) not quite the right shade for one whose ancestors were respectably Anglo-Saxon or Celtic. Goldfarb snorted bitterly as he returned the salutes. He wished his superiors thought the same way.

What am I going to do? he wondered. He knew he had to do something. Staying in a Britain slowly succumbing to the embrace of the *Reich* didn't bear thinking about. His parents had seen the writing on the wall and escaped from Poland. His wife's parents had got her out of Germany not long before the *Kristall-nacht* spelled the beginning of the end for Jews there. Waiting for trouble to land wasn't in his blood, or Naomi's, either.

Without leaving the RAF, he couldn't go to Canada, and he couldn't get out of the RAF. He didn't think he could go to the United States, either, though the secretary at the American consulate hadn't been quite so definite about it. "Have to find out," he muttered under his breath.

Suppose the Yanks said no? He didn't want to suppose that. He wanted to suppose anything but that. The way his luck was running, though—the way Basil Roundbush and his pals were helping to make his luck run— he wouldn't have bet on anything going his way.

"Where else can I go?" Another question, this one addressed to the washed-out, smoke-stained sky. The few bits of Europe the Germans didn't occupy were far more subservient to the *Reich* than the United Kingdom. The Soviet Union? He snorted again. That would be jumping back into the frying pan his parents had fled. The Russians might want him for what he knew about radars, but that didn't mean they'd treat him like anything but a damn Jew.

Goldfarb was about to climb aboard his bicycle to ride back to his flat in the officers' housing and give Naomi the bad news when he paused. If all he wanted was to escape Britain, he was leaving more than half the world out of his calculations—the part the Lizards ran.

"Well, it's no wonder I didn't think of that straight off," he said, as if someone had asserted the opposite. He'd fought the Lizards even harder than he'd fought the Nazis. He'd gone into a Polish prison carrying a Sten gun to get his cousin Moishe Russie out of there, and he'd fought with everything he could get his hands on when the Race invaded England.

And now he wanted to live under their rule?

He shook his head. He didn't want to. Living under the rule of the Race was one of the last things he wanted to do. But staying in Britain any longer was the very last thing he wanted to do.

After a moment, he shook his head again. That wasn't right. He might think it was when he was feeling down, but it wasn't. Getting arrested in Marseille had been very instructive in that regard. He would much sooner have tried to spend the rest of his life in Britain than set foot in the Greater German *Reich* again for even ten minutes—which was about how long he thought he'd last.

"And I've even got wires to pull," he murmured. These days, Moishe Russie, far from languishing in a Lizard prison, sometimes advised the fleetlord himself on how to deal with troublesome Tosevites. His cousin's influence had got him out of that Nazi gaol. Maybe it could get him out of Britain, too.

He swung onto the bicycle and started to ride. As he did so, a new name welled up in his mind. *Palestine*. His cousin Moishe lived in Jerusalem. He'd gone there after the Nazis resentfully turned him loose. What would living in Palestine be like?

Next year in Jerusalem. For how many centuries had that been a Jewish prayer? Could he make it come true?

An Austin-Healey almost ran him over. He shouted something unkind at the driver, who kept on going without a clue about the near miss. Goldfarb had had to make his way against the tide of anti-Semitism throughout his life. He'd conducted himself creditably in combat on the ground and in the air, and had the medal ribbons above his breast pocket to prove it. Against idiot drivers, though, the gods contended in vain.

After his brush with death, Goldfarb realized he'd asked himself the wrong question. He thought he had a good chance of being able to move his family to Palestine if he couldn't get to Canada or the USA. Which counted for more, freedom or simple survival?

"How much freedom will I have ten years from now if I stay here?" he mused. "How much will my children have?" He didn't like the answers he found for either of those questions. His parents had known enough to get out when the getting was good. So had Naomi's. That made up his mind for him. If traffic didn't do him in, he'd keep trying to escape, even if escape meant Palestine.

☆ 2 ☆

Little by little, Jerusalem began to settle down after the latest round of Arab rioting. Reuven Russie shook his head as he walked toward the medical college that bore his father's name. It wasn't so much that Jerusalem was settling down as that the riots had a few days between them now rather than coming one on the heels of another. When the Arabs erupted, they were as fierce as ever.

For the moment, they were quiet. An Arab woman in a long black dress with a black scarf on her head walked past Reuven. He nodded politely. So did she, though his clothes and his fair skin clearly said he was a Jew. Did something nasty gleam in her eyes despite the polite nod? Maybe, maybe not. The Arabs' riots were aimed first and foremost at the Lizards, with the Jews being secondary targets because they got on with the Race better than their Arab neighbors did.

Reuven wondered if that woman had been screeching *"Allahu akbar!"* and breaking windows or throwing rocks or setting fires during the latest round of turmoil. He wouldn't have been a bit surprised. The sour smell of old burning still clung to Jerusalem, even after a late-winter rainstorm. The rain hadn't been able to wash away all the soot streaking the golden sandstone that was the most common local building material, either.

A razor-wire security perimeter surrounded the Moishe Russie Medical College. As Reuven approached, a Lizard in a sandbagged strongpoint waved an automatic rifle at him. "Show me your authorization for entry," the Lizard snapped in his own language. No one who didn't understand that language was likely to have authorization to pass through the perimeter.

"It shall be done," Reuven said, also in the language of the

33

Race. He handed the Lizard a plastic card with his photograph. The Lizard didn't compare the photograph to his appearance. Even after more than twenty years on Earth, many males of the Race had trouble telling one human being from another. Instead, the soldier fed the card into an electronic gadget and waited to see what colored lights came on.

The result must have satisfied him, for he handed the card back to Russie when the machine spat it out. "Pass on," he said, gesturing with the rifle.

"I thank you," Reuven answered. The medical college had come under heavy attack during the fighting. He was glad the Race thought the school important enough not to be endangered so again.

He certainly thought it was that important, though he would have admitted he was biased. Nowhere else on earth did the Lizards teach people what they knew of medicine, and their knowledge was generations ahead of what humanity had understood about the art before the Race came.

Learning some of what the Lizards knew had been Moishe Russie's goal ever since the fighting stopped. Reuven was proud he'd been accepted to follow in his father's footsteps. If he hadn't passed the qualifying examinations, the name above the entrance to the block Lizard building wouldn't have meant a thing.

He went inside. The Race had built doors and ceilings high enough to suit humans, and the seats in the halls fit Tosevite fundaments. Other than that, the Race had made few concessions. Reuven carried artificial fingerclaws in a little plastic case in his back pocket. Without them, he would have had a devil of a time using the computer terminals here.

More people than Lizards bustled through the halls on the way to one class or another. The people—most of them in their mid- to late twenties, like Reuven—were students, the Lizards instructors: physicians from the conquest fleet, now joined by a few from the colonization fleet as well.

Reuven and another student got to the door of their lecture hall at the same time. "I greet you, Ibrahim," Reuven said in the language of the Race—the language of instruction at the college and the only one all the human students had in common.

"I greet you," Ibrahim Nuqrashi replied. He was lean and dark, with a perpetually worried expression. Since he came from

Baghdad, which was even more convulsed than Jerusalem, Reuven had a hard time blaming him.

They went in together, talking about biochemistry and gene-splicing. When they got inside, their eyes went in the same direction: to see if any seats were empty near Jane Archibald. Jane was blond and shapely, easily the prettiest girl at the college. No wonder, then, that she was already surrounded by male students this morning.

She smiled at Reuven and called "Good day!" in English—she was from Australia, though heaven only knew if she'd go back there once her studies were done. The Lizards were colonizing the island continent more thoroughly than anywhere else, except perhaps the deserts of Arabia and North Africa.

Nuqrashi sighed as he and Reuven sat down. "Maybe I should learn English," he said, still in the language of the Race. English was the human language most widely shared among the students, but Reuven didn't think that was why the Arab wanted to acquire it.

He didn't get much of a chance to worry about it. Into the lecture hall came Shpaaka, the instructor. Along with the other students, Reuven sprang to his feet and folded himself into the best imitation of the Race's posture of respect his human frame could manage. "I greet you, superior sir," he chorused with his comrades.

"I greet you, students," Shpaaka replied. "You may be seated." Anyone who sat without permission landed in hot water; even more than most Lizards, Shpaaka was a stickler for protocol. His eye turrets swiveled this way and that as he surveyed the class. "I must say that, until I read through this latest set of examination papers, I had no idea there were so many ways to write my language incorrectly."

Jane Archibald raised her hand. When Shpaaka recognized her, she asked, "Superior sir, is that not because we are all used to our own languages rather than to yours, so that our native grammar persists even when we use your vocabulary?"

"I think you may well be correct," Shpaaka replied. "The Race has done some research on grammatical substrates, work occasioned by our conquests of the Rabotevs and Hallessi. Our ongoing experience with the multiplicity of languages here on Tosev 3 clearly shows more investigation will be needed." His eye turrets surveyed the class once more. "Any further questions or comments? No? Very well: I begin."

He lectured as if his human students were males and females of the Race, diluting nothing, slowing down not at all. Those who couldn't stand the pace had to leave the medical college and pursue their training, if they pursued it, at a merely human university. Reuven scribbled frantically. He was lucky in that he'd already known Hebrew, English, Yiddish, and childhood pieces of Polish before tackling the Race's language; after four tongues, adding a fifth wasn't so bad. Students who'd spoken only their native language before tackling that of the Race were likelier to have a hard time.

After lecture, laboratory. After laboratory, more lecture. After that, more lab work, now concentrating on enzyme synthesis and suppression rather than genetic analysis. By the end of the day, Reuven felt as if his brain were a sponge soaked to the saturation point. By tomorrow morning, he would have to be ready to soak up just as much again.

Wringing his hand as he stuck his pen back in its case, he asked Jane, "Would you like to come to my house for supper tonight?"

She cocked her head to one side as she considered. "It's bound to be better than the food in the dormitories—though your mother's cooking deserves something nicer than that said about it," she answered. "Your father is always interesting, and your sisters are cute . . ."

Reuven thought of the twins as unmitigated—well, occasionally mitigated—nuisances. "What about me?" he asked plaintively— she'd mentioned everyone else in the Russie household.

"Oh. You." Her blue eyes twinkled. "I suppose I'll come anyway." She laughed at the look on his face, then went on, "If the riots start up again, I can always sleep on your sofa."

"You could always sleep in my bed," he suggested.

She shook her head. "You didn't sleep in mine when you spent that night in the dormitory while the fighting in the city was so bad." She wasn't offended; she reached out and took his hand. "Come on. Let's go. I'm getting hungry standing here talking."

Several students gave Reuven jealous looks as he and Jane left the campus hand in hand. They made him feel three meters tall. In fact, he was a thoroughly ordinary one meter seventy-three centimeters—in absent moments, he thought of it as five feet eight—so when he and Jane looked into each other's eyes, they did so on a level. Three or four Arab men whooped when they saw Jane. They approved of big blondes. She took no notice of them, which worked better than telling them where to go and how to get there. That only encouraged them.

"I've brought Jane home for supper," Reuven called in Yiddish as he came inside.

"That's fine," his mother answered from the kitchen in the same language. "There will be plenty." Rivka Russie, Reuven was convinced, could feed an invading army as long as it gave her fifteen minutes' notice.

His sisters came out and greeted Jane in halting English and in the language of the Race, which they were studying at school. Judith and Esther had just entered their teens; next to Jane's ripe curves, they definitely seemed works in progress. She answered them in the bits and pieces of Hebrew she'd picked up since coming to Jerusalem. Reuven smiled to himself. Like most native English speakers, she couldn't come out with a proper guttural to save her life.

Judith—he was pretty sure it was Judith, though the twins were identical and wore their hair the same way, not least for the sake of the confusion it caused—turned to him and said, "Cousin David's having more troubles. Father's doing what he can to fix things, but . . ." She shrugged.

"What now?" Reuven asked. "It's not the Nazis again, is it?"

"No, but the English don't want to let him leave," his sister answered, "and things are getting scary for Jews over there."

"*Gevalt,*" he said, and then translated for Jane.

She nodded understanding. "It's like being a human in Australia. The Lizards wish none of us were left. After what they did to our cities, it's a wonder any of us are." For her, dealing with oppression from outside had begun when she was a little girl. For Reuven, it had begun two thousand years before he was born. He didn't make the comparison, not out loud.

His father came home a few minutes later. Moishe Russie looked like an older version of Reuven: he'd gone bald on top, and the hair he had left was iron gray. Reuven asked, "What's this I hear about Cousin David?"

Moishe grimaced. "That could be a problem. The fleetlord doesn't seem very interested in helping him out. It's not as if he's in jail or about to be executed. He's just having a hard time. Atvar thinks plenty of Tosevites are having worse times, so he won't do anything about it."

He and Reuven had both spoken Hebrew, which Jane could follow after a fashion. In English, she said, "That's terrible! What will he do if he can't get out of England?"

English was Moishe Russie's fourth language, after Yiddish, Polish, and Hebrew. He stuck to the latter: "He'll have to do the best he can. Right now, I don't know how I can give him a hand."

From the kitchen, Rivka Russie called, "Supper's ready. Everyone come to the table." Reuven headed for the dining room, but discovered he'd lost some of his appetite.

The flat—they didn't call them apartments down here—in which the Lizards had set up Rance Auerbach and Penny Summers was barely half the size of the one Rance had lived in by himself in Fort Worth, and that one had been none too large.

He limped to the refrigerator, which was also about half the size of the one he'd had up in the States. Even though the flat was tiny, he was panting by the time he got there. He'd never win a footrace, not after the Lizards had shot him in the leg and in the chest during the fighting in Colorado. He supposed he was lucky nobody'd amputated that leg. He would have been a lot more certain had keeping it not meant living in pain every day of his life since.

One way or another, he did what he could to ease that pain. He took a Lion Lager out of the icebox and popped off the lid with a churchkey. At the hiss, Penny called, "Bring me one of those, too, will you?"

"Okay," he answered. His Texas drawl contrasted with her harsh, flat Kansas tone. Here in South Africa, they both sounded funny. He opened another beer and carried it out to Penny, who was sitting on a sofa that had seen better days.

She took it with a murmur of thanks, then lifted it in salute. "Mud in your eye," she said, and drank. She was a brassy blonde of about forty, a few years younger than Rance. Sometimes, she still looked like the farm girl he'd first met during the fighting. More often, though, a lot more often, she seemed hard as nails.

With a sardonic glint in her blue eyes, she raised the beer bottle again. "And here's to South Africa, goddammit."

"Oh, shut up," Auerbach said wearily. It was hot in the flat; late February was summer down here. Not too humid, though—the climate was more like Los Angeles' than Fort Worth's.

Auerbach sank down on the sofa beside her. He grunted; his leg didn't like going from standing to sitting. It liked going from sitting to standing even less. He took a pull at his Lion, then smacked his lips. "They do make pretty good beer here. I'll give 'em that."

"Hot damn," Penny said, even more sarcastically than before. She waved her bottle around. "Aren't you glad we came?"

"Well, that depends." Thanks to the bullet he'd taken in the shoulder and lung, Rance's voice was a rasping croak. He lit a cigarette. Every doctor he'd ever seen told him he was crazy for smoking, but nobody told him how to quit. After another sip, he went on, "It beats spending the rest of my life in a Lizard hoosegow—or a German one, for that matter. It beats going back to the USA, too, on account of your ginger-smuggling buddies want you dead for stiffing 'em and me for plugging the first two bastards they sent after you."

He had to pause and pant a little. He couldn't give speeches, not these days—he didn't have the wind for it. While he was re-inflating, Penny said, "You still think it beats Australia?"

If she hadn't burst back into his life, on the run from the dealers she'd cheated, he would still be back in Fort Worth . . . doing what? He knew what: getting drunk, collecting pension checks, and playing nickel-ante poker with the other ruined men down at the American Legion hall. He coughed a couple of times, which also hurt. "Yeah, it still beats Australia," he answered at last. "The Lizards wouldn't have been happy shipping us there—as far as they're concerned, it's *theirs*. And even if they did do it, they'd have their eye turrets on us every second of the day and night."

"Yeah, yeah, yeah. I know, I know, I know." Penny plucked the pack of cigarettes out of his shirt pocket and lit one herself. She smoked it in short, savage puffs, and then, when it was hardly more than a butt, aimed the glowing coal at him like the business end of a pistol. "But when you asked 'em to send us here,

Mr. Smart Guy, you didn't know it was gonna be nigger heaven, did you?"

"No, I didn't know that," Auerbach answered querulously. "How the hell was I supposed to know that? White men ran things here before the fighting. I knew that much. Tell me you heard a whole hell of a lot about South Africa in the news since the Lizards took it over. Go on. I dare you."

Penny didn't say anything. She stubbed out the cigarette and lit another one.

Rance used that pause to take a swig from the Lion Lager and to draw a couple of breaths. He went on, "I guess it makes sense, the way they did what they did. They don't give a damn about white men and black men. And there are more blacks than whites here, and the whites are the ones who fought 'em hardest, and so—"

"So it's nigger heaven." Penny rolled her eyes. "You know what? Till the Lizards came, I never even saw a nigger—not for real, I mean, only in the movies. Weren't any where I grew up. I didn't figure it'd be like this when we came here."

"Neither did I," Auerbach admitted. "How could I have? You wanted to go to a place where people speak English as much as I did. That didn't leave us a whole lot of choice, not to anywhere the Lizards were willing to send us."

"*Some* people speak English—a lot fewer than I thought." Penny aimed that second cigarette at Rance, too. "And a lot fewer than you thought, too, and you can't tell me any different about that, either. At least in the United States, the colored people can talk with you. And they mostly know their place, too." She got up from the sofa and walked quickly to the window of the third-floor flat. The stairs were hell on Rance's bad leg, but he couldn't do anything about that. Staring out onto Hanover Street, the main drag of Cape Town's disreputable District Six, Penny gestured to him. "Come over here."

Though his leg felt as if he'd jabbed a hot iron into it, Rance rose and limped to the window. He looked down and saw a trim figure in a khaki uniform and a cap like the ones British officers wore. The man had a bayoneted rifle slung on his back. "What did you get me up for?" he asked. "I've seen Potlako on his beat plenty of times before."

"He's a cop," Penny said. "He's black as the ace of spades, and he's a cop. Almost all the cops in Cape Town are black as the ace of spades."

"He's a pretty good cop, too, by what I've seen," Rance said, which made Penny give him a furious look. Ignoring it, he went on, "The Lizards aren't stupid. They tried playing blacks against whites in the USA, too, but it didn't work out so well there. A lot more smokes than white men here, and I guess the South Africans treated 'em worse than we did our colored fellows. So they're happy as you please, working for the Lizards."

"Sure they are. You just bet they are," Penny snarled. "And now they treat us like we was niggers, and I tell you something, Rance Auerbach: I don't like it for hell."

Auerbach limped into the kitchen, opened another beer, and went back to the couch. "I don't like it, either, but I don't know what I can do about it. If you can't stand it any more, I bet the Lizards would fly you back to the States after all. By now, they've probably figured out you'd last about twenty minutes after you got off the plane. That'd suit 'em fine, I bet."

She put her hands on her hips, looking, for a moment, like a furious schoolgirl. She sounded like one, too, when she wailed, "Look what you got me into!"

He was sipping from the Lion Lager. He started to laugh, and choked, and sprayed beer out his nose, and generally came closer to drowning than he ever had in his life. When he could talk again—which took a little while—he said, "Who called me out of the blue after more than fifteen years? Whose fault was it that I shot those two nasty bastards? Whose fault was it that I ended up in a Lizard jail for running ginger down into Mexico, or in a Nazi jail for trying to get Pierre the damn Turd to quit running it out of Marseille? You know anybody who fills that bill?"

By the time he got through, he was speaking in a rasping whisper, that being as much air as he could force out of his ravaged lungs. He waited to see how Penny would take a little plain home truth thrown in her face. Sometimes she went off like a rocket. Sometimes . . .

He thought she was going to ignite here. She started to: he saw that. Then, all at once, she laughed instead. She laughed as hard as she would have raged if she'd stayed furious. "Oh, you got me, God damn you," she said, wiping her eyes on the sleeve of her checked cotton blouse. "You got me good there. Okay, I had a little something to do with getting you into things, too."

"Just a little something, yeah," Rance agreed.

Penny got herself a fresh beer, too, then came over and sat down beside him, so close they rubbed together. She swigged, set down the bottle, and leaned over to look into his face from a distance of about four inches. "Haven't I done my best to make it up to you?" she asked, and ran her tongue over her lips.

"I don't know what the hell you're talking about," Rance said evenly.

For a second, he thought he'd blown it and made her angry. But, to his relief, she decided to laugh again. "Well, then, I'll just have to show you, won't I?" she said, and brought her mouth down onto his. She tasted of beer and cigarette smoke, but he did, too, so that was all right.

The kiss went on and on. Auerbach brought up his hand and tangled his fingers in her yellow hair so she couldn't pull back. Finally, he was the one who had to break away. It was either that or quit breathing altogether. She let his hand slide down to the back of her neck, where he started undoing the buttons on the blouse.

"Aren't you a sneak?" she said, as if she'd never expected he would do any such thing. She took matters into her own hands, yanking the blouse off over her head. He undid her bra and grabbed for her breasts; she still had a hell of a nice pair. When she laughed this time, it was down deep in her throat.

She unzipped his fly, pulled him out, and bent down over him. His gasp had very little to do with bad lungs. She had a hell of a mouth, too.

If she'd felt like going on that way till he exploded, he wouldn't have minded a bit—which was putting it mildly. But, after a little while, she pulled down his chinos, took off her skirt and her girdle, and swung astride him as if she intended to ride him to victory in the Kentucky Derby.

His mouth closed on her nipple. Now she grabbed his head and pressed him to her. He slipped a hand between her legs and rubbed gently. Her breath came almost as short as his, and she'd never taken a bullet in the lungs. When she gasped and shuddered and arched her back, she squeezed him inside her almost as if she had a hand of her own down there. He groaned and came and had to work very hard to remember not to bite.

"God damn," he said sincerely. "It's worth fighting with you, just on account of the way we make up."

"Who says we've made up?" Penny demanded. But, whether she wanted it to or not, her voice held a purr that hadn't been there before.

She slid off him—and dribbled on his thigh. "God damn," he said again, this time in mock anger. "I put that stuff where it was supposed to go. I'm not supposed to be wearing it."

"I don't want it staying where you put it, either," she retorted. "That'd be the last thing I need—getting knocked up at my age." She shook her head in what was either real horror or a pretty good imitation. Then, gathering up her clothes, she hurried off to the bathroom.

Auerbach sat there in just his shirt, waiting for her to come out. He wanted another cigarette. All of him except his lungs wanted one, anyhow. What with all the trouble he'd had breathing while Penny straddled him, he let them win the argument for once. Instead of the smoke, he finished the rest of the Lion Lager sitting on the table. It felt like what it was, a consolation prize, but life didn't hand out so many prizes of any sort that he could turn one down.

When Penny did come out, she smiled to see him still mostly naked. He picked up his pants and used the arm of the sofa to help lever himself to his feet. That took some of the strain off his bad leg, but made his ruined shoulder groan. "Can't win," he muttered as he limped past her toward the john. "Christ, you can't break even, either." If being in Cape Town didn't prove that, he was damned if he knew what would.

Gorppet rattled along in a mechanized combat vehicle, heading northwest toward the Tosevite city of Baghdad. Basra, where he'd been stationed, was calm these days—or so his leaders kept saying. Gorppet had seen a lot of nasty fighting after the Race landed on Tosev 3. Basra didn't feel calm to him, nor anything close. But no one had asked his opinion. He was there to do what his officers told him to do. If that turned out to be stupid, as it sometimes did, he had to make the best of it.

"Too bad about Fotsev," said Betvoss, one of the males in his squad.

"Truth—too bad," agreed Gorppet, who didn't much care for Betvoss. "He was a good male, and a good squad leader. Now you are stuck with me instead." He swung an eye turret toward Betvoss to see what the other male would make of that.

"I curse the Big Uglies," Betvoss said. "The spirits of Emperors past will surely turn their backs on them." His voice went shrill with complaint, as it did too often to suit Gorppet: "I curse them all the more for forcing ginger on the females of ours they had kidnapped, and for using the females' pheromones to lure us into that ambush."

"They are sneaky," Gorppet said. "If you forget how sneaky they are, you will regret it—if you live to regret it." He put his own worries into words: "I hope they are not quieting down in Basra to persuade us to lessen the garrison there so they can rise up again after we have weakened ourselves."

"They are not clever enough to think of something like that. I am sure of it," Betvoss said. Another reason Gorppet was less than fond of him was that he thought he knew more than he did. He went on, "Besides, if we can stamp out the rebellion in this Baghdad place, it will also fade in Basra."

That might even have been true. Baghdad was a bigger, more important Tosevite center than Basra. Even so, Gorppet didn't care to admit Betvoss could be right about anything. The squad leader said, "Until we hunt down that maniac of an agitator called Khomeini, this whole subregion will go on bubbling and boiling like a pot over too high a fire."

He wondered if Betvoss would argue about that. Since Betvoss was ready to argue about almost everything, it wouldn't have surprised him. But the other male only made the affirmative hand gesture and said, "Truth. One of the things we will have to do to carry this world fully into the Empire is to bring the Big Uglies' superstitions under our control."

"We ought to do that anyhow, for the sake of truth," Betvoss said. "Imagine believing some sort of oversized Big Ugly up above the sky manufactured the whole universe. Can you think of anything more preposterous?"

"No. But then, I am not a Tosevite," Gorppet said, speaking the last phrase with considerable relief. In an effort to be charitable, he added, "Of course, up till now, they have not known of the Emperors, and so have been forming their beliefs in ignorance rather than in truth."

"But they cling to their false notions with such persistence— we would not be going from one city to another like this if they did not," Betvoss said. "And if I never hear *'Allahu akbar!'* again, I shall not be sorry for it."

"Truth!" Every male in the rear compartment of the mechanized combat vehicle said that. Several of them added emphatic coughs, to show how strongly they felt about it.

"Truth indeed," Gorppet said. "Any male who has served where they say such things knows what a truth it is. Because it is a truth, we must stay especially alert. Remember, too many of the local Tosevites will give up their own lives if they can take us with them. They believe this will assure them of a happy afterlife."

"As you said, they know not the Emperors." Betvoss' voice dripped scorn.

Gorppet scorned the Big Uglies for their foolish beliefs, too. That didn't mean he failed to respect them as fighters, and especially as guerrilla fighters. He pressed an eye turret to the viewing prism above a firing port and looked out of the combat vehicle.

He sat on the left side of the vehicle, the one that faced away from the river, so he could see not only the farmland—worked by Big Uglies in long, flowing robes—but also the drier country where irrigation stopped. The landscape, in fact, put him in mind of Home. It was no wonder the colonists were running up so many new towns in the interior of this region, towns watered with pipes from desalination plants by the edge of the nearest sea.

Even the weather in this part of Tosev 3 was decent. The mechanized combat vehicle didn't have its heater going full blast, as it would have on most of the planet. Gorppet had fought through one winter in the SSSR. He'd told some stories about that when he went into one of the new towns. None of the newly revived colonists believed him. He'd stopped telling those stories. For that matter, he'd stopped going into the new towns. He disliked the colonists almost as much as he disliked the Big Uglies. He disliked everyone except his comrades from the

conquest fleet, and, with Betvoss beside him, he was forcibly reminded he didn't much care for some of them, either.

Before it should have, the vehicle came to a halt, tracks
rattling. "Oh, by the Emperor, what now?" Gorppet demanded.
None of his fellow infantrymales knew, of course—they were as
cooped up as he. He picked up the intercom and put the question
to the driver. If *he* didn't know, everybody was in trouble.

He had an answer, all right, but not one Gorppet cared to hear:
"The accursed Tosevites managed to sabotage the bridge we are
supposed to pass over."

"What do you mean, sabotage?" Gorppet asked irritably. "I
am in this metal box back here, remember? I cannot see straight
ahead. If I do not look out a viewing prism, I cannot see out at
all."

"They bombed the span. It fell into the river. Is that plain
enough for you, Exalted Squadlord?" The driver also sounded
irritable.

"How did they manage to bomb it?" Gorppet exclaimed,
which made the males in his squad exclaim, too. He went on,
"Whoever let that happen ought to have green bands painted on
him"—the mark of someone undergoing punishment—"and
spend about the next ten years—the next ten Tosevite years,
mind you—cleaning out the Big Uglies' stinking latrines with
his tongue."

His squadmates laughed. He was too furious to find it funny.
The driver said, "I agree with you, but I cannot do anything
about it."

"How is this column of vehicles to proceed on to Baghdad,
then, if we cannot use the bridge?" Gorppet asked.

"We shall have to go on to As Samawan and cross the river
there," the driver replied. "While it is not the route originally
planned, it should not delay us too much."

"That is good," Gorppet said. Then he paused in sudden sharp
suspicion. "Why would the Big Uglies blow up a bridge if doing
so causes us no great harm?"

"Who knows why Tosevites act as they do?" the driver said.

"I know this: they act as they do to cause us the greatest possible harm," Gorppet said with great conviction. "Either they
have an ambush waiting for us on the road to this As Samawan
place or they are going to—"

The founder of the superstition in which the local Big Uglies believed so passionately, a certain Muhammad, was said to be a prophet, a male who could see the future. The notion, like so many on Tosev 3, was alien to the way the Race thought. But Gorppet, though not pausing even for a moment, proved a prophet in his own right. He hadn't finished his sentence before bullets started slamming into the mechanized combat vehicle.

A lot of bullets were slamming into the vehicle. "They must have a machine gun out there, may the purple itch get under their scales!" he exclaimed, grabbing for his own automatic weapon.

As he spoke, the light cannon mounted atop the combat vehicle barked into life. He peered out through the vision prism. He couldn't see much. Because they were close by the river—the Tosevite name for it was the Tigris—plant life grew exuberantly, providing excellent cover for the Big Ugly raiders. Someone should have thought to trim the vegetation farther back from the roadway, but no one had. He didn't like that. How many Big Uglies were sneaking through the rank, noxiously green foliage toward the column?

There was the muzzle flash of the Tosevites' machine gun. That being the only sure target he had, Gorppet started shooting at it. If the machine gun fell silent, he would know he was doing some good. The rest of the males in his squad were also blazing away. He didn't know what the males on the far side of the combat vehicle were shooting at, but they seemed to have found something.

Before he could ask, a Big Ugly burst from the greenery and rushed toward the vehicle. He was, inevitably, shouting *"Allahu akbar!"* He carried in his right hand a bottle with a flaming wick. Gorppet had seen those in the SSSR. They were full of petroleum distillates, and could easily set even a landcruiser afire.

Gorppet sprayed the Tosevite with bullets. One of them struck the bottle. It burst and exploded into flame, which caught on the Big Ugly's robes and his flesh. He would have been in greater torment still had Gorppet's bullets—and probably those of other males as well—not toppled him and sent him quickly on the road to death.

Then a grenade flew out of the plants and exploded not far from Gorppet's vehicle. He fired in the direction from which it had come, but couldn't tell whether he'd hit the thrower. Another grenade burst on the far side of the vehicle. "We are surrounded!" Betvoss shouted in alarm.

If Betvoss could see it, it should have been obvious to anyone. Gorppet yelled into the intercom: "We had better get out of here while we still can!"

"I have no orders," the driver answered, which struck Gorppet as not being nearly reason enough to stay. Before he could say as much, the other male added, "And I will not abandon my comrades without orders."

That, unfortunately, did make sense to Gorppet. He spotted a shape moving in among the greenery and fired at it. Even through the mechanized combat vehicle's armor, he heard the shriek the Big Ugly let out. He snarled in savage satisfaction.

The vehicle did begin to back away then, which presumably meant the ones behind it in the column had already started retreating. The machine didn't have to go around any burning hulks, for which Gorppet let out a sigh of relief. Smoke dischargers helped shield the column from the Tosevites' eyes. Before long, all the combat vehicles were speeding northwest along the road to As Samawan. Gorppet wasn't the least bit unhappy to leave that marauding band of Big Uglies behind.

"Praise the spirits of Emperors past, that was not too expensive, anyhow," Betvoss said. "All they made us do was change our route."

"Now we have to hope they have not mined the highway to As Samawan," Gorppet said. Betvoss laughed, but the squad leader went on, "I was not joking. They have forced us to do something we did not plan to do. That means we are moving to their plan, not to our own. They will have something waiting for us."

Again, he proved right. The column had not gone much farther before a mine exploded under the lead combat vehicle. Fortunately, it did no more than blow off a track. The vehicle's crew scrambled out, made hasty repairs, with soldiers and the guns of the rest of the column protecting them, and got moving again. All things considered, it was, as Betvoss had said, an inexpensive journey.

As a shuttlecraft pilot, Nesseref was one of the first females revived from the colonization fleet. That meant she had more experience with Big Uglies than most of the other colonists in the new town outside Jezow, Poland. Despite that experience, she admitted—indeed, she proclaimed, whenever she got the chance—she did not understand the way the minds of the natives of Tosev 3 worked.

"Superior sir, when I began coming into this city, I could not imagine why you treated the Tosevites with such restraint," she told Bunim, the regional subadministrator based in Lodz. "Now, having spent a while on the surface of the planet, I begin to see: they are all of them addled, and many of them heavily armed. I can conceive no more appalling combination."

The male from the conquest fleet answered, "You may think you are joking, Shuttlecraft Pilot, but that is the problem facing the Race all over Tosev 3. Poland is merely a microcosm of the planet as a whole."

"In no way was I joking, superior sir," Nesseref replied. "The Poles are heavily armed. They hate the Jews, the Deutsche, us, and the Russkis, in that order. The Jews are also heavily armed. They hate the Deutsche, the Poles, the Russkis, and us, in that order. The Deutsche, off to the west, hate the Jews, us, the Russkis, and the Poles, in that order. The Russkis, off to the east, hate the Deutsche, us, the Jews, and the Poles, in that order. The Deutsche and the Russkis, of course, are even more heavily armed than the Jews and Poles. Do I have it all straight?"

"More or less," Bunim said. "You will notice, however, that in your list each group of Big Uglies hates some other group of Big Uglies more than it hates us. That is what makes our continued administration of this region possible."

"Yes, I understand as much," Nesseref said. "But I also notice that each group of Big Uglies does hate us. This strikes me as ungrateful on their part, but seems to be so."

"Truth," Bunim agreed. "That is what makes our continued administration of this region difficult. That is what makes our continued administration of this whole planet difficult. Each Tosevite faction—and there are tens upon tens of them—reckons itself superior to all the others. Each resents being administered by anyone but one of its own members. Each also resents being administered by anyone not of the Tosevite species. And, with so many explosive-metal bombs on this planet and orbiting it, we must be cautious in our actions lest we touch off a catastrophe."

"Madness," Nesseref said. "Utter madness."

"Oh, indeed." Bunim used an emphatic cough to show just how much madness he thought it was. "But it is not madness we can afford to disregard. Understanding that fact has often come hard to males and females of the colonization fleet. You show a better grasp of it than most."

"I thank you, Regional Subadministrator," Nesseref said. "Difficulties in finding land for the shuttlecraft port and in dealing with Big Ugly laborers in the construction process have proved most educational."

"I can see how they would. Everything on Tosev 3 is educational, although some of the lessons are those we would rather not learn." Bunim paused. "And you are also acquainted with the Jew Anielewicz, are you not?"

"Yes, superior sir," Nesseref answered. She also paused before continuing, "For a Big Ugly, he is quite likable." She wondered how Bunim would take that; he certainly seemed none too fond of any of the Tosevites whose territory he helped govern.

To her surprise, the regional subadministrator said, "Truth." But Bunim went on, "He is very clever, he is very capable, he is very dangerous. He plays us off against the Deutsche, the Poles, and the Russkis, and plays those groups off against one another. His own group should be the weakest among them, but I am not nearly sure it is—and if it is not, that is largely thanks to his abilities."

"Many Tosevites, I gather, are able," Nesseref said. "Your experience is greater than mine, but I would say as many Tosevites are as able as are members of the Race."

"Yes, I would say that is probably a truth," Bunim agreed. "We would have an easier time on this planet were it a falsehood." He let out a long, heartfelt sigh.

"No doubt," Nesseref said. "Many Big Uglies are able, as I say. But few are, or can make themselves be, congenial to us. Anielewicz is one of those who can. I count him a friend of sorts, even if he is not of our species— certainly more of a friend than an accursed male who sought to give me ginger to induce me to mate with him."

"I sometimes think ginger is the revenge Tosev 3 is taking on the Race for our efforts to bring this world into the Empire," Bunim said wearily. "In some ways, the herb causes us more trouble than the Big Uglies do."

"Truth," Nesseref said, with an emphatic cough. She'd tried ginger once herself, before the Race fully understood what it did to females. She'd gone straight into her season, of course, and mated with a couple of Bunim's sentries. Only luck that she hadn't laid a clutch of eggs afterwards. And only luck—luck and a strong, strong will—that the one taste hadn't led to addiction, as it had for so many males and females.

Bunim went on, "I also note that, however congenial you may find Anielewicz, by no means do all of his fellow Tosevites share your opinion. He was recently the target of an assassination attempt by one of the Big Ugly groupings with no great use for Jews. I am not certain which, but there is no shortage of such groups. You have shown you understand as much."

"Yes." Nesseref did her best to hold in surprise and dismay. Murder, especially political murder, was rare among the Race. She supposed she shouldn't have been shocked to learn it was otherwise here on Tosev 3, but she was. "An attempt, you say, superior sir? Was he injured?"

"No. Apparently fearing someone might be seeking to attack him, he dropped to the floor an instant before the assailant fired through the door of his flat. Whoever that assailant was, he escaped."

"I am relieved to hear Anielewicz was not harmed," Nesseref said.

"So was I," the regional subadministrator answered. "You cannot imagine the chaos into which a successful assassination would have thrown this area. I very likely cannot imagine it, either, and I am glad I do not have to."

He cared only about the politics involved, not about Anielewicz as an individual. Nesseref supposed she understood that. Bunim would have to go on dealing with whoever Anielewicz's successor proved to be had the Jew been killed. Still, the attitude saddened her. She returned to her own immediate business: "I do thank you for expediting inspections of the liquid-hydrogen storage system at the shuttlecraft port. An accident would be unfortunate."

"Truth." Bunim looked at her sidelong. "You have a gift for understatement, Shuttlecraft Pilot."

"I thank you," Nesseref answered. "I would be less concerned had the Race done all the construction. But, even with the

Tosevites working to our specifications, I want every possible assurance that they did the job properly."

"I understand. I shall see to it." Bunim turned one eye turret toward a chronometer. "And now, if you will excuse me, I also have other things to see to. . . ."

"Of course, superior sir." Nesseref left Bunim's office, and also left the building housing it. Having been in the hands of the Race since shortly after the arrival of the conquest fleet, it suited her kind about as well as a building originally put up by Big Uglies could. When she went outside, into the cold of the Bialut Market Square, she found herself back in a different world.

Even Tosevites had to wear layer upon layer of wrappings to protect themselves from their own planet's weather. That didn't deter them from gathering in large numbers to buy and sell. Foods of all sorts were on display (no, almost all sorts, for this was a market full of Jews, and so held no pork, which was to Nesseref's way of thinking most regrettable). So were more of the Big Uglies' wrappings. So were pots and pans and plates and the curious implements the Tosevites used to feed themselves.

And so were a good many items obviously manufactured by the Race. Nesseref wondered how they'd got there. She wouldn't have been the least bit surprised to learn it was through no legitimate means. The window in Bunim's office overlooked the market square. She wondered if the regional subadministrator or his subordinates paid any attention to the commerce the Big Uglies were conducting right under their snouts. Then she wondered if the Tosevites quietly paid some of those subordinates—with ginger, say—to turn their eye turrets in a different direction. She wouldn't have been surprised about that, either.

Big Uglies were more voluble than males and females of the Race. They shouted and whined and gesticulated and generally acted as if the world would come to an end if bargains didn't come out exactly the way they wanted them. Their frantic eagerness would have impressed and probably influenced Nesseref. The Tosevites against whom they were dickering, though, were used to such ploys, and took no notice of them—or else they too were shouting and whining and gesticulating.

Someone—a Big Ugly, by the timbre and mushy accent—called her name. She swung an eye turret in the direction from which the sound had struck her hearing diaphragm, and saw a Tosevite approaching, waving as he—she? no, he, by the wrappings and the voice—drew near. A little more slowly than she should have, she recognized him. "I greet you, Mordechai Anielewicz," she said, annoyed he'd seen and known her first.

"I greet you, Shuttlecraft Pilot," the Big Ugly said, extending his right hand in the greeting gesture common among his kind. Nesseref took it. His fingers, though large, felt soft and fleshy against hers. They also felt cool; her body temperature was a couple of hundredths higher than his. Speaking the language of the Race pretty well for one of his kind, he went on, "I hope you are well?"

"Well enough, I thank you, though I do not much care for the cold and damp. I am glad spring is coming," Nesseref replied. She wagged the eye turret with which she was looking at him, as she might have done to commiserate with one of her own kind. "I have heard from the regional subadministrator that you are having a difficult time of it."

"Why, no, the pains are no worse than—" Anielewicz caught himself. "Oh. You must mean the male with the gun. He missed me. He has not returned since. I do not worry about him . . . too much." His hand dropped to the butt of the pistol he wore on his hip.

"Who would wish to kill you?" Nesseref asked.

The Big Ugly's mouth twisted in the gesture Nesseref had come to associate with amusement, though she didn't understand why the circumstances should amuse him. "Who?" he said. "The Deutsche, the Poles, the Russkis, perhaps, and perhaps also the regional subadministrator."

"Bunim?" Nesseref made the negative hand gesture. "Impossible! The Race does not do such things. Besides, he would have mentioned it to me. He spoke of its happening through some agency other than his own."

"He would not admit to it," Anielewicz said. "Even if he arranged to have it done, he would not admit it, not to anyone who did not have to know of it."

"Why not?" Again, Nesseref was puzzled.

Again, the Tosevite smiled. Again, the shuttlecraft pilot could not see any reason to show amusement. As if speaking to a hatchling barely old enough to understand words, Mordechai

Anielewicz replied, "Because if he arranged to have it done, and if I found out he had arranged it, I would probably try to kill him in retaliation, and he knows it."

He spoke, as far as Nesseref could judge, quite calmly. She reckoned him her friend, as far as she could across the lines of species. But he'd just shown her how alien he was. Her shiver had nothing to do with the chilly weather.

Mordechai Anielewicz could tell he'd horrified Nesseref. He didn't think Bunim had tried to assassinate him. Had Bunim done so, he wasn't sure he would try to take revenge by killing the regional subadministrator. Murdering a prominent Lizard was the best way he could think of to land the Jews of Poland in serious trouble. Of course, if what he said got back to Bunim, it might keep the regional subadministrator from coming up with any bright ideas. He hoped it would.

"And how is your explosive-metal bomb?" Nesseref asked him casually.

Not for the first time, he wished he'd never mentioned the bomb to her. And now, instead of displaying his amusement, he had to hide it. The shuttlecraft pilot was trying to get information out of him the same way he was trying to give it to her. He answered, "It is very well, thank you. And how is yours?"

"I have none, as you know perfectly well," Nesseref said. "All I have to worry about is a great deal of liquid hydrogen."

Back before the invasions of first the Nazis and then the Lizards forced him into war and politics, Anielewicz had studied engineering. He whistled respectfully; he knew a little something about the kinds of problems he might be facing. And, of course, when he thought of hydrogen, he thought of the *Hindenburg*; the newsreel footage was still vivid in his mind after more than a quarter of a century. The Lizards were a lot more careful than the Germans ever dreamt of being—the Lizards were, in a word, inhumanly careful—but still. . . .

"How do you make that noise?" Nesseref asked. "I have heard other Tosevites do it, but I cannot see how."

"What, whistling?" Mordechai asked. The key word came out in Yiddish; if it existed in the Lizards' language, he didn't know it. He whistled a few bars. Nesseref made the affirmative hand gesture. He said, "You shape your lips this way. . . ." He started to pucker, then stopped. "Oh."

Once examined, the problem was simple. Nesseref couldn't pucker. Her face didn't work that way. She didn't even really have lips, only hard edges to her mouth. She could no more whistle than Anielewicz could perfectly produce all the hisses and pops and sneezing noises that went into her language. She realized that at about the same time he did, and let her mouth fall open in a laugh. "I see now," she said. "It is impossible for one of my kind."

"I fear that is truth," Anielewicz agreed. "I also fear I must shop now, or my wife"—another Yiddish word, another concept missing from the language of the Race—"will be very unhappy with me." He used an emphatic cough to show just how unhappy Bertha would be.

"Farewell, then," Nesseref told him. "I return to my new town. Perhaps you will visit me there one day."

"I thank you. I would like that." Mordechai meant it. Regardless of what they thought of the weather, lots of Lizards were colonizing Poland. He was very curious about how they lived.

But, as Nesseref went about her business, Anielewicz realized he had to go about his. Bertha would indeed be unhappy if he came home without the things she'd sent him to buy. Cabbage was easy. Several vendors were selling it; he had only to choose the one with the best price. Potatoes didn't prove any great problem, either. And he got a deal on onions that would make his wife smile.

Eggs, now . . . He'd expected eggs to be the hard part of the shopping, and they were. You could always count on plenty of people having vegetables for sale. Ever since the Nazis had been driven out of Poland, there had been enough vegetables to go around. And vegetables, or a lot of them, stayed good for weeks or months at a time.

None of that held true for eggs. You never could tell how many would be on sale when you went to the market square, or what sort of prices the vendors would demand. Today, only a couple of peasant grandmothers, scarves around their heads against the winter cold, displayed baskets of eggs.

Radiating charm, Anielewicz went up to one of them. "Hello, there," he said cheerfully. He spoke Polish as readily as Yiddish, as did most Jews hereabouts. Unlike a lot of them, he also looked more Polish than Jewish, having a broad face, fair skin, and light brown, almost blond, hair. Sometimes his looks helped him when he was dealing with Poles.

Not today. The old lady with the eggs looked him up and down as if he'd just crawled out of the gutter. "Hello, Jew," she said flatly.

Well, few *goyim* came to buy at the Bialut Market Square. During the Nazi occupation, it had been the chief market of the Lodz ghetto. The ghetto was gone, but this remained the Jewish part of town. Mordechai gathered himself. If she was going to play tough, he could do the same. Pointing to the eggs, he said, "How much for half a dozen of those sad little things?"

"Two zlotys apiece," the Polish woman said, sounding as calm and self-assured as if that weren't highway robbery.

"What?" Anielewicz yelped. "That's not selling. That's stealing, is what it is."

"You don't want them, you don't have to pay," the woman answered. "Ewa over there, she's charging two and a half, but she says hers are bigger eggs. You go on over and see if you can find any difference."

"It's still stealing," Mordechai said, and it was—even two zlotys was close to twice the going rate.

"Feed's gone up," the Polish woman said with a shrug. "If you think I'm going to sell at a loss, you're *meshuggeh*." Where he stuck to Polish, she threw in a Yiddish word with malice aforethought. A moment later, she slyly added, "And I know you Jews aren't crazy that way."

"What are you feeding your miserable chickens, anyhow? Caviar and champagne?" Anielewicz shot back. "Bread's up a couple of groschen, but not that much. *I* think you're out for some quick profit."

Her eyes might have been cut from gray ice. "I think if you don't want my eggs, you can go away and let someone who does want them have a look."

Dammit, he did want the eggs. He just didn't want to pay so much for them. Bertha would pitch a fit; then she'd make disparaging noises about the uselessness of sending a mere man to the market square. Mordechai was, or thought he was, a competent shopper in his own right. "I'll give you nine zlotys for half a dozen," he said.

For a bad moment, he thought the egg seller wouldn't even deign to haggle with him. But she did. He ended up buying the eggs for ten zlotys forty groschen, and won the privilege of picking them himself. It wasn't a victory—he couldn't pretend it was, no matter how hard he tried—but it was something less than a crushing defeat.

Weighed down by groceries, he started south on Zgierska Street, then turned right onto Lutomierska; his flat wasn't far from the fire station on that street. The backs of his legs pained him as he walked. His arms felt as if he were carrying sacks of lead, not vegetables and eggs.

Scowling, he kept on. He'd never been quite right after inhaling German nerve gas half a lifetime before. At that, he'd got off lucky. Ludmila Jäger—Ludmila Gorbunova, she'd been then—was far more crippled than he, while the gas had helped bring Heinrich Jäger to an early grave. Anielewicz found that dreadfully unfair; were it not for the German panzer colonel, an explosive-metal bomb would have blown Lodz off the face of the earth, and probably would have blown up the then-fragile truce between humans and Lizards.

Anielewicz's younger son was named Heinrich. There was a stretch of several years when he would either have laughed or reached for a rifle had anyone suggested he might name a child after a *Wehrmacht* officer.

Panting, he fought his way up the stairs to his flat. He paused in the hall to catch his breath, gathering himself so Bertha wouldn't worry, before he went inside. He also paused to examine the new door; after the would-be assassin put a submachine-gun magazine through the old one, it had become too thoroughly ventilated to be worth much. The flat also had new windows.

When he did go inside, the look on his wife's face said he hadn't paused long enough. "It must be bothering you today," Bertha Anielewicz said.

"Not too bad," Mordechai insisted. If she believed it, maybe he would, too. "And I did pretty well at the market." That won a smile from his wife. She wasn't pretty in any conventional sense of the word, but she turned beautiful when a smile lit up her face. Then, of course, she wanted details.

When he gave them to her, the smile disappeared. He'd known it would. "That's robbery!" she exclaimed.

"I know," he said. "It would have been worse robbery if I hadn't haggled hard. We did need the eggs."

"We needed the money, too," Bertha said mournfully. Then she shrugged. "Well, it's done, and the eggs do look good." Her smile returned. He smiled back, knowing full well she was letting him down easy.

Vyacheslav Molotov was not happy with the budget projections for the upcoming Five Year Plan. Unfortunately, the parts about which he was least happy had to do with the money allocated for the Red Army. Since Marshal Zhukov had rescued him from NKVD headquarters after Lavrenti Beria's coup failed, he couldn't wield a red pencil so vigorously as he would have liked. He couldn't wield one at all, in fact. If he made Zhukov unhappy with him, a Red Army–led coup would surely succeed.

Behind the expressionless mask of his face, he was scowling. After Zhukov got all the funds he wanted, the Red Army would in essence be running the Soviet State with or without a coup. Were Zhukov a little less deferential to Party authority, that would be obvious already.

The intercom buzzed. Molotov answered it with a sense of relief, though he showed no more of that than of his inner scowl. "Yes?" he asked.

"Comrade General Secretary, David Nussboym is here for his appointment," his secretary answered.

Molotov glanced at the clock on the wall of his Kremlin office. It was precisely ten o'clock. Few Russians would have been so punctual, but the NKVD man had been born and raised in Poland. "Send him in, Pyotr Maksimovich," Molotov said. Dealing with Nussboym would mean he didn't have to deal with—or not deal with—the budget for a while. Putting things off didn't make them better. Molotov knew that. But nothing he dared do to the Five Year Plan budget would make it better, either.

In came David Nussboym: a skinny, nondescript, middle-aged Jew. "Good day, Comrade General Secretary," he said in Polish-flavored Russian, every word accented on the next-to-last syllable whether the stress belonged there or not.

"Good day, David Aronovich," Molotov answered. "Take a seat; help yourself to tea from the samovar if you care to."

"No, thank you." Along with Western punctuality, Nussboym had a good deal of Western briskness. "I regret to report, Comrade General Secretary, that our attempt against Mordechai Anielewicz did not succeed."

"Your attempt, you mean," Molotov said. David Nussboym had got him out of his cell in the NKVD prison. Otherwise, Beria's henchmen might have shot him before Marshal Zhukov's troops overpowered them. Molotov recognized the debt, and had acquiesced in Nussboym's pursuit of revenge against the Polish Jews who'd sent him to the USSR. But there were limits. Molotov made them plain: "You were warned not to place the Soviet government in an embarrassing position, even if you are permitted to use its resources."

"I did not, and I do not intend to," Nussboym said. "But, with your generous permission, I do intend to continue my efforts."

"Yes, go ahead," Molotov said. "I would not mind seeing Poland destabilized in a way that forces the Lizards to pay attention to it. It is a very useful buffer between us and the fascists farther west." He wagged a finger at the Jew, a show of considerable emotion for him. "Under no circumstances, however, is Poland to be destabilized in a way that lets the Nazis intervene there."

"I understand that," David Nussboym assured him. "Believe me, it is not a fate I'd wish on my worst enemies—and some of those people are."

"See that you don't inflict it on them," Molotov said, wagging that finger again: Poland genuinely concerned him. "If things go wrong, that is one of the places that can flash into nuclear war in the blink of an eye. It can—but it had better not. No debt of gratitude will excuse you there, David Aronovich."

Nussboym's features were almost as impassive as Molotov's. The Jew had probably learned in the gulag not to show what was on his mind. He'd spent several years there before being recruited to the NKVD. After a single tight, controlled nod, he said, "I won't fail you."

Having got the warning across, Molotov changed the subject: "And how do you find the NKVD these days?"

"Morale is still very low, Comrade General Secretary," Nussboym answered. "No one can guess whether he will be purged next. Everyone is fearful lest colleagues prepare denunciations against him. Everyone, frankly, shivers to think that his neighbor might report him to the GRU."

"This is what an agency earns for attempting treason against the workers and peasants of the Soviet Union," Molotov said harshly. Even so, he was disquieted. He did not want the GRU, the Red Army's intelligence arm, riding roughshod over the NKVD. He wanted the two spying services competing against each other so the Party could use their rivalry to its own advantage. That, however, was not what Georgi Zhukov wanted, and Zhukov, at the moment, held the whip hand.

"Thank you for letting me continue, Vyacheslav Mikhailovich." Nussboym got to his feet. "I won't take up any more of your time." He used another sharp nod, then left Molotov's office. Molotov almost wished he'd stayed longer. Anything seemed preferable to returning to the Five Year Plan.

But then the intercom buzzed again, and Molotov's secretary said, "Comrade General Secretary, your next appointment is here: the ambassador from the Race, along with his interpreter."

Next to confronting an irritable Lizard—and Queek was often irritable—the Five Year Plan budget suddenly looked alluring. *Bozhemoi!* Molotov thought. *No rest for the weary.* Still, his secretary never heard the tiny sigh that fought its way past his lips. "Very well, Pyotr Maksimovich," he answered. "I will meet them in the other office, as usual."

The other office was identical to the one in which he did most of his work, but reserved for meetings with the Race. After he left it, he would change his clothes, down to his underwear. The Lizards were very good at planting tiny electronic eavesdropping devices. He did not want to spread those devices and let them listen to everything that went on inside the Kremlin: thus the meeting chamber that could be quarantined.

He went in and waited for his secretary to escort the Lizard and his human stooge into the room. Queek skittered in and sat down without asking leave. So did the interpreter, a stolid, broad-faced man. After the ambassador spoke—a series of hisses and pops—the interpreter said, "His Excellency conveys the usual polite greetings." The fellow had a rhythmic Polish accent much like David Nussboym's.

"Tell him I greet him and hope he is well," Molotov replied, and the Pole popped and hissed to the male of the Race. In fact, Molotov hoped Queek and all his kind (except possibly the Lizards in Poland, who shielded the Soviet Union from the Greater German *Reich*) would fall over dead. But hypocrisy had always been an essential part of diplomacy, even among humans. "Ask him the reason for which he has sought this meeting."

He thought he knew, but the question was part of the game. Queek made another series, a longer one, of unpleasant noises. The interpreter said, "He comes to issue a strong protest concerning Russian assistance to the bandits and rebels in the part of the main continental mass known as China."

"I deny giving any such assistance," Molotov said blandly. He'd been denying it for as long as the Lizards occupied China, first as Stalin's foreign commissar and then on his own behalf. That didn't mean it wasn't true—only that the Race had never quite managed to prove it.

Now Queek pointed a clawed forefinger at him. "No more evasions," he said through the interpreter, who looked to enjoy twitting the head of the USSR. "No more lies. Too many weapons of your manufacture are being captured from those in rebellion against the rule of the Race. China is ours. You have no business meddling there."

Had Molotov been given to display rather than concealment, he would have laughed. He would, in fact, have chortled. What he said was, "Do you take us for fools? Would we send Soviet arms to China, betraying ourselves? If we aided the Chinese people in their struggle against the imperialism of the Race, we would aid them with German or American weapons, to keep from being blamed. Whoever gives them Soviet weapons seeks to get us in trouble for things we haven't done."

"Is that so?" Queek said, and Molotov nodded, his face as much a mask as ever. But then, to his surprise and dismay, Queek continued, "We are also capturing a good many American weapons. Do you admit, then, that you have provided these to the rebels, in violation of agreements stating that the subregion known as China rightfully belongs to the Race?"

Damnation, Molotov thought. *So the Americans did succeed in getting a shipload of arms through to the People's Liberation Army.* Mao hadn't told him that before launching the uprising. But then, Mao had given even Stalin headaches. The interpreter grinned offensively. Yes, he enjoyed making Molotov sweat, imperialist lackey and running dog that he was.

But Molotov was made of stern stuff. "I admit nothing," he said stonily. "I have no reason to admit anything. The Soviet Union has firmly adhered to the terms of all agreements into which it has entered." *And you cannot prove otherwise . . . I hope.*

For a bad moment, he wondered if Queek would pull out photographs showing caravans of weapons crossing the long, porous border between the USSR and China. The Lizards' satellite reconnaissance was far ahead of anything the independent human powers could do. But the ambassador only made noises like a samovar with the flame under it turned up too high. "Do not imagine that your effrontery will go unpunished," Queek said. "After we have put down the Chinese rebels once and for all, we will take a long, hard look at your role in this affair."

That threat left Molotov unmoved. The Japanese hadn't been able to put down Chinese rebels, either Communists or Nationalists, and the Lizards were having no easy time of it, either. They could hold the cities—except when rebellion burned hot, as it did now—and the roads between them, but lacked the soldiers to subdue the countryside, which was vast and heavily populated. Guerrillas were able to move about at will, almost under their snouts.

"Do not imagine that your colonialism will go unpunished," Molotov answered. "The logic of the historical dialectic proves your empire, like all others based on the oppression of workers and peasants, will end up lying on the ash heap of history."

Marxist terminology did not translate well into the language of the Race. Molotov had seen that before, and enjoyed watching the interpreter have trouble. He waited for Queek to explode, as Lizards commonly did when he brought up the dialectic and its lessons. But Queek said only, "You think so, do you?"

"Yes," Molotov answered, on the whole sincerely. "The triumph of progressive mankind is inevitable."

Then Queek startled him by saying, "Comrade General Secretary, it is possible that what you tell me is truth." The Lizard startled his interpreter, too; the Pole turned toward him with surprise on his face, plainly wondering whether he'd really heard what he thought he had. With a gesture that looked impatient, the Lizard ambassador continued, "It is possible—in fact, it is likely—that, if it is truth, you will regret its being truth."

Careful, Molotov thought. *He is telling me something new and important here.* Aloud, he said, "Please explain what you mean."

"It shall be done," Queek said, a phrase Molotov understood before the interpreter translated it. "At present, you Tosevites are a nuisance and a menace to the Race only here on Tosev 3. Yet your technology is advancing rapidly—witness the Americans' *Lewis and Clark.* If it should appear to us that you may become a risk to the Race throughout the Empire, what is our logical course under those circumstances?"

Vyacheslav Molotov started to lick his lips. He stopped, of course, but his beginning the gesture told how shaken he was. Now he hoped he hadn't heard what he thought he had. Countering one question with another, he asked, "What do you believe your logical course would be?"

Queek spelled it out: "One option under serious consideration is the complete destruction of all independent Tosevite not-empires."

"You know this would result in the immediate destruction of your own colonies here on Earth," Molotov said. "If you attack us, we shall assuredly take vengeance—not only the peace-loving peasants and workers of the Soviet Union, but also the United States and the *Reich.* You need have no doubts about the *Reich.*" For once, he was able to use the Germans' ferocity to his advantage.

Or so he thought, till Queek replied, "I understand this, yes, but sometimes a mangled limb must be amputated to preserve the body of which it is only one part."

"This bluff will not intimidate us," Molotov said. But the Lizards, as he knew only too well, were not nearly so likely to bluff as were their human opposite numbers.

Again, their ambassador echoed his unhappy thoughts, saying, "If you think of this as a bluff, you will be making a serious mistake. It is a warning. You and your Tosevite counterparts—who are also receiving it—had better take it as such."

"I shall be the one who decides how to take it," Molotov replied. He concealed his fear. For him, that was easy. Making it go away was something else again.

☆ 3 ☆

Up until now, the only time since the Japanese overran her village just before the little scaly devils came that Liu Han had lived in a liberated city was during her visit with her daughter to the United States. Now . . . Now, in exultation, she turned to Liu Mei and said, "Peking remains free!"

"I never thought we would be able to drive out the scaly devils' garrison." Liu Mei's eyes glowed, though the rest of her long face remained almost expressionless. The scaly devils had taken her from Liu Han just after she was born, and for more than a year set about raising her as if she were one of theirs. They had not smiled—they could not smile—back at her when she began to smile as a baby. Without response, her ability to smile had withered on the stalk. That was one reason, and not the least of reasons, Liu Han hated the little scaly devils.

"Shanghai is still free, too," Liu Han went on. "So is Kaifeng."

"They are still free of the little devils, yes, but they aren't in the hands of the People's Liberation Army, the way Peking is," Liu Mei said. Her revolutionary fervor burned hotter than her mother's. "We share them with Kuomintang reactionaries, the way we share Harbin and Mukden up in Manchuria with pro-Japanese reactionaries. But Peking is *ours*."

"Next to the little scaly devils, the fighters from the Kuomintang aren't reactionaries. They're fellow travelers," Liu Han answered. "Next to the scaly devils, even the jackals who want to turn Manchuria back into Manchukuo and make it a Japanese puppet again are fellow travelers. If we don't have a common front together against the little devils, we are bound to lose this struggle."

"The logic of the dialectic will destroy them in their turn," Liu Mei said confidently.

Liu Han was confident that would happen, too, but not so confident about when. Had she replied just then, Liu Mei wouldn't have been able to hear her; killercraft piloted by scaly devils screamed low above their rooming house in the western part of Peking's Chinese City. Cannons roared. Bombs burst close by with harsh roars—*crump! crump!* Window frames rattled. The floor beneath Liu Han's feet quivered, as if at an earthquake.

Down on the ground, machine guns rattled and barked as the men—and a few women—of the People's Liberation Army tried to bring down the scaly devils' airplanes. By the way the jet engines of the killercraft faded in the distance, Liu Han knew the machine guns had failed again.

Her mouth twisted in vexation. "We need more antiaircraft weapons," she said. "We need better antiaircraft weapons, too."

"We only got a few guided antiaircraft rockets from the Americans, and we've used most of those," Liu Mei answered. "With the fighting the way it is, how can they send us any more?"

"I would take them from anyone, even the Japanese," Liu Han said. "We need them. Without them, the little scaly devils can pound us and pound us from the sky, and we can't hit back. I wish we had more mortars, too, and more mines we could use against their tanks." *While you're at it, why not wish for the moon?* she thought—not a Chinese phrase, but one she'd picked up in Los Angeles.

Before Liu Mei could answer, a new cry pierced the shouts and screams that mingled with the gunfire outside. The cry was raw and urgent and came from the throats of both men and women: "Fire!"

Liu Han rushed to the window of the room she shared with her daughter. Sure enough, a column of black smoke rose from a building only a block or so away. Flames leapt up, red and angry. Turning to Liu Mei, she said, "We'd better go downstairs. That's a big fire, and it will spread fast. We don't want to get stuck in here."

Liu Mei didn't waste time answering. She just hurried for the door. Liu Han followed. They went down the dark, rickety stairs together. Other people in the rooming house, some of them also prominent Communists, were scurrying to the ground floor, too.

When Liu Han got down there, she ran out into the *hutung*—the cramped alleyway—onto which the rooming house opened. Peking was a city of *hutung*s; between its broad thoroughfares, alleys ran every which way, packed with shops and eateries and shacks and rooming houses and taverns and everything else under the sun. *Hutung*s were commonly packed with people, too; in a country as crowded as China, Liu Han hadn't particularly noticed that till she went to the USA—before then, she'd taken it for granted. Now, every so often, she didn't.

This *hutung*, at the moment, was so packed, people had a hard time running. The wind—as usual, from out of the northwest, from the Mongolian desert—blew smoke through the alley in a choking cloud. Eyes streaming, Liu Han reached out for Liu Mei's hand. By what was literally blind luck, she seized it. If she hadn't, they would have been swept apart, two different ships adrift on the Hwang Ho River. As things were, they drifted together.

"No one will be able to get through to fight the fire." Liu Mei had to scream to make herself heard in the din, though her mother's ear was only a couple of feet from her mouth.

"I know," Liu Han said. "It will burn till it stops, that's all." Peking had seen a lot of fires since the uprising against the little scaly devils began. A lot of them had ended that way, too. Fire trucks were all very well for blazes on the larger streets, but hadn't a prayer of pushing their way into the *hutung*s, and bucket brigades weren't much good against the massive fires combat caused. Even a bucket brigade would have had a hard time breasting this tide of fleeing humanity.

More smoke billowed over Liu Han and Liu Mei. They both coughed horribly, like women dying of consumption. Behind them, people shrieked in panic. Above the shrieks came the crackle of flames. "The fire is moving faster than we are," Liu Mei said, fear in her voice if not on her impassive face.

"I know," Liu Han answered grimly. She had a knife in a hidden sheath strapped to her ankle; she didn't go anywhere unarmed these days. If she took it out and started slashing at the people ahead of her, would it clear a path so she and Liu Mei could outrun the flames? The only thing that kept her from doing it was the cold judgment that it wouldn't help.

And then, without warning, the pressure eased. Like melon

seeds squeezed between the fingers, she and Liu Mei popped out onto a wider street, one with cobblestones rather than just dirt. She hadn't even known it was close by, for she couldn't see over the backs of the people ahead. Liu Mei hadn't seen it either, though she was a couple of inches taller than her mother—Bobby Fiore, her American father, had been a big man by Chinese standards.

Now people could move faster. Liu Han and Liu Mei fled the fire, and gained on it. "Gods and spirits be praised," Liu Han gasped, even though, as a good Marxist-Leninist, she wasn't supposed to believe in gods or spirits. "I think we'll get away."

Liu Mei looked back over her shoulder. She could do that now without so much fear of getting trampled after a misstep. "The rooming house must be burning," she said in a stricken voice.

"Yes, I think so," Liu Han said. "We are alive. We will stay alive, and find another place to live. The Party will help us, if we need help. Things are not important. We didn't have many things to lose, anyhow." Having grown up in a peasant village, she needed few things to keep her going.

But tears streamed down Liu Mei's expressionless, soot-streaked (and, yes, rather big-nosed) face. "The photographs we got in the United States," she said in a broken voice. "The photographs of my father and his ancestors."

"Oh," Liu Han said, and put a consoling arm around her daughter. Ancestors mattered in China; filial piety ran deep, even among Party members. Liu Han had never imagined that Liu Mei would be able to learn anything about Bobby Fiore and his family, even after leaving China for the United States. But Yeager, the expert on scaly devils with whom she'd talked, had turned out to be a friend of Fiore's, and had put her and Liu Mei in touch with his family. Everything the Fiores had sent was indeed bound to be going up in flames. Liu Han sighed. "You know what you know. If peace comes back"—she was too honest to say, *When peace comes back*—"we can get in touch with the Americans again."

Liu Mei nodded. "Yes, that's true," she said. "Thank you, Mother. That does make it easier to bear. I thought my family was being all uprooted."

"I understand." No one had tended the graves of Liu Han's ancestors for a long time. She didn't even know if the village near

Hankow had any people left in it these days. How many times had the red-hot rake of war passed through it since the little scaly devils carried her off into captivity?

A roar in the air that might have come from a furious dragon's throat warned her the little devils' airplanes were returning for another attack run. All over Peking, machine guns started shooting into the air even though their targets weren't yet in sight. Before long, those bullets would start falling back to earth. Some would hit people in the head and kill them, too.

All that passed through Liu Han's mind in a couple of seconds. Then the scaly devils' killercraft roared low overhead. One of their pilots must have spied the swarm of people in the street because of the fire, for he cut loose with his cannon. When one of those shells struck home, it tore two or three people into bloody gobbets of flesh that looked as if they belonged in a butcher's shop, then exploded and wounded another half a dozen. In that tight-packed crowd, the little scaly devil had a target he could hardly miss.

The attack itself lasted only a moment. Then the killercraft that had fired was gone, almost as fast as the sound of its passage. The horror lasted longer. Men and women close by Liu Han and Liu Mei were ripped to bits. Their blood splattered the two women. Along with its iron stink, Liu Han smelled the more familiar reek of night soil as shells and their fragments ripped guts open. The wounded, those unlucky enough not to die at once, shrieked and howled and wailed. So did men and women all around them, seeing what they had become.

Liu Han shouted: "Don't scream! Don't run! Help the injured! People must be strong together, or the little scaly devils will surely defeat us."

More because hers was a calm, clear voice than because what she said made sense, people listened and obeyed. She was bandaging a man with a shattered arm when the roar of jet engines and the pounding of machine guns again cut through every other sound. Though she ground her teeth, she kept on working on the injured man. Peking was a vast city. Surely the killercraft would assail some distant part.

But they roared right overhead. Instead of ordinary bombs, they released swarms of little spheres. "Be careful of those!" Liu Han and Liu Mei cried together. Some of the spheres were tiny mines that were hard to see but could blow up a bicycle or a man unlucky enough to go over them. Others . . .

Others started squawking in Chinese: "Surrender! You cannot defeat the scaly devils! Give up while you still live!" Someone stomped one of those to silence it. It exploded, a sharp, flat bark. The woman stared at the bloody stump that had replaced her foot, then toppled screeching to the ground.

"Even if we hold Peking, I wonder if anyone will be left alive inside the walls," Liu Han said glumly.

"That is not a proper revolutionary sentiment," Liu Mei said. Her mother nodded, accepting the criticism. But Liu Han, twice her daughter's age, had seen far too much to be certain proper revolutionary sentiment told all the truth there was to tell.

As Lieutenant Colonel Johannes Drucker stopped his Volkswagen at one of the three traffic lights Greifswald boasted, drizzle began to fall. That was nothing out of the ordinary in the north German town: only a few kilometers from the Baltic, Greifswald knew fog and mist and drizzle and rain with great intimacy. It knew snow and ice, too, but the season for them was past—Drucker hoped so, anyhow.

He pulled the windshield-wiper knob. As the rubber blades began traveling streakily across the glass in front of him, he rolled up the driver's-side window to keep the rain out of the automobile. His wife, Käthe, did the same thing on the passenger's side.

With the two of them in the front, and with Heinrich, Claudia, and Adolf squeezed into the back, the inside of the hydrogen-burning VW's windows began to steam up. Drucker turned on the heater and vented the warm air up to the inside of the windshield. He wasn't sure how much good it did, or if it did any good at all.

The light turned green. "Go, Father," Heinrich said impatiently, even as Drucker put the auto into first gear. Heinrich was sixteen now, and learning to drive. Had he known half as much about the business as he thought he did, he would have known twice as much as he really did.

As the Volkswagen went through the intersection—no more slowly than anyone else—a great roar penetrated the drizzle and the windows. Peenemünde was only about thirty kilometers east of Greifswald. When a rocket went up, everybody in town knew about it.

"Who would that be, Father?" Adolf asked, sounding as excited as any eleven-year-old would have at the prospect of blasting into space.

"It's Joachim's—uh, Major Spitzler's—turn in the rotation," Drucker answered. "Unless he came down with food poisoning"—a euphemism for getting drunk, but Adolf didn't need to know that—"last night, he's heading for orbit right now."

"When do you go up again?" Claudia sounded wistful, not excited. She enjoyed having her father down on the ground.

Drucker enjoyed it, too. But, as he had to be, he was intimately familiar with the duty roster. As the roar from the A-45 slowly faded, he said, "I'm scheduled for next Thursday." Claudia sighed. So did Käthe. He glanced over at his wife. "It won't be so bad."

She sighed again. He prudently kept driving. She knew how much he loved going into space; he knew better than to rhapsodize about it. He even enjoyed weightlessness, which put him in a distinct minority. And coming back after being away gave him several honeymoons a year. *Abstinence makes the heart grow fonder,* he thought, cheerfully butchering Shakespeare—an American spaceman had taught him the pun, which didn't work in German.

When they got back to their neat, two-story home on the outskirts of Greifswald, the children hurried to the door and went inside. Drucker didn't bother locking it unless everyone was going to be away longer than for an hour's shopping. Greifswald had few thieves. Few people were rash enough to want to risk falling foul of the Ministry of Justice.

"Let's get the packages out of the boot," Käthe said.

"You have to wait for me—I've got the key," Drucker reminded her. He pulled it from the ignition switch and walked up to the front of the car. As he walked, his mouth twisted. He, or rather Käthe, had fallen foul of the Ministry of Justice. They'd found out she had, or might have had, a Jewish grandmother—which, under the racial-purity laws of the *Reich*, made her a Jew, and liable to liquidation.

Because Drucker was a *Wehrmacht* officer, and one with important duties, he'd been able to pull strings. The *Gestapo* had set Käthe free, and given her a clean bill of racial health. But pulling those strings had cost him. He'd never rise above his present rank, not if he served his country till he was ninety. From what the commandant at Peenemünde said, he was lucky he hadn't been thrown out of the service altogether.

He opened the boot. Käthe scooped up the bundles—clothes for the children, who outgrew them or, with the boys, wrecked them faster than he thought they had any business doing. He didn't really want to think about clothes, though. He slipped an arm around his wife's waist. Käthe smiled up at him. He leaned over and planted a quick kiss on her mouth. "Tonight . . ." he murmured.

"What about it?" By the smile in her voice, she knew just what he had in mind, and liked the idea, too.

Before he could answer, the telephone rang inside the house. He let out a snort of laughter. "We don't have to worry about that. It'll be Ilse calling Heinrich or else one of Claudia's school friends. Nobody bothers with old folks like us."

But he was wrong. Claudia came hurrying to the door, pigtails flying. "It's for you, Father—a man."

"Did he say which man he was?" Drucker asked. Claudia shook her head. Drucker scratched his. That eliminated everyone military, and most of his civilian friends, too—though his daughter would have recognized their voices. Still scratching, he said, "All right, I'm coming." He slammed down the Volkswagen's boot lid and went inside.

He'd shed his overcoat by the time he got to the phone; the furnace kept the house toasty warm. Picking up the handset, he spoke briskly: "Johannes Drucker here."

"Hello, Hans, you old son of a bitch," said the voice on the other end of the line. "How the hell are you? Been a goddamn long time, hasn't it?"

"Who is this?" Drucker demanded. Whoever he was, he sounded not only coarse but more than a little drunk. Drucker couldn't place his voice, but couldn't swear he'd never heard it before, either.

Harsh, raucous laughter dinned in his right ear. "That's how it is, all right," the—stranger?—said. "People go up in the world, they forget their old pals. I didn't think it would happen with you, but fuck me if I'm too surprised, either."

"Who *is* this?" Drucker repeated. He was beginning to be sure this fellow was looking for some other Hans. Drucker had given his last name, but how often did drunks bother to listen?

He turned out to be wrong again. The other fellow said, "How many Lizard panzers did we blow to hell and gone in Poland, you driving and me at the gun?"

No wonder the voice seemed as if he might have known it before. "Grillparzer," he said in slow wonder. "Gunther Grillparzer. Christ, man, it's been close to twenty years."

"Too goddamn long," agreed the gunner with whom Drucker had shared a Panther panzer through the most desperate fighting he'd ever known. "Well, we'll make up for lost time, you and me. We're going to be buddies again, damned if we're not. Just like the old days, Hans—except maybe not quite." His laugh was almost a giggle.

Drunk, all right, Drucker thought. "What do you mean?" he asked sharply. When Grillparzer didn't answer right away, he found another, more innocuous, question: "What have you been doing since the fighting stopped?" Käthe was giving him a curious look. "Old army pal," he mouthed, and she nodded and went away.

"What have I been doing?" Grillparzer echoed. "Oh, this and that, old son. Yeah, that's about right—a little of this, a little of that, a little of something else now and again, too."

Drucker sighed. That meant the panzer gunner was a bum or a petty criminal these days. Too bad. "So what can I do for you?" he asked. He owed Grillparzer his neck. He wouldn't begrudge him five hundred or even a thousand marks. He could afford it, and Gunther was plainly down on his luck.

"Like I say, you've come up in the world," the gunner said. "Me, I wasn't so lucky." His voice turned into a self-pitying whine.

"How much do you need?" Drucker asked patiently. "I'm not what you'd call rich—nobody with three kids is likely to be—but I'll do what I can for you."

He'd expected—he'd certainly hoped—Grillparzer would babble in sodden gratitude. That didn't happen, either; it wasn't his day for guessing right. Instead, the ex-gunner said, "Do you remember the night we went after those black-shirted pigdogs with our knives?"

Ice prickled up Drucker's back. "Yes, I remember that," he said. Toward the end of the fighting, the SS had arrested the regimental commander, Colonel Heinrich Jäger, in whose panzer Drucker and Grillparzer had both served. The panzer crew had rescued him before he got taken away from the front, and had bundled him into the airplane of a Red Air Force senior lieutenant—a pretty woman, Drucker recalled—bound for Poland. No one but the panzer crew knew what had happened to those SS men. Drucker wanted to keep it that way. "Don't talk about it on the phone. You never know who might be listening."

"You're right—I don't," Grillparzer agreed with good humor that struck Johannes Drucker as put on. "I might lose my meal ticket if people start hearing things before I want 'em to. Can't have that, can we, Hans?" He laughed out loud.

Drucker was feeling anything but cheerful. "What do you want from me?" he asked, hoping against hope it wasn't what he thought.

But it was. "Whatever you've got, and then another fifty pfennigs besides," Grillparzer answered. "You've lived high on the hog these past twenty years. You're an officer and everything, after all. Now it'll be my turn."

After a look around the living room to make sure nobody in his family could hear, Drucker pressed his mouth against the phone and spoke in a low, urgent voice. "My arse. If you bring me down, I'll sure as hell take you with me. If you don't think I'll sing when they start working me over, you're out of your goddamn mind."

But Gunther Grillparzer laughed again. "Good luck," he said. "You're the first fellow who's called me Gunther in a devil of a long time. Name got too hot for me to keep wearing it. The papers I've got with this one are damn good, too. All I have to do is write the *Gestapo* a letter. I don't even have to sign it—you know how those things go."

That Drucker did, only too well. The *Reich* ran on anonymous accusations. And he was already in a bad odor with the *Gestapo* and with his own higher-ups because of the accusations against Käthe. Regardless of whether there was any truth in Grillparzer's letter, Drucker couldn't stand another investigation. It would mean his neck, and no mistake—and probably his wife's neck, too, after he couldn't protect her any more.

He licked his lips. "How much do you want?" he whispered.

"Now you're talking like a smart boy," Grillparzer said with another nasty chuckle. "I like smart boys. Five thousand for starters. We'll see where it goes from there."

Drucker let out a silent sigh of relief. He could make the first payment. Maybe Grillparzer aimed to bleed him to death a little at a time, not all at once. After that first payment . . . He'd worry about that later. "How do I get you the money?" he asked.

"I'll let you know," the ex-gunner answered.

"I'm going up next week," Drucker warned. "My wife doesn't know anything about this, and I don't want her to. Don't mix her up in this, Grillparzer, or you'll get trouble from me, not cash."

"I'm not afraid of you, Hans old boy," Grillparzer said, but that might not have been altogether true, for he went on, "All right, we'll play that your way—for now. You'll hear from me." He hung up.

Käthe chose that moment to come into the living room. "And how is your old army buddy?" she asked indulgently.

"Fine," Drucker answered, and the lie survived his wife's long and intimate acquaintance with him. He nodded, ever so slightly. Now he had a little stretch of time in which to plan how best to commit a murder.

Ttomalss had been studying the Big Uglies ever since the conquest fleet came to Tosev 3. Sometimes he thought he understood this world's strange inhabitants as well as anyone not hatched among them could. He certainly had that reputation among the Race. He was, after all, the only male who'd ever successfully reared a Tosevite hatchling from its earliest days to the approach of maturity. He was, so far as he knew, the only male addled enough even to try such a mad venture.

But, despite that success, despite endless other research, despite endless study of others' research on the Big Uglies and even their research on themselves, he sometimes thought he didn't understand them at all. He'd had a lot of those moments since coming to the Greater German *Reich*. Now he found himself facing another one.

A Big Ugly named Rascher, who called himself a physician— by Tosevite standards, maybe he was one, but Tosevite standards were low, low—spoke in the tones of calm reason that so often characterized officials of the *Reich* at their most outrageous: "Of course these individuals deserve death, Senior Researcher. They are a weakness in the fabric of the Aryan race, and so must be plucked from it without mercy."

He used the language of the Race. As far as Ttomalss was concerned, that only made the horror underlying his words worse. The researcher said, "I do not understand the logic behind your statement." *I ought to learn that phrase in the language of the Deutsche,* Ttomalss thought. *Spirits of Emperors past know I use it often enough.*

"Is it not obvious?" Dr. Rascher said. "Does the Race not also punish males who mate with other males?"

Ttomalss shrugged; that was a gesture the Race and Tosevites shared. "I have heard of such matings happening among us," he admitted. "During the mating season, we are apt to become rather frantic. But the occurrences are rare and accidental, so what point to making a fuss, let alone punishing the behavior?"

"It is not rare and accidental among us," the Big Ugly said. "Some misguided males deliberately pursue it. They must be rooted out, exterminated, lest they pollute us with this unnatural behavior."

"I do not understand," Ttomalss said again. "If they mate among themselves, they cannot have hatchlings. This in itself eliminates them from your gene pool. Where is the need to root out and exterminate?"

"Mating among males is filthy and degenerate," Dr. Rascher declared. "It corrupts the young in the *Reich.*"

"Even if what you say is true—and I have seen no evidence to that effect—do you not believe the problem to be self-correcting?" Ttomalss asked. "I repeat, these males are unlikely to breed, and so, except for new mutations—assuming this trait to be genetically induced, about which I have seen no evidence either for or against—will in the course of centuries gradually tend to diminish. You Deutsch Tosevites, if you will forgive me for saying so, have always struck the Race as being impatient even for your species."

He had been around Big Uglies long enough to recognize Dr. Rascher's glower for what it was. The Deutsch physician snapped, "And the Race has always struck us Aryans as being in-sanely tolerant. If you are daft enough to put up with degeneracy in your own kind for centuries or millennia on end, that is your affair. If we choose to take direct action in uprooting it, that is ours."

Plainly, Ttomalss wouldn't get anywhere with this line. The Race, to its dismay, had got nowhere in attempting to dissuade the Deutsche from slaughtering the Jews in their not-empire for no other reason than that they *were* Jews. Since they were as determined to slaughter males with different mating habits, they would go on doing that, too. Males . . . That sparked a thought in Ttomalss' mind. "Have you also females who mate with females? If so, what do you do with them?"

"Exterminate them when we catch them, of course," Dr. Rascher replied. "We are consistent. Did you expect anything different?"

"Not really," Ttomalss said with a sigh. Unless he was mistaken, Rascher's face bore an expression of smug self-satisfaction. The researcher hadn't been familiar with that expression in his work in China, but had seen it on a great many Deutsch officials. *They are ideology-mad,* he thought. *Too many Big Uglies are ideology-mad. They are as drunk on their ideologies as they are on their sexuality.*

"You should not have," Dr. Rascher said, and added an emphatic cough. "It is most important for the Aryan race to preserve its purity and to prevent its defilement by such elements as these."

"I have heard you Deutsche use this term 'Aryan' before," Ttomalss said. "Sometimes you seem to use it to refer to yourselves and yourselves alone, but sometimes you seem to use it in a different way. Please define it for me." He knew how important precise definitions were. The Deutsche, all too often, preferred arguing in a circle to precision, though they vehemently denied that was the case.

Dr. Rascher said, "I will define it with great pleasure, taking the definition from the words of our great Leader, Adolf Hitler. Aryans have been and are the race which is the bearer of Tosevite cultural development. It is no accident that the first cultures arose in places where the Aryan, in his encounters with lower races, subjugated them and bent them to his will. As a conqueror, he regulated their practical activity, according to his will and for his aims. As long as he ruthlessly upheld the master attitude, not only did he really remain master, but also the preserver and increaser of culture, which was based on his abilities. When he gives up his purity of blood, he loses his place in the wonderful world which he has made for himself. This is why we so oppose the idea of mingling races."

"You Deutsche see yourselves as Aryans, then, but not all Aryans are necessarily Deutsche—is that correct?" Ttomalss asked.

"It is, although we are the most perfect representatives of the Aryan race anywhere on Tosev 3," Rascher replied.

"Fascinating," Ttomalss said. "Most fascinating indeed. And what is your evidence for these assertions?"

"Why, I told you," Dr. Rascher said. "In his writings, Hitler sets forth the doctrine of the Aryans in great detail."

"Yes, you did tell me that," Ttomalss agreed. "But what was Hitler's evidence? Did he have any? What do Tosevite historians say about these questions? What does archaeology say about them? Why do you accept Hitler's word and not the statements of those who disagree with him, if there are any?"

Behind corrective lenses that magnified them, Dr. Rascher's eyes—they were of a washed-out gray, a very ugly color to Ttomalss—grew larger still, a token of astonishment. "Hitler was the Leader of the *Reich*," the Deutsch physician exclaimed. "But naturally, his writings on any subject are authoritative."

"Why?" Ttomalss asked in genuine puzzlement. "He must have known something about leading, of course, or he would not have led your not empire, but how much did he understand about these other things? How much could he have understood? He spent most of his time leading or getting ready to lead, did he not? What chance did he have to study these other issues in any sort of detail?"

"He was the Leader," Dr. Rascher replied. "He knew the truth *because* he was the Leader." He tacked on another emphatic cough.

Ttomalss and he stared at each other in perfect mutual incomprehension. After a long, long pause, Ttomalss let out another sigh. He'd had a lot of these moments with Big Uglies. Trying to get past this one, he said, "You claim this as revealed belief, then, not as scientific knowledge. You hold it as a superstitious opinion, like the ones expressed in . . . what is the local one here? Ah, Christianity, yes." He was pleased he'd remembered the name.

But Rascher shook his head. "This is scientific truth. Christianity, on the other fork of the tongue, is a belief similar to your veneration of the spirits of Emperors past."

He might know the idioms of the Race's language, but he was an ignorant, barbarous Big Ugly, and did not cast down his eyes when mentioning the Emperors. And he mentioned them in insulting fashion, too. "You have no business speaking of that which you are too foolish to comprehend," Ttomalss snapped. Dr. Rascher laughed a yipping Tosevite laugh, which further infuriated the researcher.

"Neither have you," the Big Ugly retorted.

Now Ttomalss and he stared at each other in perfect mutual loathing. "Whatever the veneration of the spirits of Emperors past may be"—Ttomalss lowered his eye turrets toward the ground; *he* was no ignorant barbarian—"we do not shape the policy of the Empire around it."

Even as he spoke, he realized that wasn't completely true. After its first two planetary conquests, the Race had encouraged Emperor-veneration among the Rabotevs and Hallessi, using it as one means of binding the subject peoples to the Empire. Plans had been developed to do the same here on Tosev 3. So far, however, none of those plans had come to anything.

Dr. Rascher said, "Whether the Race lives according to its principles is of no concern to me. The *Reich*, I am proud to say, does."

"These principles seem to include slaughtering anyone your famous Leader happened to dislike." Ttomalss was too nettled to stay anywhere close to diplomatic. "How fortunate for you that his dislikes did not include doctors."

He'd succeeded in making the Big Ugly as angry as he was. Rascher sprang to his feet and pointed toward the door. "Get out!" he shouted. "Get out, and never show your ugly snouted face outside your embassy again!" He punctuated that with another emphatic cough. "Your kind deserves extermination far more than any Tosevites."

Ttomalss also rose, with more than a little relief: he found the Big Ugly–style chair in which he'd been sitting imperfectly comfortable. "I never thought any intelligent race or subgroup deserved extermination," he said. "You Deutsche, though, tempt me to believe I may have been mistaken."

Having got the last word, he returned to the Race's embassy in something approaching triumph. He was still studying his recorded notes, trying to find anything resembling sense in the *Reich*'s policies, when the telephone circuitry in his computer hissed for attention. On activating the telephone, he found himself looking into Veffani's face. The ambassador said, "I have received a complaint of you from the Deutsche."

"It could be, superior sir," Ttomalss said. "I have a good many complaints against them, too." He summarized his conversation with Dr. Rascher, including the Big Ugly's revolting comments about the veneration of the spirits of Emperors past.

"They *are* revolting," Veffani agreed. "But you have insulted them to such a degree that they insist you leave the *Reich* immediately. By the usages of diplomacy on Tosev 3, they are within their rights to make such a demand."

"It shall be done." Ttomalss did his best to sound as if he were obeying an order he didn't care for. Inside, though, he felt like skittering for joy, mad and carefree as a hatchling.

"I want you to know one thing, Senior Researcher," Veffani said.

"What is that, superior sir?" Ttomalss asked, as he knew he should.

"It is very simple: by the Emperor, how I envy you!"

Kassquit passed Tessrek in a corridor of the orbiting starship where she'd spent almost her entire life. Tessrek, she knew, loathed her for what she was and for what she had so nearly become. But the male was a colleague of Ttomalss, and so Kassquit bent into the best posture of respect she could and said, "I greet you, superior sir."

"I greet you," Tessrek replied, and went on his way without so much as turning an eye turret back in her direction. It was the minimum possible politeness, but Kassquit did not feel insulted. On the contrary: most of what she'd had from Tessrek over the years were insults. He'd given them to Ttomalss, too; he was a thoroughly bad-tempered male. After she'd insulted him in return, though, he'd become a lot more wary—she'd gone from target to possibly dangerous foe.

"That will do," Kassquit murmured as she let herself into her own cubicle. "Let him hate me, so long as he fears me a little, too."

Once inside, she went over to the computer terminal and sat down in front of it. Before she began to use it, she took a set of artificial fingerclaws from a drawer below the keyboard and put them on. She could not use voice commands; as she'd seen time and again, the machine stubbornly refused to understand her.

A glance at her reflection in the computer screen told her why, as if she hadn't known. No way around it: though Ttomalss had raised her as a hatchling and then as a female of the Race, she was a Big Ugly. The computer knew—it couldn't follow the mushy way in which she pronounced the language of the Race. It was the only language she knew, and she couldn't speak it properly. That struck her as most unfair.

She shaved the hair on her head. Since her body matured, she'd shaved the hair under her arms and between her legs, too. Having the stuff at all disgusted her. Getting rid of it didn't make her soft, smooth hide much like the scaly skin a female of the Race should have had. Even her color was wrong: she was golden, not a proper greenish brown.

Her eyes were too small and too narrow and did not lie in moving turrets. She had no proper snout. She had no tailstump, either, and when she stood, she stood far too erect. She'd tried leaning forward all the time like a proper member of the Race, but it made her back hurt. She'd had to give it up.

"I am not a proper member of the Race," she said, rubbing it in. "I am very ugly. But I am civilized. I would rather be what I am—and what I almost am—than a wild Big Ugly down on Tosev 3."

As she turned on the computer and colors filled the screen, she let out a sigh of relief. For one thing, those colors made her own reflection harder to see, which made it easier to imagine she really was a female of the Race. For another, the computer gave her access to the Race's information and opinion network. There, she might as well have been a female of the Race. No one could tell otherwise, not by the way she wrote. Her views were worth as much as anyone else's—sometimes more than someone else's, if she could argue better.

She wondered what males and females of the Race would

think if they knew the person who challenged their views was in fact an overtall, overstraight, soft-skinned, small-eyed Big Ugly. Actually, she didn't wonder. She knew. Whatever respect she'd earned for her brains would vanish, dissolved in the scorn and suspicion the Race felt toward Tosevites.

She felt the same scorn and suspicion toward Tosevites herself. She'd learned it from Ttomalss, who'd raised her since hatchlinghood; from every other male—and, since the coming of the colonization fleet, female—of the Race she'd met in person; and from every bit of video and writing the Race had produced about Tosev 3.

But having it aimed at her hurt almost too much to bear.

She checked for new comments and speculations about which independent Tosevite not-empire had attacked and destroyed more than ten ships from the colonization fleet not long after they took up their orbits around this world. The Race had delivered token punishments to each of the three suspects—the SSSR, the USA, and the *Reich*—because it could not prove which of them had done the murderous deed. That didn't stop males and females from speculating endlessly, but the speculations, as far as Kassquit could see, had reached the point of diminishing returns. And the less the speculators knew, the more strident they were about advancing their ill-informed claims.

With more than a little relief, she escaped that area and went to one nearby: one where the Race discussed the American spacecraft known, for no reason she could fathom, as the *Lewis and Flark*. No. She corrected herself: the *Lewis and Clark*. Changing the name made it no more meaningful to her.

Here, too, discussion had died down. The *Lewis and Clark* had been a mystery when the American Big Uglies were fitting out their former space station to travel through this solar system. They'd done so in such ostentatious secrecy that they'd aroused everyone's suspicion and alarm. Most males and females had feared they were turning it into some immense, and immensely dangerous, orbital fortress.

It had even aroused the Big Uglies' suspicions. Somehow or other, a Tosevite going by the name of Regeya had wormed his way onto the Race's network, to learn what he could of what the Race thought and had learned about the space station. No one had recognized him for what he was till Kassquit did.

I should be proud of that, she thought. *I got him expelled from areas of the network where he had no right to go.*

With a sigh, Kassquit made the negative hand gesture. She was proud ... but then again, she wasn't. The Tosevite who called himself Regeya had had a more interesting way of looking at things and expressing himself than most of the males and females with whose opinions she'd become all too familiar. The network was a duller place without him on it.

It is a more secure place without him on it, Kassquit told herself. That consoled the part of her which devoted itself to duty: a very large part, thanks to Ttomalss' training. But it wasn't all of her. The rest craved fun and amusement. She sometimes wished it wouldn't, but it did.

Some of the curious part of her also wished Regeya remained on the network. Before she'd recognized him as a Big Ugly, he'd come close to doing the same in reverse. She didn't know how; her command of the Race's written language was perfect, which his wasn't quite. But he had. He'd asked to talk to her by telephone. She couldn't do that, not without giving away what she was.

"Fun," she said aloud. "Amusement." She went to a new area on the network, one that offered both of those: the area devoted to discussion of the best ways to nurture hatchlings. The conquest fleet had been all-male; not till the colonization fleet arrived did that area become necessary.

How do you make hatchlings not bite when you feed them? someone—a harassed someone—had written since Kassquit last checked there.

Someone else, evidently a voice of experience, had given a three-word reply to that: *You do not.* The responder had also added the Race's conventional symbol for an emphatic cough.

The next message was a glyph of an open mouth, the conventional symbol for laughter. Kassquit's mouth fell open, too. She laughed like that when she remembered to. Sometimes, though, amusement made her yip the way a Big Ugly was biologically programmed to do.

A few messages further on, someone named Maargyees wrote, *This is my very first clutch of eggs. I wish I had never laid them. Not being able to talk to the hatchlings is driving me out of my scales. What do I do about that?*

Live with it, answered the cynic who'd replied to the earlier message.

We all do, someone else added. *Sooner or later, they turn into civilized beings. We did, you know.*

Maargyees wasn't easily quelled. *Sure seems like later to me,* she wrote.

How is it that you are so ignorant of hatchlings and their ways? a male asked.

Me? Maargyees answered. *I was hatched in a barn myself. I do not know anything. Know? I do not even suspect anything.*

That sent several laughter signs up onto the computer screen. Kassquit added one of her own. Maargyees had a flippant, irreverent way of looking at the world, very different from the endless run of boring comments from most males and females. Kassquit hadn't seen anything like it for quite a while. She hadn't seen anything like it, as a matter of fact, since . . .

She paused with her artificial fingerclaws poised above the keyboard. "Since Regeya," she said aloud. And she knew only too well who, or rather what, Regeya had turned out to be.

Could the obstreperous Big Ugly, having been booted off the network once, have found a new disguise under which to return? Kassquit decided to do a little checking. No messages from anyone named Maargyees appeared anywhere until some time after Regeya had been removed. That didn't prove anything, but it was suggestive. Maargyees sounded more like a name a Rabotev should carry than one belonging to a female of the Race, but that didn't prove anything, either—some members of the Race hatched on Rabotev 2 had local names.

As she had for the falsely named Regeya, Kassquit checked the records. Sure enough, a Maargyees had come with the colonization fleet—a Maargyees with a personal identification number different from the one this female was using.

"Well, well," Kassquit murmured. She knew she ought to report the wild Big Ugly's return to the network, but had trouble bringing herself to do it. Things had been dull since Regeya vanished from the network. And Kassquit had a hard time seeing how asking questions about hatchlings constituted any sort of danger for the Race.

She could always report the Tosevite later. For now, she sent him—him, not her—an electronic message: *I greet you, Maar-gyees. And how is the life of a senior tube technician these days?* That was the fictitious occupation the equally fictitious Regeya had said he used.

If she didn't get an answer, Kassquit vowed she would report that the Tosevite was roaming the network again. But one came back before long: *I greet you, Kassquit. And how is the life of a snoopy nuisance these days?* With the words, he used the symbol suggesting he didn't intend to be taken seriously.

Very well; I thank you, Kassquit answered. *And have you truly laid eggs?*

Oh, yes, Regeya—so she thought of him—answered. *A big square green one and a little purple one with orange spots.*

Kassquit stared at the words on the screen, imagining a Big Ugly producing such a preposterous clutch. She dissolved in Tosevite-style noisy giggles. The picture was too deliciously absurd for anything else. *I like you,* she wrote. *I really do.*

You must, Regeya wrote back. *Why else would you get me in so much trouble?* Kassquit cocked her head to one side. How in the name of the Emperor was she supposed to take *that*?

Straha jumped when the telephone rang. The exiled shiplord laughed at himself as he went to answer it. He'd been living in the United States more than forty years now: more than twenty of Tosev 3's slow turns about its star. After all that time, ringing telephones could still sometimes startle him. By rights, phones were supposed to hiss, as they did back on Home.

He reached for the handset with a small, scornful hiss of his own. Tosevite telephones were good for little more than voice communication: not nearly so sophisticated as the flexible instruments the Race used. *This is what you get—this is part of what you get—for casting your lot with the local primitives,* he thought. But he'd been sure Atvar would give him worse had he stayed. Defying the fleetlord—defying him but not overthrowing him—had a price.

So did exile. He'd paid, again and again. He would go on paying till the day he died—and maybe after that, if the spirits of Emperors past turned their backs on him for his betrayal.

He picked up the telephone. "I greet you," he said in his own language. By now, he spoke and understood English quite well, but his native hisses and pops went a long way toward getting rid of annoying Big Uglies who wanted nothing more than to sell him something.

"I greet you, Shiplord, and hope you are well." That was a Big Ugly speaking, all right, but one whose voice was familiar and welcome in Straha's hearing diaphragm.

"I greet you, Sam Yeager," Straha answered. Yeager might inhabit a Tosevite body, but he was good at thinking like a male of the Race—better than any other Big Ugly Straha knew. "And what would you like today?"

What do you want from me? was really what he meant. As exiles had to do, he'd earned his keep by telling the rulers of his new home everything they wanted to know about his old one. He'd known he would have to do that when he fled the *206th Emperor Yower* in a shuttlecraft. He'd been doing it ever since.

But all Yeager asked was, "How does the Race ever manage to civilize its hatchlings? Far as I can see, predators are welcome to them."

Straha laughed. "We do eventually improve. You Tosevites are liable to be less patient than we are, as your hatchlings develop language faster than ours. In every other way, though, ours are more advanced."

"Shiplord, that is a big exception." The Tosevite used an emphatic cough.

"I suppose so," Straha said indifferently. "As for myself, I never had much interest in trying to civilize hatchlings. I never had much interest in trying to civilize anyone. Maybe that is why I have not had too much difficulty living among you Big Uglies." He used the Race's imperfectly polite name for the Tosevites without self-consciousness; when they were speaking English, Yeager called him a Lizard just as casually.

"You came down in the right not-empire, Shiplord—that is what it is," Yeager said. "Suppose you had landed in the Soviet Union. Whatever sort of time you are having here, it would be worse there."

"So I am given to understand," Straha answered. "At the time, it was a matter of luck: I had a friend stationed in this not-empire, which gave me a plausible excuse for coming here, so I instructed Vesstil to bring me down not far from that other male's ship. Had he been in the SSSR, I would have gone where he was."

By everything he'd learned since, he would indeed have regretted that. The Russkis seemed interested in nothing but squeezing males dry and then discarding them. The Americans had squeezed him dry, but they'd rewarded him, too, as best they could. He had this house in the section of Los Angeles called the Valley, he had a motorcar and a Tosevite driver (who was also bodyguard and spy) at his disposal, and he had the society—such as it was—of other males of the Race living in this relatively decent climate. They weren't exiles, but former prisoners of war who'd decided they liked living among the Big Uglies. They could, if they chose, travel to areas of Tosev 3 where the Race ruled. Straha couldn't, not while Atvar remained fleetlord.

And he had ginger. The Americans made sure he had all he wanted. Why not? It was legal here. The local Big Uglies wanted him happy, and ginger made him that way—until he crashed down into depression, even into despair, as the effects of each taste wore off.

Thinking about tasting made him want to do it. It also made him miss a few words of what Yeager was saying: "—do not guess you are the right male to come to for advice about the little creatures, then."

"No, I fear not," Straha said. "Why are you suddenly interested in them, anyhow? As I said, I am not so very interested in them myself."

"I am always curious about the Race and its ways," the Tosevite replied, an answer that was not an answer. "You may find out more than that one of these days, but the time is not right yet. I hope you will excuse me now, but I have other calls to make. Goodbye, Shiplord."

"Farewell, Sam Yeager." Straha swiveled an eye turret in perplexity. Why was Yeager asking questions about hatchlings? The only time Straha had thought about them since coming to Tosev 3 was after he'd mated with a female who'd tasted ginger at a former prisoner's home: he'd wondered if his genes would go on in the society the Race was building here on Tosev 3, even though he couldn't.

Well, if Yeager had got an itch under his scales, that was his problem, not Straha's. Big Uglies had more curiosity than they knew what to do with. What Straha had was a yen for ginger.

The house in which he lived was built to Tosevite scale, which meant it was large for a male of the Race. He kept his supply of the powdered herb at the back of a high cupboard shelf. If he didn't want a taste badly enough to go to the trouble of climbing up onto a chair and then onto a counter to get the jar, then he would do without.

He was perfectly willing to go clambering today. A breathy sigh of anticipation escaped him as he got down and set the jar on the counter. He took a small measuring spoon out of a kitchen drawer, then undid the lid to the jar. He sighed again when the ginger's marvelously spicy aroma floated up to his scent receptors. One hand trembled a little as he took a spoonful of the herb from the jar and poured it into the palm of his other hand.

Of itself, his head bent. His tongue shot out and lapped up the ginger. Even the flavor was wonderful, though it was the least part of why he tasted. Almost before he knew it, the herb was gone.

And, almost before he knew it, the ginger went straight to his head. Like that of mating, its pleasure never faded. He felt twice as tall as a Big Ugly, full of more data than the Race's computer network, able to outpull a landcruiser. All that (or almost all of it—he really did think, or thought he thought, faster with the herb than without it) was a ginger-induced illusion. That made it no less enjoyable.

Experience had taught him not to try to do too much while he was tasting. He really wasn't infinitely wise and infinitely strong, no matter what the herb told him. During the fighting, a lot of males had got themselves and their comrades killed, for ginger made them think they could do more than they really could.

Straha simply stood where he was, eyeing the ginger jar. Before long, the herb would leave his system. Then he would feel as weak and puny and miserable as he felt wonderful now. And then, without a doubt, he would have another taste.

He was still feeling happy when the telephone rang again. He picked it up and, speaking as grandly as if he were still the third most senior male in the conquest fleet rather than a disgraced exile, he said, "I greet you."

"And I greet you, Shiplord."

This time, the telephone wire brought Straha the crisp tones of a male of the Race. "Hello, Ristin," he said, grandly still. "What can I do for you?"

Ristin had been one of the first infantrymales captured by the Americans. These days, he might almost have been a Big Ugly himself, so completely had he taken on Tosevite ways. He said, "No, Shiplord, it is what I can do for you."

"Ah? And what is that?" Straha asked. He did not altogether like or particularly trust Ristin. While he himself lived among the Big Uglies, he had not abandoned the ways of the Race: he still kept his body paint perfect, for instance, and often startled males and females who saw him without realizing for a moment which shiplord he was. Ristin, by contrast, wore and wore proudly the red, white, and blue prisoner-of-war body paint the Big Uglies had given him in Hot Springs, Arkansas. His housemate Ullhass was the same way. Straha found them in large measure unfathomable.

But then Ristin said, "Shiplord, I can get you several prime ssefenji cutlets. Are you interested?"

"I am. I cannot deny it, and I thank you," Straha said. "I had heard that the colonization fleet was beginning to bring down domestic animals, but I did not know the meat was available yet. Ssefenji!" He let out a soft exclamation redolent of longing. "I have not tasted ssefenji since before we left Home."

"Neither had I," Ristin answered. "It is as good—well, very nearly as good—as I remembered, too. I have some in the freezer. I will bring it to you today or perhaps tomorrow. May you eat it with enjoyment. And may you eat it with Greek olives—they go with it very well."

"I shall do that. I have some in the house," Straha said.

"I thought you would," Ristin said.

Straha made the affirmative hand gesture, though the other male couldn't see that, not over a primitive, screenless Tosevite telephone. Males—and females—of the Race found a lot of the food Big Uglies ate on the bland side. Ham, salted nuts, and Greek olives were welcome exceptions. Straha said, "So there are herds of ssefenji roaming Tosev 3 now, eh? And azwaca and zisuili, too, I should not wonder."

"I believe so, Shiplord, though I have not been able to get any of their flesh yet," Ristin answered.

"Perhaps I can manage that," Straha said. His connections within the American army and the American government ought to be able to arrange it. "If I can do it, of course I shall make you a return gift."

"You are gracious, Shiplord," Ristin said, for all the world as if Straha were still his superior.

"Ssefenji," Straha said dreamily. The ginger was wearing off now, but he didn't feel so depressed as he would have otherwise. "Azwaca. Zisuili. Good eating." The herb still sped his wits to some degree, for he went on, "And not only good eating, but also a sign that we are beginning to make this planet more Homelike. High time we had our own beasts here."

"Truth. And my tongue quivers at the thought of fried azwaca." Ristin sounded dreamy, too.

In musing tones, Straha said, "I wonder how our animals and the local ecology will interact with each other. That is always the question in introducing new life-forms to a world. The results of the competition should be interesting."

"Our beasts and plants prevailed on Rabotev 2 and Halless 1," Ristin said. "No doubt it will be the same here."

"You are likely to be right." Perhaps it was the onset of after-tasting depression that made Straha add, "But this is Tosev 3. You never can tell."

Jonathan Yeager's alarm clock woke him at twenty minutes before six. He sat up in bed and rubbed his eyes. He hated getting up so early, but he had an eight o'clock class in the language of the Race at UCLA and chores to do before then. With a grunt, he got out of bed, turned on the ceiling light, and put on a pair of tight-fitting blue jeans and an even tighter-fitting flesh-colored T-shirt adorned with a fleetlord's body paint.

He'd showered just before he went to bed, so he ran a hand over his scalp and his chin. His face needed shaving; his scalp didn't. That saved him a little time in the bathroom.

He went out to the kitchen as quietly as he could. His parents—lucky them!—were still asleep. He poured himself a big glass of milk and cut a slab off the coffee cake in the refrigerator. Inhaling breakfast was a matter of moments. He ate like a shark and never gained any weight. Over the years, the things his father said about that had grown increasingly rude.

That thought made Jonathan laugh. His old man was an old man, all right, even if he did know a hell of a lot about the Lizards. Jonathan washed his glass, his plate, and the silverware he'd used and set everything in the dish drainer by the sink. The hard time his mom would have given him if he'd left the stuff for her made that more trouble than it was worth.

Then he muttered to himself. He was going to have to get another knife dirty. He got a cooked ham out of the refrigerator, cut off a couple of thick slices, and cut them into inch-wide strips. He put those strips on a paper towel, took a pair of leather gloves from a drawer and put them on, and went down the hall to the room in which the baby Lizards lived.

Before he opened the door to that room, he shut the door at the end of the hall. Every so often, the Lizards didn't feel like eating—instead, they would run past him and try to get away. They were much easier to catch in the hall than when they got into places where they could skitter under or behind furniture.

Jonathan sighed. "Mom and Dad never had to do *this* when I was little," he muttered as he opened the door to the Lizards' room and flipped on the light. Now, closing the door behind him, he spoke aloud: "Come on, Mickey. Wake up, Donald. Rise and shine."

Both baby Lizards were holed up in a corner, behind a chair that had been ragged before they hatched and that their sharp little claws had torn up further. They often slept back there; it wasn't quite a hole in the ground or a cave, but it came pretty close.

They came out at the light and the sound of Jonathan's voice. Donald was a bit bigger and a bit more rambunctious than Mickey; he (if he was a he; the Yeagers didn't know for sure) was also a little darker. He and his brother—sister?—both made excited hissing and popping noises when they saw the ham strips Jonathan was carrying.

He squatted down. The Lizards were a good deal bigger than they had been when they hatched, but their heads didn't come anywhere close to his knee. He held out a piece of ham. Donald ran up, grabbed it out of his hand, and started gulping it down.

Mickey got the next one, Donald the one after that. Jonathan talked to them while he fed them. They were pretty much used to him and to his mother and father by now, and associated humans with the gravy train. Feeding them, these days, was a lot like feeding a dog or a cat. Jonathan wore the gloves more because the Lizards got excited when they ate than because they were trying to nip him.

After a while, Donald finished a piece in nothing flat and tried to get the next one even though it was Mickey's turn. "No!" Jonathan said in English, and wouldn't let him have it. Jonathan wanted to use the language of the Race—the noises the baby Lizards made clearly showed where its sounds came from—but his father would have pitched a fit. The idea here was to make the Lizards as nearly human as possible, not that they'd be speaking any language themselves for quite a while.

Seeing Mickey get the strip of ham he'd wanted, Donald went over and bit his sibling on the tailstump. They started fighting like a couple of puppies or kittens. That was another reason Jonathan wore leather gloves: to break up squabbles without getting hurt in the process.

"No, no!" he said over and over as he separated them. Like puppies or kittens or small children, they didn't hold grudges: they wouldn't start up again after he left the room. Sooner or later, with luck, they'd learn that "No, no!" meant they were supposed to stop what they were doing. Then he wouldn't need the gloves any more. That wasn't close to happening yet, though.

When the ham was gone, Mickey and Donald kept on looking expectantly at him. He wondered what was going on inside those long, narrow skulls. The hatchlings had no words, so it couldn't be anything too complex. But was he only room service for them, or did they like him, too, the way a puppy liked its master? He couldn't tell, and wished he could.

Before he left, he used a strainer to sift through the cat box in another corner of the Lizards' room. They'd figured that out even faster than a cat would have, and rarely made messes on the floor. Even when they did, the messes weren't too messy: their droppings were firm and dry.

Chores done, he shut the door on the Lizards, went back to his own room, grabbed his books, and hopped in the jalopy he drove to school: a gasoline-burning 1955 Ford, an aqua-and-white two-tone job that seemed almost as tall as he was. It got lousy mileage and drank oil, but it ran . . . most of the time. As he started it up, the tinny car radio blared out the electrified country music that was all the rage these days.

The Westside Freeway was new, and cut travel time from Gardena to UCLA almost in half. Now that he was a sophomore, he'd gained an on-campus parking permit. That saved him a good part of the hike he'd had to make from Westwood every day during his freshman year.

A lot of students had early classes. Some of them carried coffee in waxed-cardboard cups. Jonathan had never got that habit, which amused his father to no end. He often got the idea his dad thought he had life pretty soft. But he didn't have to listen to the "When I was your age . . ." lecture too often, so he supposed things could have been worse.

A few students wore jackets and slacks. The rest were about evenly divided between guys who kept their hair and wore ordinary shirts and their female counterparts in clothes their mothers might have worn on the one hand (*on the one fork of the tongue,* Jonathan thought, using the Lizard idiom) and those like him on the other: fellows and coeds who made the Race their fashion, wearing body paint or, with the weather cool, body-paint T shirts. A lot of the fellows in that crowd shaved their heads, but only a few of the girls.

No girls went bare-chested on campus, either—there was a rule against it—though a good many did at the beach or even on the street. Jonathan didn't mind the lack too much; he had plenty to watch anyhow.

He trudged up the broad expanse of Janss Steps to Royce Hall, a big Romanesque red-brick building with a colonnade in front, in which he had his class in the language of the Race. He wasn't surprised to see Karen sitting under the colonnade, her pert nose in the textbook. "Hi," he said in English, and then switched to the Race's tongue. "I greet you."

"And I greet you," she answered in the same language before she looked up. When she saw the shirt he'd chosen, she smiled and added, "Exalted Fleetlord."

"Oh, yes, I am an important male," he said with an emphatic cough that told just how important he imagined he was. Karen's expression said he wasn't so important as all that. Tacitly admitting as much, he went on, "Are you ready for today's quiz?"

"I hope so," she said, which made him chuckle. He spoke the language of the Race pretty fluently—given what his parents did, he had no excuse not to—but she understood the way the grammar worked better than he did. She also studied harder, which she had ever since high school. Closing her book, she got to her feet. "Shall we go see how it is?"

"Sure," Jonathan said in English, and tacked on another emphatic cough. A lot of his conversations with his friends mixed his own language and the Lizards'. That kept most of the older generation—though not, worse luck, his own mother and father—from knowing what they were talking about.

He took Karen's hand. She squeezed his, hard. They hadn't just been studying together since high school; they'd been dating since then, too. Giving him a sidelong glance, she asked, "Have you heard anything from Liu Mei since she went back to China?"

"No," Jonathan answered, which made Karen squeeze his hand again—in relief, probably. He'd been taken with the daughter of the Communist envoy who'd come to the USA for weapons. They'd been able to talk with each other, too, because Liu Mei knew the language of the Race. But she was gone, and Karen was still around. He did add, "With all the fighting over there, I hope she's okay."

Karen considered that, with some reluctance decided it was unexceptionable, and nodded. She went on, "And how are your little friends?"

"They're fine," he said. He didn't want to say too much more than that, not in a crowded hallway where anybody might be listening. An officer's son, he understood the need for security, even if he wasn't always perfect enough about it to delight his father. "They're getting bigger." He could tell her that safely enough. "If you want, you can feed them next time you're over."

"Okay." Karen giggled. "That's the funniest way to get a girl to come over to your house I ever heard of. And you know what's funnier? It'll work."

"Good," Jonathan said as they went upstairs together. He stopped in front of a door with 227 painted on a rippled-glass window in blocky, old-fashioned numbers. The oval brass doorknob, polished by countless students' palms, was old-fashioned, too; Royce Hall dated from the 1920s.

Before the Lizards came, Jonathan thought. *A whole different world.* He tried to imagine what it would have been like then, with people smugly convinced they were alone in the universe. He couldn't do it, even though his folks talked about those times as if they'd happened day before yesterday. *It must have been boring,* was the first thing that always sprang to mind. No televisors, no computers, no satellite networks to bring the whole world into your living room . . . From what his father said, they'd barely even had radio. He shook his head. *I couldn't have lived like that.*

The chimes in the Powell Library bell tower, across the square from Royce Hall, announced eight o'clock. As soon as the last note died, the instructor rapped a pointer down on the lectern. "I greet you, class," he said.

"I greet you, superior sir," Jonathan chorused along with everyone else.

By his body paint, the instructor, a male named Kechexx, had once served in the artillery. Now, like a lot of captured Lizards who'd chosen not to rejoin their own kind, he made his living by teaching humans about the Race. His eye turrets swiveled this way and that, taking in the whole class. "It was to be a quiz today. Did you think I would forget?" His mouth fell open in a laugh. "Did you perhaps hope I would forget? I have not forgotten. Take out a leaf of paper."

"It shall be done," Jonathan said with his classmates. He hoped he wouldn't forget too much.

☆ **4** ☆

The train rattled east over the dry South African plain. Rance Auerbach and Penny Summers sat side by side, staring out the window like a couple of tourists. They *were* a couple of tourists; this was the first time they'd been out of Cape Town since the Lizards sent them into exile there.

"Looks like New Mexico, or maybe Arizona," Rance said. "Same kind of high country, same kinds of scrubby plants. I went through there a couple of times before the fighting started." He shifted in his seat, trying to find the least uncomfortable position for his bad leg and shoulder.

"New Mexico? Arizona?" Penny looked at him as if he'd gone out of his mind. "I never heard of antelopes out there, by God, bouncing along like they've got springs in their legs, or those big white plumy birds standing in the fields—"

"Egrets," Auerbach supplied.

"Those are the ones," Penny agreed. "And we saw a *lion* half an hour ago. You ever hear of a goddamn lion in Arizona?"

"Sure," he said, just to watch her eyes get big. "In a zoo." He wheezed laughter. Penny looked as if she wanted to hit him with something. He went on, "The country looks that way. I didn't say anything about the animals."

He might as well not have spoken. "Even the cows look funny," Penny said; having grown up in western Kansas, she spoke of cows with authority. "Their horns are too big, and they look like those what-do-you-call-'ems—Brahmas, that's what I want to say."

"They look like longhorns to me," Auerbach said. That wasn't quite right, but it was as close as he could come; he knew horses better than cattle. With a chuckle, he added, "They used to have longhorns in New Mexico. Maybe they still do, for all I know."

"Hot damn," Penny said, unimpressed. She held out a peremptory hand. "Give me a cigarette."

"Here." He took the pack out of his shirt pocket and handed it to her. After she lit one, he found himself wanting one, too. He stuck one in his mouth and leaned toward her so she could give him a light. He sucked in smoke, coughed a couple of times—which hurt—and said, "Just like in the movies."

"How come all the little stuff is like it is in the movies and all the big stuff really stinks?" Penny asked. "That's what I want to know."

"Damn good question," Rance said. "Now all we need is a damn good answer for it." He stared out the window at what looked like a big hawk on stilts walking across the landscape. The train swept past before he got as good a glimpse of it as he would have liked.

He and Penny weren't the only ones smoking in the railway car; far from it. Smoke from cigarettes and cigars and a couple of pipes turned the air bluer than Penny's language. Everybody smoked: whites, blacks, East Indians, everybody. A couple of rows ahead, a black kid who couldn't have been more than eight was puffing on a hand-rolled cigarette about twice the size of the store-bought one Rance was smoking.

His sigh turned into another cough. Everybody rode together, too. It hadn't been like that back in the United States. Despite everything he'd already seen in South Africa, he hadn't expected it to be like that here, either. But the only ones who got special privileges on trains in this part of the world were the Lizards, and they didn't ride trains very often.

The car might have been the Tower of Babel. African languages dominated—some with weird clicking noises that seemed more as if they belonged in the Lizards' speech than in anything human, others without. But Auerbach also heard the clipped sounds of the British-style English some whites spoke here, the harsher gutturals of Afrikaans, and the purring noises the little brown men and women from India used.

Every so often, the train would stop at a tiny, sunbaked town not much different from the tiny, sunbaked towns of the American Southwest. And then, at last, the conductor shouted, "Beaufort West! All out for Beaufort West!" He repeated himself in several different languages.

In spite of all the repetition, Rance and Penny were the only ones who got off at Beaufort West. It wasn't a tiny town; it had advanced to the more exalted status of small town, and lay on the northern edge of the Great Karoo. Auerbach shrugged. He didn't know exactly what a karoo was, but the country still put him in mind of west Texas or New Mexico or Arizona.

"Drier than Kansas," Penny said, shading her eyes with her hand. "Hotter, too—even if it's not as hot as it was on the train. Looks like the middle of nowhere. No two ways about that."

"Well, that's what we came for, isn't it?" Auerbach answered. "We can rent a car or get somebody to drive us around and look at lions or whatever the hell else lives around here." He wondered if he'd see one of those tall, funny hawks close up.

"Okay." Penny shrugged and picked up their suitcases; she carried things better than Rance did. "Now all we have to do is find the Donkin House."

It was only a block away: logically, on Donkin Street, which looked to be Beaufort West's main drag, such as that was. It was hardly out of the motel class, which didn't surprise Auerbach. He registered himself and Penny as Mr. and Mrs.; South Africans were even more persnickety about that than Americans.

Beef stew at a little café across the street from the Donkin House wasn't anything like what Rance's mother had made, but wasn't bad. A bottle of Lion Lager improved his outlook on the world. "We'll take it easy tonight," he said, "and then tomorrow morning we'll go out and see what there is to see."

"Miles and miles of miles and miles," Penny predicted.

"Miles and miles of miles and miles with lions and antelopes and maybe zebras, too." Auerbach poked her in the ribs. "Hey, you're not in Kansas any more."

"I know." Penny grimaced. "I'm not wearing ruby slippers, either, in case you didn't notice."

As things turned out, nobody in Beaufort West had a car to rent. The locals, even the ones who spoke English, looked at Rance as if he were mad for suggesting such a thing. The only taxi in town was an elderly Volkswagen whose engine coughed worse and louder than Auerbach. The driver was a middle-aged black man named Joseph Moroka.

"You speak English funny," he remarked as he drove Rance and Penny out of town onto the karoo.

Auerbach thought the cabby was the one with the funny accent, but Penny said, "We're from the United States."

"Oh." Up there in the front seat, Moroka nodded. "Yes, that is what it is. You talk like films I have seen at the cinema." He got friendlier after realizing they weren't native South African whites. That no doubt said something about the way things had been here before the Lizards came.

He found his passengers lions. They were sleeping in the shade of a tree. He found plenty of gemsbok and kudu—he almost ran over a gemsbok that bounded across the road. He found a fox with ears much too big for its head. And Auerbach discovered that his hawk on stilts was called a secretary bird; it had a couple of plumes sticking up from its head that looked like pens put behind a man's ear.

"It is a good bird," Moroka said seriously. "It eats snakes."

Here and there, cattle roamed the countryside, now and then pausing to graze. "Need a lot of land to support a herd here," Auerbach said. That was true in the American Southwest, too. Joseph Moroka nodded again.

"Shall we head back toward town?" Penny said.

Rance gave her a dirty look. "If you just want to sit around in the room, we could have done that back in Cape Town," he said.

"Well, we can go out again tomorrow, if there's anything different to see than what we just looked at," she answered. Had they been by themselves, she likely would have told him where to head in. But, like most people, she was less eager to quarrel where outsiders could listen.

And compromise didn't look like the worst idea in the world to Rance, either. "All right—why not? We're going to be here a week. No point to doing everything all at once, I guess." He tapped the driver on the shoulder. "You can take us back to the hotel, Joe."

For the first time, the black man got huffy. "You please to call me Mr. Moroka. Most white men here, they never bother learning blacks have names until the Lizards come. Now they have to learn, and learn right." He spoke with quiet pride.

It had been like that in the American South, too. *Boy!* would do the job, or *Uncle!* for an old Negro. Things were changing there; things had been forcibly changed here. Auerbach rolled with the punch. "Okay, Mr. Moroka." His great-grandfather, a Confederate cavalryman, wouldn't have approved, but great-granddad had been dead a long time.

Moroka looked back and grinned. "Good. I thank you." If Auerbach showed manners, he'd show them, too. Rance supposed he could live with that. The cabby turned the VW around— there wasn't any other traffic on this stretch of narrow, poorly paved road—and started jouncing back toward Beaufort West.

He topped a low rise and had just begun the long downgrade on the other side when Rance and Penny both cried out at the same time: "Wait! Hold up! Stop the damn car!" Auerbach added the last word that needed to be said, "What the *hell* are those things?"

"Dinosaurs," Penny said in astonishment, and then, "But dinosaurs are supposed to all be dead. Extinct." She nodded in satisfaction at finding the right word.

"They *are* dinosaurs," Rance said, his eyes bugging out of his head. "A whole herd of dinosaurs. What the hell else can they be?"

They were bigger than cows, though not a whole lot. Their scaly hides were a sandy yellow-brown, lighter than those of the Lizards. They went on all fours, and had big, broad heads with wide, beaky mouths. As Rance took a longer look at them, though, he noticed that their eyes were mounted in big, upstanding, chameleonlike turrets. That gave him his first clue about what they had to be.

Joseph Moroka breaking into peals of laughter gave him his second. "The Lizards call them zisuili," he said, pronouncing the alien name with care. "They use them for meat and blood and hide, like we use cattle. These things give no milk, but I hear they lay eggs like hens. They are new here." He laughed again. "The lions have not yet decided if they are good to eat."

"They don't graze like cattle." Again, Penny spoke with expert assurance. "They graze more like sheep or goats. Look at that, Rance—they don't hardly leave anything behind 'em. They crop everything right on down to the ground."

"You're right," Auerbach said. He could see from which direction the herd of zisuili was coming by the bare, trampled dirt behind them. "Wonder how the antelopes are going to like that—and the real cows, too."

Moroka wasn't worrying about it. He was still laughing. "But the Lizards, they do not use their cows to buy wives, oh no. They have no wives to buy. I should be like a Lizard, eh?" He found that funny as hell.

Auerbach hadn't thought about the Lizards' having their own domestic animals back on their home planet. He supposed it made sense that they would. They didn't have trouble with much Earthly food, so . . . He tapped Joseph Moroka one more time. "Anybody tried eating these things yet?"

"We are not supposed to," the cabby replied. Auerbach coughed impatiently. That wasn't an answer, and he knew it. After a moment, Moroka went on, "I hear—I only hear, now; I do not know—I hear they taste like chicken."

Atvar studied a map of the subregion of the main continental mass called China. "We make progress," he said in some satisfaction.

"Truth, Exalted Fleetlord," replied Kirel, the shiplord of the *127th Emperor Hetto*, the bannership of the conquest fleet. "We have taken Harbin back from the rebellious Tosevites, and this other city, this Peking, cannot hold out against us much longer."

"I should hope not, at any rate," Atvar said. "The Chinese have no landcruisers and no aircraft to speak of. Without them, they can still be most troublesome, but they cannot hope to defeat us in the long run."

"Truth," Kirel said again. He was solid and conservative and sensible; Atvar trusted him as far as he trusted any male on Tosev 3. Back during the fighting, Kirel had had his chances to overthrow the fleetlord, especially during Straha's uprising after the Tosevites detonated their first explosive-metal bomb. He hadn't used them. If that didn't establish his reliability, nothing would.

Thinking of explosive-metal bombs in that context made the fleetlord think of them in this one as well. "These Big Uglies, the Emperor be praised, cannot lure a great part of our forces forward and then destroy them with a single blast."

Kirel cast down his eyes. "Emperor be praised, indeed," he said. "You speak truth again, Exalted Fleetlord: they are too primitive to create explosive-metal bombs. Some other Tosevite not-empire would have to provide them with such weapons before they could use them."

Atvar swung both eye turrets toward the second most senior male from the conquest fleet. "Now that is a genuinely appalling thought. The Chinese must understand that, if they did such a thing, we would bomb them without mercy in retaliation. Unlike the independent not-empires, they could not hope to respond in kind."

"Even so." Kirel gestured in agreement. "We could destroy half their population without doing the planet as a whole severe damage."

But the fleetlord remained worried. "I wonder how much they would mind. Along with India, which presents its own problems, China is the subregion that reminds me most urgently of how many Big Uglies there are, and how few of us. The Chinese Tosevites are liable to be willing to accept the loss of half their number in the hope that doing so would damage us more in the long run."

"Exalted Fleetlord, when have you ever known Big Uglies to think of the long run?" Kirel asked.

"Well, that is also a truth, and a good thing for us that it is, too," Atvar said. "Even so, you have given me something new to worry about. After so long here, I thought I had exhausted the possibilities."

"I am sorry, Exalted Fleetlord." Kirel bent into the posture of respect. "Do you think warning the independent not-empires against pursuing such a course would be worthwhile?"

After brief consideration, Atvar made the negative hand gesture. "I fear it would be likelier to give them ideas that have not yet occurred to them, although I admit that ideas of a troublesome sort very readily occur to Big Uglies."

"So they do." Kirel used an emphatic cough. "Still, though, in spite of the difficulties the Tosevites pose, we do make progress all over this world."

"Some. Not enough," Atvar said. Kirel had put him in a fretful mood. "I would give a great deal—I would give almost anything I can think of—to know, for instance, which of the not-empires did in fact attack the colonization fleet. That, by the Emperor, would be a vengeance worth taking."

"Indeed it would." Kirel sighed. "But, knowing the enormity

of the crime they were committing, those Big Uglies took pains to conceal their footprints."

"One day, we shall know. One day, they will pay," Atvar said. "And that will be progress, too, a step we can measure."

"Indeed it will," Kirel agreed. "I was, I confess, thinking of smaller steps: for instance, it is good to taste the flesh of our own domestic animals again, after so long living on solely Tosevite rations."

"I will not say you are wrong, for I think you are right. The thought of grilled azwaca cutlets makes my mouth water." Atvar had always been especially fond of azwaca. He walked over to the window of his suite and looked west across the great river toward the pyramidal funerary monuments that passed for ancient on Tosev 3. In the green strips between the monuments and the river, azwaca were grazing, though without magnification he could not see them.

"I am more partial to zisuili myself, but the taste of every one of the beasts is a reminder of Home," Kirel said.

"Truth. But do you know what?" Atvar asked. He waited for Kirel to make the negative hand gesture, then continued, "I have already begun receiving complaints from Tosevite agriculturalists and pastoralists to the effect that our domestic animals graze so thoroughly, no fodder is left for any of theirs."

"I had not heard of such complaints, but they do not surprise me," Kirel said. "Tosevite grazers have evolved in an environment of relative abundance. Because moisture is more widespread here than back on Home, so is vegetation. Tosevite animals can afford to leave some behind and still flourish. Our own beasts, by the nature of the terrain to which they are adapted, have to be more efficient."

"Over the course of time, it will be interesting to see what they do to the ecosystems in which they find themselves," Atvar said. "They may well make large stretches of this world resemble Home more closely than is now the case."

"Do we have analysts examining the issue?" Kirel asked.

"I do not," Atvar answered. "Reffet should: this is, after all, more properly an issue involving the colonization of this planet than its conquest. But what Reffet should be doing and what he is doing are too often not one and the same." He scribbled a note to himself. "I shall send an inquiry."

"He will resent it," Kirel said.

"He resents everything I do and everything I do not do," the fleetlord said scornfully. "Let him resent this, too. But if Tosevite ecosystems become more Homelike, that will aid in assimilating this world into the Empire, will it not? I can justify the query on those grounds."

"No doubt you can, Exalted Fleetlord. Fleetlord Reffet will still resent it." Kirel had long since made plain that his opinion of the head of the colonization fleet was not high. That had not failed to endear him to the head of the conquest fleet. He added, "Since you are rationalizing it as a conquest issue, perhaps our experts *should* also examine it."

"Perhaps they should." Atvar sighed. "We are stretched very thin. We have been stretched very thin—thinner than anyone ever imagined we would be—since we came to Tosev 3 and discovered the inadequacies of the data our probe sent us. Well, perhaps we can stretch a little thinner yet."

"We have said that a good many times, and we have always succeeded in stretching up till now," Kirel said. "We should be able to stretch once more."

"So we should," Atvar said. "I keep worrying that we will eventually snap and break, but it has not happened yet. *Why* it has not happened yet, I cannot imagine, given what this world is, but it has not."

Before Kirel could answer, Atvar's telephone hissed for attention. When he activated the screen link, his adjutant stared out at him. "What is it, Pshing?" he asked suspiciously. Pshing, being one of his principal links to Tosev 3, was also one of his principal sources of bad news.

"Exalted Fleetlord—" the adjutant began, and then broke off.

Atvar's heart sank. This was going to be one of those times. Like an itch, the certainty burrowed under his scales. "You had better tell me," he said heavily.

"It shall be done, Exalted Fleetlord," Pshing said. Yes, he was gathering himself. Yes, that meant he needed to gather himself. After a deep pause, he went on, "Exalted Fleetlord, there has been an attack on the desalination plants supplying fresh water to the new towns in this region."

A map appeared on the screen beside his face. It showed the eastern coast of the peninsula the Big Uglies called Arabia that depended from the main continental mass. "Tell me more," Atvar said. "How serious is this attack? Is it the work of the local Tosevites springing from their superstitious fanaticism, or are the independent not-empires using them as a cloak for their own larger designs against us?"

"Those two need not be inseparable," Kirel pointed out.

Atvar made the hand gesture of agreement, but then waved the shiplord to silence; he wanted to hear what Pshing had to say. "One of the plants is destroyed, another badly damaged," the adjutant reported. Red dots appeared on the map to show the affected desalination plants; the others remained amber. "Our defense forces have slain a large number of Tosevites, all of whom appear to be native to the vicinity. Whether they were inspired or aided by other groups of Big Uglies as yet remains to be determined."

"They were surely aided in one way or another," Atvar said. "They do not produce the weapons they use against us."

"Truth," Kirel said. "But whether the Deutsche or the Americans or the Russkis furnished weapons for this particular attack is another matter."

"Indeed it is." Atvar's voice was grim. "Adjutant, were there, for example, rockets fired at these installations?"

"There do appear to have been some, yes, Exalted Fleetlord," Pshing replied, "but only those of the common and primitive type manufactured in the SSSR and known as *Katyushas*." He had as much trouble with the Tosevite word as Big Uglies did with the language of the Race.

"*Those* things." Kirel spoke in disgust. "They are as common as sand, and are easy to carry on the backs of beasts. Even if they were supplied especially for this assault, the independent not-empires will be able to deny it and still seem plausible."

"They have done that too often," Atvar said. "We shall have to seek ways to punish them nevertheless." He swung an eye turret back toward Pshing. "One plant destroyed, you said, and one damaged? How severe is the impact on the new towns in the area?"

"Production loss is about fifteen percent, Exalted Fleetlord," Pshing replied. "The damaged plant will return to full operation in about forty days, as a preliminary estimate. That will reduce losses to about ten percent. Rebuilding the wrecked plant will take three times as long—assuming no more attacks from Khomeini's fanatics."

"Ah—you did not mention that maniac before," Atvar said. "So these Big Uglies profess his variant of the local superstition?"

"They do," Pshing said. "Those captured proudly proclaim it during interrogation."

"We would be better off if he were dead," Kirel said. "We have not been able to eliminate him, and rewards have failed to turn any Big Uglies against him." Now he sighed. "The Tosevites will betray us whenever they see the chance. It seems most unfair."

"So it does." Atvar knew he sounded unhappy, but couldn't help it. "I shall increase the size of the reward—again."

With a long, resigned sigh, Monique Dutourd sat up in bed. She reached for the pack of Gauloises on the nightstand, lit one, and turned to Dieter Kuhn, who sprawled beside her. "There," she said. "Are you happy?"

He rolled over and grinned at her, a large, sated male grin of the sort she found particularly revolting. "Now that you mention it, yes," he answered. "Give me a smoke, will you?"

She handed him the pack and the book of matches. What she wanted to do after that was go into the bathroom and soak in the tub for an hour, or perhaps for a week: long enough to get the feel of him off her body. If he'd cared what she wanted, though, he wouldn't have made her go to bed with him in the first place.

After a long, deep drag on the cigarette, he asked, "And how was it for you?"

Monique shrugged. It made her bare breasts bounce a little. His eyes went to them. She'd been sure they would draw his notice, and felt vindicated to find herself right. Now—how to answer the question? "Well," she said, "it was, I suppose, better than being hauled off to the Palais de Justice and tormented, if that's what you mean."

"Your praise overwhelms me," he said. He didn't sound too angry. Why should he have? He'd got it in, after all. He'd had a fine time. And if she hadn't—too bad.

He hadn't deliberately tried to hurt her. She gave him that much. She'd dreaded worse when he made it very plain she could either come across or face another stretch of interrogation.

If she'd let him have her because she liked him rather than acquiescing to a polite rape, she might have enjoyed herself. As things were . . . well, it was over.

"Going to bed with me won't get you any closer to my brother," she warned. "If he finds out I did, it will only make him trust me even less than he does now, and he doesn't trust me very far as is."

"So you say. But blood, in the end, is thicker than water." Speaking French as a foreign language, Kuhn was fond of clichés. They let him say what he wanted without having to think too much about it. He went on, "Your dear Pierre does stay in touch with you. We know that, even if we don't always know what he says."

"You never know what he says," Monique replied, stubbing out her cigarette in the glass ashtray on the nightstand while wishing she could put it out on some of the more tender parts of the SS man's anatomy. As long as Pierre stayed tight with the Lizards, they gave him gadgets that defeated the best electronic eavesdroppers mere humans could build.

But Kuhn's smug look now was different from the one he'd worn after grunting and spurting his seed into her. "We know more than you think," he said. Monique was inclined to take that as a boast to get her to tell the German more than he already knew. But then he went on, "We know, for instance, that he told you the other day he was going to eat a big bowl of stewed mussels for his supper."

"Oh, I am sure that will help you catch him," Monique said sardonically. Under the sarcasm, though, she worried. Pierre had mentioned the mussels. That meant the Nazis could unscramble some of what he said to her. Did it also mean they could unscramble some of what he said to other people, or to Lizards? She didn't know. She would have to find a way to make her brother aware of the risk without letting Kuhn and his pals find out she'd done it.

"One never knows," he said, giving her a smile she was sure he was sure was charming. She remained uncharmed. Kuhn got up on his knees and leaned across her to put out his own cigarette, which he'd smoked down to a very small butt.

Instead of drawing his hand all the way back, he let it close over her left breast. He twiddled her nipple between his thumb and forefinger, as if he were adjusting the dial on a wireless. He probably thought that would inflame her. She knew better. His hand slid down to the joining of her legs. He rubbed insistently. He could have rubbed forever without doing anything but making her sore.

But, after a little while, apparently satisfied he'd done his duty, he drew her to him. She had to suck him before he would rise for his second round. She particularly hated doing that, and hated it worse after he laughed and murmured, "Ah, the French," as he held her head down.

If he'd spent himself in her mouth, she would have done her best to vomit on him. But, after a while, he rolled from his side to his back and had her get on top of him. She hadn't known an SS man was allowed to be so lazy. She did what he wanted, hoping he would finish soon. He finally did.

Afterwards, he got dressed and left, though "See you again soon" wasn't the sort of farewell she wished she'd had from him. Monique used the bidet in the bathroom, then did climb into the tub. She didn't feel like a woman violated, if a woman violated was supposed to feel downtrodden and put upon. What she felt like was a woman infuriated. But how to get revenge on a Nazi? In long-occupied Marseille, that wouldn't be easy.

Suddenly, Monique laughed out loud. Dieter Kuhn wouldn't have been happy to hear that laugh, not even a little. She didn't care what would make the SS man happy. She didn't care at all. She had, or might have, connections to which the average woman of Marseille could not aspire.

She couldn't call her brother from the flat, not when the Germans had proved they truly could hear some of those conversations. She didn't dare. Even more than she didn't want to see Kuhn again erect while lying down, she didn't want to revisit the Palais de Justice. She didn't think the *Gestapo* had learned much from its interrogation of her. But what she'd learned about man's inhumanity to man—and to woman—made her certain she never wanted to see the inside of that building again.

Phoning from a telephone box was risky, too. She didn't know whether the Nazis had their listening apparatus on her telephone (no—she didn't know whether they had it *only* on her phone, for they surely had it there) or on Pierre's line as well. She couldn't write a letter, either; had the postman known her brother's address, the Germans would have known it, too.

"Merde," she said, and shifted so the water sloshed in the tub. Even with unusual connections, getting what she wanted—getting Dieter Kuhn's naked body lying in a ditch with dogs and rats gnawing on it—wouldn't be so easy, not unless she wanted to endanger not only herself but also whoever might try to help her.

She got her own naked body, which was beginning to resemble a large, pink raisin, out of the tub. She dried as vigorously as she ever had in her life, especially between her legs. However hard she scrubbed at herself, the memory of the German's fingers and privates lingered. *Maybe I feel violated after all,* she thought.

Three nights later, Kuhn knocked on her door again. She enjoyed that visit no more than she had the earlier one, but not a great deal less, either—he didn't turn vicious. He just wanted a woman, and instead of hiring a tart he got himself a politically suspect professor for free. That was not the sort of Teutonic efficiency about which the Nazis boasted, but it served him well.

The next afternoon, Monique stopped at a greengrocer's for some lettuce and onions on the way back from the university. She was about to take her vegetables over to the proprietor when a woman a year or two older than she was—short and dumpy, with the distinct beginnings of a mustache—came into the shop. "Monique!" she exclaimed. "How are you, darling?" She had a throaty, sexy voice altogether at odds with her nondescript looks.

"Bonjour, Lucie," Monique said to her brother's lady friend. "I was hoping to run into you before too long. I have so much to tell you." She did her best to sound like a woman getting ready to swap gossip with an acquaintance.

"I'm all ears, and I've got some things to tell you, too," Lucie answered in like tones. "Just let me get some garlic and I'll be right with you." She chose a string of fragrant heads while Monique was paying for what she wanted. Monique went out to her bicycle and waited by it. She could speak more freely outside than anywhere indoors. Who could guess where the Nazis might have planted microphones?

Lucie came out a couple of minutes later, grumbling about the prices the grocer charged. They weren't that bad, but Lucie liked to grumble. She reached into her handbag and took out a pair of sunglasses. Maybe she thought they made her look glamourous. In that case, she was wrong. Maybe, on the other hand, she just wanted to fight the glare. Even in early spring, Marseille's sun could give a foretaste of what brilliant summer days would be like.

Monique looked around. Nobody was paying any more attention than what people usually gave a couple of women chatting on the street. A man riding by on a bicycle whistled at them. He was easy to ignore. Taking a deep breath, Monique said, "The Germans can tap your phone, at least when you and Pierre talk with me."

"Ah." Lucie nodded. "I knew that. I wanted to warn you of it." She frowned. "The Nazis turn into bigger nuisances every day."

"Oh, don't they just!" Monique said. Lucie had given her the perfect opening for the rest of what she had in mind, and she proceeded to use it: "Everyone would be better off without one Nazi in particular, I think."

"Dieter Kuhn." Lucie spoke the name without hesitation and with great assurance: so much so that Monique wondered if Pierre and his friends—human and otherwise—had microphones in her flat, too. Lucie went on, "Perhaps that can be arranged. I do not say it surely can be, but perhaps. It depends on whether we can find a way that does not point straight back at ourselves."

"If you can do it, that would be wonderful," Monique said. "If not, I will try to think of something else."

"Some people need killing," Lucie said matter-of-factly. Monique found herself nodding before she wondered what she was doing associating with people who said things like that. She'd had no choice, but that wouldn't be enough to satisfy her priest—not that she'd been to confession in a good long time. And besides, she was the one who wanted the German dead.

But she might not be the only one who wanted him dead. "If you could arrange for the Lizards to do the job . . ."

"It could be," Lucie said. "They have not always the stomach for killing, but some of them do, without a doubt. They differ less, one from another, than people do, I think, but they are not all the same, either. I may know a male or two who would do better business without this nosy Nazi poking into their affairs."

Just then, a Lizard came by on the other side of the street. Lucie shut up with a snap. Monique wondered if he was one of the males Pierre's companion had in mind. Before she could ask, she stared at something else: the Lizard was walking a long-necked, four-legged, scaly creature on a leash, for all the world as if it were a poodle or a greyhound. Pointing toward it, she said, "For heaven's sake, what is that thing?"

"It has a name. I've heard it, but I forget what it is," Lucie answered. "The males of the conquest fleet were here to tend to business. The colonization fleet has also brought farm animals and pets like that one."

"Ugly little thing, isn't it?" Monique said.

"Which, the Lizard or the pet?" Lucie asked, and startled a laugh out of Monique. Her brother's lady friend went on, "I do business with them, but that doesn't mean I have to love them. *Au contraire*." Monique nodded, and then looked thoughtfully at Lucie. That was the first confidence, no matter how small, she could remember getting from her. Was Lucie starting to trust her at last? And if Lucie was, what did that say about Monique? That she was the kind of person a drug smuggler's woman would trust? She'd hoped she might think of herself as something better than that.

Like what? she jeered. *A Nazi's whore?* She reached out and set a hand on Lucie's arm. All at once, being her confidante didn't look so bad.

With a hiss of glee, Nesseref strode into the new shop that had opened in the Race's new town outside of Jezow. "Pets!" she exclaimed. "Now this truly makes me think I am back on Home!"

"I am pleased I am finally able to open," replied the female in charge of the place. "The animals, of course, were almost all brought here as frozen fertilized ova. At last, we have been able to begin thawing them and letting them come to maturity."

"One small step after another, we do advance on this world," the shuttlecraft pilot said. "When I talk with males from the conquest fleet, they often seem amazed at how far we have come."

"When I talk to males from the conquest fleet, I am amazed at how little those ragamuffins have done," the other female declared. "They should have delivered all of Tosev 3 to us, not just patches of the planet. And this place!" Her eye turrets waggled in exasperation. "It is so chilly and wet, I might as well be back in cold sleep."

"When I was first revived, I was furious to discover the conquest incomplete, too," Nesseref said. "As I have come to see more of the Big Uglies and the things they can do, I have more sympathy for the conquest fleet."

"I do not care to see more of the Big Uglies," the female said, and used an emphatic cough. "I have already seen more than I like. Not only are they barbarians, they are dangerous barbarians. The only worthwhile thing this planet produces has been made illegal, and where is the justice in that?"

"Ginger, do you mean?" Nesseref asked, and the other female made the affirmative hand gesture. Nesseref said, "The stuff has been made illegal for good reasons. It tears up our society as nothing else has ever done."

"When I taste it . . . uh, that is, when I did taste it"—the female in the shop was being cagey, not knowing exactly who Nesseref was—"I did not care about the society of the Race. All I care, uh, cared about was how good I felt."

"Yes, I understand as much." Nesseref decided to let it go. Pretty plainly, the female in the shop was still tasting, laws or no laws. As plainly, nothing Nesseref said would make her change her mind. Nesseref hadn't come into the shop to argue about ginger, anyhow. She said, "I want to see your tsiongyu."

"Most males and females are more interested in my befflem," the other female replied. She was going to score points off Nesseref any way she could, for Nesseref had tried to score points off ginger.

Patiently, the shuttlecraft pilot answered, "Befflem need care every day. My work can take me away from here for days at a time. Tsiongyu are better at fending for themselves when their owner is away."

The pet-shop keeper sighed. "I wish my work took me away from this frigid place for days at a time. I would love to go somewhere, anywhere, with decent weather." She seemed to remember she needed to do business. "Come with me. You will have to walk past the befflem, I am afraid. I have them in front, because they are in greater demand."

Befflem turned their eye turrets toward Nesseref as she went by. They wanted to be bought; every line of their small, sinuous bodies proclaimed how much they wanted to be bought. They opened their mouths and squeaked endearingly. Nesseref was tempted to change her mind. No doubt about it: befflem were more friendly, more responsive, than tsiongyu.

But a beffel without companionship from the Race would not be happy, and was liable to turn destructive. Nesseref did not want to come back to her apartment and find it torn to pieces by an animal with nothing better to do.

"Here are the tsiongyu," the other female said, as if she didn't expect Nesseref to recognize them without help.

Where the befflem were eager to make friends with any female or male who came near, the larger tsiongyu sat aloof in their cages. Each one was as proudly drawn up as if it were the Emperor. Nesseref pointed to one with striking red-brown stripes. "May I see that male, please?"

"It shall be done," the proprietor answered, and opened the cage. When she reached for it, the tsiongi hissed in warning, as its kind had a way of doing. Had it tried to bite and scratch, Nesseref would have asked to see another. Even after so many millennia of domestication, about one tsiongi in four remained convinced it was by rights a wild animal.

After hissing, though, this one allowed the female to pick it up and take it out of its cage. When she set it on the floor, it stood there on all fours lashing its tail, as if to show how irate it was at being handled, but did not streak for the door, as many of its kind might have. Here and there back on Home, feral tsiongyu, no less than befflem, made pests of themselves.

Nesseref extended a hand toward the animal. It hissed once more, not so loudly as it had before, but again did not try to bite. Instead, it extended its tongue in the direction of the hand. Nesseref waited, knowing its scent receptors were telling it what to think of her.

"It seems to accept you," the female from the shop said. By her tone, she might have wished the tsiongi had taken a bite out of Nesseref.

"So it does," Nesseref said. "I will buy it, and I will need supplies for its care. At least it will not have parasites here, which will make things easier."

"Truth," the proprietor said. "You will need a leash, a container for its wastes, and absorbent for the container, at least until you train it to use your own waste-disposal unit. Will you also require a supply of food?"

"This would come from the flesh of Tosevite animals?" Nesseref asked.

"Yes, of course," the other female replied. "Eventually, we will use our own beasts, as we do back on Home, but that time is not yet here—like the pets, the food animals are only now coming to Tosev 3."

"I will feed it table scraps, then," Nesseref decided. The petshop proprietor's tailstump quivered in poorly concealed annoyance: she would get less from Nesseref than she'd hoped. Nesseref wondered how much she was spending on ginger, and how badly she needed more. Well, that, fortunately, was not the shuttlecraft pilot's worry.

She picked up the tsiongi, moving slowly and carefully so as not to take the animal by surprise. It stuck out its tongue again and studied her with its large eyes, very much like those of the Race. She took it up to the front of the shop, past the befflem. They tried to leap through the bars of their cages; they did not like tsiongyu. The tsiongi eyed them with lordly disdain, as if to say it knew it could dispose of three or four befflem without working very hard.

"Here are the other things you will require," the shopkeeper said. "If you will let me have your card, so I can make the charge against your account . . . I thank you. And here is the statement of what you have purchased."

"And I thank you." Nesseref examined it to make sure the other female hadn't charged her for tsiongi food or anything else she hadn't bought. Satisfied, she tucked the bit of paper into one of the pouches she wore on her belt. Then she set the tsiongi on the floor and fastened the leash onto its long, flexible neck. It endured the indignity of being leashed with the air of a prisoner enduring interrogation from the Deutsche or some equally fierce Big Uglies. But when Nesseref started out of the shop, the tsiongi trotted along at her heels.

When she got to the door, she turned back and said to the shopkeeper, "If I had bought a couple of befflem, they would already have tangled their leashes around my legs three different times."

"Befflem are not hatched to be led on leashes," the other female replied. "Their free spirits are what make them enjoyable."

"Their free spirits are what make them nuisances," Nesseref said. "If they had any brains and weren't so friendly, they'd be Tosevites." The female in the pet shop drew back, obviously insulted. Nesseref left before that female found anything to say. The tsiongi stayed right with her. The wild ancestors of tsiongyu had hunted in pairs, a leader and a follower. In domesticating them, the Race had in effect turned its own males and females into pair leaders.

Nesseref proudly led her new pet through the streets of the new town. Several males and females exclaimed over it; a couple of them asked where she'd bought it. She told them about the pet shop. The tsiongi, meanwhile, accepted the attention as nothing less than its due.

Its air of restrained nobility lasted till it caught sight of a feathered Tosevite flying creature, a plump beast with a metallic green head and a grayish body, walking along looking for tidbits. The tsiongi turned an eye turret toward Nesseref, plainly expecting her to attack this thing that could only be prey. When she didn't, when she just kept walking, the tsiongi gave what sounded like a male or female's hiss of irritation. Then it sprang for the flying creature itself.

The leash, which Nesseref hung on to, brought the tsiongi up short. The Tosevite creature flew away with a whir and a flutter of wings. The tsiongi stared as if it couldn't believe its eye turrets. Maybe it couldn't; fewer animals flew back on Home than here on Tosev 3, and tsiongyu didn't hunt flying creatures there. It had probably thought this one couldn't do anything but slowly walk along. The feathered creature had given it a surprise, as all manner of Tosevite creatures had given the Race unpleasant surprises.

"Come along," Nesseref told it. "I will feed you something, even if you could not catch that animal." Still looking as if it thought it had been cheated, the tsiongi reluctantly followed.

Half a block farther on, it saw another bird. Again, it tried to attack. Again, the bird flew away. Again, the tsiongi seemed astonished. That happened twice more before Nesseref got back to her apartment building. By then, she was laughing at the tsiongi—all the more so because the beast's native dignity seemed so frazzled.

She had got the tsiongi almost back to the apartment building when a beffel—naturally, not on a leash—ran past. The male to whom it more or less belonged called, "Careful there, Golden-scale!" Goldenscale didn't feel like being careful. It infuriated Nesseref's tsiongi in a way the birds hadn't. And the beffel wanted to fight, too. Nesseref had to drag her pet the rest of the way to the entrance.

"You had better be careful," she called to the male with the beffel. "Your little friend there will be someone's supper if you are not."

"Befflem do what befflem do," the male answered with a shrug, which had some truth to it. He raised his voice: "Come, Goldenscale! Come!" Despite his emphatic cough, the beffel went on doing what it did, which in this case involved antago-nizing Nesseref's tsiongi.

The tsiongi tried to slam through the glass entryway door to get at the obnoxious beffel. It slammed into the glass instead, and looked even more bewildered than it had when the birds flew away. Nesseref took it to the elevator. Once the tsiongi couldn't see the beffel any more, it regained its dignity. Even so, Nesseref wondered if she would ever be able to take it out on the street for a walk.

Flight Lieutenant David Goldfarb was going through the motions, and he knew it. The Canadian consulate in Belfast had lost interest in having him as an immigrant once he proved unable to retire from the RAF. Officials at the American consulate hadn't formally told him no yet, but they hadn't shown any signs of saying yes, either.

And the Lizards, on whom he'd pinned such a great part of his hopes, had let him down. From what Cousin Moishe said, he'd done his best to get the fleetlord interested in the plight of an op-pressed British Jew, but his best hadn't been good enough. Gold-farb believed Moishe had indeed done his best. He just wished that best had been better.

Since it hadn't been, he was left to keep an eye on the radar screens that watched the sky and space above Belfast. He was doing just that, and trying not to doze off inside the darkened room that housed the radar displays, when an aircraftman first class came in and said, "Telephone call for you, sir."

"Thanks," Goldfarb replied, and the enlisted man saluted. Goldfarb turned to Sergeant Jack McDowell, his partner on the shift. "Will you keep an eye on things, Jack? I doubt I'll be long."

"Aye, sir, I'll do it," McDowell replied in his rich burr. He didn't look down his nose at Goldfarb for being Jewish— or if he did, he kept it to himself. He didn't even have to do that; his place in the RAF was odds-on to be more secure than Goldfarb's.

Not caring to dwell on such things, David tapped the aircraftman on the shoulder. "Lead on, Macduff," he misquoted, and followed the youngster down the hall and into an office where a telephone lay with the handset off the hook. Goldfarb eyed it with the warm affection a bird gave a snake. It was, he feared, all too likely to be Basil Roundbush trying to get him into fresh trouble—as if he didn't have enough already. With a sigh, he picked up the telephone. "Goldfarb here."

"Hullo, old man," said a cheerful voice on the other end of the line. Three words were plenty to tell Goldfarb the owner of that voice had gone to Oxford or Cambridge, and to one of the best public schools before that. Roundbush, his tormentor, had done all those things, but this wasn't Roundbush's voice. It wasn't any voice with which David was immediately familiar. Its owner went on, "Haven't seen you in a long time—not since we went trolling for barmaids together back in Dover, eh?"

"Jerome Jones, by God!" Goldfarb burst out. They'd worked side by side on radar sets through the Battle of Britain, and then during the onslaught of the Lizards—till radar-seeking missiles had taken out their sets and reduced them to using field glasses and field telephones right out of the First World War. "What the devil are you doing with yourself these days?"

"I'm in the import-export business," Jones answered, and David's heart sank. If that wasn't a euphemism for smuggling ginger, he would have been astonished. And if Jones wasn't going to try to use him some way or other, he would have been more astonished still. Sure enough, his former comrade went on, "I hear you've come on a spot of trouble lately."

"What if I have?" Goldfarb asked tightly. Jerome Jones

wasn't in Her Majesty's forces; David could tell him where to head in without worrying about getting court-martialed—not that he'd let that bother him when he'd finally told Roundbush where to go and how to get there. Even though Jones' father had headed up a bank, dear Jerome would be hard-pressed to land Goldfarb in worse trouble than he'd already found for himself.

"Why, I wanted to lend you a hand, if I possibly could," Jones said, sounding surprised David would have to ask.

"What sort of hand?" Goldfarb remained deeply suspicious. He knew the kind of answer he expected. *If you need to put a few hundred quid in your pocket,* Jones would say, *you can take this little shipment to Buenos Aires for me.* Or maybe it would be *to Warsaw* or *to Cairo* or even, God help us, *to Nuremberg.*

Jerome Jones said, "Unless the little bird I've been listening to has it altogether wrong, there are some people giving you a bit of difficulty about leaving the country."

"That's true." Goldfarb kept on answering in monosyllables, waiting for the sales pitch. He remained sure it was coming. What would he do if good old Jerome promised to help him emigrate after he did his former pal one little favor that would, undoubtedly, turn out not to be so little? Also undoubtedly, good old Jerome had the clout, if he could be persuaded to use it.

"It's bloody awful, is what it is." Jones sounded indignant. How smooth was he these days? Back when Goldfarb had known him, he'd been distinctly callow. But he was a captain of industry these days, not a puppy still wet behind the ears. "You've done more for Britain than Britain wants to do for you. We're still a free country, by God."

"From where you sit, maybe," David said. From where he sat himself, the United Kingdom tilted more toward the Greater German *Reich* with every passing day. With most of the British Empire in the Lizards' scaly hands, with the USA still rebuilding after the fighting, and with the *Reich* just across the Channel, he supposed that tilt was inevitable. That didn't mean he thought it was anything but disastrous.

"I also hear your superiors have taken unfair advantage of you. Officers are nasty that way—think they're little tin gods, what?" Jones chuckled. "I always thought that. Back when I was wearing RAF blue, though, there was damn all I could do about it. Things are different now. If I ring the minister of defense, I expect he'll listen to me. He'd damn well better; his son is married to my first cousin."

"My God." Goldfarb's voice was hoarse. "You really mean it."

"Well, of course I do," Jones answered. "What's the point of having influence if you don't get to use it? I'd have rung you up sooner, but I only heard of your difficulties a few days ago."

"That's all right," David said vaguely. Back when they'd served in the RAF together, he'd thought about Jerome Jones' secure upper-class upbringing and his own roots in East End London. Then he'd thought the most he could aspire to was a little wireless-repair shop. After the fighting ended, staying in the RAF looked like a road to a better life. It had been, for a little while.

"I'll ring you back directly I know something," Jones told him. "Be good in the meanwhile." He hung up. The line went dead.

Goldfarb stared at the telephone handset before slowly returning it to the cradle. The young aircraftman was long gone. Goldfarb went back to the radar screens by himself, his head whirling.

A few days later, he was watching the glowing green screens again. They showed a Soviet spacecraft passing north of the U.K. The Americans and Germans—and likely the Race, too—laughed at the craft the Russians flew; the Americans called them flying tin cans. Because of the limits to their craft, Soviet spacemen couldn't do nearly so much up there as their counterparts from the USA and the *Reich*. But they were flying. Britain had no spacemen. Watching everyone else go by above his head, Goldfarb acutely felt the lack.

He was about to remark on it to Sergeant McDowell when a fresh-faced enlisted man stuck his head into the room and said, "The base commandant's compliments, Flight Lieutenant, and he'll see you in his office fast as you can get there."

Taking the privilege of long acquaintance, McDowell asked, "What have you gone and done now, sir?"

"I don't know," David answered, "but I expect I'll find out before long. Don't let that Russian land in Belfast—people would talk." Before the Scotsman could find a comeback, Goldfarb headed for Group Captain Burton Paston's office.

Paston was doing paperwork when he walked in. The commandant's face, normally dyspeptic, now grew less happy still.

"Oh, it's you, Goldfarb," he said, as if he'd been expecting someone else—perhaps the Spanish Inquisition—instead.

"Reporting as ordered, sir," Goldfarb said, coming to attention and saluting as he waited to discover what sort of new trouble he was in.

"Yes." Distaste filled Paston's voice, too. "Some little while ago, you attempted to resign from the Royal Air Force."

"Yes, sir, I did, but I've performed my duties since to the best of my ability," Goldfarb said. If Group Captain Paston thought he'd be able to hang a bad-conduct discharge on him, he had another think coming.

But Paston waved that away. "You seem to have friends as well as enemies in high places," he remarked. "Why so many people would get themselves exercised over a flight lieutenant up from the ranks is beyond me, but that's neither here nor there. The point of the matter is, I have been instructed in no uncertain terms to reconsider your resignation. Having done so, I've elected to accept it after all."

"Have you, sir?" David breathed. No matter what Jerome Jones said, he hadn't dreamt his old pal really did have so much clout, nor that he could work so fast. He also noted that Paston had tacitly admitted he'd been under pressure to reject the resignation before. Gloating would have felt good, but wouldn't have helped; Goldfarb could see as much. All he said was, "Thank you very much."

"I'm not nearly certain you're welcome," the base commandant answered. "You're the most experienced radar operator we've got, and I'm damned if I know where we'll come up with another one even half as good."

If he'd put something like that on a fitness report, Goldfarb might have risen higher than flight lieutenant. On the other hand, he couldn't do anything about being a Jew, so he might not have, too. He said, "I do appreciate this, from the bottom of my heart." Now that he'd got what he wanted, he could afford to be gracious. He couldn't very well afford to be anything else.

Burton Paston shoved forms across the desk at him. "I'm going to need your signature on all of these."

"Yes, sir." David signed and signed and signed.

When he was done, the base commandant handed him a copy of one of the forms. "If you take this to the Canadian consulate, it will serve to notify them that you have in fact separated yourself from the RAF, and that no impediment stands in the way of your emigration."

"That's splendid. Thanks." Goldfarb reflected on what influence could do. Before, Paston would sooner have thrown him in the guardhouse than let him leave Her Majesty's service. Now, he was practically laying down a red carpet to help speed Goldfarb out the door. So much cooperation got Goldfarb worried. "Suppose, sir, that the blokes who don't like me so much have got to the Canadians. If they turn me down, will I be able to rescind this resignation? I don't fancy being down and out with no hope for any job in sight."

"If they and the Yanks turn you down, yes," Paston answered. "Your friend already considered that possibility. You're lucky to have so many people looking out for your interests."

"I suppose I am, sir," David said. He didn't point out to Paston that, since he was a Jew, he automatically had a lot more people doing their best to give him a knee in the ballocks. The group captain wouldn't understand that, and wouldn't believe it, either. Goldfarb shrugged. He knew what he knew. And one of the things he knew was that he was getting out. At last, he was getting out.

One thing Johannes Drucker appreciated about his long service to the *Reich*: he had no trouble getting his hands on a firearm. Rifles and especially pistols were hard to come by for civilians in the *Reich*. Every officer, though, had his own service weapon. Drucker would have preferred a pistol not so easily traced back to him, but, with any luck, no one would associate Gunther Grillparzer's untimely demise with him anyhow.

He tried to read a copy of *Signal* as the train rolled southwest toward Thuringia. By what the magazine said, everyone in Europe was delighted to live under the benevolent rule of the *Reich* and to labor to make Germany greater still. Drucker hoped that was true, which didn't necessarily mean he believed it.

As usual, the compartment was tightly shut up against the outside air. The atmosphere was full of smoke from cigarettes and a couple of cigars. In the forward compartment of this car, there'd been a screaming row earlier in the trip. Someone—a foreigner, without a doubt—had had the nerve to open up a window. Everyone else had pitched a fit till a conductor, quite properly, shut it again and warned the miscreant he'd be put off the train if he opened it again.

The interior remained unsullied by fresh air until a conductor came through the car calling, "Weimar! All out for Weimar!" as the train slowed to a stop at the station. Drucker grabbed his carpetbag—all the luggage he had with him—and descended from the car.

Weimar's station had a shabby, run-down look to it. As Drucker carried the bag out to the street to flag a taxi, he saw that the whole town looked as if it had seen better days. The *Reich* and the National Socialists did not love the place where the preceding unhappy German republic had been born.

Drucker discovered he didn't need a cab after all. He could see the Hotel Elephant from where he was standing. He hurried toward and into it. A clerk nodded to him from behind the desk. "Yes, sir. May I help you?"

"I am Johann Schmidt," Drucker said, using the voice an officer used toward an enlisted man to hide his nervousness. "I have a room reserved."

That tone worked wonders, as it so often did in the *Reich*. The desk clerk flipped pages in the register. "Yes, sir," he said, nodding. He handed Drucker a key. "You'll be in 331, sir. I hope you enjoy your stay with us. We've been here on the Marktplatz for more than two hundred years, you know. Bach and Liszt and Wagner have stayed here."

Not wanting to drop his air of lordly superiority, Drucker said, "I hope the plumbing is better now than it was in those days."

"Oh, yes, sir, *Herr* Schmidt," the clerk said. "You will find everything to your satisfaction."

"We'll see." Having established a personality, Drucker played it to the hilt. "Oh. One thing more. Where is the central post office?"

"On Dimitroffstrasse, sir, just west of the square here," the desk clerk answered. "You can't miss it."

That seemed worth another sneer. Having delivered it, Drucker climbed the hotel's sweeping staircase to the third floor. Once he got there, he discovered the bath was at the end of the hall. He felt like going down and complaining. It would have been in character. With a shrug, though, he let himself into the room. Except for the lack of private bath, it seemed comfortable enough.

He changed into fresh shirt and trousers and as nondescript a jacket as he owned. The jacket's one virtue was that it had big, roomy pockets. He put the pistol in one and a paperbound book in another, then went downstairs and headed across the square to Dimitroffstrasse.

For a wonder, the clerk had got it right: he couldn't have missed the post office, for it lay only a couple of buildings away from the Gothic church that dominated Weimar's skyline. The post-office building, on the other hand, was severely utilitarian. Drucker sat down inside on a bench that gave him a good look at the bank of postal boxes, pulled out the book, and began to read.

A Postal Protection NCO in field-gray uniform with orange piping strolled by and eyed him. The *Postschutz* was a branch of the SS, and had been since a couple of months before the Lizard invasion. Drucker kept on reading with a fine outward appearance of calm. The NCO paused between one step and another, then shrugged and walked on, his booted feet clicking on the marble floor. Drucker wasn't a bum or a drunk. He didn't look as if he intended causing trouble. If he felt like reading in a post office . . . well, there was no regulation against it.

Drucker kept a surreptitious eye on Box 127. He'd mailed Gunther Grillparzer—or rather, Grillparzer's alias, Maxim Kipphardt—his first payment two days earlier; it should be reaching Grillparzer today. By the way Grillparzer had sounded, he wouldn't let it sit around in the postal box for long. No, he'd spend it, either to keep a roof over his head or, perhaps more likely, on schnapps.

Maybe I should have worn a disguise, Drucker thought. But the idea of putting on false whiskers had struck him as absurd. And all the false whiskers he'd ever seen *looked* false. In the end, he'd decided that being what he was—an ordinary-looking middle-aged German in ordinary clothes—made as good a disguise as any. The ex-panzer gunner wouldn't have seen him for more than twenty years, after all.

The Postal Protection NCO tramped past him again. Drucker not only pretended to be absorbed in his book—a study of what people knew, or thought they knew, about Home—but actually got interested in it. That was an acting triumph of which he hadn't thought himself capable. The *Postschutz* man didn't even bother pausing this time. He'd accepted Drucker as part of the landscape.

A fat man came up and opened a postal box. It wasn't 127. When the fat man pulled out an envelope, he muttered something sulfurous under his breath. Drucker couldn't see the envelope. Was it a past-due bill? A letter from an ex-wife? A writer's rejection slip? He'd never know. Still muttering, the fat man went away. Drucker returned to his book.

When someone did come to Box 127, Drucker almost didn't notice: it wasn't Gunther Grillparzer but a blond woman—quite a good-looking one—in her mid- to late twenties. She took out an envelope—*the* envelope, the one Drucker had sent—and left the post office.

"Scheisse," Drucker muttered under his breath as he got to his feet, stuck the book in his pocket, and went out after the woman. Things weren't going as he'd planned. *No plan survives contact with the enemy,* he thought, all the while wishing Grillparzer hadn't found a way to complicate his life.

He hadn't been trained in shadowing people. Had the woman looked back over her shoulder, she would have spied him in the blink of an eye. But she didn't. She stood at a street corner, waiting for the trolley. Drucker decided to wait for the trolley, too. *What am I supposed to do now?* he wondered. He had no qualms about killing Gunther Grillparzer, none whatever. But a pretty stranger who might not even know what she was carrying in her handbag? That was a different business.

Here came the streetcar, clanging its bell. She got on. So did Drucker. He didn't know the right fare, and had to fumble in a pocket—not the one that held the pistol—for change. The trolley driver gave him a severe look. Feeling absurdly sheepish, he went back and sat down beside the young woman. She nodded politely and then ignored him. He marveled that she couldn't hear his heart pounding in his chest.

The streetcar rattled along for several blocks, heading into as seedy a part of town as Weimar had. When it stopped, the woman murmured, "Excuse me," and walked past Drucker and out. He didn't get out with her. That would have been giving himself away. Instead, he stared out the window, hoping to see where she headed.

He got lucky. A lorry on the cross street blocked the intersection for fifteen seconds or so. No matter how angrily the motorman clanged, the truck didn't—likely couldn't—move. That let Drucker see the woman go into a block of flats whose brick front was streaked with coal soot.

He got out at the next stop and hurried back to the apartment building. In the lobby, as he'd expected, he found a brass bank of mailboxes. None said *Gunther Grillparzer*. None said *Maxim Kipphardt*, either. Before he started knocking on doors at random—a desperation ploy if ever there was one—Drucker noticed that the one for 4E did say *Martin Krafft*. In detective novels, people often used aliases whose initials matched their real names. Martin Krafft wasn't Grillparzer's real name, but he'd said he'd been using a false one for a while. Without any better ideas—without any better hopes—Drucker started up the stairs.

Panting a little, wishing the place had a lift, he stood in the fourth-floor hallway, which smelled of cabbage and spilled beer. There was 4E, opposite the stairway. Drucker slipped his right hand into the pocket with the pistol. He thought fast as he advanced on the doorway and used his left hand to knock.

"Who is it?" The woman's voice. His knees sagged with relief: one right guess.

Drucker grimaced. Now he had to take another chance. "Telegram for Herr Krafft," he said. If Grillparzer wasn't there, life would get more difficult still. But, a moment later, the door opened and there stood the ex-panzer gunner, middle-aged and podgy fat and looking more than a little bottle-weary. He needed a couple of seconds to recognize Drucker, and that was a couple of seconds too long: by then, the pistol was aimed at his face. "Let me in, Gunther," Drucker said. "Don't do anything stupid, or you'll never do anything at all ever again. Keep your hands where I can see them."

"You won't get away with this," Grillparzer said as he backed away. Drucker came in and kicked the door shut behind him. His former comrade went on, "I thought you'd be a smart boy and pay me off. When I denounce you—"

Drucker laughed in his face. He tapped one of the buttons on his coat. "You fool—the SS is listening to you run your mouth now, thanks to my transmitter here." Grillparzer looked horrified. Drucker *was* horrified—at the bluff he was running. But, as Hitler had said, the bigger the lie, the better. "I *am* the SS, and you, my friend, have cooked your own goose—and your girlfriend's, too."

If the woman standing in back of Grillparzer had been his wife or his kid sister, Drucker wouldn't have looked infallible, and he might have had to start shooting. But the ex-gunner only grimaced. "Christ, what a pack of lies you must have told to get yourself into the SS, you murdering bastard."

"I don't know what you're talking about, and you can't prove I do—it's your word against mine," Drucker answered. "I do know, and I have evidence"—he tapped the button again—"that you've tried to blackmail me. Cough up the cash. You can't use it, anyhow. The banks have the serial numbers of all the notes on their watch list. As soon as you spent one, it'd just be another nail in your coffin."

He sounded convincing as hell. He would have believed himself. And Grillparzer believed him—or believed the pistol. Turning his head, he said, "Hand it over, Friedli. The son of a bitch has got us, dammit."

The woman had only to reach onto the cheap pine table behind her to retrieve the envelope. Drucker took it by one corner with his left hand. "Both your fingerprints are on this now, of course," he said cheerfully. The envelope had been opened, but still weighed about what it had when he'd posted it. Grillparzer and—Friedli?—hadn't had the chance to do much plundering. "Remember, if you even think of giving me grief again, you'll be sorrier than you can imagine."

"Christ, why didn't you just tell me over the phone you were a blackshirt along with being a spaceman?" Grillparzer asked. By the look in Friedli's eyes, he was going to be sorrier than he could imagine even if Drucker had nothing to do with it.

Cheerful still, Drucker answered, "You'll remember the lesson longer this way. *Auf wiedersehen*." And out the door he went.

☆ 5 ☆

Sam Yeager sighed. He'd drafted his son to feed Mickey and Donald breakfast, and Jonathan often gave the Lizard hatchlings supper, too. For their lunch, though, the kid was at school. That meant Sam needed to do the job himself.

Well, he could have given it to Barbara, but his pride prevented that. President Warren had assigned him the job of raising the baby Lizards, so he couldn't very well palm all of it off on his family. Besides, the critters were interesting. "I've been in the Army too long," he said as he stood in the kitchen slicing ham. "Even if it's fun, I don't want to do anything I have to."

"What did you say, honey?" Barbara called from their bedroom, which was at the other end of the house.

"Nothing, really—just grousing," he answered, a little embarrassed that she'd heard him. He looked at how much meat he'd cut. Just after the Lizards hatched, it would have kept them going for a couple of days. Now it was just one meal, or would be after he put a couple of more slices on the plate. Donald and Mickey were almost five months old now, and a lot bigger than when they'd fought their way out of their eggshells.

He took the plate piled high with ham down the hall to the Lizards' room. They still liked to bolt whenever they got the chance, so he shut the door at the end of the hall before opening theirs. These days, they didn't quite make the mad dash for freedom they had when they were smaller. It seemed more a game of the sort puppies or kittens might play. No matter what it was, though, he didn't feel like running after them, not at his age he didn't.

When he did open the door to their room, he found them rolling on the floor clawing and snapping at each other. They

126

rarely did any damage: again, they could have been a couple of squabbling puppies. From what he'd learned on the Race's computer network, these brawls were normal for hatchlings of their age. He didn't give his leather gauntlets a workout by pulling them apart, the way he had the first few times he'd caught them tangling.

Even though he didn't try to separate them, they sprang apart when he stepped inside. "You know I don't like you doing that, don't you?" he said to them. He talked to them whenever he fed them—whenever he had anything to do with them at all. They didn't pick up language and meaning as readily as human babies did. But he'd already seen they were a lot smarter than dogs or cats. That did make sense. By the time they grew up, they'd be at least as smart as he was, maybe smarter.

For the time being, they were more interested in him as the dinner wagon than in him as a person. Their eye turrets focused on the plate of sliced ham to the exclusion of everything else. They let out little excited hisses and snorts. Maybe it was Sam's imagination, but he thought he caught some humanlike sounds among their noises. Were they trying to imitate him and his family? He supposed he would have to listen to a comparison recording of the noises of Lizard-raised hatchlings to be certain.

"Come and get it, boys," he said, though Mickey and Donald might have been girls for all he knew. He crooked his finger in the come-here gesture people used.

It wasn't a normal Lizard gesture. When they wanted to tell someone to come, they used a twist of the eye turret to get the message across. But Yeager watched Mickey crook one of his skinny, scaly, claw-tipped tiny fingers in just the same way as he hurried forward to get his lunch.

Sam felt like cheering. Instead, he gave Mickey the first piece of ham. That usually went to Donald, who was a little larger and a little quicker. Mickey made the ham disappear in a couple of quick snaps. He cocked his head to one side and turned an eye turret up at Yeager, who was feeding Donald his first slice of meat.

What wheels were spinning inside Mickey's head? Sam had wondered that since the day the Lizard hatched. Lizards thought as well as people, but they didn't think like people in a lot of ways. And did hatchlings, could hatchlings, really think at all in the strict sense of the word when they had no words with which *to* think?

Quite deliberately, Mickey bent his finger into that purely human come-here gesture again. "You little son of a gun!" Yeager exclaimed. "You figured out that that means you get extra, didn't you?" He rewarded the hatchling with another piece of ham.

Donald had one eye turret on Sam, the other on Mickey. He saw the reward his—brother? sister?—had got. When he crooked his finger, he was imitating Mickey, not Yeager.

"No, you fellows aren't dumb at all," Sam said, and gave Donald some meat. From then on, both Lizards kept making come-hither gestures till Yeager ran out of ham. "Sorry, boys, that's all there is," he told them. They didn't understand that, any more than puppies or kittens would have. But their little bellies bulged, so they weren't in imminent danger of starving to death. He looked from one of them to the other. "I don't know. I have the feeling you guys may start talking sooner than you would if you were around a bunch of other Lizards. What have you got to say about that?"

They didn't have anything to say about that. Jonathan wouldn't have had anything to say about it at five months old, either. Physically, the Lizards were a long way ahead of where Jonathan had been at their age—he couldn't even sit up unsupported then, let alone run and jump and fight. Yeager had always thought they were developing more slowly when it came to mental processes.

Now, suddenly, he wasn't so sure. All right: maybe they wouldn't talk as fast as a human baby would. But, plainly, a lot was going on inside their heads. It might not come out in words. One way or another, though, it looked as if it would come out.

"See you later," Sam told them, and waved goodbye. To his disappointment, they didn't try to imitate that. Of course, it didn't have food attached to its meaning. Maybe the big difference between the way they thought and the way people thought was just that they were a lot more practical.

He went back to the kitchen, washed the plate, and set it in the dish drainer. Then he went back to the bedroom. "Those little guys are getting smarter," he told Barbara, and explained what the hatchlings had done.

"That *is* interesting," she said. "I think you're right. Something is definitely going on inside their heads—more than I would have expected, since they don't have words with which to form concepts."

"I was thinking the same thing," Sam answered: not surprising, considering that they were married and considering that he'd learned from her a lot of what he knew about the way languages worked. Something else was on his mind. "When do you suppose we can start letting them go around the house more?"

"When we can teach them not to tear up the furniture so much," Barbara replied promptly, as if she were talking about a couple of kittens that enjoyed sharpening their claws on the sofa. She went on, "If you're right, though, we really might be able to start trying to teach them."

"Might be worth doing. They'd enjoy it." Yeager was about to say something more, but paused, hearing footsteps on the front porch. If he could hear them, whoever was making them could hear him. A moment later, the mail slot in the front door opened. Envelopes landed on the rug. The footsteps went away. Sam said, "Let's see . . . to whom we owe money today." He wagged a finger under Barbara's nose. "You were going to nail me if I said, 'who we owe money to today.' "

"Of course I was," she answered. "That kind of grammar deserves it." But she was laughing; she didn't take herself too seriously, and didn't mind teasing about what she admitted to be her obsession. They went out together to check the mail.

"No bills," Yeager said with some relief, shuffling the envelopes. "Just ads and political junk."

"I won't be sorry to see the primary come," Barbara said. "It's still six weeks away, and look at everything we're getting. 'Junk' is right."

Yeager held up a flyer extolling the virtues of President Warren. "I don't know why his people bother to mail this stuff. He's going to get reelected in a walk, let alone renominated. Christ, I wouldn't be surprised if he won the Democratic primary, too."

"He's done a good job," Barbara agreed.

"I'll vote for him again, no doubt about it," Sam said. "And one of the reasons I'll vote for him again is that he doesn't take a lot of chances—which is probably why he has his people send this stuff out in carload lots."

"I suppose you're right," Barbara said. "But, since we already know what we're going to do . . ." She took the political flyers and the advertising circulars into the kitchen and pitched them in the trash.

"Good for you," Sam called after her. She was death on traveling salesmen, too. If they didn't back away in a hurry, they'd get their noses smashed when she slammed the door in their faces. Having grown up on a farm, where such visitors were always made welcome, Sam liked to chat with them. Half the time, he'd buy things from them, too. Barbara and he didn't have many arguments, but that could touch one off.

He went into the study and turned on the human-built computer that shared desk space with—and used more of it than—the Lizards' machine he preferred. But the Lizards didn't have access to the rather fragmentary network that had grown up in the United States over the past few years. He certainly hoped they didn't, anyhow. Still, if he could sneak around through their electronic playground, they were bound to be trying to sneak around through the USA's.

Waiting for the screen to come to life (which also took longer than it did in the Lizard-built computer), he wondered how good his country's electronic security really was. He'd got in Dutch when he poked his nose in where it didn't belong—he'd bought himself a royal chewing-out from a three-star general when he tried to find out what was going on with the *Lewis and Clark* before the United States was ready to let anybody know the answer.

With any luck at all, the Race would have as much trouble. But he hadn't tried to be sneaky. He supposed the Lizards would. And they'd been using computers as long as people had been counting on their fingers. How sneaky could they be if they put their minds to it?

That wasn't his problem. No: it *was* his problem, but he couldn't do anything about solving it. He had other things on his mind, anyway. In his spare time—a concept ever more mythical, now that Mickey and Donald were around—he kept poking around, trying to find leads that would show either the *Reich* or the USSR had blown up the ships from the colonization fleet. If he ever did find anything, he intended to pass it on to the Lizards. As far as he was concerned, that attack had been murder, and could have touched off a nuclear war. He wouldn't shed a tear if the Nazis or the Reds got hammered on account of it.

Thanks to his dealings with the Race, he had a security clearance that let him go almost anywhere on the U.S. network (not quite, as he'd found out when he went snooping after data on the *Lewis and Clark*). He'd found a couple of interesting archives of signals received just after the orbiting weapon, whoever it was, launched its warheads at the orbiting ships of the colonization fleet.

The screen went dark. After a moment, a message appeared: CONNECTION BROKEN. PLEASE TRY AGAIN. Disgustedly, he whacked the computer. That happened all too often with it. "Miserable half-assed piece of junk," he growled.

Few men in the history of the world—no, of the solar system—had enjoyed the view Glen Johnson had now. There was Ceres below him: mostly dust-covered rock, with a little ice here and there. It was the biggest asteroid in the whole damn belt, but not big enough to be perfectly round; it looked more like a roundish potato than anything else. The landscape put Johnson in mind of the heavily cratered parts of the moon. Rocks of all sizes had been slamming into Ceres for as long as it had been out there.

Colonel Walter Stone had a different way of looking at things. "That's the worst case of acne I've ever seen," he said.

"Yeah, any kid with that many zits wouldn't like high school a whole hell of a lot," Johnson agreed.

"None of the other asteroids can tease Ceres, though," his mentor observed. "They're all just as ugly and just as pockmarked—or if there are any that aren't, we haven't found 'em yet. Still, no matter how ugly it is, we're in business here, and that's what counts."

"We've been in business for a while, too," Johnson observed. "I can't believe how fast we got here."

"Just a couple of months." Stone sounded as complacent as if he'd got out behind the *Lewis and Clark* and pushed. "You have to remember, Glen old boy"—he put on a British accent too fruity to be real—"this isn't one of those old-fashioned *rocket* ships. They're as out of date as buggy whips, don't you know."

"And we could have been a little faster, too, if we hadn't swung wide to keep from coming too close to the sun." Johnson shook his head in slow wonder. "I wouldn't have believed how quick we could get here if I hadn't done the math—well, had the math done for me, anyhow."

"And if we hadn't been hanging around here in orbit for the past three and a half months," Stone added. "Except we're not really hanging around. We're going exploring. That's what it's all about."

"Finding that big chunk of ice only a few hundred miles away was a lucky break," Johnson remarked.

"That's not a chunk of ice—it's an asteroid," Walter Stone said. "And it was only part luck. There are lots of chunks of—uh, icy asteroids floating around here. The first exploration team saw that. No reason why one of 'em shouldn't be someplace where we can get at it."

Lieutenant Colonel Mickey Flynn, a large, solidly built fellow who let nothing faze him, floated into the control room. "I'm here a couple of minutes early out of the goodness of my heart," the *Lewis and Clark*'s second pilot said, "so you poor peasants can get an early start on supper. I expect nothing in return, mind you. Worship isn't necessary. Even simple adoration seems excessive."

"You're what seems excessive," Stone said with a snort. Being senior to Flynn, he could sass him with, if not impunity, at least something close. "And why should we trust anybody who's named after a knockout drop?"

"That's Finn, my cousin," Flynn said in dignified tones. "Sassenachs, the both of you. And Sassenachs wasting their time getting out of here by giving a hard time to a son of Erin who never did 'em any harm."

Johnson undid his harness. "I'll go to supper," he said, unsnapping his safety belt. Now that the *Lewis and Clark* was in orbit around Ceres, he didn't even have .01g to hold him in his seat. He pushed off, grabbed the nearest handhold, and then swung on to the next. Still snorting, Stone followed him.

Because of the banter they'd traded with their relief, the mess hall was already crowded when they got to it. Then the banter started up again. A woman called, "If you're here, who's flying the damn ship?"

"Nobody," Johnson shot back. "And if you don't believe me, go ask Flynn. He'll tell you the same thing."

"No, he'd say that was going on during the shift before his," somebody else returned. Walter Stone said something pungent. Johnson mimed being wounded. In spite of that, he was grinning. When he first involuntarily came aboard the *Lewis and Clark*, people wouldn't give him the time of day. They treated him like a spy. A lot of people had thought he was a spy.

Now he was one of the crew. He might not have helped build the spaceship, but he'd helped fly her. And even if he was a spy, he couldn't very well telephone whoever he was spying for, not from a quarter of a billion miles away he couldn't. What he could do, better than Stone or Flynn or anybody else, was fly the little hydrogen-burning rockets the *Lewis and Clark* used to explore the asteroids in Ceres' neighborhood. They weren't just like *Peregrine*, the upper stage he'd flown countless times in Earth orbit, but they weren't very far removed, either. He understood them, the way his grandfather had understood horses.

He didn't fully understand the dynamics of chow lines in weightlessness, not yet. At last, though, he drifted up in front of the assistant dietitian, who gave him chicken and potatoes that had been frozen and dried out and were now reconstituted with water. They tasted like ghosts of their former selves.

With them, he got a squeeze bulb full of water and a lidded plastic cup full of pills: vitamins and calcium supplements and God only knew what all else. "I think we carry more of these than we do of reaction mass," he said, shaking the pills.

The assistant dietitian gave him a dirty look. "What if we do?" she said. "If we get here but can't finish the mission because we're malnourished, what's the point of coming at all?"

"Well, you've got me there," Glen said, and drifted away. There weren't any tables or chairs—they were no good in weightlessness, or even in .01g. Instead, he snagged a handhold and started gossiping with some people who looked interesting—which was to say, at least in part, some people who were female.

More women had come along in the *Lewis and Clark* than he'd expected when he came aboard: they made up something close to a third of the crew. Very few of them were married to male crew members, either. Come to that, very few of the men were married. Johnson was divorced, Walter Stone a widower, Mickey Flynn a bachelor, and they were pretty typical of the crew.

And military rules about fraternization were a dead letter. The *Lewis and Clark* wasn't going home again. More people might come out, but nobody here was going back. People had to do the best they could with their lives out here, and to hell with Mrs. Grundy. So far as Johnson knew, nobody'd got pregnant yet, but that wasn't through lack of effort.

"Hi, Glen," said the mineralogist, a brunette named Lucy Vegetti. She was on the plump side, but he liked her smile. He liked any woman's smile these days. She went on, "Have you heard about the latest samples up from Ceres?"

He shook his head. "Nope, sure haven't. What's the new news?"

"Plenty of aluminum, plenty of magnesium, plenty of all the light metals," she said. "All we need is energy, and we can get them out of the rocks."

"We've got energy, by God—we've got more energy than you can shake a stick at," Johnson answered, pointing back toward the engine on its boom at the rear of the *Lewis and Clark.* "Just have to worry about getting it out." He was also worrying about getting it in, but not to the point where it made him stupid. Any man who lived by himself and didn't take advantage of the five-finger discount was a damn fool, as far as he was concerned.

One of the ship's three doctors—everything aboard the *Lewis and Clark* was as redundant as anybody could figure out how to make it—said, "But we can't build everything we'll need for the project out of aluminum and magnesium."

Johnson listened to Miriam Rosen with careful attention. He told himself he would have listened to her the same way even if she weren't a redhead who wasn't half bad-looking. Sometimes, for little stretches of time, he even believed it.

Lucy Vegetti said, "No, we can't build everything, but we can sure build a heck of a lot." She doubled in brass as an engineer, and was learning more about that part of her business every day. Redundancy again. Johnson was just glad he had one skill anybody aboard found useful. If he hadn't, he might have gone out the air lock instead of coming along for the ride.

"Can we really do this?" he asked. "Or will we all die of old age out here before it happens?"

For a little while, silence reigned around him. He grimaced. He'd asked the question too bluntly, and stuck his foot in it.

People knew they were never going to see Earth again, but they didn't like to think about that when they didn't have to. Just when the pause threatened to become really awkward, Dr. Rosen said, "We'll probably find plenty of things besides old age to die of."

That produced another silence, but not one aimed at Johnson. He smiled his thanks toward her. She didn't smile back. He'd got to know she was like that: she spoke the truth as she saw it.

"I think we can do it," Lucy Vegetti said. "I really do. Oh, we'll need more help from back home, but we'll get that. The *Lewis and Clark* showed that we could make constant-boost ships. The next one that comes out will be better. We'll have a good start on things by then, too. Pretty soon, we'll be mining a good stretch of the asteroid belt. I think we'll find most of the metals we need, sooner or later."

"What about uranium?" Miriam Rosen asked. "Not likely we'll find much of that here, is it?"

Lucy shook her head. "We'd have to get lucky, I think. The asteroids aren't as dense as rocks back on Earth, which means there are fewer heavy metals around. But you never can tell."

Was she looking at Johnson when she said "get lucky"? He wasn't sure, and he didn't want to foul up a chance for later by messing up now. The rules on the *Lewis and Clark* hadn't fully shaken out yet, but one thing was already clear: the ladies did the choosing. Maybe things would have been different if there'd been two gals for every guy, but there weren't.

A couple of other male optimists came floating up to join the conversation. Johnson took his squeeze bags and lidded cup now empty of pills back to the assistant dietitian. Nothing got thrown away on the *Lewis and Clark*; everything was cleaned and reused. That included bodily waste water: one more thing the crew preferred not to think about. A spaceship beat even a nuclear-powered submarine as a self-contained environment.

Swinging out of the galley, Johnson went to the gymnasium. He logged in, strapped himself onto an exercise bicycle, and grimly began pedaling away. That helped keep calcium in his bones. He wondered why he was bothering. If he wasn't going back to Earth and Earth's gravity, who cared if his bones were made of calcium or rubber bands?

But orders prescribed at least half an hour of exercise every day. He'd been in the Army too long to think orders had to make sense. They were just there, and they had to be obeyed. On he pedaled, going nowhere.

In his time in Lodz, Mordechai Anielewicz had heard a lot of strange noises coming from alleys. Once, he'd foiled a robbery, though he hadn't caught the robber: the fellow had leaped over a wall—an Olympic-quality jump—and got away. Once, he'd surprised a couple making love standing up in a doorway. He'd felt like leaping over a wall himself then; Bertha still didn't know about that.

More often than not, though, noises down alleys meant animal fights: dog-dog, cat-cat, cat-dog. These furious snarls were of that sort, and under most circumstances Mordechai would have paid them no special attention. But, as he walked past the mouth of the alley, some of the noises proved to have a stridency the likes of which he'd never heard before. Almost before he knew what he was doing, he craned his neck to see what the devil was going on.

He was surprised enough to stop in midstride, one foot off the ground, till he noticed and made it come down. The alley was just an alley: cobblestones, weeds pushing up among them, a couple of dead vodka bottles. One of the beasts down it was a cat, sure enough; it was clawing at its foe like a lioness ripping the guts out of a zebra. But that foe . . .

"*Gevalt,* what is that thing?" Mordechai exclaimed, and hurried past a battered trash barrel toward the fight to find out. Whatever it was, he'd never seen anything like it. It was clawing at the cat, too, but it was also biting, and it had a very big mouth full of sharp teeth. Pretty plainly, it was getting the better of the fight, for the cat's claws and even its needle-sharp canines had trouble piercing its scaly hide.

Anielewicz stooped and grabbed a stick—always handy to have when breaking up a fight between animals—before advancing on the cat and the . . . thing. He hadn't taken more than a couple of steps toward the beasts when the cat decided it had had enough. It broke free of the fight and levitated up a wooden fence, leaving only bloodstains behind to prove it had been there.

The other animal was bleeding, too, though not so badly. Now that Mordechai got a good look at it, he saw it was smaller than the cat it had just mauled. It stuck out a long, forked tongue and licked a couple of its worst wounds. It was looking at him, too; while it tended to itself, one turreted eye swung in his direction to make sure he didn't mean trouble.

Realization smote him. "It must be from the Lizards' world!" he exclaimed: either that, or he was hallucinating. He shook his head; he couldn't have imagined anything so funny-looking. And he did remember hearing that the colonization fleet had brought along some of the Lizards' domesticated creatures. He hadn't expected his first meeting with one to be in an alley, though.

Now that it wasn't fighting, the Lizardy thing—he didn't know what else to call it—seemed to relax. When Mordechai didn't wave the stick or do anything else untoward, the animal turned both eye turrets toward him and let out an absurdly friendly squeak.

He laughed. He couldn't help himself. Snarls and hisses were one thing. He would have expected noises like those from a small creature that could take on a cat and win. He hadn't expected the thing to sound like a rubber squeeze toy.

Whatever he thought of the noises the animal made, it didn't like the ones he made. It streaked past him, nimble as a champion footballer getting past a midfielder who only stepped onto a soccer pitch as a weekend amusement. It was, he thought, even faster and more agile than a cat, though it had shown no signs of being able to climb.

Out on the street, someone exclaimed in surprise: "What was *that*?" "What was what?" somebody else—a woman—said. "I didn't see anything."

Anielewicz laughed again as he threw down the stick and walked out of the alley. Some people were always unlucky enough to miss things. He wondered if this lady would ever have another chance to see an animal from another planet.

He also wondered, in a different and more urgent way this time, what an animal from another planet was doing in an alley in Lodz (besides fighting a cat, that is). He hadn't intended to go by the Bialut Market Square—Bertha was reluctant to let him anywhere near the place, too, after his fiasco with the peasant woman selling eggs—but Bunim's headquarters looked out onto it. He didn't suppose the Lizards would mind talking about the animals they'd brought to Earth.

As he started for the market square, he laughed again. He wasn't likely to have much immediate interest in animals from Home, and neither was any other Polish Jew. How likely were they to divide the hoof and chew a cud? Not very, which put them beyond the pale as far as he was concerned.

People and a few Lizards crowded the square. Since Mordecai wasn't shopping, he ignored the frantic haggling in Yiddish and Polish and, every now and then, the hisses and pops of the language of the Race. He strode up to the building from which the Lizards administered this stretch of Poland—along with the shadow governments of the Jews and Poles. The guards in front of the building were alert, as they had reason to be. "What do you want?" one of them asked in passable Polish.

The male didn't recognize him. Well, that was all right; he had trouble telling one Lizard from another. "I just saw an animal . . ." he began, also sticking to Polish—he could do a better job of describing the creature in that tongue than in the Race's.

"Ah," the guard said when he was through. "That is a beffel. They *will* run wild. 'Crazy as a beffel on a leash' is a saying in our language."

"A beffel," Mordecai repeated—now he had a name for the beast. "What good is it? Do you eat it, or is it just a pet?"

"Eat a beffel? What an ignorant Tosevite you are." The guard's mouth dropped open in amusement. So did his partner's. "No. It is only a pet, as you say."

"All right. I *am* ignorant—I'd never seen one till now. It was fighting a cat," Anielewicz said. "Are they going to start running loose all over the place now?"

"I would not be surprised," the guard replied. "They get to be nuisances back on Home. So do tsiongyu."

"What's a tsiongi?" Mordecai asked.

"Another kind of pet, larger," the guard said. "You speak some of our language, to know the singular when you hear the plural."

"Truth," Anielewicz answered, shifting to the language of the Race. "So: are we to be overrun with animals from Home?"

"If we so choose," the Lizard replied. "We rule this part of

Tosev 3. We have the right to bring in the beasts on which we feed—and we are doing that, too—and the beasts that are our friends. What business do you have to say otherwise?"

That was a pretty good question, although the male sounded arrogant even for one of his kind. Mordechai didn't try to answer it. Instead, he asked a question of his own: "How will your animals like the winters here in Poland?"

By the way both guards winced, he knew he'd struck a nerve. "We cannot know that until we find out by experiment," said the one who was doing the talking. "The hope is that they will do well. I certainly hope this. Our beasts are better eating than your Tosevite animals."

"Truth." The other guard proved he could talk.

Anielewicz wondered if he needed to go inside and talk with Bunim. He decided he didn't. He'd learned everything he needed to know from the regional subadministrator's guards. Bunim wouldn't stop bringing his kinds of animals into Poland just because Mordechai asked him to. Europeans had brought cows and pigs and dogs and cats to America and Australia. Why wouldn't the Race bring its creatures to Earth? The Lizards had come to stay, after all.

And the Poles probably wouldn't mind the new domestic animals one bit. They didn't have to worry about keeping kosher. Mordechai chuckled, wondering how soon some strange meat would start turning up in Polish farmwives' pots and how soon Polish leather makers would start tanning new kinds of hide. *Sooner than the Lizards expect,* he thought. Yes, the Poles were very likely to turn into—what did the Westerns imported from the United States call cattle thieves? *Rustlers,* that was it. And an old joke about the recipe for chicken stew floated through his mind. *First, steal a chicken. . . .*

"Do you need anything else?" the first guard asked.

If that wasn't a hint for Anielewicz to clear out, he'd never heard one. "No. I thank you for your time," he said, and made his way back across the Bialut Market Square. These days, he was always in the habit of keeping an eye open for possible assassins: amazing what a burst of submachine-gun fire through the door would do. Now, though, he also kept an eye out for befflem and tsiongyu. He wouldn't have known a tsiongi if it walked up and bit him, not really, but any sort of alien animal that wasn't a beffel would do for one till he knew better.

No doubt because he was on the lookout for the Race's pets, he saw none as he went back to the flat. All the way there, though, he kept thinking about how the beffel had laid up that cat. Cats were tough; not many Earthly animals their size could take them on and win. What did that say about how rugged other beasts from Home were liable to be? Did it say anything at all? Nobody could predict a cow from a cat, so why was he trying to figure out what the Race's equivalent of a cow would be like from extremely brief acquaintance with a beffel?

Then he paused, smiling in spite of himself. The Lizardy creature had squeaked most endearingly. He wondered what sort of pet a beffel would make for a human being. Would it accept a person as a master, or would it think he was a large, fearsome wild animal?

His son Heinrich would like to know the answer to that question, too. Heinrich couldn't see a stray dog without saying, "Can we keep it?" The answer, in a flat none too big for the people who lived in it, was inevitably no, but that didn't keep him from asking.

Over supper—chicken soup with dumplings—Mordechai talked about the beffel. Sure enough, Heinrich exclaimed, "What a great-sounding animal! I want one! Can we get one, Father?"

Before Anielewicz could answer, Heinrich's older sister Miriam said, "A thing that looks like a little Lizard? That's disgusting! I don't want anything that looks like a Lizard here." She made a horrible face.

"A beffel looks about as much like a Lizard as a cat or a dog looks like a person. It's about so long"—Mordechai held his hands thirty or forty centimeters apart—"and goes on all fours."

"Like a regular lizard—not like one of the Race, I mean?" His daughter sounded no happier. "That's even worse."

"No, not like a regular lizard, either," Anielewicz said. "Sort of like what a dog or a cat would be if a dog or a cat had scales and eye turrets." Predictably, that entranced Heinrich and even interested his older brother David, but left Miriam cold.

"There's no point in worrying about these creatures now," Bertha Anielewicz said, spreading warning looks all around.

"We don't have them, and as far as we know, we can't get them. We don't even know"—she eyed Heinrich—"if we'd want one."

"*I* know!" her younger son exclaimed.

"You've never even seen one," Bertha said.

But that was the wrong way to go about things, and Mordechai knew it. "For now, I don't think people can have bef-flem, so there's nothing we can do about that," he told Heinrich. "Anyhow, I just saw this one by luck. I don't know if I'll ever see another one, so there's no point worrying about it, is there?"

"If I find one, can I keep it?" Heinrich asked.

"I don't think you're going to," his mother said, "but all right." Heinrich grinned from ear to ear. Bertha looked confident. Mordechai wished she would have given him the chance to speak first. But she hadn't, and now they were both stuck with her answer.

Kassquit was as happy as the anomalous combination of her birth and her upbringing let her be. She hadn't fully realized how much she missed Ttomalss till he returned from the Greater German *Reich*. Of all the males of the Race, he came closer to understanding her than any other. Having him around, having him here to talk to, was far better than staying in touch by telephone and electronic message.

"In a way, though," he said as they sat down together in the starship's refectory, "my absence may well have helped you mature. You might not have confronted Tessrek had I been here, for instance; instead, you would have left the disagreeable task to me. But you did it, and did it well."

"Only because I had to," answered Kassquit, who would indeed have preferred not to confront a male of superior years and rank.

"Exactly my point." Ttomalss picked up his tray. "And now I hope you will excuse me. I have many reports to organize and write. My stay among the Deutsche proved most informative, if not always very pleasant."

"I understand, superior sir." Kassquit did her best to hide her disappointment. She was not a hatchling any more, and could not hope to monopolize Ttomalss' time as she had when she was smaller and more nearly helpless. She could not hope to, but she could wish.

After Ttomalss left, she finished her meal in a hurry. She did not enjoy the company of large numbers of the Race; seeing so many males and females together always acutely reminded her of how different she was. Back inside her cubicle, she was simply herself, and did not need to make comparisons.

She was simply herself on the electronic network, too. What she looked like, what she sounded like, didn't matter there. Only her wit mattered—and that, she had seen, was a match for those of most males and females. No wonder she spent so much time in front of the screen, then.

She was heading toward the area where males and females discussed the new generation of the Race that had been hatched on Tosev 3 when the telephone attachment hissed for attention. With a sigh, she arrested her progress on the network and activated the phone connection. "Kassquit speaking. I greet you."

"And I greet you, superior female." No image appeared on the screen; the conversation remained voice-only. The male on the other end of the line—a male with a voice of odd timbre—went on, "I needed to do a little of this and a little of that before I was able to call you, but I managed."

"Who is this?" Kassquit asked in some annoyance. Whoever he was, he had a very strange voice: not only deeper than it had any business being, but also mushy, as if he were talking with his mouth full.

"What?" he said, and somehow managed to make his interrogative cough sound sarcastic. "You mean you do not recognize the voice of your old not-quite-friend, the senior tube inspector?"

Ice and fire chased each other through Kassquit. "Oh, by the Emperor," she whispered, and cast down her eyes. "You are a Tosevite." She was talking with a wild Big Ugly. Somehow, he'd found her telephone code and arranged access to a phone connected to the Race's communication system.

"I sure am," answered the Big Ugly male she thought of as Regeya. "I bet you could tell the instant I opened my mouth. I cannot make some of your sounds the way . . ." His voice trailed off. With dull horror, Kassquit knew what was coming next. Regeya was no fool. He'd heard her speak. She reached for the recessed key that would break the connection, but her hand faltered and stopped. The tongue was out of the mouth any which way. If the worst was coming, she might as well hear it. And it was. In slow wonder, Regeya went on, "You have trouble with the same sounds I do. Are you by any chance a Tosevite yourself, Kassquit?"

Kassquit thought she spoke much better than the wild Big Ugly. Not only did he have trouble with some of the pops and special hisses of the Race's tongue, but he also spoke it with an odd syntax and accent: shadows, no doubt, of his own Tosevite language. But that had nothing to do with anything. "I am a full citizen of the Empire," she answered proudly.

Despite the pride, it was an evasion, and Regeya recognized as much. "You did not answer my question," he said. "*Are* you a Tosevite?" He answered it himself: "You must be. But how did it happen? What made you throw in your lot with the Race?"

He thought she was a Tosevite traitor, as some males of the Race from the conquest fleet had turned traitor after the Big Uglies captured them. She proceeded to disabuse him of the notion. "I would not be anything but a citizen of the Empire," she declared. "The Race has raised me since earliest hatchlinghood."

Regeya said something in his own language that she didn't understand, then let out several barking yips of Tosevite laughter. When at last he returned to the language of the Race, his only comment was, "Is that a fact?"

"Yes, it is a fact," Kassquit said with more than a little irritation. "Why in the name of the Emperor"—calling on him made her feel more secure—"would I waste my time lying to you? You are on the surface of Tosev 3, while I orbit above it. Since you must remain there, what can you possibly do to me?"

She'd nipped the Big Ugly's pride, but not quite as she'd expected. "I have been farther from Tosev 3 than you," he answered, "for I have walked on the surface of the moon. So I might visit you one day."

I hope not, was the first thought that went through Kassquit's mind. The idea of coming face to face with a wild Big Ugly terrified and horrified her. Nor would she tolerate Regeya's scoring points off her. "You may have gone from Tosev 3 to its moon," she said, "but the Race has come from its sun to the star Tosev."

"Well, that is a truth," the Big Ugly admitted. "Pretty proud of the Empire, eh?" That last grunt was almost an interrogative cough in its own right.

"I am part of it. Why should I not feel pride in it?" Kass-quit said.

"All right—something to that, too," Regeya said. "How old are you, Kassquit? How old were you when the Race took you from the female who bore you?"

"I was taken away when I was newly hatched," Kassquit answered. "Had I been brought up as a Big Ugly, even in part, I would have had more trouble becoming as fully a part of the Race as I have. The male who raised me began the project not long after the fighting stopped."

"So you would be close to twenty now?" Regeya said, half to himself. Kassquit began to correct him, but then realized he naturally reckoned by Tosevite years rather than those of the Race. Laughing again, he went on, "Well, well, quite a head start." Kassquit didn't know what that meant. Regeya was still talking: "Did the male who raised you tell you that you were not his first attempt?"

"Oh, yes," Kassquit replied at once. "He had to return one hatchling to the Tosevites because of political considerations, and was kidnapped while seeking to obtain another. With me, however, he succeeded." *As much as he could, as much as anyone could,* she thought. But she would not let the Big Ugly see what lay in her mind.

"He was honest with you, at any rate. That is something," Regeya said. "And you may be interested to know that I have met the Tosevite whom your male released. She is a normal young adult female in most ways, except that her face has no motion in it to speak of."

"Neither has mine," Kassquit said. "Here among the Race, that is of small account."

"Yes, I suppose it would be," Regeya said. "It is different among us Big Uglies." He wasn't shy about using the Race's nickname for his—and Kassquit's—kind. "You may also be interested to know that she—this other female—is one of the leaders in the rebellion against the Race in China."

"No, that does not interest me at all," Kassquit answered. "In the long run, rebellions will not matter. All of Tosev 3 will become part of the Empire. Males and females will be proud citizens, as I am."

"That is possible," the Big Ugly on the other end of the line said, which surprised her. He went on, "But I do not think it is certain. Our kind"—by which, to Kassquit's annoyance, he had to mean his and hers—"is different from the Race in important ways. For instance, we are sexually receptive all the time, and the Race is not. Do you not agree that that is an important difference? How do you deal with it, there by yourself?"

"None of your business," Kassquit snapped. She felt blood rising to her face, as it did when she was embarrassed. Having continuous sexuality among beings who did not was extremely embarrassing. She had learned that stroking her private parts brought relief from the tension that sometimes threatened to overwhelm her, but she'd been humiliated to find out Ttomalss knew what she did, even if he intellectually understood her need. She wished she were like the Race in that regard, but she wasn't.

To her relief, Regeya did not press her. He said, "I am going to go now. I am using a telephone at the Race's consulate in Los Angeles, and it is expensive for me. If you want to get in touch with me again, my name is Sam Yeager. I decided to call just to say hello. I tell you the truth when I say that I had no idea I would be speaking with another Tosevite."

"I am not a Tosevite, not in the same sense you are," Kassquit said, once more with considerable pride. "As I told you, I am a citizen of the Empire, and glad of it." Now she broke the connection. She did not think it would offend the Big Ugly—the *other* Big Ugly—for Sam Yeager (not Regeya) had already said he was going.

A wild Tosevite . . . Her hand moved in the gesture of negation. The two of them might be similar genetically, but in no other way. His accent, his alien way of looking at things, made that perfectly clear.

But, in some ways, genetics and genetic predispositions did matter. Regeya had, for instance, unerringly focused on her sexuality as an important difference between herself and the Race. Ttomalss, looking at the issue from the other side of the divide, had proved far less perceptive.

Kassquit wondered what the Big Ugly looked like.

It does not matter, she told herself. He probably had hair all over his head, which would make him even uglier than Tosevites had to be. His face would be snoutless, his skin scaleless. He could not help being ugly, given all that. But she remained curious about the details.

On the telephone, he seemed much as he did in his electronic messages: clever, and possessed of a quirky wit very different from the way males and females of the Race thought. She should have despised him for being what he was. She tried, but could not do it. He intrigued her too much.

He is a relation, she thought. *In a way, he is the closest relation with whom I have ever spoken.* She shivered, though the air in her chamber was not cold, or even cool: it was adjusted to the warmth the Race found comfortable. She'd never known air of a different temperature. She'd never known anyone but males and females of the Race, either—not till now, she hadn't. She shivered again.

Over lamb chops and carrots and mashed potatoes, Jonathan Yeager listened to his father in fascination. "That's amazing," he said. "They're holding her prisoner up there, and she doesn't even know she is one."

His father shook his head. "Are Mickey and Donald prisoners?"

"No," Jonathan said. "We're raising them to see how much like people they'll turn into. They're guinea pigs, I guess, but they're not . . ." Shoveling in another forkful of potatoes let him make the pause less awkward than it might have been otherwise. "Okay. I see where you're going."

"The girl up there is a guinea pig, too," his mother said.

"That's right." Now his father nodded. "Twenty years ago, the Lizards started doing what we're doing now. I wonder what sort of experiments they've run on her." He sipped from a glass of Lucky Lager. "Makes me think twice about what we're doing with the baby Lizards—seeing the shoe on the other foot, I mean."

"It certainly does," Jonathan's mother said. "That poor girl—brought up to be as much like a Lizard as she could?" She shuddered. "If she's not completely out of her mind, it's God's own miracle."

"She sounded sensible enough," his father said. "She doesn't know what being a human is like. What bothers her most, I think, is that she can't be as much like the Race—like the rest of the Race, she'd probably say—as she'd like."

"If that's not crazy, what is?" his mother returned. His father took another sip of beer, in much the same way as Jonathan had eaten those mashed potatoes.

"We ought to set her free," Jonathan exclaimed: the idea blazed in him. "We—the United States, I mean—ought to tell the fleetlord we know they've got her and they have to let her go."

He expected his mother and father to catch fire, too. Instead, they looked at each other and then at him. "I don't think that would be a good idea, Jonathan," his mother said after a moment.

"What? Why not?" he demanded. "If I'd been living up there all this time, I'd sure want to be free."

"No." His father shook his head in a way that could only mean he was ready to lock horns on this one. "If you'd been living up there all this time, you'd want what Kassquit wants: to be more like a Lizard. You play games about imitating the Race. With her, it's not a game. It's the real thing."

Jonathan started to get angry at that. A couple of years earlier, he would have for sure. His old man had a lot of damn nerve saying his study of the Race was only a game. But, he had to admit, trying to live like the Lizards wasn't the same as never having seen, never even having talked to, another human being in his life. "Well, maybe," he said grudgingly—from him, a large concession.

His father must have seen that he'd been on the point of blowing up, because he leaned across the kitchen table and set a hand on Jonathan's for a moment. "You're growing up," he said, which almost caused trouble again, because Jonathan was convinced he'd already grown up. But then his dad said something that distracted him: "Besides, if you look at it the right way, Kassquit's our ace in the hole."

"Huh?" Jonathan said.

"I don't follow that, either," his mother added. With a pointed look at Jonathan, she went on, "I'm more polite about the way I say it, though."

His father grinned. He always did when he put one over on Jonathan's mom, not least because he didn't do that very often. He said, "Suppose the Race finds out we've got Mickey and Donald. What will the fleetlord do? Scream his head off, that's what, and probably tell us to give 'em back before he sends in the Lizard Marines."

"Oh, I get it!" Jonathan said excitedly. "I get it! That's hot, Dad! If he says, 'Give 'em back,' we can answer, 'Why should I? You've had this girl for years.' " His old man could be sneaky, no two ways about it.

But Jonathan's mother said, "I don't like that, Sam. It turns the girl into nothing but a pawn."

"Hon, we both just told Jonathan that Kassquit's never, ever going to have a normal life or anything close to it," his father said. "She's been the Lizards' pawn ever since they got hold of her. If she turns out to be our pawn, too, what's so bad about that?"

"I don't know," his mother answered. Her gaze went down the hall toward Mickey and Donald's room. "It's different somehow, thinking of that being done to a human being rather than a Lizard."

"That's what the Race would say, too, Mom, except they'd put it the other way round," Jonathan said.

"He's not wrong, hon," his father said. His mother still didn't look happy, but she finally nodded. His father went on, "And speaking of Mickey and Donald . . ." He got up from the table and put his dishes in the sink, then pulled a knife from the drawer next to it and opened the refrigerator. "Time they had their supper, too."

Jonathan also got up. "I'll feed 'em, Dad, if you want me to."

"Thanks." His father nodded. "I'm glad you help with the chores around here, believe me I am, but I'll take care of this. I was the one who got ordered to raise them, after all, so I will."

"Well, I'll come along, if that's okay," Jonathan said. "I like Lizards, in case you hadn't noticed." He tapped himself on the chest. With the weather warm, he didn't bother wearing a shirt. This week, his body paint declared him an electronic instruments repairmale.

His father paused while slicing corned beef. (Jonathan sometimes thought the hatchlings ate better than he did. But then, the government paid for all their food, while his folks had to shell out for what went down his throat.) "Sure. Come right ahead. Be good for the little guys to know people visit sometimes, that we aren't just the gravy train."

As they walked down the hall toward the Lizards' room, Jonathan asked, "Aren't you going to shut that door?"

"Hmm? Oh. Yeah." His dad did, but then said, "It won't be too long, or I hope it won't, before we don't have to do that any more. We'll be able to start letting them loose in the house. I hope we will, anyhow."

"You don't think they'll rip the furniture to ribbons?" Jonathan said. "Mom won't be real happy if they do."

"Well, neither will I—we've talked about that," his father answered as he opened the door to Mickey and Donald's room. "But heck, you can teach a cat to use a scratching post—most of the time, anyhow—so I figure we can probably teach these guys to do the same thing. They're smarter than cats, that's for darn sure."

The hatchlings had been playing some sort of game with a red rubber ball—an active one, by the way they stopped and stood there panting when Jonathan and his father came in. The ball was about golf-ball size. A human baby would have stuck it in his mouth and likely choked to death. Jonathan wouldn't have known something like that for himself, but his parents both insisted it was true. Mickey and Donald were different, though. Unlike human babies, they knew from the very beginning what was food and what wasn't; at need, they could catch their own.

Donald did something with the ball no cat could: he picked it up and threw it at Jonathan. Jonathan tried to catch it, but it bounced off his hand and away. Both Donald and Mickey sprang after it. His father clicked his tongue between his store-bought teeth. "Have to score that one an error, son."

"Yeah, I know," Jonathan said in mild annoyance. He was sure that, had the baby Lizard thrown the ball at his father, he would have caught it even though he had only one free hand. Jonathan was stronger than his dad these days, but he still wasn't half the ballplayer his father was. That got under his skin when he let himself think about it.

But he preferred thinking about Mickey and Donald. "Come and get it," his father told them, and they didn't waste much time abandoning the ball for corned beef. He and Jonathan both talked to them, and with each other. *Letting them get used to the idea of language,* Jonathan's dad always called that. Turning to Jonathan, he remarked, "They aren't stupid—they're just different."

"Uh-huh." Jonathan could get away with grunts and even split infinitives around his father, where his mother would come down on him like a ton of bricks. He sometimes wondered if his dad found talking around his mom hard, too. But that wasn't anything he could ask. Instead, he pointed to Mickey, who had a little shred of corned beef hanging from one corner of his mouth, and said, "You're a little pig, you know that?"

One of the hatchling's eye turrets swung to follow his pointing finger: it might have been danger, or so evolution warned. Mickey's other eye kept watching Jonathan's father, who at the moment emphatically was the source of all blessing. Sure enough, he offered Mickey another strip of corned beef, and the little Lizard leaped forward to take it.

"I wonder what he and Donald will be like in twenty years," Jonathan's father said, and then, more than half to himself, "I wonder if I'll be around to see it."

Jonathan had no idea how to respond to that last sentence, and so he didn't. He said, "I wonder what that—Kassquit, was that her name?—is like now. She'd be somewhere close to my age, wouldn't she?"

"Maybe a little younger—she said the Lizards got her after the fighting stopped," his father answered. "She's smart—no two ways around that. But as for the rest . . . I just don't know. Pretty strange. She can't help that."

"I'd like to talk with her myself," Jonathan said. "It would be interesting." He used an emphatic cough, forgetting he wasn't supposed to do that around Mickey and Donald.

"Don't know if I could arrange it," his father said, in tones suggesting he had no intention of trying. But then his gaze sharpened. "You know, it might not be so bad if I could, though, especially with the video hooked up. You look like a Lizard, you know what I mean?—or as much as a person can."

"That might make her feel easier," Jonathan agreed, and then, "What does she look like?"

His father laughed. "I don't know. She didn't have her video on, either."

"Okay, okay. I just asked, that's all." But Jonathan was glad Karen hadn't been around to hear that question. She wouldn't have taken it the right way. He was sure of that. *Women are so unreasonable,* he thought, and never stopped to wonder how he would have felt had she asked whether some man was good-looking.

Donald and Mickey were both looking at his father. "Sorry, boys," Sam Yeager told them. "That's all there is—there ain't no more." He winked at Jonathan, as if to say he knew he was putting one over on Jonathan's mother by using bad grammar behind her back. The baby Lizards didn't understand anything about that, but they'd put away enough corned beef that they weren't too disappointed not to get any more.

"Bye-bye," Jonathan said to them, and waved. His father echoed him with word and gesture. And, a little tentatively, a little awkwardly, the hatchlings waved back. Even a couple of weeks before, they hadn't known to do that. Excitement tingled through Jonathan. The Lizards couldn't talk. Heaven only knew when they would. But they'd started to communicate without words.

"Slowly," Ttomalss said. "Tell me slowly about the conversation you had with this Big Ugly." He was most careful not to say, *with this other Big Ugly.*

"It shall be done, superior sir," Kassquit said, but a moment later she was babbling again, her words falling over one another in their eagerness to come forth. Ttomalss tried to decide whether that eagerness sprang from glee at surviving the encounter or from Kassquit's desire to talk with the Tosevite— *the other Tosevite*—again as soon as she got the chance. He couldn't.

I shall have to check the recording of the conversation myself, the researcher thought. Kassquit didn't know her telephone was constantly monitored. Ttomalss knew he would have to take care not to reveal any undue knowledge. That would destroy Kassquit's spontaneity and lessen her value as an experimental subject.

When she finally slowed down, Ttomalss asked her, "And how do you feel about this encounter?"

Her face, unlike those of Big Uglies raised by their own

kind, revealed little of what she thought. That made her seem a little less alien to Ttomalss. After a pause for thought, she said, "I do not precisely know, superior sir. In some ways, he seemed to understand me remarkably well."

Like calls to like, Ttomalss thought. But he did not say it, for fear of putting thoughts in Kassquit's mind that she hadn't had for herself. What he did say was more cautious: "In some ways, you say? But not in all?"

"Oh, no, superior sir, not in all," Kassquit answered. "How could that be possible? I have been raised among the Race, while he is only a wild Big Ugly."

Unmistakable pride rang in her voice. Ttomalss understood that; he wouldn't have wanted to be a wild Big Ugly, either. He asked, "Are you interested in holding further conversations with this—what did you say the Tosevite's name was?"

"Sam Yeager." Kassquit, naturally, pronounced the alien syllables more clearly than Ttomalss could have done. "Yes, superior sir, I think I am—or willing, at any rate. You have spoken of me as a link between the Race and the Tosevites. I know the Race's side of this link well. Except for my biology, though, I know next to nothing about the Tosevite side."

Her ignorance was deliberate on Ttomalss' part; he'd wanted to integrate her as fully into the Race as he could. Now it was time to see how well he'd done. But something else sprang to mind first. "Sam Yeager?" he said, knowing he was botching the name but wanting to bring it out as well as he could. "That is somehow familiar. Why is it somehow familiar?"

"I do not know, superior sir," Kassquit answered. "It was not familiar to me."

But Ttomalss hadn't asked the question of her, not really; he'd been talking to himself. He went over to his computer terminal and keyed in the name. The answer came back almost at once. "I thought so!" he exclaimed, skimming through the information on the screen. "This Yeager is one of the Big Uglies' leading experts on the Race, and has done considerable writing and speaking on the subject."

"As if the Big Uglies could have experts on the Race!" Kassquit said scornfully.

"They seek to learn about us, as we seek to learn about them," Ttomalss answered. "I am, in some measure, an expert on Tosevites, so this Big Ugly may be my counterpart in the not-empire known as the United States."

After some thought, Kassquit made the affirmative gesture. "It could be so," she said. "He appeared on our computer network for some time without drawing suspicion. No one with only a little familiarity with the Race could have done that."

"Truth," Ttomalss said; he would not have cared to try to impersonate a Big Ugly, even if only electronically. "In his way, then, he too may be a link between the Tosevites and the Race. Perhaps further conversations between you may indeed be of value. I am glad you are willing to hold them."

"I suppose I am," Kassquit agreed. "We must make arrangements before we can do that, of course. His telephone is not fully integrated into our network; he came to our consulate in his city to call me. I can exchange messages with him by computer, but that is not quite the same thing."

"No—it lacks immediacy," Ttomalss agreed. "But it will do to set up a time for another conversation. Feel free to make those arrangements."

"Very well, superior sir." Kassquit assumed the posture of respect. "I depart." She left his compartment, ducking her head a little to get out through the doorway.

Ttomalss wondered if he ought to get in touch with this Yeager himself. After the Deutsche, a Tosevite who showed some understanding of the Race would prove a refreshing change. In the end, though, he refrained. *Let Kassquit handle it,* he thought. *Best to learn how she will fare in this new situation.* She had the right of it; he had brought her up as a link between the wild Tosevites and the Empire, between Tosev 3's past and its future. An unused link was useless.

And it was very interesting indeed that the Big Uglies were developing links of their own to the Race. Ttomalss spoke into the computer: "The Tosevites consistently demonstrate coping skills far superior to those the Rabotevs and the Hallessi showed after their initial contact with the Race. This no doubt hatches from the intense competition among groups of Big Uglies prior to the arrival of the Race. The Tosevites have come to view us as if we were one more of their not-empires: dangerous to them, but not necessarily of overwhelming superiority."

He stabbed out a fingerclaw and turned off the recording

mechanism. Nevertheless, he continued speaking out loud. It helped him put his thoughts in order: "And how do the Tosevites' coping skills compare to those of the Race? Unless I am badly mistaken, they outdo us to the same degree as they do the Rabotevs and Hallessi. They are used to dealing with powerful rivals and to adapting themselves to changing circumstances. Both these things are unfamiliar to us, or were unfamiliar to us before we came to Tosev 3."

He sighed. That was, if anything, an understatement. Back on Home and throughout the Empire, the Race viewed change with active suspicion. It occurred slowly, over centuries, so that it was rarely visible in the course of a male or female's lifetime. Things weren't like that on Tosev 3—another understatement.

With the recorder still off, Ttomalss continued, "And the Big Uglies have had an altogether unexpected influence on the Race. Because the Tosevites have proved so strong and so quick to change, they have forced the males of the conquest fleet to become far more changeable than is our norm. This is also proving true for the males and females of the conquest fleet, but to a lesser degree. Indeed, the difference in outlook between veterans of Tosev 3 and the far more numerous newcomers has caused considerable friction between the two groups."

He'd seen that firsthand, not least in his dealings with Felless. She had learned a good deal since her revival, but still did not really appreciate just how changeable the Big Uglies were, because she was not very changeable herself . . . except when she'd tasted ginger.

"Ginger," Ttomalss muttered. Before he said anything else, he checked to make sure he truly had turned off the recorder. Talking about ginger was nearly as dangerous as talking about explosive metal. Once he'd satisfied himself no one but he would ever hear his words, he went on, "Ginger is another change agent here on Tosev 3. That was true before the colonization fleet came, but it is even more true now, thanks to the herb's effects on females. Tosev 3 disrupts even our sexuality, pushing us closer to Tosevite norms. This will have profound consequences for the relationship between this world and the rest of the Empire for a very long time to come."

No, he couldn't have said any of that in a place where it

might have become public. From things he'd gathered down at the embassy to the *Reich*, discussions on these subjects were under way at the highest levels. If the fleetlords and shiplords and ambassadors wanted his opinions, they would ask for them. His title might be senior researcher, but he was not senior enough to offer his views unsolicited. Nor would those above him be delighted if his unsolicited views went out over the computer network.

He sighed. Hierarchy and concern for status were and always had been hallmarks of the Race. Back on Home, where everyone played by the rules, they worked fine and contributed to the stability of society. On Tosev 3 . . . Here, Ttomalss feared they made the Race less adaptable than it should have been.

"Adaptable," he muttered. "Coping skills." The Race shouldn't have had to adapt. It shouldn't have had to cope. The Big Uglies should have been the ones doing all the coping. By now, they should have accepted the conquest. They should have been learning the language of the Race in place of their own multitude of tongues. They should have begun to venerate the Emperor, as Ttomalss did himself.

Instead, they stubbornly preferred their own superstitions. Some of them even presumed to mock the veneration of Emperors past, even if it had served the Race well for a hundred thousand years and more, and the Rabotevs and Hallessi since they were conquered. Ttomalss hissed angrily, remembering the arrogant Dr. Rascher in the *Reich*.

Out shot his fingerclaw again. This was for the record: "My view is that we should go forward as aggressively as possible with programs to acquaint the Big Uglies with the spiritual benefits of Emperor veneration. Bringing them to a belief system more congruent to the truth than are their own superstitions can only help in assimilating them into the Empire."

With an emphatic cough, he turned off the recorder once more. That opinion *needed* to get into the Race's data stream. He felt so strongly about it, he added an emphatic cough. The sooner fanatics like Khomeini could no longer use the local superstitions to rouse the Big Uglies against the Race, the better.

And then Ttomalss had an inspiration. He turned on the recorder for the third time. "Economic incentives," he said, getting the main idea out, and then amplified it: "If Tosevites are taxed for the privilege of continuing to adhere to their native superstitions but not if they agree to venerate the spirits of Emperors past, the truth will be more readily propagated among them."

Almost of itself, his hand shaped the affirmative gesture. If adhering to their superstitions cost the Tosevites under the Race's rule money, they would be more inclined to drop those superstitions and adopt the correct usages that prevailed on the other three planets of the Empire. They would not be compelled to do so, which was apt to spark fanatical resistance. They would simply come to see it was in their own best interest to conform to standard practice.

"How splendidly devious," Ttomalss said. What better way to get rid of superstition than to tax it out of existence?

Now he was going to have to look for males and females in positions of authority to support his scheme. He wanted to skitter with glee and excitement. He hadn't had such a good idea since he'd decided to raise a Tosevite hatchling among the Race.

Then he remembered what had happened to him after he took his second hatchling. He was lucky Liu Han hadn't murdered him after his kidnapping. But surely the Big Uglies would not get so excited about taxes as they did about their own offspring.

☆ 6 ☆

Gorppet liked Baghdad no more than he'd liked Basra. If anything, he liked it less than he'd liked Basra, because it was a bigger city with more Big Uglies in it. And all of those Big Uglies were united in their hatred of the Race.

His squad always moved together. That was a standard order in Baghdad. Males could not travel these narrow, winding streets by ones and twos. They simply disappeared when they did, disappeared or were ambushed and slain. Whole squads had perished that way, too. Gorppet didn't like to dwell on that.

"How do we tell what is a street and what is not?" Betvoss asked peevishly—he could always find something to complain about. "With so much rubble strewn everywhere, what used to be streets and what used to be houses look the same."

"Just follow me," Gorppet answered, and pressed on. He had trouble telling streets from houses, too, but wasn't about to admit it. He picked what looked like the easiest route through the cratered landscape. His eye turrets tried to look every which way at once. The rubble showed that the Big Uglies had fought hard hereabouts. Enough was left standing to give their diehards lots of hiding places, too. And there were plenty of diehards.

Someone had scrawled something in the sinuous local script on a whitewashed stretch of mud-brick wall that hadn't been knocked down. "What does that say, superior sir?" one of Gorppet's troopers asked.

"Spirits of Emperors past turn their backs on me if I know," he answered. "I've learned to speak some of this miserable language—Arabic, they call it—but I can't read a word. Each sound has one character if it is at the beginning of a word,

157

another one in the middle, and still another if it is at the end. More trouble than it is worth."

"It probably just says, *'Allahu akbar!'* anyhow," Betvoss said. "I do not think these Tosevites know how to say anything else."

Shouts—Tosevite shouts—came from ahead. Gorppet swung his rifle toward them. "We advance—cautiously," he said. He envisioned all sorts of dire possibilities as he took advantage of piled rubble to climb up and see what was going on without exposing most of himself to gunfire.

"What is it, superior sir?" Even Betvoss sounded anxious. Anyone who wanted another fight with the Big Uglies was addled, or so Gorppet thought. He reckoned Betvoss addled, all right, but not so addled as that.

And then, when he could see what was going on, he laughed in relief. "Nothing but a pack of Tosevites kicking a ball around a flat stretch of ground," he said. "We can go on."

Kicking a ball around was the Big Uglies' favorite sport hereabouts. It was, from what Gorppet had heard, the Big Uglies' favorite sport in almost all the lands the Race ruled. Gorppet couldn't see much point to it himself, but then—the Emperor be praised!—he was no Big Ugly.

The Tosevites looked up warily as he and his comrades approached. "Go on," he said in the guttural local language. "Play. We do not trouble you if you do not trouble us."

If the Big Uglies did feel like causing trouble . . . But one of them spoke in the language of the Race: "It is good." He said the same thing in Arabic, so his fellow Tosevites would understand. They started kicking the ball again, their robes flapping as they ran after it.

Still wary, Gorppet led his males past the Big Uglies. But they were intent on their sport, and paid the squad little attention. Gorppet wondered how many of them had been fighting hereabouts till the Race brought in enough soldiers to reduce the latest uprising from boil to sizzle. Quite a few, unless he missed his guess.

As if getting by the pack of Tosevites were a good omen, the rest of the patrol also went smoothly. Gorppet brought his squad through the perimeter of razor wire and back to the barracks without any untoward incidents. "If only it were this easy all the time," he said.

"It probably means the Big Uglies are plotting something," Betvoss said. Gorppet wished he could quarrel with that, but he couldn't.

As things turned out, the Race was plotting something. An officer harangued the patrol leaders: "One of our experts on the Big Uglies has come up with a way to bring them round toward reverencing the spirits of Emperors past—making them pay if they do anything else. We are ordered to collect coins outside the houses of their superstition. If they do not pay, they are not to be admitted."

Gorppet stuck out his tongue, calling for attention. When the officer granted him leave to speak, he said, "Superior sir, do you mean to say that we are becoming tax collectors rather than soldiers?"

"We are becoming tax collectors *and* soldiers," the officer replied, and Gorppet realized the fellow's fancy body paint didn't keep him from being very unhappy about the orders he'd received. "I do not say this will be easy, for I do not believe that for a moment. But it is what we are required to do, and so it shall be done."

"Superior sir, have you any idea what the Big Uglies are likely to do if we try to make them pay before we let them enter the houses of their superstition?" Gorppet demanded. He had such an idea, and did not care for it at all.

"We are also going to move a landcruiser or mechanized combat vehicle up before each of the said houses by tomorrow morning," the officer answered, which proved he did indeed have some idea. The way he ignored the nearly insubordinate tone of Gorppet's questioning proved the same thing. He went on, "This policy, you must understand, is not regional in scope. It shall be done over all the areas of Tosev 3 under the Race's rule. The sooner the Big Uglies begin venerating the spirits of Emperors past as we do, the sooner they will become contented citizens of the Empire."

Gorppet supposed that made sense, at least in the long run. The Race habitually thought in terms of the long run, and had succeeded by pursuing long-term strategies . . . until Tosev 3. Such strategies might yet succeed here, too, but they were apt to end up unpleasant for the poor males who had to put them into motion right at the moment.

Another squad leader had to be thinking along those same lines, for he said, "I expect we can count on Khomeini and the other fanatics to exploit our policy to the greatest possible degree."

"I think that is likely to be truth," the officer agreed unhappily. "We shall have to see whether the results of the policy justify the difficulties it will bring with it. We are all veterans here, every single male from the conquest fleet. We know our dealings with the Tosevites are full of experiments and improvisations. Maybe this one will work. Maybe it will not. We shall have to wait and see." He made a peremptory gesture. "You males are dismissed."

So much for being veterans together, Gorppet thought. He went back to the barracks and told the males of his squad what the new plan was. None of them had much to say about it. Betvoss was too startled—perhaps too appalled—even to complain. An orderly came by with the locale of the house of superstition to which the squad was assigned. That confirmed Gorppet's words and left everyone glummer than ever.

When morning came, all the males made sure they were carrying plenty of ammunition. They also made sure their body armor did the best possible job of covering their vitals. It might not hold out a high-powered bullet, but it was the best hope they had.

To Gorppet's relief, the house of superstition where his squad had to collect fees wasn't far from the barracks. The troopers got there just before sunrise. A landcruiser had already arrived, which made the squad leader feel better. He devoutly hoped its immense bulk and formidable gun would make the Big Uglies think twice about any trouble.

A Tosevite in wrappings and head cloth was expostulating at the landcruiser commander, who stood up in his cupola watching and waiting. That male either spoke no Arabic or preferred to pretend he didn't. The Big Ugly rounded on Gorppet. "What are you doing here?" he demanded.

"Collecting money," Gorppet answered. "If your males and females do not pay half a dinar each, they do not go in."

"Half a dinar?" the Big Ugly howled. "Half a dinar at each of five daily prayers? You will make beggars of us!"

"I have my orders," Gorppet said stolidly. He gestured with

his rifle barrel toward the landcruiser. "I have the power to make orders good."

"You are wicked. The great Satan will burn you in the fires of hell forever!" the Big Ugly said. "Why do you torment us? Why do you persecute us?"

As far as Gorppet was concerned, Tosevites tormented the Race far more than the other way round. Before he could say as much, amplified screeches from the towers at the corners of the house of superstitions summoned the local Big Uglies to the day's first petitions to the imaginary all-powerful Big Ugly beyond the sky.

Gorppet positioned his males in the entranceway. Since he knew more Arabic than the others, he made the announcement: "Half a dinar to go inside. If you do not pay, go home and venerate the spirits of Emperors past."

His fellow males backed him up with rifles aimed at the Big Uglies coming to worship. The landcruiser backed him up with its cannon and machine gun and intimidating massiveness. Despite all that, he thought he would have to start firing into the building crowd. The Tosevites screamed and cursed and waved their arms in the air and jumped up and down. But they had been taken by surprise, and had not thought to bring firearms to the house of superstition.

Some of them threw down coins or fluttering pieces of paper also in circulation as money. Gorppet wasn't sure all of those payments were half-dinars. He didn't check very closely. Any payment was enough to satisfy him. He used the barrel of his rifle to beckon into the house of superstition those who gave money of any sort.

Some of the others kept angrily milling about. Others headed back toward their homes. He hoped they were relieved to have an excuse to go away, and were not going to return later with weapons.

Rather to his surprise, the Big Uglies didn't start shooting. Betvoss said, "Well, we got away with it. I would not have believed that we could."

"We got away with it *this time*," Gorppet said. "These Tosevites come here to pray five times a day, remember. We are going to have to charge them this fee every time they come. Who knows how long they will tolerate it?" He sighed. "If only they would venerate the spirits of Emperors past, life would be easier for us."

"Truth," Betvoss said. "But they have all these houses for their own superstition, and none for the truth. How can we expect them to venerate the Emperors if they have nowhere to do it?"

Gorppet stared at the other male in surprise. Like any malcontent, Betvoss was full of ideas. As with any malcontent, most of them were bad. But this one struck Gorppet as quite good. He said, "You ought to pass that along to the authorities, Betvoss. It might get you a bonus or a promotion."

If it got Betvoss a bonus, that might improve his sour attitude. Stranger things had happened—on Tosev 3, plenty of stranger things had happened. And if it got Betvoss a promotion, Gorppet wouldn't have to worry about him any more. Gorppet swiveled his eye turrets this way and that. He wouldn't have to worry about much of anything—not till the next call for worship at this house of superstition, anyhow.

Along with his family, Reuven Russie walked toward the synagogue a few blocks away for Friday evening services. He was less devout than his parents, and sometimes felt guilty about it. They'd suffered because of their Judaism even before the Nazis invaded Poland. For him, being a Jew had been pretty easy through most of his life: the Lizards generally preferred Jews to Muslims. He wondered if his faith needed strengthening in the fire of persecution.

On the other hand, Judith and Esther took their belief more seriously than he did his, and they'd never been persecuted at all. They chattered with their mother as the family rounded the last corner on the way to the synagogue. Maybe they just hadn't yet been exposed to the flood of secular knowledge he'd acquired.

But his father was full of secular knowledge, too, and still believed. Reuven scratched his head. Plainly, he didn't understand everything that was going on.

Moishe Russie pointed toward a crowd of Jews gathered in front of the synagogue. That was unusual. "Hello," he said. "I wonder what's going on."

Whatever it was, a lot of people were excited. Angry shouts in Yiddish and Hebrew reached Reuven's ears. Rivka Russie pointed, too. "Look," she said. "There's a Lizard standing in front of the entrance. What's he doing there?"

"Maybe he wants to convert," Esther said. Judith giggled.

Reuven leaned toward his father and murmured, "How would we circumcise him?" Moishe Russie let out a strangled snort. He waggled a reproachful finger at Reuven, but his heart wasn't in the gesture. It was the sort of joke any doctor or medical student might have made.

As Reuven got closer to the synagogue, the shouting began turning into intelligible words. "An outrage!" someone cried. "An imposition!" someone else exclaimed. "We won't put up with this!" a woman warned shrilly. Reproach filled a man's voice: "After all we've done for you!"

The Lizard—who was armed and wearing body armor—kept speaking hissing Hebrew: "I have my orders. I cannot go against my orders."

"What are your orders?" Reuven asked in the language of the Race, pushing through the crowd toward the doorway.

As he'd hoped, the male responded to hearing his own tongue. "Perhaps you will explain it to these Tosevites better than I can," he replied. "My orders are that no one may enter this house of superstition without first paying five hundred mills."

"Half a pound?" Reuven exclaimed. "Why? What is the purpose of this order? How can I explain it if I do not understand it?"

"It is to reduce superstition," the Lizard told him. "If you Tosevites have to pay a tax to gather together to celebrate what is not true, the hope is that you will turn toward the veneration of the spirits of Emperors past, which is true."

A woman grabbed at Reuven's arm. "What's he saying?" she demanded.

Reuven translated the male's words. They brought a fresh storm of protest. Some of the language in which the protest was couched made Esther and Judith exclaim, whether in horror or in admiration, Reuven couldn't quite tell. "A tax on religion?" someone said. "Who ever heard of a tax on religion?"

But an old man with a white beard answered, "I came to Palestine when the Turks still ruled here. They used to tax Jews, and Christians, too. Only Muslims got off without paying."

Understanding that, the Lizard said, "We tax Muslims, too. We tax all who do not venerate the Emperors."

"They're trying to convert us!" a woman said indignantly.

The Lizard understood that, too, and made the negative hand gesture. "You may follow your superstition," he said. "If you do, though, you have to pay."

Moishe Russie took out his wallet. "I am going to pay," he said, and gave the male a two-pound note and another worth five hundred mills. "This is for all my family."

"Pass on," the Lizard said, and stood aside to let the Russies into the synagogue. Reuven discovered they were not the first to go in. He and his father sat on the right side of the aisle, his mother and sisters on the left. All the conversation, among men on the one side and women on the other, was about the tax.

"How will poor Jews pay it?" a fat man asked. "It is not a small fee."

"Maybe we can get the Race to lower it," Reuven's father said. "If we can't, the rest of the congregation will have to pay for the Jews who can't pay for themselves. How could we spend money in a way more pleasing to God?"

The fat man didn't look as if he wanted to spend money at all, whether it pleased God or not. Reuven set a hand on his father's arm. "I'm proud of you," he said.

Moishe Russie shrugged. "If we don't help one another, who's going to help us? The answer is, nobody. We've seen that too many times, over too many hundreds of years. We have to take care of our own."

A couple of rows in front of the Russies, a scholarly look-ing man with a fuzzy gray beard was saying, "The Romans worshiped their Emperors, too. They didn't try to make the Jews do it."

"The Lizards aren't trying to make us worship their Em-perors, either," somebody else answered. "They're just trying to make it expensive for us if we don't."

"True enough." The man who looked like a scholar nodded. "But that wasn't quite my point. Who worships dead Roman Emperors nowadays?"

Reuven burst out laughing. He couldn't help himself. "There we go!" he exclaimed. "We'll convert *all* the Lizards to Judaism, and then we won't have to worry about paying the tax any more."

That got a laugh, even from his father. But the gray-bearded man said, "And why not? 'Hear, O Israel, the Lord our God, the Lord is one.' That doesn't say what He looks like; He doesn't look like anything. He is as much the Lizards' God as He is ours. Nothing holds them back from becoming Jews: we don't talk about God having a human son."

Reuven almost repeated the crack about circumcising Lizards, but held his tongue; it didn't seem to fit, not inside the synagogue. Thoughtfully, his father said, "They could become Muslims as easily as Jews." That brought on a glum silence. No one liked the idea at all.

The scholarly looking man said, "They could, but they won't, not as long as the Muslims keep rising against them. And, pretty plainly, they want us to forget our own religions and worship their Emperors. That would make it easier for them to rule us."

"Politics and religion," Moishe Russie said. "Religion and politics. They shouldn't mix. Trouble is, too often they do." He sighed. "For a while here, we just got to worship as we pleased. I suppose it was too good to last."

Before anyone could say anything to that, the rabbi and the cantor took their places at the front of the congregation. Singing in the welcome for the Sabbath made Reuven forget about the tax his father had paid to enter the synagogue . . . for a little while, anyhow.

But, after the service was over, after Reuven and his father rejoined his mother and twin sisters, he said, "If the Muslims have to pay half a pound five times a day, all the rioting we've been through so far is going to look like nothing in particular. This town will go up like a rocket."

"We have enough groceries to last a while," his mother said. "We've been through this before. We can do it again, even if the riots will be worse. Whatever the Arabs do, they can't be worse than the Nazis were in Warsaw."

"That's true," Reuven's father agreed, and added an emphatic cough for good measure. "I thought the *Reich* would have fallen apart from its own wickedness by now, but I was wrong. Back when we were living in London, that fellow named Eric Blair who used to broadcast with me called the Nazis and the Russians a boot in the face of mankind forever. I used to think he was too gloomy, but I'm not so sure any more."

"You mention him every now and then," Reuven said. "Do you know what happened to him after we left England?"

"He's dead—ten or fifteen years now," Moishe Russie answered, which took Reuven by surprise. His father went on, "Tuberculosis. He had that particular soft cough even back when I knew him—but as far as I know, he never let it get in the way of his broadcasting." He sighed. "It's too bad. He would still have been a young man, and he was one of the most honest people I ever met."

They walked on through the quiet streets back toward their house. Moths fluttered around street lamps. The day's heat had faded; the night air made Reuven glad he had on a sweater. A mosquito landed on his hand. He slapped at it, but it buzzed away before he could squash it.

"When the muezzins call for prayer tomorrow morning . . ." he began.

"We'll find out what happens," his father said. "No point to borrowing trouble. We get enough of it anyhow."

Because the next morning was Saturday, Reuven didn't have classes. The Race thought humanity's seven-day cycle absurd, but had given up trying to impose their own ten-day rhythm on the medical college. *Weekend* was an English word the Lizards had had to borrow. Their custom was to rotate rest days through the week, so ninety percent of them were busy at any given time. They reckoned the Muslim Friday day of rest, the Jewish Saturday, and the Christian Sunday equally inefficient.

Reuven slept through the amplified sunrise calls to prayer from mosques in the Muslim districts of Jerusalem, and no gunfire awakened him, either. He ate bread and honey for breakfast, and washed it down with a glass of milk. The relief he felt at the silence in the city was sweeter than the honey, though.

It didn't last. He'd hoped it would, but hadn't expected it to, not down deep. He and his family were heading toward Saturday morning services when, as the call to prayer drifted in from the Muslim districts, gunfire rang out: not just rifles but automatic weapons and, a moment later, cannon.

Moishe Russie stopped in his tracks. "We go back," he said, and his tone brooked no contradiction. "God only knows what the streets will be like when services are done, and I don't care to find out by experiment."

"God will also know why we didn't go to *shul* this morning," Rivka Russie agreed. She set a hand on each twin's shoulder. "Come on, girls. Back to the house." The gunfire started up anew, this time much closer. Esther and Judith's mother gave them a shove. "And hurry."

By the time they got home, emergency vehicles were racing along the streets, those of human make clanging bells and those with Lizards inside hissing urgently to clear the right of way. Reuven hurried toward the telephone. Before he could pick it up, it rang. He grabbed it. "Hello?"

"Are you all right?" Jane Archibald asked.

"Yes, we're fine here," he answered, adding, "I was just about to call you. Is the dormitory safe?"

"So far, yes," she answered. "No trouble here yet. This is all aimed at the Lizards, not at us. But everyone is worried about you and your family."

That deflated Reuven; he'd hoped Jane had called only because she was worried about him. But he repeated, "We're fine. I hope there'll be something left of the city when all this dies down again."

"If it ever does," Jane said. "And I'm not half sure the Lizards hope the same thing. They may be looking for another excuse to slaughter the people who don't like them and have the nerve to stand up to them." Because of what the Race had done to Australia, she naturally thought the worst of them. But, as a helicopter flew low over the house and began pouring rockets into a target bare blocks away, Reuven had a hard time telling her she was bound to be wrong.

Liu Han, Liu Mei, and Nieh Ho-T'ing peered north from a four-story building the little scaly devils somehow hadn't yet managed to knock down. Through smoke and dust, Liu Han spied the column of tanks advancing on Peking. Another column was coming up from the south. The People's Liberation Army had done everything it could to throw back the scaly devils. In the end, everything it could do hadn't been enough.

"What now?" Liu Han asked Nieh.

"Now?" the People's Liberation Army officer echoed, his face grim. "Now we try to escape to the countryside and carry on the revolutionary struggle there. We cannot hold this city, and there will surely be a great bloodbath of a purge after the little devils retake it."

"Truth," Liu Han said in the scaly devils' language. After their uprising succeeded, the Communists had meted out summary punishment to every collaborator they could catch. Liu Han was sure the enemy would not be so foolish as to fail to return the favor.

One of the advancing tanks started pumping rounds into the city from its big gun. Every explosion wrecked a little more of Peking—and drove home to the people left inside that they could not hope to halt the little scaly devils' advance.

But the People's Liberation Army kept fighting. Peking's defenders had no real artillery with which to oppose the little devils' tanks. They did have mortars; the tubes were hardly more than sheet metal, and artisans could make the bombs they fired. Those bombs began bursting among the tanks.

Liu Han cheered. So did Liu Mei, though she didn't change expression. Nieh looked as sour as if he were sucking on a lemon. "That will do no good," he said, "and it will tell the enemy where our weapons are positioned."

Sure enough, the little scaly devils, who had been shooting more or less at random, began concentrating their fire on the places from which the mortars had opened up. One after another, the mortars fell silent. Liu Han hoped at least some of them were shamming, but she had no way to know.

Nieh Ho-T'ing said, "And if we are going to leave, we had better leave now. If we wait till the little devils are in the city, it will be too late. They will set up checkpoints, and they will have collaborators with them, people who are liable to recognize us no matter what stories we tell."

Again, he assumed the scaly devils would follow the pattern the Party had used. Again, Liu Han found no reason to disagree with him. But Liu Mei asked, "Can we do anything more here before we have to leave?"

"No," Nieh answered. "If we had a radio, we might direct fire—for a little while, till the scaly devils triangulated our position and flattened this building. That would not take long, and it would not help the cause. The best thing we can do is survive and escape and fight on."

"He's right," Liu Han told her daughter. To prove she thought so, she started down the stairs. Nieh Ho-T'ing followed without hesitation. Liu Han looked back over her shoulder, fearful lest Liu Mei, in a fit of revolutionary fervor, stay behind to court martyrdom. But her daughter was following, though shaking her head in regret. Seeing Liu Mei made Liu Han go faster. When they got to the ground, she asked, "Which way out?"

"The scaly devils are coming from the north and south," Nieh answered. "We would be wise to go east or west."

"West," Liu Mei said at once. "We're closer to the western gates."

"As good a reason as any, and better than most," Nieh Ho-T'ing said, while Liu Han nodded. Nieh went on, "The last thing we want is to get stuck in the city when it falls. That can be very bad."

"Oh, yes. It can be bad in a village, too," Liu Han said, remembering what had happened to her village at the hands of first the Japanese and then the little scaly devils. "It would be even worse in a big city, though."

"So it would," Nieh agreed. "It would indeed."

A couple of youths ran past, both with shaved heads and wearing tight-fitting shirts with the patterns of body paint printed on them. They looked and sounded frightened, not of the people around them but of the little scaly devils whom they aped. Now they were discovering where their loyalties truly lay.

Some of their number, though, would be joining the collaborators who'd escaped the purges in welcoming the little scaly devils back into Peking. Liu Han was sure of that. Some of them, before too long, would be marked down for liquidation. She was sure of that, too.

Liu Mei said, "I'm afraid I don't really know how to live in the countryside. I haven't gone out there very often."

"It's not like the city—that's true," Liu Han said, and this time Nieh nodded in response to her words. "But we'll get along. One way or another, we will." She set a hand on her daughter's shoulder. "You're not afraid to work. As long as you keep that in mind, you'll do all right."

The walls that in earlier years had shielded Peking from the world around it were now battered by the little scaly devils' bombardment. People weren't fleeing only at the gates; they were also scrambling out through breaches in the wall. Thousands—tens of thousands—of men and women would be descending on the villages around the city.

"Eee!" Liu Han said unhappily. "They will be like so many locusts—they will eat the countryside bare. There will be famine."

That word, heard too often in China, was enough to make two women also hurrying toward the gate whip their heads around in alarm. Liu Mei said, "Would we do better trying to stay, then?"

"No." Nieh Ho-T'ing and Liu Han spoke at the same time. Nieh continued, "Once we get among people who know who and what we are, we will not starve. They will set food aside for the leaders of the struggle against the little devils' imperialism."

"That is not as fair as it might be." Had Liu Mei been able, she would have frowned. Her revolutionary fire burned very bright, very pure.

Nieh Ho-T'ing shrugged. "I could justify it dialectically. Maybe I will, when we have more time. For now, all I'll do is say I don't feel like starving, and I don't intend to. When your belly cries for noodles or rice, you won't feel like starving, either."

That quelled Liu Mei till she and Liu Han and Nieh hurried out through the *Hsi Chih Mên*, the West Straight Gate. It led to the great park called the Summer Palace, a few miles northwest of Peking, but the fugitives did not go in that direction. Instead, they fled through suburbs almost as battered as the interior of the city until, at last, buildings began to thin out and open fields became more common.

By then, the sun was sinking ahead of them. The moon, nearly full, rose blood red through the smoke and haze above Peking. Nieh said, "I think we had better sleep under trees tonight. Any building will already have snakes in it—two-legged snakes. We'd better keep a watch through the night, too." He wore a pistol on his hip, and tapped it with his right hand.

"Good idea," Liu Han said. They weren't really in the countryside, not yet, but the very air around her felt different from the way it had back in Peking. She couldn't have told how, but it did. She cocked her head to one side. "Come on," she said, pointing. "There will be water over there."

"You're right," Nieh said. "I can tell by the way the bushes grow." Liu Mei looked from one of them to the other as if they'd started speaking some foreign language she didn't understand.

Unlike Nieh Ho-T'ing, Liu Han hadn't consciously known why she was so sure they would find water in that direction. She'd spent half her life in Peking. So much she'd taken for granted when she was young would seen strange now, to say nothing of unpleasant. But she hadn't forgotten everything. She might not have known how she knew water was there, but she had.

"It tastes funny," Liu Mei said after they drank.

"You're not used to drinking it when it hasn't come out of pipes," Liu Han said. For her, water straight from a little stream was a taste out of childhood. Nieh took it for granted, too. But for Liu Mei, it was new and different. Liu Han hoped it wouldn't make her daughter sick.

They found a place where pine trees screened them from the road, and settled down to rest there. Liu Han took the first watch. Nieh Ho-T'ing handed her the pistol, lay down among the pine needles, twisted a few times like a dog getting comfortable, and fell asleep. Liu Mei had never tried sleeping on bare ground before, but exhaustion soon caught up with her.

The late spring night was mild. Explosions kept rocking Peking. Careless of them, owls hooted and crickets chirped. Flashes on the eastern horizon reminded Liu Han of heat lightning. Fugitives streamed away from the doomed city, even in darkness. Liu Han hung on to the pistol. She hoped nobody else would try to rest here among the trees.

No one did, not while she was on watch. In due course, she woke Nieh, gave him back the automatic, and went to sleep herself. She didn't think she'd been asleep very long when three gunshots hammered her out of unconsciousness. Screams and the sound of pounding feet running away followed those thunderclaps.

"Somebody who thought he'd try being a bandit, to see what it was like," Nieh said lightly. "I don't think he cared for it as well as he expected to. Bandits never think victims are supposed to have guns of their own."

"Did you hit him?" Liu Mei asked—she was sitting up, too.

"I hope so," Nieh Ho-T'ing answered. "I'm not sure, though.

I know I scared him off, and that's what matters. Go back to sleep, both of you."

Liu Han doubted she could, but she did. When she woke, birds were chirping and the sun was rising through the smoke above Peking. Her belly was a vast chasm, deeper than the gorges of the Yangtze. She went back to the little stream and drank as much water as she could hold, but that didn't help much. "We have to have food," she said.

"We'll get some." Nieh sounded confident. Liu Han hoped his confidence had some basis. Had she been a peasant villager, she wouldn't have wanted anything to do with refugees from the city.

When they came to a village, the peasants greeted them with rifles in hand. "Keep moving!" one of them shouted. "We have nothing for you. We haven't got enough for ourselves."

But Nieh Ho-T'ing said, "Comrade, is that the proper revolutionary spirit?" He went up to the peasant leader and spoke to him in a low voice. Several other peasants joined the discussion. So did a couple of their womenfolk. At one point, Nieh pointed to Liu Han and spoke her name. The women exclaimed.

That seemed to turn the argument. A few minutes later, Liu Han and Liu Mei and Nieh Ho-T'ing were slurping up noodles and vegetables. A woman came up to them. "Are you really the famous Liu Han?" she asked.

"I really am," Liu Han answered. "Now I am also the hungry Liu Han."

But the woman didn't want to take the hint. "How did you get to be the way you are?" she persisted.

Liu Han thought about that. "Never give up," she said at last. "Never, ever, give up." She bent her head to the noodles once more.

Straha made the negative hand gesture even though Sam Yeager couldn't see it, not with the primitive Tosevite telephone he was using. "No," the ex-shiplord said, and added an emphatic cough. "I was not aware of this. It did not come to my attention before I, ah, decided to leave the conquest fleet and come to the United States."

"Okay," Yeager answered, an English word he sometimes threw into conversations even in the language of the Race, just as he sometimes used emphatic and interrogative coughs while speaking English. "I did wonder, and thought you might know."

"I did not," Straha said. "That we should attempt to rear Tosevite hatchlings makes sense to me, however. How better to learn to what degree your species can come to conform to our usages?"

He waited for the Big Ugly to wax indignant. Tosevites—especially American Tosevites—often got very shrill about the rights of their kind, especially when they thought the Race was violating those rights. If they or their fellow Big Uglies violated them, though, they were much less strident.

To Straha's surprise, all Yeager said was, "Yes, I can see how that would make sense from your point of view. But I have the feeling it is liable to be hard on the hatchling you are rearing."

"That is part of the nature of experiments—do you not agree?" Straha said. "It is unfortunate when the experiments involve intelligent beings, but I do not see how it is avoidable. Sometimes such things are necessary."

Again, he expected Sam Yeager to get angry. Again, Yeager failed to do so. "You may have something there, Shiplord," he replied. Straha had to fight down a small, puzzled hiss. He'd known this Big Ugly longer than almost any other, and thought he knew him better than any other save perhaps his own driver. Now Yeager wasn't responding as he should have. Straha knew the Tosevites were a highly variable species, but Yeager usually thought so much like a male of the Race that the ex-shiplord had expected him to maintain a respectable consistence.

"How did you happen to make the acquaintance of this Tosevite reared under the tutelage of the Race?" Straha asked, trying to find what lay behind Yeager's curious indifference to the experiment.

"She identified me as a Big Ugly by the way I wrote," Yeager answered. "I had no idea she was one till I heard her speak. You know we have trouble with some sounds in your language because of the way our mouths are made."

"Yes, just as we do in Tosevite tongues," Straha agreed. Yeager didn't seem inclined to be very forthcoming, for which Straha could hardly blame him. That being so . . . "Have you anything else?"

"No, Shiplord. I thank you for your time," the Big Ugly said, and broke the connection.

Straha also hung up the Tosevite-style telephone. He did let out the discontented hiss he'd held in before. Something was going on under his snout, and he didn't know what it was. That annoyed him. He walked from the kitchen into the front room, where his driver sat leafing through a Tosevite news magazine.

"I greet you, Shiplord," the Big Ugly said. As far as grammar and pronunciation went, he spoke the language of the Race as well as Yeager. He didn't think like a male of the Race, though. His next question was sharp, not deferential. "What was that all about on the telephone?"

"That was Sam Yeager, the soldier and student of the Race," Straha answered. His driver was not just an aide; the Tosevite was charged with monitoring what Straha did. The English description for such a male, which Straha found expressive, was *watchdog*.

"Ah," the driver said. "Sam Yeager has a gift for sticking his snout where it does not belong. What was he trying to learn from you that is none of his business?"

"Nothing, as a matter of fact," Straha said tartly. "In my humble opinion"—a bit of sarcasm all too likely to sail past the Tosevite—"a female of your kind who has been raised by the Race from hatchlinghood to maturity is very much within Yeager's area of responsibility."

"Oh—that. Yes. Truth, Shiplord," the driver said. Then he let out several barks of Big Ugly laughter. "More truth than you know about, as a matter of fact."

"Suppose you enlighten me, then," Straha suggested.

To a male of the Race, such a suggestion would have been as good as an order. The driver shook his head, and then, for good measure, also used the Race's negative hand gesture. "Suppose I do *not*, Shiplord." His tone was so emphatic, he didn't bother with a cough. "You do not need to know that."

Straha understood security without having a Big Ugly explain it to him. He also understood the driver had slipped. "Then you should not have alluded to such a thing," he said. "Now my curiosity is aroused."

"You speak truth, Shiplord—I should not have mentioned it,"

the Tosevite admitted. "Since I did, I must ask you to pretend I did not."

"Next I suppose you will ask a female to unlay an egg," Straha snapped. "What would happen if I went back to the telephone and asked Sam Yeager to tell me what you will not?"

"He might do it. He has a way of talking too much," the driver said. "But, Shiplord, I very strongly ask you not to do that." Now he did use an emphatic cough.

He was not simply asking, Straha realized. He was giving an order, and expected to be obeyed. That the driver presumed to do such a thing spoke of who had power here and who had none. With an emphatic cough of his own, Straha said, "I am not your servant. Nor am I going to betray whatever I may learn to the Race. Nor is the Race likely to try to kidnap me, not after all these years."

"Perhaps not," the driver replied. "But the Race may well be monitoring your telephone line, and Yeager's. I would be, were I a male from the conquest fleet's intelligence service." Straha hissed unhappily; his driver made a good point. The Big Ugly went on, "And we still do not know at whom the miscreants were shooting when you visited Yeager's house while the Chinese females were also there. It could have been them. It could have been Yeager. But it could also have been you, Shiplord."

"Me?" Straha swung both eye turrets sharply toward the driver: such was his surprise. "I assumed those females were the targets. The Race is not in the habit of using assassination as a weapon."

"The Race has picked up all sorts of bad habits since coming to Tosev 3," his driver answered. To compound his insolence, the Tosevite bent his head over one hand and pretended to taste ginger.

But what he said, while it held enough truth to be infuriating, did not hold enough to be convincing. "I am not involved in the ginger trade, except as one more male who tastes," Straha said. "And, since you are giving forth with nonsense, who would want to murder Yeager, and why?"

"Who would want to kill Yeager?" Straha's driver echoed. "Someone who got tired of his habit of sticking his snout where it does not belong, that is who. I assure you, he has made enemies doing so."

"And are you one of those enemies?" the ex-shiplord asked. "You certainly speak as if you have considerable knowledge of them."

I shall have to find some way to warn Sam Yeager, Straha thought. Yeager had always behaved in a proper manner toward him. Like any well-trained male of the Race, Straha understood that loyalty from below created obligations in those above. Yeager had left Straha in his debt, and debt required repayment.

"In some ways, at some time, I may be an enemy of Yeager's," the driver answered evenly. "I had nothing to do with the shots fired at his home, however. Indeed, if you will recall, I shot at the shooters."

"Yes, I do recall," Straha said, wondering if the driver had opened fire to make himself appear innocent.

"All things considered, I still believe the attack was most likely aimed at the Chinese females," the Big Ugly said. "An assault on you or on Yeager would have been better planned and would also have been more likely to succeed."

"You so relieve my mind." Straha's voice was dry.

"I am so happy to hear it." So was his driver's. Straha would have taken most Tosevites literally. With this one, he knew better. The driver continued, "It is, however, one more reason for you not to telephone Yeager."

"It may be, if what you say is truth," Straha said. "You have not proved that; you have only mentioned it as a possibility."

The driver sighed. "Shiplord, is this your day to be particularly difficult?"

"Perhaps it is," Straha answered. "And perhaps we can compromise. At a time convenient to Sam Yeager, will you drive me to his house, so we can discuss these things without fretting over insecure telephone lines?"

"It shall be done," the Tosevite said, and sighed again. He was not happy about Straha's request, but evidently saw no way to evade it. Gradually, over the long years of his exile, the ex-shiplord had come to learn the subtleties of the Big Uglies' responses. When setting out for Tosev 3, he hadn't imagined such knowledge would be useful—but then, the Race hadn't imagined a great many things about Tosev 3.

Since his driver was also in some measure his keeper, and was his link to the Tosevite authorities of the United States, Straha decided conciliation might be a wise course. "Will you eat with me?" he asked: that was an amicable gesture among the Big Uglies, as it was among the Race. "I have some zisuili chops defrosting in the kitchen."

"Will they poison me?" the driver asked.

"I doubt it," Straha answered. "Few Tosevite foods have proved poisonous to us." He thought of ginger. "And sometimes, when they do poison us, we enjoy it."

"Even so, Shiplord, I think I will decline," the Tosevite said. "I have not found appetizing the odors that come from your meats."

"No?" Straha shrugged, then thought on how best to manipulate Big Uglies, particularly the males of the species. "If you have not the courage to try new things, I will enjoy a larger meal of my own."

In due course, he and the driver sat down at the table together. The Tosevite ate a small bite of zisuili meat, then paused in thought of his own. "Not so bad," he said at last. "Are all your meats as salty as this, though?"

"Yes," Straha answered. "To us, as you well know, uncured Tosevite meats seem unpleasantly bland. More potato chips?"

"I thank you, but no," the driver said. "I will make do with what I have here." He did dutifully finish the portion Straha had given him. When he was through, he gathered up his dishes and Straha's and began to wash them.

Having an intelligent being perform such a service for Straha took him back to the most ancient days of the Race. Most of the time, he would have reckoned it a reversion to barbarism. This once, he found it no less than his due.

Vyacheslav Molotov's secretary stuck his head into the Kremlin office Molotov most commonly used. "Comrade General Secretary, the ambassador from the Race has arrived," the fellow said.

"Thank you for informing me, Pytor Maksimovich," Molotov answered. He had no great desire to see Queek, but could hardly refuse his request for an interview. "Tell him I shall be there directly." The secretary hurried away. Molotov nodded to himself as he rose. If he found an interview with Queek unpleasant, he was determined that the Lizard should not enjoy it, either.

Having promised to come at once, he deliberately took his time in walking to the office where the ambassador and his interpreter waited. Queek sat impassively, but the Pole who did his talking for him sent Molotov a dirty look. The general secretary savored that, as he would have savored a particularly delicate tea.

"To business," he said, as if he had not delayed at all. "I must tell you that the peace-loving peasants and workers of the Soviet Union again reject out of hand the invidious assertions the Race has made in regard to our alleged collaboration with the freedom-loving peoples of those parts of the world you now occupy."

Queek spoke at some length. The interpreter summed up his first couple of hissing sentences in one word: *"Nichevo."*

"It doesn't matter, eh?" Molotov said. "In that case, why did your principal demand this meeting?"

After the interpreter had done his job, Queek spoke again. The Pole turned his words into Russian: "I wanted to inform you personally that Peking is once more in the hands of the Race. This effectively brings to an end the rebellion the Soviet Union fomented and abetted."

"I deny fomenting the rebellion of the freedom-loving Chinese people and their People's Liberation Army," Molotov answered—truthfully, for Mao would have risen up against the Lizards without any encouragement from Moscow. "And I also deny assisting the rebellion in any way." That was a great thumping lie, but the Race had never—quite—been able to prove it.

Unusually, Queek didn't try to prove it now. He just said, "Your claims are noted. They are also, as I say, irrelevant. China is ours. China will remain ours. The same applies farther west on the main continental mass. Our cities in that region do not suffer to any great degree despite the damage inflicted on the seaside desalination plants thereabouts."

"We had nothing to do with that damage, either," Molotov said. That wasn't the whole truth, but it wasn't a lie, either. The Soviet Union did smuggle arms down into the Middle East, but the locals there used them as they saw fit, not as the USSR desired. Mao was a nationalist, but he was also a Communist. The Arabs and Persians hated Moscow's ideology almost as much as they hated the Race.

"Your rockets called *Katyusha*s were among the weapons employed against the desalination plants," Queek said.

"*Katyusha*s have been in production for more than twenty years," Molotov said blandly. "Many were captured by the fascists in their invasion of the Soviet Union, and others by the Race. These weapons are also widely imitated."

"You always have excuses and denials," Queek said. "Do you wonder that the Race has trouble taking them seriously?"

"What I have is a complaint, and the Race had better take it seriously," Molotov said—he was indeed intent on making sure Queek went away unhappy.

"We shall treat it with the seriousness it deserves, whatever that proves to be," the Lizard answered. "I do find it intriguing that this not-empire, the cause of so many complaints, is now issuing one. Say on. I hope you intend no frivolity."

"None whatsoever," said Molotov, to whom frivolity was as alien as satyriasis. The ironic style Queek affected was also the one he preferred; he flattered himself that he was better at it than the Lizard. He went on, "My complaint—the Soviet Union's complaint—is that your alien domestic animals have begun straying from the border regions of the territory you occupy into land unquestionably under the jurisdiction of the Soviet Union. I demand that the Race do everything in its power to curb these incursions, and that you pay compensation for damage to our crops and livestock."

"Animals, unfortunately, know nothing of political borders. They go where they can find food," Queek said. "We shall have no complaints if you drive them back over the frontier. We shall also have no complaints if you slay them when you find them on your territory. Compensation for damages does not strike me as unreasonable, provided your claims are not exorbitant."

It was a softer answer than Molotov had expected, and so one that left him disappointed. He said, "Some of your beasts are devouring the crops that will yield the bread that feeds the Soviet people. Others kill chickens and ducks, and have even been known to kill cats and dogs as well."

The translation took a little while; Molotov guessed that the interpreter had to explain to the Lizard what sort of animals he was talking about. Finally, Queek said, "You would be referring to befflem, I suppose, in the matter of your livestock, befflem and possibly tsiongyu."

Molotov cared very little about the Race's names for its annoying creatures. He was about to say as much, but checked himself. Queek would surely respond that the names of proper Earthly animals did not matter to him, either. Forestalling an opponent could be as important as counterattacking after a sally. The Soviet leader contented himself with observing, "Whatever else these creatures may be, they are pests, and they will be exterminated from Soviet soil."

"I wish you good fortune in your efforts along those lines," Queek said: yes, he did have a sardonic turn of phrase. "The Race has been making similar efforts since long before the establishment of the Empire. Some few have been partially successful. Most, however, were undoubted failures."

Molotov studied the Lizard. He reluctantly concluded Queek, despite the sarcasm, was not joking. He thought about feral cats that lived off pigeons and mice and squirrels and such, and about packs of wild dogs that scavenged in the cities and sometimes killed cattle and sheep out in the countryside. "You have released a new plague on us, you are telling me," he said.

Queek shrugged after that was translated. "You have your domestic animals, and we have ours. They have accompanied us as the Empire has grown. We see no reason why Tosev 3 should be different from any other world in this regard."

"You have not conquered us, as you conquered these other worlds," Molotov said. "Your animals have no business on our soil."

"I repeat: we are willing to discuss reasonable compensation," the ambassador from the Race said. "But I also repeat that you are unreasonable if you expect us to keep perfect control over all our animals at all times. I am certain your own notempire is unable to do this, so why do you assume we can?"

For that, Molotov found no good answer. He shifted his ground: "It appears to me that you are seeking to win through environmental change what you could not win at the battlefield or at the negotiating table."

"Our intention is to colonize this world. We have never said otherwise," Queek replied. "We are not at war with the Soviet Union or with any other independent Tosevite not-empire, but we do hope and expect to bring all of Tosev 3 into the Empire in the fullness of time."

"That shall not happen," Molotov declared.

"Perhaps you speak truth," the Lizard told him. "I do not deny the possibility. But, as I said at a previous meeting, this is not necessarily to your advantage. If you become a threat to the Empire as a whole, rather than merely to peace and good order here on Tosev 3, we shall be as ruthless as circumstances require. Do not doubt that I mean this with complete sincerity."

However much Molotov wanted to, he didn't doubt that. "We must also be able to protect ourselves from you," he warned. "You want us to abandon technical progress. As I have said before, that is impossible." The USSR didn't just have to protect itself from the Race, either. The *Reich* and the USA remained potential enemies. So did Japan, in a more limited way. Molotov had been a boy during the Russo-Japanese War, but he still remembered his country's humiliation. One day, the Soviet Union would settle scores against all its neighbors, human and otherwise.

Queek said, "It appears, then, that we are on a collision course. In that case, squabbles over domestic animals suddenly become less important, would you not agree?"

Molotov shrugged. "Since we are not in combat, my view is that we had best behave as if we were at peace."

"Ah," the Lizard said. "Yes, that is a sensible attitude, I must admit. I would not have expected it of you." The Polish interpreter's eyes gleamed as he turned that into Russian.

"Life is full of surprises," Molotov said. "Have we anything further to discuss?"

"I think not," Queek replied. "I have delivered the statement required of me by my superiors, I have heard your complaint and suggested a possible resolution, and I have listened to your bluster pertaining to your not-empire's technical prowess. Nothing more remains that I can see."

"Bluster travels on both sides of the street," Molotov said icily, and rose from his desk. "This meeting is at an end. The guards will escort you back to your limousine. Good day." He didn't say *good riddance*, but his manner suggested it.

After the Lizards' ambassador and his interpreter had left, Molotov went into the antechamber to one side of the office.

There he changed all his clothes, down to socks and underwear. If Queek or his human stooge had smuggled electronic eavesdropping devices into the office, they would go no farther than the antechamber. Molotov wondered if the Race knew he entertained human visitors in another office. He wouldn't have been surprised. He didn't mind offending the Lizards—or anyone else—but didn't care to do so inadvertently.

Once back in clothes sure to be uncontaminated, Molotov returned to the regular office. No sooner had he got there than the telephone rang. He picked it up. "Marshal Zhukov on the line," his secretary said.

Molotov's expression did not change, but he grimaced inside. Zhukov knew altogether too much about his comings and goings. No doubt the marshal had a spy among Molotov's aides. "Put him through," Molotov said, suppressing a sigh, and then, "Good day, Georgi Konstantinovich. And how are you?"

"Fine, thank you, Comrade General Secretary," Zhukov replied, outwardly deferential. But, a blunt soldier, he had little patience with small talk. "What did the Lizard want?"

"To brag that the Race has suppressed the uprising in China," Molotov said. "He labored under the delusion that we did not already know."

"Ah," Zhukov said; Molotov could imagine his nod even if he couldn't see it. The marshal went on, "When the Chinese are ready themselves or when we can stir them up, they will rise again, of course. You had a countercomplaint ready, I assume?"

"Oh, yes—the matter of these animals from Home on our soil," Molotov said. Zhukov would hear it from someone else, if not from him. "They do threaten to become a nuisance in our border regions, but Queek proved conciliatory on the matter of compensation."

"I wish you had found something stronger," Zhukov grumbled, "but I suppose foreign affairs *is* your bailiwick." *For as long as I feel like letting it be your bailiwick.* Marshal Zhukov didn't always say everything he thought, either. But then, he didn't always have to. That was what holding power meant.

Felless felt isolated and useless and frustrated at the Race's embassy to the *Reich*. With Ttomalss gone, she had no one there with whom she could really have a conversation grounded in her professional expertise. Most of the males and females at the embassy dealt with the Deutsch Tosevites in a purely pragmatic way, caring nothing for the theoretical underpinnings of interspecies relations.

The Deutsche cared nothing for those underpinnings, either, so far as Felless could tell. As time went on, they grew less and less willing to discuss with her the rationale behind their strange not-empire. She had had trouble enough grasping even what they were willing to discuss. Now that new information came in more slowly than it had before, she despaired of ever making sense of their system.

She'd thought about insulting some Deutsch official to the point where his government would expel her from the not-empire, as Ttomalss had been lucky enough to manage. She'd not only thought about it, she'd tried to do it a couple of times. That had involved her in shouting matches with Big Uglies, but no expulsion order came, worse luck. She remained stuck here in Nuremberg, stuck without escape and hating every moment of it.

Her office was her refuge. She could analyze such data as she had, and she could reach out to the wider world of the Race through the computer network. And . . .

Sometimes she would stay in her office for days at a time, bringing food back from the refectory, storing it in a little refrigerator, and reheating it in an even more compact radar oven. The locked door there was a shield against a world far more unpleasant than she had imagined on waking from cold sleep. Behind that shield, she could do her best to make the world go away.

After finishing the first of several meals she had waiting in the refrigerator, she went over to her desk, opened one of the drawers, reached behind several file folders, and took out a small plastic vial half full of brownish powder. "By the Emperor," she said softly, "ginger is the only thing that makes Tosev 3 even close to being a world worth living on."

Her fingers trembled in anticipation as she took off the stopper. She couldn't taste as often as she craved the herb, not with the punishments to which males and females—especially females—were liable these days. Only when she was sure no one would disturb her till she no longer reeked of pheromones did she dare shake powdered ginger into the palm of her hand, bend her head low over it, and flick out her tongue.

Ginger's hot, spicy flavor was marvelous enough, but what the herb did when it coursed through her blood and set her brain afire made the flavor seem a small thing. When she tasted ginger, she was as near omnipotent as made no difference. Somewhere back inside her mind, she knew both the omnipotence and the delight that came with it were illusions. She knew, but she didn't care.

She also knew the euphoria she got from ginger wouldn't last long enough to suit her. It never did. The only way it could have lasted long enough to suit her was never to end. But the herb didn't work that way, however much she wished it did.

All too soon, she began to slide down into the depression that was the price she paid for the euphoria. She hissed in despair and walked over to the desk. She knew that if she tasted again, the depression would only be worse and deeper after that second taste. Again, she knew but she didn't care. That would be later. She felt bad enough now to want to escape.

And escape wasn't far away. She didn't have to think to yank the top off the vial of ginger, pour some more of the herb into the palm of her hand, and lap it up. She sighed and shuddered with pleasure. Again she was brilliant, strong, invincible. Again she could—

The telephone hissed. She strode over to it as if she were the Emperor at a ceremonial function. She didn't mind talking on the telephone while ginger lifted her; it made her feel more clever than the caller, whoever he might be. This time, she saw as she turned an eye turret toward the screen, it was Ambassador Veffani. "I greet you, superior sir," she said, and assumed the posture of respect.

"And I greet you, Senior Researcher," Veffani answered. "Please come to my office immediately. Several males and females have come from Cairo to discuss our present relations with the *Reich*, and your contributions would be valuable."

Felless stared at him. "But, superior sir—" she began, and discovered the difference between feeling brilliant and actually being brilliant. If she went out of her office now, she would turn the whole embassy topsy-turvy, let alone that chamber full of males and females with fancy body paint. But what sort of excuse could she find for not coming when the ambassador required her presence? The ginger didn't give her any marvelous ideas. She tried her best: "Superior sir, could I not participate by telephone? I am in the midst of an exacting report, and—"

"No," Veffani broke in. "Conference calls with too many participants quickly grow confusing. Please come and give your insights in person."

He said *please*, but he meant it as an order. "But, superior sir . . ." Felless repeated. "That might not be the best idea right now." Veffani knew she had a ginger habit—or rather, he knew she had had one. She hoped he would be able to hear what she wasn't saying.

If he could, he didn't choose to. He said, "Senior Researcher, your presence is required here. I will see you directly."

Felless let out a long, hissing sigh. Had he forgotten about the herb, or was he going to use this opportunity to show her up and expose her to punishment? It didn't really matter. He'd left her no choice. She sighed again. "It shall be done, superior sir," she said, and broke the connection.

She knew what would happen when she stepped out into the corridor and headed for Veffani's office. The only question was where and with whom. As things happened, she hadn't gone more than half a dozen steps before she saw Slomikk, the science officer.

He saw her, too. "I greet you, Senior Researcher. How are you tod . . . ?" His voice trailed away as the pheromones she couldn't help emitting reached his scent receptors. Almost at once, he straightened till he stood nearly as erect as a Big Ugly. The scales of his crest rose along the crown of his head, too, as they did at no other time than during a mating display.

And his visual cues affected Felless just as her scent cues affected him. She bent down till her snout all but touched the floor: the mating posture was not so far removed from the posture of respect. "Hurry," she said with the small part of her rational mind that still functioned. "I must see the ambassador."

Slomikk wasn't listening. She hadn't expected that he would be. He took his place behind her. Of itself, her tailstump moved up and out of the way. The science officer thrust his mating organ into her cloaca. The pleasure she felt was different from what she got with ginger, though she couldn't have said how.

She remembered from earlier matings that the pleasure would ease the slide down from the heights of ginger. Slomikk hissed in delight as he finished. Felless straightened up and hurried on toward Veffani's office.

Another male mated with her on the way there. Veffani's secretary was a female, and so did not notice the pheromones coming off Felless in waves. All she said was, "Go right into the conference chamber, superior female. The ambassador is expecting you."

"So he is," Felless said. *But not like this.* She sighed, wondering if she would lay another clutch of eggs. Matings after ginger seemed less likely to lead to gravidity than those of the normal mating season, but they easily could. She knew that from experience.

Bracing herself for what she knew would happen, she went into the conference chamber. Veffani turned an eye turret toward the opening door. "Ah, here she is now," he said. "Senior Researcher, I was just telling the males and females here from Cairo of the strides you have made in unraveling the . . ."

As Slomikk's had, his voice trailed away. The ventilation system swept her pheromones toward him and toward the other males and females of the Race. The females didn't notice. The males did. Almost in unison, they sprang from their seats and stood straight up. Their crests rose. This time, they were displaying to warn off one another as well as to make Felless assume the mating posture.

Assume it she did. One of the females from Cairo exclaimed, "Oh, by the Emperor, she has been tasting ginger!"

Felless cast her eyes down to the ground on hearing the Emperor's name. Since the carpet was very close to the tip of her snout, she got an excellent view of it. A male—she couldn't tell if it was Veffani or one of the visitors from Cairo—stepped up behind her and began to mate. Two other males brawled, sending chairs flying every which way. And yet another male, inflamed by her pheromones, went into a mating display in front of a female who was not in her season. The female exclaimed in disgust.

Felless thought every male in the chamber had coupled with her by the time the ginger ebbed from her system. Even as she straightened out of the mating posture, one of the males from

Cairo was sidling around behind her to try to mate again. "Enough," she said, and hoped she sounded as if she meant it.

"Yes, enough." That was Veffani, who sounded shaken to the core. Looking round the conference chamber, Felless could hardly blame him. One chair lay on top of the table. A male was rubbing at clawmarks that scored his flank, another nursing a bitten arm that dripped blood.

Turning to Veffani, Felless assumed the posture of respect—carefully, so none of the males would take it for the mating posture. "I apologize, superior sir," she said. "I knew something like this would happen when I came here, but you required it of me, and I had no choice but to obey."

"You have been tasting ginger," Veffani said.

"Truth." Felless admitted what she could hardly deny. Now the after-tasting depression was on her. Whatever the ambassador chose to do to her, at the moment she felt she deserved every bit of it and more besides.

"We depend on high-ranking females to set an example for those below them," Veffani said. "Senior Researcher, you have failed in this fundamental obligation."

"Truth," Felless repeated. Veffani was making her feel even worse than she would have anyhow. "Do with me as you will, superior sir. I do not seek to evade my responsibility."

Veffani swung both eye turrets toward her. "I know you have not been happy here, Senior Researcher. Accordingly, the most severe punishment I can mete out to you is that requirement that you continue your duties and your investigation of the Deutsche exactly as before."

"It shall be done, superior sir," Felless said dully. Even in the depths of her depression, she had trouble believing she deserved to be punished *that* harshly.

☆ **7** ☆

Lieutenant Colonel Johannes Drucker was walking past Peenemünde's liquid-oxygen plant when loudspeakers throughout the
enormous rocketry complex began blaring out his name: "Lieutenant Colonel Drucker! Lieutenant Colonel Johannes Drucker!
Report to the base commandant's office immediately! Lieutenant Colonel Drucker . . . !"

"Donnerwetter!" Drucker muttered. "What the devil has
gone wrong now?" He couldn't remember the last time he'd
heard anyone so summarily summoned to Lieutenant General
Dornberger's office.

He couldn't report there immediately, either, not when he was
closer to the Peene River side of Peenemünde's flat, muddy
peninsula while the commandant's office lay a couple of kilometers away, hard by the Baltic. He started down the road toward
the office, hoping to flag a lift along the way.

No such luck. He made the journey by shank's mare, and arrived about as sweaty as he could get in a cool, clammy climate
like northern Germany's. "Reporting as ordered," he told Dornberger's adjutant, a skinny major named Neufeld who always
looked as if his stomach pained him.

"Yes, Lieutenant Colonel. One moment, please." Major
Neufeld pressed the intercom switch and spoke two words:
"He's here."

"Send him in," Walter Dornberger said, and Neufeld waved
Drucker past him and into the commandant's sanctum.

Walter Dornberger was in his late sixties, bald but still erect
and vigorous. He'd been in the artillery during the First World
War, and in charge of Peenemünde since before the start of

World War II. He knew as much about rockets and space flight as any man alive.

"*Heil* Himmler!" Drucker said, and shot out his arm in the Party salute that had also become the Army salute. "Reporting as ordered, sir."

"*Heil,*" General Dornberger returned, though his answering salute was more nearly a wave. "Close the door behind you, Drucker, and then take a seat."

"Yes, sir," Drucker said, and obeyed. He tried to look brisk and capable and—most of all—innocent. He wondered if he was innocent. If he wasn't, looking as if he were became all the more urgent. He tried to sound innocent, too, asking, "What's up, sir?"

"A letter mentioning your name in unusual circumstances came to me." Dornberger shoved a piece of paper across the desk at him. "Tell me what you think of this, if you'd be so kind."

Even before Drucker picked it up, he knew what it would be. And it was: a denunciation from the pen of Gunther Grillparzer. Maybe Grillparzer hadn't believed he was an SS man after all. Or maybe he had, and decided to get him in trouble with the *Wehrmacht. I should have killed him when I had the chance,* Drucker thought, *him and his girlfriend, too.*

"Well?" General Dornberger asked when Drucker set the paper down again.

"Well, what, sir?" Drucker answered. "If you want my head on a bloody platter, this gives you the excuse to take it. If you don't, throw it in the trash can where it belongs and let's go about our business."

Dornberger tapped the letter with a nicotine-stained fingernail. "So you deny these accusations, then?"

"Of course I deny them," Drucker exclaimed. "Only a man who wanted to commit suicide would admit to them." He'd been brought up to fear God and tell the truth. The second sentence was nothing but the truth . . . and he feared the *Gestapo*, too.

"This fellow includes some circumstantial details," the commandant at Peenemünde observed. "If he wasn't there, if this didn't happen as he says, how could he make them up? I have done a little checking. This Colonel Jäger was supposed to have been arrested. Somehow, he wasn't—somehow, he escaped, apparently to Poland. It's believed he died there."

"Is it?" Drucker fought the chill of fright that ran through him. Dornberger didn't want his head on a platter; the commandant had already proved that. But he was a conscientious man, or maybe just a good engineer—he wanted to get to the bottom of things. Drucker had never heard what had happened to his regimental commander after the lady flier from the Red Air Force took him away.

"Yes, it is." General Dornberger tapped Gunther Grillparzer's letter once more. "I ask you again, Hans—what about this? What do I say when the pointy-nosed SS men come around here and start asking me the questions I'm asking you now?"

That was a fair question—more than a fair question, if Dornberger wanted to be able to protect him. Drucker thought fast, as he had in the hallway outside Grillparzer's flat in Weimar. "Sir," he said, "it's pretty plain somebody in the SS doesn't like me, isn't it? The way they went after my wife . . ."

"Yes," Dornberger said, nodding. Drucker didn't tell him—Drucker wouldn't tell anybody, not to his dying day—that Käthe truly did have a Jewish grandmother. Whoever'd found that out had been right, even if Drucker and Dornberger between them had managed to quash the investigation. The commandant went on, "You are suggesting this is another hoax?"

"Yes, sir," Drucker answered. "One way to put all sorts of details in a letter is to just make them up. The SS knows my service record; it knows the names of the men I served with. This letter makes it sound like Grillparzer was as much a murderer as I was. Do you think anybody who really did something like that would give you or the blackshirts the whole story?"

"A point—a distinct point," General Dornberger said.

Drucker nodded, doing his best to look as well as sound convincing. He was convinced Gunther Grillparzer wouldn't be in that Weimar flat any more if he or the *Gestapo* came knocking. The ex-gunner would probably have shed his alias and his girlfriend, too, though Friedli had been worth hanging on to. Nothing, though, was worth the risk of kicking your life away at the end of a piano-wire noose after some highly ingenious men spent a long time making you wish you were dead.

Dornberger paused to light a cigar. He aimed it at Drucker as if it were a pistol. "You realize that, if your enemy in the SS wants you badly enough, he will simply come and take you away regardless of anything I can do."

"Yes, sir, I understand that," Drucker said. He knew he sounded worried—he *was* worried. But anyone with a powerful enemy in the SS had every right to be worried. More than a generation of German history proved as much.

"All right, then." General Dornberger picked up Grillparzer's letter, folded it in thirds, as it had been in the envelope, and then slowly and methodically tore it to pieces. "I think we will be able to carry on on that basis. You understand that Neufeld has also seen this?"

"I would have expected that, yes, sir," Drucker said, nodding. "But, sir, Major Neufeld wouldn't tell his granny her own name if she happened to ask him for it."

Dornberger chuckled, coughed, and chuckled some more. "I won't say you're wrong. I will say that's one of the reasons he's so useful to me. If your unfriend has sent copies of this letter to people besides me—which it makes sense that he would do—we shall try to deal with them as you've suggested." He took another puff on the cigar, then set it in an ashtray. Exhaling smoke, he went on, "You are dismissed, Lieutenant Colonel."

Drucker sprang to his feet and saluted. "*Heil* Himmler!" he said, as he had when he came in. For once, the words were not automatic. He wondered what he was doing hailing the man who, along with heading the *Reich*, also headed the outfit that had tried to execute Käthe, the outfit that had done its best to get him drummed out of the *Wehrmacht*, the outfit that would no doubt take another shot at him now, thanks to Gunther Grillparzer.

But that couldn't be helped. As long as he lived in the Greater German *Reich*, he had to conform to its outward usages. He made a smart about-turn and strode out of General Dornberger's office. In the antechamber, Major Neufeld's face revealed nothing but dyspepsia. Drucker nodded to him and walked out.

He was just leaving the administrative center when a black Mercedes pulled to a halt in front of it. A couple of *Gestapo* men got out of it and hurried into the building. They took no special notice of him, but he would have bet Reichsmarks against pfennigs they hadn't come to Peenemünde on any other business.

To hell with you, Grillparzer, you son of a bitch, Drucker thought. *If you drag me down, I'll take you with me.* He knew the alias under which the ex-panzer gunner had been living in Weimar. If the *Gestapo* couldn't track the bastard with that much to go on, the boys in the black shirts weren't worth much.

As Drucker walked away from the administration building, he wondered if the loudspeakers would blare out his name again. The SS had wanted his scalp ever since he managed to get Käthe out of their clutches. If Dornberger couldn't convince them to leave him alone . . .

What would he do then? Take out his pistol and go down fighting? Take it out and kill himself, so he wouldn't suffer whatever the blackshirts wanted to inflict on him? If he did either of those things, how would he avenge himself on Gunther Grillparzer? And what would happen to his family afterwards? But if he didn't do it, would that save his wife and children? And what horrid indignities would be waiting for him?

The loudspeakers kept quiet. Drucker stayed where he could keep an eye on that black Mercedes. After about forty-five minutes, the *Gestapo* men came out of the administrative center and got back into the car. By the way they slammed the doors, they weren't happy with the world. The Mercedes leaped away with a screech of tires, almost flattening a couple of enlisted men who'd presumed to try to cross the road. The soldiers sprang out of the way in the nick of time.

Drucker watched it go with the same savage joy he'd known when he stuck a pistol in Grillparzer's face. Before then, he hadn't felt that particular delight since taking out a Lizard panzer during the fighting. Somebody'd tried to ruin him, tried and failed. That was how things were supposed to work, but things didn't work that way often enough.

Whistling, Drucker went into the officers' club, ordered a shot of schnapps, and knocked it back with great relish. The fellow behind the bar, a young blond corporal straight out of a recruiting poster, grinned at him. "Something good must have happened to you, sir," he said.

"Oh, you might say so. You just might say so," Drucker agreed. "Let me have another one, why don't you? There's nothing in the world to match the feeling you get when somebody shoots at you and misses, you know that?"

"If you say so, sir," the bartender answered. "I'm sorry, but I haven't seen combat myself, though." Polite puzzlement was on his face: what sort of combat would Drucker have seen lately?

But Drucker knew—and combat it was, even without a literal shot being fired. "Don't be sorry, son," he said. "Count yourself lucky. I wish I could say the same thing."

"Germans!" Monique Dutourd snarled as she walked up to her brother in the Jardin Puget, a few blocks south of Marseille's Old Harbor. Not far away, sweaty kids booted a football toward one side's goal.

"Don't start talking yet," Pierre warned. He looked around to make sure no one else in the park was taking any notice of him, then pulled from his pocket a gadget plainly not of Earthly manufacture. Only after waving it at her and examining the lights that glowed and flickered at one end did he nod. "All right. The *Boches* have not planted any ears on you."

"Germans," Monique said again; even the usual scornful French nickname for them didn't let her get rid of enough anger to be satisfying. Only by calling them exactly what they were could she vent even part of the loathing she'd come to feel for the occupiers.

To her intense annoyance, her older brother chuckled. "You just went about your business as long as they didn't bother you too much. It's only after they start annoying you personally that you discover you've hated them all along, eh?"

"Oh, shut up, damn you," Monique said. Pierre had been content to let her think for twenty years that he was dead; she saw little point wasting politeness on him. "This is business. If we can get the Lizards to rub out Dieter Kuhn—"

"I get him off my back and you get him off your belly," Pierre broke in, which almost made Monique turn on her heel and stalk out of the park. He went on, "Well, neither of those things would be so bad."

"Nice of you to say so." Monique glared. She was sick to death of Kuhn on her belly, and inside her, and in her mouth. But it wasn't her death she wanted; it was the *Sturmbannführer*'s. She lusted for that as she would never lust for the Nazi alive.

Pierre waggled a finger at her. He was sad-eyed and plump, not at all the young *poilu* who'd gone off to fight the *Reich* in 1940—not that she was a little girl any more, either. He said,

"You have to understand, I don't hate the Germans just because they're Germans. I do business with quite a few of them, and I make a nice piece of change off them, too."

Monique tossed her head. "Never mind the advertisements, dammit. We both want this one dead, and we want it done so we can't be blamed. You have the connections with the Lizards to arrange it, and—" She broke off.

"And what?" her brother prompted.

Unwillingly, she went on, "And, since he comes to my flat every couple of nights, we have a place where the Lizards can lie in wait."

"Ah," Pierre said. "You want him to die happy, I comprehend."

"I want him to die dead," Monique ground out. "I don't care how. He won't stay happy, by God."

"I suppose not," Pierre said, with the air of a man making a sizable concession. He sat down on a wooden bench with rusty iron arm rests. Monique stood there, hands on hips; in his own way, her brother could be almost as infuriating as Dieter Kuhn. Pierre continued, "Well, I will see what I can do. When will the Nazi be at your flat again? Tonight?"

Monique grimaced. Having to admit that Kuhn came there at all was humiliating enough. Having to admit that she knew his schedule was somehow worse. But she did, and could hardly pretend otherwise. Reluctantly, she answered, "No, he was there last night, and that means he isn't likely to be back till tomorrow, and then a couple of days after that, and so on."

"Nice regular fellow, eh?" Pierre chuckled. Monique wanted to hit him. In that moment, she wouldn't have minded seeing him dead. But then he said, "All right, my little sister, I'll pass the word along. And who knows? It could be that, one day before too long, someone scaly will be waiting for your German when he comes outside."

"He's not my German, and you can go straight to hell if you call him that again," Monique said. She didn't have to worry about keeping Pierre sweet. He had his own good reasons for wanting Kuhn dead. That let Monique take a certain savage pleasure in turning her back on him and stamping past the oleanders that screened the traffic noise and out of the Jardin Puget.

She would have taken even more pleasure if she hadn't heard Pierre laughing as she stalked away.

Since she didn't have to entertain Dieter Kuhn that evening, she actually managed to get some research done. Reading Latin, especially the abbreviation-filled Latin of her inscriptions, helped ease some of her fury. Scholars would be poring over these texts a thousand years from now, long, long after she and Dieter Kuhn were both dead. Thinking in those terms gave her a sense of proportion.

She bared her teeth in something that wasn't a smile. With any luck at all, a thousand years from now Dieter Kuhn would be dead a great deal longer than she was. *Outliving him is the best revenge,* she thought. But she shook her head a moment later. Revenge was the best revenge.

When he knocked on her door a night later, she was almost eager to see him. He'd brought along a bottle of red wine, too; he didn't try to make himself hateful to her. He could only have succeeded, though, by leaving her alone. He didn't feel like doing that.

As usual, she endured his attentions without enjoying them. As usual, that bothered him not in the least. *Men,* she thought. She'd known a couple of Frenchmen who'd cared for her pleasure as little as Dieter Kuhn did. But she hadn't had to go to bed with them, and she'd stopped going to bed with them as soon as she realized what sort of men they were. The German didn't give her that choice.

Monique didn't mind drinking his wine. Having him spend a few Reichsmarks was revenge of a sort, even if only of the tiniest sort. It turned out to be pretty good wine, too. And, if she got a little drunk, if her thinking got a little blurry, so much the better.

"Well, my dear," Kuhn said as he buttoned the fly to his trousers, "I must be off. I will see you again day after tomorrow, I think."

I am not your dear, Monique thought. She hadn't got so blurry as to be confused about that; there wasn't enough wine in the world to leave her confused about that. *With any luck at all, I'll never see you again, except, it could be, your bleeding corpse.*

"Yes, I suppose you will," she answered aloud, and gave him a sweet smile. *"Au revoir."*

"Au revoir," the SS man answered, and he smiled, too. "You

see, you are coming to care for me after all. I knew you would, even if it took a while."

Monique didn't say anything to that. She couldn't, not unless she cared to give the game away. She did manage another smile. It was a smile of gloating anticipation, but Dieter Kuhn didn't need to know that.

He finished dressing, smugly kissed her, even more smugly fondled her, and, at last, headed for the door. Monique, still naked, stayed in the bedroom. That was what she always did when Kuhn left. If she did anything different tonight, she might rouse his suspicions. The last thing she wanted was to rouse Kuhn in any way.

He turned the knob. Hinges creaked as the door swung open. Back in the bedroom, Monique hugged herself in glee. She didn't know it would be tonight, but she hoped, she even prayed . . .

A burst of gunfire shattered the quiet of the street outside, gunfire and a scream. *"Gott im Himmel!"* Dieter Kuhn exclaimed. Still in German, he went on, "That was a Lizard weapon, or I'm a Jew." He slammed the door shut behind him and ran down the hall.

"No," Monique said, shaking her head back and forth. "No, no, no." She had a horrible feeling she knew what had happened. The Race had as much trouble telling human beings apart as people did telling one Lizard from another. If the would-be assassin had been told to kill whoever came out of the block of flats at such-and-such a time, and if some luckless fellow had chosen just that time to go out for a stroll or a glass of wine . . . if that had happened, the fellow's blood was on her hands.

A couple of minutes later, someone pounded on her door. *Kuhn,* she thought, and then, *Dammit.* She threw on a nightgown and went to open the door. The SS man pushed past her and into the flat. "I need to use your telephone," he said.

"What happened?" Monique asked, though she feared she knew only too well.

"Someone just shot a man to death outside this building with a Lizard automatic rifle," Kuhn answered. *"Merde alors,* if I had gone out a couple of minutes sooner, that could have been me." He was dialing the telephone as he replied, and began speaking into it in German, too fast and excited for Monique to follow more than one word in three.

"Quel dommage," she said distantly. If the SS man heard her, she thought he would think she meant it was a pity the other fellow had got shot, not that he himself hadn't.

After a couple of minutes, Kuhn hung up. He turned back to her. "They are on their way," he said, returning to French. "As long as you have some clothes on, come downstairs with me and see if you can identify the body. The fellow may live here. If we know who he is, we may be able to find out why someone with a Lizard weapon—maybe even a Lizard—wanted him dead."

Monique gulped. "Do I have to?" she asked. She knew perfectly well why the poor fellow out there on the street was dead: because of her, and because the drug-dealing Lizard who'd shot him didn't know what the devil he was doing. Seeing the result of her failed revenge was the last thing she wanted.

But Dieter Kuhn, as she knew all too well, didn't care what she wanted. "Come on," he repeated, and grabbed her by the arm. He wasn't the typical hulking German; by his looks and compact, wiry build, he might more readily have been French. But he was much stronger than Monique. When he dragged her along with him, she had no choice but to come.

A little crowd of the curious and the ghoulish had gathered around the corpse on the sidewalk just in front of Monique's block of flats. Blood, black in the moonlight, streamed down into the gutter. A man had a startling amount of blood in him. Monique could smell it, and the latrine stench that had come when the dead man's bowels let go.

Sirens yowled in the distance, rapidly coming closer. Kuhn took a little flashlight off his belt and shone it in the dead man's face. "Do you know him?" he asked.

"Yes," Monique answered, trying not to look at the wound that had torn away one side of his jaw. "That's Ferdinand Bonnard. He lives—lived—downstairs from me, on the second floor. He never bothered anyone that I heard of." *And I killed him, as sure as if I'd pulled the trigger myself.* She wondered if she'd be sick.

Kuhn wrote the name in a little notebook he fished from a trouser pocket. "Bonnard, eh? And what did he do?"

"He sold fish in a little shop on the Rue de Refuge, not

far from the harbor," Monique answered as a couple of SS vehicles squealed to a stop and uniformed Germans spilled out of them. Everyone but Monique suddenly found urgent business elsewhere.

"Dealt with fishermen, did he? Maybe he was a smuggler, too," Kuhn said, and started talking to his Nazi colleagues. He might have forgotten about Monique. But when she started to go back inside the apartment building, Kuhn shook his head. "No—you will come with us to the Palais de Justice and answer more questions." She must have looked as horrified as she felt, for he added, "It will not be as bad as it was last time. You have my word of honor."

And it wasn't—quite.

Once he started getting used to it, Rance Auerbach discovered Cape Town's District Six wasn't such a bad place after all. Yes, he had to treat Negroes as if they were as good as anybody else. He even had to take orders from them every now and then. That wasn't easy for a Texan. But after he leaped the hurdle, he started having a pretty fair time.

Everybody in District Six, black and white and colored (a distinction between full-blooded blacks and half-breeds the USA didn't bother drawing) and Indian, was hustling as hard as he or she could. Some people had honest work, some work that wasn't so honest. A lot of people had both kinds of jobs, and ran like maniacs from long before the sun rose over Table Mountain till long after it set in the South Atlantic.

Rance couldn't have run like a maniac even if he'd wanted to. Getting up and down the stairs to the flat he and Penny Summers shared was plenty to leave him sore and gasping. When he shuffled along the streets near the apartment building where he lived, kids of all colors laughed at his shuffling gait. They called him Stumpy, maybe because of his stick, maybe just because of the way he walked.

He didn't care what they called him. Kids back in the States had thought he walked funny, too. Hell, even he thought he walked funny. But he could get to the Boomslang saloon a couple of blocks from his apartment building, and most of the time that was as far as he wanted to go.

Boomslang, he found, meant *tree snake*, and one particular, and particularly poisonous, kind of tree snake at that. Considering some of the rotgut the place served up, he could understand how it got its name. But it was close, it was cheap, and the crowd, despite being of all colors, was as lively and interesting as any he'd ever found in a bar.

To his surprise, he found he was interesting to the Boomslang's other patrons. His American accent made him exotic to both whites and blacks. So did his ruined voice. When people discovered he'd been wounded fighting the Lizards, he won respect for courage if not for sense.

But when they found out how he'd wound up in South Africa, he won . . . interest. One evening, somewhat elevated from a few hours at the saloon, he came home and told Penny, "Half the people in this goddamn country are either in the ginger-smuggling business or want to be, if you listen to 'em talk."

His girlfriend threw back her head and laughed. "You just figured that out, Rance? Hell, sweetheart, if I'd've wanted to, I could've gotten back into business long since. But I've been taking it easy, you know what I mean?"

"You?" Auerbach felt the whiskey singing in him. It didn't make him stupid, but it did make him care less about what he said. "Since when did you ever believe in taking it easy?"

Penny Summers turned red. "You really want to know? Since those damn Nazis pointed every gun in the world right at my head and carted you and me off to that jail in Marseille, that's when." She shuddered. "And then, after the Lizards got us back, they could've locked us up in their own jail and thrown away the key. So I'm not real hot to give 'em another shot at doing that. Thanks, but no thanks."

Auerbach stared. Of all the things he'd expected, Penny cautious was among the last. "You mean you like living like this?" His wave took in the cramped little flat. If he hadn't been careful, he would have barked his knuckles on the wall.

"Like it? Hell no," Penny answered. "Like it better than a nice, warm, cozy cell with nothing but Lizards to look at for the rest of my days? Hell, yes."

"I'll be damned," he said wonderingly. "They really did put the fear of God in you, didn't they?"

She walked up to him and set her hands on his shoulders. It wasn't the prelude to a kiss, as he'd hoped at first it might be.

"Listen to me," she said, as serious as he'd ever heard her. "Listen to me good. We caused those scaly bastards a lot of trouble, I mean a *lot* of trouble. If you don't think they're keeping an eye on us to make sure we're good little boys and girls, you're smack out of your mind. Want to bet against me? How much have you got?"

Auerbach thought about it. He thought slower than he should have, but still thought pretty straight. When he was done, he shook his head, even though it made his ruined shoulder ache. "Nope. That'd be like raising with a pair of fives against a guy who's got four diamonds showing."

Now Penny did kiss him, a peck on the lips that had nothing to do with lust and everything to do with gratitude. "See, Rance?" she said. "I knew you weren't dumb."

"Only about you," he answered, which made her laugh, though he hadn't been more than half joking. He sighed and went on, "But if you listen to them, half the guys in the Boomslang have sold the Lizards a taste one time or another."

Penny laughed again. "How much have you had to drink, babe? Must be a hell of a lot, if you're dumb enough to believe what a bunch of barflies say. And even if they have sold some poor damn Lizard a taste or two, so what? That's nickel-and-dime stuff. If I ever do start playing the game down here, it won't be for nickels and dimes, and you can bet your bottom dollar on that."

"If you get in trouble, you want to get in a whole lot of trouble—that's what you're telling me." Now Rance nodded; that did sound like the Penny Summers he'd known for the past twenty-odd years. Penny . . . you could say a lot about her, but she never did things by halves.

She knew it, too. "I stiffed my pals for plenty before I came running back to you," she said. "If I ever take a shot at it again, I'll do it once—once and then it's off to Tahiti or one of those other little islands the Free French run."

Free France was a joke, but a useful joke. The Japanese Empire could have run the French off their South Pacific islands. So could the USA. So could the Lizards, flying out of Australia. Nobody bothered. Neutral ground where nobody asked a whole lot of questions was too useful to everyone.

"I could go for that," Rance agreed. The ginger he and Penny had run down into Mexico should have got them a stash that would have taken them to Tahiti. Auerbach liked the notion of island girls not overburdened with clothes or prudery. But things hadn't worked out the way they'd had in mind, and so. . . .

Penny said, "I'll tell you one more time, sugar: you won't find anything that could head us toward Free France there in the goddamn Boomslang. And if you do find it in the Boomslang, it's dollars to doughnuts somebody's trying to set us up. You want to be a sucker, go ahead, but leave me out, okay?"

"Okay," Auerbach said, and then he yawned. "Let's go to bed."

"How do you mean that?" Penny asked.

"Damned if I know," he answered. "Meet me in the bedroom and we'll both find out." Five minutes later, two sets of snores rose from the bed.

A couple of evenings afterwards, Rance and Penny went to the Boomslang together. She didn't go with him all the time, but then, she wasn't in constant pain, either. When she did come into the saloon, she always drew admiring glances, not just from whites but from blacks as well. That was one more thing Auerbach had had to get used to in a hurry here. Those kinds of looks from Negroes in Texas might have touched off a lynching bee. He gathered the same thing had been true in South Africa before the Lizards came. It wasn't true any more.

Rance drank scotch that had never been within five thousand miles of Scotland. Penny contented herself with a Lion Lager. A barmaid took one of the other regulars upstairs. "Don't even think about it, buster," Penny murmured.

"I won't," Rance promised. "She's homely." Penny snorted.

After a while, a big, broad-shouldered black fellow whom Auerbach knew only as Frederick—emphatically *not* as Fred—came over and sat down beside him. "It is the ginger man," he said in a rumbling bass. His smile was broad and friendly. Too broad and friendly to be convincing? Rance had never quite figured that out, which meant he stayed wary where Frederick was concerned. The black man inclined his head to Penny. "And this is the ginger lady?"

His musical accent made the question less offensive than it might have been otherwise. Penny tossed her head. "There's plenty of ginger in me, pal," she said, "but I'm spoken for." She put a hand on Rance's arm.

In a way, Rance was annoyed that she thought she needed to say such a thing, especially to a Negro. In another way, he was relieved. He wouldn't have wanted to tangle with Frederick even if he'd had two good arms and two good legs. With things as they were, the black man could have broken him in half without working up a sweat.

But Frederick shook his head. "No, no, no," he said. "Not that kind of ginger, dear lady. The kind that makes the Lizards dance."

"Ixnay," Rance muttered to Penny. South African English was different enough from the kind he'd grown up with that he didn't worry about Frederick's knowing what that meant.

Penny nodded slightly, but leaned forward so she could see Frederick around Rance and said, "Yeah, I've done that. But so what? If I hadn't done it, I wouldn't have ended up here, and so I'm not going to do it any more."

If the Negro was a plant, if the Lizards were looking to get Rance and Penny in more trouble, that would put sugar in their gas tank. But all Frederick said was, "No doubt you are wise. Still, though, do you not miss the excitement of never knowing when things might turn . . . interesting?"

Damn him, Auerbach thought. He'd made a shrewd guess there. Penny liked living on the edge. Once upon a time, Rance had known that feeling, too. Before Penny could answer, he said, "You lose excitement in a hurry the first time somebody puts a couple of bullets through you."

"Yeah," Penny said. If she sounded a little disappointed, then she did, that was all. Tahiti remained tempting—to her and to Auerbach both—but only if the potential gain made the risk worthwhile. And she was dead right about that being unlikely for any deal made in a no-account District Six saloon.

Frederick spoke a sentence in whatever African language he'd grown up with, then translated it into English: "Who is a hunter after the lion bites?" He beamed. "You see? We are not so very different, you people from a far land and me."

"Maybe not," Auerbach said. He didn't want to start a brawl. A couple of bullets had ruined his taste for that, too. Penny nodded, which eased his mind. She was still looking for her big chance; she just didn't think she'd find it here.

And damned if Frederick wasn't doing the exact same thing. With a sigh full of longing, he said, "If only I could find enough ginger and the right Lizards, all my worries would be over."

"Yeah," Penny said, that same longing in her voice.

"Hell of a big if," Rance said, and hoped she was listening to him.

Engine rumbling, Jonathan Yeager's elderly Ford came to a stop in front of Karen's house. He killed the engine, jumped out of the car, and hurried toward the door. Summer nights could be chilly in Southern California, but that wasn't the only, or even the main, reason he wore his T-shirt striped with the fleetlord's body paint. Karen's parents were nice people—*for old fogies,* he added to himself, as he did whenever the thought occurred to him—but they weren't the sort of folks who took bare chests for granted.

He rang the doorbell. A moment later, the door opened. "Hello, Jonathan," said Karen's father, a burly man whose own red hair was going gray. "Come on in. She'll be ready in two shakes, I promise."

"Okay, Mr. Culpepper. Thanks," Jonathan said. He looked around the living room. The Culpeppers didn't have so many books as his family did, but nobody he knew had as many books as his family did.

"Would you like a Coke, Jonathan?" Mrs. Culpepper asked, coming out of the kitchen. She was a blonde herself, but Karen looked more like her than like her husband. As far as Jonathan was concerned, that was all to the good.

But he shook his head now. "No, thanks. Karen and I will get our sodas and popcorn and candy at the movie."

Karen came into the front room just then. "Hi!" she said brightly, and wrinkled her nose at Jonathan. She switched to the language of the Race, saying, "I greet you, Exalted Fleetlord," and dropped into the posture of respect. Then, laughing, she straightened up again. Her own body paint said she was a senior mechanized combat vehicle driver. Her halter top didn't hide much of it—didn't hide any, in fact, because she'd continued the pattern on the fabric in washable paint.

Her parents looked at each other. Jonathan saw them roll their eyes. They didn't take the Race for granted, the way Karen and he did. Well, even his own folks didn't do that, but they knew how important the Race was. The Culpeppers didn't seem to get that, either, or to want to get it.

"Have fun at the movie," Mrs. Culpepper said.

"Don't get back too late," Mr. Culpepper added. But his voice didn't have a growl in it, the way it had when Karen and Jonathan first started dating. He approved of Jonathan, as much as any middle-aged man could approve of the lout going out with his precious daughter.

As soon as the car got moving east up Compton Boulevard, Karen turned to Jonathan and said, "Okay, now you're going to tell me why you're so hot to see *The Battle of Chicago*. I didn't think war movies were your taste of ginger." By her tone, if war movies were his taste of ginger, she was wondering whether she'd made a mistake by having anything to do with him.

But Jonathan answered, "Sure, I'll tell you. It's because my dad and mom were *in* the Battle of Chicago, or at least the first part of it. Their ship got shot up when it took them and everybody else who was working on our explosive-metal bomb out of Chicago when it looked like the Lizards would break in."

"Oh." Karen thought about it, then nodded. "Okay. I guess I can put up with it for that. But it won't be much like what really happened, you know."

"Of course it won't—it's a movie." Jonathan stopped at the light at Vermont, waited for a couple of southbound cars to go by, and turned right to follow them. On the radio, a fellow with a soft drawl shouted above twanging electric guitars. Jonathan's parents found modern music raucous—all the more reason for him to like it.

He drove with his left hand for a couple of seconds so he could poke Karen in the ribs with his right forefinger. As she squeaked, he went on, "And don't tell me you're just putting up with it, either, not when you'll be drooling all over everything every time James Dean shows up—and since he's the star, he'll show up most of the time."

She made a face at him. "Like you won't be leering at that French chippie, whatever her name is—you know, the one who keeps trying to fall out of her clothes all the time. What was *she* doing in the battle of Chicago?"

"Decorating it?" Jonathan suggested. Karen poked him in the

ribs for that, which made him swerve the car and almost nail a station wagon in the next lane. The fellow in the station wagon sent him a dirty look. Jonathan gave Karen one, too, and added, "You were the one who said it wouldn't be much like what really happened."

"I didn't mean like *that*," Karen said. They kept teasing each other till they got to the Vermont drive-in, a little past Artesia. Houses were thin that far south; some of the little farms and orchards and nurseries that had been there since before the war still survived. The drive-in movie theater made a raucous addition to the air of rural charm.

Jonathan chose a parking space well away from the snack bar, though a good many closer to it were open. Karen raised an eyebrow—she knew what he had in mind aside from watching the movie. She stuck out her tongue at him, but didn't say anything. If she had said something, he might have moved the car. As things were, he said, "I'll be right back," and headed off to bring back a cardboard carton full of grease and salt and chocolate and fizzy, caffeinated water and other nutrients essential to human life.

When he got back, he found that Karen had mounted the little speaker on the window of the front driver's-side door. She was waiting in the back seat, and opened the rear door for him so he wouldn't have to put down the carton and maybe spill all the goodies.

They grinned at each other as they started eating Milk Duds. She hadn't come along with him just to watch the movie, either. They didn't do anything but grin, not yet; cars were still coming in, the glare of headlights blasting into their faces every few seconds. Jonathan didn't even put his arm around her. They'd have plenty of time for that later.

By luck—and also by Jonathan's strategic choice of parking space—nobody parked close to the Ford. He looked out at the white lines painted on the asphalt as if he'd never expected such a thing. "How about that?" he said.

"Yeah, how about that?" Karen did her best to sound stern— that was one of the rules of the game—but a giggle lurked somewhere down at the bottom of her voice. They'd been going out for a good long while now. Sure enough, she knew what he had in mind, and he knew she knew, and had it on her mind, too. It wasn't as if they'd just started discovering each other.

They'd made a good-sized dent in the big bags of popcorn when the screen lit and music blared out of the tinny speaker. An announcer's voice followed: "Here are scenes from our coming attractions!"

Now Jonathan slipped his arm around Karen's shoulder. Her flesh was warm and smooth under his hand. She slid closer to him—carefully, so as not to disturb the surviving food and what was left of the sodas. One of the coming features had dinosaurs that looked remarkably like overgrown Lizards tearing up the landscape, one was a tear-jerking love story, and one had Red Skelton and Bing Crosby wisecracking, strutting their stuff, and outwitting real Lizards (one of whom Jonathan thought he recognized) left and right.

"My father would like that one," Karen said with a sigh.

"Uh-huh," Jonathan said. "So would mine, even if he spent half the time telling everybody else in the car with him what all was wrong with it."

"How are Mickey and Donald?" Karen asked as the cartoon came on—a rascally rabbit who eluded Lizards and bumbling human hunters at every turn.

"Growing like weeds," he answered. "Eating us out of house and home." Clichés were safest when he talked about the hatchlings. His father surely wished he wouldn't talk about them at all, but hadn't ordered him not to do it. He tried not to betray the trust he'd earned. Adding, "They keep learning things all the time, too," seemed safe enough.

"And now, our feature presentation," the announcer boomed. Karen snuggled closer to Jonathan. He let his hand close on the smooth skin of her shoulder rather than just resting there. Quite involuntarily, he took a deep breath. He had to remind himself they weren't in a hurry: for one thing, it was a three-hour movie.

Spaceships filled the enormous screen. "That's terrific trick photography," Karen said.

"No, it's not—it's real Lizard newsreel footage. I've seen it before," Jonathan answered. "I wonder how much MGM had to pay the Race to use it."

They watched the movie for a while, though the view from the backseat wasn't so good as it would have been from up front.

Jonathan soon discovered the film was even hokier than he'd feared; just from things his folks had said, he soon found half a dozen absurdities. But some of the battle sequences looked very gritty and realistic. They were newsreel footage, too, human-filmed black-and-white footage turned into color with the help of computers. Watching how the director cut back and forth from them to the actors and the story he was shooting himself kept Jonathan half interested for a while. James Dean aside, Karen hadn't much cared to begin with. Before long, they found other things to do.

Jonathan untied the bow that held her little halter top on. It was so small, nobody coming by in the dark would notice whether she was wearing it, anyhow. And . . . "You did the body paint under there, too!" he exclaimed.

Karen smiled at him. "I thought you might find that out," she answered as he caressed her. She turned toward him. He kissed her, then lowered his face to her breasts. She sighed and pressed him to her. They sank down onto the seat together.

Neither of them had the nerve to go all the way in the drive-in, but Jonathan's hand glided along her thighs and then dived under the waistband of her shorts and inside her panties. He kissed her breasts and her mouth as he rubbed her. His lips were pressed against hers when she let out a little mewling cry a couple of minutes later. He'd made sure he would be kissing her just then; he knew she got noisy at such times.

"Sit up," she said. She unzipped his fly, reached in, and pulled him out. His breath came ragged. Her touch seemed sweeter than ever as she stroked him. And then, instead of finishing him with her hands the way she usually did, she bent over him and took him in her mouth. She'd never done that before. He was as-tonished at how good it felt. She didn't have to do it very long, either—he exploded almost instantly. Karen pulled back, wheez-ing and gulping and choking a little, too. She grabbed a napkin from the cardboard carton and wiped at her chin. "Sorry," she told him. "You caught me by surprise."

"You caught me by surprise, too." Jonathan was amazed the whole drive-in couldn't hear his thudding heart. "What made you decide to do that?" Whatever it was, he hoped it would make her decide to do it again.

"I don't know." Her eyes sparkled with mischief. "But my

mother did tell us to have a good time, remember." Their laughter came closer to disturbing the people a few spaces over than anything else they'd done.

Like any Tosevite, Kassquit used metabolic water to cool herself. She used a lot of it aboard her starship, which was of course kept at the temperature the Race found comfortable. Never having known any other, she took that temperature for granted. Intellectually, she knew it was warmer than the mean down on Tosev 3, but that meant little to her. It was the temperature she was used to.

Sweating, of course, made her unique on the starship. The very idea disgusted most males and females of the Race. Because it disgusted them, it disgusted Kassquit, too. She wished she could pant as they did. But that wasn't how her kind had evolved, so she was stuck with being clammy a lot of the time.

She'd also noticed that she put forth more metabolic water when stressed. She felt stressed now, as stressed as she ever had in her life. She was expecting another telephone call from the wild Big Ugly named Sam Yeager. This time, at Ttomalss' urging, she was going to leave the video on.

"If you are going to serve as a link between the Race and the Tosevites, you cannot fear to look at them, or to have them look at you," her mentor had said.

"Truth," she'd answered, for a truth it obviously was. And Sam Yeager was what passed for an expert on the Race among the Tosevites. She'd seen as much from his comments on the electronic network—and even from his gaining access to the network in the first place.

But sweat poured off her now. Her heart pounded in her chest. She wished she'd never agreed to this. She wished she could hide. She wished she could flee. She wished the video unit in the computer terminal would malfunction. She wished something would happen to the Tosevite so his call couldn't come through.

None of those wishes, none of the prayers she breathed to spirits of Emperors past, came true. At precisely the appointed time, her screen lit. She muttered a worried curse under her breath—had the spirits of Emperors past forsaken her because she was so irrevocably a Big Ugly herself?

Her internal torment did not show on her face. Nothing much

showed on her face. She knew that set her apart from other Tosevites as much as sweating set her apart from the Race, but she
didn't want Tosevites perceiving her thoughts and feelings anyhow.

"I greet you, Sam Yeager," she said, and then stopped in surprise, for not one but two Tosevite faces peered out of the screen
at her.

"I greet you, superior female," one of the Big Uglies said. His
skin had wrinkles in it that almost made him look scaled. He had
yellowish gray hair on his head and wore cloth wrappings. "I am
Sam Yeager. I also present to you my hatchling here. His name is
Jonathan Yeager."

"I greet you, superior female," the other Big Ugly said. He
spoke a little less fluently than his father, but Kassquit had no
trouble understanding him. She eyed him in some surprise. Like
her, he shaved his head. And, like her, he wore body paint rather
than wrappings—at least, on as much of him as she could see.

"I greet you, Jonathan Yeager," she replied, doing her best to
say the name as Sam Yeager had. "Are you truly a missile radar
technician?"

"No, superior female," he answered, still speaking the language of the Race slowly and carefully. The corners of his mouth
turned upward. That, Kassquit had learned, was an expression of
amiability. He went on, "I wear the body paint for decoration
and amusement, no more."

"I see," Kassquit said, though not at all sure she did. She continued, "And I greet you, Sam Yeager. You are surely senior to
your hatchling, so I am remiss in making my greetings out of
order. I apologize."

"Do not fret about it. I am not offended," Sam Yeager replied.
"I am not such an easy fellow to offend. I brought my hatchling
along with me so you could see that we also have bridges between the Race and the Tosevites."

"You are such a bridge yourself, I am given to understand,"
Kassquit said.

"Yes, that is also a truth," Sam Yeager agreed. "We have realized the Race is going to be on Tosev 3 for a long time to come.
That means we are going to have to deal with it one way or another. And besides . . ." He glanced over to Jonathan Yeager.
Like Kassquit, he had to turn his whole head to do it; he couldn't
just flick one eye turret toward the other Tosevite in the screen.

Far more than his words, that motion reminded her she was his biological kin. "Besides, he is ignorant enough to think the Race is a whole lot of fun."

Was that an insult? Kassquit looked toward Sam Yeager's hatchling. The corners of Jonathan Yeager's mouth turned up again. "Truth," he said, and added an emphatic cough.

"What sort of truth?" Kassquit asked, bewildered. "That you are ignorant?"

"He will never admit that," Sam Yeager said with a barking Tosevite laugh.

Another insult? Evidently not, for Jonathan Yeager laughed, too, laughed and said, "No—truth that things having to do with the Race are fun."

"Fun." Kassquit chewed on the word. She knew what it meant, of course, but she'd never thought of applying it to the Race or the way the Race lived. More bewildered than ever, she asked, "Why?"

"Good question," Sam Yeager said cheerfully. "I never have been able to figure it out myself." Then he waved one of his hands—one of his fleshy, soft-skinned hands, so like hers—back and forth, palm out. "I do not intend you to take that seriously."

"You never intend anyone to take anything you say seriously," Jonathan Yeager said, and both Big Uglies laughed. Then the younger one turned his face back toward Kassquit. He too had to move his whole head. Kassquit watched in fascination. The wild Tosevites took such motions utterly for granted, while she'd never failed to feel self-conscious about them. But then, they all used those motions, while she was the only individual she knew who did. Jonathan Yeager went on, "Of course the Race is fun. It is new and exciting and fascinating. Is it any wonder that I think as I do?"

Alien, Kassquit thought. She might share biology with these Big Uglies—every move they made reminded her she *did* share biology with them—but she would never have put *new* and *exciting* and *fascinating* all in the same sentence. "I do not understand," she confessed.

"Do not worry about it," Sam Yeager said. "It is a wonder that my hatchling thinks at all, let alone that he thinks in any particular way."

"Thank you," Jonathan Yeager said, with an emphatic cough

obviously intended to mean he was doing anything but thanking the older Tosevite. No male of the Race would have used the cough that way, but Kassquit understood it.

So did Sam Yeager, who started laughing again. He said, "A lot of Tosevite males and females of about my hatchling's age feel the same way about the Race as he does. The Race *is* new on Tosev 3, which to many Big Uglies automatically makes it exciting and fascinating. And the Race is powerful. That makes it exciting and fascinating, too."

Kassquit understood the connection between power and fascination. That connection had helped make the Rabotevs and Hallessi into contented citizens of the Empire. It would, she hoped, help do the same for the Big Uglies. The connection between novelty and fascination still eluded her. So did another connection: "Why would Tosevites"—she didn't want to call Big Uglies *Big Uglies*, even if Sam Yeager casually used the term—"be so interested in the Race, when you are constantly concerned with reproduction, which matters to the Race only during the mating season?"

"I am sorry, superior female, but I did not follow all of that," Jonathan Yeager said.

"I did. I will translate," Sam Yeager said. Turning to his hatchling, he spoke in their own language—English, Kassquit had learned it was called. Jonathan Yeager coughed and flushed; his change in color was easily visible on the monitor. Sam Yeager returned to the language of the Race: "I think you embarrassed him, partly because, at his age, he *is* constantly concerned with reproduction"—the younger Yeager let out another indignant, wordless squawk, which the older one ignored—"and partly because it is not our usual custom to talk so frankly about reproductive matters with strangers."

"Why not?" Kassquit was confused again. "If they concern you all the time, why do you not talk about them all the time? And why did you yourself talk about them with me in our last conversation?"

"Those are good questions," Sam Yeager admitted. "As for the second, I guess I was taken by surprise when I found out you were a Tosevite like me. For the first, I do not have an answer as good as I might like. One reason is that we mate in private, I suppose. Another is that we usually form mating pairs, and try to make those pairings permanent. Mating outside a pair is liable to destroy it."

"Why?" Kassquit asked again.

"Because it shows a lack of trust inside the pair," Sam Yeager answered. "Since the Race raised you, you probably would not understand."

"Maybe I do," Kassquit said slowly. "You are speaking of a competition for attention, are you not?" She remembered how jealous she'd been of Felless when the female of the Race began taking away Ttomalss' attention, which she'd largely had to herself till the colonization fleet arrived.

"Yes, that is exactly what I am speaking of," Sam Yeager replied. "Perceptive of you to grasp it when you have not known it yourself."

"You think not, do you?" Kassquit said. "This proves only that you do not know everything there is to know." She did not hide her bitterness. Part of her didn't want to show it to a couple of wild Big Uglies. The rest didn't care about the embarrassment in that. After all, when would she see them or deal with them again? Who else that she knew would ever see them or deal with them? And showing someone, anyone, that bitterness was such a relief.

Sam Yeager bared his teeth in the Tosevite expression of amiability. "I never said I did know everything, superior female. I have spent a lot of years having it proved to me that I do not. But I know I am ignorant, which puts me ahead of some of the males and females who think they are smart."

"You speak in paradoxes, I see," Kassquit answered, which for some reason made the Big Ugly laugh again. Annoyed, Kassquit said, "I must go, for I have an appointment. Farewell." Abruptly, she broke the connection.

After a moment, she sighed in relief. It was over. But then she stood up, and stood taller and straighter than usual. No small pride filled her. She had given as good as she'd got. She was sure of that. She had seen the wild Big Uglies face-to-face, and she had prevailed.

As Sam Yeager and his son left the Race's consulate in Los Angeles and headed for his car, he turned to Jonathan and asked, "Well, what did you think of that?"

"It was pretty strange, Dad," Jonathan answered, and Sam could hardly disagree. His son went on, "It was interesting, too, I guess. I got to practice the language some more. That's always good."

"You spoke well. And you look a lot more like a Lizard than I do, too," Yeager said. "That's one of the big reasons I brought you along: to give her somebody who might look halfway familiar to deal with. Maybe it helped some. I hope so." He shook his head. "That poor kid. Listening to her, seeing her, makes me feel terrible about what we're doing to Mickey and Donald."

"Her face is like Liu Mei's," Jonathan said as they got to the car. "It doesn't show anything."

"Nope," Sam agreed, sliding behind the wheel. "I guess what they say is, you have to learn how to use expressions when you're a baby, or else you don't. Since the Lizards' faces don't move much, the kids they took couldn't do that." He glanced over at his son. "Were you just looking at her face?"

Jonathan coughed and spluttered a little, but rallied fast: "I've seen lots of bare tits before, Dad. They're not such a big deal for me as they would have been for you when you were my age."

And that was undoubtedly true. Sam sighed as he started the engine. "Having 'em out in the open so much takes away some of the thrill, I think," he said. His son looked at him as if he'd started speaking some language much stranger than that of the Race. So he was: to Jonathan, he was speaking the language of the nostalgic old-timer, a tongue the young would never understand.

Proving as much, Jonathan changed the subject. "She seems pretty smart," he said.

"Yeah, she does." Sam nodded as he got on the southbound freeway for the ride back to Gardena. "That probably helps her. I bet she'd be a lot crazier if she were stupid."

"She didn't seem all that crazy to me," his son said. "She acts more like a Lizard than a person, yeah, but heck, half my friends do that." He chuckled.

So did Sam Yeager, but he shook his head while he did it. "There's a difference. Your friends are acting, as you said." He'd been married to Barbara for quite a while, and most of the time he automatically kept his grammar clean. "But Kassquit isn't—acting, I mean. The Race is all she knows. As best I can tell, we're the first Big Uglies she's ever seen face-to-face. We're at least as strange to her as she is to us."

He watched Jonathan think about that and slowly nod. "No ordinary person would have come out and talked about, uh, reproduction like that."

"Well, it would have been surprising, anyhow," Sam said. "But she thinks about it the way the Lizards would. She can't help that—they've taught her everything she knows." He took a hand off the wheel to remove his uniform cap—he'd gone to the consulate in full regalia—and scratch his head. "Still, she's not made the way they are. She can't even be as old as you are, Jonathan. If she's like anybody else your age, she's going to get urges. I wonder what she does about them."

"What can she do, up there by herself?" Jonathan asked.

"What anybody by himself, or by herself, can do." Sam raised an eyebrow. "Sooner or later, you find out it doesn't grow hair on the palm of your hand."

That made Jonathan turn red and clam up for the rest of the drive back home. Sam used the quiet to do some thinking of his own. Not only seeing Kassquit, but also listening to her trying so hard to be something she couldn't be, did bring on guilt about Mickey and Donald. No matter how hard he and his family tried to raise them up as people, they would never be human beings, any more than Kassquit could really be a Lizard.

And what would happen when they met Lizards, as they surely would one day? Would they be as confused and dismayed as Kassquit had been at the prospect of talking with a couple of genuine human beings? Probably. He didn't see how they would be able to help it.

It wasn't fair. They hadn't asked to be hatched in an incubator on his service porch. But nobody, human or Lizard, had any say about where he got his start in life. Mickey and Donald would have to make the best of it they could, as did everybody else on four worlds. And Sam and his family would have to help.

He hoped he'd stay around to help. Being fifty-seven had a way of putting that kind of thought in his mind. He was in pretty good shape for his age, but every time he shaved in the morning the first glance in the mirror reminded him he wouldn't be here forever. Barbara could take over for him if he went too soon (somehow, contemplating his own death was easier than thinking about hers), and Jonathan, and whomever Jonathan married. He hoped that would be Karen. She was a good kid, and she and Jonathan had been thick as thieves lately.

After a moment, he shook his head. "Back to business," he muttered. Business was getting a summary of the conversation Jonathan and he had had with Kassquit down on paper, and adding his impressions to it. He was glad he'd talked with his son. It helped him clarify his own thoughts.

He had to use the human-made computer to draft his report. With the one he'd got from the Lizards, he couldn't print in English, but was stuck with the language of the Race. Kassquit might have found a report in the Lizards' language interesting, but it wouldn't have amused his superiors.

When he finished the report and pressed the key that would print it, a glorified electric typewriter hammered into life. The printer hooked up to the Lizard-built computer was a lot more elegant, using powdered carbon and a *skelkwank* light to form the characters and images it produced. You needed a powerful magnifier to tell its output was made up of tiny dots and didn't come from a typewriter or even from set type.

He read through the report, made a couple of small corrections in ink, and set it aside. The printer kept humming till he turned it off. He started to turn off the computer, too, but changed his mind. Instead, he hooked himself up to the U.S. network. He hadn't tried visiting the archive that stored signals traffic from the night the colonization fleet was attacked for quite a while. The more he learned about that, the better his chances of nailing the culprit and passing what he knew on to the Lizards.

They'll never figure out whether it was the Nazis or the Russians, not on their own they won't, he thought. The Lizards were less naive than they had been when they came to Earth, but humans, long used to cheating one another, still had little trouble deceiving them. And, because the Lizards weren't human, they often missed clues that would have been obvious to a person.

"There we go," Sam muttered, as the name of the archive appeared on his screen. He waited for the table of contents to come up below it, so he could find exactly which transcripts would be most useful to him. The list took its own sweet time appearing; compared to the Race's machine, this one was slow, slow.

Instead of the contents list, he got a blank, dark screen. Pale letters announced, CONNECTION BROKEN. PLEASE TRY AGAIN.

"You cheap piece of junk," he snarled, and whacked the side of the case that held the screen. That didn't change the message, of course. It did go a little way toward easing his annoyance. The Lizards' computer worked all the time. The machine made in the USA broke down if he looked at it sideways.

But he was a stubborn man. He wouldn't have spent eighteen years riding trains and buses through every corner of the bush leagues if he hadn't been stubborn. He wouldn't have risen to lieutenant colonel, either, not when he'd joined the Army as a thirty-five-year-old private with full upper and lower dentures. And he wouldn't have got so far with the Lizards, either.

And so, even though he kept swearing under his breath, he patiently reconnected the computer to the network and navigated toward that archive again. This time, he didn't even get the archival name before he lost his connection.

He scowled and stared at the dark screen with the now familiar message on it. "Junk," he repeated, but now he sounded less sure whether the fault lay inside his computer. Maybe the chain connecting him to that distant archive—actually, he didn't know how distant it was, only that it existed—had some rusty links in it.

He wondered if he ought to report the problem. He didn't wonder for long, though. While his security clearance was high enough to give him access to that archive, he had no formal need-to-know. Nobody above him would be happy to find out he'd been snooping around in things that were formally none of his business. The powers that be would frown all the harder because he'd already established a reputation for snooping.

"Hell with it," he said, and this time he did turn off the computer. Maybe the simplest explanation was that somebody somewhere had made a tidy profit selling the U.S. government—or would it be the phone company?—some lousy wiring.

He was making himself a bologna sandwich (he'd got sick of ham) when a car stopped in front of the house. The sound of the closing door made him look up from pickles and mayonnaise. A young man he'd never seen before was walking across the lawn toward the front porch. Another one sat in the car, waiting.

The one coming up to the house had his right hand in the

pocket of his blue jeans. After somebody had taken some pot-shots at the house, that triggered an alarm bell in Sam. He hurried to the hutch in the front room and pulled out his .45.

Barbara came into the front room from the direction of the bedroom. She'd spotted the guy, too, and was going to find out what he wanted. When she saw the automatic in Sam's hands, her eyes opened enormously wide. He used it to motion her away.

Up on the porch came the stranger. Before he could knock, Sam opened the front door and stuck the .45 in his face. "Take that hand out of your pocket real nice and slow," he said pleasantly, and then, over his shoulder, "Honey, call the cops."

"Sure, Pop, anything you say," the young man answered. "You've got the persuader there, all right." But his hand moved swiftly, not slowly, and had a pistol in it as it cleared his pocket.

He must have thought Yeager would hesitate long enough to let him shoot first. It was the last mistake he ever made. The .45 jerked against Sam's wrist as he fired. The young man went down. He wouldn't get up again, either, not after taking one between the eyes at point-blank range. He kept jerking and twitching, but that was only because his body didn't know he was dead yet.

Tires screaming, the car in which he'd come roared away. Barbara and Jonathan came dashing out at the sound of the shot. "Thank God," Barbara said when she saw Sam standing. She turned away from the corpse on the porch. "Christ! I haven't seen anything like that since the fighting. The police are on the way."

"Good. I'll wait for 'em right here," Sam said.

They arrived a couple of minutes later, lights flashing, siren yowling. "What the hell happened here?" one of them asked, though he was talking more about why than about what—that was obvious.

"Somebody shot at this house from the street last year, Sergeant," Yeager answered. He explained what he'd seen and what he'd done, finishing, "He tried to draw on me, and I shot him. His pal took off as soon as I did."

"Okay, Lieutenant Colonel, I've got your side of it," said the sergeant, who'd been taking notes. He turned to his partner. "See just what the guy was holding, Clyde."

"Right." The other cop used his handkerchief to pick up the weapon. It was a .45 nearly identical to Sam's. Clyde looked up at Yeager. "He was loaded for bear, all right. Lucky you were, too." He glanced over at the sergeant. "If this isn't self-defense, I don't know what the devil it is."

"A hell of a mess on this guy's porch," the sergeant said. He looked back to Yeager. "No charges I can see, Lieutenant Colonel. Like Clyde says, this one looks open-and-shut. But don't leave town—we're going to have about a million questions for you, maybe more once we find out who this character is and what he had in mind."

"If I get orders to go, I'll have to follow them," Yeager said. "I've got to report this to my superiors, too."

"If you do have to leave, let us know where you're going and how long you'll be there," the police sergeant said. "And if I was your CO, I'd give you a medal. If you didn't do what needed doing, you wouldn't be able to report to him now, that's for damn sure." He raised an eyebrow. "You think this guy had anything to do with the shots last year?"

"Damned if I know," Sam answered. "Maybe we'll be able to find out."

☆ **8** ☆

Ttomalss was happily busy. Not only did he have endless work to do on his stint in the *Reich* (a stint that had only seemed endless), but his long experiment with Kassquit had entered a new and fascinating phase. "Now that you have made the acquaintance of these Tosevites through electronic messages and by telephone, would you be interested in meeting them in person?" he asked.

"No, superior sir," Kassquit answered at once, "or at least not yet."

His Tosevite hatchling perched awkwardly on the chair across the desk from his own. Not only was it the wrong shape for her posterior, but it was also too small. Ttomalss remembered when she could hardly even climb up into it—he remembered when she'd hardly been able to do anything but suck up nutrient fluid, make horrid excretions, and yowl. He had to remind himself she wasn't like that any more. She was, these days, startlingly far from foolish.

Still, she needed guiding. "I have reviewed the recording of your conversation with these two Big Uglies," he said—this recording had been made with her knowledge and consent. "For their kind, they do indeed seem remarkably sophisticated about the Race. This makes sense, since the senior male named Yeager is one of their experts on us. If you are ever to meet Tosevites not under our rule, they seem good candidates."

"I understand that, superior sir," Kassquit said, "but I am not yet ready to endure such a meeting. Even talking with them by telephone was most disturbing: more than I expected it to be."

"Why?" Ttomalss asked. He was recording this conversation, too.

219

"Why, superior sir?" Yes, Kassquit was ever more her own person these days; she gave the counterquestion a fine sardonic edge. "It was disturbing to talk to beings who look like me. It was also disturbing to talk to beings who think nothing like me. To have both sets of circumstances combined was more than doubly disturbing, I assure you."

"I see," Ttomalss said. And, after a little intellectual effort, he did. "I suppose hatchlings of the Race raised by the Big Uglies, if there were such unfortunates, would be disturbed by their first meeting with true males and females of their own species."

"Yes, I suppose they would," Kassquit agreed. "If there were any such, I would be interested in talking with them, if we had some language in common. It would be intriguing to learn whether their experiences paralleled mine here."

Now Ttomalss looked at her with alarm and dismay. She didn't usually speak of herself as being apart from the Race, even though she was. Contact with the wild Big Uglies truly had disturbed her. He did his best to reassure her: "This is a circumstance unlikely to arise. The Tosevites lack the patience needed to carry out such a long-term project."

After he'd spoken, he wondered if he was right. The Big Uglies might be impatient, but they owned boundless curiosity. If they could somehow get their hands on eggs . . . But, unlike Tosevites, he didn't show his thoughts on his face. Kassquit could have no notion of what went through his mind.

Her own thoughts were taking a different trajectory. "It would not happen for some years, at any rate. They could not have even attempted to raise hatchlings until the colonization fleet arrived."

"As I say, there is no evidence, none, that they have attempted to do such a thing," Ttomalss replied. "Now, shall we withdraw from hypotheticals and return to what can in fact be established?"

"As you wish, superior sir." Unlike an independent Big Ugly, Kassquit had learned proper subordination.

Ttomalss asked her, "Under what circumstances might you eventually agree to a direct meeting with these Big Uglies?"

"I need further conversations with them," Kassquit answered. "Only then will I be able to decide if I want to take that step."

"Not unreasonable," Ttomalss admitted. Now that he thought on it, he was not altogether sure he wanted to risk her, either. She had never been exposed to or immunized against Tosevite diseases. There were many of those, and the Race was not well equipped to combat them. Losing Kassquit would be a devastating setback. "I think I may need further·conversations with our physicians before permitting the meeting, too. I must plan with all possible forethought."

"Certainly," Kassquit said. "What other course to take?"

Ttomalss did not reply, not to a question obviously rhetorical. Had he been a Big Ugly, though, his features would have twisted themselves into the expression that showed amiability. *You are not altogether a Tosevite,* he thought. *My teaching—the Race's teaching—has made you far less headstrong than you would be otherwise. What has succeeded with you can succeed with your whole species.*

Kassquit said, "May I go now, superior sir?"

"Yes, of course," Ttomalss answered. "I thank you for your efforts in this matter. You must now determine whether you are willing to attempt a physical meeting with these Big Uglies, and I must determine how dangerous to your health such a meeting might be."

After Kassquit had left his compartment, the senior researcher permitted himself a long sigh of relief. He was very glad Kassquit had declined his offer to get her a wild male Tosevite with whom she could relieve the tensions of her continuous sexual drive. He had not considered the possible medical consequences of such a meeting before he made the offer. Had she accepted, he would have felt duty-bound to carry it out. Had she fallen ill on account of anything so trivial as sexuality, he would never have forgiven himself.

He went through the recording of her conversation with the Big Uglies again. The younger Tosevite named Yeager particularly fascinated him. As far as appearance went, he might almost have hatched from the same egg as Kassquit. But his accent and his limited understanding made it plain he was only a wild Tosevite.

Ttomalss knew there were Big Uglies who imitated the Race every way they could. That encouraged him. As far as he was concerned, it marked a step toward assimilation. He had seen no such Tosevites in the *Reich*. The leaders there, having evidently come to the same conclusion, had banned body paint and shaved heads in the territory they held. Considering what passed for justice in that territory, Ttomalss found it unsurprising that few Tosevites there dared flout the law.

Though the younger Big Ugly was more interesting to look at, Ttomalss slowly realized the older one was much more interesting to hear. Like Jonathan Yeager, Sam Yeager spoke the language of the Race with a curious accent and with odd turns of phrase. But, listening to him, Ttomalss found that he did—or at least could—think like a male of the Race. The senior researcher wondered if he understood Big Uglies anywhere near as well as the older Yeager understood the Race. He was honest enough to admit that he didn't know. He himself was capable—he didn't denigrate his own abilities—but the Tosevite seemed inspired.

How, he wondered, could a Big Ugly have prepared himself to become an expert on another intelligent species when his kind hadn't known there were any other intelligent species to meet? If he ever conversed with the elder Yeager, he would have to ask that question.

He was contemplating other questions when the telephone hissed. He'd been forming a clever thought. It disappeared. That made him hiss, in annoyance. Resignedly, he said, "Senior Researcher Ttomalss speaking—I greet you."

"And I greet you—you who have escaped from the *Reich*," said Felless, whose image overlay the now muted views of Kassquit and the two Big Uglies named Yeager. "You have no idea how lucky you are."

"You are mistaken, superior female," Ttomalss answered with an emphatic cough. "I know exactly how lucky I am. Spirits of Emperors past grant that you soon find yourself able to make a similar escape."

Felless cast down her eyes. In a miserable voice, she said, "It shall *not* be done." She sighed. "You transgressed against the Deutsche and were ordered out of the *Reich*, while I transgressed against our own kind and was ordered to stay in this accursed place. Where is the justice in that?"

"Transgressed against our—?" Ttomalss began, but his confusion quickly faded. "They caught you with your tongue in the ginger jar, did they?"

"You might say so," Felless said bitterly. "Veffani and most of a team of senior officials from Cairo mated with me when I was summoned to a meeting in the ambassador's office just after I had tasted."

Now there was a scandal to keep the embassy buzzing for a long time! Ttomalss had to work to keep from laughing in Felless' face. That would be cruel—tempting, but cruel—after she'd disgraced herself. "I do not understand why you were ordered to stay there," he said.

"As punishment," she snapped. "I was hoping you would have a sympathetic hearing diaphragm, but I see that is too much to ask for."

"I am lucky enough not to have acquired the ginger habit," he said. "And it is a less urgent matter with me, since I am a male."

"Unfair," Felless exclaimed. "I did not ask to release pheromones after tasting. I wish I would not. I also wish I were not going to lay another clutch of eggs. But wishes are pointless, are they not?"

Ttomalss remembered the extravagant wishes he'd made while Liu Han held him in captivity. "No, not always," he said. "They can help keep hope alive, and hope matters most when things look worst."

"Hope?" Felless said. "My only hope is to get away from this dreadful place, and that is what I cannot do." She paused. "No, I take that back. My other hope is to be able to get more ginger before my present supply runs out. That, at least, I expect I will be able to accomplish." Her image disappeared from the screen.

Ttomalss stared for a little while at the soundless pictures of the two wild Big Uglies and of Kassquit. With a sigh, he ended the playback of that recording, too; he couldn't concentrate on it. Poor Felless! For all her expertise, she hadn't adapted well to Tosev 3. She'd expected it to be far more like Home than it really was.

If she'd stayed aboard a starship or gone to one of the new towns on the island continent or on the main continental mass, she might have done well enough. But her field of specialization involved dealing with the alien natives of Tosev 3 . . . who had proved far more alien than the Race could possibly have imagined before setting out from Home.

Well, I know all about that, Ttomalss thought. He knew it in more intimate detail than he'd ever imagined, thanks to his captivity in China and thanks to his raising Kassquit. One way or another, everyone in the conquest fleet had learned the lessons with which the males and females of the colonization fleet were still grappling.

The colonists didn't want to adapt. There were so many of them, they didn't have to adapt to the same degree as had the males of the conquest fleet. *They have it easy,* Ttomalss thought. *We did the real work, and they do not appreciate it.* He wondered if the older generation of the Big Uglies ever had such thoughts about their dealings with the Race, and if the younger ones were as ungrateful as the males and females of the colonization fleet. He doubted it.

Atvar studied a map of the regions of Tosev 3 the Race ruled. Some parts of it were a tranquil yellow-green, others angry red, still others in between. He turned to Pshing, his adjutant. "Fascinating how little correlation there is between this map and the one reflecting active rebellion," he observed.

"Truth, Exalted Fleetlord," Pshing agreed. "The subregions of the main continental mass known as China and India accept veneration of the spirits of Emperors past almost without complaint, as do large stretches of the region known as Africa. Yet China and India still seethe with political strife, while Africa is largely tranquil. Intriguing."

"So it is." Atvar pointed to another section of the map. "Yet the southern part of the lesser continental mass is afire with resentment against us because of this measure, and that had also been one of the areas where our administration was least difficult and annoying. It is a puzzlement."

"We do not yet understand everything we should about the Big Uglies," Pshing said. "A world, I have discovered since our arrival here, is a very large place to get to know in detail."

"That is indeed a truth." The fleetlord's emphatic cough told how much of a truth he thought it was. He followed the cough with a sigh. "And, of course, there is this central region of the main continental mass, where rebellion and resistance to veneration of the spirits of Emperors past skitter side by side."

Pshing also sighed. "Such a pity, too, because this region really is among the most Homelike on the whole planet. I have actually come to enjoy Cairo's climate. It could easily be that of a temperate region back on Home. Now if only the Tosevites were temperate."

"Expect temperance from a Big Ugly and you are doomed to disappointment," Atvar said. His mouth came open and he waggled his lower jaw from side to side in a wry laugh. "Expect anything from a Big Ugly and you are doomed to disappointment. What have we had on Tosev 3 but one surprise after another?"

"Nothing," his adjutant replied. "We can only hope we have also succeeded in giving the Tosevites a few surprises." He turned one eye turret back toward the map. "I truly do wonder what accounts for the differences in response to our edict."

"Part of it, I suppose, springs from the differences in local superstition," Atvar said, "but the role these differences play still baffles me. The followers of the Jewish superstition, for instance, have always been well disposed to us, but they are among those who most strongly resist venerating spirits of Emperors past. They bombard me with petitions and memorials. Even Moishe Russie does nothing but complain about it."

"I know, Exalted Fleetlord," Pshing said. "I have shielded you from several of his calls, too."

"Have you? Well, I thank you," Atvar said. "So many of the Big Uglies are so passionately convinced of their own correctness, they are willing to die, sometimes eager to die, to maintain it. This is one of the things that makes them such a delight to govern, as you must be aware."

As if to underscore his words, the Tosevite howling that was the call to prayer of the Muslim superstition floated through the open windows of his office—except during the worst of the rioting, when he needed the armor glass as protection against assassins, he saw no point to closing those windows against the fine mild air of Cairo. Here and there, spatters of gunfire accompanied the howling. No, the locals were not reconciled to paying a tax for the privilege of keeping their foolish beliefs.

"With rational beings, lowering the tax, as we did, would also have lowered the resentment," he grumbled. "With Big Uglies . . ."

Before he could go on fulminating, the telephone started making a racket. At Atvar's gesture, Pshing answered it. No sooner had the caller's image appeared on the screen than the adjutant assumed the posture of respect, saying, "I greet you, Exalted Fleetlord."

"And I greet you, Pshing," Reffet said, "but I need to speak with your principal at once—at once, do you hear me?"

"One moment, please," Pshing replied, and muted the sound. Still down in the posture of respect, he asked Atvar, "What is your pleasure, Exalted Fleetlord?"

Speaking with his opposite number from the colonization fleet was not exactly Atvar's pleasure, but it was sometimes necessary. Maybe this would be one of those times. He strode up to the telephone, touched the sound control, and said, "I greet you, Reffet. How now?"

"How now indeed?" Reffet returned. "How many more males and females from the colonization fleet will face assault and perhaps assassination because of your efforts to tax Tosevite superstitions?"

No, Atvar did not care for the fleetlord from the colonization fleet, not even a little bit. With a certain sardonic relish, he replied, "You have complained because we did not, in your view, do enough to bring Tosev 3 into the Empire. Now that we are taking a step to do exactly that, you are complaining again. You cannot have it on both forks of the tongue at once."

"Answer my question and spare me the rhetoric, if you would be so kind," Reffet said. "We are suffering. Can you not perceive that?"

Unimpressed, Atvar answered, "My own males, the males of the conquest fleet, are suffering more, I remind you. They are the ones who actually have to enforce the new edict, and who face the dangers inherent in doing so. Colonists, if they are prudent, should not be at great risk. They do need to remember that Big Uglies, even in areas we rule, are not fully acclimated to us."

"Are, in other words, wild beasts," Reffet said, sarcastic in his own right. "Or would be wild beasts, did they not have the cleverness of intelligent beings. And either you do not know what you are talking about in respect to relative danger or you have not heard of the latest Tosevite outrage, word of which just reached me."

Atvar knew a sinking feeling in the middle of his gut. He'd known that feeling too many times on Tosev 3; he kept hoping not to have it again, and kept being disappointed. "I have not heard the latest," he admitted. "You had better tell me."

"Tell you I shall," Reffet said. "One of the new towns in this region of the main continental mass, the one near the attacked desalination plants"—an image on the screen showed the area known as the Arabian Peninsula—"has just suffered a devastating attack. A Tosevite drove a large truck loaded with explosives into the center of the place and touched them off, killing himself and an undetermined but large number of males and females. Physical damage is also extensive."

"By the Emperor!" Atvar said, and cast down his eyes. "No, I had not yet heard. The only thing I will say in aid of this is that it is cursedly difficult to thwart an individual willing to pay with his own life to accomplish some goal. This is not the least of the problems we face in attempting to consolidate our control on this world, for the Big Uglies are far more willing to resort to such behavior than any other species we know."

"They are, no doubt, especially willing to resort to it when you incite them," Reffet said. As he spoke, words crawled across the bottom of the screen, informing Atvar of the bombing incident all over again. Atvar read them with one eye while looking at Reffet with the other.

A detail caught the attention of the fleetlord of the conquest fleet. "How did this Big Ugly manage to drive his vehicle into the center of the new town without being searched?"

"The inhabitants must have assumed he was there to deliver something or perform a service," Reffet answered. "One does not commonly believe a Big Ugly in a truck is come on a mission of murder."

"In that part of Tosev 3, with the present stresses, why not?" Atvar asked. "The males of the conquest fleet cannot do everything for you, Reffet. A checkpoint outside the town might have saved the colonists much sorrow."

"Colonists are not soldiers," Reffet said.

"Colonists can certainly be police," Atvar answered, "and we have already begun to discuss the need for colonists to become soldiers. The males of the conquest fleet cannot carry the whole burden forever. Before all that long, we shall grow old and die. If the Race has no soldiers left after that, who will keep the Big Uglies from eating us up?"

"If we have a permanent Soldiers' Time on this world, how can we be a proper part of the Empire?" Reffet returned. "The meaning of the Empire is that we have soldiers only in emergencies and for conquests."

"When is it not an emergency on Tosev 3?" Atvar asked, a question for which Reffet could have no good answer. "Before the Empire unified Home, it always had soldiers, for it always needed them. That seems to be true on this world as well. You may regret it—I certainly regret it. But can you deny it?"

"Colonists will scream if you seek to make some of them into soldiers," the fleetlord of the colonization fleet said. "Can you deny that?"

"How loud are they screaming because of those killed or wounded in the new town?" Atvar asked.

Reffet sighed. "This is not the world they were told to anticipate when they went into cold sleep back on Home. Many of them are still having difficulty adjusting to that. I understand, for I am still having difficulty adjusting to it myself."

"Really? I never would have noticed," Atvar said. It sounded like praise. Reffet knew it wasn't. He glared at Atvar. The fleetlord of the conquest fleet went on, "Colonists can deal with Tosev 3 as they imagined it to be, or they can deal with it as it is. I know which of those courses is likely to produce more satisfactory results. I wish more colonists would come to the same conclusion, rather than screaming because things are not as they would prefer."

"That is unfair," Reffet said. "We have labored long and hard to establish ourselves on this planet since our arrival here. You do not give us enough credit for it."

"And you do not give us enough credit for all the labor—yes, and all the dying, too—we of the conquest fleet did so you would have a world you could colonize, even in part," Atvar replied. "All we get is blame. Who back on Home would have thought the Big Uglies would have either trucks or explosives to load aboard them? And yet you colonists shout abuse at us for botching the war. You still cannot see how lucky we were to come away with a draw."

"My males and females are not meant to be soldiers," Reffet said stubbornly.

"Are they then meant to be victims?" Atvar inquired. "That

seems to be the only other choice. I grieve that this terrorist assault against them succeeded. They will have to play a part if
they want to keep others from succeeding."

"You ask too much," Reffet said.

"You give too little," Atvar retorted. In perfect mutual
loathing, they both broke the connection at the same time.

As Straha's driver pulled to a halt in front of the house Ristin
and Ullhass shared, the Big Ugly said, "Well, Shiplord, it seems
as though you will have your chance to talk to Sam Yeager here
instead of having to go all the way to Gardena."

"Why do you say that?" Straha peered through the windows
in the front part of the house. He did not see Yeager or any other
Tosevite.

The driver barked laughter. "Because that is his automobile
there, parked just in front of us."

"Oh." Straha felt foolish. He had never noticed what sort of
motorcar Yeager drove. All he had noticed about American
motorcars was that they came in far more varieties than seemed
necessary. He undid his safety belt and opened the door. "Will
you come in and join us? Ullhass asked that you be included in
the invitation, if you so desired."

"I thank you, but no," the Big Ugly answered. "For one thing,
I do not much care for crowds, whether of the Race or of Tosevites. And, for another, I can do a better job of protecting you
from out here than from in there. I am assuming you will be in
less danger from guests than from uninvited strangers."

"I believe that is a valid assumption, yes," Straha said. "If it is
not, I have more and more diverse difficulties than I would have
thought. I shall return in due course. I hope you will not be bored
waiting for me."

"It is my duty," the driver said. "Enjoy yourself, Shiplord."

Straha slammed the car door shut and headed for the house.
He intended to do just that. Ullhass and Ristin always had good
alcohol and plenty of ginger. They also had interesting guests,
no matter what the driver thought. Because they were only
small-scale traitors, the Race had long since forgiven them.
Males and females from the land under the Race's control could
visit here without opprobrium, where they would have caused a
scandal by coming to see Straha.

At the doorway, Ullhass folded himself into the posture of respect. "I greet you, Shiplord," he said, as deferential as if Straha still commanded the *206th Emperor Yower*. "I am always pleased when you honor my home by your presence."

"I thank you for inviting me," Straha replied. On the whole, that was true: these gatherings were as close as he could come to the society of his own kind. And if Ullhass, like Ristin, chose to wear red-white-and-blue body paint that showed he was a U.S. prisoner of war in place of the proper markings of the Race . . . well, he'd been doing that for a long time now, and Straha could overlook if not forgive it.

"Come in, come in," Ullhass urged, and stood aside to let Straha do just that. "You have been here before—you will know where we keep the alcohol and the herb and the food. Help yourself to anything you think will please you. We are also doing some outdoor cooking in back of the house, with meats both from Tosev 3 and from Home."

Sure enough, odors of smoke and of hot meat reached Straha's scent receptors. "The smells are intriguing indeed," he said. "I must be careful not to slobber on your floor." Ullhass laughed.

Straha went into the kitchen and poured himself some rum—like most of the Race, he had no use for whiskey. He loaded a small plate with Greek olives and salted nuts and potato chips, then went out through the open sliding glass door into the back yard. Sam Yeager stood out there offering helpful advice to Ristin, who was cremating meat on a grill above a charcoal fire.

"I greet you, Shiplord," Yeager said to Straha, and raised his glass in a Tosevite salute. "Good to see you."

"How can you stand to drink that stuff?" Straha asked—Yeager's glass did hold whiskey. "What is it good for but removing paint?"

The Big Ugly sipped the nasty stuff. "Removing troubles," he answered, and sipped again.

That startled a laugh out of Straha, who took a drink of rum himself. "Well, but why not remove troubles with something that tastes good?" he asked.

"I like the way whiskey tastes just fine," Yeager answered. "I have spent a lot of time getting used to it, and I see no point in wasting the accomplishment."

That made Straha laugh, too; he enjoyed Yeager's off-center way of looking at the world. "Have it as you will, then," he said. "Every beffel goes to its own hole, or so the saying has it."

"Befflem, yes." Yeager's head bobbed up and down. "All of your animals here now. Some of them smell very tasty." He pointed back to the grill on which Ristin was cooking. "But others . . . Do you know about the rabbits in Australia, Shiplord?"

"I know what rabbits are: those hopping furry creatures with long flaps of skin channeling sound to their hearing diaphragms," Straha answered. Yeager nodded once more. Straha continued, "And I know of Australia, because it is one of our principal centers of colonization—not that I will ever get to see as much, of course." For a moment, his bitterness at exile showed through. "But, I confess, I do not know of any connection between rabbits and Australia."

"Until a little more than a hundred years ago, there were no rabbits in Australia," the Tosevite told him. "None used to live there. The settlers brought them. Because they were new, because they had no natural enemies to speak of, they spread all over Australia and became great pests. Your animals from Home are liable to do the same thing on big stretches of Tosev 3."

"Ah. I see your concern," Straha replied. After another sip of rum, he shrugged. "I do not know what to say about this. I do not know that there is anything to be said about it. Your settlers, I presume, brought their animals with them and transformed the ecology of the areas in which they settled till it suited them better. Our colonists are doing the same thing here on Tosev 3. Did you expect them to do otherwise?"

"If you want to know the truth, Shiplord, I did not think much about it one way or the other," Sam Yeager said. "I do not think any Tosevites thought much about it till the colonization fleet came. Now reports from all over Tosev 3 are beginning to reach me. I do not know how big a problem your animals will turn out to be, but I think they will be a problem."

"I would not be surprised if you were right—from a Tosevite point of view, of course," Straha said. "To the Race, these animals are a convenience, not a problem."

As if to prove what a convenience the Race's domesticated animals could be, Ristin chose that moment to shout—in English—"Come and get it!" Straha let out a small snort of dismay. He knew Ristin and Ullhass had taken on as many Tosevite ways as they could, but a call like that offended his sense of dignity.

He was not so offended, however, as to keep from taking chunks of azwaca still sizzling from their time above the coals. Sam Yeager did the same. Unlike Straha's driver, he showed no reluctance about trying the Race's foods. After his first bite, he waved to get Ristin's attention and spoke in English: "That's pretty damn good."

"Glad you like it," the former infantrymale answered, again in the same tongue. Sure enough, he was nothing but a Big Ugly with scales and eye turrets.

But he did have good food. Straha tried the ssefenji next: a grainier, tougher meat then azwaca, and less sweet to the tongue. He didn't like it so well, but it too was a taste of Home. And it turned out to go very well with cashews. Straha walked back into the house to get some more nuts, and filled up his glass of rum while he was there.

He glanced out the kitchen window. There sat his driver in the motorcar, looking, as best Straha could tell, bored. But the Big Ugly was in fact alert; Straha had never known him when he wasn't alert. Seeing Straha in the window, he waved and saluted. Not many Tosevites could have recognized the ex-shiplord from such a brief glance, but he did. Straha waved back, in grudging but genuine respect.

Then he headed outside once more for another helping of ssefenji ribs. He caught Sam Yeager's eye again. "And how is the Tosevite raised by the Race?" he asked.

"Well enough," Yeager answered. "My hatchling and I spoke with her again, not so long ago, and with video this time. She would be a very attractive female, did she not shave off all her hair—and were her face more lively, of course."

"Attractive? How could you judge over the telephone?" Before Yeager could answer, Straha did it for him: "Never mind. I forgot that you Big Uglies judge such matters as much by sight as by odor."

"More by sight, I would say," Yeager answered.

"Our females are the same, in judging a male's mating display, but with males it is a matter of scent." Straha looked for a way to change the subject; when not incited by pheromones, he did not care to discuss matters pertaining to mating. Having seen his driver put a new thought in his mind: "Are you aware that you have made enemies by poking your snout into places where it is not welcome? I quote someone in a position to know whereof he speaks."

"I bet I can guess who he is, too," Yeager said. Straha neither confirmed nor denied that. The Big Ugly's laugh was harsh. "Yes, Shiplord, you might say I am aware of that. You just might. I killed a man last week, to keep him from killing me."

"By the Emperor!" Straha exclaimed. "I did not know that. Why did he want to do such a thing?"

"He is too dead to ask, and his pal escaped," Yeager answered. "I wish I knew."

Straha studied him. "Has this incident any connection to the Big Uglies who fired shots at your home last year when the Chinese females and I were visiting?"

"I do not know that, either, and I wish I did," Sam Yeager said. "As a matter of fact, I was wondering if you ever found out anything more about those Big Uglies."

"Myself personally? No," Straha replied. "Assassination is a tactic the Race seldom employs. My driver is of the opinion that the Chinese females were the likeliest targets for the Big Uglies. He is also of the opinion that you may have been a target yourself, this due to your snout-poking tendencies."

"He is, is he?" Yeager's mobile mouth narrowed till he seemed to have hardly more in the way of lips than a male of the Race. "Your driver has all sorts of interesting opinions. One of these days, I may have to sit down with him for a good long talk. I might learn a few things."

"On the other fork of the tongue, you might not," Straha told him. "He is not in the habit of revealing a great deal. I, for one, am certain he knows a great deal more than he says."

"That does not sound much like a Big Ugly," Sam Yeager remarked, and now his mouth stretched wide to show amusement. But his expression quickly became more nearly neutral. "It does sound like a particular kind of Big Ugly—one in the business of intelligence, for instance."

"Are you surprised at that?" Straha felt an exile's odd sort of pride. "I am an intelligence resource of some value to your not-empire."

"Well, so you are, Shiplord. You—" Sam Yeager began.

But Straha stopped listening just then. As had happened before at Ullhass and Ristin's gatherings, a female from the colonization fleet must have decided to try a taste of ginger, which was legal here in the United States. As soon as her pheromones floated outside, Straha, along with the rest of the males in the back yard, lost interest in everything else. He hurried into the house, hoping for a chance to mate.

When Mordechai Anielewicz came up to the door of his flat, he heard shouting inside. He sighed as he raised his hand to knock on the door. Both Miriam and David were old enough to have strong opinions of their own these days, and young enough to be passionately certain their opinions were the only right and proper ones, those of their parents being idiotic by assumption. No wonder life sometimes got noisy.

He knocked. As he did so, he cocked his head to one side and listened. One eyebrow rose. This wasn't Miriam or David arguing with his wife. This was Heinrich, and he sounded even more passionate than either of his older siblings was in the habit of doing. Not only was he the youngest, he was also usually the sunniest. What could have made him . . . ?

As David Anielewicz opened the door, Mordechai heard a squeak. It wasn't a squeak from hinges that wanted oiling. It was much too friendly and endearing for that.

"He didn't," Anielewicz exclaimed.

"He sure did," his older son answered. "He brought it home about an hour ago. Mother's been trying to make him get rid of it ever since."

No sooner had Anielewicz shut the door than Heinrich, doing an excellent impersonation of a tornado, dashed up to him shouting, "She said I could keep him! She said if I got one, I could keep him! She *said*, Father! And now I did, and now she won't let me." Tears streaked the tornado's cheeks—mostly, Mordechai judged, tears of fury.

"Take it easy," he said. "We'll talk about it." Back inside the flat, the beffel squeaked again. It sounded as if it wanted to stay, but who—who human, anyway—could know how a beffel was supposed to sound?

His wife strode into the short entry hall a moment later. It was getting crowded in there, but no one seemed to want to move away. "That thing, that horrible thing, has got to go," Bertha declared.

"It's not horrible," Heinrich said. The beffel let out yet another squeak. It didn't sound like a horrible thing. It sounded like a squeeze toy. Heinrich went on, "And you said that if I caught one, I could keep him. You did. You *did*."

"But I didn't think you'd really go and do it," his mother said.

"That doesn't matter," Anielewicz said. Bertha looked appalled. Mordechai knew he would hear more—much more—about this later, but he went on, "You didn't have to make the promise, but you did. Now I'd say you've got to keep it."

Heinrich started dancing. There wasn't room for that in the narrow hallway, but he did it anyhow. "I can keep him! I can keep him! I can keep him!" he sang.

Anielewicz took him by the shoulder and forcibly stopped the dance. "You can keep him," he agreed, ignoring the dismay that still hadn't left his wife's face. "You can keep him, as long as you take care of him, and as long as he doesn't cause trouble. If he makes horrible messes, or if he starts biting people, out he goes on his ear." Befflem didn't have ears, but that had nothing to do with anything.

"I promise, Father." Heinrich's face shone.

"You have to keep your promise, just like Mother has to keep hers," Mordechai said, and his son nodded eagerly. He went on, "And even if you do, the beffel goes if he turns out to be a nuisance."

His younger son nodded again. "He won't. I know he won't." A Biblical prophet listening to the word of God could have spoken no more certainly.

Squeak! Mordechai chuckled. He couldn't help himself. "Well, let me have a look at this fabulous beast."

"Come on." Heinrich grabbed his arm. "He's great. You'll see." He led Mordechai into the front room. The beffel was under the coffee table. One of its eye turrets swiveled toward Anielewicz and his son. It squeaked and trotted toward them. Heinrich beamed. "There! You see? It likes people."

"Maybe it does at that." Anielewicz crouched down and held out his hand to the beffel, as he might have to give a strange dog or cat the chance to smell him. He was much more ready to jerk that hand back in a hurry than he would have been with a dog or a cat, though.

But the beffel acted as friendly as it sounded. After one more of those ridiculous squeaks, it stuck out its tongue at him. The end of the long, forked organ, amazingly like a Lizard's, brushed the back of his hand. The beffel cocked its head to one side, as if trying to decide what to make of something unfamiliar. Then, with yet another squeak, it butted Anielewicz's leg with its head.

"You see?" Heinrich said. "You see? He likes you. Pancer likes you."

"Pancer, eh?" Mordechai raised an eyebrow. "You're going to call him Tank in Polish?"

"Sure," his son replied. "Why not? With scales all over him, he's armored like a tank."

"All right. You've got all the answers, it seems." In an experimental sort of way, Anielewicz scratched the beffel's head. "What do you think of that, Pancer?"

"He likes this better," Heinrich said, and rubbed the beffel under the chin. The beffel put its head up so he could rub it more easily. Its tail thumped the carpet. If it wasn't enjoying itself, it put on a mighty fine act. Maybe Heinrich really did have all the answers.

"How did you find out it likes that?" Mordechai asked.

"I don't know." His son sounded impatient. "I just did, that's all." He rubbed Pancer some more. In ecstasy, the beffel rolled over onto its back. Heinrich scratched its belly, whose scales were a couple of shades paler than those on its back. It wriggled around and let out several more preposterous squeaks.

David watched all this in fascination, Bertha with an expression that said she was a long way from reconciled to having the creature in the flat. Miriam chose that moment to come home from her music lesson. Pancer squeaked at her, too. She didn't squeak. She squawked. She squawked even louder when she found out the beffel would be staying.

"Oh, Mother, how could you?" she cried, and retreated to her room. The beffel started to follow her. Heinrich held on to it. That was one of the wiser things he'd done in his young life.

Anielewicz asked, "Since you magically know all about this creature, do you happen to know what it eats?"

"I gave it some salted herrings," Heinrich answered. "It liked them fine. I bet it'll eat chicken, too."

"I wouldn't be surprised," Mordechai admitted. "All right, we'll feed it like a pet and see how things go." He remembered the first beffel he'd seen, and what it had been doing when he saw it. "If that doesn't work, we can start giving it the neighbors' cats."

His wife said: "One more thing: if we find out that it belongs to some particular Lizard who wants it back, we'll give it back to him. We'd do the same thing if we took in a stray cat or dog."

Heinrich sent a look of appeal to Anielewicz. But Mordechai only nodded. "Your mother's right. That's fair." And if Bertha had sounded a little too hopeful such a thing might happen, then she had, that was all.

Pancer ate boiled beef with enthusiasm. The beffel wouldn't touch carrots, but ate potatoes with the same almost thoughtful air it had had after licking Mordechai: as if it wasn't sure what to make of them but would give them the benefit of the doubt. Having eaten, the little scaly creature prowled around under the dining-room table. Toward the end of supper, Miriam squealed and sprang up out of her chair. "It licked my ankle," she said in a high, shrill voice.

"This is not the end of the world," Anielewicz told her. "Sit down and finish eating."

She didn't. "You don't care," she burst out. "You don't care at all. We've got this ugly, horrible, Lizardy *thing* in here, and you think it's funny." She stormed off to her room again. The rest of the meal passed in silence, punctuated by occasional squeaks.

To Bertha's obvious disappointment, no Lizard posted a notice offering a reward for the return of a missing beffel. Mordechai wondered if the beast had got lost in Lodz, or if it had wandered into the city from one of the new Lizard settlements to the east. From what he'd seen of the other one in the alley, befflem were more than able to take care of themselves.

As one day followed another, he got used to having Pancer around. Heinrich was in heaven, and didn't even mind changing the cat box the beffel quickly learned to use. David liked the creature, too. Even Bertha stopped complaining about it. Only Miriam stayed unhappy. Anielewicz had trouble understanding why she did; it was as good-natured a pet as anyone could have wanted.

"It's ugly," she said the one time he asked her about it, and said no more. He gave up. The beffel didn't strike him as ugly, but he didn't think anything he said along those lines would make her change her mind.

A couple of nights after that, Heinrich shook him out of a sound sleep. "Father, I think there's a fire in the building," the boy said urgently. "Pancer woke me up. He's never done that before. I was going to be mad at him, but then I smelled smoke."

Anielewicz smelled it, too. Bertha was sitting up beside him. "Get out to the fire escape," he told her. "Take Heinrich with you."

"And Pancer," Heinrich said. "I've got him right here."

"And Pancer," Mordechai agreed. "I'll get the other children."

"David's already getting Miriam," Heinrich said, which made Anielewicz feel useless and inefficient.

But he didn't just smell smoke. He could see flames now—they were burning through the door. "Go on, then, both of you—and Pancer," he said, and ran up the hall to make sure David and Miriam were coming. They were; he had to stop abruptly to keep from running into them. "Come on," he said. "We've got to get out of here."

Bertha's feet and Heinrich's were already rattling on the cast iron of the fire escape. Mordechai shoved his older son and daughter out onto the escape ahead of him. He hurried after them; flames were starting to lick across the carpet, and the smoke was getting thick.

As he stepped out of the flat, he paused a moment, sniffing. Along with the smoke, he smelled something else, something familiar, something he didn't expect to smell inside the block of flats. After a heartbeat's worth of puzzlement, he recognized it. *"Gottenyu!"* he exclaimed. "That's gasoline!"

He didn't know if anyone heard him. His family—and other people in the block of flats—were hurrying down the iron stairs. They let down the last leg of the stairway with a screech of un-oiled metal and reached the street. More people spilled out the front door, but cries and shrieks from above warned that not everyone who lived in the building would be able to get out.

A clanging announced the arrival of the fire engine, which had to come from only a couple of blocks up Lutomierska Street. The firemen started playing water on the blazing building. Mordechai turned to Bertha and said, "That fire didn't just happen. Somebody set it." He explained what he'd smelled and what it had to mean.

"Vey iz mir!" his wife exclaimed. "Who would do such a thing?"

"Well, I don't know," he answered, "but whoever tried to shoot me not so long ago is a pretty good guess, I'd say. And I'd also say the *mamzer*, whoever he is, doesn't care how many other people he kills as long as he gets me." In the flickering light of the flames, Bertha's eyes were wide with horror as she nodded.

Heinrich, meanwhile, rounded on Miriam. "If it hadn't been for Pancer, we might never have woken up at all," he said, and thrust the beffel in Miriam's face. After a moment's hesitation, she bent down and gave it a quick kiss on the snout. Pancer squeaked.

Nesseref was glad she had her tsiongi. He was better company than a lot of the males and females she knew. He didn't argue with her. He didn't try to get her to taste ginger so he could mate with her. He didn't give her stupid orders. He lived contentedly in her apartment, and enjoyed going for walks when she took him out.

She'd named him Orbit, partly because she was a shuttlecraft pilot, partly because he had at first liked to walk around her on his leash if she gave him the chance. Little by little, she was training him out of that unfortunate habit. Pretty soon Orbit would be as fine a companion on the street as he was in the apartment—with a couple of other exceptions.

One of those exceptions was as ancient as the history of domestication back on Home. Ever more befflem roamed the streets of the new town outside Jezow. Whenever Orbit saw one of them, the tsiongi seemed to think he was duty-bound to try to kill the little squeaking beast. As often as not, the befflem were ready to squabble, too.

That, Nesseref could have dealt with. The Race had been dealing with squabbling tsiongyu and befflem since before civilization hatched from the egg of barbarism. She had more trouble with Orbit's encounters with Tosevite flying creatures.

She supposed she could hardly blame the tsiongi. The little feathered beasts were so slow and awkward on the ground, they looked as if they ought to be the easiest prey imaginable. And so, joyously, Orbit would rush at them—and they would fly away.

The tsiongi would leap at them, miss, and then turn an indignant eye turret toward Nesseref, as if to say, *They are not supposed to be able to do that.* To Orbit, the unexpected abilities of the birds were as confusing and demoralizing as the unexpected abilities of the Big Uglies had been to the males of the conquest fleet.

Once, one of the gray feathered creatures with green heads waited so long before taking to the air that Orbit's leap after it was even higher and more awkward than usual, though no more successful. The tsiongi crashed back to the pavement with a piteous screech.

As the disgruntled beast picked itself up, a male called, "Does he think he is going to learn to fly, too?" His mouth gaped wide; he plainly enjoyed his own wit.

Nesseref didn't. "He has a better chance of learning to fly than you do of learning to be funny," she snapped.

"Well, pardon me for existing," the male said. "I did not know the Emperor had come to Tosev 3."

"There are, no doubt, a great many things you did not know," Nesseref said acidly. "By the evidence you have shown so far, you demonstrate this every time you speak."

She and the male were eyeing each other's body paint before they exchanged more insults. The male was only a data-entry clerk; Nesseref outranked him. If he tried coming back at her again, she was ready to blister his hearing diaphragms. He must have seen as much; he turned and skittered away.

Orbit kept on trying to catch birds. So did the other tsiongyu Nesseref saw in her walk along the streets of the new town. Noting that made the shuttlecraft pilot feel better, though it did nothing for her pet.

And then, as she was heading back toward her apartment building, a beffel trotted past with one of those plump gray birds in its mouth. Orbit saw the beffel—and the prize the beffel had, the prize the tsiongi hadn't been able to get—an instant before Nesseref did. That instant was all Orbit needed. The tsiongi streaked after the beffel and, catching Nesseref by surprise, jerked the leash out of her hand.

"No! Come back!" she shouted, and ran after Orbit. The tsiongi, unfortunately, ran faster than she did. Tsiongyu also ran faster than befflem. The beffel, looking back with one eye turret, saw Orbit gaining on it. Hoping to distract its pursuer, it spat out its prey.

The ploy worked. The beffel dashed away as Orbit stopped in front of the feathered Tosevite creature and stuck out his tongue to find out what it smelled like before devouring it. Only then did the tsiongi discover the beffel had seized the bird without killing it. With a flutter of wings, the bird, though hurt, managed to get into the air and fly off. Orbit snapped at it but missed, even though its flight was as slow and awkward as that of a badly damaged killercraft.

Before the tsiongi could go after it, Nesseref came dashing up and grabbed the end of the leash. "No!" she said once more when Orbit tried to break loose. This time, because she had hold of the leash, Orbit had to listen to her.

Nesseref scolded the tsiongi all the way back to the apartment building. That probably didn't do much good as far as Orbit was concerned: he was going to keep right on chasing befflem and trying to catch birds. But it did make the shuttlecraft pilot feel better.

When she got into the apartment building, she discovered the day's mail had come. She didn't expect much; most things where time mattered came electronically instead. But some of the local shops advertised themselves on paper, and she'd already found a couple of good bargains by paying attention to their flyers. Maybe she would be lucky again today.

Along with the bright-colored printed sheets, her box held a plain white envelope of peculiar size. The paper was strange, too: of coarser manufacture than she'd ever seen before. When she turned it over, she understood, for it had her address written not only in the language of the Race but also in the funny-looking characters the local Big Uglies used. Something had been pasted in one corner of the envelope: a small picture of a Tosevite in a lorry partly obscured by a rubber stamp with more Tosevite characters. Nesseref needed a moment to remember that was how the Big Uglies showed they'd paid a required postage fee.

"Why would a Tosevite want to write me?" she asked Orbit. If the tsiongi knew, he wasn't talking; his experience with all things Tosevite had been less than happy. Nesseref scratched him below his hearing diaphragm. "Well, let's go up and find out."

Once she'd closed the door to the apartment behind her, she opened the envelope—awkwardly, because it wasn't made quite like the ones the Race used. She tore the letter inside, but not badly. After she got it unfolded, she turned both eye turrets to the page.

I greet you, superior female, she read. *Mordechai Anielewicz here. I do not often try to write your language, so I am sure this will have many mistakes. I am sorry, and I hope you will excuse them.* She had already noted and discounted a couple of misspellings and some strange turns of phrase, and had dismissed them—she couldn't have written Anielewicz's language at all.

He went on, *The reason I am writing to you is that I want you to find for me whatever sort of treat a beffel might like most. My hatchling brought one home, and it may have saved our lives, because it woke him when a fire started in the building where I lived. We lost our goods, but otherwise escaped without harm. We are very grateful to the beffel, as you will understand.*

Nesseref turned one eye turret toward Orbit; the tsiongi had gone to rest on the couch. "It is a good thing you do not understand what is in this letter," she said. Orbit, fortunately, didn't understand that, either.

Whatever you find, please mail it to me at my new address, Anielewicz wrote. *Here it is, in characters a Tosevite postal delivery male will understand. You have only to copy them.* He'd printed the characters very plainly. Nesseref thought she could imitate them well enough to let a Big Ugly make sense of them—or she could scan them into her computer and print them out. Her Tosevite friend finished, *Let me know what this costs and I will arrange to pay you back.*

Exchange between the Big Uglies and the Race was often problematical. That didn't matter, though, not here. Nesseref wouldn't have expected repayment from a male or female of the Race for such a favor, and saw no reason to expect it from Anielewicz, either.

She went to the computer and wrote, *I greet you. I am glad to be able to greet you. How strange that an animal from Home should have saved you from the fire. How did it start?* That question loomed large in her mind. The Race's buildings were nearly fireproof, and were equipped with extinguishing systems in case a blaze did somehow break out. She'd seen, though, that the Big Uglies didn't build to anything like the same standards.

With this letter I will send a cloth animal full of ssrissp seeds, she continued. *Befflem like the scent very much. You need not pay me back; it is my pleasure. I am glad you are safe. You write my language well.* That was an overstatement, but she had been able to understand him.

After printing the letter, she scrawled her name below it. "How strange," she said to Orbit. One of the tsiongi's eye turrets turned toward her. He knew she was talking to him, but not why. She explained: "Who would have thought a Big Ugly would take charge of a beffel?"

Orbit rolled onto his back and stuck his feet in the air. Maybe he followed more than she thought, for every line of his body said that he cared nothing for befflem—or for Big Uglies, either. He'd always ignored the rubbish collectors and other Tosevites he sometimes saw on the streets of the new town.

Even so, Nesseref went on, "And who would have thought a beffel could—or would—save a Tosevite's life?"

Still on his back, the tsiongi opened his mouth in an enormous yawn. He probably would have been just as well pleased to learn that a lot of Big Uglies had burned, so long as that meant the beffel went up in flames with them. Nesseref understood the attitude, but didn't sympathize with it.

The next day, after she got back from the shuttlecraft base not far outside the new town, she visited the pet store where she'd bought Orbit. When she chose a ssrissp-seed animal, the female who ran the place remarked, "I hope you know that tsiongyu care nothing for these toys."

"Of course I know that," Nesseref said indignantly. "Do you think I hatched out of my eggshell yesterday? This is not for me—it is for a friend who has a beffel. Does that meet with your approval, superior female?"

Nesseref was in fact of far higher rank than the other female. But the pet-shop proprietor seemed to have trouble recognizing sarcasm. She answered, "I suppose you can get one if you really want to."

"Thank you so much," Nesseref said. "My friend, by the way, is a Tosevite. He likes his beffel very much."

"A Big Ugly with a beffel?" The other female stared in undisguised horror. "What is this world coming to?"

She meant it as a rhetorical question, but Nesseref answered it anyhow: "Something no one on Home expected—a true blending of the Race and the Tosevites."

"I do not like it," the other female said firmly.

Although Nesseref wasn't so sure she liked it, either, she said, "It may just turn out to be . . . interesting."

David Goldfarb thought the Canadian shipping line that ran the *Liberty Hot Springs* might have changed the ship's name after acquiring her from the USA, but no one had bothered. He asked a sailor about it one day as the ship steamed west across the Atlantic.

"No, we wouldn't do that," the fellow answered. "Hadn't been for the Americans, we'd be bowing down to the Emperor five times a day, too, or whatever it is the Lizards do."

He sounded like an American himself, at least to Goldfarb's ear. The RAF officer—*no, the ex-RAF officer,* he reminded himself—could gauge the home region and status of anyone from the British Isles just by listening to him for a couple of minutes. But American accents only put him in mind of evenings at the cinema, and all Yanks seemed to him to talk the same way.

But when he remarked that the sailor sounded like an American screen actor, the fellow laughed at him. "You can tell the difference once you learn how," he said. "We say *zed* and *shedule,* the same as you do in England. On the other side of the border, they say *zee* and *skedule.* And when they go through a door, they go *owt*"—he exaggerated the pronunciation—"but we go *oat.*"

"Now that you tell me, I can hear the difference," Goldfarb admitted, "but I wouldn't have noticed otherwise."

The Canadian shrugged. Was that rueful? Resigned? Amused? Something of all three? Goldfarb wasn't sure. The sailor said, "Getting harder and harder for us to tell differences these days. Since the fighting stopped, we've looked more and more south to the USA and less and less across the ocean to England. Meaning no offense, pal, but you've had other things on your mind than us."

"I know," Goldfarb said bitterly. "Britain's looking south more and more these days, too—south across the Channel to the Greater German *Reich.* The UK is turning into a pack of little Nazis because it's next door to the big ones."

"Yes, it's a shame," the sailor said. He sounded sympathetic but distant—what happened to the United Kingdom didn't matter much to him. And the *Reich* wasn't the biggest danger loose in the world, and hadn't been for a long time. Next to the Lizards, who cared about Germans?

And, next to the sailor's duties, he didn't care much about keeping a passenger entertained. Oh, he was polite; he tipped his cap as he went on his way. But go on his way he did, leaving Goldfarb alone on the deck of the *Liberty Hot Springs*, with the Atlantic all around him.

The only long sea voyages he'd made before were to Poland and back during the fighting, when he'd rescued his cousin Moishe Russie from a Lizard gaol. He'd gone by submarine then, and hadn't had much—hadn't had any—chance to look out. Traveling from Liverpool to Belfast for his last RAF posting hadn't been the same, either, for he'd hardly gone out of sight of land. Now . . .

Now, for the first time in his life, he got a sense of how truly vast the ocean was. The ship didn't seem to move on it. Nothing came up over the western horizon, nothing vanished below the eastern horizon. From what his senses told him, the *Liberty Hot Springs* might sail on forever without seeing land again.

Goldfarb wondered if it was the same out in space. Airplanes were different. He knew about them. The sense of motion was never absent in them; neither was the sense that the journey, which by the nature of things could last only hours, would soon end. Traveling across the solar system as the *Lewis and Clark* had done, or from star to star as the Lizards did . . . Those were wider oceans than the *Liberty Hot Springs* was meant to sail.

A couple of other sailors hurried past him, intent on business of their own. On this ship, passengers were an afterthought. On a liner, they wouldn't have been, but Goldfarb wouldn't have been able to afford passage across the Atlantic on a liner. Serving his country all his adult life hadn't made him rich.

He wondered what serving his country all his adult life had got him. In some small ways, he'd helped make sure Britain wouldn't be occupied by the Germans or the Lizards, but he doubted that would have changed much had he stayed in London's East End instead of volunteering for the RAF.

Of course, if he'd played along with the ginger smugglers in the RAF, he might well be on his way toward getting rich now. But that wasn't why he'd joined. He might not know many things, but he was certain of that.

Some sort of bird flew by the ship. Pointing to it, a passing sailor said, "Land in a couple of days."

"Really?" Goldfarb said, and the Canadian nodded. Goldfarb felt foolish; he knew when the journey had started and how long it was supposed to last, and shouldn't have needed the bird to remind him when they would approach Canada. Using it as a sign took him back to the days before steam engines, back even to the days before chronometers, when accurately gauging a ship's position was impossible and such portents really mattered.

Naomi came up from below and looked around. Seeing Goldfarb, she waved and made her way over to him. She'd always been very fair; in the moderately rough seas they'd met earlier in the journey, she'd gone pale as skimmed milk. She didn't have a whole lot of color now, either, come to that.

"Won't be too much longer," David said, and spoke of the bird as if it, and not the steady thud of the ship's engine, meant they would be coming to Canada soon.

Naomi accepted the news in the spirit with which he'd offered it. *"Danken Gott dafür,"* she said. "It's seemed like forever." A voyage that had been timeless in one sense for Goldfarb had been timeless in a very different sense for her. She gathered herself and went on, "The children will be disappointed."

"Yes, they've had a fine time," Goldfarb agreed. "They won't want to get off the ship when we get to Montreal."

Naomi rolled her eyes. "If I have to, I'll drag them off," she said. "Who would have thought my children would turn out to be good sailors?" She sounded as if they'd betrayed her by not getting sick.

When the *Liberty Hot Springs* reached Canadian waters, Goldfarb got another surprise: the scale of the country. The Gulf of St. Lawrence, protected from the greater sea by Newfoundland and the headland of Nova Scotia, was impressive, but nothing had prepared him for the St. Lawrence River itself. He had trouble seeing both banks at the same time when the ship first entered it: where gulf stopped and river began seemed very much a matter of opinion. Even when it eventually narrowed, it remained awe-inspiringly large.

"There must be as much water going through here as there is in all the rivers in England put together," Goldfarb remarked to a sailor.

"Oh, more than that," the Canadian said smugly.

And, fighting against the St. Lawrence's fierce current, the *Liberty Hot Springs* took two and a half days to get to Montreal after entering the river. That journey alone was about as far as it was from the Isle of Wight in southern England to the Orkneys off the northern coast of Scotland—but it took in only a small bite of the vastness that was Canada. Goldfarb's notions of scale got revised again.

Only Montreal itself failed to overwhelm him. It was a fair-sized city, sure enough. But to a man born and raised in London, that was all it was. Britain might be small, but it had plenty of people.

When longshoremen tied the ship up at a quay, he gave a long sigh of relief. "We're here," he said to Naomi. "We can start over now."

"Let's not be so happy till we get through customs," his wife answered. She'd been a refugee before, fleeing the *Reich*. If that wasn't enough to ingrain pessimism in someone, Goldfarb didn't know what would be.

But he said, "Well, our papers are in order, so we shouldn't have any trouble." As she had up on deck a few days before, his wife rolled her eyes.

Clutching papers and suitcases and children, he and Naomi went over the gangplank, off the ship, and onto Canadian soil. He'd wondered if, in Montreal, he would have to deal with officials who spoke French. But the fellow to whose post he came wore a name badge that said v. WILLIAMS and used English of the same sort as the sailors on the *Liberty Hot Springs*.

"So you are immigrating to our country, eh?" he said, examining passports and immigration forms.

"Yes, sir." A lifetime in the RAF had taught Goldfarb the shortest answers were the best.

"Reason for leaving Great Britain?" Williams asked.

"Too many people getting too chummy with Himmler," Goldfarb said dryly.

Whatever Williams had expected by way of reply, that wasn't it. He was about Goldfarb's age; he might well have seen action against the Germans himself. "Er, yes," he said, and scribbled a note on the form in front of him. "So your claim would involve political liberties, then? We don't often see that from the mother country."

Naomi said, "You will see more of it, I think, as England comes closer to the *Reich*."

"It could be so, ma'am," the immigration officer said, and wrote another note. He turned back to David. "Now, then—what skills do you bring to Canada?"

"I'm just retired from the RAF," Goldfarb answered. "I served since 1939, and I've been working with radars all that time. I'll gladly pass along anything I happen to know that you don't, and I'll be looking for civilian work in electronics or at an airport."

"I see." Williams turned away and shuffled through some papers. He pulled one out, read it, and nodded. "I thought your name was familiar. You're the fellow who was involved in that ginger-smuggling mess last year, aren't you?"

"Yes, that's me," Goldfarb answered with a sinking feeling. His old chum Jerome Jones had managed to clear away the obstacles to his emigration from Britain. What obstacles had Basil Roundbush and his pals managed to throw up against his immigration into Canada?

Williams tapped the eraser end of his pencil against his front teeth. "You and your family are to be permitted into the country," he said, still eyeing that sheet of paper. "You are to be permitted entry, but you are also to be transported to Ottawa for a thorough interrogation. Until that interrogation is completed to the satisfaction of the authorities, you are to remain under the authority of the Canadian government."

"What precisely does that mean?" Goldfarb asked. *I should have known this wouldn't be easy. Gevalt, Naomi knew it wouldn't be easy.*

"What it says, more or less," the immigration officer answered. "You are not free to settle until this process is finalized." He sounded every inch a bureaucrat.

Voice brittle, Naomi asked, "And how long is that likely to take?"

Williams spread his hands. "I'm sorry, but I haven't the least idea. That's not my bailiwick at all, I'm afraid." Yes, he was a bureaucrat, all right.

"We're prisoners, then," David Goldfarb said.

"Not prisoners—not exactly, anyhow," Williams answered.

"But not free, either."

The immigration officer nodded. "No, not free."

☆ 9 ☆

Glen Johnson peered out through the spacious glass canopy of his hot rod. That was the name that seemed to have stuck on the little auxiliary rockets the crew of the *Lewis and Clark* used to go exploring in the neighborhood of Ceres. He had radar and an instrument suite almost as complete as the one aboard *Peregrine*, but the Mark One eyeball was still his instrument of first choice.

Just for a moment, he glanced toward the shrunken sun. It showed only a tiny disk, barely a third the size it would have from Earth's orbit. Lots of pieces of rock in the neighborhood looked bigger.

He watched the rocks and he watched the radar screen. At the moment, he was out ahead of Ceres, and moving away from it. Most of what he had to worry about was stuff he was approaching. He'd have to be more careful on the return trip, when he'd be swimming against the tide, so to speak. Hot rods were built to take it, but he didn't want to put that to the test.

From the back seat, Lucy Vegetti said, "That dark one over to the left looks like it ought to be interesting. The one that looks like a squash, I mean."

To Johnson, it looked like just another floating chunk of rock, with a long axis of perhaps a quarter of a mile. He shrugged. "You're the mineralogist," he said, and used the hot rod's attitude jets to turn toward the little asteroid. "What do you hope we'll find there?"

"Iron, with luck," she answered.

He chuckled. "Here I am, alone with a pretty girl"—all the women on the *Lewis and Clark* looked good to him by now, even the sour assistant dietitian—"and all she wants to do is talk about rocks."

"This is work," Lucy said.

"Well, so it is." Johnson glanced to the radar screen. He grunted in surprise, looked out the canopy, and grunted again. "What the devil?" he said.

"Is something wrong?" Lucy Vegetti asked.

"I dunno." He looked down at the radar screen again. "The instruments are reporting something my eyes aren't seeing." He scratched his chin. "As far as I can tell, the set's behaving the way it's supposed to."

"What's that mean?" she asked.

"Either it's misbehaving in a way I don't know about, or else my eyes need rewiring," he answered.

Lucy laughed, but he wasn't kidding, or not very much. He didn't like it when what his eyes saw didn't match what the radar saw. If the instrument was wrong, it needed fixing. If it wasn't wrong . . . He rubbed his eyes, not that that would do a whole lot of good.

"If you don't mind, I'm going to try to find out what's going on," he said. "No offense, but your rock isn't going anywhere."

"Go ahead," Lucy Vegetti said, though she had to know he'd asked her permission only as a matter of form.

Ever so cautiously, Johnson goosed the hot rod toward what the radar insisted was there but his eyes denied. And then, after a bit, they stopped denying it. "Will you look at that?" he said softly. "Will you just look at that? Something's getting in the way of the stars." He pointed to show Lucy what he meant.

She nodded. "So it is. I see it, now that you've shown it to me, but I didn't before. What do you suppose it could be?"

"I don't know, but I intend to find out." As *Peregrine* had back in Earth orbit, the hot rod mounted twin .50-caliber machine guns. He had teeth. He didn't know if he'd need to use them, but knowing they were there helped reassure him. He slowed the hot rod's acceleration—whatever this thing was, it didn't seem to be under acceleration itself.

"No wonder we couldn't see it before," Lucy breathed as they got closer and the mystery object covered more and more of the sky. "It's all painted flat black."

"It sure is," Johnson agreed. "And that's a better flat black than anything we could turn out, which means . . ."

The mineralogist finished the sentence for him: "Which means the Lizards have sent something out to take a look at what we're up to."

When the hot rod got within a couple of hundred yards of the spacecraft, Johnson stopped its progress and peered through binoculars. From that range, he could see the sun sparkling off lenses here and there, and could also make out antennas aimed back toward Earth—much smaller and more compact than those the *Lewis and Clark* carried.

"What are you going to do about it?" Lucy asked.

Johnson's first impulse was to cut loose with the machine guns the hot rod carried. He didn't act on that impulse. Pulling a sour face, he answered, "I'm going to ask Brigadier General Healey what he wants me to do." He didn't like Healey, not even slightly. The commandant of the *Lewis and Clark* had hauled him aboard for the crime of excess curiosity, a crime that had just missed being a capital offense.

He had no trouble raising the *Lewis and Clark*; he would have been astonished and alarmed if he had. But convincing the radioman he really did need to talk to the commandant took a couple of minutes. At last, Healey said, "Go ahead, Johnson. What's on your mind?"

His suspicions about the pilot had eased, but hadn't gone away. Johnson got the idea Healey's suspicions never went away. Well, he was going to feed one that had nothing to do with him. "Sir," he answered, "I've found a Lizard spy ship." He explained how that had happened.

When he was done, Healey let out a long, clearly audible sigh. "I don't suppose we ought to be surprised," the commandant said at last. "The scaly sons of bitches have to be wondering what we're up to out here."

"Shall I shoot it up, sir?" Johnson asked. "That would give 'em a good poke in the eye turret."

To his surprise, Healey said, "No. For one thing, we don't know if this is the only machine they've sent out. They're suspenders-and-belt . . . critters, so odds are it isn't. And if you do, they'll know what's happened to it. We don't want to give them any excuse to start a war out here, because odds are we'd lose it. Hold fire. Have you got that?"

"Yes, sir. Hold fire," Johnson agreed. "What do I do, then? Just wave to the Lizards and go on about my business?"

"That's exactly what you do," Healey answered. "If you'd opened up on it without asking for orders, I would have been very unhappy with you. You did the right thing, reporting in." Maybe he sounded surprised Johnson had done the right thing. Maybe the radio speaker in the hot rod was just on the tinny side. Maybe, but Johnson wouldn't have bet on it.

He asked, "Sir, can we operate in a fishbowl?"

"It's not a question of *can*, Johnson," Brigadier General Healey answered. "It's a question of *must*. As I said, we shouldn't be surprised the Lizards are conducting reconnaissance out here. In their shoes, I would. We'll just have to learn to live with it, have to learn to work around it. Maybe we'll even be able to learn to take advantage of it."

Johnson wondered if his superior had gone out of his mind. Then he realized that Lizard spaceship he was next to wasn't just taking pictures of what the *Lewis and Clark* and its crew were up to. It also had to be monitoring the radio frequencies people used. Maybe Healey was trying to put a bug in the Lizards' ears—or would have been, if they'd had ears.

If that was what he was up to, Johnson would play along. "Yes, sir," he said enthusiastically. "They can look as much as they please, but they won't be able to figure out everything that's going on."

Brigadier General Healey chuckled, an alien sound from his lips. "That wouldn't be so bad, would it?"

"No, sir," Johnson said. "I wouldn't mind at all." Behind him, Lucy Vegetti snickered. He turned around and gave her a severe look. She laughed at him, mouthing, *You can't act for beans.*

"Anything else?" Healey barked. When Johnson said there wasn't, the commandant broke the connection. That was in character for him, where the chuckle hadn't been—hadn't even come close.

"So we just go on about our business?" Lucy asked. "That won't be so easy, not for some of the things we'll need to do sooner or later."

Johnson shrugged; his belt held him in his seat. He'd spent his adult life in the service; he knew how to evaluate military problems. "Yes and no," he said. "If you know the other guy is watching, you can make sure he only sees what you want him to see, and sometimes you can lead him around by the nose. What's really bad is when he's watching and you don't know he's there. That's when he can find out stuff that hurts you bad."

"I can see how it would be." The mineralogist sounded thoughtful. "You make it seem so logical. Every trade has its own tricks, doesn't it?"

"Well, sure," Johnson answered, surprised she needed to ask. "If we hadn't had some notion of what we were doing, we'd all be singing the Lizard national anthem every time we went to the ballpark."

She laughed. "Now there's a picture for you! But do you know what? Some of the Lizard POWs who ended up settling in the States like playing baseball. I saw them on the TV news once. They looked pretty good, too."

"I've heard that," Johnson said. "I never saw film of them playing, though."

"More important to worry about what they're doing out here," Lucy said. "And whatever it is, they'll have a harder time doing it because you were on the ball. Congratulations."

"Thanks," he said in some confusion. He wasn't used to praise for what he did. If he carried out his assignments, he was doing what his superiors expected of him, and so didn't particularly deserve praise. And if he didn't carry them out, he got raked over the coals. That was the way things worked. After a moment, he added, "I never would have spotted it if you hadn't sent me out this way, so I guess you deserve half the credit. I'll tell General Healey so, too."

They spent the next little while wrangling good-naturedly about who deserved what, each trying to say the other should get it. Finally, Lucy Vegetti said, "The only reason we did come out here was to get a look at that asteroid shaped like a zucchini. Can we still get over there?"

Johnson checked the gauges for the main tank and the maneuvering jets, then nodded. "Sure, no trouble at all." He chuckled. "Now I can't stop halfway there and say, 'I'm sorry, sweetheart, but we just ran out of gas on this little country road in the middle of nowhere.' "

They were in the middle of nowhere, all right, far more so than they could have been anyplace on Earth. The very idea of a road, country or otherwise, was absurd here. Lucy said, "I didn't figure you for that kind of guy anyway, Glen. You're not shy if you've got something on your mind."

"I've got something on my mind, all right," he said.

"Maybe I've got something on mine, too," she answered. "Maybe we could even find out—after we give this asteroid the once-over and after we get back to the *Lewis and Clark*."

"Sure," Johnson agreed, and swung the nose of the hot rod away from the Lizard spy craft and toward the asteroid that interested Lucy.

Vyacheslav Molotov had disliked dealing with Germans longer than he'd disliked dealing with Lizards. On a personal level, he disliked dealing with Germans more, too. He made allowances for the Lizards. They were honestly alien, and often were ignorant of the way things were supposed to work on Earth. The Germans had no such excuses, but they could make themselves more difficult than the Lizards any day of the week.

Paul Schmidt, the German ambassador to Moscow, was a case in point. Schmidt was not a bad fellow. Skilled in languages— he'd started out as an English interpreter—he spoke good Russian, even if he did always leave the verb at the end of the sentence in the Germanic fashion. But he had to take orders from Himmler, which meant his inherent decency couldn't count for much.

Molotov glared at him over the tops of his reading glasses. "Surely you do not expect me to take this proposition seriously," he said.

"We could do it," Schmidt said. "Between us, we could split Poland as neatly as we did in 1939."

"Oh, yes, that *was* splendid," Molotov said. Schmidt recognized sarcasm more readily than a Lizard would, and had the grace to flush. Molotov drove the point home anyhow: "The half of Poland the *Reich* seized gave it a perfect springboard for the invasion of the Soviet Union a year and a half later. How long would we have to wait for your panzers this time? Not very, unless I miss my guess."

"*Reichs* Chancellor Himmler is prepared to offer an ironclad guarantee of the integrity of Soviet territory after this joint undertaking," the German ambassador told him.

He didn't laugh in Schmidt's face. Why he didn't, he couldn't have said: some vestige of bourgeois politesse, perhaps. "In view of past history, the Soviet Union is not prepared to accept German guarantees," he said.

Schmidt looked wounded. Like any Nazi, he thought a wave of the hand sufficed to relegate history to the rubbish bin. *A miracle the Americans haven't gone Nazi,* Molotov thought. But Schmidt said, "Surely you cannot say you like having the aliens on your western border."

"I do not," Molotov admitted. The German ambassador brightened—until Molotov added, "But I vastly prefer them to the *Reich*. They form a useful buffer. And what do you suppose they would do if we were rash enough to fall on their colony in Poland? They would not sit quiet, I assure you."

"I think they might," Schmidt said, and then qualified that by adding, "*Reichs* Chancellor Himmler thinks they might. They have no adjoining territory. Once lost, Poland would be difficult for them to regain. What could they do but acquiesce to the *fait accompli*?"

"Drop nuclear weapons on the Soviet Union and the *Reich* till both countries glow for the next thousand years," Molotov answered. "In my considered opinion, that is exactly what they would do at such an outrageous provocation."

"Chancellor Himmler believes otherwise," Schmidt said. This time, he didn't say anything about what he believed. Molotov nodded to himself. He'd pegged the ambassador for an intelligent man. He might present Himmler's proposal as part of his duty, but that didn't mean he thought it was a good idea.

"If Chancellor Himmler believes otherwise, he is welcome to launch this attack against Poland by himself," the Soviet leader said. "If he succeeds, he is welcome to all the spoils. I will congratulate him." *I will also begin fortifying our western frontier more strongly than ever.*

"Our two great nations have cooperated before, first in rectifying the frontiers of eastern Europe in 1939 and then in the struggle against the Lizards," Schmidt said smoothly. "What we have done once, we can do again."

"We have also fought each other to the death in the interval between those times," Molotov said icily. "When your predecessor, Count Schulenberg, announced that your nation had wantonly invaded mine, I asked him, 'Do you believe that we deserved this?' He had no answer. I do not believe you have an answer, either."

He had never had a worse moment in his life than when the German envoy announced the start of hostilities on 22 June 1941. Stalin had never thought that day would come, which meant no one under Stalin had dared think it might come. Had the Lizards not landed, who could guess which of the two giants in Europe would have been left standing when the fighting was done?

Schmidt did his best, as his masters in Berlin would have wanted him to do. Voice still smooth, he said, "That was twenty years ago, Comrade General Secretary. Times change. Both of our governments view the Race as the greatest menace facing humanity these days, would you not agree?"

"The Race is the greatest enemy facing humanity, yes. I would agree with that." Molotov shot out a forefinger to point at the German ambassador. "But the *Reich* is without a doubt the greatest menace to the peace-loving people of the Soviet Union."

"Chancellor Himmler does not think the Soviet Union is the greatest menace to the *Reich*," Paul Schmidt told him. "That is why he invited you—"

"To share in his own destruction," Molotov broke in. "Do you know what would likely happen even if the *Reich* and the USSR did succeed in wresting Poland from the Race?"

"You have expressed your view on the matter with great clarity," Schmidt said.

Molotov shook his head. "The view I expressed was, as you say, mine. If anything, it was also unduly optimistic. If we ousted the Lizards from Poland, they might conclude we were drawing ahead of them technically. Do you know what they might do if they came to that conclusion?"

"Respect us. Fear us," Schmidt answered. He might be a decent enough fellow. He might be a clever fellow. But Nazi ideology had corroded his thought processes, sure enough. *Too bad,* Molotov thought.

"They might indeed do those things," he said aloud. "Most

especially, they might fear us. And, if they fear us enough, their ambassador here in Moscow has made it clear that they will seek to destroy us altogether so we cannot possibly become a menace to the Empire as a whole. Has not the Lizard ambassador in Nuremberg conveyed a similar message to your leaders?"

"If he has, I am not aware of it." Schmidt looked thoughtful, an unusual expression to find on a German's face.

Here, Molotov believed him. Regardless of the warnings the Race might have given the Nazi bigwigs, they were unlikely to take them seriously. In their arrogance, the leaders of the *Reich*, like so many spoiled children, still thought they could do whatever they wanted simply because they wanted to do it. Unlike spoiled children, though, they could wreck the world if they tried.

Schmidt licked his lips. "I think I had better send that message back to Nuremberg with some urgency. If it has already been communicated to my superiors, it will do no harm. If it has not, it may do some good."

"I hope so," Molotov said. "Considering the adventurism your government has displayed up to this point, though, I would not bet any sizable sum on that, however. Perhaps you had better go attend to it at once—unless, that is, you have any less reckless proposals to lay on the table before me."

"I have made the proposal I came here to make," Schmidt said. He rose, bowed, and took his leave.

Molotov's secretary looked into the office. "Your next appointment, Comrade General Secretary, is—"

"I don't care who it is," Molotov said. "I need to consult the foreign commissar. Have Comrade Gromyko come here at once."

"But it's Marshal Zhukov!" the secretary wailed.

"I don't care," Molotov repeated, though he cared very much. But he had to do this for the safety of the country. "Give him my regrets, say the matter is urgent, and tell him I will see him as soon as it is convenient. Go on, Pyotr Maksimovich. He won't eat you." *Though if he is unhappy enough, he may eat me.*

By the look on the secretary's face, he was thinking the same thing. But he said, "Very well, Comrade General Secretary," and disappeared. Molotov might not be more powerful than Zhukov—he feared he wasn't—but he could still tell his secretary what to do. Silently, he cursed Lavrenti Beria. If the NKVD chief hadn't tried to overthrow him, he wouldn't be beholden to the Red Army now.

But Zhukov didn't choose to eat Molotov, at least not then. And Gromyko got to the Soviet leader's office inside ten minutes. Without preamble, the foreign commissar said, "And what has gone wrong now?"

Molotov appreciated Gromyko's style, not least because it came so close to matching his own. "I will tell you what has gone wrong, Andrei Andreyevich," he said, and recounted the exchange he'd just had with Paul Schmidt.

"Bozhemoi!" Gromyko exclaimed when he was through. "The fascists are serious about this?"

"I would say so, yes, unless they are merely trying to lure us to our own destruction," Molotov answered. "But surely even the Nazis could not reckon us so naive. My question for you is, how do we respond, beyond rejecting the proposal?"

"One obvious thing we could do is tell the Lizards what the *Reich* has in mind," Gromyko said.

"We could indeed do that. Whether we should is one of the things I wanted to ask you," Molotov said. "The question, of course, is whether the Lizards would believe us. We and the Germans spend a good deal of time spreading misinformation about each other. That could prove a nuisance now."

"So it could," the foreign commissar agreed. "But I think that, in this case, the effort would be worthwhile. The Nazis are surely contemplating the use of nuclear weapons here: they could not hope to conquer Poland without them. This is not a trivial matter."

"No, indeed," Molotov replied. "I warned Schmidt about what Queek has told me: that the Race may seek to exterminate mankind if we present a large enough danger to them."

"And how did he respond?" Gromyko inquired.

"With surprise," Molotov answered. "But who can truly say what goes on inside a German's head? Who can truly say if anything goes on in a German's head? Your view is that we should inform the Race?"

"Yes, I think so," Gromyko replied. "I think we should also be conspicuous about *not* moving troops into areas near Lizard-held Poland. They must not think we are trying to deceive them and preparing our own surprise attack."

"A distinct point, and one I shall have to raise with Marshal Zhukov," Molotov said. *And if he fusses, I will ask him how well prepared he is for a nuclear exchange with the Lizards. With a little luck, I may be able to begin to exert a little control over the Red Army after all.* He nodded to Gromyko. The foreign commissar nodded back, and even managed something of a smile. He probably knew what was on Molotov's mind.

"I really do not see why you require my presence here, superior sir," Felless said to Veffani as the motorcar that carried them pulled up in front of the residence the not-emperor of the Greater German *Reich* used as his own.

The Race's ambassador to the *Reich* turned an eye turret toward her. "Because he is a Tosevite," Veffani answered. "Because you are alleged to be an expert on Tosevites. I want your views on what he says and on how he says it."

"And you want to continue punishing me for the incident in your conference room," Felless added.

Veffani was unabashed. "Yes, I do, as a matter of fact. Count yourself lucky that I let you remove the green bands denoting punishment: I do not wish to advertise your disgrace to the Deutsche. Now come with me. The matter over which we visit the Deutsch not-emperor is, or at least has the possibility of being, of considerable importance."

"It shall be done," Felless said miserably, and got out of the heated motorcar and into the chilly atmosphere that passed for summer in Nuremberg.

Up the stairs she went. The not-emperor's residence, like most official architecture in the capital of the *Reich*, was on a scale designed to dwarf even Big Uglies, to make them feel insignificant when measured against the power of their leaders. It trivialized males and females of the Race even more effectively. So did the immensely tall Deutsch sentries at the head of the stairs.

A shorter, unarmed Big Ugly stood between the sentries. "I greet you," he said in the language of the Race, and favored Veffani with the posture of respect. "And your colleague is . . . ?"

"Senior Researcher Felless," Veffani answered.

"Very well," the Deutsch male said, and inclined his head to Felless. "I am Johannes Stark, Senior Researcher. I shall interpret for you with the *Reichs* Chancellor. He will be able to see you shortly."

"He should see me now," Veffani said. "This is the time set for our appointment."

"The meeting he is currently attending is running long," the Big Ugly said.

"Delay is an insult," Felless said.

Stark shrugged. "Come with me. I will take you to an antechamber where you can make yourselves comfortable."

Felless doubted she would be able to make herself comfortable in any Tosevite building, and she proved right. The chamber was chilly. The seats in it were made for Big Uglies, not for the Race. A servant did come in with refreshments, but they tasted nasty. Felless endured. What choice had she?

After what seemed like forever, the Big Ugly named Stark returned and said, "The *Reichs* Chancellor will see you now. Please follow me."

The Big Ugly named Himmler sat behind a desk so large, a starship might have landed on it. On one wall of his office was an enormous hooked and tilted cross, the emblem of his faction. On the other wall hung an equally enormous portrait of another Tosevite, this one with the hair on his upper lip cut in a pattern different from the one Himmler chose. Felless gathered that was his predecessor as not-emperor of the *Reich*.

Against all that immensity, Himmler himself seemed strangely shrunken. Even for a Big Ugly, he was unprepossessing, with a round, flat, soft-fleshed face with corrective lenses in front of his immobile eyes. He spoke in the guttural language the Deutsche used among themselves. Johannes Stark translated: "The *Reichs* Chancellor greets you and inquires why you have requested this meeting."

"I greet him as well," Veffani said. "I asked to see him to warn him and to warn this whole not-empire against taking any course that would jeopardize the long-standing truce on Tosev 3."

Stark translated that, too. Felless wished she had some ginger. It would have made time pass more quickly. Of course, it would also have made Veffani mate with her on the spot, which might have entertained the Tosevites but would not have advanced diplomacy. Listening to Himmler and the interpreter drone on in their own language made it hard for her to care. At least she wouldn't have been bored.

Himmler said, "On behalf of the *Reich*, I must tell you that I have no idea what you are talking about."

"On behalf of the Race, I must tell you that that had better be so," Veffani answered. "Any movement against Poland, any attack on Poland, will lead at once to the harshest and most stringent retaliation."

"I deny that the Greater German *Reich* intends any attack on Poland," Himmler said.

"Do you deny proposing to the SSSR a joint attack on Poland, your two not-empires to divide the region between you?" Veffani asked.

"Of course I do," the Big Ugly replied.

Felless spoke up: "But you would deny it whether it was true or not, because it is in your interest to do so. Why should the Race take your denials seriously?"

Behind the corrective lenses, Himmler's eyes swung her way. She had dealt with him before, but not often. Only now did she get the strong impression that his stare said he wished she were dead, and also that he wished he could arrange her death. Considering the policies of the *Reich*, he doubtless meant that literally. Had she been subject to his whimsy, she would have been terrified. Even as things were, that measuring gaze disturbed her.

"I repeat: I deny it," Himmler said. "And I speak the truth when I tell you this." His features moved very little as he spoke; for a Big Ugly, he showed scant visible expression.

"Do you also deny troop movements toward the frontier between the *Reich* and Poland have taken place?" Veffani demanded.

"I do not deny that there have been such movements, no," Himmler said. "I deny that there is anything in the least aggressive about them, however. The *Wehrmacht* and the *Waffen-SS* conduct exercises as best suits them."

"They would be well advised—very well advised—to conduct them elsewhere in the *Reich*," Veffani said.

"You cannot give me orders," Himmler said. "The *Reich* is a sovereign and independent not-empire."

"I am not giving you orders. I am giving you a warning," Veffani said. "Here is another one: if you attack Poland, the Race will destroy you."

"If you attack the *Reich*, we will also destroy you," Himmler said. "We can wreck this world, and we will do it."

"He means what he says, superior sir," Felless whispered to Veffani. "The ideology of this faction—perhaps of all the Deutsche—is full of images of battle destroying both sides."

"I also mean what I say," Veffani answered. He swung his eye turrets back toward the Tosevite leader. "That does not matter. If we are destroyed to ensure your destruction, we shall pay the price."

"It would be the end for you. Do you not understand that?" Himmler said.

"No, it would not." Veffani made the negative hand gesture. "It would be a setback for us. It would be an end for us on this world. But the Empire would continue on its other three worlds. For you Tosevites, though, it would indeed be the end. Please carry that thought in your mind at all times."

"If we could reach your other worlds, you would regret this arrogance and insolence," Himmler said. "That time may come, and sooner than you think."

"The better the chance you have of reaching our other worlds, the likelier it is that we will find it necessary to destroy you first," Felless said.

Indeed, Himmler wished her dead. He said, "We are the master race, and not to be trifled with."

"We crossed the space between the stars to come to Tosev 3," Veffani said. "You cannot match that. Who then are the masters?"

Felless thought—hoped—that would make Himmler lose his temper. She had read of the spectacular rages that would seize the not-emperor's predecessor, and had viewed video of a couple of them. Even across species lines, they were appalling in their intensity and ferocity.

But the present *Reichs* Chancellor seldom seemed to get very excited about anything. Through his interpreter, he answered, "You have a much longer history than we do. We had almost caught you by the time you came here. We are closer now than we were then. Before long, we shall surpass you. If this is not the mark of the master race, what is?"

His certainty was in its way as frightening as his predecessor's volcanic wrath. And he raised good points, alarming points. Where *would* the Tosevites be in a few hundred years? *All over the Empire,* was the thought that sprang into Felless' mind. And if they came to Home or to Rabotev 2 or Halless 1, they would come as conquerors. The thought chilled her worse than the weather on Tosev 3.

But Veffani said, "Have you not listened to a word I told you? If you are on the point of becoming a menace to the Empire as a whole rather than merely to this planet, we will destroy you and ourselves here rather than allowing that to happen."

To Felless' dismay, Himmler yawned. "By the time you perceive the threat, you will not be able to destroy it. We will have gone too far ahead of you by then. You of the Race had best bear that in mind and behave accordingly. Your time is passing away. Ours is coming."

Before Veffani could speak, Felless did: "Then the best thing we could do would be to destroy you now, while you cannot hope to prevent us from doing it."

That got through to the Big Ugly. Himmler fixed her with a glare that warned he did know rages like his predecessor's, even if he didn't show them on the outside. He said, "If you try, we shall have our vengeance on you."

"And yet, despite your knowledge of the ruin that would fall on your not-empire, you planned an attack against the Race," Veffani said. "You need to consider very carefully the likely consequences of your actions."

"I have already denied your allegations," Himmler said. "I deny them again." But his tone when he spoke his own language carried no conviction, and neither did the interpreter's in the language of the Race.

"See that your denial becomes and remains a truth," Veffani said, rising from the uncomfortable Tosevite chair. He assumed the posture of respect, then straightened. "I bid you farewell." He left the *Reichs* Chancellor's office, Felless following him.

"Will he listen?" Felless asked when they had returned to

the comfortably heated motorcar and begun the return journey to the Race's embassy.

"Who can say? You are the expert on Big Uglies," Veffani replied, which was disingenuous; having come to this world with the conquest fleet, he had more experience with Tosevites than she did. But then he went on, "You did well there, Senior Researcher. Your remarks to me were germane, and, while you irked Himmler, you did so without attempting to be deliberately inflammatory."

"I thank you, superior sir," Felless answered. "What point to being inflammatory? You would not let me leave even if I were."

"High time you begin to realize such things," Veffani said in what sounded more like approval than anything she'd heard from him since disgracing herself with him and the visiting males from Cairo. Maybe his measured praise should have made her pleased at doing her duties well. To a degree, it did. But thinking about her disgrace also made her think about how much she wanted another taste of ginger.

"I greet you." Gorppet waved to a female walking down a Baghdad street toward one of the markets that had recently been declared safe for the Race once more. "How would you like a taste of ginger?"

He felt like mating, even though it wasn't the proper season. Here and there in Baghdad, females had been tasting ginger. He could smell the pheromones: not strongly enough to drive him into a frenzy, but enough to leave an itch at the back of his mind, almost like the itch he had for ginger. Maybe that was the way Big Uglies worked all the time.

Whether it was or not, though, it wasn't the way the female worked. "I do not use that illegal herb," she declared, and went on her way with her tailstump quivering in indignation.

"A pestilence take her," Betvoss muttered. He raised his voice and called, "Your pheromones probably stink, anyhow!" The female's tailstump quivered harder, but she did not turn back.

Gorppet laughed. "There you go." This time, he was glad to see Betvoss disagreeable, because the other male's venom wasn't aimed at him.

Betvoss said, "I hope the Big Uglies in the marketplace cheat her out of all her money."

"So do I," Gorppet said. His eye turrets hadn't once stopped their wary swiveling, even while he was talking to the female. He wasn't sure how much good it would do; swaddled in robes as they were, the local Big Uglies had little trouble concealing weapons. Still . . . "I would rather patrol the marketplace than collect coins at a house of superstition." He used an emphatic cough.

"Truth!" Betvoss used another one. "That is one duty I too am just as well pleased to escape. Here in the marketplace, at least, I am a moving target."

That made Gorppet laugh again. Then he wondered why he was laughing. Betvoss had probably spoken a truth. Gorppet said, "The other thing being on the edge of wanting to mate all the time does to me is, it makes me mean. I want to claw something or bite something or shoot something."

"Plenty of Big Uglies around," Betvoss said. "Go ahead. I will not mind. None of your other squadmales will mind." He lowered his voice a little. "Of course, that could be ginger talking, too."

And he was right again. *Twice in one day,* Gorppet thought. *Who would have imagined it?* Wanting to taste ginger made a male—or a female—jumpy. And when a male tasted ginger, he did things before he finished thinking about them, which also led to trouble.

Biting a Big Ugly, or even shooting one, felt tempting right now. After the riots and uprisings he'd helped quell, after the hatred the local Tosevites showed whenever they had to pay to enter their houses of superstition, he wished he could go off somewhere that had no Tosevites for a little while—say, for the next couple of hundred years.

A mechanized combat vehicle moved slowly and carefully through the market square. It had speakers mounted above it. Through the speakers came the recorded voice of a Tosevite. His voice boomed forth in the local language: "Come reverence the spirits of Emperors past! Next offering of reverence in one hour's time. Come reverence the spirits . . ."

"Be ready," Gorppet warned the males in his squad.

The warning was hardly necessary. Whenever the Big Uglies

heard the recording, they pelted the combat vehicle with rocks and fruit and rotten eggs. Sometimes they did worse than that: sometimes they started shooting. That didn't happen so often as it had, though, not when the Race hit back so hard.

"I wonder where the Big Ugly who made that recording is hiding," Gorppet said. "If his fellow Tosevites ever find out who he is, his life expectancy is about as long as an azwaca rib's at a feast."

"What I wonder is why we bother with the combat vehicle," Betvoss said. "How many Big Uglies come to reverence the spirits of Emperors past in this part of the world? How many of them live to come give reverence more than once?"

"Some," Gorppet said. "Not many. Not enough. But our superiors say we have to keep trying."

No sooner were the words out of his mouth than the radio on his belt hissed for attention. "Report to the shrine to the spirits of Emperors past," said the male on the other end of the line. "We have heard there may be disturbances above and beyond the ordinary there today."

"It shall be done, superior sir," Gorppet said resignedly, and passed the order on to his squad. "We have to keep trying," he repeated.

"Waste of time," Betvoss grumbled. "Liable to be a waste of us, too." But he obeyed Gorppet, as Gorppet had obeyed the dispatching officer. Gorppet wondered what would have happened had he told that officer he was sick of Big Uglies and would sooner go to Australia. He sighed. Either he needed another taste of ginger or his wits were addling from all the tastes he'd already had.

The shrine for giving reverence to the spirits of Emperors past was a bit of Home dropped down not far from the center of Baghdad: a plain cube of a building, looking achingly familiar against the masonry and mud brick of local Tosevite architecture. But the razor-wire perimeter around the building did not come from Home; it was an effort to keep hostile Big Uglies far enough away so they couldn't use truly large weapons against the building.

Despite what Betvoss had said, a few Tosevites had passed through the perimeter and were heading toward the shrine when the squad got there. Many more, though, crowded up against the wire, aiming curses and abuse and occasional bits of offal at those who presumed to follow the ways of the Empire instead of their own preposterous superstition. It was, in fact, a pretty typical day.

"I wonder what the males heard to make them think there would be extra trouble here," Gorppet said.

"For all we know, it may be a drill," Betvoss said. "They like to keep us half addled all the time."

"It could be," Gorppet agreed. But, though he didn't waste time arguing with Betvoss, he doubted it. A lot of males had come from all over Baghdad and were prowling along the perimeter. It didn't have the feeling of a drill, though Gorppet supposed that could have been intentional on the part of the officers who'd called it.

He watched not only the males from the conquest fleet but also the Big Uglies. He wanted to have every chance he could of shooting first if this wasn't a drill—or even if it was and things got out of hand.

His squadmales were doing the same. "All these cursed Tosevites look alike," Betvoss complained.

"Not alike, exactly," Gorppet said. "But certainly similar." Males of the Race had always had trouble telling one Tosevite from another. That male with the gray hair growing out of his face, for instance, looked a good deal like the badly wanted preacher named Khomeini, but how likely was he to be the fearsome Big Ugly male in fact?

Gorppet stopped. That male looked very much indeed like Khomeini. Gorppet had a photograph of Khomeini with him. He examined it, then turned an eye turret toward the male. *No,* he thought. *Impossible.* But the higher-ups had had a warning of trouble, and so. . . .

He hissed to his squadmales—not a hiss with words in it, in case any nearby Big Uglies understood the Race's language, but one to draw their attention. Once he had it, he gathered the males together so he could speak in a low voice: "By the Emperor, I think that fellow there in the black robe with the white head rag is the accursed Khomeini. We are going to seize him. We are going to hustle him into the shrine. We are going to shoot any Tosevite who tries to stop us. Have you got that?"

"What if that is not the fearsome Khomeini?" Betvoss asked.

"Then our superiors will turn him loose," Gorppet answered. "But if it is, we are all heroes, every one of us, and we do the Race a great service by stopping his poison. Now come on. Back me."

After making sure he had a round in the chamber of his rifle and the safety off, he hurried up to the gray-whiskered Big Ugly. In Arabic, he said, "You are under arrest. Come with me."

"What?" The tufts of hair above the Tosevite's eyes were still black. They leaped upward, a sign of surprise or alarm. "I have done nothing."

"You will be questioned. If you have done nothing, you will be freed." Gorppet went back to the language of the Race: "Seize him—and then on to the entranceway."

Before the Big Ugly could move, the squad of soldiers swarmed over him. Though he was bigger than any of them, together they hustled him toward the guarded entry. A couple of Tosevites who'd been with him shouted and made as if to try to rescue him, but Gorppet and the other males pointed their rifles at them and they fell back.

"What is this?" asked a trooper at the entranceway.

"I think it is Khomeini," Gorppet answered, which made the other male's eye turrets jerk in surprise. "We will find out. This building is secure, not so?"

"Considering what it is and where it is, it had better be," the trooper said. "Everyone in this city wants to destroy it, but it is the most secure building here."

Gorppet waited to hear no more. "Come on, you," he said in Arabic, and gestured to the males in his squad to get the Big Ugly moving again. As they hurried him down the covered way toward the shrine, cries of fury rang out among the Tosevites beyond the razor-wire barriers. They made Gorppet begin to hope he really had seized Khomeini. Would the Tosevites have got so excited for anyone less?

The shrine, Gorppet discovered, had an armored door. In spite of that, peace flowed through him when he walked in and saw the tiny holographic images of all the Emperors who had reigned since the unification of Home. The interior *was* Home, or felt like it, and the presence of a few Tosevites didn't change that.

A male came hurrying up to the squad. "You should not enter this place bearing weapons," he said, as if to a half-trained hatchling.

"We would not have, superior sir, did I not believe this Big Ugly here to be the agitator named Khomeini," Gorppet replied.

As it had at the entrance to the perimeter around the shrine, that name worked wonders. Several males came hurrying forward. They took charge of the Tosevite. Very much as an afterthought, one of them added, "You soldiers wait here while we attempt to identify this fellow."

"It shall be done, superior sir," Gorppet said. His eye turrets flicked from one Emperor's image to another. So many Emperors to enfold and cherish his spirit when it finally left his body.

And then the males came back, far more excited than they should have been inside the shrine. "It *is*!" one of them exclaimed. "We were almost certain ourselves, and then one of our Tosevite converts positively identified him for us. It *is* Khomeini." Awe of a new and different sort washed over Gorppet. He'd never been a hero before, nor thought he wanted to be. Now he discovered it wasn't so bad.

Over the weeks since fleeing from Peking, Liu Han had discovered how much she'd forgotten about farming and about farming villages since leaving her own village near Hankow. What she'd forgotten mostly involved two things: how uncomfortable village life was and how much work it involved.

She'd thought she remembered, but she was wrong. Memory had failed to warn her about how exhausted she would be, staggering home from the fields at sunset every evening. Maybe that was because they grew wheat and barley and millet in these northern lands, not the rice that had sprung up in the paddies around her old village. Maybe, but she doubted it. More had to do with memory's being like opium and blurring how bad things had been. And more still was her being twice as old as she had been back then. Things she could have done easily in those days left her stiff and sore and aching now.

Living in a straw-roofed stone hut didn't help her recover. She and Liu Mei had more space to themselves than they'd enjoyed back in the Peking rooming houses in which they'd lived, but that was the only advantage she could see. A dirt floor meant everything was filthy all the time. The well was far away. The water that came from it was unpurified, too. It had given her a flux of the bowels, and had given her daughter a nastier one.

But worse than all that was the feeling of emptiness, of disconnectedness, she had. Ever since she'd come to Peking, she'd been at the center of the revolutionary struggle against the imperialist scaly devils. News from all over the city, from all over China, from all over the world, had flowed in to her. Now she heard nothing but village gossip. One other thing her memory had failed to hold was how boring and picayune village gossip was.

To her annoyance, Nieh Ho-T'ing seemed to drop into the narrow world of the village as if he'd never seen Peking a day in his life. He was older than she, and came from a wealthier family than she did. But he fit right in, and she didn't.

He laughed at her when she complained. "You have lived among the bourgeoisie too long," he said. "A little reeducation will do you good."

"Oh, yes, it will be splendid—if I live through it," Liu Han answered. "I don't want my bones to end up here, where nobody knows or cares who I am. And I certainly don't want Liu Mei to have to stay here for the rest of her life to tend to my grave. She would be buried here even more than I was."

"I don't think you need to worry about that," Nieh said. "When things calm down, we'll be moving on. We'll get in touch with the others who got out of Peking, too, and with the ones who weren't in Peking at all, and we'll start up the struggle again. We don't need to hurry. The dialectic is certain."

"The dialectic is certain," Liu Han repeated. She believed that, as she'd believed in the endless gods and spirits of the countryside back when she was nothing but a peasant. But the gods and spirits of the countryside had failed against both the Japanese and the little scaly devils, and the dialectic, however much she believed in it, did not seem to be holding its own against the little devils. She said what was in her heart: "Losing Peking hurt."

"Of course it did," Nieh said. "The People's Liberation Army has been hurt before, though, and worse than this. Chiang and the Kuomintang reactionaries thought they'd destroyed us a generation ago, but we made the Long March and kept fighting. And we will keep fighting here, too, till we win, however long it takes."

"However long it takes." Liu Han repeated that, too. She saw time stretching out as a river before her, a river longer than the Yangtze. Where along that river lay the port named Red Victory? Was there such a port at all, or did the river of time just flow into the sea called Forever? She wondered if she'd live long enough to find out.

She didn't share the conceit with Nieh Ho-T'ing. He might accuse her of trying to set up as a poet. That she could deal with. But he might also accuse her of defeatism, an altogether more serious business.

Next morning, just before sunrise, a motorcar rolled into the village. Music, both Chinese-style and the raucous noise the little scaly devils enjoyed, blared from the speakers mounted on top of the car. A man's voice—a recording, Liu Han realized after a moment—called out, "Come see how much we are all alike, little scaly devils and human beings! Come see! Come see!"

"This is a new sort of propaganda," Liu Mei observed, spooning up the last of her barley porridge.

"So it is." Liu Han sipped tea, then sighed. "I suppose we'd better go find out what kind of new propaganda it is."

She set down her cup and stepped out of the hut where she'd been living. Liu Mei followed. The motorcar, Liu Han saw, was of the scaly devils' manufacture, and was of a make she knew to be armored. It carried several little devils with body armor and rifles, and one who came out unarmed.

"I greet you, people of this village," that one said, speaking Chinese as well as Liu Han had ever heard a little scaly devil do. "For too long, your kind and mine have been enemies. Part of the reason we have fought, I think, is that we have believed we are more different than is so."

"A very new sort of propaganda," Liu Mei murmured. Liu Han nodded. The scaly devil reminded her of the fast-talking merchants of Peking, who all did their best to sell people things they neither wanted nor needed. But what was this little devil selling?

He didn't leave her in suspense for long. "You Chinese people reverence your ancestors," he said. "Is it not so?" Here and there in the crowd that had gathered around the motorcar, people nodded. Liu Han found herself nodding, too, and made herself stop with a grimace of annoyance. If only she hadn't been talking with Nieh Ho-T'ing the day before. The scaly devil went on, "We, too, give reverence to the spirits of our Emperors, our Emperors dead. Their spirits comfort us when we die. They can comfort your spirits when you die, if only you will also give them reverence while you are still living."

Having thought of Nieh, Liu Han looked around for him. There he was, looking like a peasant who was starting to get old. She caught his eyes. One of his eyebrows rose a little. She'd known him a long time, and understood what that meant—he was taking seriously what the scaly devil said.

"We have big shrines in big cities," the little devil went on. "But in a village like this, we do not need a big shrine. A small one will do. We have one here." He gestured to the armed scaly devils. Two of them opened the motorcar's boot and took out what looked like a large, polished-metal headstone for a Christian grave. The little devil who spoke Chinese said, "Where is the village headman?"

No one said anything. No one came forward. Liu Han took that as a good sign. Had the village headman admitted who he was, his next step at collaboration might have been to tell the scaly devil Communists were hiding there.

"I mean no harm to anybody," the scaly devil said. When silence stretched, he continued, "Somebody, anybody, then, please tell me, where can we plant this shrine in the ground in the village without angering anyone? We do not wish to cause anger. Our spirits and yours should be together."

Liu Han had never heard language like that from a little scaly devil. It was good propaganda, very good propaganda. If they'd used propaganda like that from the moment they came to Earth, many more people would have been reconciled to their rule. She stared around the crowd with worry in her eyes.

To her vast relief, people still stood silent. The little devil who spoke Chinese gave a very humanlike shrug. He said, "All right, then, if you do not tell me, we will place it here, near the edge of this little square. As I say, we do not mean to anger anyone. I will also tell you one other thing. We will know how you treat this shrine. We will know if you offer to it. You do not have to do that, but we wish you would. We will know if you harm it, too. If you do that, we will come back and punish you. You need to understand that."

He turned an eye turret to the males holding the shrine and spoke in his own language. A couple of the males took the shrine over to one edge of the square, where it would be visible but would not get in the way. The one who spoke Chinese had chosen well. The other two planted the shrine in the ground. Then all the little scaly devils got back into the armored motorcar and drove away.

As soon as they were gone, villagers crowded around Liu Han, Liu Mei, and Nieh Ho-T'ing. "You come from the city," a woman said to Liu Han. "Can it be true, what the ugly scaly devil told us? If we take down that piece of polished metal and smash it, will the little devils know?"

"I don't know if they will, but they might," Liu Han admitted reluctantly. "They are very good at making tiny machines that tell them all sorts of things."

A man asked, "Are they putting up one of these shrines in every village?"

"How can I know that? Am I in every village?" Liu Han knew she sounded irritable, but she couldn't help it. Yes, she felt cut off from the world, here in a village without even a wireless set or a telegraph line. And she was worried. If the scaly devils had put up a shrine in one no-account village, they were surely putting up shrines in a lot of them if not in all.

Another man said, "The scaly devils are strong. Their ancestors must be strong, too. How can it hurt if we burn paper goods in front of their shrine, the way we do for our own ancestors? Maybe the spirits of the little devils will like us if we do that. Maybe they will help us if we do that."

"You will be doing what the little devils want if you make offerings to the spirits of their dead," Liu Han said. Listening, she heard her daughter and Nieh Ho-T'ing saying the same thing, saying it ever louder and more stridently.

But the villagers didn't listen. "If we do this, the little devils are more likely to leave us alone," one of them said. Before long—even before people went out to the fields—automobiles and big houses and liquor bottles and other offerings, all made of paper, went up in smoke before the metal shrine.

Sick with defeat, Liu Han went out to grub away weeds in the millet fields around the village. She tore them from the ground with savage ferocity. Her ancestors got no offerings, but the dead Emperors did. Where was the justice in that?

And if the villagers made offerings to the dead Emperors, wouldn't that lead them toward accepting the little scaly devils as their rightful rulers? The scaly devils had to think so, or they wouldn't have come out with all these shrines. They had a long history of oppressing and co-opting people—or rather, other kinds of devils—they'd beaten in war. Liu Han knew that.

The dialectic said the little devils were doomed: progressive forces would overwhelm them. "But when?" Liu Han asked the millet waving gently in the breeze. "When?" She got no answer. The millet would be there regardless of whether people or little scaly devils ruled the land. Cursing, Liu Han got back to work.

These days, the Russies had to pay only a pound to admit the whole family into services on a Friday night or Saturday morning. "See, it is cheaper now," said one of the Lizards collecting the fee at the door. "Nothing to get upset about."

Moishe Russie went past the male without a word. Reuven, younger, was more inclined to argue. "It isn't right that we should have to pay anything," he said. "People should be free to worship any way they please."

"No one stops you," the Lizard answered in hissing Hebrew. "You worship any way you please. But if you do not go to the shrine to Emperors past, you have to pay. That is all. It is a small thing."

"It's wrong," Reuven insisted.

"It's wrong to block the door," someone behind him called. "That's what's wrong." Muttering, Reuven went into the synagogue.

As usual, he and his father sat together in the men's section. As usual, lately before services, conversation centered on the worship tax. Someone asked, "Has anybody actually gone to see what sort of shrine the Lizards have for their Emperors?"

"I would never even look," somebody else said. "I wouldn't go to a church, I wouldn't go to a mosque, and I don't see how this is any different."

That drew several nods of agreement, Moishe Russie's among them. But the man who'd asked the question said, "The Lizards never persecuted us, the way Christians and Muslims have. If it weren't for the Lizards, a lot of us in this room would be dead. If that isn't different, what is it?"

"It isn't different *enough*," insisted the other fellow who'd spoken. That started a fine, almost Talmudic, discussion of degrees of difference and when different was different enough.

With the argument going on, services seemed almost irrelevant. And, sure enough, as soon as they were done, the discussion picked up again. "Confound it, Russie, you're supposed to be able to fix *tsuris* like this," somebody said to Reuven's father. "Why haven't you gone and done it?"

"Do you think I haven't tried?" Moishe Russie said. "I've talked to the fleetlord. And I've talked even more to his adjutant, because Atvar is sick of talking with me. All I can tell you is, the Lizards aren't going to change their minds about this."

"Does anybody actually go to the shrine they built here?" someone else asked.

"I've seen some people do it," Reuven said. "A few Christians, a few Muslims . . . a few of us, too."

"Disgraceful." Three men said the same thing at the same time.

"I don't think the world will end," Reuven said. "I wouldn't care to do it myself, though."

"The world may not end if a few Jews go to this shrine," Moishe Russie said heavily, "but we haven't got so many Jews that we can afford to waste even a few." Reuven had a hard time disagreeing with that.

And then, the next Monday, he'd just got into his seat at the medical college when the Lizard physician named Shpaaka said, "You Tosevites here are an elite. You have the privilege of learning from us medical techniques far more sophisticated than any your own kind would have developed for many years to come. Is this not a truth?"

"It is truth, superior sir," Reuven chorused along with the rest of the young men and women in his class.

"I am glad you concede this," Shpaaka told them. "Because you are an elite, more is expected from you than from other Tosevites. Is this not also a truth?"

"It is truth, superior sir," Reuven repeated with his classmates. He wondered what the Lizard was getting at. Most days, almost all days, Shpaaka simply started lecturing, and heaven help the students who couldn't keep up.

Today, though, he continued, "Because you are privileged, you also have responsibilities beyond the ordinary. Another truth, is it not so?"

"Another truth, superior sir," Reuven said dutifully. He wasn't the only one puzzled now. Half the class looked confused.

"One of the responsibilities you have is to the Race," Shpaaka said. "In learning our medicine, you also learn our culture. Yet you do not participate in our culture as fully as we would like. We are going to take steps to correct this unfortunate situation. I realize we should have done this sooner, but we have only just reached consensus on the point ourselves."

Jane Archibald caught Reuven's eye—not hard, because his gaze had a way of sliding toward her every so often anyhow. *What's he talking about?* she mouthed. Reuven shrugged one shoulder. He didn't know, either.

A moment later, Shpaaka finally got around to the point: "Because you are privileged to attend the Moishe Russie Medical College and learn the Race's medical techniques, we do not think it unjust that you should also learn more of the Race's way of doing things. Accordingly, from this time forward, you shall be required to attend the shrine in this city dedicated to the spirits of Emperors past at least once every twenty days as a condition for attending this college."

Shpaaka insisted on decorum in his lecture hall. Normally, he had no trouble getting it and keeping it. This was not a normal morning. Instead of holding up their hands and waiting to be recognized, his human students shouted for attention. Reuven was as loud as any of them, louder than most.

"Silence!" Shpaaka said, but he got no silence. "This is most unseemly," he went on. The racket just got louder. He spoke again: "If there is no silence, I shall end lectures for today and for as long as seems necessary. Are you more attached to the pursuit of knowledge or to your superstitions?"

In answer to that, Reuven shouted loud enough to make himself heard through the din from his fellow students: "Are *you* more attached to teaching your knowledge or to teaching *your* superstitions?"

Shpaaka drew back behind his lectern, plainly affronted. "We teach the truth in all matters," he declared.

"How many spirits of Emperors past have returned to tell you so?" Reuven shot back. "Have you ever seen one? Has anybody ever seen one?"

"You are impertinent," Shpaaka said. He was right, too, and Reuven wasn't the only one being impertinent, either—far from it. The Lizard went on, "Anyone refusing to give reverence to the spirits of Emperors past shall not continue at this college. I dismiss you all. Think on that."

He left the lecture hall, but the clamor didn't die down behind him. Some of the students, the ones without much religion of their own, didn't care one way or the other. Others did care, but cared more about what would happen to them if they were forced from the medical college.

Reuven and the Muslim students seemed most upset. "My father will kill me if I go home to Baghdad without finishing my medical studies," Ibrahim Nuqrashi said. "But if I bow before idols, he will torture me and then kill me—and I would not blame him for doing it. There is no God but Allah, and Muhammad is His prophet."

No one would kill Reuven, or torture him, either, if he went to the shrine the Lizards had built here in Jerusalem. Even so, he couldn't imagine such a thing, not for himself. The Nazis had wanted to kill his family and him for being Jews. He couldn't slough that off like a snake shedding its skin.

He made his way over toward Jane Archibald. She nodded to him. "What are you going to do?" she asked, seeming to understand his dilemma.

Except it wasn't a dilemma, not really. "I'm coming to say goodbye," he answered. "I'm not going to stay. I can't stay."

"Why not?" she asked—no, she didn't understand everything that was on his mind. "I mean, it's not as if you believe everything that's in the Bible, is it?"

"No, of course not," he answered. He bit his lip; he didn't know how to explain it, not so it made rational sense. It didn't make rational sense to him, either, not altogether. He tried his best: "If I went to the Lizards' shrine, I'd be letting down all the Jews who came before me, that's all."

Jane cocked her head to one side, studying him. "I almost feel I ought to be jealous. I can't imagine taking the Church of England so seriously."

"So you'll go to the shrine, then?" Reuven asked.

"Why not?" she said with a shrug. "If I don't believe in what I grew up with and I don't believe in this, either, where's the difference?"

That was perfectly logical. Part of Reuven wished he could see things the same way. Part of him was relieved he hadn't got intimately involved with Jane. And part of him—a bigger part—wished he had. He said, "Good luck to you."

When he said no more, she nodded as if he'd passed a test, or perhaps as if he'd failed one. She found another question for him: "What will your father say when he finds out about this?"

"I don't know," he answered. "I'll find out when he gets home tonight. But I don't see how I can do it. And even if I don't finish here, I know more about medicine than anyone who just went to a human university."

Jane nodded again, then hugged him and kissed him, which had to drive every male student in the class wild with envy. "I'll miss you," she said. "I'll miss you a lot. We might have—" Now she shook her head. "Oh, what's the use?"

"None," Reuven said. "None at all." He left the lecture hall, he left the cube of a building that housed the medical college named for his father, and he left the razor-wire perimeter around the building.

One of the Lizard sentries at the perimeter said, "It is not time for you Tosevites to be leaving your classes."

"Oh, yes, it is," Reuven answered in the language of the Race. "It is time for me; in fact, it is past time for me." The sentry started to say something to that, then shrugged and waved Reuven out into the world beyond the perimeter—*the real world,* he thought as he headed home.

His mother exclaimed in surprise when he walked in. "What are you doing here?" she demanded. "You should be in class." He laughed a little at how much she sounded like the Lizard. But then he explained. His mother's face got longer and longer as she listened. After he finished, she let out a long sigh. "You did the right thing."

"I hope so." He went into the kitchen, took a bottle of plum brandy off a pantry shelf, and poured himself a good dose. He didn't usually do that in the middle of the day, but it wasn't a usual day, either.

"Your father will be proud of you," Rivka Russie said.

"I hope so," Reuven repeated. He hefted the bottle of slivovitz. His father wouldn't be proud of him if he drank himself blind, which was what he felt like doing. Instead, with a sigh, he put the bottle away.

The twins also exclaimed when they got home from their school and discovered Reuven there ahead of them. He made his explanations all over again. Judith and Esther's faces grew unwontedly serious by the time he was through.

And he explained one more time when his father came home. "No, you can't do that," Moishe Russie said gravely. "Or you could, but I'm glad you didn't. Till we see what else we can arrange, how would you like to help me in my practice?"

"Thank you, Father!" Reuven let out a long sigh of relief. "That would be very good." As good as staying at the college? He didn't know. He had his doubts, in fact. But it would do.

"Dammit, I want another chance at him!" Monique Dutourd said in a savage whisper as she examined tomatoes in the green-grocer's.

"Not right now," Lucie answered, choosing one for herself. "If things change, then yes, certainly. But we don't want to draw too much heat from the Nazis down on our heads, not for a bit."

"Easy for you to say. You don't have to sleep with him." Monique knew she sounded bitter. Why not? She damn well was.

"No, I'm sleeping with your brother." Lucie's voice made the prospect sound extraordinarily nasty, even though she and Pierre Dutourd were both on the dumpy side. "And getting the Lizards to do things isn't so easy, whether you know it or not. They were very unhappy when they rubbed out that fishmonger."

"Not half so unhappy as I was," Monique said mournfully. "I had my hopes up—and then the miserable fool started shooting too soon. And I'm still stuck with Kuhn."

Lucie shrugged. "If you want to put arsenic in his wine, I won't tell you not to do it, but you're liable to get caught. The advantage of the Lizards is, if they do the job, you get away scot free."

"So do you. So does Pierre." Monique put a tomato into her string bag. "The only reason Kuhn started bothering me was to get at Pierre—and I didn't even know Pierre was alive then."

"Only an American would expect life to be fair all the time," Lucie said. "It isn't as though the *Boches* gave us no trouble."

That was undoubtedly true. It didn't make Monique feel any better. It didn't keep Dieter Kuhn out of her bedroom, either. "Maybe I will put arsenic in his wine," she said. "And after they arrest me for it and start working me over, I'll tell them it was your idea."

"They already want to get their hands on me," Lucie said with a shrug. "Giving them one more reason isn't so much of a much."

Monique was tempted to throw a tomato at her. But if she angered Lucie, her own brother might stop having anything to do with her. What would she do then? Stay an SS man's unwilling mistress till the end of time? That was intolerable. "I want to get away!" she cried, loud enough to make the greengrocer look up from what he was reading—a girlie magazine, by the cover.

"Well, then, why don't you?" Lucie said. "If you stay in your flat and let the Nazi come over whenever he chooses and do whatever he wants, why do you think you deserve anything in the way of sympathy?"

Again, Monique felt like hitting her. "What am I supposed to do, sneak out of my flat, throw away my position at the university, and sell drugs with you in Porte d'Aix?" Without waiting for an answer, she took her vegetables up to the shopkeeper. He gave her an unhappy look; totting up what she owed made him put down the magazine. She paid, got her change, and went out into the warm air of late summer. The sun didn't stand so high in the sky as it had a couple of months before. Autumn was coming, and then winter, though winter in Marseille wasn't the savage beast it was farther north.

Monique was swinging aboard her bicycle when Lucie came out, too. Her brother's mistress said, "If you want to disappear, Pierre and I can arrange it. It's easier than you think, as a matter of fact. And if it gets that German out of your hair and out of your bed, why not?"

"You must be crazy," Monique said. "I've spent my whole life training to be a Roman historian. Now that I finally am, I can't just throw that over."

"If you say so, dearie," Lucie answered. "But I'm damned if I see why not." She got on her own bicycle and pedaled away.

With a muttered curse, Monique rode back to her own block of flats. No bloodstains remained to show where the luckless fish seller had been gunned down instead of *Sturmbannführer* Dieter Kuhn, but she saw them in her mind's eye. *But I'm damned if I can see why it wasn't him.* The words gnawed at her as she went upstairs.

They gnawed even more after Kuhn paid her a visit that evening. As usual, he enjoyed himself and she didn't. "I wish you would leave me alone," she said wearily as he was getting dressed to leave again.

He smiled at her—a smile both sated and something else, something less pleasant. "I know you do. That is one of the things that keeps me coming back, sweetheart. *Bonne nuit.*" He turned on his heel and walked out, jackboots thumping on her carpet.

After he was gone, she got up, cleaned herself off—the bidet didn't seem nearly enough—put on a robe, and tried to read some Latin. None of her inscriptions seemed to mean anything. She fought them for a while, then sighed, scowled, and gave up and went to bed.

She slept late the next morning: it was Sunday. Church bells clanged as she made her morning coffee. Along with a croissant and strawberry jam, it made a good breakfast. She lit a cigarette and sucked in harsh smoke.

A flat full of books, a university position where promotion would be slow if it ever came at all, a German lover she loathed. *This is what I've made of my life?* she thought, and the notion was far harsher than the smoke.

She didn't want to go back into the bedroom even to dress; it reminded her too much of Dieter Kuhn's odious presence. As soon as she had dressed, she left and manhandled her bicycle down the stairs. She couldn't stand staying cooped up in there, wrestling with a dead language and with dead hopes. Off she rode, away from her troubles, away from Marseille, up into the hills back of the city that rose steeply from the Mediterranean Sea.

The Germans had placed antiaircraft-missile batteries in those hills. Otherwise, though, she had a surprisingly easy time escaping from civilization. Presently, she pulled off a dirt track and sat down on a flat yellow stone. Somewhere a long way off, a dog barked. Skippers flitted from dandelion to thistle to clover. *If only I didn't have to go home*, Monique thought.

Here and there in the hills, men scratched out a living from little farms. Others herded sheep and goats. *One of them is bound to be looking for a wife.* Monique laughed at herself. Not going home was one thing. Spending the rest of her life as a peasant woman was something else again. Next to that, even Dieter Kuhn looked less appalling . . . didn't he?

Monique didn't have to think about the German now. She didn't have to think about anything. She could lean back on the stone and close her eyes and let the sunshine turn the inside of her eyelids red. She wasn't free. She knew she wasn't, but she could pretend to be, at least for a little while.

A bee buzzing round her head made her open her eyes. Another bicyclist was coming up the dirt track toward her. She frowned. Company was the last thing she wanted right now. Then she recognized the man on the bicycle. She stood up. "How did you find me?" she demanded angrily.

Her brother smiled as he stopped. "There are ways."

"Such as?" Monique said, hands on hips. Pierre's smile got wider and more annoying. She thought for a moment. Then she got angry for another reason. "You put some miserable Lizard toy on my bicycle!"

"Would I do such a thing?" Her brother's amiability was revoltingly smug.

"Of course you would," Monique answered. She looked at the bicycle that had betrayed her. "Now—did the Germans do the same thing? Will that dog of a Kuhn come pedaling up the road ten minutes from now?" If anything, she would have expected the SS man to get out from Marseille faster than her brother. However much she despised Dieter Kuhn, he was in far better shape than Pierre.

"I don't think so." Pierre still sounded smug. "I would know if they had."

"Would you?" Monique didn't trust anyone any more. *I wonder why*, she thought. "Remember, the Nazis are starting to be able to listen to your talk on the telephone, even though you didn't think they could do that. So are you sure the gadgets you have from the Lizards are as good as they say?"

To her surprise, her brother looked thoughtful. "Am I sure? No, I'm not sure. But I have a pretty good notion with this one."

Monique tossed her head. No matter how good a notion he had, she didn't particularly want him around. She didn't want anyone around. Why else would she have come all the way out here? "All right, then," she said grudgingly. "What do you want? You must want something."

"I should resent that," Pierre said. Monique shrugged, as if telling him to go ahead. He laughed, annoying her further, and went on, "There you have me."

"Say your say, then, and leave me what's left of the day. Monday morning, I have to be a scholar again."

Pierre clicked his tongue between his teeth. "And Monday night, very likely, you will have another visit from the fellow you love so well."

She spent the next minute or so cursing him. One of the main reasons she'd come up here was to forget about Dieter Kuhn for a little while. It didn't seem she could even do that.

Her brother waited till she ran down, then said, "If you want to be rid of him for good, you really should come down to the Porte d'Aix. He won't bother you there, I promise you that, and you might be very useful to me."

"I don't care whether I'm useful to you or not," Monique flared. "All I want is to be left alone. I haven't had much luck with that, and it's your fault."

He bowed, more than a little scornfully. "No doubt you are right. Do you care about whether the *Boche* comes to your bedroom tomorrow night?"

"Damn you," Monique said. If it weren't for Kuhn—and it wouldn't have been for Kuhn except for Pierre . . . "All I want is to be left alone." She'd already said that. Saying it again underlined it in her own mind.

Saying it again did nothing for Pierre, though. "You can't have that. It might be nice if you could, but you can't. You can have the Nazi up your twat, or you can have the Porte d'Aix. Which will it be?"

Monique looked around for a rock. There by her feet lay a good one, just the size of her hand. If she bounced it off her brother's head, she might shut him up for good. It wasn't so simple. It couldn't be so simple. If she stayed where she was, that didn't just mean Kuhn. It meant her classes, her research, her friends at the university—not that she'd had time for them lately. And her research had gone to hell; she'd thought that the night before. As for her classes, Kuhn had got to know her through them. So what did that leave her?

Nothing, which was exactly what her life had become. *How could it be worse, down there in the Porte d'Aix?* One word and she'd find out how it could be worse. The past couple of years had taught her such things were always possible.

"Porte d'Aix," she said wearily. If it was worse, it was worse, that was all. At least she'd escape Dieter Kuhn.

Pierre beamed. "Oh, good. I won't have to tell my friends to put all that stuff back into your flat." She glared furiously. He kept right on beaming. "Little sister of mine, I knew you would see sense when someone pointed it out to you."

"Did you?" Monique said. Her brother nodded. She asked another question: "Did I?" Pierre couldn't answer that one. Neither could she. But she'd find out.

Nesseref bustled about, making sure everything in her apartment was just the way she wanted it to be. She didn't have guests all that often, and these would be special. She'd even borrowed a couple of chairs for the occasion.

She swung an eye turret toward Orbit. The tsiongi wasn't too happy about being on a leash inside the apartment. Maybe she'd be able to let him off later on. But maybe she wouldn't. She wouldn't know for a bit, and didn't feel like taking chances: very much a shuttlecraft pilot's view of the world.

When the knock came, she knew at once who it had to be: no male or female of the Race would have knocked so high on the door. Few males or females would have knocked at all; most would have used the hisser set into the wall by the door frame. But using the hisser required a fingerclaw, and her guests had none.

She opened the door. "I greet you, Mordechai Anielewicz," she said. "Come in. And this is your hatchling?"

"I greet you, Nesseref," the Tosevite said. "Yes, this is my hatchling. His name is Heinrich." He said something to the younger Big Ugly in their own language.

"I greet you, superior female," Heinrich Anielewicz said in the language of the Race. "I learn your speech in school."

He didn't speak very well, even for a Big Ugly. But she could understand him. As she did with Mordechai Anielewicz's use of the Race's written language, she made allowances. Speaking as if to a youngster of her own species, she said, "I greet you, Heinrich Anielewicz. I am glad you are learning my speech. I think it will be useful for you later in life."

"I also think so," Heinrich said, whether because he really did or because that was an easy way to answer, Nesseref did not know. Then the gaze of the small Big Ugly—he was just about Nesseref's size—fell on Orbit. "What is that?" he asked. "It is not a beffel."

Nesseref laughed. Orbit would have been insulted had he understood. "No, he is not a beffel," the shuttlecraft pilot agreed. "He is called a tsiongi."

"May I . . ." Heinrich cast about for a way to say what he wanted; he plainly didn't have much in the way of vocabulary. But he managed: "May I be friends with it?" Without waiting for a reply, he started toward the tsiongi.

"Be careful," Nesseref said, to him and to Mordechai Anielewicz as well. "I do not know how the tsiongi will react to Tosevites coming up to him. None of your species has ever done that before."

Mordechai Anielewicz followed his hatchling, ready to snatch him back from danger. The younger Big Ugly, rather to Nesseref's surprise, did what a male or female of the Race might have done: he stretched out a hand toward the tsiongi to let the beast smell him. Orbit's tongue shot out and brushed his fleshy little fingers. The tsiongi let out a discontented hiss and deliberately turned away.

Although Nesseref didn't know all she might have about how Tosevites reacted, she would have bet that Heinrich Anielewicz was discontented, too. Mordechai Anielewicz spoke to his hatchling in their own language. Then he returned to the language of the Race for Nesseref's benefit: "I told him this animal might smell on him the odor of the beffel we have at home. Some of our own animals do not like the smell that others have, either."

"Ah? Is that a truth? How interesting." Nesseref saw no reason why things like that shouldn't be so, but that they might be hadn't occurred to her. "In some ways, then, life on Tosev 3 and life on Home are not so very different." She turned her eye turrets toward Heinrich Anielewicz. "And how did you get a beffel of your own?"

"I find it in the street," he answered. Then he started speaking his own language.

Mordechai translated: "He says he gave it something to eat and it followed him home. He says he likes it very much. And you know how the beffel helped save us when the fire started."

"Yes, I know that. You wrote of it," Nesseref said. "What I find hard to imagine is having a fire starting in a building where males and females of your species live."

"When I see this building, I understand why you find it hard to imagine." The larger Anielewicz used an emphatic cough. "But our buildings are not like this. And this fire was set on purpose, to try to kill me, or so I think." He spoke quickly there, doing his best to make sure his hatchling couldn't follow what he said.

He succeeded in that, and, in any case, Heinrich Anielewicz seemed more interested in Orbit than in Nesseref. The shuttlecraft pilot said, "You have vicious enemies."

"Truth." Mordechai's shrug was much like one from a male of the Race. "Do you see why I would rather talk about befflem?"

"Befflem?" Heinrich understood that word. "What about befflem?"

"What interests me about befflem," Nesseref said, "is that they have so quickly begun to run wild here. I hear this is true of several kinds of our animals. We begin to make Tosev 3 into a world more like Home through them."

Heinrich didn't get all of that. Mordechai did. He said, "For you, this may be fine. For us, I do not think it is."

Before Nesseref could answer that, the timer in the kitchen hissed. "Ah, good," she said. "That means supper is ready. I have made it from the meat of Tosevite animals, as you asked, and made sure none of it was from the one you call 'pig.' I do not understand why you cannot eat other meats, but I am not quarreling with you."

"We Jews can eat other meats, but we may not," Mordechai Anielewicz said. "It is one of the rules of our . . . superstition, is what the Race calls it."

"Why have such rules?" Nesseref asked. "Do they not pose a nutritional hardship?"

"Nor really, or not very often," Mordechai answered. "They do help remind us that we are a special group of Tosevites. Our belief is that the one who created the universe made us his chosen group."

Nesseref had learned that all Big Uglies were on the prickly side when it came to their superstitions. Picking her words with care, she asked, "Chosen for what? For disagreements with your neighbors?"

Mordechai Anielewicz translated that into his own tongue. He and Heinrich both let out yips of barking Tosevite laughter. In the language of the Race, Mordechai said, "It often seems so."

"Well, you and your hatchling and I are not disagreeing," Nesseref said. "Let us sit down and eat together. I have alcohol for you, if you would care for it. Afterwards, we can talk more about these things."

"Good enough," Mordechai said. "Can I do anything to help?"

"I do not think so," Nesseref said. "I have chairs for your kind, and I also have your style of eating utensils. Let us use them now."

Heinrich Anielewicz went straight through the doorway into the eating area. Mordechai Anielewicz had to duck his head to get through, as he'd had to duck his head to enter Nesseref's apartment. She'd wondered if he would be able to stand straight inside the apartment, but his head didn't quite brush the ceiling.

Even so, he said, "Now I understand why the Race calls us Big Uglies. In a place made for the Race, I feel very large indeed." He spoke in his own tongue to his hatchling, who answered him in the same language. The older Tosevite translated: "Heinrich says he thinks this place is just the right size."

"For him, it would be." Nesseref corrected herself: "For him, it would be now. When he is full grown, it will seem cramped to him, too. Here, sit down, both of you, and I will bring the food and the alcohol."

"Only a little alcohol for my hatchling," Mordechai Anielewicz said. "It is not our custom to let hatchlings become intoxicated."

"Nor ours," Nesseref agreed, "but a little will do no harm." The elder Anielewicz's head went up and down, the Tosevite gesture of agreement.

After a moment, Nesseref brought bowls of stew from the kitchen to the table. Nothing in the stew would offend Mordechai and Heinrich's sensibilities: it was of the local meat called beef, and had more vegetables in it than Nesseref would have used had she been cooking for herself. Tosevites, she'd learned, preferred more calories from carbohydrates and fewer from proteins and fats than did the Race.

As everyone began to eat, a problem developed. Mordechai Anielewicz said, "Superior female, may we please have knives as well as forks and spoons? Some of these pieces are rather large for us."

"It shall be done." Nesseref hurried back into the kitchen and returned with the utensils. As she handed one to each of the Tosevites, she said, "You have my apologies. I cut the meat and the vegetables in portions that would fit my mouth, forgetting that yours are smaller."

"No harm done," Mordechai Anielewicz said. "We have creatures called 'snakes' that can take very large bites, but we Tosevites cannot."

The Big Uglies' smaller mouthparts didn't keep them from finishing the supper at about the same time as Nesseref did. "Is it enough?" she asked anxiously. "I do not know just how much you eat at a meal. If you are still hungry, plenty more is in the pot."

After the elder and younger spoke back and forth, Mordechai said, "My hatchling tells me he has had enough. You gave him about what he would eat at home. I would thank you for a little more, if it is no trouble."

"It is no trouble at all." Nesseref used an emphatic cough. She brought the bigger Big Ugly another bowl of stew, and also took a smaller second helping for herself. To the growing hatchling, she said, "You may play with the tsiongi while we finish, if he will permit it. Please be careful, though. If he does not, just watch him. I do not want you bitten."

Heinrich Anielewicz followed that without need for translation. "I thank you, superior female," he said. "It shall be done." He brought out the stock phrases more fluently than he spoke while trying to shape his own thoughts in the Race's language. Pushing back his chair, he returned to the front room. Nesseref listened for sounds of alarm, but none came.

Mordechai Anielewicz sipped at his alcohol. He too seemed to be listening to make sure Heinrich and Orbit were getting on well. When things had stayed quiet for a little while, he said, "May I ask you a question, superior female?"

"You may ask," Nesseref said. "I may not know the answer, or I may know and be unable to tell you. That depends on the question."

"I understand," the Big Ugly said. "Here it is: Do you know how close the Deutsche came to launching an attack on Poland recently?"

"Ah," Nesseref said. "No, I do not know how close, not for a certainty. For that, you would have to talk with the males of the conquest fleet. I do know my shuttlecraft port was placed on heightened alert, and that the alert was abandoned a few days later. The Race, I would say, judges any immediate danger past."

"The Race, I would say, is too optimistic," Anielewicz answered. "But I thank you for the information. It confirms other things I have learned. We may have been very lucky there."

Nesseref asked a question of her own: "And if we had not been? What would you have done with your explosive-metal bomb then?" She still didn't know if he had one, but she thought he might.

"Do you know the Tosevite story of Samson in the, uh, house of superstition?" Anielewicz asked. When the shuttlecraft pilot made the negative hand gesture, the Big Ugly said, "Count yourself lucky." He added an emphatic cough.

Atvar turned an eye turret toward Pshing with more than a little annoyance. "*Must* I see the accursed Tosevite now?" he said.

"Exalted Fleetlord, it *is* a scheduled appointment," his adjutant answered. "Having conceded these not-empires their independence, we seem to have little choice but to treat them as if we meant it."

"I am painfully aware of that," Atvar answered. "If you will recall, I recently suffered through a harangue from the American ambassador, who seemed shocked we would presume to swing an eye turret in the direction of what his not-empire is doing with its spaceship. Truculent, arrogant . . . Maybe I should retire and let Reffet see how he likes taking on this whole burden."

"Please do not do that, Exalted Fleetlord," Pshing said earnestly. "You would leave us at the mercy of the colonists. They still show little true understanding of the realities of Tosev 3."

"Well, there you have spoken a truth," Atvar said, flattered. "But it is a temptation, nonetheless. I have done too much for too long. Kirel might manage as well—or as poorly—as I have."

In Atvar's opinion, the thing most likely to limit Kirel's effectiveness was Kirel himself. He kept that to himself; he would not cast aspersions on the senior shiplord of the conquest fleet to amuse his adjutant. "Send in the Deutsch ambassador," he said. "The sooner I have heard his absurd, outlandish complaints, the sooner I can dispose of them."

"It shall be done." Pshing went out into an antechamber and returned with a Big Ugly named Ludwig Bieberback.

Atvar preferred dealing with Bieberback to trying to deal with his predecessor, Ribbentrop. This Tosevite had some elementary understanding of the world around him. He also spoke the language of the Race; going through interpreters had often been enough to give Atvar the itch.

"I greet you, Exalted Fleetlord," the Deutsch male said now, assuming the posture of respect.

"And I greet you, Ambassador," Atvar replied. "Please be seated." He waved the Big Ugly to a chair made for his kind.

"I thank you." After Bieberback had sat down, he said, "Exalted Fleetlord, I am here to protest the arrogant and highhanded way in which the Race's ambassador to the *Reich* presumed to pass judgment on our movements of soldiers within our own territory."

"He did so at my express order," Atvar said; he had learned from painful experience that rudeness worked better with the Deutsche than tact, which they took for weakness. "If you try to attack Poland, we will smash you flat. Is that plain enough for you to understand?"

"We deny that the *Reich* intended to do any such thing," Ludwig Bieberback said. "We have a legitimate right of selfdefense, and we were exercising it in a nonprovocative manner."

"No, you were not, or I would not have had my warning delivered to you," Atvar said. "And we do not find your denials credible. The *Reich* has carried on a covert conflict with the Race since the fighting stopped. To have that break into open war would not surprise us in the least, and you would not find us unprepared to take the harshest measures against your not-empire."

"This presumption of yours is intolerable," Bieberback said. "Is it any wonder so many Tosevites seek to be free of your rule?"

"Nothing Tosevites do is much of a wonder," Atvar said. "Is it any wonder that the Race has to keep both eye turrets toward all Tosevite not-empires at all times, to make sure we are not treacherously assailed?"

"That is not how the Race operates in practice," Bieberback answered, a whine coming into his mushy voice. "In practice, you persecute the *Reich* more than all others put together."

"You have spoken an untruth," the fleetlord told him. "And if we do keep a particularly close watch on the *Reich*, it is because the *Reich* has shown itself to be particularly untrustworthy."

"Now you have spoken an untruth," Ludwig Bieberback said, a discourtesy no one from the Race except Reffet would have presumed to offer Atvar. "If we cannot live in peace, we will have to see how else the Deutsche can obtain their legitimate rights from you."

"If you try to take what you imagine to be your legitimate rights by force, you will discover how easy your not-empire is to devastate," Atvar said.

"What gives you the right to make such threats?" Bieberback demanded.

"The power to make them good," Atvar replied. "You and your not-emperor would be wise to remember it."

Bieberback rose and bowed, the Tosevite equivalent of assuming the posture of respect. "I think there is little point to continuing these discussions," he said. "The *Reich* will act in accordance to its interests."

"Yes, the *Reich* would be wise to do that," Atvar agreed. "It would also be wise to bear in mind that antagonizing the Race is not in its interest. Antagonize the Race enough and the *Reich* will abruptly cease to be."

With another bow, the Big Ugly said, "We shall defend ourselves against your aggression to the best of our ability. Good day." Without waiting for the fleetlord's leave, he walked out of the office.

Atvar let out a long sigh. Pshing came in a moment later. The fleetlord said, "We shall have to keep ourselves at increased alert against the *Reich*. Plainly, the Deutsche have belligerent intentions."

"Shall I prepare orders to that effect?" Pshing asked.

"Yes, do so," Atvar answered. "So long as these Big Uglies see they cannot take us by surprise, they are unlikely to attack us. If we ignore them, we put ourselves in danger."

"Truth," Exalted Fleetlord," Pshing said. "I shall draft the orders for your approval."

"Very good." Atvar made the affirmative hand gesture. "And when you transmit them to the males of the conquest fleet in Poland and in space, do not do so over the channels with the greatest security."

His adjutant let out a startled hiss. "Exalted Fleetlord? If I follow that order, the Deutsche are only too likely to intercept our transmission. Much as I hate to say it, they are beginning to gain the technology required to defeat some of our less sophisticated scrambler circuits."

"Yes, so I understand from some of the reports reaching us from the part of the *Reich* known as France," Atvar replied. "In most circumstances, this is a nuisance—worse than a nuisance, in fact. But here, I want them to intercept the order. I want them to know we are alerted to the possibility of unprovoked attack from them. I want them to know that they will pay dearly if they make such an attack."

"Ah." Pshing assumed the posture of respect. "Exalted Fleetlord, I congratulate you. That is deviousness worthy of a Big Ugly."

"I thank you," Atvar said, even if the form of the compliment was not what he might have liked. "The Deutsche will feel they have genuinely important information if they think they are stealing it from us. If we give it to them, on the other fork of the tongue, they will think we want them to have it, and so will discount it."

"Ah," Pshing repeated. He turned an eye turret toward the fleetlord. "No one from the colonization fleet could possibly have such a deep understanding of the way Big Uglies think."

That was a compliment Atvar could appreciate in full. "And I thank you once more," he said. "By now, we of the conquest fleet have more experience of the Tosevites than anyone could want."

"Even so," Pshing said with an emphatic cough. "In aid of which, have you yet decided what we ought to do with the rabble-rouser named Khomeini now that he is finally in our hands?"

"Not yet," Atvar said. "By the Emperor, though, having his

hateful voice silenced is a relief. He is far from the only fanatical agitator in this part of the main continental mass, but he was among the most virulent and the most effective."

"His followers are among the most virulent, too, even among those who follow the Muslim superstition," Pshing said. "If he remains imprisoned, they are liable to stop at nothing in their efforts to free him."

"I am painfully aware of this," Atvar said. "We have, to our sorrow, seen too many such efforts—and too many of them have succeeded. I have made matters more difficult for the Big Uglies by ordering Khomeini transferred to a prison in the southern region of the lesser continental mass. The Big Uglies there speak a different language and follow the Christian superstition, so his influence among them should be much less than it would were we to have kept him incarcerated locally."

"This also shows considerable understanding of Tosevite psychology," his adjutant remarked.

"So it does, but I cannot take full credit for it," Atvar said. "Moishe Russie suggested it to me. This Khomeini is almost as antithetical to the Big Uglies of the Jewish superstition as he is to us, so, as against the Deutsche, Russie was able to make the suggestion in good conscience."

"Excellent," Pshing said. "We do our best when we can turn the Tosevites' differences among themselves to our advantage."

"The only trouble being, too often they abandon those differences to unite against us," Atvar said. "They might even do that in the case of Khomeini, which is the main reason why I am considering ordering his execution."

Both of Pshing's eye turrets swung sharply toward him. "Exalted Fleetlord?" he said, as if wondering whether he'd heard correctly.

Atvar understood that. The Race had not used capital punishment since long before Home was unified. But he said, "This is a barbarous world, and ruling it—or ruling our portion of it—requires barbarous measures. During the fighting, did we not match the Big Uglies city for city with explosive-metal bombs?"

"But that was during the fighting," Pshing answered.

"So it was," Atvar agreed. "But the fighting on Tosev 3 has never truly stopped; it has only slowed." He sighed. "Unless it comes to a boil again and destroys this world, it is liable to continue at this low level for generations to come. If we do not adopt our methods to the ones widely used and understood here, we will suffer more as a result."

"But what shall we become if we do adapt our methods to those the Big Uglies use and understand?" Pshing asked.

"Barbarized." Atvar did not flinch from the answer. "Different from the males and females on the other worlds of the Empire. Ginger contributes to such differences, too, as we know all too well." He sighed once more. "Perhaps, over hundreds and over thousands of years, we will become more like those we have left behind." After a moment, he sighed yet again, even less happily. "And perhaps not, too."

The frontier between Lizard-occupied Poland and the Greater German *Reich* was less than a hundred kilometers west of Lodz. Mordechai Anielewicz used bicycle trips to the frontier region to keep himself strong—and to keep an eye on what the Nazis might be up to.

As he neared the border, he swung off the bicycle to rest and to try to rub the stiffness out of his legs. He wasn't too sore; the poison gas he'd breathed all those years before sometimes dug its claws into him much harder than this. It was hot, but not too muggy; sweat didn't cling as it might have on a lot of summer days. He stood on top of a small hill, from which he could peer west into Germany.

Even with field glasses, which he didn't have, he couldn't have seen a great deal. No tanks rumbled toward the border from the west, as they had in 1939. The only visible German soldiers were a couple of sentries pacing their routes. One of them was smoking a cigarette; a plume of smoke drifted after him.

In a way, the calm was reassuring: the *Wehrmacht* didn't look ready to come charging toward Lodz. In another way, though, this land was war's home. It was low and flat and green—ideal country for panzers. In front of the smoking sentry lay barbed wire thicker than either side had put down in the First World War. Concrete antitank obstacles stood among the thickets of barbed wire like great gray teeth. More of them farther from the frontier worked to channel armored fighting vehicles to a handful of routes, at which the German troops no doubt had heavy weapons aimed.

This side of the frontier, the Polish side, was less ostentatiously fortified. The Nazis went in for large, intimidating displays; the Race didn't. More of the Lizards' installations were camouflaged or underground. But Mordechai knew how the Race could fight, and also knew both the Poles and the Jews would fight at the Lizards' side to keep the *Reich* from returning to Poland.

He raised his eyes and looked farther west, past the immediate border region. Mist and distance blocked his gaze. He wouldn't have been able to see the German rockets aimed at Poland anyhow—rockets tipped with explosive-metal bombs. The Jews and Poles couldn't do anything about them. Anielewicz hoped the Lizards could, either by knocking down the German rockets or by sending so many into the *Reich* as to leave it a lifeless wasteland.

With such gloomy thoughts in his mind, he didn't hear the mechanized combat vehicle coming up behind him till it got very close. It was much quieter than a human-made machine of the same type would have been; the Lizards had had not a couple of decades but tens of thousands of years to refine their designs. They were splendid engineers. An engineering student himself back in the days before the world went mad, Anielewicz understood that. But they moved in little steps, not the great leaps people sometimes took.

The combat vehicle stopped at the top of the hill. A Lizard—an officer, by his body paint—got out and peered west as Mordechai had been doing. He had field glasses, of odd design by human standards but perfectly adapted to the shape of his head and to his eye turrets.

After lowering the binoculars, he turned one eye toward Anielewicz. "What are you doing here?" he asked in fair Polish.

"Looking at what the enemy may be up to—the same as you, I suspect," Anielewicz answered in the language of the Race.

"If there is any trouble, we will defend Poland," the Lizard said, also in his own language. "You need not concern yourself about it."

Anielewicz laughed in the arrogant male's face. The Lizard, plainly startled, drew back a pace. Anielewicz said, "We Tosevites fought alongside you to expel the Deutsche from this region." They'd also helped the Germans against the Race in a nasty balancing act Mordechai hoped never to have to try again. Not mentioning that, he went on, "We will fight alongside you if the Deutsche attack now. If you do not understand that, you must be very new to the region."

He almost laughed at the Lizard again. Had the male been a human being, he would have looked flabbergasted. The Race had less mobile features, but the way the officer held himself proclaimed his astonishment. He asked, "Who are you, to speak to me so?"

"My name is Mordechai Anielewicz," Anielewicz answered, wondering if the Lizard was so new to Poland that that wouldn't mean anything to him. But how could he be, if he spoke Polish?

And he wasn't. "Ah, the Tosevite fighting leader!" he exclaimed. "No wonder you have an interest in the Deutsche, then."

"No wonder at all," Anielewicz agreed dryly. "What I do wonder about is your foolish insistence before that Tosevites were not fighters. I hope you know better. I hope your superiors know better."

"I am sorry," the Lizard said, a rare admission from his kind. Then he spoiled it: "I took you for an ordinary, lazy Big Ugly, not one of the less common sort."

"Thank you so much," Mordechai said. "Are you sure you are a male of the Race and not a male of the Deutsche?" Few Germans could have been more open in their scorn for Polish and Jewish *Untermenschen*—but the Lizard applied his scorn to the whole human race. *Remember, he's an ally*, Anielewicz reminded himself.

"Of course I am sure," the male said; whatever he was, he had no sense of humor and no sense of irony. "I am also sure that the Deutsche will not dare attack us, not after the warnings we have given them. You may take this to your fighters and tell them to rest easy."

"There have been warnings, then?" Mordechai asked, and the Lizard made the affirmative hand gesture. That was news Anielewicz hadn't heard before—and, as far as he was concerned, good news. He said, "The one thing I will tell you is that the Deutsche can be treacherous."

"All Big Uglies can be treacherous," the male answered. "We have learned this, to our sorrow, ever since the conquest fleet came to Tosev 3."

To him, that obviously included Anielewicz. He had some

reason for his suspicions, too: with luck, he didn't know how much. Mordechai said, "We Jews will fight with the Race against the Deutsche."

"I know this. This is good. You will fight harder against the *Reich* than you would against the SSSR," the Lizard officer said. "But the Poles, while they will also fight for us against the *Reich*, might well fight harder against the SSSR. Is this not a truth? You will know your fellow Tosevites better than I can."

"You know them well enough, or so it seems," Anielewicz said—the Lizard had a good grasp of local politics. "Some of us reckon one side a worse enemy, some the other. We all have reasons we think good."

"I know that." The male let out a hiss of discontent. "This trying to deal with every tiny grouping of Tosevites as if it were an empire has addled a good many of us. It is but one way in which you are such a troublesome species."

"I thank you," Anielewicz said, straight-faced.

"You *thank* me?" After his interrogative cough, the Lizard spread his hands to show more perplexity. "I do not understand."

"Never mind," Mordechai said resignedly.

"Is it a joke?" No, the Lizard wasn't able to tell. He went on, "If it is, I warn you to be careful. Otherwise, one day the joke will be on you." Before Anielewicz could come up with an answer for that, the officer continued, "Since you are who you are, I suppose you have come to the border here to spy on the Deutsche."

"Yes, as a matter of fact, I have." Mordechai saw no point in denying the obvious. "You may tell your superiors that you met me here, and you may tell them that we Jews are in the highest state of readiness with all our weapons. We will resist the Deutsche with every means at our disposal—every means."

As he'd intended, the male got his drift—this was indeed an alert, clever Lizard, even if one without a sense of humor. "Does that include explosive-metal weapons?" he asked.

"I hope both you and the Deutsche never have to find out," Anielewicz answered. "You may tell that to your superiors, too." After more than twenty years, he didn't know whether the bomb the Nazis had meant for Lodz would work, either. He too hoped he would never have to find out.

Most Lizards would have kept on grilling him about the explosive-metal bomb. This one didn't. Instead of pounding away at an area where he wouldn't get any answers, he adroitly changed the subject. Pointing west, he asked, "Do you observe anything that, in your opinion, requires special vigilance on our part?"

"No," Mordechai admitted, not altogether happily. He laughed at himself. "I am not altogether sure whether coming to the border was a waste of time, but I did it anyhow. Still, you of the Race can observe from high over the heads of the Deutsche." He pointed up into space. "You can see far more than I could hope to from this little hill."

"But if you saw something, you would be more likely to do so with full understanding," the officer said. "We have been deceived before. No doubt we shall be deceived again and again, until such time as this world at last fully becomes part of the Empire."

Just when Anielewicz began to think this Lizard did understand people after all, the male came out with something like that. "Do you really believe the Race will conquer the independent not-empires?"

"Yes," the Lizard answered. "For you Tosevites, a few years seem a long time. Over hundreds of years, over thousands of years, we are bound to prevail."

He spoke of the Race's triumph with the certainty a Communist would have used to proclaim the victory of the proletariat or a Nazi the dominance of the *Herrenvolk*. Anielewicz said, "We may not think in the long terms as well as the Race does, but we also change more readily than the Race does. What will happen if, before hundreds or thousands of years pass, we go ahead of you?"

"You had better not," the Lizard replied. "This is under discussion among us, and you had better not."

He sounded as if he were warning Anielewicz in person. "Why not?" the Jewish fighting leader asked. "What will happen if we do?"

"The consensus among our leaders is, we will destroy this entire planet," the male said matter-of-factly. "If you Tosevites are a danger to the Race here on Tosev 3, you are an annoyance—a large annoyance, but an annoyance nonetheless. If you seem likely to be able to trouble the other worlds of the Empire, you are no longer an annoyance. You are a danger, a deadly danger. We do not intend to let that happen." He added an emphatic cough.

"What about your colonists?" Mordechai asked, ice running through him. Not even the Germans spoke so calmly of destruction.

He'd seen before that Lizards shrugged much as men did. "That would be most unfortunate. We might have done very well on this world. But the Empire as a whole is more important."

Humans would have had a hard time thinking so dispassionately. Anielewicz stared after the officer, who got back into his vehicle. As it clattered off, Mordechai looked east after it, and then into the *Reich* once more. He shivered. He'd suddenly got a brand-new reason to worry about the Germans.

Gorppet bent into the posture of respect. "After so many years as a simple infantrymale, superior sir, I never expected to be promoted to officer's rank."

"You have earned it," answered the officer sitting across the table from him. "By capturing Khomeini, you have earned not only the promotion, not only the stated reward, but almost anything else you desire."

"For which I thank you, superior sir." Gorppet knew he'd have a harder time collecting on the promise than the officer did making it. But he was going to try, anyhow. "I have served in this region of the main continental mass since what is called the end of the fighting, and I fought in the SSSR before that."

"I know your record," the officer—*the other officer,* Gorppet thought—said. "It does you credit."

"And I thank you once more, superior sir." As far as Gorppet was concerned, his record showed he remained alive and intact only by a miracle. "Having served in such hazardous posts, what I would like most of all is a transfer to an area where the conditions are less intense."

"I understand why you say this, but could I not persuade you to ask for a different boon?" the officer said. *I knew it,* Gorppet thought. The other male went on, "Your experience makes you extremely valuable here. Without it, in fact, you would hardly have been able to recognize and capture the wily Khomeini."

"No doubt that is a truth, superior sir, but I am beginning to feel I have used up about all the luck I ever had," Gorppet answered. "You asked what I wanted. I told you. Are you telling me I may not have it?"

The officer sighed and waggled his eye turrets in a way that suggested Gorppet was asking for more than he had any right to expect. The newly promoted trooper held his ground. The officer sighed again. He had not expected Gorppet to request a transfer or to insist on getting it. Gorppet didn't care what the officer had expected. He knew what he wanted. If he had a chance for it, he would grab with both hands.

With one more sigh, the officer turned his swiveling chair half away from Gorppet to use the computer. Gorppet turned his eye turrets toward the screen, but he was too far away and at too bad an angle to be able to read anything on it. And the officer did not speak to the machine, but used the keyboard. Gorppet's suspicions rose. If the other male told him no posts elsewhere were available, he would raise as big a fuss as he could. He wished he'd been wise enough to record this conversation. He might well need the evidence to support his claims of promises denied.

But, at last, the officer turned back to him. "There is a position available in the extreme south of the main continental mass," the male said unwillingly.

"I will take it, superior sir," Gorppet said at once. "Get my acceptance into the computer, if you would be so kind."

"Very well." No, the officer did not sound happy. "How much do you know about this place called South Africa?" he asked as he clicked keys.

"Nothing whatsoever," Gorppet answered cheerfully. "But I am sure it cannot possibly be worse than Basra and Baghdad."

"The climate is worse," the officer warned. "As far as climate goes, this is one of the best parts of Tosev 3."

"No doubt you are right, superior sir," Gorppet said—openly disagreeing with a superior did not do . . . and the other male *was* right. This area of Tosev 3 did have good weather. Still, Gorppet continued, "As far as the Big Uglies go, though, this is one of the worst parts of the planet. I have had more than enough of them."

"I doubt you will find the Big Uglies in South Africa much of an improvement," the officer said. "The ones with light skins hate and resent us for making the ones with dark skins, who outnumber them, their equals. The ones with the dark skins hate and resent us because we do not let them massacre the ones with the light skins."

"I am willing to take my chances with them, dark and light," Gorppet said. "As long as they are not so fanatical as to kill themselves so they can harm us, they are an improvement on the

Tosevites hereabouts." He pushed things a little: "I very much look forward to receiving my transfer orders."

With a snorted hiss full of angry resignation, the officer turned back to the computer, although he kept one eye turret on Gorppet, as if afraid Gorppet would steal something if he gave the machine all his attention. After a little while, a sheet of paper came out of the printer by the computer. The officer thrust it at Gorppet. "There is a flight from Baghdad to Cairo tomorrow. You will be on it. There is a flight from Cairo to Cape Town the day after. You will be on it, too."

Gorppet read the travel document to make sure it said what the officer told him it did. He'd stopped taking officers' words on trust shortly after he started fighting in the SSSR. That was one of the reasons the spirits of Emperors past hadn't yet greeted his spirit. These orders, however, read as they were supposed to.

"I thank you for your help, superior sir," he said, though the officer had done everything he could to thwart him. "I will be on that flight tomorrow."

"See that you are," the other male said distantly, as if he were doing his best to forget Gorppet had ever stood before him. "I dismiss you."

Gorppet went back to the barracks and packed his belongings. That wasn't a hard job; everything he owned—except for his new and much improved credit balance—he could sling on his back. Just for a moment, he wondered if that was a fitting reward for having gone through so much danger. He shrugged. That wasn't the sort of question a soldier's training made him fit to answer.

He said his goodbyes to his squad. He would miss some of them, though not all: if he ever thought of Betvoss again, it would be with annoyance.

He was at the airfield long before his aircraft would leave. *Nothing must go wrong,* he thought, and nothing did. The flight took off on time, had little turbulence, and landed in Cairo on time. He got ground transport to a transient barracks to wait for his next flight. The Big Uglies on the streets of this city might have come from Baghdad. A couple of them, concealed by the crowd, threw stones at the vehicle in which Gorppet was riding.

"Does that happen very often?" he asked the driver.

"Only on days when the sun comes up in the morning," the

other male assured him. They both laughed, and spent the rest of the journey through the crowded streets swapping war stories.

More Big Uglies threw rocks at the vehicle that took Gorppet back to the Cairo airfield the next day. "You ought to teach them manners with your machine gun," he told the male at the wheel of this machine.

"Orders are to hold our fire unless they start using firearms against us," the driver answered with a resigned shrug. "If we started shooting at them for rocks, we would have riots every day."

"Or else they might learn they are not supposed to do things like that," Gorppet said. The driver shrugged again, and did not reply. Gorppet outranked him—*now* Gorppet outranked him—but he had to do as local authority told him to do.

No one fired at the vehicle. Gorppet carried his gear into the aircraft that would take him to this place called South Africa. He wondered what it would be like. *Different from Baghdad* was what he wanted. The officer back there had told him the Big Uglies in the new place were different. That was good, as far as he was concerned. The officer had also told him the weather was different. That wasn't so good, but couldn't be helped. After a winter in the SSSR, Gorppet doubted anything less would unduly faze him.

Peering out the window, he saw the aircraft pass over terrain desolate even by the standards of Home. Afterwards, though, endless lush green vegetation replaced the desert. Gorppet stared down at it in revolted fascination. It seemed almost malignant in the aggressiveness of its growth. Only a few scattered river valleys and seasides back on Home even came close to such fertility.

So much unrelieved green proved depressing. Gorppet fell asleep for a while. When he woke again, the jungle was behind him, replaced by savanna country that gave way in turn to desert once more. Then, to his surprise, more fertile country replaced the wasteland. The aircraft descended, landed, and came to a stop.

"Welcome to South Africa," the pilot said over the intercom to Gorppet and to the males and females who'd traveled with him. "You had better get out. Nothing but sea after this, sea and the frozen continent around the South Pole."

Gorppet shouldered his sack and went down the ramp black-skinned Big Uglies had wheeled over to the aircraft. He'd seen few of that race up till now. They looked different from the lighter Tosevites, but were no less ugly. When they spoke, he discovered he couldn't understand anything they said. He sighed. Knowing what the Big Uglies back in Basra and Baghdad were talking about had helped keep him alive a couple of times. He would have to see how many languages the local Tosevites spoke and how hard they were to learn.

Sack still shouldered, he trudged toward the airfield terminal. The weather *was* on the chilly side; the officer back in Baghdad hadn't lied about that. But Gorppet didn't see any frozen water on the ground, and even the broad, flat mountain to the east of the airfield and the nearby city was free of the nasty stuff. *It will not be too bad,* he told himself, and hoped he was right.

In the terminal, as he'd expected, was a reassignment station. A female clerk turned one eye turret toward him. "How may I help you, Small-unit Group Leader?" she asked, reading his very new, very fresh body paint.

After giving his name and pay number, Gorppet continued, "Reporting as ordered. I need quarters and a duty assignment."

"Let me see whether your name has gone all the way through the system," the female said. She spoke to the computer and examined the screen. After a moment, she made the affirmative hand gesture. "Yes, we have you. You are assigned to Cape Town, as a matter of fact."

"And where in this subregion is Cape Town?" Gorppet asked.

"This city here is Cape Town," the clerk answered. "Did you not study the area to which you would be transferred?"

"Not very much," Gorppet admitted. "I got the order a couple of days ago, and have spent my time since either traveling or staying in transit barracks."

"No reason you could not have examined a terminal there," the female clerk said primly. "I would have thought an officer would show more interest in the region to which he has been assigned."

That took Gorppet by surprise. He wasn't used to being an officer. He wasn't used to thinking like an officer, either. As an infantrymale, he'd gone where he was ordered, and hadn't worried about it past that. Fighting embarrassment, he spoke gruffly: "Well, I am here now. Let me have a printout of my billet and assignment."

"It shall be done," the clerk said, and handed him the paper.

He rapidly read the new orders. "City patrol, is it? I can do that. I have been doing it for a long time, and this is a relatively tranquil region."

"Is it?" the clerk said. "If you are coming from worse, I sympathize with you." She got very insulted when Gorppet laughed at her.

Ttomalss studied the report that had come up from the Moishe Russie Medical College. *Based on our present knowledge of Tosevite physiology and of available immunizations,* the physician named Shpaaka wrote, *it seems possible, even probable, that the specimen may, after receiving the said immunizations, safely interact with wild Tosevites. Nothing in medicine, however, is so certain as it is in engineering.*

With a discontented mutter, Ttomalss blanked the computer screen. He'd hoped for a definitive answer. If the males down at the medical college couldn't give him one, where would he get it? *Nowhere,* was the obvious answer. He recognized that Shpaaka was doing the best he could. Psychological research was also less exact than engineering. That still left Ttomalss unhappy.

After more mutters, he telephoned Kassquit. "I greet you, superior sir," she said. "How are you this morning?"

"I am well, thank you," Ttomalss answered. "And yourself?"

"Very well," she said. "And what is the occasion of this call?"

She undoubtedly knew. She could hardly help knowing. That she asked had to mean she was unhappy about proceeding. Even so, Ttomalss explained the news he'd got from the physician down on the surface of Tosev 3. He finished, "Are you willing to undergo this series of immunizations so you are physically able to meet with wild Big Uglies?"

"I do not know, superior sir," Kassquit replied. "What are the effects of the immunizations likely to be on me?"

"I do not suppose there will be very many effects," Ttomalss said. "Why should there be? There are no major effects to immunizations among the Race. I had most of mine in early hatchlinghood, and scarcely remember them."

"I see." Kassquit made the affirmative hand gesture to show she understood. But then she said, "Still, these would not be immunizations from the Race. They would be immunizations from the Big Uglies, for Tosevite diseases. The Big Uglies are less advanced than the Race in a great many areas, and I am certain medicine is one of them."

"Well, no doubt that is a truth." Ttomalss admitted what he could hardly deny. "Let me inquire of Shpaaka. When he gives me the answer, I shall relay it to you." He broke the connection.

On telephoning the physician, he got a recorded message telling him Shpaaka had gone to teach and would return his call as soon as possible. His own computer had the same kind of programming, which didn't make him any happier about being on the receiving end of it. Concealing annoyance over such things was part of good manners. He recorded his message and settled into some other work while waiting for Shpaaka to get back to him.

After what seemed forever but really wasn't, the physician did call back. "I greet you, Senior Researcher," Shpaaka said. "You asked an interesting question there."

"I thank you, Senior Physician," Ttomalss replied. "The question, however, does not come from me. It comes from my Tosevite ward, who is of course most intimately concerned with it."

"I see. That certainly makes sense," Shpaaka said. "I had to do some research of my own before I could give the answer: partly by asking Big Ugly students of their experience with immunizations, partly having some of them consult Tosevite medical texts so they could translate the data in those texts for me."

"I thank you for your diligence," Ttomalss said. "And what conclusions did you reach?"

"That Tosevite medicine, like so much on this planet, is primitive and sophisticated at the same time," the physician told him. "The Big Uglies know how to stimulate the immune system to make it produce antibodies against various local diseases, but do so by brute force, without caring much about reducing symptoms from the immunizations. Some of them appear to be unpleasant, though none has any long-term consequences worthy of note."

"I see," Ttomalss repeated, not altogether happily. If the immunizations were likely to make Kassquit sick, would she want to go forward with them?

Shpaaka said, "I tell you this, Senior Researcher: finding your answer has been one of the more pleasant, enjoyable, and interesting things I have had to do lately."

"Oh?" Ttomalss said, as he was plainly meant to do. "And why is that?"

"Because the medical college has been cast into turmoil, that is why," the physician replied. "You may or may not know that some miserable individual who thought he was more clever than he really was devised the *brilliant* plan of making the Big Uglies pay for the privilege of exercising their superstitions, which has provoked disorder over wide stretches of Tosev 3."

"Yes, I do recall that," Ttomalss said in faintly strangled tones. Shpaaka's sarcasm stung. Fortunately, the other male didn't know he was talking to the originator of the plan he scorned.

"You do? Good," Shpaaka said. "Well, someone then decided on the converse for the medical college: that no one who failed to give reverence to the spirits of Emperors past would be allowed to continue. What no one anticipated, however, was that many Big Uglies—including some of the most able students, and even including the hatchling of the Big Ugly for whom the medical college was named—would be so attached to their superstitions that they would withdraw instead of doing what we required of them."

"That is unfortunate, both for them and for relations between the Race and their species," Ttomalss said.

Shpaaka made the affirmative hand gesture. "It is also unfortunate for the Tosevites these half-trained individuals will eventually treat. They would have done far better by choosing to stay."

Ttomalss hadn't thought about infirm Big Uglies. He'd seen plenty in China—rather fewer in the *Reich*, where the standards of medicine, if not high, were higher. "Well, it cannot be helped," he said after a brief pause.

"Oh, it could be," Shpaaka said. "All we have to do is rescind the idiotic policy we are now following. But I do not expect that, and I shall not take up any more of your time advocating it. Good day to you."

"Good day," Ttomalss answered, but he was talking to a blank screen: the physician had already gone.

He thought about telephoning Kassquit with the news, but decided to wait and take a meal with her at the refectory so he could pass it along in person. Among the Race, males and females had a harder time saying no in person than they did over the telephone.

Ttomalss idly wondered if the same held true among the Big Uglies—those of them who had telephones, that is. Eventually, the Race would get around to researching such things. He doubted the time would come while he remained alive, though.

At the next meal, he put Shpaaka's opinion to Kassquit. "How do you feel about the notion of bodily discomfort?" he asked.

"I really do not know," she answered. "I have known very little bodily discomfort in my life here. The notion of illness seems strange to me."

"You are fortunate—far more fortunate than the Big Uglies down on the surface of Tosev 3," Ttomalss said. "You have never been exposed to the microorganisms that cause disease among them, and those of the Race do not seem to find you appetizing."

"If I were to meet with wild Big Uglies, I would need these immunizations, would I not?" Kassquit asked.

"I would strongly recommend that you have them, at any rate," Ttomalss said. "I would not wish to see you fall ill as a result of such a meeting." *And I certainly would not wish you to die, not after I have put so much hard work into raising you up to this point.*

Kassquit might have plucked that thought right out of his head. She said, "Yes, it would be inconvenient to you if I died in the middle of your research, would it not?" After a moment, she added, "It would also be most inconvenient to me." She used an emphatic cough.

"Of course it would," Ttomalss said uncomfortably. "If you do decide to meet with these wild Tosevites in person, you would be wise to receive these immunizations first."

"You very much want me to meet with them, is that not so?" Without waiting for Ttomalss' reply, Kassquit gave one herself: "It must be so. Why else would you have gone to all the trouble of raising me?" She sighed. "Well, if I am going to be an experimental animal, I had best be a good one. Is that not a truth, superior sir?" She waved a hand at the refectory full of males and females. "For all your efforts, and for all mine, I can never fully fit in here, can I?"

"Perhaps not fully, but as much as a Rabotev or a Hallessi." Ttomalss spoke with care. As Kassquit reached maturity, so did her sense of judgment.

She proved that by making the negative hand gesture. "I believe you are mistaken, superior sir. From all I have been able to learn—and I have done my best to learn all I could, since the matter so urgently concerns me—the Hallessi and Rabotevs are far more like the Race than Tosevites are. Would you agree with that, or not?"

"I would have to agree," Ttomalss said, wishing he could do anything but, yet knowing he would forfeit her confidence forever if he lied. "But I would also have to tell you that, when the day comes when all Tosevites are as acculturated to the ways of the Empire as you are now, the Race will have no difficulty in ruling this planet."

"May it be so," Kassquit said. "And you need me to help you make it so, is that not also a truth?"

"You know it is," Ttomalss answered. "You have known it ever since you grew old enough to understand such things."

Kassquit sighed again. "Truth, superior sir: I have known that. And the best way for me to make it so is for me to begin meeting with Big Uglies in person. You have wanted me to do so since my first telephone conversation with Sam Yeager, and you were surely planning such a thing even before the Big Ugly precipitated matters. Can you truthfully tell me I am mistaken?"

"No," Ttomalss said. "I cannot tell you that. But I can tell you I have not tried to force you onto this course, and I shall not do so. If you do not wish it, it shall not be done."

"For which I thank you—but it needs to be done, does it not?" Kassquit asked bleakly. Again, she did not wait for Ttomalss to reply, but answered her own question: "It does indeed need to be done. Very well, superior sir. I shall do it."

There in the crowded refectory, Ttomalss rose from his seat and assumed the posture of respect before Kassquit. His Tosevite ward exclaimed in surprise. So did a good many males and females, who also stared and pointed. He didn't care. As far as he was concerned, what he'd done was altogether appropriate. As he rose once more, he said, "I thank you."

"You are welcome," Kassquit answered. "You may give whatever orders are necessary to begin the immunization process."

"I shall do that," Ttomalss said. He'd almost answered, *It shall be done.* Kassquit was not his superior. Somehow, though, she'd made him feel as if she were. He wondered how she'd managed to do that.

☆ **11** ☆

In her life aboard the Race's starship, Kassquit had known little bodily discomfort. Oh, she'd had her share of bumps and bruises and cuts—more than her share, as she saw things, for her skin was softer and more vulnerable than the scaly hides of the Race—but none of them had been bad. And, since her body reached maturity, she'd also had to deal with the cyclic nature of Tosevite female physiology. It made her resent her origins—the Race certainly had no such problems—but, with the passage of time, she'd grown resigned to it.

These immunizations brought a whole different order of unpleasantness. One of them raised a nasty pustule on her arm. Up till then, her knowledge of infections had been purely theoretical. For a while, as the afflicted region swelled and hurt, she wondered if her immune system could cope with the microorganisms from the planet on which her kind had evolved. But, after a few days, the pustule did scab over, even though the scar it left behind looked as if it was liable to be permanent.

Other injections proved almost as unpleasant as that one. They made her arm or her buttock sore for a couple of days at a time. Some of them raised her body temperature as her immune system fought the germs that stimulated it. She'd never known fever before, and didn't enjoy the feeling of lassitude and stupidity it brought.

As a physician readied yet another hypodermic, she asked, "By the Emperor, how many diseases *are* there down on Tosev 3?"

"A great many," the male answered, casting down his eyes for a moment. "Even more than there are on Home, by all indications— or perhaps it is just that the Big Uglies can cure or prevent so few of them. This one is called cholera, I believe. It is not an illness

310

you would want to have, and that is a truth." He used an emphatic cough. "This immunization does not confer perfect resistance to the causative organism, but it is the best the Tosevites can do. Now you will give me your arm."

"It shall be done," Kassquit said with a sigh. She did not flinch as the needle penetrated her.

"There. That was very easy," the physician said, swabbing the injection site with a disinfectant. "It was, in fact, easier than it would have been with a male or female of the Race. Here, your thin skin is an advantage."

"How nice," Kassquit said distantly. She did not want to be different from the Race. With all her heart, she wished she could be a female like any other. She knew what such wishes were worth, but couldn't help making them.

Except for the one that had raised the pustule, the injection for the disease called cholera proved the most unpleasant Kassquit had endured. She enjoyed neither the pain nor the fever. They seemed to take forever to ebb. If the disease was worse than the treatment that guarded against it, it had to be very nasty indeed.

Sam Yeager telephoned Kassquit while she was recovering from the immunization. Not feeling up to dealing with the Big Ugly, she refused the call. Before long, he sent her a message over the computer network: *I hope I have done nothing to cause offense.*

That was polite enough to require a polite answer. *No*, she replied. *It is only that I have not felt well lately.*

I am sorry to hear it, he wrote back promptly. *I did not think it would be easy for you to get sick up there, away from all the germs of Tosev 3. I hope you get better soon.*

I have been free of the germs of Tosev 3, Kassquit answered. *That is the cause of my present discomfort: I am being immunized against them, and some of the immunizations have unpleasant aftereffects.*

Again, Sam Yeager wrote back almost at once. He had to be sitting by his computer as Kassquit was sitting by hers. *Are you getting immunized so you can meet Big Uglies in person?* he asked. *If you are, I hope that my hatchling and I are two of the Big Uglies you will want to meet. We certainly want to meet you.* He used the conventional symbol that represented an emphatic cough.

Despite its breezily informal syntax, Kassquit studied that message with considerable respect. Wild Big Ugly Sam Yeager might be, but he was anything but a fool. *Yes, that is why I am being immunized,* Kassquit told him, her artificial fingerclaws clicking on the keyboard. *And yes, you and your hatchling are two of the Tosevites I am interested in meeting.*

Sam Yeager's hatchling, Jonathan Yeager, intrigued her no end. She had never seen anyone who resembled her so closely. Living as she did among the Race, she had never imagined that anyone could resemble her so closely. He even shaved his head and wore body paint. It was as if he and she were two ends of the same bridge, reaching toward the middle to form . . . what?

If this world has a future as part of the Empire, she thought, *its future will be as whatever forms in the middle of that bridge.*

Once more, Sam Yeager wasted no time in replying. *We very much look forward to it, superior female,* he wrote. *Shall we start setting up arrangements with the Race?*

Part of Kassquit—probably the larger part—dreaded the idea. The rest, though, the rest was intrigued. And she agreed with Ttomalss that such a meeting would bring advantage to the Race. And so, in spite of a sigh, she answered, *Yes, you may do that, and I will do the same. I do not know how long the negotiations will take.*

Too long, Sam Yeager predicted.

Kassquit laughed. *You are intolerant of bureaucracy,* she observed.

I hope so, the wild Big Ugly wrote, which made Kassquit laugh again. Sam Yeager went on, *Bureaucracy is like spice in food. A little makes food taste good. Because it does, too many males and females think a lot will make the food taste even better. But cooking does not improve that way, and neither does bureaucracy.*

Some regulation is necessary, Kassquit wrote. She had known nothing but regulation throughout her life.

I said as much, Sam Yeager answered. *But when does some become too much? Tosevites have been arguing that question for as long as we have been civilized. We still are. I suppose the Race is, too.*

No, not really. Kassquit keyed the characters one by one. *I have never heard such a discussion among the Race. We have, for the most part, the amount of regulation that suits us.*

I do not know whether to congratulate the Race or offer my sympathy, the Tosevite responded. *And as for you, you are with the Race but not of it, the way hatchlings of the Race would be if Big Uglies raised them.*

I would like to meet such hatchlings, if there were any, Kassquit wrote. *I have thought about that very possibility, though I do not suppose it is likely. Even if it were, such hatchlings would still be very small.*

So they would, Sam Yeager replied. *And I have another question for you—even if you did meet these hatchlings when they were grown, what language would you speak with them?*

Why, the language of the Race, of course, Kassquit wrote, but she deleted the words instead of sending them. The Big Ugly had thought of something she hadn't. If his kind were raising hatchlings of the Race to be as much like Tosevites as possible, they would naturally teach them some Tosevite tongue. Kassquit had trouble imagining males and females of the Race who didn't know their own language, but it made sense that such hatchlings wouldn't. And why not? She was a Big Ugly by blood, but spoke not a word of any Tosevite tongue.

What she did transmit was, *I see that you have done a good deal of thinking on these matters. Do I understand that you have been dealing with the Race since the conquest fleet came to Tosev 3?*

Yes, the Tosevite answered. *In fact, I was interested in non-Tosevite intelligences even before the conquest fleet got here.*

Kassquit studied the words on the screen. Sam Yeager wrote the language of the Race well, but not as a male of the Race would have: every so often, the syntax of his own language showed through. That was what had first made her suspect he was a Big Ugly. Did his message mean what it looked to mean, or had he somehow garbled it? Kassquit decided she had to ask. *How could you have known of non-Tosevite intelligences before the conquest fleet came?* she wrote. *Big Uglies had no space travel of their own up till that time.*

No, we had no space travel, Sam Yeager agreed. *But we wrote a lot of fiction about what it might be like if Tosevites met all different kinds of intelligent creatures. I used to enjoy that kind of fiction, but I never thought it would come true till the day the Race shot up the railroad train I was riding.*

"How strange." Kassquit spoke the words aloud, and startled herself with the sound of her own voice. The more she learned about the species of which she was genetically a part, the more alien it seemed to her. She wrote, *Such things would never have occurred to the Race before spaceflight.*

So I gather, Sam Yeager replied. *We speculate more than the Race does, or so it seems.*

Is that good or bad? Kassquit wrote.

Yes. The unadorned word made her stare. After a moment, in a separate message, Sam Yeager went on, *Sometimes differences are not better or worse. Sometimes they are just different. The Race does things one way. Big Uglies do things a different way— or sometimes a lot of different ways, because we are more various than the Race.*

If it hadn't been for that variability, Kassquit knew the Race would easily have conquered Tosev 3. The majority of the planet's inhabitants, the majority of the regions of its land surface, had fallen to the conquest fleet with relatively little trouble. But the minority . . . The minority had given, and continued to give, the Race enormous difficulties.

Before Kassquit could find a way to put any of that into words, Sam Yeager wrote, *I have to leave now—time for my evening meal. I will be in touch by message and by telephone—if you care to talk with me—and I hope to see you in person before too long. Goodbye.*

Goodbye, Kassquit answered. She got up from her seat in front of the computer, took off the artificial fingerclaws one by one, and set them in a storage drawer near the keyboard. It wasn't time for her evening meal, or anywhere close to it. All the ships in the conquest fleet—and now in the colonization fleet, too—kept the same time, independent of where in their orbit around Tosev 3 they happened to be. Intellectually, Kassquit understood how time on the surface of a world was tied to its sun's apparent position, but it had never mattered to her.

She hoped she would hear from Sam Yeager again soon. Such hope surprised her; she remembered how frightened she'd been at first of the idea of communicating with a wild Big Ugly. But he looked at the world in a way so different from the Race, he gave her something new and different to think about in almost every message. Not even Ttomalss did that.

And Sam Yeager, just because he was a Big Ugly, knew her and knew her reactions, or some of them, better than even Ttomalss could. In some ways, Kassquit suspected Sam Yeager knew her better than she knew herself. She made the negative hand gesture. *No. He knows what I would be, were I an ordinary Big Ugly.*

But wasn't she some of that anyhow? She shrugged helplessly. How was she supposed to know?

Reuven Russie had thought he knew a good deal about medicine. His father was a doctor, after all; he'd had the benefit of insight and training no one starting from scratch could hope to equal. And he'd attended the Moishe Russie Medical College, learning things from the Race that human physicians wouldn't have discovered for themselves for generations. If that didn't prepare him for practice, what could?

After his first few hectic weeks of working with his father, he began to wonder if anything could have prepared him for the actual work of medicine. Moishe Russie laughed when he complained about that, laughed and remarked, "The Christians say, 'baptism by total immersion.' That's what you're going through."

"Don't I know it?" Reuven said. "The medicine itself isn't all that different from what I thought it would be. The diagnostic tests work the same way, and the results are pretty clear, even if the lab you use isn't as good as the one attached to the college."

"Isn't it?" Moishe Russie's eyebrows rose in surprise.

"Not even close," Reuven told him. "Of course, the technicians are only human." He didn't realize how disparaging that sounded till he'd already said it.

Now his father's laugh held a wry edge. "You'd better get used to dealing with human beings, son. We mostly do the best we can, you know."

"Yes, I do," Reuven said. He glanced around his father's office, where they were talking. It was a perfectly fine place, with palm trees swaying in the breeze just outside the window; with Moishe Russie's diplomas, one of them in the language of the Race, in frames on the wall; with shelves full of reference books; with a gleaming microscope perched on a corner of the desk.

And yet, to Reuven's eyes, it was as if he'd fallen back through time a century, maybe even two. The plaster on the walls was uneven and rough. It was at home, too, but he noticed it more here because he contrasted it to the smooth walls of the Moishe Russie Medical College. The microscope seemed hopelessly primitive next to the instruments he'd used there. And books . . . He enjoyed reading books for entertainment, but electronics were much better for finding information in a hurry. His father had access to some electronics, but didn't display them where his patients could see them. He didn't seem to want people to know he used such things.

That was part of the problem Reuven had been having in adjusting: pretending to know less than he did. The other part lay in the patients themselves. He burst out, "What do I do about the little old men who come in every other week when there's nothing wrong with them? What I want to do is boot them out on the street, but I don't suppose I can."

"No, not really," Moishe Russie agreed. "Oh, you could, but it wouldn't do you much good. They'd come back anyhow: either that or they'd go bother some other doctor instead."

"I've been looking over the files," Reuven said. "Looks like we've got some patients other doctors have run off."

"I'm sure we do," his father said, nodding. "And they have some of ours, too—I try to be patient, but I'm not Job. Sometimes all the little old men and women really want is for someone to tell them, 'Don't worry. You're really all right.' And"—he grinned at Reuven—"you're a hero to a lot of them, you know."

Reuven shrugged in some embarrassment. "Yes, I do know. I don't think it's worth making a fuss over."

"I know you don't, but you have to remember: you grew up here in Jerusalem, not in Warsaw or Minsk or Berlin," Moishe Russie said. "Being a Jew is easy here. It wasn't so easy back in Europe, believe me. And a Jew who walks away from something important so he doesn't have to go worship the spirits of Emperors past"—he used the language of the Race for the phrase— "deserves to have people notice."

"If we had advertisements, you could use it in them: 'genuine Jewish doctor,' I mean," Reuven answered. "But it doesn't make me any smarter. If it does anything, it makes me stupider."

His father shook his head. "It may make you a little more ignorant, but not stupider. And it makes you honest. That's important for a doctor."

Reuven snorted. "If I were honest, I'd tell those people to *geh kak afen yam.*"

"Well, you can't be a hundred percent honest *all* the time." Moishe Russie chuckled, but then sobered. "And the other thing to remember is, you can't take anything for granted. Just the other day, I found a lump in Mrs. Berkowitz's breast. She's been coming in here three, four times a year for the past ten years, and I never noticed anything worse than varicose veins wrong with her up till then. But you have to be careful."

"All right," Reuven said. By the unhappy expression on his father's face, he suspected that Moishe Russie wished he'd found the lump sooner. Knowing his father, he'd probably been kicking himself ever since he did discover it. Reuven continued, "And it feels strange to have a chaperone of some sort in the room whenever I examine a woman, even if she's older than the Pyramids."

"You have to be careful," his father repeated, this time in a different tone of voice. "I know a couple of men who ruined their careers because they weren't. Why take chances when you don't have to?"

"I don't," Reuven answered, knowing his father would land on him like an avalanche if he did. "It still seems like something out of the Middle Ages, though."

"Maybe it is, but that doesn't mean it's not real," Moishe Russie said. "Our Arab colleagues have a harder time with it than we do. Sometimes they can't touch their female patients at all. They have to do the best they can by asking questions. If they're lucky, they get to ask the woman. If they're not, they have to ask her husband."

"Yes, I know about that," Reuven said. "There's a fellow named Nuqrashi who resigned from the college about the same time I did. He's back in Baghdad now, I suppose, getting his practice going. I wonder if he's having those kinds of troubles."

"Worse troubles than those in Baghdad nowadays," his father said. "Sometimes they spill over here, too. If I never hear anybody shouting *'Allahu akbar!'* again, I won't be sorry." Moishe Russie's eyes went far away. "Not long after we first came to

Palestine, I tried to help a wounded Arab woman in the streets of Jerusalem, and an Arab man thought I was going to violate her. He did change his mind when he realized what I was doing, I will say that."

"What happened to her?" Reuven asked.

His father looked bleak. "She bled to death. Torn femoral artery, I think."

Before Reuven could answer that, the receptionist tapped on the door and said, "Dr. Russie—young Dr. Russie, I mean— Chaim Katz is here for his appointment. He's complaining about his cough again."

"Thanks, Yetta." Reuven got to his feet. As he started for the examination room, he glanced back at his father, who was lighting a cigarette. In disapproving tones, he said, "Katz would do a lot better if he didn't smoke like a chimney. As a matter of fact, you'd do better, too."

Moishe Russie looked innocent. "I'd do better if Katz didn't smoke? I don't see that." He inhaled. The end of the cigarette glowed red.

"Funny," Reuven said, though he thought it was anything but. "You know what the Lizards have found out about what tobacco does to your lungs. They think we're *meshuggeh* for using the stuff."

"Among other reasons they think we're *meshuggeh*." His father breathed out smoke as he spoke. He looked at the cigarette between his index and middle fingers, then shrugged. "Yes, they've found out all sorts of nasty stuff about tobacco. What they haven't found is how to make somebody quit using the stuff once he's got started." He raised an eyebrow. "They haven't figured out how to make themselves stop using ginger, either."

That struck Reuven as more rationalization than reasoned defense, but he didn't have time to argue—not that arguing was likely to make his father stub out that cigarette and never smoke another one. All he said was, "You can't be having as much fun with tobacco as the Lizards do with ginger." Moishe Russie laughed.

In the examination room, Chaim Katz was working a cigarette down to a tiny butt and coughing between puffs. He was about sixty, stocky, bald, with a gray mustache and tufts of gray hair sprouting from his ears. "Hello, Doctor," he said, and coughed again.

"Hello." Reuven pointed to an ashtray. "Will you please put that out and take off your shirt? I want to listen to your chest." He reached for his stethoscope, which hung beside his father's. Even as he set the ends in his ears, he knew he wouldn't be hearing everything he might. The Race had electronically amplified models.

He didn't need anything fancy, though, to dislike what he heard in Chaim Katz's chest. He marveled that the older man got any air into his lungs at all: wheezes and hisses and little whistling noises filled his ears. *"Nu?"* Katz said when he put the stethoscope away.

"I want you to make an appointment with Dr. Eisenberg for a chest X ray," Reuven told him. Back at the medical college, he could have sent the man for an X ray then and there, and learned the results in a few minutes. Unfortunately, things weren't so simple here. "When I see the film, I'll have a better idea of where we stand." *I'll find out whether you've got a carcinoma in there, or just a running start on emphysema.*

"That'll be expensive," Katz complained.

Reuven said, "How expensive is being sick, Mr. Katz? You've had this cough for a while now. We need to find out what's going on in there." The stocky little man made a sour face, but finally nodded. He put on his shirt, buttoned it, and pulled out the pack of cigarettes in the breast pocket. Reuven pointed to them. "You'll probably get some relief if you can give those up. They don't call them coffin nails for nothing."

Chaim Katz looked at the cigarettes—a harsh Turkish blend—as if just consciously noticing he was holding them. He stuck one in his mouth and lit it before answering, "I like 'em." He took a drag, then continued, "All right, I'll talk to Eisenberg. Tell your old man hello for me." Out he went, leaving a trail of smoke behind.

With a sigh, Reuven ducked into his own office—smaller and a good deal starker than his father's—and wrote up the results of the examination. He was just finishing when the telephone rang. He looked at it in mild surprise; his father got most of the calls. "Miss Archibald for you," Yetta said.

"Put her through," Reuven said at once, and then switched

from Hebrew to English: "Hullo, Jane! How are you? So you still remember me even though I escaped? Do you remember me well enough to let me take you to supper tomorrow night?"

"Why not?" she said, and laughed. Reuven grinned enormously, though she couldn't see that. She continued, "After all, you're a man of money now, with your own practice and such. Since you've got it, why shouldn't you spend it on me?"

Had he thought she meant that in a gold-digging way, he would have hung up on her. Instead, he laughed, too. "Only goes to show you haven't had a practice of your own yet. How are things back there?" He still longed for news, even after severing himself from the medical college.

"About what you'd expect," Jane answered. "The Lizards keep muttering about Tosevite superstitions." She dropped into the language of the Race for the last two words. "I don't think they expected nearly so many people to resign."

"Too bad," Reuven said with more than a little relish. "Even after all these years, they don't understand just how stubborn we are."

"Well, I know how stubborn you are," Jane said. "I'm still willing to go out to supper with you. What time do you think you'll be by the dormitory?"

"About seven?" Reuven suggested. When Jane didn't say no, he went on, "See you then," and hung up. Maybe if he was stubborn enough, she'd be willing to do more than go out to supper with him. Maybe not, too, but he could hardly wait to find out.

Every time Sam Yeager went to Little Rock, the new capital of the United States seemed to have grown. It also seemed as gawky as Jonathan had during the years when he was shooting up like a weed. He thought the president's residence—the papers called it the Gray House, in memory of the White House that was, these days, slightly radioactive ruins—lacked the classic dignity of its predecessor. People said it was more comfortable to live in, though, and he supposed that counted, too.

Posters on the telephone poles outside the Gray House shouted, REELECT WARREN & STASSEN! They were printed in red, white, and blue. The Democrats' posters were black and gold. HUMPHREY FOR PRESIDENT! was their message, along with a picture of the beaky, strong-chinned governor of Minnesota. Yeager had nothing much against Hubert Humphrey or Joe Kennedy, Jr., but didn't intend to vote for them. President Warren was a known quantity. At Sam's stage of life, he approved of known quantities.

A receptionist at the front entrance to the residence nodded politely to him as he came up. "May I help you, Lieutenant Colonel?" she asked.

"Yes, ma'am." Yeager gave his name, adding, "I have an eleven o'clock appointment with the president."

She checked the book in front of her, then looked carefully at the identification card he showed her. When she was satisfied his image matched his face, she nodded again. "Go to the waiting room, sir. He'll be with you as soon as he finishes with the Russian foreign commissar."

"Thanks," Yeager said, and grinned in bemusement as he headed down the hall. The Russian foreign commissar, then him? He'd never expected to be mentioned in the same breath with such luminaries, not back in the days when he was bouncing around the mid- to lower minor leagues. Then his idea of big shots was fellows who'd had a cup of coffee in the majors before dropping down again.

He grinned once more when he got to the waiting room. One of the things set out for people, along with *Look* and *U.S. News and Interspecies Report*, to read was the *Sporting News*. The Los Angeles Browns were two days away from squaring off with the Phillies in the World Series. His heart favored the Browns. If he'd had to put money on the Series, though, he would have bet on the Phils.

I might have made it to the big time as a coach, he thought. *I might have. If I had, I might have been standing in the first-base box two days from now.* Instead, he was sitting here waiting to talk with the president of the United States. It wasn't what he'd had in mind as a younger man, but it wasn't so bad, either.

Out came Andrei Gromyko. He didn't look happy, but he had the sort of face that wasn't made for looking happy. "Good day," he said to Yeager in excellent English. He strode out of the room without waiting for a reply.

In his wake, a flunky in an expensive suit emerged from President Warren's office. He gave Sam a smile wide enough to make up for the one he hadn't got from the Russian. It also made him want to check to be sure his wallet was still in his hip pocket. The flunky said, "The president will see you in a few minutes. He wants to finish writing up his notes first."

"Okay by me," Sam answered—as if Warren needed his permission to do some work before summoning him. He returned to the *Sporting News*. Like Budweiser beer, it had survived the Lizard occupation of St. Louis.

He almost went past the necrology listing for Peter Daniels, who'd caught briefly for the Cardinals before the First World War. Then his eyes snapped back. Peter Daniels, more commonly known as Mutt, had been his manager at Decatur in the I-I-I League when the Lizards invaded the USA, and had gone into the Army with him. So Mutt had made it to almost eighty. That wasn't a bad run, not a bad run at all. Sam hoped he'd be able to match it.

Here came the flunky again. "The president will see you now, Lieutenant Colonel."

"Thanks." Yeager got to his feet, walking into the office, and saluted his commander in chief. "Reporting as ordered, sir."

"Sit down, Yeager." Earl Warren didn't believe in wasting time. "We have a couple of things to talk about today."

"Yes, sir." Sam sat. A houseman brought in coffee on a silver tray. When the president took a cup, Yeager did, too.

President Warren picked up a fat manila folder. "Your reports on the Lizard hatchlings—Mickey and Donald: I like that—have been fascinating. I've enjoyed reading them not only for what they tell me about Lizard development but also for the way they're written. You could have been published, I think, had you chosen to try to go in that direction."

"Maybe, Mr. President, and thanks, but I hope you'll excuse me for saying that I have my doubts," Sam answered. He added, "I was also smart enough to marry a good editor. She makes me sound better than I would otherwise."

"A good editor can do that," Warren agreed. "A bad one . . . But back to business. In many ways, these two hatchlings seem to be progressing far faster than human children would."

"They sure are, sir." Yeager nodded. He almost added an emphatic cough, but wasn't sure the president would understand. "Of course, they're born—uh, hatched—able to run and grab onto things. That gives them a big head start. But they understand faster than babies do, the way puppies or kittens would."

"But they aren't short-lived, as dogs and cats are," President Warren said.

"Oh, no, sir. They live as long as we do. Probably longer." Yeager eyed the president with respect. Warren saw the implications of things. "The only thing they don't do is, they don't talk. They understand hand signals. They're even starting to understand expressions, which is funny, because they don't have any of their own to speak of. But no words yet. Nothing even really close."

"A lot of babies are just starting to say 'mama' and 'dada' at nine or ten months," the president pointed out. His stern face softened. "It's been a while, but I remember."

"I know, sir, but there isn't anything in the noises they make that's even close to 'dada' or 'mama,' " Sam answered. "The one thing I will say is that there are more human-sounding noises in the babbling than there were when they first came out of their eggs. They're listening to people, but they aren't ready to start talking to people yet. We've got a ways to go before that happens."

"All right, Lieutenant Colonel. You sound as if you're doing a splendid job there," Warren said. "And all that is in accordance with what you've been able to learn about hatchlings from the Lizards, isn't it?"

"Oh, yes, sir, it sure is," Yeager said. "I've had to be careful about that, though. You made it clear we don't want them finding out what we're up to there." He didn't mention the hypothetical he'd offered to Kassquit. He wished he hadn't done it, but too late now.

"It may turn out to be a smaller problem than we believed at first," the president replied. "That brings me to the next thing on the agenda, your upcoming meeting with this"—he opened the folder and flipped through it to find the name he needed—"this Kassquit, yes."

"That's right sir." Sam nodded, oddly relieved to find Warren thinking about her, too. "Turns out the Lizards did unto us before we had the chance to do unto them. Kassquit is for them what Mickey and Donald will be for us in twenty years or so.

She's been raised as a Lizard, she wishes she were a Lizard, but she's stuck with a human being's body."

"Yes." The president flipped through more pages. "I've read your reports on your conversations with her with great interest— even if you were less than perfectly discreet, considering what you just said now." No, Warren didn't miss much. But he didn't make an issue of it, continuing, "Do you think there's any chance of teaching her she really is a human being and ought to be loyal to mankind instead of the Race?"

"No, Mr. President." Yeager spoke decisively. "She's a naturalized citizen of the Empire, you might say. We're just the old country to her, and she'd no more choose us over them than most Americans would choose Germany or Norway or what have you over the USA, especially if they came here as tiny babies. She's made her choice—or had it made for her by the way she was brought up."

"Your point is well taken," Warren said. "I still judge the meeting worthwhile, and I'm glad you and your son are going forward with it. Even if we have no hope of turning her, we can learn a lot from her." He went back to the manila folder, which apparently held copies of all of Sam's reports for quite some time. "Now—you raised another interesting point here: this note about the possibility of the Lizards' domestic animals making themselves more at home on Earth than we wish they would."

"I got to thinking about rabbits in Australia," Sam answered. "There are other cases, too. Starlings, for instance. There weren't any starlings in America seventy-five years ago. Somebody turned loose a few dozen of them in New York City in 1890, and now they're all over the country."

"The year before I was born," Warren said musingly. "I see we may have a problem here. I don't see what to do about it, though. We can hardly go to war with the Race over the equivalents of dogs and cows and goats."

"I wouldn't think so, sir," Yeager agreed. "But these creatures are liable to damage big chunks of the world."

"From the reports that have come in from certain areas—our desert southwest among them—that may already be starting to happen," the president replied. "As I say, it may be a problem, and it may well get worse. But not all problems have neat, tidy solutions, however much we wish they would."

"I used to think they did," Yeager said. "The older I get, though, the more it looks as if you're right."

"You've had some problems of your own," President Warren observed. "If you weren't fast with a pistol, I suspect I'd be talking with someone else right now."

"Somebody tried to take a shot at me, sure enough." Sam shrugged. "I still don't have the faintest idea why."

"One thing you keep doing, Lieutenant Colonel, is looking into matters that aren't really any of your concern," Warren answered. "I've had to mention this to you before. If you didn't, you might not have had such difficulties."

Sam Yeager started to say something, then stopped and studied the president. Was Warren trying to tell him something? Was it what it sounded like? Had that punk tried to punch his ticket because he'd shown he was too interested in the space station that became the *Lewis and Clark* or in the data store that held information about the night the colonization fleet was attacked?

This is the United States, he thought. *Things like that don't happen here . . . do they? They can't happen here . . . can they?*

"Do you understand what I'm telling you?" the president asked, sounding like the kindly, concerned grandfather he also looked like.

"Yes, sir, I'm afraid I do," Sam said. He wished he hadn't put it like that, but that did him as much good as wishing he hadn't swung at a curve down in the dirt.

"Nothing to be afraid of," President Warren said easily. "You're doing a wonderful job. I've said so all along. Keep right on doing it, and everything will be fine." He closed the manila folder, an obvious gesture of dismissal.

Yeager got to his feet. "Okay, sir, I'll do that," he said. But, as he turned to go, he knew damn well it wasn't okay. And he knew something else. It wouldn't matter for beans come November, but he'd just changed his mind: he'd vote for Hubert Humphrey anyway.

When the telephone rang, Straha answered it in the language of the Race: "I greet you." He enjoyed the confused splutters that commonly caused among Big Uglies. Most of them hung up without further ado. He also enjoyed that.

This time, though, he got an answer in the same tongue: "And I greet you, Shiplord. Sam Yeager here. How are you today?"

"I thank you—I am well," Straha said. "I telephoned your home the other day, but learned you were out of the city."

"I have returned," the Tosevite said. Straha thought he sounded unhappy, but had trouble figuring out why. Any male should have been glad to complete a mission and come home once more. In that, the Big Uglies were similar to the Race.

Or maybe, Straha thought, *I am simply misreading his tone.* Although he had lived among the Big Uglies since defecting from the conquest fleet, he did not always accurately gauge their emotions. He felt no small pride at reading them as well as he did: his diligence had, in most instances, overcome billions of years of separate evolution.

"And what do you want from me today?" he asked. He assumed Yeager wanted something. Few if any Big Uglies were in the habit of calling him simply to pass the time of day. As a defector, he understood that. He was likelier to be a source of information than a friend. And yet, among the Tosevites, Sam Yeager was as close to a friend as he had. He sighed sadly, even though he despised self-pity.

"I was just wondering if anything new about Kassquit had bounced off your hearing diaphragms," Yeager said. "You remember: the Big Ugly being raised as a female of the Race."

"Of course," Straha said, though he was glad Sam Yeager had reminded him who Kassquit was. "I regret to have to tell you, I have heard nothing."

"Too bad," Yeager said. "Anything I can find out would help a lot. If we can work things out with the Race, my hatchling and I will be going up into space to meet her. The more we know, the better off we will be."

"If I hear anything of interest, you may rest assured I will inform you of it," Straha said. "But I cannot tell you what I do not know."

"Truth," Yeager admitted. "It would make things a lot easier if you could. Well, I thank you for your time." He shifted into English for two words—"So long"—and hung up.

Not altogether by chance—very likely not at all by chance—Straha's driver strolled into the kitchen a moment later. "That was Sam Yeager, wasn't it?" he asked.

"Yes," Straha answered shortly.

"What did he want?" the driver asked.

Straha turned both eye turrets toward him. "Why are you so curious whenever Yeager calls?" he asked in return.

The driver folded his arms across his chest and replied, "My job is being curious." *Your job is giving me the answers I need,* was his unspoken corollary.

And, by the rules under which Straha had to live, the driver was right. With a sigh, he said, "He was making inquiries about Kassquit."

Unlike the ex-shiplord, his driver didn't need to be reminded who that was. "Oh. The female Tosevite up in space." He relaxed. "All right. No problem there."

That roused Straha to indignation: "If you Big Uglies have problems with your finest expert on the Race, my opinion is that you have severe problems indeed."

As usual, he failed to irk his driver. The fellow shifted into the language of the Race to drive home his point: "Shiplord, you were one of the best officers the conquest fleet had. That did not mean you always got on well with your colleagues. If you had, you and I would not be talking like this now, would we?"

"It seems unlikely," Straha admitted. "Very well. I see what you mean. But if Yeager is as great a nuisance to his colleagues as I was to mine, he is a very considerable nuisance indeed." He spoke in tones of fond reminiscence; if he hadn't made Atvar's blood boil, it wasn't for lack of effort.

His driver said, "He is," and used an emphatic cough.

"I see," Straha said slowly. He'd known Yeager had occasional trouble with the American authorities, but hadn't really believed they were of that magnitude. *No wonder I sometimes feel as if he and I were hatched from the same egg,* he thought.

"Kassquit, though, is legitimate business for him," the driver said. "He should stick to legitimate business. He would do better if he did." With that, he turned on his heel and strode away.

Arrogant, egg-addled . . . But Straha cursed the driver only mentally, and even then the curse broke down half formed. The Big Ugly was anything but addled, and the ex-shiplord knew it. Indeed, his effortless competence was one of the most oppressive things about him.

When the driver had gone round the corner, Straha opened a

drawer, took out a vial of ginger, poured some into the palm of his hand, and tasted. Even as pleasure surged through him, he carefully put the vial back and closed the drawer. The driver knew he tasted, of course. The driver got ginger for him. But he did not like to taste in front of the Big Ugly. He treated the Tosevite as he would have treated one of his own aides: no high-ranking officer cared to do something unseemly while his subordinates were watching.

Tasting ginger, of course, was legal under the laws of the United States. But those laws mattered only so much to Straha. He lived under them, yes, but they weren't *his*. The whole snout-counting process by which the Big Uglies in the USA chose their lawmakers had never failed to strike him as absurd. Emotionally, he still adhered to the regulations of the conquest fleet, and under them tasting ginger was a punishable offense.

With the herb blazing in him, he followed the driver out to the front room. The Big Ugly had just settled down with a magazine, and seemed somewhat surprised to have to deal with Straha again so soon. "Can I help you with something, Shiplord?" he asked.

"Yes," Straha answered. "You can tell me whose snout you intend to choose in the upcoming snoutcounting for the leader of your not-empire."

"Oh, I think I'll vote to reelect President Warren," the driver answered in English.

Straha didn't blame him for shifting languages; the Big Uglies' tongue was better suited to discussing this strange quadrennial rite of theirs. The ex-shiplord also used English: "And why is that?"

"Well, the country's doing okay, or better than okay," the Tosevite said. "Warren's made sure we're strong, and I like the way he's handled relations with the Race. We have a saying: don't change horses in midstream. So I figure staying with the man we've got is probably the best way to go."

That sounded cautious and conservative. It might almost have been a male of the Race speaking, not a Big Ugly. As a Tosevite might have stuck out his index finger, Straha stuck out his tongue. "Suppose Warren loses, though. Suppose more American Tosevites choose the snout of this other male, this . . . Humpty?"

"Humphrey," his driver corrected. His sigh sounded like the

sigh of a male of the Race. "Then they do, that's all. Then Humphrey becomes president, and we all hope he does as good a job as Warren did. I'd support him. I'd follow his orders. I'd have to."

"But you would still think all the time that this other male, the one you have leading you now, would be able to do the job better," Straha persisted.

"Yes, I probably would," the driver said.

"Then why would you follow Humphrey?" Straha took care to pronounce the name correctly.

"Because more people would have voted for him than for Warren," the Big Ugly replied. "We've been over this before, Shiplord. With us, the government is more important than the names of the people in the top slots. Things go on any which way."

"Madness," Straha said with conviction. "What would happen if some large number of American Tosevites decided they did not like the way the snoutcounting—uh, the election—turned out, and refused to obey the male who was chosen?"

To his surprise, the driver answered, "We had that happen once, as a matter of fact. It was just over a hundred years ago."

"Oh? And what was the result?" Straha asked.

"It was called the Civil War," the driver said. "You may have noticed some of the anniversary celebrations we've been having." Straha made the negative hand gesture. Lots of things went on around him that he didn't notice. With a shrug, the driver went on, "Well, whether you've noticed or not, the war caused so much damage that we've never come close to having another one over an election."

So Big Uglies *could* learn from history. Straha wouldn't have bet on it. The Tosevites were most adept technically; had they not been, this planet would be a firmly held part of the Empire. But they'd been doing their best to destroy one another when the conquest fleet arrived.

Straha wondered what would have happened if the Race had waited another couple of hundred years before sending out the conquest fleet. The Big Uglies had already been working on explosive-metal bombs. Maybe they would have committed suicide. *Or maybe,* Straha thought unhappily, *not a single ship from the conquest fleet would have managed to land on Tosev 3.*

The ginger was leaving him. So was the euphoria it had brought. Imagining the Race ambushed by fearsome Big Uglies came easy at such times. It had come too close to happening as things were.

"Is there anything else, Shiplord?" The driver returned to the language of the Race, a sure sign he considered the conversation on snoutcounting at an end.

"No, nothing else," Straha answered. "You may return to your reading. What publication have you got there?"

By the way the driver hesitated, Straha knew he'd hit a nerve. He thought he knew what kind of nerve he'd hit, too. Sure enough, when the driver showed him the magazine, he found it to be one featuring female Big Uglies divested of most of the cloth wrappings they customarily used.

"I do not mind your titillating your mating urge if that does not interfere with your other duties, and it does not seem to," Straha said.

Despite that reassurance, the driver closed the magazine and would not open it again while Straha was in the room. He was as embarrassed about openly indulging his sexuality as Straha was about tasting ginger in front of him. While different in so many ways, Big Uglies and the Race shared some odd things.

Straha said, "Never mind. I will leave you in privacy. And I will not hold it against you that you are so reluctant to extend me the same privilege."

"Shiplord, my job is to keep you safe first and happy second," the driver answered. "It is much harder for me to keep you safe if I do not know where you are and what you are doing."

"But it would be much easier for you to keep me happy under those circumstances," Straha said. The driver only shrugged. He had his priorities. He'd spelled them out for the ex-shiplord. And Straha, like it or not, was stuck with them: one more delight of exile.

Arguing with Heinrich Himmler hadn't got Felless tossed out of the *Reich*. From that, she reluctantly concluded nothing she would do would get her expelled. The proper attitude under those circumstances was to buckle down and do her job in Nuremberg as well as she could.

Felless cared very little for the proper attitude. She was

gloomily certain she could do her job here without an error for the next hundred years and Veffani would still refuse to transfer her to a starship or even to a different Tosevite not-empire. And she could not appeal to Cairo for relief from such high-handed treatment, not after several leading officials from the Race's administrative center on Tosev 3 had mated with her in the ambassador's conference chamber.

Among the Big Uglies, mating created bonds of affection. Among the Race, all it seemed to create was resentment, especially when it was an out-of-season, ginger-induced mating. Felless sighed. Just what she didn't want: a reason to wish she were a Tosevite.

What she did want was another taste of ginger. The craving gnawed at her like an itch deep under her scales that she couldn't hope to scratch. She had several tastes waiting in her desk. The battle she fought wasn't to keep from tasting. It was to wait till she had the best chance of going long enough after her taste to keep from exciting males with her pheromones when she left her office.

It was also a losing battle. Her eye turrets kept sliding away from the monitor and toward the desk drawer where she'd hidden the ginger. *You are nothing but an addict, dependent on a miserable Tosevite herb,* she told herself severely. That should have shamed her. Back when she'd first started tasting, it had shamed her. It didn't any more. Now she knew it was nothing but a statement of fact.

Like her eye turrets, the chair swiveled. Before she quite knew what she'd done, she turned the chair away from the computer table and toward the desk. She'd just started to rise when the telephone circuitry inside the computer hissed for attention.

She turned back with a hiss of her own, one that mixed frustration and relief. "I greet you," she said, and then, when she saw Veffani's image on the screen, "I greet you, superior sir."

"And I greet you, Senior Researcher," the ambassador to the *Reich* replied. "Come to my office immediately."

"It shall be done," Felless said, and switched off. If she was busy, she could keep her mind—or some of her mind—off her craving. Had Veffani waited a little longer before calling, she would have created fresh scandal by poking her nose outside her office.

Maybe the call was a test. If it was, she would pass it. She'd passed other, similar, tests before. If she passed enough of them . . . odds were it still wouldn't matter. Veffani had made it all too clear he wouldn't let her go no matter what she did.

As she had on that disastrous day when the ambassador summoned her after she'd tasted, she walked by Slomikk in the hall. The science officer turned an eye turret in her direction, no doubt wondering whether mating pheromones would reach his scent receptors in a moment. When they didn't, he kept on walking. Felless felt as if she'd won an obscure victory.

Pheromones didn't matter to Veffani's secretary, a female from the colonization fleet. Even so, after Felless' previous fiasco, the female was wary. "I trust there will be no problem when you go in to see him?" she said.

"None," Felless said, and walked past the secretary too fast for her to get in any more digs.

Veffani turned an eye turret toward her. "I greet you, Senior Researcher. You are commendably prompt."

"I thank you, Ambassador." Felless fought to hold her temper. Nothing she did here would get her a commendation, and she knew it only too well. "How may I serve the Race?"

When Veffani didn't answer right away, hope began to rise in her. If the ambassador didn't like what she had to say, maybe it would do her some good. At last, he said, "As you no doubt know, you were reckoned the colonization fleet's leading expert on alien races when your fleet set out from Home."

Felless made the affirmative gesture. "Yes, superior sir. I did not know then how much of my training would be useless here on Tosev 3."

"This world has surprised all of us," Veffani said, which was an undoubted truth. "The point I am trying to make, however, is that Fleetlord Reffet still reckons you a leading expert on the Big Uglies, no matter how little you deserve that recognition when compared to various males from the conquest fleet."

Now hope did surge, hot and strong, in Felless. Being a fleetlord himself, Reffet could cancel out Atvar and the males from the conquest fleet—even Veffani. He could . . . provided he wanted to badly enough. Felless had to fight to keep a quiver from her voice as she asked, "What does the exalted fleetlord require of me?"

"I cannot tell you, because no one has informed me." Veffani didn't sound very happy to tell her that. He went on, "The fleet-lord's representative, a certain Faparz, will be coming down by shuttlecraft to inform you personally. He is due to arrive this evening."

"By shuttlecraft?" Felless knew she sounded surprised, but the ambassador could scarcely blame her for that, no matter what else he blamed her for. "Why does he not communicate by telephone or electronic message?"

"That I can answer," Veffani replied. "The accursed Deutsch Tosevites are becoming altogether too good at reading and de-coding our signals. And they are not the only ones, are they? Do I not recall your telling me an American Big Ugly succeeded for some time in masquerading as a male of the Race on the com-puter network?"

"Yes, superior sir, that is correct." Felless knew another stab of jealousy about Ttomalss—one that, for a change, had nothing to do with his escape from the *Reich*. His project involving the Tosevite hatchling kept paying handsome dividends. Felless might have thought of doing such a thing herself, but Ttomalss, having come with the conquest fleet, had an enormous head start on her . . . as he did in all matters Tosevite. She forced her thoughts back to the matter directly in front of her: "Then what-ever message Faparz bears is one where security is an important concern?"

"I should think so, yes," Veffani answered. "My I offer you a word of advice, Senior Researcher?"

"I rather think I know what you are about to say," Felless replied.

"Duty requires me to say it anyhow." It wasn't just duty, ei-ther: Veffani looked as if he was enjoying himself. "Do not taste ginger between now and then. Faparz is not a Big Ugly male, and you will not win favor with him because he has mated with you. The reverse is likelier to be true."

"Believe me, superior sir, I understand that," Felless said stiffly. She would crave ginger, and this evening felt a long way off. But the ambassador was undoubtedly right, even if he took too much pleasure in rubbing her snout in her own disgrace.

"For your sake, I hope you do," he said now. "I would just as soon see your punishment continue; in my opinion, you deserve it. You will prove that if you humiliate yourself with the representative of the fleetlord of the colonization fleet as well as with those from the conquest fleet." Felless did her best to hide her resentment, part of which sprang from Veffani's being right. The ambassador went on, "I dismiss you."

"I thank you, superior sir." Felless did not in fact feel in the least thankful, but even Big Uglies recognized how hypocrisy lubricated social wheels. She hurried away before Veffani found any more pungent advice for her.

As was her habit, she retreated to her office. That proved a mistake; her eye turrets kept going back to the drawer where she kept her precious vials of ginger. But fleeing the office would have meant mingling with the rest of the embassy staff, most of whom where members of the conquest fleet and most of whom had no more use for her than did Veffani. *Except when I've been tasting ginger,* she thought. *They have a use for me then, but not one that makes them like me or respect me any more afterwards.*

All that made perfect sense . . . in her mind. But she'd been on the point of tasting when Veffani summoned her to his office. No matter what made sense in her mind, her body craved ginger. It let her know it craved ginger, too, and in no uncertain terms. Every moment seemed an eternity. She wanted to call Veffani back and ask him when in the evening Faparz was scheduled to arrive, but made herself hold back. The ambassador would surely understand why she made such a call: would understand, and would scorn her more than ever.

She was trembling with the desperate urge to taste when the intercom unit connected to her door hissed for attention. "Enter," she called, and the male waiting in the corridor did come in.

"I greet you, Senior Researcher," Faparz said. The body paint on one side of his torso and one arm was plainer than Felless'. That on his other side was as colorful and ornate as anyone on or near Tosev 3 possessed.

"I greet you, Fleetlord's Adjutant," Felless replied. Veffani hadn't told her Reffet was sending his adjutant, and Felless hadn't expected it. Maybe the ambassador hadn't known. But maybe he'd been hoping she would taste, and would end up in trouble because of it. Well, she hadn't. Pride helped fight her desire for the Tosevite herb—helped a little, anyway. "How may I serve the commander of the colonization fleet?"

"We are seeking to make colonization more effective, and to spread safely over broader areas of Tosev 3," Faparz replied. "Your insights into this process will be valuable, and most appreciated."

"I shall of course do whatever I can to aid this worthy effort," Felless said. "One thing that occurs to me is using animals native to Home to make portions of Tosev 3 more Homelike. This is, I gather, already beginning to occur informally; systematizing it could yield good results."

"I agree," Faparz said. "This notion has already been proposed, and is likely to be implemented." Felless hid her disappointment. But Reffet's adjutant went on, "That is the sort of idea we are seeking. That you can find such a scheme on the spur of the moment shows you are likely to be valuable to the project."

"Spirits of Emperors past look kindly on you for your praise!" Felless exclaimed. Then her own spirits grew gloomy, almost as if ginger were ebbing from her system. "But I must tell you, Fleetlord's Adjutant, that removing me from the *Reich* may prove difficult. Ambassador Veffani has . . . formed a grudge against me, and desires that I stay here to work among Big Uglies."

"I am aware of the nature of this, ah, grudge," Faparz said primly, and Felless' spirits tumbled down into her toeclaws. Then Reffet's aide continued, "Still, I believe we may accommodate the ambassador while still involving you. Some of this research is being conducted at a consular site that, while within the boundaries of the *Reich*, is relatively close to territory the Race rules, and the climate there is certainly more salubrious than in this miserable, cold, dank, misty place."

"If you are offering me a new assignment, superior sir, I gladly accept." Felless had to swallow an emphatic cough that would have shown how glad she really was. Now she felt almost as if she'd had the taste of ginger she'd forgone waiting for Faparz. Wherever he—and Reffet—sent her, it couldn't possibly be worse than Nuremberg. Of that she had not a doubt in the world, not a doubt in the whole wide Empire.

Lieutenant Colonel Johannes Drucker floated weightless in *Käthe*, the reusable upper stage of the A-45 that had blasted him into orbit from Peenemünde. He was glad to be a couple of hundred kilometers above the weather, even more glad than usual: fogs rolling in off the Baltic had twice delayed his launch. Here in space, he still felt like a man serving his country. Down on the ground, he had trouble feeling like anything but a man his country was trying to get.

Gently, he patted the instrument panel. A lot of fliers named their upper stages for wives or girlfriends. How many, though, named them for wives or girlfriends who were, or might be, a quarter part Jew? Well, no one had tried making him change the name. That was something, a small something. Since the SS had had to give Käthe back to him, perhaps the official thinking was that she couldn't really have had any Jewish blood at all. Or perhaps the powers that be simply hadn't noticed till now, and a technician with a can of paint would be waiting when Drucker came down.

He didn't want to think about that. He didn't want to think about anything of the sort. Instead, he looked outward. Somewhere out there, in the asteroid belt past the orbit of Mars, the Americans aboard the *Lewis and Clark* were doing . . . what? Drucker didn't know. Neither did anyone else in the Greater German *Reich*.

What he did know was that he was enormously jealous of the Americans. They'd gone out there in a real spacecraft, not just an overgrown Roman candle like the one he'd ridden into orbit. "We should have done that," he muttered. Germany had been ahead of the USA in rocketry during the fighting against the Lizards; it struck him as unconscionable that the *Reich*'s lead had been frittered away.

His gaze grew hungry, as hungry as those of the wolves that had once prowled around Peenemünde. The Americans had taken a long step toward building a real starship. If the *Reich* had such ships, the Lizards would be shaking in the boots they didn't wear. If the *Reich* had starships, they would be vengeance weapons, and the Race had to know it.

The radio crackled to life: "Spaceship of the Deutsche, acknowledge this transmission at once!"

It was, of course, a Lizard talking. No human being would have been so arrogant. No human nation could have afforded to be so arrogant to the Greater German *Reich*. But the Race could.

However strong the *Reich* was, the Race was stronger. Every trip into space rubbed Drucker's nose in that unpalatable fact.

"Acknowledging," he said, shortly, using the language of the Race himself. Some of the Lizards with whom he dealt were decent enough sorts; with them, he went through the polite *I greet you*s. To the ones who only snapped at him, he snapped in return.

"Your orbit is acceptable," the Lizard told him. The Lizard would have been not just arrogant but furious had his orbit been anything else.

"You so relieve my mind," Drucker responded. That was sarcasm and truth commingled. Weapons were tracking him now. They would have been ready to go after *Käthe* had an unannounced orbital change made the Race nervous.

"See that you stay where you ought to be," the Lizard said. "Out."

Drucker chuckled. "Not even a chance to get the last word." He chuckled again. "Probably a female of the Race." The real Käthe, had she heard that slur on womankind, would have snorted and stuck an elbow in his ribs. He probably would have deserved it, too.

He glanced down at Earth below. He was sweeping along above the western Pacific; a nasty storm was building there, with outlying tendrils of cloud already stretching out over Japan and reaching toward China. The *Reich*, the Americans, and the Race all sold meteorological photos to countries without satellites of their own. Back when Drucker was a child, people had been at the mercy of the weather. They still were, but to a lesser degree. They couldn't change it, but at least they had some idea of what was on the way. That made a difference.

Down toward the equator *Käthe* flew at better than 27,000 kilometers an hour. The velocity sounded enormous, but wasn't enough to escape Earth orbit, let alone travel from star to star. That bothered Drucker more than usual. He wanted to go out farther into the solar system, wanted to and couldn't. Some German spacecraft had gone to Mars, but he hadn't been aboard any of them. And they were only rockets, hardly more potent than the A-45 that had lifted him into orbit.

"Calling the German spacecraft! Calling the German spacecraft!" Another peremptory signal, but this one in German, and one he was glad to answer.

"*Käthe* here, with Drucker aboard," he said. "How goes it, *Hermann Göring*?"

"Well enough," the radio operator aboard the German space station replied. "And with you?"

"Not too bad," Drucker said. "And when do you take off and start rampaging through outer space?"

"Would day after tomorrow suit you?" The radioman laughed. So did Drucker. Up above them, some Lizard listening to their transmission would probably have started tearing out his hair, if only he'd had any to tear.

"Day after tomorrow wouldn't suit me at all," Drucker said, "because then I couldn't be aboard when you left. And I want to go traveling."

"I don't blame you," the radio operator said. "The frontier is out this way. If the Americans are going to explore it, we had better do the same."

"Not just the Americans," Drucker said, and said no more. The Lizards already knew the *Reich* mistrusted them. For that matter, the mistrust ran both ways, no doubt with good reason.

Drucker wondered just how soon the *Hermann Göring* really would be leaving Earth orbit for something more worthwhile. Sooner than it would have if the Americans hadn't lit a fire under the *Reich*'s space program—he was sure of that. He was also sure the Race would be horrified to have not one but two Earthly nations on the way toward genuine spacecraft.

A little later, he passed about twenty kilometers below the German space station. Through Zeiss field glasses, it seemed almost close enough to touch. The job of converting it to a spaceship was going much more smoothly than it had for the Americans. But they'd kept what they were up to a secret, while the *Reich* was making no bones about what it had in mind. If the Lizards didn't like it, they could start a war. Such was Himmler's attitude, anyhow.

The swastikas painted on the space station were big enough to be easily visible. Straining his eyes, Drucker imagined he could read Göring's name above them, but he really couldn't, or not quite. He chuckled a little. Down on Earth, the late *Reichsmarschall* was a bad joke, the *Luftwaffe* moribund and subservient to the *Wehrmacht* and the SS. But Göring's name would go traveling farther than the pudgy, drug-addled founder of the German air force could ever have imagined.

And the Lizards couldn't—or at least they'd better not—try to forbid a German spacecraft from going where an American one had already gone. That would mean trouble, big trouble. It might even mean war.

Back when he'd been driving a panzer against the Lizards, Drucker would have given his left nut to control the kind of firepower he had at his fingertips now. He'd been so outgunned then . . . and he was outgunned up here, too. He sighed. The Lizards had more and better weapons. Odds were they would for a long time to come. But the *Reich* could hurt them. That was the essence of German foreign policy. And he, Johannes Drucker, could hurt them with his nuclear-tipped missiles.

He hoped he wouldn't have to. They would surely blow him out of the sky the instant after he launched. The one thing he didn't think they'd do was try to blow him out of the sky before he could launch. They'd attacked Earth without provocation, but hadn't staged any unprovoked assaults since the fighting ended.

Maybe that made them more trustworthy than human beings. Maybe it just made them more naive. Drucker never had figured that out.

His radio crackled into life. "Relay ship *Hoth* to spacecraft *Käthe*. Urgent. Acknowledge."

"Acknowledging," Drucker said. *"Was ist los, Hoth?"* The relay ship, down in the South Atlantic, kept spacecraft in touch with the *Reich* even when they were out of direct radio range. All the spacefaring human powers used relay ships. The Lizards, with their world-bestriding lands, didn't have to.

"Urgent news bulletin," the radio operator down below answered.

"Go ahead." Drucker did his best to hide the alarm that surged through him. But surely his superiors wouldn't order him into battle with a news bulletin . . . would they?

Plainly reading from text in front of him, the radio operator said, "Radio Nuremberg has announced the death of Heinrich Himmler, Chancellor of the Greater German *Reich*. The Chancellor, on duty to his last breath, suffered a coronary thrombosis while working on state papers. No date for services celebrating his life has yet been set, nor has a successor been named."

"Gott im Himmel," Drucker whispered. Things would be hopping down in Nuremberg now. Even more than Hitler before him, Himmler had stayed strong because he let no one around

him have any strength. *Nor has a successor been named* was liable to cover some vicious infighting in the days to come.

"Have you got that, *Käthe*?" the radioman asked.

"I've got it," Drucker said. *This is liable to be the safest place I could find,* he thought. He almost said it aloud, but thought better of that.

And then the fellow down below said it for him: "Staying a few thousand kilometers away when the big boys squabble isn't so bad, eh?"

"That's the truth, sure enough," Drucker answered. "Well, I don't give orders. All I do is take them. Whoever the new *Führer* is, he'll tell me what to do and I'll do it. That's the way things work."

Without a doubt, someone aboard the *Hoth* was recording every word he said. Without a doubt, the *Gestapo* would be listening to make sure he sounded properly loyal to the *Reich* and to its *Führer*, whoever that turned out to be. Drucker knew as much. He was no fool. He also knew his loyalty was liable to be suspect. That meant he had to be especially careful to say all the right things.

And the radioman aboard the *Hoth* said, "That's how we all feel, of course. Our loyalty is to the state, not to any one man."

He said all the right things, too. And Drucker made a point of agreeing with him: "That's how it is, all right. That's how it has to be."

As he flew along, as the signal from the *Hoth* faded, he wondered who would take over for the late, unlamented (at least by him) Heinrich Himmler. The SS would naturally have a candidate. So would the *Wehrmacht*. And Joseph Goebbels, passed over when Hitler died, would want another try at ruling the *Reich*. There might be others; Drucker did his best not to pay attention to politics. Maybe that was a mistake. More and more these days, politics kept paying attention to him. His orbit swept him up toward the *Reich*. By the time his tour ended, everything was likely to be over.

☆ **12** ☆

Vyacheslav Molotov felt harassed. That was not the least common feeling he'd ever had, especially after Marshal Zhukov rescued him while smashing Beria's coup. Every American presidential election made him nervous, too. The prospect of dealing with a new man every four years was enough to make anybody nervous when that man could start a nuclear war just by giving an order. But Warren seemed likely to beat Humphrey, which would give Molotov a breathing space before he had to start getting nervous about the USA again.

Now, though, Himmler had had to go and die. Molotov thought that most inconsiderate of the Nazi leader. Himmler had been a bastard, no doubt about it. But, on the whole (the recent aborted lunge at Poland aside), he'd been a predictable bastard. Who would manage to throw his fundament into the seat he'd occupied?

What sort of madman will I have to deal with next? was how Molotov phrased the question in his mind. American presidential candidates, at least, spelled out what they had in mind before taking office. You could plan for a man like that, even if he looked likely to be unfortunate. But the only qualification for *Führer* that Molotov could see was a quick, sharp knife.

He did not dwell on how a German politico might view the process of succession in the USSR. He took his own country, his own system, for granted.

His secretary looked into the office. "Comrade General Secretary, the foreign commissar is here for his ten o'clock appointment."

As usual, Molotov glanced at the clock on the wall. Gromyko was precisely on time. He always was. Few Soviet officials

341

imitated him. Despite two generations of Soviet discipline, most Russians seemed constitutionally unable to take the notion of precise time seriously. "Send him in, Pyotr Maksimovich," Molotov said.

Gromyko, craggy features impassive as usual, strode past the secretary and into the office. He leaned across the desk to shake hands with Molotov. "Good day, Vyacheslav Mikhailovich," he said.

"And to you, Andrei Andreyevich," Molotov replied. He waved Gromyko to a chair. They both lit cigarettes, Molotov's Russian-style in a long paper holder, Gromyko's an American brand. After a couple of puffs, Molotov said, "You will, no doubt, have a good notion of why I want to see you."

"What ever gave you that idea?" Gromyko had a good deadpan, all right. "It's not as if the *Reich* were of any great concern to us."

"No, of course not." Molotov wouldn't let the foreign commissar win the palm for irony without a fight. "Why, for the past generation Germany has scarcely mattered to us at all."

"Even so." Gromyko stretched out an arm to tap his cigarette into an ashtray on Molotov's desk. After another drag on the cigarette, his manner changed. "I wonder what we do have to look forward to."

"That is the reason I asked to speak with you," Molotov replied. "You will be flying off to Nuremberg for the state funeral day after tomorrow. I await your impressions of the potential German leaders."

"Goebbels we know," Gromyko said, and Molotov nodded. The foreign commissar went on, "Manstein we also know. He is the likeliest of the generals to come to the top. By all accounts, an able man."

Molotov nodded again. "Zhukov respects him," he said. By his tone, by his expression, no one would have known how much having to acknowledge Zhukov's opinion pained him. "As you say, he too is a known quantity."

"But the SS officials under Himmler . . ." Gromyko's voice trailed away. He stubbed out the cigarette and lit another one.

"Yes, they are the trouble," Molotov agreed. "None of them has been able to show what he can do, for Himmler has held power there firmly in his own hands. If one of them can grab it, who knows in which direction he might go?"

"It could be worse," Gromyko said. Molotov raised an eyebrow. The foreign commissar explained: "The Lizards might have landed a few days earlier. Then, perhaps, the British would not have assassinated Heydrich."

After pondering that, Molotov discovered he had to nod. "Yes, you are right—although I doubt Heydrich would have waited for Himmler to die of natural causes before making his bid for the top spot. Go on to Nuremberg, then, Andrei Andreyevich. Learn what you can and report back to me."

"Very well, Comrade General Secretary." Gromyko's shaggy eyebrows twitched. "I do hope the Nazis can keep from starting their civil war until Himmler's funeral is over."

"Yes, that would be good, wouldn't it?" After a moment, Molotov realized the foreign commissar hadn't been joking. He glanced at the smoke spiraling up from his own cigarette, which he hadn't crushed quite well enough. "Do you really think it will come to that?"

"I hope not," Gromyko answered. "But in the *Reich* there is only one way to tell who is the stronger: by conflict. When Hitler died, Himmler was inarguably the strongest man left. Who is strongest now is not so clear, which makes struggles over the succession more likely."

"You could be right," Molotov said. Guile and intrigue had got him the top spot in the Soviet Union after Stalin died. He wondered who would succeed him, and how. The question wasn't idle—far from it. Now he did think about similarities between the USSR and the Greater German *Reich*. His own country had no more formal system for succession than did Germany. Beria's failed coup had rubbed everyone's nose in that. The failed coup had also made it all too likely that Molotov's successor would be Marshal Zhukov, a distinctly unappetizing prospect for an *apparatchik*.

Smoking yet another cigarette, Gromyko left the office. Molotov lit a new one from his own packet. The Americans and the Lizards both claimed tobacco cut years off your life. Having already passed his threescore and ten, Molotov found that hard to believe. If tobacco was poisonous, wouldn't it have killed him by now? In any case, he was inclined to doubt claims from the Race or from the USA on general principles.

He could have watched Himmler's funeral on television. In these days of relay satellites, news went around the world as soon as it happened. He didn't watch. He knew the Nazis were good at melodramatic spectacle. As far as he was concerned, their rule depended in no small measure on keeping the masses mystified through spectacle so they would have no chance to contemplate either their oppression or rising against it.

And, when Gromyko returned from the German capital, Molotov asked no questions about the last rites for the dead *Führer*. Instead, he came straight to the point: "Who is in charge in Nuremberg?"

"Vyacheslav Mikhailovich, I do not precisely know." Gromyko sounded troubled at the admission. "I don't think the Germans know, either."

"That is not good," Molotov said, with what he judged considerable understatement. "Where no one is in charge, anything can happen." It wasn't a proverb, but it sounded like one.

Gromyko accepted it as if it were. "What they have in place now is something they call the Committee of Eight. It has soldiers on it, and SS functionaries, and Nazi Party officials, and a couple of Goebbels' men, too."

Scornfully, Molotov clicked his tongue between his teeth. "All that means is that they are putting off the bloodletting till someone is ready to start it."

"Of course," Gromyko agreed. No veteran of Communist Party infighting could fail to recognize such portents.

"Now we have an interesting question," Molotov said. "Do we prod the Germans while they are weak and confused, or do we leave them severely alone till they sort themselves out?"

"If we prod them, we may gain advantages we could not have managed against Himmler." The foreign commissar spoke in musing tones. "On the other hand, we may only succeed in uniting the members of this committee against us, or in bringing one of them to the top."

Molotov nodded. Gromyko had laid out the alternatives as neatly as a geometry teacher proving a theorem on the blackboard. "If we leave them alone, they are likely to stay disorganized longer than they would otherwise. But so what, if we gain nothing from their disorganization?"

"In that case, at least, we do not run the risk of conflict with them," Gromyko said.

"Conflict with them is inevitable." There Molotov knew he was on firm ideological grounds. But, ideology or no ideology, he temporized: "With the weapons they and we have, conflict with them is also liable to be suicidal."

"Yes," Gromyko said, and then, greatly daring, "This is a problem I fear neither Marx nor Lenin anticipated."

"Possibly not," Molotov said. The admission made him as nervous as if he were the Pope airing doubts about the Trinity. He backed away from it: "But if we cannot rely on Marx and Lenin, on whom can we rely?"

"Lenin extended Marx's doctrine into areas on which Marx did not speak," the foreign commissar replied. "It is up to us to extend Marxist-Leninist thought into the new areas that have come to light over the past forty years."

"I suppose so." Again, Molotov thought of the Pope. "We cannot say we are changing the doctrine, of course—only strengthening it." How had the papacy dealt with the theory of evolution? *Carefully,* was the answer that sprang to mind.

"Of course," Gromyko echoed. "That was what Stalin said, too. It gave him the excuse he needed to do whatever he pleased—not that he needed much of an excuse to go and do that."

"No," Molotov agreed. Stalin was more than ten years dead now, but his shadow lingered over everyone who'd ever had anything to do with him. Molotov had never been shy about ordering executions, but he knew he lacked Stalin's relentless ruthlessness. In a way, that knowledge made him feel inadequate, as if he were a son conscious of not being quite the man his father was.

Gromyko said, "Have you yet decided what we ought to do, given the changed conditions inside the *Reich*?"

Stalin would have decided on the spur of the moment. He would have followed through on whatever he decided, too: followed through to the hilt. He might not have been right all the time—Molotov knew only too well he hadn't been right all the time—but he'd always been sure. Sometimes being sure counted for as much as being right. Sometimes it counted for more than being right. If you were sure, if you could make other people sure, you might easily end up right even when you'd been wrong before.

Molotov also knew he lacked that kind of decisiveness. He said, "We can try prodding at Romania and Finland and see how they react—and how the *Reich* reacts. If the fascists' puppet states show weakness, that will be a sign the *Reich* itself is on the way to the ash-heap of history to which the dialectic consigns it."

Gromyko considered, then nodded. "Good enough, I think, Comrade General Secretary. And if the Germans show they are still alert in spite of this collective leadership, we can pull back at little risk to ourselves."

"Yes." Molotov permitted himself a small, cold smile of anticipation. "Just so. And it will be pleasant to pay them back in their own coin for the troubles they continue to cause us in the Ukraine. That will make Nikita Sergeyevich happy, too." He dismissed Gromyko, then spent the next twenty minutes wondering whether he wanted to make Khrushchev happy or not.

As the airliner droned on toward Kitty Hawk, Jonathan Yeager turned to his father and asked, "Do you think Mom is up to . . . taking care of what needs taking care of till we get back?"

He didn't want to mention Mickey and Donald. His father nodded approval that he hadn't, then answered, "She'll do fine—because she has to." He grinned. "She put up with you when you were a baby, so she ought to be able to manage the other."

Hearing about himself as a baby never failed to embarrass Jonathan. He changed the subject: "Four more years for President Warren, eh?"

"Sure enough," his father said. "I thought he'd win. I didn't think he'd take thirty-nine states." He didn't look so happy that Warren had taken thirty-nine states, either.

"Neither did I," said Jonathan, who knew his father had soured on the president but didn't know why. He clicked his tongue between his teeth. "I wish the election had come a couple of months later. Then I could have voted, too." Having to wait till he was almost twenty-five to help pick a president struck him as dreadfully unfair. He tried to make the best of it: "One vote wouldn't have mattered much this time around, anyhow."

"No, but you never can tell when it will," his father said. "As for that, you're lucky. When I was your age, I was living somewhere different every year. I never put down enough roots to be able to register and vote, so I never did, not till after the fighting stopped and I settled down with your mother."

Jonathan hadn't thought about that. Lord, his father had been an old man by the time he finally got the chance to vote. Before Jonathan could say anything about it, the pilot announced they'd be landing soon. This was Jonathan's first flight. His father took airplanes for granted, so he did his best to do the same. It wasn't easy. Watching the ground rush up, feeling the jounce as the plane hit the runway . . .

And you'll be going into space in a couple of days, he thought. *If you're getting excited about airplanes, what will you do when you blast off?*

A trim captain halfway between his age and his father's took charge of them when they got off the plane. The captain gave Jonathan's shaved a head a couple of glances, but didn't say anything.

The officer drove through drizzle to a barracks. The quarters the two Yeagers got struck Jonathan as spartan. His father accepted them with the air of a man who'd known worse. Sometimes Jonathan wondered what all his old man had been through in the days before he'd reached the scene himself. His father didn't talk about that much.

When they went to the mess hall, some of the soldiers there also gave Jonathan's shiny skull and casual civilian clothes odd looks. He ignored them. He wished he could have ignored the food. You could eat as much as you wanted, but he couldn't see why anybody would want to eat any of it.

Along with his father, he spent the time till he went into space getting lectured about everything that could go wrong and what to do if anything did. The short answer seemed to be, *If anything fails, you probably die.* The long answers were more complicated, but they added up to the same thing.

People did die going into space. He thought about that as he boarded the upper stage with REDTAIL painted on its nose. He didn't think about it for long, though. At not quite twenty-one, he didn't really believe he could die.

"Going to pay a call on the Lizards, eh?" said the pilot, a Navy lieutenant commander named Jacobson. "I'll get you there and I'll bring you home again—as long as we don't blow up."

"If we do, it'll be over in a hurry," Jonathan's father said. "Plenty of worse ways to go, believe you me."

"Oh, yeah." The Navy man glanced over at Jonathan. "First time I ever took up a guy dressed like a Lizard, I'll tell you that."

Jonathan knew his dad would defend him if he didn't speak up for himself. But he figured he was old enough to do that, even if he hadn't hit twenty-one yet: "One of the reasons I'm going up is that I dress this way. It's supposed to set their minds at ease, I guess you'd say." He still kept quiet about Kassquit; the lieutenant commander didn't need to know about her.

"Okay, kid," Jacobson said. "You're on the manifest, so you're going. Strap in good there. I know your old man's done this before, but you haven't, have you?"

"No, sir." Jonathan tried not to be nervous as he settled himself on the foam-padded seat. He didn't know how much good the safety harness would do, but he fastened it.

"Been a while for me," his father said. "But I know I'd rather go up there in just body paint and shorts than in my uniform here. The Race likes it hot."

"That's what I've heard," Jacobson said. "Well, get as comfy as you can, because we've got an hour to kill now, waiting for launch time."

That hour seemed to Jonathan to stretch endlessly. At last, though, the countdown, hallowed by endless books and films, reached zero. The rocket motor roared to life beneath him; all at once, it felt as if three or four guys had piled onto his chest. He'd had that happen in football games. But here, the guys didn't get up. They couldn't—they were him, his own body weight multiplied by acceleration. Though it was only a matter of minutes, the time felt as long as the hour's wait before blastoff.

Beside him, his father forced out a sentence a word at a time: "Watch that first step—it's a lulu."

"You all right, Dad?" Jonathan asked: wheezed, actually. He wasn't having too much trouble with the acceleration, but his father—heck, his father was practically an old man.

"I'll manage," Sam Yeager answered. "I reckon I was born to hang."

Before Jonathan could answer that, he stopped weighing several hundred pounds. In fact, as the rockets cut off, he stopped weighing anything at all. He discovered another reason for his safety harness: to keep him from floating all over the *Redtail's* cramped little cabin. He also discovered his stomach was trying to climb up his gullet hand over hand. Gulping, he did his best to get it back where it belonged.

Lieutenant Commander Jacobson recognized that gulp. "Air-sick bag to your right," he said. "Grab it if you need it. Grab it before you need it, if you please."

"I'll try," Jonathan said weakly. He found the bag, but discovered he didn't have to clap it over his mouth, at least not right away. The pilot, meanwhile, was talking in the language of the Race and getting answers from the Lizards. Every so often, he'd use the *Redtail's* motors to change course a little. Jonathan was too sunk in misery to pay much attention. His father was also quiet and thoughtful.

"We dock at the central hub of the Lizard ship," Jacobson said after a while. "They spin most of their vessels for artificial gravity, but the axis stays weightless, of course."

Again, Jonathan didn't much care. The ship the *Redtail* approached looked big enough to have respectable gravity just from its own mass. Clanks and bangs announced contact. "Very neat," his father said. "Very smooth." It hadn't felt smooth to him, but he had no standards of comparison.

"I'll be waiting for you when the Lizards bring you back," Jacobson said. "Have fun." By his snort, he found that unlikely.

When the hatch opened, it revealed a couple of Lizards floating in a corridor. "The two Tosevites for the interview will come with us," one of them said.

Jonathan undid his harness and pushed himself toward the Lizards. He flew as easily as if in a dream, but in a dream he wouldn't have been fighting nausea. His father followed him. Sure enough, it was hot and dry in the spaceship, as hot and dry as it got in L.A. with the devil winds blowing.

Little by little, as Jonathan and his father followed the Lizards outward from the hub, weight, or a semblance of it, returned. By the time they got to the second deck out, they were walking, not floating. Jonathan approved. His stomach approved even more. The curved horizon of each deck seemed as surreal as something out of an Escher painting, but bodily well-being made him willing to forgive a lot.

At last, when his weight felt about the way it should have, the Lizard guides stopped using stairs and led his father and him along a corridor to a chamber with an open doorway. "The female Kassquit awaits within," he said.

"We thank you," Jonathan's father replied in the language of the Race. He dropped back into English for Jonathan: "Let's do it."

"Okay, Dad," Jonathan said, also in English. "You go in first—that's how they do things." He was pleased he remembered some of what he'd learned.

"Right." His father squared his shoulders and entered the chamber. As Jonathan followed, his father went back to the language of the Race: "I greet you, superior female. I am Sam Yeager; here with me is my hatchling, Jonathan Yeager."

"I greet you, superior female," Jonathan echoed. He had to work to hold his voice steady, but thought he managed. He'd known Kassquit would be naked, but knowing and experiencing were two different things, especially since she wasn't just naked but shaved, not only her head but on all of her body.

"I greet you," she said. She took her nudity altogether for granted. Her face showed nothing of what she thought. "How strange to make the acquaintance of my own biological kind at last." She pointed to the body paint on Jonathan's chest. "I see you are now wearing the marking of a psychological researcher's assistant."

"Yes," Jonathan answered. "It is a true marking, for I assist my father here." He tried to eye her paint without eyeing her breasts. "It is not much different from yours."

"It is an accurate marking," Kassquit said. "But it is not a true marking, for the Race did not give it to you." She was as fussily precise as any real Lizard Jonathan had ever met.

His father asked, "How do you feel about meeting real Big Uglies at last?"

"Sore," Kassquit replied at once. Jonathan was wondering whether he'd understood her correctly when she went on, "I had to be immunized against many Tosevite diseases before taking the risk of physical contact."

"Ah," Sam Yeager said. "Yes, you wrote to me about that. I respect your courage. I hope we bring you no diseases."

"So do I," Kassquit said. "I have never known illness, and have no desire to make its acquaintance."

Jonathan gaped. He couldn't help himself. She'd never been sick a day in her life? That hardly seemed possible. He wondered what his father was thinking—his father who'd almost died in the influenza epidemic of 1918, and who complained these days that colds hung on a lot longer than they had when he was younger. Not wanting to contemplate his father's mortality, he wondered if Mickey and Donald would grow up disease-free, too, because they wouldn't meet any adult Lizards. He also wondered how many diseases Lizards had. They had doctors—he knew that much.

Kassquit said, "And what do you Big Uglies think of me?"

"You are an attractive young female," Jonathan's father answered. Jonathan would have agreed with that. His generation was a lot more relaxed about showing skin than his old man's had been, but not so altogether oblivious about its even being an issue as Kassquit was. He had to work to keep his eyes on her face, not her breasts or the shaved place between her legs. His father went on, "The biggest differences between you and a wild Big Ugly are that you shave all your hair and that your face does not move much."

"Your hatchling also shaves his hair," Kassquit said.

"Uh—not as much of it as you do," Jonathan said, and felt his face heat in a way that had nothing to do with the temperature of the chamber. "I try to look like a member of the Race."

"So do I—with rather more reason than you." Kassquit could be tart when she chose. She went on, "As for my face, my caregiver, Ttomalss, speculates that I needed to see moving faces when newly hatched to learn to move mine as wild Tosevites do. Since his face cannot move, I never acquired the art myself. I do not miss it." She shrugged. Her breasts were so small and firm, they hardly jiggled. Jonathan couldn't help noticing that.

His father asked, "From what you know of life down on Tosev 3, what do you miss about it?"

"Nothing!" Kassquit used an emphatic cough. "Except genetically, I am not of your kind."

"But that is a large exception," Jonathan's father said. "It means you can never be fully of the Race, either. What is it like, staying forever betwixt and between?"

What was going on behind Kassquit's impassive mask? Jonathan couldn't tell. At last, she said, "I was made to be a bridge between my kind and Big Uglies." She pointed at Jonathan. "He—your hatchling—is a bridge between your kind and the Race. So are you, Sam Yeager—or should I say, Regeya? We reach from opposite sides toward each other."

"To the Race, you are a Big Ugly, too," Jonathan's father pointed out.

Kassquit shrugged again. "I am of the Empire. You are not. Males and females of the Race, Rabotevs, Hallessi—they are my kind. You are not."

"Look in a mirror," Jonathan suggested. "Then try to say that. See if it is truth."

For the first time, Kassquit raised her voice. "This interview is over," she said sharply, with another emphatic cough. She strode out of the chamber through a side door Jonathan hadn't noticed till she used it. He glanced over at his father, wondering if he'd horribly botched things. Only when his dad winked back at him did he relax—a little.

If Ottawa wasn't the end of the line, you could see it from there. So thought David Goldfarb, at any rate, as he and his family stayed and stayed and stayed at the detention center for immigrants about whom the Canadians weren't certain. People who'd come in after the Goldfarbs had already gone on their way, but the authorities remained dissatisfied with him.

He was dissatisfied with them, too, and with their country. Ottawa lay six degrees of latitude south of London, ten degrees south of Belfast. But, as 1964 drifted toward 1965, he thought he'd chosen to emigrate to Siberia. He'd never known such cold as he found every time he stuck his nose outdoors. Schoolchildren learned about what the Gulf Stream did for Britain's climate, but he'd never had to think about it outside of school till now.

"How long?" Naomi asked one day after the children had

gone to sleep. "How long can they keep us like this in—in purgatory, is that the word?"

"That's the word, all right," Goldfarb told his wife. It was, all things considered, not the worst of purgatories—the flat where they'd been installed was bigger and boasted more amenities than the one they'd had in married officers' quarters back in Belfast. Still . . . "I just wish they'd let me get on with my life, dammit." He'd wished that since summer. It hadn't happened yet.

"Can your friend Jones do nothing about this?" she asked.

"If he could, I think he would have by now," Goldfarb answered gloomily. "It's not that I haven't written him, you know. Trouble is, I haven't just got friends in high places. I've got enemies there, too—too bloody many of them."

"We're here," Naomi said. "I will thank God for that. There is no Canadian fascist party, and I will thank God for that, too. Canada looks to the USA, not to the *Reich*. I have been through pogroms once in my life. Once is too often."

"I know," he said. "Believe me, I know. I went to Poland during the fighting, remember. And I saw Marseille, and what was left of the synagogue there."

"But you didn't see how things turned," Naomi told him. "When I was a little girl in Germany, before Hitler, having a different religion wasn't anything special—well, not too special, anyhow. And things . . . everything changed. I don't want our children to go through that. And my family got out before the worst." Her laugh was shaky. "If we hadn't got out before the worst, we wouldn't have got out at all."

"That won't happen here," Goldfarb said. "That's something. Whenever I feel the walls closing in around me, I remind myself we got out of Britain. Sooner or later, they have to get sick of holding us here and turn us loose." He wondered if he was whistling in the dark. He'd been saying the same thing for months now, and it hadn't happened yet.

Before Naomi could answer, the telephone jangled in the front room. "I'll get it," she said; her side of the bed was closer to the door. "Who could be calling at this hour?" Flannel nightgown swirling around her, she hurried away. Goldfarb came up with several possibilities, none of them pleasant. His wife returned a moment later. "It's for you—someone from the RCAF."

"At half past ten?" Goldfarb raised an eyebrow. "Someone calling to harass me, more likely. Well, I can always hang up on the blighter." He got out of bed and went to the telephone. "Goldfarb here." His voice was hard with suspicion.

Whoever was on the other end of the line sounded more like an Englishman than a Canadian; to Goldfarb's unpracticed ear, Canadians, however much they pointed out the differences in accent, still sounded like Yanks. "You're the Goldfarb who used to mess about with radars, isn't that right?"

"Yes, that's me," Goldfarb agreed. "Who's this?"

He didn't get a straight answer; he'd grown resigned to not getting straight answers. "You have an appointment at the Defense Ministry at eleven tomorrow. You'd do well to show up fifteen or twenty minutes early."

"Who is this?" Goldfarb repeated. This time, he not only got no answer, but the line went dead. He scratched his head as he hung up the telephone.

"Who was it?" Naomi asked when he came back to bed.

"Hanged if I know," he answered, and gave her the abbreviated conversation.

"Are you going to do what he told you?" she asked when he'd finished.

"I don't know that, either," he admitted, not very happily. "Fellow might have been trying to set me up." He saw in his mind's eye a couple of gunmen waiting outside the Defense Ministry. But they could be waiting as easily at eleven o'clock as at a quarter till. He sighed. "I suppose I will. I don't see how things could get any worse if I do. Now, though . . ." He turned out the light on the nightstand. "Now, I'm going to bed."

And, when he left the next morning, he left early enough to get to the Defense Ministry building near the Ottawa River well before the time scheduled for his latest round of grilling. Frigid air smote his face and burned in his lungs as soon as he left the block of flats where he'd been quartered. He turned up his greatcoat collar to protect some of his face from the ghastly weather, but the garment hadn't really been made to stand up against a Russian-style winter.

Had he been going more than half a dozen blocks up Sussex Drive, he would have tried to flag a taxi. But he might have stood there waiting for one—and, incidentally, freezing—longer than the walk would take him. Ottawa was a national capital, but it was nowhere near so richly supplied with cabs as London, or Belfast, either.

Even the ten-minute walk showed him many other differences between the capital of the country he'd left and that of the country that wasn't sure it wanted him as a part of it. Most of Ottawa was laid out on a sensible grid pattern, and all of it, to Goldfarb's eye, was new. No pubs dating back to the fifteenth century—and some looking as if they hadn't been swept up since—here. It was less than a hundred years since Victoria had chosen this town—till then a little lumbering village—as the capital of the new Dominion of Canada. Everything dated since then, and most since the turn of the century.

Off to the west, on Parliament Hill by the Ottawa River, stood the splendid buildings where the Canadian government deliberated. They weren't, in Goldfarb's no doubt prejudiced opinion, a patch on the Houses of Parliament in London, but they did stand out from the square boxes that dominated the city's architecture.

The Defense Ministry was one of those boxes. It replaced what had probably been a more imposing structure till the Lizards bombed it during the fighting. Ottawa hadn't suffered too badly then. Nor, for that matter, had most of Canada; just as the winter weather was too chilly to suit Goldfarb's overcoat, it was also too chilly to suit the Race. The USA had taken a worse beating.

A sentry in a uniform about halfway between U.S. and British styles took Goldfarb's name at the entrance. After checking it against a list, he nodded. "Yes, sir," he said. "They'll want you in room 327. Go to the west wing, then take the stairs or the elevator."

"Thanks," Goldfarb said, reminded anew he was in a foreign country; back home, someone would have urged him onto the lift. But, back home, too many people would have urged him to a very warm clime indeed because of who his ancestors were.

He hadn't been to room 327 before, and had to wander the corridors for a little while before he found it. When he went through the door with the frosted-glass window with 327 on it, he found himself in an antechamber. A fellow in RCAF uniform a few years older than he sat there, leafing through a magazine. The officer looked up, then got to his feet, a smile on his face. "Goldfarb, isn't it?" he said, sticking out his hand.

"Yes, sir," Goldfarb said. The man's rank badges proclaimed him a colonel, which still struck Goldfarb as odd; the Canadians had gone their own way on air force ranks a few years before. There were more urgent things he didn't know, though, such as why this bloke recognized him. "I'm afraid I can't quite . . ." He stopped and took a second, longer, look at the officer. His jaw dropped. "George Bagnall, by God! Good to see you, sir!" He pumped the proffered hand with enthusiasm.

"That's right," Bagnall said, smiling more widely. He was good-looking in the horsey British way, and had the proper accent, too, only slightly diluted by however long he'd spent in Canada. "Been a while since you shoved one of your bloody radars into the Lanc I was flight officer for, hasn't it?"

"You might say so, yes, sir," Goldfarb answered. "You were in Russia after that, weren't you? We met in a Dover pub. Some of the stories you were telling would make anybody's knees knock."

"And you joined the infantry when the Lizards invaded England," Bagnall said, "so you've got stories of your own. But that's all water over the dam. Rather more to the point here, I was in Russia with a certain—often very certain—chap by the name of Jerome Jones."

Something unfamiliar ran through Goldfarb's spirit. After a moment, he recognized it: hope. He wondered if he ought to let himself feel it. Disappointment, he knew, would only hurt more now. But he couldn't help asking, "So you're in touch with Jones, are you, sir?"

"I wasn't," Bagnall answered. "Hadn't been for years. I came over to this side of the Atlantic in '49; I could see the writing on the wall even then. Come to think of it, I was on one of the first ships—maybe *the* first ship—carrying heavy water from German-occupied Norway to England, though I hadn't the faintest notion what heavy water was in those days. So I knew the *Reich* and the U.K. were getting friendly, and I didn't like it worth a damn."

"Who did?" Goldfarb said. But the trouble was, altogether too many people did. He made himself stick to the business at hand: "You weren't in touch with Jones, you said. But you are now?"

"That's right." George Bagnall nodded. "He hunted me down, wrote me about the trouble you'd been having with the ginger smugglers, and about how they'd bollixed up your trip over here."

That *was* hope, by God; nothing else could produce such a pounding in the chest, such a lump in the throat. But, despite hope, asking the question that wanted asking took every ounce of courage Goldfarb had: "Can you . . . Can you do anything about it, sir?"

"Possibly, just possibly," Bagnall said, with such maddening English reserve that Goldfarb wasn't sure whether to take him literally or to think things were in the bag. Then he went on, "You're here to see Colonel McWilliams, aren't you?"

"That's right," David said. "You know him?"

"Possibly, just possibly," Bagnall repeated, but this time he couldn't keep the smile from sneaking back. "He was best man at my wedding, and I was a groomsman at his—his brother was best man for him."

"God bless Jerome Jones," David Goldfarb murmured. He'd intended it for a joke, but it came out sounding quite reverent.

Bagnall chuckled. "I hope God's listening—He probably doesn't hear that very often. But now, let's go have a word with Freddy, shall we?" He steered Goldfarb toward Colonel McWilliams' office, and Goldfarb was glad to let himself be steered.

Rance Auerbach shook his finger at Penny Summers. "You're getting itchy," he said. "I can *feel* you getting itchy, goddammit. It's summertime down here, and you're looking to make a deal. You're sweating to make a deal, any old kind of deal."

"Of course I'm sweating." Penny took off her straw hat and fanned herself with it. "It's hot outside."

"Not so bad," Auerbach said. "It's a dry kind of heat, more like L.A. than Fort Worth." He coughed, which hurt, and which also brought him back to what he'd been saying. "You're not going to distract me. You want to make a deal with you-know-who for you-know-what."

He wished he could have been more specific than that, but—

when he remembered to—he operated on the assumption that the Lizards were likely to be listening in on whatever Penny and he said in their apartment. So did she; she exclaimed, "I'd never do any such thing. I've learned my lesson."

Lizards often missed the tone in human conversations. Any Lizard monitoring this one, though, would have to be extraordinarily tone-deaf to miss the obvious fact that Penny was lying through her teeth. Rance didn't miss it. His rasping laugh turned into a rasping cough that felt as if it were going to tear his chest apart from the inside out. One day, maybe it would. Then he'd stop hurting.

"Serves you right," Penny said, which showed him how much sympathy he was likely to get from her.

"Bring me a beer, will you?" he asked, and she went and got him a Lion Lager from the icebox, and one for herself, too. He took a long pull at his. It helped cool the fire inside him. Then he lit a cigarette. That started it up again, but he didn't care. He offered Penny the pack—the packet, they called it here in Cape Town. She took one, leaning forward to light it from his.

After a couple of puffs, she said, "You know I wouldn't do anything stupid like that, Rance."

He laughed. "There's a hot one. You'd do anything you thought you could get away with."

"Who wouldn't?" Penny said. "But if I don't think I can get away with it, I'm not going to try it, right?"

"Well, yeah," Rance admitted. "Trouble is, you always think you're going to get away with it. If you were right all the damn time, we'd still be in Texas, or more likely in Tahiti."

She gave him a dirty look. "I didn't hear you telling me not to run that ginger down into Mexico. I didn't see you staying back in Texas when I did it, neither. If you had, you'd still be in that apartment by your lonesome, pouring your life down a bottle one day at a time."

"Maybe," he said, though he knew damn well she wasn't wrong. "So I'm here instead. If I hadn't been along, you'd probably still be in a Lizard jail. Of course, if I hadn't been around, you'd probably be dead now, but you don't think about that, not any more you don't."

Penny's scowl got fiercer. "All right, I've screwed some up before, but I really don't see what can go wrong this time."

Rance laughed again—he laughed till it hurt again, which didn't take long. "So there's nothing going on, and there's nothing that can go wrong with whatever is going on. I like that, I'll go to hell if I don't."

"God damn you," she said furiously. "You weren't supposed to know anything about it." They were both barely remembering the microphones they figured the Lizards had hidden in the apartment, if they were remembering at all.

"That's what the gal who's cheating on her husband always says, too, and she never thinks he's going to find out," Auerbach said. He didn't have the energy to get as mad as she was. "Just remember, if your boat springs a leak down here, I drown, too. And I don't feel like drowning, so you'd better level with me."

He could tell what was going on behind her blazing blue eyes. She was deciding whether to stay where she was and talk or walk out the door and never come back. Rather to his surprise, she kept on talking to him, even if what she had to say didn't directly bear on the argument. "Come on down to the Boomslang," she said. "We can hash it out there."

"Okay," he answered, and limped over to pick up his stick. He didn't feel like hobbling to the tavern, but he didn't feel like having the Lizards listen in on an argument about smuggling ginger, either. Even with the cane, his bad leg gave him hell as he went downstairs, and kept on barking when he got down onto the sidewalk. It would do worse when he had to go back upstairs, and he knew it. *Something to look forward to,* he thought.

A Lizard patrol was coming up the street toward him. The male in charge was even newer in town than he and Penny were. Auerbach waved; there were good Lizards and bad Lizards, same as there were good people and bad people, and this male seemed to be a pretty good egg. "I greet you, Gorppet," Rance called in the language of the Race.

"And I greet you, Rance Auerbach," the Lizard said. "You are easy to recognize because of the way you walk." He waved, too, and then led the patrol past Rance and away along the street.

As soon as the Lizards were out of earshot, Penny said, "If you know Gorppet, what are you getting your bowels in an uproar about over this ginger deal? He's not the kind of Lizard who'd rat on us. Anybody can see that."

"You're cooking up a deal with *him*?" Rance said, and Penny nodded. He stopped in his tracks; standing still hurt marginally less than walking. Before he said anything more, he paused to think. Penny wasn't wrong. Gorppet struck him as a Lizard who'd done a lot and seen a lot and wouldn't blab any of it. Still . . . "He's not that high-ranking. If he makes a deal with you, can he hold up his end of it?"

"Has he got the cash, you mean?" Penny asked, and Rance nodded. She said, "You don't have to be a general to be a big-time ginger smuggler, sweetie. A lot of the big ones are just clerks. They don't buy the stuff with their salaries—they buy it with what they make selling it to their buddies."

"Okay," Auerbach said after more thought. "I guess that makes sense. But Gorppet doesn't strike me as the type who'd do a lot of tasting. Didn't he get transferred down here on account of he's some kind of hero?"

"Yeah, but that doesn't mean he hasn't been tasting for years—I asked him," Penny said. *You would,* Rance thought. She went on, "He hasn't been in the selling end of the business till now, though. You're right about that. Part of what he got for being a hero, along with this transfer and his promotion, was a hell of a big reward for catching some Arab or other."

"Can he turn it into any kind of cash we can use?" Rance inquired.

"We, huh?" Penny said, and he felt foolish. She let him down easy by answering the question: "It's not that hard here in South Africa, you know. Everything turns into gold if you work it a little."

She was right about that. He couldn't deny it. "Only trouble with gold," he said slowly, "is that it's heavy if we've got to leave town in a hurry."

"It's heavy, yeah, but it doesn't take up much space," Penny replied. All of a sudden, she grabbed him and kissed him. A little black kid walking past smoking a cigarette giggled around it. She took no notice. When she was done with the kiss, she said, "And now you're starting to sound like somebody who might be interested in this deal after all."

"Who, me?" Auerbach looked back over his shoulder, as if

Penny might be talking to somebody else. She made as if to hit
him in the head. He ducked, then winced when his shoulder
twinged. "I don't know what the devil gave you that idea."

"Can't fool me—I know you too well," Penny said. Since
that was probably true, he didn't answer. She went on, "We can
do it—I know we can. And when we do, Tahiti here we come."

Not for the first time, Rance thought of warm, moist tropical
breezes and warm, moist native girls. But his long-ago West
Point days made him also think of logistics. "How do we get
there from here? Either way we go, it's through Lizard-held territory. They sent us down here to be good little boys and girls,
remember? They're liable not to want to let us loose again."

"If we've got the cash to get to Free France and live there,
we'll have the cash to pay off whoever we need to pay off to get
us the hell out of here," Penny said, and Rance could hardly
deny that was odds-on to be true. She continued, "Come on,
let's get over to the Boomslang. I've got to talk to Frederick."

Alarm bells clanged in Auerbach's mind. "What do you need
to talk to him about?" He didn't like Frederick much, not least
because he thought the Negro might like Penny a little too well.

She set her hands on her hips. "I've got to get the ginger
from somebody, don't I?" she said patiently. "Frederick's got
ginger, but he doesn't have the connections with the Lizards for
anything more than nickel-and-dime deals. I damn well do."

"Frederick's got connections with the local tough guys,
though," Rance said, "or I figure he does, anyhow. He probably
would have woke up dead one morning if he didn't. How's he
going to like you pulling off a big score on his home turf?"

"He'll get enough to keep him sweet—plenty for everybody,"
Penny said. "Rance, honey, this'll work. It *will*."

Her confidence was infectious—and Rance didn't feel like
living in South Africa for the rest of his life. It might be better
than a Lizard jail, but it wasn't a patch on the States. "Okay," he
said. "Let's go to the Boomslang." He wondered how much
trouble he was getting into. He'd find out. He was all too sure
of that.

Penny kissed him again. Nobody on the street snickered this
time. "You won't be sorry," she promised.

"I'm sorry already," Rance said, which wasn't quite true but
wasn't quite a lie, either.

Frederick wasn't in the saloon when Rance and Penny went inside. That surprised him; from everything he'd seen, Frederick damn near lived in the Boomslang. But, sure enough, the big black man breezed in before they'd got very far into their drinks. He sat down beside them as if he expected to talk business. And so he probably did—Penny must have started setting up this deal a while ago.

"So . . . we go forward?" he said.

"We go forward," Rance answered before Penny could say anything, "as soon as you convince us you're not going to sell us out to the Lizards or try to do us in and keep all the loot for yourself."

Frederick laughed as if those were the funniest ideas in the world. Auerbach didn't find them so amusing. Frederick might be greedy for cash, or he might want to screw them over because they were white. But then the Negro started to talk. He had a good line; Rance had to admit as much. The longer he listened, the more convinced he got—and the more he wondered how big a fool he was being this time.

No one in the village where Liu Han, Liu Mei, and Nieh Ho-T'ing had taken refuge dared destroy the altar to the spirits of Emperors past the little scaly devils had set up at the edge of the square. Despite protests from the three Communists, the villagers went right on burning offerings in front of the altar, as if it commemorated their ancestors and not forward-slung creatures with eye turrets.

"They are ignorant. They are superstitious," Liu Mei complained to her mother.

"They are peasants," Liu Han answered. "Living in Peking, you never really understood what the countryside is like. Now you're finding out." Living in Peking, she'd forgotten how abysmally ignorant the bulk of the Chinese people were, too. Returning to a village reminded her in a hurry.

"We have to instruct them," Liu Mei said.

"Either that or we have to get out of here," Liu Han said unhappily. "We probably should have already. The little devils are learning to use propaganda better and better. Before too long, the peasants in this village—and the peasants in too many villages all through China—will take sacrificing to the spirits of the little devils' dead Emperors as much for granted as they do sacrificing to the spirits of their own ancestors. It will help turn them into contented subjects."

"What can we do?" Liu Mei demanded. "How can we start a counterpropaganda campaign?"

It was a good question. It was, in fact, the perfect question. Liu Han wished she had the perfect answer for it. She wished she had any answer this side of flight for it—and how much good would flight do, if other villages were like this one? She didn't, and knew as much. "If the Lizards punish villages that harm the altars, no one will harm altars," she said. "Burning paper goods in front of them seems too cheap and easy to be very bothersome."

"But it enslaves," Liu Mei said, and Liu Han nodded. Her daughter went on, "How do we know the little scaly devils really are watching those altars, the way they say they are?"

"We don't," Liu Han admitted. "But they could be doing it, and who has the nerve to take a chance?"

"Someone should," Liu Mei insisted.

"Someone should, yes—but not you," Liu Han said. "You're all I have left in the world. The little devils already took you away from me once, and they tore my heart in two when they did. I couldn't stand it if they took you again."

Reproof in her voice, Liu Mei said, "The revolutionary cause is more important than any one person."

Liu Mei had been around revolutionary rhetoric all her life. She took it seriously—as seriously as the scaly devils took their spirits of Emperors past. Liu Han took revolutionary rhetoric seriously, too, but not quite in the same way. She was willing to fight for the Communist cause, but she didn't care to be a martyr for it. Maybe that was because she'd come to the Party as an adult. She believed its teachings, but she didn't believe *in* them the way she believed in the ghosts and spirits about whom she'd learned in childhood. Liu Mei did.

Liu Han didn't say any of that; Liu Mei would have ignored it. What Liu Han did say was, "What happens to people matters, too. I probably wouldn't have become a revolutionary if the little scaly devils hadn't kidnapped you."

"Even if you hadn't, the cause would go on." Liu Mei's logic was perfect—and perfectly irritating.

"I think it has gone on better with me in it," Liu Han said. Yes, she could hear the anger in her own voice.

And, for a wonder, Liu Mei heard it, too. "Well, maybe it has," she said, and walked out of the hut the two of them shared.

Staring after her, Liu Han stayed where she was: on the *kang*, the raised hearth where she spent as much time as she could during the winter. She'd been in the north more than twenty years now, and never had got used to the wretched weather. The wind off the Mongolian desert blew hot and dusty in the summer and sent blizzard after blizzard down on the countryside in winter. If Liu Mei wanted to stamp through snow, that was her business. She took it as much for granted as she did revolutionary fervor. After growing up near Hankow, Liu Han didn't.

She wondered what Liu Mei was doing out there. Glaring at the memorial tablet the scaly devils had set up, more than likely. Liu Han bit her lip. Her daughter wasn't going to listen to her. She could feel that in her bones. What would happen when Liu Mei took a hatchet to the tablet or smashed it with a rock or did whatever else she was thinking of doing?

Maybe nothing. Maybe the little devils were bluffing. Their propaganda was better these days than it had been—maybe they were paying more attention to their Chinese running dogs. But maybe they weren't bluffing. The spirits of Emperors past played a big role in their ideological system. Liu Mei didn't understand that. She thought superstitions were unimportant because they were false. She didn't understand the power they could hold over people's—and scaly devils'—minds.

Would she listen to Nieh Ho-T'ing if he told her the same things Liu Han had been telling her? Unfortunately, Liu Han doubted it. Liu Mei would do whatever she would do. She lacked the almost blind respect for her elders Liu Han had had at the same age. That lack of filial piety sprang from revolutionary rhetoric, too. Most of the time, Liu Han applauded it; it made Liu Mei freer than she had been. This once, Liu Han would have been content—would have been delighted—with a little old-fashioned blind obedience.

That evening, Liu Mei carried the chamber pot out to dump it in the snow. She was gone longer than Liu Han thought she should have been. Liu Han craned her neck, listening for smashing noises. None came, but she didn't rest easy. The next morning, she went out herself to make sure the memorial tablet was still there. When she saw it, she breathed a long, foggy sigh of relief. She said nothing of that to her daughter. Silence seemed wiser.

Less than a week later, she bitterly regretted that silence. Excited exclamations in the village square brought her out of her hut, hastily fastening the toggles of her quilted, cotton-stuffed jacket. Sure enough, it was just as she'd feared: someone had overturned and wrecked the memorial tablet.

"Eee!" the village headman squealed, looking about ready to tear his hair. He rounded on Liu Han and Nieh Ho-T'ing. "If the scaly devils come down on us, it will be your fault! Yours, do you hear me?"

"I don't think the scaly devils will do one thing," Liu Han said, much more calmly than she felt. Standing in front of his own hut, Nieh nodded. The headman subsided. Having important Communists in his village had taught him there were authorities greater than his.

All Liu Han could do was hope she'd been right. That she did, for the village's sake, and her own, and most of all her daughter's. She didn't know Liu Mei had destroyed the memorial tablet, but couldn't think who else might have. She didn't want to ask her daughter, either, for fear interrogators might tear the truth from her if she knew it.

The day passed quietly. So did the night. In the morning, helicopters that looked like flying tadpoles came thuttering toward the village from the east, from the direction of fallen Peking. They landed in the frozen, snow-covered fields. Little scaly devils, looking miserably cold, got out of them. Almost all the little devils carried weapons. Liu Han's heart sank.

One of the little devils, an unarmed one, spoke Chinese. "Let everyone assemble!" he shouted. "A crime has been committed here, a vile crime, and justice shall be done on the criminals."

"How do you even know who the criminals are?" someone shouted. "You weren't here. You didn't see."

"We were not here," the scaly devil agreed. "But we did see." He set down a machine he'd been carrying. Liu Han had seen its like in Peking: the little devils used them to display images. "This will show us who the criminal was," the little scaly devil declared, sticking a clawed forefinger into a control on the side of the machine.

As Liu Han had expected, a three-dimensional image sprang to life above the device. Several of the villagers exclaimed; even though they lived close to Peking, they'd never seen, never imagined, such a thing. They'd probably never even seen a human-made motion picture. Liu Han kept hoping some other villager had decided to wreck the memorial tablet. No such luck: there came Liu Mei, advancing on the tablet with a pick-axe handle in her hand and smashing it till it abruptly stopped recording. She must have done that during the night, but the image was as clear as if it were daylight.

Numbly, Liu Han waited for the little scaly devils to seize her daughter, or perhaps to shoot her down on the spot. But the one who spoke Chinese said, "Now you will tell us who this person is, and tell us immediately."

They have as much trouble knowing one person from another as we do with them, Liu Han thought. Hope surged in her. It grew even higher when no one gathered there in the snowy square said a word.

Then the scaly devil said, "You will tell us who this person is, and nothing bad will happen to this village." Yes, his kind were learning ruthlessness.

But still no one spoke. Some of the little devils hefted their weapons. Others examined the crowd, doing their best to identify the person in the recording, which kept repeating over and over. They didn't seem to be having any luck, though. Some of the villagers started to laugh at them.

The little scaly devil who spoke Chinese said, "You tell us who this person is, and you take everything this person has."

They were indeed learning. There was always someone, someone full of greed, who would pounce on an offer like that. And, sure enough, someone pointed at Liu Mei and shouted, "She did it! She's the one! She's a Red!"

Little scaly devils skittered forward to seize Liu Mei. Liu Han vowed a horrible revenge on the traitor. Maybe he also thought of that, for he kept right on pointing. "And there's her mother, and there's her mother's comrade! They're both Reds, too!" If he could remove the Communist presence from the village, maybe he could escape vengeance.

More scaly devils aimed their rifles at Liu Han. Numbly, she stuck her hands in the air. A little devil frisked her, and found a pistol in her pocket. That raised a fresh alarm. The scaly devils tied her hands behind her back, and served her daughter and Nieh Ho-T'ing the same way. Then they marched them back toward their helicopters.

I was captured once before, Liu Han thought. *Eventually, I got away. I can do it again.* She didn't know if she would, but she could. She was sure of it. Because of that, she didn't give way to despair, however tempted she might have been. *Something will turn up.* But, as she climbed into the helicopter, she couldn't imagine what.

Glen Johnson grimly pedaled away on one of the *Lewis and Clark*'s exercise bicycles. Sweat flew off him and floated in little, nasty drops in the exercise room. His wasn't the only sweat floating around in the chamber, either. Several other crewmen and -women also exercised there. In spite of the ventilation currents that also eventually got rid of the sweat, the place smelled like a locker room right after a big game.

After what seemed like forever, an alarm chimed. Panting, Johnson eased up on the pedals. His heart pounded in his chest. It usually took things easy in weightlessness, and resented having to go back and work for a living. But he'd keep on living longer if it did, so he exercised. Besides, he'd get in trouble with the powers that be if he didn't.

He unhooked the belt that held him onto the bike. The rest of the people in the chamber were doing the same. One of the troubles with strenuous exercise was that it made him look at a sweaty, tousled woman and not think of anything except how tired he was.

Lucy Vegetti, the sweaty, tousled woman in question, was looking at him, too. He wondered what that meant, and hoped to find out some time when his interest wasn't quite so academic. But the mineralogist, after wiping her face on her sleeve, told him at least some of what was on her mind: "I heard last night that somebody had spotted another Lizard spy ship."

"News to me," Johnson answered. People were gliding out of the chamber to change and sponge off in the two adjoining smaller rooms, one for men, the other for women. In five minutes, another shift of exercisers would mount the bikes.

Lucy looked worried. "How are we supposed to do what we came out here to do if the Race keeps spying on us?"

She'd asked the same question when she and Johnson discovered the first Lizard spy craft. He shrugged. "We've got to do it. If we don't, we might as well pack up and go home."

She shook her head. "No, that would be worse than not trying at all. It would be giving up. It would tell the Lizards they're stronger than we are."

"Well, they are stronger than we are," Johnson said. "If they weren't, we wouldn't have to worry about any of this folderol." Reluctantly, he pushed off toward his changing room, adding, "See you," over his shoulder.

"See you," Lucy said. Johnson sighed. He hadn't seen as much of her as he would have liked. She kept him thinking she was, or could be, interested, but things had gone no further than that. She didn't tease; that wasn't her style. But she was cautious. As a pilot, Johnson approved of caution—in moderate doses. As a man, he wished Lucy'd never heard of it. But, by the rules that had shaped up aboard the *Lewis and Clark*, the choice was all hers.

A damp sponge made a poor substitute for a hot shower, but it was what he had. After he'd cleaned up and put on a fresh pair of coveralls, he was about to go to his cubicle and either read or grab a little sack time when the intercom blared to life: "Lieutenant Colonel Johnson, report to the commandant's office immediately! Lieutenant Colonel Glen Johnson, report to the commandant's office immediately!"

"Oh, shit," Johnson muttered under his breath. "What have I done now? Or what does that iron-assed son of a bitch think I've done now?"

He got no answer from the intercom. He hadn't expected one. He wished Brigadier General Healey had yelled for him a couple of minutes earlier. Then, in good conscience, he could have reported to the commandant all sweaty and rank from his exercise period. He wondered if Healey kept close enough tabs on his schedule to know when he'd have sponged off. He wouldn't have been surprised. Healey seemed to know everything that happened aboard the *Lewis and Clark* as soon as it happened, sometimes even before it happened.

Alone among the officers on the spaceship, the commandant boasted an adjutant. "Reporting as ordered," Johnson told him. He half expected the spruce captain to make him cool his heels for half an hour before admitting him to Healey's august presence. *Hurry up and wait* had been an old army rule in the days of Julius Caesar. It was older now, but no less true.

But Captain Guilloux said, "Go on in, sir. The commandant is expecting you."

Since Healey had summoned him, that wasn't the biggest surprise in the world. But Johnson just nodded, said, "Thanks," and glided past Guilloux and through the door into the commandant's office. Saluting, he repeated what he'd told the adjutant: "Reporting as ordered, sir."

"Yes." As usual, Healey looked like a bulldog who wanted to take a bite out of somebody. He'd wanted to take a bite out of Johnson when the pilot came aboard—either take a bite out of him or boot him out the air lock, one. He still wasn't happy with Johnson, not even close. But Johnson wasn't his biggest worry. His next words showed what was: "How would you like to stick a finger in one of the Lizards' eye turrets?"

He couldn't mean it literally—so far as Johnson knew, there were no live Lizards within a couple of a hundred million miles. But what he likely did mean wasn't hard to figure out: "Have we got permission from Little Rock to blast their spy ship to hell and gone, sir?"

"No." Healey looked as if having to give that answer made him want to bite, too. "But we have got permission to explore the possibility of covering the damn thing with black-painted plastic sheeting or aluminum foil or anything else we can spare that'll make it harder for them to monitor us."

Johnson nodded. "I've heard there's a second ship in the neighborhood, too."

Before he could say anything else, Brigadier General Healey pounced: "Where did you hear that, and from whom? It's not supposed to be public news." Johnson stood—or rather, floated— mute. He wasn't about to rat on Lucy Vegetti, even if she hadn't given him a tumble yet. Healey made a sour face. "Never mind, then. What you heard is true. We can only hope there aren't any others we haven't found."

"Yes, sir." Johnson considered. "Well, if that's so, how much trouble can we give them? Blind 'em, sure, but can we jam their radar and their radio receivers? If we can't, is throwing a sack over them worth the trouble we'll get into for doing it?"

Now Healey turned the full power of that high-wattage glare on him. "If you're yellow, Lieutenant Colonel, I can find somebody else for the job."

"Sir, as far as I'm concerned, you can go to the devil," Johnson said evenly.

Healey looked as if he'd just got a punch in the nose. Unless Johnson missed his guess, nobody'd told the commandant anything like that in a hell of a long time. He wished he'd said something worse. *Goddamn military discipline,* he thought. After a couple of deep, angry breaths, Healey growled, "You are insubordinate."

"Maybe so, sir," Johnson replied, "but all I was trying to do was figure the angles, and you went and called me a coward. You've got my war record, sir. If that doesn't tell you different, I don't know what would."

Brigadier General Healey kept on glaring. Johnson floated in place, one hand securing him to the chair bolted to the floor in front of the commandant's desk, the chair in which he'd be sitting if there were gravity or a semblance of it. When he didn't buckle or beg for mercy, Healey said, "Very well, let it go." But it wasn't forgotten; every line of his face declared how unforgotten it was.

Trying to get back to business, Johnson asked, "Sir, *is* it worth it to do whatever we can to those ships if we don't destroy them? If it is, send me. I'll go."

"As yet, we are still evaluating that," Healey said gruffly. "Not all the variables are known."

"Well, of course we can't know ahead of time what the Lizards will do if . . ." Johnson's voice trailed away. Healey's face had changed. He'd missed something, and the commandant was silently laughing at him on account of it. And, after a moment, he realized what it was. "Oh. Do we know if these ships are armed, sir?"

"That's one of the things we're interested in finding out," the commandant answered, deadpan.

"Yes, sir," Johnson said, just as deadpan. So Healey was thinking about turning him into a guinea pig, eh? That didn't surprise him, not even a little bit. "When do you want me to go out, and which one do you want me to visit?"

"We haven't prepared the covering material yet," Healey said. "When we do—and if we decide to—you will be informed. Until then, dismissed."

After saluting, Johnson launched himself out of the commandant's office. He glided straight past Captain Guilloux, then used the handholds in the corridor to pull himself back to his tiny cubicle. The only thing his bunk and the straps securing him to it did that a stretch of empty air couldn't was to make sure he didn't bump up against anything while sleeping.

He kept waiting for the order to climb into a hot rod and go blind one of the Lizards' spy ships. The order kept on not coming. He didn't want to ask Brigadier General Healey why it didn't come. After a week or so, he broached the subject to Walter Stone in an oblique way.

Stone nodded. "I know what you're talking about. I don't think you have to worry very much."

"I wasn't worried," Johnson said, which would do for a lie till a better one came along. "I was curious, though; I'll say that."

"Sure you were." Stone grinned at him, there in the privacy of the *Lewis and Clark*'s control room. Johnson grinned back. The spaceship's chief pilot had been through the mill, even if he was an Army Air Force man and not a Marine. He knew the feeling of going out on a mission from which you didn't expect to come back. He went on, "You don't know this officially because I don't know it officially, but we got, uh, discouraged from going on with that."

"Oh, yeah?" Johnson leaned forward in his seat. "I'm all ears."

"That's not what Healey thinks—he figures you're all mouth and brass balls," Stone answered with a chuckle. "Anyway, this is all scuttlebutt, and you haven't heard it from me." Solemnly, Johnson crossed his heart, which made the number-one pilot laugh out loud. "What I heard is, we did a dry run, with a hot rod under radio control. Whoever was in charge of the beast inched it up to the spy ship, and when it got close enough . . ."

"Yeah?" Johnson said. "What happened then?" Stone had hooked him, sure as if he'd been telling a hell of a dirty joke.

"Then the damn thing—the spy ship, not the hot rod—broke radio silence, or that's what they say," Stone told him. "It sent out a recorded message in the Lizards' language, something like, 'You come any closer or do anything cute and we count it as an act of war.' And so they backed up the hot rod and sent it home, and nobody's said a word about it since."

"Is that a fact?" Johnson said.

"Damned if I know," Stone answered. "But it's what I've heard."

No wonder Healey isn't sending for me, Johnson thought. Then something else crossed his mind: *I'm damn glad I didn't open up on the lousy thing.*

Jonathan Yeager sprawled across his bed, working on the chemistry notes and problems he'd missed because he'd gone into space. Karen sat in the desk chair a couple of feet away. The bedroom door remained decorously open. That was a house rule. Now that he'd finally turned twenty-one, Jonathan had proposed to his folks that they change it. They'd proposed to him that he keep his mouth shut as long as he lived under their roof.

He pointed to a stretch of Karen's notes he had trouble following. "What was Dr. Cobb saying about stoichiometry here?"

Karen pulled the chair closer and bent over to see what he was talking about. Her red hair tickled his ear. "Oh, that," she said, a little sheepishly. "I didn't quite get that myself."

He sighed. "Okay, I'll ask after lecture tomorrow." He made motions that would have implied tearing his hair if he'd had any hair to tear. "I don't think I'm ever going to get all caught up, and I was only gone a week."

"What was it like?" Karen asked. She'd been asking that ever since he got back from Kitty Hawk. He'd tried several different ways of explaining, but none of them satisfied her—or him, really.

After some thought, he took another shot at it: "You've read Edgar Rice Burroughs, right?" When Karen nodded, he went on, "You know how the apes raised Tarzan but he still turned out to be a man pretty much like other men?" She nodded again. Jonathan said, "Well, it was *nothing* like that. I mean, nothing at all. Kassquit looks like a person, but she doesn't act like a person. She acts just like a Lizard. My dad was right." He laughed a little; that wasn't something he said every day. "We just play at being Lizards. She's not playing. She wishes she had scales—you can tell."

Karen nodded again, this time thoughtfully. "I can see that, I guess." She paused, then found a different question, or maybe a different version of the same one: "How did it feel, talking about important things with a woman who wasn't wearing any clothes?"

Was *that* what she'd been getting at all along? Jonathan answered, "For me, it felt funny at first. Kassquit didn't even think about it, and I tried not to notice—you know what I mean?" He'd tried; he hadn't succeeded too well. Not wanting to admit as much, he added, "I think it flustered my dad worse than it did me."

"That's how it works for people that old," she agreed with careless cruelty. Jonathan felt he'd passed an obscure test. He'd been attracted to Liu Mei when she visited Los Angeles, so now Karen was nervous about every female he met. Here, he thought she was wasting worry. UCLA boasted tons of pretty girls, all of them far more accessible and far more like him than one raised by aliens who'd spent her whole life on a starship.

Interesting, now—Kassquit was certainly interesting. Fascinating, even. But attractive? He'd seen all of her, every bit; she was no more shy of herself than a Lizard was. He shook his head. No, he didn't think so.

"What?" Karen asked.

Before Jonathan could answer, one of the Lizard hatchlings skittered down the hall. He stopped in the doorway, his eye turrets swinging from Jonathan to Karen and back again. They lingered longer on Karen, not because the hatchling found her attractive—a really preposterous notion—but because he saw her less often. Jonathan waved. "Hello, Donald," he called.

Donald waved back. He and Mickey had got good at gestures, though the sounds they made were nothing but hissing babbles.

"I greet you," Karen called to him in the language of the Race.

He stared at her as if he'd never heard such noises before. And, except from himself and Mickey, he hadn't. "Don't do that," Jonathan told Karen. "My dad would go through the roof if he heard you. We're supposed to raise them like people, not like Lizards. When they learn to talk, they'll learn English."

"Okay. I'm sorry," Karen said. "I knew that, but I forgot. When I see a Lizard, I want to talk Lizard talk."

"Mickey and Donald won't be Lizards, any more than Kassquit is really a person," Jonathan said. Then he paused. "Still and all, I think there's a little part of her that wants to be a person, even if she doesn't know how."

Karen didn't want him talking about Kassquit any more. She made a point of changing the subject. She made a literal point: pointing at Donald, she said, "He sure is getting big."

"I know," Jonathan said. "He and Mickey are an awful lot bigger than human one-year-olds would be." His mother would have flayed him if he'd said *Mickey and him*. However he said it, it was true. The baby Lizards weren't babies any more, not to look at they weren't. They'd grown almost as if inflated by CO_2 cartridges, and were closer in size to adult Lizards than to what they'd been when they came out of their eggs.

Liu Mei never learned to smile. Neither did Kassquit, Jonathan thought. *I wonder what sorts of things Mickey and Donald will never be able to do because we're raising them instead of Lizards*. He didn't know. He couldn't know. And he didn't feel like broaching the subject to Karen, not when she plainly didn't want him thinking about Liu Mei or Kassquit.

After another wave, Donald scurried back up the hall. Karen said, "I wonder why they grow so much faster than people do."

"Dad says it's because they take care of themselves so much more than human babies do," Jonathan answered. "If you're on your own, the bigger you are, the fewer the things that can eat you and the more things you can eat."

"That sounds like it makes pretty good sense," Karen said. Jonathan automatically turned that *like* to *as if* in his mind. Karen was lucky enough not to have parents who got up in arms over grammar.

With a grin, he said, "Yeah, I know, but it's liable to be true anyhow." Karen started to nod, then noticed what he'd said and made a face. He made one back at her. With the air of somebody granting a great concession, he went on, "The things Dad says usually make pretty good sense."

"I know," Karen said. "You're so lucky. At least your parents know we're living in the twentieth century. My folks think we're still back in horse-and-buggy days. Or if they don't think so, they wish we were."

Jonathan didn't reckon himself particularly lucky in his

choice of parents. Very few people his age did, but that never crossed his mind. He thought Mr. and Mrs. Culpepper were pretty nice, but he didn't have to try to live with them. Pretty soon, he wouldn't have to try to live with his own folks, either. Part of him eagerly looked forward to that. The rest of him wanted to stay right here, in the bedroom where he'd lived so long.

If he did stay, he couldn't very well share the bedroom with Karen. That was the best argument he could think of for leaving the nest.

His mother looked in on them. "You kids are working hard," she said. "Would you like some cookies and a couple of Cokes to keep you going?"

"Okay," Jonathan said.

"Sure, Mrs. Yeager. Thanks," Karen said.

The look Jonathan's mother sent him said what she wouldn't say in words: that he had no manners, but his girlfriend did. Getting away from looks like that was another good reason for striking out on his own.

Chocolate-chip cookies and sodas eased his annoyance. Were he living by himself, he'd have had to get up and fetch them himself. *If I were married, I could ask my wife to bring them,* he thought. He glanced over at Karen. Looking at her made him think of some of marriage's other obvious advantages, too. That *she* might ask *him* to fetch Cokes and cookies didn't cross his mind.

While Jonathan and Karen were eating cookies, Mickey came into the room. He watched them in fascination. Before he and Donald were allowed to go outside their room, they hadn't seen the Yeagers eating. For all Jonathan knew, they might have thought they were the only ones who did.

They knew better now. They'd also had to learn that grabbing whatever they wanted off people's plates was against the rules. That had produced some interesting and lively scenes. Now they were good—most of the time, anyhow.

Mickey was good more often than Donald. His eye turrets followed a cookie from the paper plate on the bed by Jonathan to Jonathan's mouth. Watching, Karen snickered. "You ought to put sunglasses on him and give him a little tin cup," she said.

"I'll do better than that." Jonathan snapped his fingers, the signal his family had worked out after trial and error to let the little Lizards know they could come up and have some of the food a human was eating. Mickey advanced, hand outstretched. Jonathan held out a cookie. Mickey took it with surprising delicacy. Then, delicacy forgotten, he stuffed it into his mouth.

Jonathan waited to see how he liked it. Lizards were more carnivorous than people, and Mickey and Donald were as emphatic as any human babies or toddlers about rejecting things they didn't care for. But Mickey, after a couple of meditative smacks, gave a gulp, and the cookie was gone. He pointed to the paper plate, then rubbed his belly.

Karen giggled. "He's saying he wants some more."

"He sure is. And he's not trying to steal it, either. Good boy, Mickey." Jonathan held out another cookie. "You want this?"

Mickey's head went up and down in an unmistakable nod. "He's really learning," Karen said. "The Lizards use a hand gesture when they mean yes."

"He doesn't know what the Lizards do, though," Jonathan said. "He just knows what we do. That's the idea." He gave Mickey another cookie. This one disappeared without meditation. Mickey rubbed his belly again. Jonathan laughed. "You're going to get fat. You give him one, Karen."

"Okay," she said. "That way you get to keep more of yours, huh? See, I'm on to you." But she held out a cookie. "Here, Mickey. It's all right. You can have it."

Mickey hesitated. He was shier than Donald. And neither hatchling was as used to Karen as he was to the Yeagers. But the lure of chocolate chips seduced Mickey, as it had so many before him. He skittered forward, snatched the cookie out of Karen's hand, and then scuttled away so she couldn't grab him.

"You like that?" Karen said as he devoured the prize. "I bet you do. You want another one? I bet you do." Mickey stood there, eye turrets riveted on the cookie in her hand. "Come on. You want it, don't you?"

Mickey opened his mouth. That alarmed Jonathan. Was the hatchling going to take the cookie that way? He'd mostly outgrown such behavior—and Jonathan didn't want him biting Karen. But, instead of going forward, Mickey stood there; he quivered a little, as if from intense mental effort. At last, he made a sound: "Esss."

"Jesus," Jonathan said softly. He sprang to his feet. "Give him the cookie, Karen. He just said, 'Yes.' " He hurried past her. "I'm going to get my folks. If he's started talking, they need to know about it."

The motorcar pulled to a halt in front of a house not much different from the one in which Straha lived. By now, the ex-shiplord had grown used to stucco homes painted in bland pastels with swaths of grass in front of them. They seemed to be the local Tosevites' ideal. He'd never been able to figure out why—taking care of grass struck him as a waste of both time and water—but it was so.

"Here we are," his driver said. "You may have a more interesting time than you expect."

"Why?" Straha asked. "Do you think someone will start shooting at the house, as happened on an earlier visit to Sam Yeager?"

"No, that is not what I meant," the driver answered. "If that happens, I will do my best to see that no harm comes to you. But the surprise I had in mind is not likely to be dangerous."

"What is it, then?" Straha demanded.

His driver smiled. "If I told you, Shiplord, it would not be a surprise any more. Go on. The Yeagers will be waiting for you. And who knows? You may not be surprised at all."

"Who knows?" Straha said irritably. "I may one day have a driver who does not enjoy annoying me." The driver laughed a loud, braying Tosevite laugh, which annoyed Straha more than ever. He got out of the motorcar and slammed the door. That only made the driver laugh louder.

Tailstump quivering with irritation he couldn't hide, Straha went up onto the front porch and rang the bell. He could hear it chime inside the house. He never had liked bells; he thought hisses the proper way to gain attention. But this was not his world, not his species. If the American Big Uglies liked bells and pastel stucco and grass, he had to accommodate himself to them, not the other way round.

The door opened. There stood Barbara Yeager. She briefly bent into the posture of respect. "I greet you, Shiplord," she said in the language of the Race. "How are you?"

"Fine, thanks," Straha answered in English. "And you?"

"We are also well," Sam Yeager's mate answered. She shifted to English, too: "Sam! Straha's here."

"I'm coming, hon," Yeager called. Straha listened with mingled amusement and perplexity. Despite having lived so long among the Big Uglies, he didn't—by the nature of things, he couldn't—fully understand the way their family relationships worked. Neither the Race, the Rabotevs, nor the Hallessi had anything similar, so that was hardly surprising. The former shiplord found endearments like the one Yeager had used particularly hard to fathom. They struck him as informal honorifics, a contradiction in terms if ever there was one. But the Big Uglies didn't seem to find it a contradiction; they used them all the time.

Sam Yeager came into the front room. "I greet you, Shiplord," he said, as his mate had before. "I hope things are not too bad."

"No, not too," Straha answered. With Sam Yeager, he stuck to his own language; more than with any other Big Ugly, even his driver, he felt as if he were talking with another male of the Race. That *I hope things are not too bad* proved how well Yeager understood his predicament. Any other Tosevite would have said, *I hope things are good.* Things weren't good. They couldn't be, not in exile. They could be not too bad.

"Come on into the kitchen, then," Yeager said. "I have a new kind of salami you might want to try. I have rum and vodka— and bourbon for Barbara and me. And I have ginger, if you care for a taste."

"I shall gladly try the salami," Straha said. "If you pour me the glass of rum, I expect it will manage to empty itself. But I shall decline the ginger, thank you."

"Whatever suits you," Sam Yeager said, turning and walking through the front room and dining room toward the kitchen. His mate and Straha followed. Over his shoulder, Yeager went on, "Shiplord, you had better know by now that I do not mind if you taste ginger, any more than I mind if you drink alcohol. No Prohibition here." The second word of the last sentence came out in English. By Yeager's chuckle, it was a joke.

Straha didn't get it. "Prohibition?" he echoed, confused.

"When I was young, the United States tried to prohibit the drinking of alcohol," Yeager explained. "It did not work. Too many Tosevites like alcohol too well. I wonder if that will happen with the Race and ginger."

Addicted to the Tosevite herb though he was, Straha said, "I hope not. I can drink a little alcohol and have my mood slightly altered, or I can drink more for greater changes. Ginger is not like that. If I taste ginger, I *will* enjoy the lift it gives me, and I *will* suffer the depression afterwards. I have far less control with it than I do with alcohol, and the same holds true for other tasters."

"All right," Yeager said. "That makes better sense than a lot of things I have heard." Once in the kitchen, he got out glasses, poured rum into Straha's, and put ice and whiskey into the ones for his mate and himself. He raised his in salute. "Mud in your eye." That was in English, too.

The Race also used informal toasts. After drinking to Yeager's, Straha returned one: "May your toeclaws tingle." Yeager drank to that, then started slicing salami. Straha went on, "I never have understood why you Big Uglies do not freeze up, what with all the ice you use."

He had been teasing the Yeagers about that for a long time. "We like it," Barbara said. "If you are too ignorant to appreciate it, that only leaves more for us."

"We have no reason to like ice," Straha said. "If this planet did not have so much snow and ice, we would have had a better chance of conquering it. Of course, if I had been made fleetlord instead of failing in my effort to overthrow Atvar, we would also have had a better chance of conquering it."

After more than twenty Tosevite years, he seldom let his bitterness show so openly. Sam Yeager said, "We Big Uglies are glad you failed, then. Here, see how you like this." He gave Straha a plate full of salami slices.

After trying one, the ex-shiplord said, "It is certainly salty enough. Some of the Tosevite spices I enjoy, while others are harsh on my tongue." He turned an eye turret toward the wrapper in which the salami had come. He found English spelling a masterpiece of inefficiency even by Tosevite standards, but he could read the language well enough. "Hebrew National?" he asked. "Hebrew has to do with the Big Uglies called Jews, is it not so? Is this salami brought into the United States from regions the Race rules?"

"No, we have plenty of Jews here, too," Yeager told him.

"This salami is made only with beef. Jews are not supposed to eat pork."

"One more superstition I shall never understand," Straha said.

Yeager shrugged. "I am not a Jew, so I cannot say I understand it, either. But they follow it."

Back in the days before the Empire unified Home—long before the Empire unified Home—males and females of the Race had held such preposterous beliefs. They'd all been subsumed in the simple elegance of reverencing the spirits of Emperors past. Only scholars knew any details of the ancient beliefs. But here on Tosev 3, the Big Uglies had developed a formidable civilization while keeping their bizarre hodgepodge of superstitions. It was a puzzlement.

Before Straha could remark on what a puzzlement it was, he heard a loud thump from down the hall, and then another. "What was that?" he asked.

"That?" Sam Yeager said. "That was . . . a research project."

"What kind of research project goes thump?" Straha asked.

"A noisy one," the Big Ugly answered, which was no answer at all. After yet another thump, Yeager added, "A very noisy one."

Straha was about to insist on some sort of real explanation when he got one, not from Sam Yeager but again from down the hall. Though they came only faintly, as if through a door, the hisses and squawks he heard were unmistakable. "You have other males or females of the Race here!" he exclaimed. "Are they prisoners?" He cocked his head to one side, listening intently. Try as he would, he could make out no words. Then he realized there were no words to make out. "Hatchlings! You have hatchlings!"

Sam and Barbara Yeager looked at each other. That was much more obvious among Big Uglies than in the Race, for the Tosevites had to turn their whole heads. In English, Barbara Yeager said, "I told you we should have put them out in the garage."

"Yeah, you did," Sam answered in the same language. "But the neighbors might have seen them when we moved them, and that would have been worse." He swung back toward Straha. "The shiplord here, he's a soldier. He knows how to keep secrets."

His tone implied that Straha had better know how to keep

secrets. Straha hardly noticed. He was still too astonished. "How did you get hold of hatchlings?" he asked. "Why did you get hold of hatchlings?"

Sam Yeager regathered his composure and returned to the language of the Race: "I cannot tell you how we got the eggs, for I do not know myself. You understand that, Shiplord: what I do not know, I cannot betray. Why? So we can raise them as Big Uglies, or see how close they can come to being like us."

Just for a moment, Straha felt as if he were a shiplord of the Race once more. To have his own kind raised by these Tosevite barbarians, never to know their own heritage . . . "It is an outrage!" he shouted, tailstump quivering with fury.

"Maybe it is," Yeager said, which surprised him. The Big Ugly went on, "But if it is, how is it anything different from what you have done with Kassquit?"

"But these are ours," Straha said automatically. Even he realized that wasn't a good enough answer. Some of the blind anger that had filled him began to seep away. He was glad he hadn't tasted ginger. If he had, he probably would have bitten and clawed first and talked later, if at all.

"We are free. We are independent. We have as much right to do this as you do," Sam Yeager said. Logically, he was right.

But logic still had a hard time penetrating. "You have robbed them of their heritage," Straha burst out.

"Maybe," Yeager said, "but maybe not, too. We have had them a little more than two of your years, and they are already starting to talk."

"What?" Straha stared. "That is impossible."

"It is a truth," Sam Yeager said, and the ex-shiplord found him impossible to disbelieve.

Another realization exploded within Straha: his driver had known about this all along. He'd known, and never said a word. No, not quite never. Now some of the things he'd said that hadn't made sense to Straha did. Straha wondered what he could do to take revenge on the Big Ugly. Nothing came to mind, not right away, but something would, something would. He was sure of that.

"This is all quite astonishing," he said at last.

"I would sooner you had not learned," Yeager said, "but they got too boisterous." He ruefully spread his hands. "And you

understand security, so it is not so bad." Was he trying to convince himself? Probably.

"Yes, I understand security," Straha agreed. But his thoughts
were far away. He knew he would need something approaching a
miracle to get back into Atvar's good graces and be allowed to
rejoin the Race. Reporting a couple of hatchlings kidnapped by
the Big Uglies . . . would that be enough? He didn't know. He
couldn't know—but it was worth thinking about.

Gorppet wasn't so sure he'd been smart in coming to South
Africa after all. It was a lot more easygoing than his longtime
former posting, that was certain. Of course, that would have
been true of anywhere the Race ruled. But the weather, as far as
he was concerned, left a lot to be desired. In what was allegedly
summer in this hemisphere, it was tolerable, he supposed, but
what would winter be like? Not good—he was sure of that. He
hoped it wouldn't be as bad as the SSSR. The males stationed
here said it wouldn't, but Gorppet had learned the hard way not
to trust what others said without testing it.

He sighed as he tramped through the streets of Cape Town's
District Six. However atrocious the Big Uglies in the district
known as Iraq had been, he'd enjoyed the weather there. Every
so often, he'd even felt hot. He didn't think he would do
that here.

Black and brown and pinkish-tan Big Uglies filled the streets
around him. They chattered in several languages he didn't understand. Learning Arabic had come in handy in Iraq, but did
him no good here. Even this script was different from the one
they'd used there. He hadn't been able to read Arabic writing, but
he'd got used to the way it looked. These angular characters
seemed wrong somehow.

He paused at a street corner. More motorized vehicles were
on the streets here than in Basra or Baghdad—many more driven
by Big Uglies. More bicycles were on the road, too. They were
ingenious contraptions, and made individual Tosevites into little
missiles.

A male Big Ugly came up to the corner at a slow limp, leaning
on a stick. "I greet you, Gorppet," he said, speaking the language
of the Race with a thick accent.

"And I greet you, Rance Auerbach," Gorppet replied. "How are you today?"

"Bad," Auerbach answered, as he usually did. He used an emphatic cough, and then several that showed nothing but infirmity. "Very bad. That hurts."

"I believe it. It sounds as if it should," Gorppet said. "A wound from the fighting, you told me?"

"That is right." Auerbach nodded. "One of your miserable friends put a couple of bullets in me, and I have never been the same since." He shrugged. "And some of your friends may limp on account of bullets I put in them back then. That is how things were. I only wish the male would have missed me."

"I can understand that." Gorppet liked Rance Auerbach, liked him better than he'd expected to like any Big Ugly. Auerbach was able to greet him and deal with him without rancor in spite of what had happened during the fighting. Gorppet thought he himself would have been able to do the same with the Soviet Tosevites he'd faced then. They'd all been doing what they'd been told to do, and doing it as best they could. How could you hate anyone who'd only been doing his best?

Auerbach said, "Come on. Let us go to the Boomslang. Penny and Frederick will be waiting for us."

"All right," Gorppet said. "I will listen to what all of you have to say." He paused, then added, "I am less sure I would listen to the others if you were not with them."

"Me?" Auerbach said, and Gorppet knew he'd startled the Big Ugly. "Why me? Penny found you. Of all of us involved in the deal, I am the least."

Gorppet made the negative hand gesture. "No. You are mistaken. I understand you in ways I do not understand the female and the black-skinned male. We have been through many of the same things, you and I. It gives us something of a bond."

"Maybe." Auerbach didn't sound convinced.

But Gorppet wanted to convince him. "It is a truth," he said earnestly. "Did you never feel, back in those days, that you had more likenesses to the males you fought than to your own high officers and to the Tosevites who were not fighting?"

Rance Auerbach stopped walking so abruptly, Gorppet took a couple of paces before realizing the Big Ugly wasn't with him any more. The male turned an eye turret back toward Auerbach.

Hoarsely, the Tosevite said, "I had that feeling more times than I could count. I did not know it worked the other way."

"Well, it did," Gorppet said. "We were sent here, to a world about which, as it turned out, we knew less than nothing. We were told conquering it would be easy, a walk in the sand. We were told all sorts of things. Not one of them turned out to be truth. Is it any wonder that we were not always happy with those who led us and those who sent us forth?"

"No wonder at all," Auerbach said with another emphatic cough. This time, he managed not to add any involuntary coughs of his own.

When he and Gorppet walked into the Boomslang together, the place got very quiet all at once. It was a dangerous sort of quiet. Having come from Basra and Baghdad, Gorppet knew that sort of quiet all too well. He let a finger slide toward the safety on his rifle. If anyone wanted trouble, he was ready to give plenty.

But then the black male named Frederick spoke in one of the local languages, and everybody else relaxed. "I greet you," he called to Gorppet from the table he shared with the female with gaudy yellow hair. His accent was different from hers and Auerbach's, more musical. "Come—have something to drink and we shall talk."

"Good enough," Gorppet said. The chair in which he sat was made for Tosevite posteriors, but he had survived such seats before and knew he could again. "I do not want that nasty brown stuff you two are drinking there—the alcohol straight from the fruit tastes better to me."

"Wine!" Penny Summers called to the Big Ugly who served drinks, and Gorppet sipped from the glass with something not too far removed from enjoyment.

Rance Auerbach had some of the vile brownish liquor the Big Uglies seemed to enjoy so much. After he'd finished it and waved to the Tosevite behind the bar for a refill, he said, "Now. Down to business."

"Down to business," Gorppet answered. "You have ginger. I want it. If you can get it for me, I will pay you what it is worth and make it back by selling what I do not keep to taste for myself."

As much ginger as I could ever want, he thought. He wasn't sure there was that much ginger on all of Tosev 3, but he intended to find out. The reward he'd got for capturing Khomeini had included a credit transfer as well as a promotion. What was money for, if not for spending?

"It is not quite so simple," Frederick said. "We have to be certain you are not a decoy for the Race."

"In theory, I understand this," Gorppet said, making the affirmative gesture. "In practice, it is absurd. I want the ginger for myself and my comrades and friends. If I were a decoy, the males handling me would take the herb. They would get it all, and leave me with nothing. I want more than nothing."

"So you say," Penny remarked. "We have to be sure we can believe you. The Race does not like Tosevites who sell ginger."

"It does not like males of the Race, or females, either, who buy it," Gorppet pointed out. "We all run risks here."

Rance Auerbach spoke up in a local language. Gorppet understood not a word he was saying. He returned to the language of the Race: "I told them I think you are worth trusting—and I thought they were addled when this scheme began to take shape."

"I thank you," Gorppet said. "I also do not believe you are tools of the Race, aiming to entrap me."

"I should hope not!" exclaimed the female with the yellow hair. "The Race has entrapped us before, but we would never entrap anyone for the Race."

Gorppet wondered if she was protesting too much. What would his superiors do to him if they found out he'd spent his reward to buy ginger? Nothing pleasant—he was sure of that. But how could they do anything worse than demoting him to simple infantrymale and sending him back to Baghdad for the rest of his days? As far as he was concerned, they couldn't. And, but for a minor difference in rank, how was that different from what he would have been doing had he not recognized the fanatic called Khomeini? Simple—it wasn't. And so . . .

Gamble, he thought. *Why not? If you lose, you only go back to what you were before—the Race does not have so many trained infantrymales that it can afford to imprison one for a crime that has nothing to do with combat effectiveness. And if the gamble pays off, it will make what your superiors paid you look like nothing but the money you would use to buy a narration to make the time pass by.*

He'd never really thought about being rich before. What infantrymale did? None that had any sense—except the few sharp fellows who'd got into the ginger trade early on. But if the chance for riches came his way, was he fool enough not to turn his eye turrets toward it?

"If we do this," he said slowly, "how do you want to be paid? I have heard it is difficult for Tosevites to use our credit, though I know there are ways around this."

"Oh, yes, there are ways," the dark-skinned male called Frederick said. The other two Big Uglies made the head motion that was their equivalent of the affirmative hand gesture. Frederick went on, "But we do not want your credits. We want gold."

He spoke the word with as much reverence as Khomeini gave to his imaginary Big Ugly beyond the sky. And, by the way Rance Auerbach and Penny Summers said, "Truth," in a sort of crooning whine, they were as reverent as the other Tosevite.

Gorppet understood that. The Tosevite economy was far less computerized than that of the Race. Money wasn't just an abstract concept here; it was often a real thing, traded at a standard rate of value for other real things. And gold was the principal medium of exchange here.

"I think that can be done," Gorppet said.

"I know a male Tosevite who will take your credit and give you gold for it," Frederick said.

"Not so fast," Gorppet told him. "First, let us settle on a price in credit. Then let us settle on a rate of exchange between credit and gold. And then let me make my own quiet inquiries and see if I can find a dealer with a better rate than your friend."

"This is not a good way to do business," Frederick protested. "It shows no trust."

"There is no trust." Gorppet stressed that with an emphatic cough. "There is only business. Business that deals in lots of ginger and money is dangerous to begin with, in the middle and at the end. Anyone who thinks different came from his eggshell addled."

Frederick started to say something more—probably another protest. But Rance Auerbach spoke first: "This is also truth. If we get through this dealing without trying to kill one another, we shall be ahead of the game." He swung his head toward Frederick. In his rasping, ruined voice, he went on, "This is what we all have to think: *my share of what we get here is enough*. Do you understand what I am telling you? You could try for all. Penny and I could try for all. Gorppet here could try for all. Someone might win. But, more likely, everyone would lose."

"I understand," Frederick said in that musical accent of his. "Have I been anything but a proper partner?"

"Not yet," Auerbach answered.

"No, not yet." Gorppet made the affirmative gesture to show he agreed with Auerbach. "But betrayal was not in your interest before. Now . . . I hope it still is not. It had better not be."

Rance Auerbach didn't like the pistol he was carrying. After the heavy solidity of an Army .45, this cheap little .38 revolver felt like a toy. But it was what he'd been able to get his hands on, and it was a damn sight better than nothing. He nodded to Penny. "Ready, sweetheart?"

"You bet," she said, and pulled her own .38 out of her purse to show she understood what he meant. Inside their apartment—the apartment that, with luck, they'd never see again after tonight—she said no more. They'd never been able to prove the Lizards listened to them, but they didn't want to take any chances, either.

"Let's see what happens, then." Auerbach stubbed out a cigarette and immediately lit another one. His mouth would have been dry even without the harsh smoke. He felt like a man going into combat. And this might be three-sided combat—he and Penny had one interest, Gorppet another, and Frederick yet another.

His eyes slid over to Penny. It might even turn into four-sided combat, if she decided to double-cross him. Would she? He didn't think so, but the idea that she might wouldn't leave his mind. She'd had her eye on the main chance for a long time now. If she decided she wanted all the loot . . .

She might be planning to double-cross him with Frederick, too. Rance didn't really think she was, but he didn't ignore the possibility, either. His Army days had taught him to evaluate all the contingencies.

Out they went. Rance fought his way down the stairs. Once he got outside, the very chirps of the insects reminded him he was a long way from home. If this went through, he'd still be a long way from home, but he'd be someplace he wanted to be, not where the Lizards dumped him.

If it didn't go through . . . "Shoot first, babe," he told Penny. "Don't wait. If you think you might be in trouble, chances are you're already there."

"I gotcha," she said, sounding as if she'd come out of a gangster movie. She'd been through these deals before, he knew, and every one of them outside the law. But this one was further outside than most—and she didn't have any hired muscle along except for him. He snorted and fought back a cough. Hired muscle that could hardly walk without a cane. If it came to rough stuff, the home team was in trouble.

They walked through the narrow, winding streets of District Six. This late at night, Rance worried less about being a white man in a largely black part of town. Hanover Street and a few of the other main drags were well lit. Away from them, though, it was too dark and gloomy for anybody to tell whether he and Penny were white, black, or green.

Music that sounded like U.S. jazz with something different, something African, mixed in blared out of a little hole-in-the-wall club. A black woman leaning against the wall stepped out and spoke to Rance in her own language. He didn't understand a word of it. Then the woman noticed he already had a companion. She said something else. He didn't understand that, either, but it sounded scornful. He and Penny kept walking. The woman went back and leaned against the wall again, waiting for someone else to come along.

A couple of blocks later, screams floated down from an upper floor of a rickety block of flats. Auerbach tried to make a joke of it: "Somebody teaching his wife to behave."

"You try teaching me like that, big boy, and you'll eat your dinner through a straw for the next year, on account of I'll break your jaw," Penny said, and she didn't sound as if she were joking at all.

After about half an hour, they came to the little park where gold and ginger would change hands. Everything seemed quiet and peaceful. Rance trusted neither peace nor quiet. "Stay well back of me," he said. "If anything goes wrong and we get separated, we try and meet on the docks, okay?"

"I know what we're supposed to do," Penny told him. "You hold up your end, I'll hold up mine, and we hope everybody else holds up his."

"Yeah, we hope," Rance said bleakly. He glanced at his glowing watch dial. Five to one. They were early.

A hiss came out of the darkness, followed by more hisses that were words in the language of the Race: "I greet you, Rance Auerbach."

"Gorppet?" Rance stood very still. He knew the Lizards had gadgets that let them see in the dark. Human soldiers—maybe human cops, too—also had them these days. But he didn't, and somehow hadn't expected the male to be using one. It felt like cheating.

"Who else would know your name?" the Lizard asked, to which he had no good answer. Gorppet went on, "I have the payment ready. Now we await the Tosevites with the herb."

"They will be here," Auerbach said. "The deal cannot go on without all of us." That wasn't strictly true, which worried him. The deal couldn't have got started without Penny and him, but they weren't essential any more. If the others wanted to take them out . . . He didn't worry too much about Gorppet; Lizards generally played straight. But he didn't trust Frederick any farther than he could throw him.

"I greet you, my friends." Frederick, in Rance's opinion, spoke the Lizards' language with a funny accent. "I have some of what we need. You, brave male, you have the rest of what we need. Let us now make the exchange."

He didn't say a word about Rance and Penny having anything they needed. That bothered Auerbach. Set gold in the scales against gratitude, and figuring out which one weighed more wasn't tough.

Now Penny walked past Auerbach. Gold didn't take up much room, but it was heavy. With a bad shoulder and a bad leg, he couldn't carry so much. If she got their share of the loot and ran off . . . What could he do about it? Not much. He didn't like that, either. Penny ate, drank, and breathed trouble. She might try to run off, as much for the hell of it as anything else.

"I have males covering me," Gorppet warned, so Rance wasn't the only imperfectly trusting soul here.

"I have males covering me," Frederick said, as if he took the idea altogether for granted.

"And I have males covering me," Penny said. Auerbach looked around to see if he'd grown a twin—or, even better, quintuplets. No such luck, though. He knew that too damn well.

"The exchange," Gorppet said. Rance peered through the darkness. He could hardly see a thing.

"Now," Frederick said, and the gloating triumph in his voice made Rance realize he was going to try to hijack all the gold. Rance filled his ruined lungs to shout a warning—

And another shout came from the edge of the park, a shout in an African language. A shot followed it, and then another, and then a stuttering roar of gunfire. Screams rang out, not just from human throats but from those of the Race. "Surrender!" a Lizard called, his voice amplified. "You cannot escape!"

By then, Rance was already on the ground, rolling toward cover. Old reflexes took over, modified only by the need to hang on to his cane. Bullets snarled not far enough above his head. "Who says we cannot escape?" Frederick shouted. "We shall smash you!" He shouted again. Rifles barked. Submachine guns chattered. He had to have brought a young army with him. By the volume of fire his men were laying down, he had the Lizards outnumbered and very nearly outgunned.

He wouldn't have brought so many if he hadn't intended to cut Rance and Penny out of the deal, to say nothing of punching their tickets for good. And he'd probably intended to rub out Gorppet and whatever pals the Lizard had along, too. Having that patrol come into the park just when it did looked to have been good luck for everybody but the black man, and Auerbach wasted no pity on him.

What they had now was a nasty three-cornered gunfight, with Rance in the middle of it. He shouted Penny's name, but his best shout wasn't very loud, and noise filled the air. She didn't hear him—or if she did, if she shouted back, he couldn't hear her.

He crawled toward her, or toward where he thought she was. Muzzle flashes sparked here and there, putting him in mind of giant, malignant lightning bugs—or of the fight in Colorado where he'd got himself ruined. He'd never thought he would wind up in anything like that again. He wished to Jesus he hadn't.

Somebody ran toward him—or maybe just toward the gold. Everyone human would be making a beeline for that. All the Lizards would be rushing toward the ginger, either to taste it or to grab it as evidence. Getting himself in deeper was the last thing he wanted to do, but Penny was there somewhere, and he'd been trained never to let the folks on his side down.

The running figure was about to run over him. He rose up onto his elbows and fired a round from his .38. With a soft grunt, the man toppled. His weapon clattered to the ground right in front of Rance, who grabbed it. His hands told him at once what he had: a Sten gun, about as cheap a way to kill lots of people in a hurry as humanity had ever made. He stuffed the pistol into a trouser pocket for a backup weapon; the submachine gun suited him a lot better now.

"Rance!" That was Penny, not very far away. He crawled toward her. One of his hands went into a pool of something warm and sticky. He exclaimed in disgust and jerked the hand away. "Rance!"

"I'm here," he answered, and then, "Get down, goddammit!" What was she doing still breathing if she didn't have the sense to hit the deck when bullets started flying? Another burst of gunfire from off to the right underscored his words. That was the direction from which Gorppet and his pals had come. They were making their getaway now, and doing a good, professional job of it. He wondered if they'd been able to nab the ginger before they started out of the fighting.

"Jesus Christ," Penny said, this time sounding as if she was on the ground. "You still alive, hon?"

"Yeah, I think so," Auerbach answered. "Where's the gold? Where's Frederick?" The African worried him more than the Lizards did. The Lizards played by their own rules. Frederick was liable to do anything to anybody.

"Fred's dead, or I think so, anyway," Penny said. "I sure to God shot him—I know that. Double-crossing son of a . . . You told him, Rance, but he didn't want to listen. Gorppet's worth a dozen of the likes of him."

"Yeah." But Auerbach remembered Penny had got herself in

trouble by double-crossing her pals in a ginger deal. And . . .
"Where's the gold?" he repeated, more urgently this time.

"Oh. The gold." Penny laughed, then switched to the language
of the Race: "I have it here, or some of it. How much can you
carry?"

"I do not know," Rance said in the same language—good security. "But I can find out, and that is a truth."

"Suits me fine," Penny said, reverting to English. "Here."

She pushed something at Rance. It wasn't a very big package,
but it weighed as much as a child. He grinned. "Let's see if we
can slide out of here," he said. "Without getting killed, I mean."

"Yeah, that's the best way." Penny surprised him with a kiss.
He wondered if they could make it. As long as Frederick's pals
and the Lizards kept a no-man's-land between them, they had a
chance. He also wondered how he would lug the gold and his
cane and the Sten gun. Wishing for another pair of hands, he set
off to do his best.

Atvar turned one eye turret from the computer screen toward
his adjutant. "Well, *this* is a shame and a disgrace and a first-
class botch," he remarked.

"To what do you refer, Exalted Fleetlord?" Pshing asked. He
approached the computer terminal. "Oh. The report on the unfortunate incident down at the southern end of the main continental mass."

"Yes, the unfortunate incident." Atvar's emphatic cough said
just how unfortunate an incident he thought it was. "When we
discover a deal for ginger in progress, it is generally desirable to
capture the guilty parties, the herb, and whatever was being exchanged for it. Would you not agree?"

His tone warned Pshing he had better agree. "Truth, Exalted
Fleetlord," he said.

Atvar pointed to the screen. "By this report, did we do any of
those things in this incident? Did we accomplish even one of
them?"

"No, Exalted Fleetlord," Pshing said unhappily.

"No," Atvar agreed. "No. *No* is the operative word; indeed it
is. No suspects, or none to speak of—only hired guns. No
ginger. No gold—it was supposed to be gold, I gather. Two males
killed, three wounded, and who can say how many Big Uglies?

We have had a great many fiascoes in the fight against ginger,
but this one is worse than most."

"What can we do?" Pshing asked.

That was indeed the question. It had been the question ever
since the Race discovered what ginger did to males, and had
even more urgently been the question since the Race discovered
what ginger did to females. No one had found an answer yet.
Atvar wondered if anyone ever would. Not about to admit that to
his adjutant, he said, "One thing we can do is make sure we do
not disgrace ourselves in this fashion again."

"Yes." Pshing used the affirmative gesture. "Have you any
specific orders to achieve that end, Exalted Fleetlord?"

"Specific orders?" Atvar glared at Pshing, wondering how to
reply to that. He'd been giving very specific orders against
ginger ever since it became a problem. It remained a problem,
and was a worse problem now that the colonization fleet was
here. Even in Cairo, even at this administrative center that had
once been a Tosevite hotel, females sometimes tasted ginger.
Atvar would get a distant whiff—or sometimes a not-so-distant
whiff—of pheromones, and thoughts of mating would go
through his mind, addling him and rendering him all but useless
as far as work went for annoyingly long stretches of time.

He wondered if that was what Big Uglies were like all the
time, forever distracted by their own sexuality. If it was, how did
they ever manage to get anything done? Mating was good
enough in the proper season, but thinking about it all the time
was definitely more trouble than it was worth.

He also realized he hadn't answered Pshing's question. "Specific orders?" he repeated. "For this case, yes: every effort is to
be made to track down the members of the Race and the Big
Uglies responsible for this horrendous crime, and all are to be
punished with maximum severity when apprehended."

"It shall be done," Pshing said. "It would have been done in
any case, but it shall be done with all the more vigor now."

"It had better be," Atvar snarled. He went back to the report.
After a moment, he snarled again, this time in raw fury. "The Tosevites involved in this crime, or some of them, are believed to
be the ones we resettled in that area after their failure to help us
as fully as they should have in Marseille? This is how they repay

our forbearance? They must be punished—oh, indeed they must."

"Their involvement is not proved," Pshing said. "It is only that they have not been seen or overheard by monitoring devices in their apartment since the gun battle took place."

"Where have they gone? Where could they have gone?" Atvar raged. "They are pale-skinned Big Uglies; they cannot find it easy to hide in a land where most have dark skins. That is one reason we sent them to this particular portion of the territory we control."

His adjutant spoke consolingly: "We are bound to find them soon."

"We had better," Atvar said. "And our own males, involved in gun battles against each other? Disgraceful!"

"The criminals could even have been females," Pshing said.

"Why, so they could," Atvar said. "That had not occurred to me. But they handled weapons as if they were familiar with them, which makes it more likely they were males from the conquest fleet."

"Were you not due to discuss with Fleetlord Reffet plans for the training of the colonists to aid the conquest fleet?" Pshing asked.

"Yes, I was." Had Atvar been a Big Ugly, his face would have assumed some preposterous expression. He was sure of that. Fortunately, though, he didn't have to show so much of what he thought. What he did show was bad enough; Pshing drew back a pace. But Atvar knew it needed doing, however little he relished it. "I had better take care of it," he said, though he would sooner have faced a surgeon's scalpel without anesthesia.

He made the call, consoled by the thought that Reffet would be as unhappy to talk with him as he was to talk with the fleetlord from the colonization fleet. In a matter of moments, Reffet's image stared at him out of the screen. "What is it now, Atvar?" the other fleetlord demanded.

"I think you know," Atvar replied.

"I know what you will ask for, yes," Reffet said. "What I do not know is how I can hope to build a successful colony here on Tosev 3 if you take my males and females from their productive tasks and turn them into soldiers."

By his tone, he had nothing but contempt for the males of the

Soldiers' Time. Atvar's tailstump quivered with fury. "I do not know how you can hope to build a successful colony if the Big Uglies kill your males and females."

"They should not be able to," Reffet snapped.

"Well, they can. They can do a great many things we did not anticipate," Atvar said. "High time you finally figured that out. In fact . . ." He paused, all at once much more cheerful. "Is it not a truth that we obtain many more manufactured goods from To-sevite factories than we anticipated?"

"Of course it is a truth," Reffet said. "We did not anticipate the Big Uglies' having any factories at all."

"Does this not mean, then, that there are surplus workers from the colonization fleet who could be turned into soldiers without greatly disrupting the colonization effort?" Had Atvar been a beffel, he would have squeaked with joy.

Reffet paused before answering, from which Atvar concluded the other fleetlord hadn't thought about that, and neither had his advisors. Maybe they hadn't wanted to think about it, since doing so would have made them reexamine the way they looked at the colonists and at life on Tosev 3. Refusing to look at the unpleasant was a more common failing of Big Uglies than of the Race, but males and females from Home were not altogether immune.

At last, Reffet said, "This proposal may have some merit, if you think you can shape what is liable to be unpromising material into soldiers."

"We can do that," Atvar said. "We shall have to do that, since it is the material we have available. I guarantee we can. Send us the males—send us the females, too—and we shall make soldiers of them. We have been through the training of a Soldiers' Time. We can duplicate it here."

"You guarantee it? On the strength of no evidence?" Reffet said. "Merely on your unsupported word, you expect me to turn over to you males and females by the thousands? You have been dealing with Big Uglies too long, Atvar; you think like one yourself."

Somehow, Atvar kept his temper under his command. Voice tight with the rage he was holding in, he said, "Well, if you will not turn them over, what brilliant idea for their use do you have?"

"Your notion may perhaps have some merit." Reffet spoke with the air of a male granting a large concession. "I propose establishing a committee to study the matter and see how—and if—that notion might be implemented. Once we examine all possible factors impacting the proposal, we can make an informed decision on whether to go forward. Such is the way of the Race." He sounded as if he thought Atvar needed reminding.

He was probably right about that. Atvar had got used to the headlong pace of life on Tosev 3. "Splendid, Reffet—splendid indeed," he said, letting out the sarcasm he'd held in its eggshell till then. "And your magnificent committee will, no doubt, bring in its recommendations about the time the last male of the conquest fleet dies of old age. I am afraid that will be rather late, especially given the recent threats from the Deutsche. How long do you think our colonies can stay safe without soldiers to defend them?"

"I will tell you what I think," Reffet snapped. "I think you see the males of the conquest fleet dying out and hope to gain power over some part of the colonization fleet so you will not fade into obscurity with their passing."

"Eventually," Atvar said, "you will review this conversation and realize what an addled cloaca you have been through the whole of it. When that time comes, I shall be glad to speak to you. Until then, however, I have no such desire." He broke the connection, and felt like breaking the monitor, too.

"He does not understand," Pshing said.

Up in Reffet's spaceship, the other fleetlord's adjutant was doubtless saying the same thing about Atvar. Atvar didn't care what males or females from the colonization fleet thought. "Of course he does not. We do not fully understand the Big Uglies or the entire situation on Tosev 3, and we have been here a great deal longer than the colonists. But they know everything—and if for some reason you do not believe me, you have only to ask them."

"What will you do about recruiting soldiers from the colonization fleet?" Pshing asked. "I think you are correct that a committee would be impossibly slow."

"I know I am correct about that," Atvar said. "What shall I do?" He thought, then began to laugh. "One thing I shall do at once is begin to accept volunteers for training. Reffet cannot possibly object, and I think there may be a fair number of colonists who would sooner do something with themselves than sit around in their apartments watching videos all day."

"I hope you are right, Exalted Fleetlord," Pshing said. "I think that a reasonable calculation myself. Will you truly include females as well as males among these new soldiers?"

"Why not?" Atvar said. "Females and males mix in almost every aspect of the Race's life; it was only for the convenience of avoiding mating issues that the conquest fleet was made all-male. Those will arise now—and will be worse, thanks to the accursed Tosevite herb—but I think we will manage quite well. Accepting females also means we have a larger group of potential recruits. We need them, and we shall get them. It is as simple as that." Atvar hadn't the slightest doubt he was right.

As day followed day, Monique Dutourd discovered she had lived her whole life in Marseille without knowing half her city, maybe more. When she told that to Pierre, her older brother laughed at her. "You kept up the family's *petit bourgeois* respectability too well," he said. "You wouldn't have wanted to have much to do with the black market or anything of that sort."

"Everybody does a little," Monique said. "One has to, to live; without the black market, especially in the days not long after the fighting, the whole city would have starved, the way the *Boches* stole everything in sight."

"Everybody does a little," Pierre echoed, laughing still. "But you never *approved*, did you, little sister? And now, whether you approve or not, you're part of it. Is it really so bad?"

Looking at the flat in which he lived, the flat in which she occupied a spare room these days, Monique had a hard time saying no. The flat was far larger and far airier than the one from which she'd escaped. And it held every sort of electronic gadget, mostly Lizard-made, under the sun: more modern conveniences than people could even imagine. Still . . .

"How do you stand living like a hunted animal all the time?" she burst out.

Her brother looked back at her, for once without a hint of irony on his plump, pouchy features. "I'd sooner live as a hunted animal than as one in a cage, where the keeper could reach in and pet me—or do anything else he wanted—whenever he chose."

That held enough truth to sting. But Monique said, "I'm still in a cage, only now it's yours and not the SS man's."

"You can go back any time you please," Pierre said easily. "If you would rather do what he wants than what I want, go right ahead."

"I'd sooner do what *I* want," Monique said. She'd said that a good many times, to anyone who might listen. It hadn't done her much good, and didn't seem likely to do her much good this time, either.

And so it didn't. Her brother, at least, didn't laugh at her any more. Voice serious now, he answered, "If that is what you would rather have, you need to make yourself strong enough to be able to get it. No one will give it to you. You have to take it."

Monique clenched her fists till her nails bit into her flesh. "You talk like you just came back from the revival of *The Triumph of the Will*."

"I saw it," he said, which made her glare harder than ever. Since he'd come back into her life, she'd never been able to faze him. He went on, "It's marvelous propaganda. Even the Lizards say so. They study it to see how to make people do what they want. If it's good enough for them, why shouldn't it be good enough for me?"

Before Monique could answer, someone knocked on the front door. Pierre didn't just open it. Instead, he checked a little television screen connected to an even littler camera hooked up to look out on the front hall. He nodded to himself. "Yes, those are the Lizards I'm expecting." Turning to Monique, he said, "Why don't you go shopping for a couple of hours? Spend as much of my money as you want. I've got some business to take care of here."

By his tone, he was as convinced he had the right to send her away as Dieter Kuhn was that *he* had the right to tell her to take off her clothes and lie down on the bed. One fine day, and it wouldn't be long, she'd have something pointed to say about that. But it wouldn't be today. She grabbed her handbag and left the flat as soon as the Lizards outside had come in.

Except for the clothes the people wore, Porte d'Aix always made her think of Algiers as much as France. It reminded her of the unity the Mediterranean had known during Roman times and even later; Professor Pirenne's famous thesis said the rise of first Muhammad and then Charlemagne had set the two sides of the sea moving in different directions. Scholars of Monique's generation worked to refute Pirenne, but she, not a medievalist herself, thought he made good points.

A walk through this part of Marseille certainly supported his views of the way history worked. Streets here were short and winding and narrow—most too narrow for automobiles, quite a few too narrow for anyone but a madman to try on a bicycle. But plenty of madmen were loose; Monique had to flatten herself against brick or stone walls every few steps to keep from getting flattened as they whizzed past.

Shops and taverns and eateries were tiny, and most of them did as much business out on the street as back in the buildings that supposedly housed them. A tinker sat on a chair, a cigarette dangling from the corner of his mouth, as he soldered a patch onto a cracked iron pot that might almost have dated back to Roman days. His legs stuck out into the street, so that Monique had to step over them.

He moved the pot and patted his lap. "Here, sweetheart, you can have a seat if you care to."

"You can solder your fly shut, if you care to," Monique told him, "and your mouth to go with it." Bristling, she strode on. Behind her, the tinker laughed and, without any undue haste, went back to work.

In the course of the three blocks that lay between Pierre's flat and the local market square, she heard several dialects of French, German, Spanish (or was it Catalan?), Italian, English, and the language of the Race spoken by both men and Lizards. People changed tongues more readily than they changed trousers. As a scholar—*as a former scholar,* she reminded herself—she wished she could go back and forth from one language to another as readily as did some of these traders and tapmen and smugglers.

As always, the market was packed. Some merchants had stalls their families had held for generations. Others guided pushcarts through the crowds, shouting abuse and lashing out to keep people from getting too many free samples of their cooked squid or lemon tarts or brass rings polished till they looked like gold but sure to start a finger turning green in a week if you were rash enough to buy one.

Monique hung on to her purse with both hands. Plenty of thieves in the market square were a lot less subtle than the ones who sold rings. No sooner had that thought crossed her mind than a German soldier in field-gray let out a guttural bellow of fury at discovering his pocket picked. The fingersmith was sure to be long gone. Even if he hadn't been, Monique saw no police, French or German, anywhere.

Some of the Lizards who skittered through the largely human crowd were as much at home here as any people. Monique would have guessed they were males from the conquest fleet, veterans who understood people as well as any Lizard could and were liable to be up to something shady themselves.

Then there were the Lizard tourists. They were as obvious and as obnoxious as any travelers from an English-speaking land. They all carried video cameras and photographed everything that moved and everything that didn't. Monique kept her head down. She was wearing a new bouffant hairdo and makeup far more garish than she would have dared—or even wanted—to use while teaching at the university, but she didn't care to be recognized if she showed up on some Lizard's pictures.

She wondered how many of the hissing tourists were spies for the Race. A moment later, she wondered how many were spies for the Nazis. Ginger, from what she'd seen, was a great corrupter. She wished her brother had never got into the trade, even if it had made him rich. If he hadn't, she wouldn't have needed to have anything to do with the Nazis, either.

One of the Lizards, one with fairly fancy body paint, bumped up against her. It spoke in its own language. "I'm sorry, but I don't understand," Monique said in French. Along with her own tongue, she had Latin. She had Greek. She had German and English and some Italian. But very little classical scholarship was conducted in the language of the Race.

To her surprise, the Lizard handed her a card printed in pretty good French. It read, *You may already be a winner. To find out if you are, come to the consulate of the Race, 21 Rue de Trois Rois. Many valuable prizes.*

"What kind of winner?" she asked. "What kind of prizes?"

The Lizard tapped the card with a fingerclaw and said something else in its own language. Evidently it knew no more French than she did of its language. It reached out and tapped the card again, as if certain the little rectangle held all the answers.

"I don't have the faintest idea what you're trying to tell me," Monique said with a shrug. The Lizard shrugged, too, in what seemed to her a sad way. Then it vanished into the crowd.

Monique stared at the card. Her first impulse was to crumple it up and let it fall to the ground, to be trampled underfoot. The Lizards' consulate was bound to be the most intently spied-upon building in Marseille. If she ever wanted to remake the acquaintance of Dieter Kuhn, that struck her as the way to go about it. All she wanted for Kuhn was a horrible death far away from her.

But, from somewhere, that miserable Lizard had come up with magic words. *You may already be a winner.* Was the Race running a contest, the way rival laundry-soap makers did when business got slow? Laundry-soap makers sold soap. What were the Lizards selling? She had no idea, but the very notion of the Lizards selling anything piqued her curiosity.

Many valuable prizes. It sounded more like something Americans would say than anything the Lizards were likely to do. What would a Lizard think a valuable prize was? Just how valuable a prize would it be? Valuable enough to let her get away from her brother as she'd got away from Dieter Kuhn? Were there any prizes that valuable?

She didn't know. But she wanted to find out. She wondered if she could manage it. She started to let the card drop—she knew where the consulate was—but then hesitated. Maybe she would need it. She looked at it again. By what she could see, any French printing house could have done up such cards by the tens of thousands. But she didn't know what she couldn't see.

Thoughtfully, she dropped the card into her handbag. *If I get the chance, maybe I will go over there.* She wondered how many cards the Lizard was giving out, and how many Lizards were giving out cards. If she did go to the Rue de Trois Rois, would she find half of Marseille there ahead of her? And would the valuable prize turn out to be aluminum pans or something else every bit as banal?

She knew she shouldn't leave the Porte d'Aix for any reason. If she was safe anywhere in Marseille, this was the place. The

Germans came in here, yes, but they came in to buy and sell, not to raid and plunder. They didn't know a half, or even a quarter, of what went on under their noses. And the Lizard authorities didn't know half of what went on under their snouts, either, or Pierre wouldn't have thrown her out so he could meet with those two shady, scaly characters.

"Lady, you going to stand there till you grow roots?" somebody demanded in loud, irritable tones.

"I'm sorry," Monique said, though she wasn't, not really. She moved, and the annoyed man pushed past her. Then she sank into abstracted study once more. What *were* the Lizards doing? Did she dare to find out? On the other hand, did she dare not to find out?

☆ **14** ☆

Felless looked down from a third-story window at the crowd that had gathered in front of the Race's consulate in Marseille. The male who stood beside her was a researcher from the conquest fleet named Kazzop. "Save that these Big Uglies have black hair, this puts me in mind of a Tosevite work of fiction called 'The Red-headed League,' " he said.

"Tosevite literary allusions leave me uninterested," Felless said. "The question is, will this accomplish what we desire?"

"We have certainly stimulated the Big Uglies, superior female," Kazzop said. "I do not think the Deutsche or the Français have the least idea how to control this swarm of Tosevites."

"In that case, they will start brutalizing them soon," Felless predicted. "It is not what you had in mind for this experiment, but does seem to be the standard Tosevite procedure in case of insecurity."

"Truth," Kazzop said. "Of course, the Deutsch Tosevites need little excuse for brutalizing the Français in any case. They rule them more through forcing fear than through promoting affection."

"I suppose it is because they only conquered this province of their not-empire shortly before the conquest fleet arrived," Felless said. "It strikes me as counterproductive, but a great deal the Deutsche do strikes me as counterproductive, so this would be nothing out of the ordinary there."

"Indeed it would not," Kazzop said. "We had better go down there and get things under way, or else the Deutsche will disperse that crowd before we can get any use out of it."

"I suppose so," Felless said unhappily. This wasn't her project; she'd been brought here at the bidding of others, just as she'd been sent to Nuremberg. She remained inside the borders of the Greater German *Reich*. Here, though, she had at least a chance to escape the disgrace that had hovered over her in the capital. That should have made her more enthusiastic about cooperating.

To a point, it did. But only to a point. She had to keep coming out of her office and working not only with Big Uglies but also with females and males of the Race. Working with Big Uglies was merely annoying, though less so than it had been in Nuremberg. Working with females of her own kind was innocuous. Working with males of her own kind she hated, because it meant she dared not taste ginger.

She wanted a taste. How she wanted a taste! As she never had before, she understood what addiction meant. She would crave ginger even on her deathbed, regardless of whether she had another taste between now and then. She knew that. If only she could get a couple of days doing research and data correlation inside the cubicle they'd given her. Maybe that would be long enough to let her taste and to let her raging pheromones subside afterwards.

And maybe she would taste and taste and then humiliate herself with the males who coupled with her after she emerged from the cubicle. She'd done that before. She'd done it more than once, in fact. She was all too likely to do it again.

She still wanted a taste.

Down on the ground floor, males had cordoned off all the passages leading away from the front entrance. Others stood in front of those cordoned-off passages with weapons in hand, to make sure no snoopy Big Uglies went down them in spite of the barricades.

Boxes full of prizes stood in back of tables just behind the closed front doors. Felless sighed. "I am not ideally suited for this task," she said, "because I speak neither the Deutsch language nor that of the local Français, which I understand is different."

"Quite different," Kazzop said. "But do not let it worry you. Most of us have at least some knowledge of one or both of these languages. While you are part of the project proper, your most important role will be data analysis. It is simply that we lack the personnel to restrict you to analysis alone, Senior Researcher."

With a martyred sigh, Felless said, "I understand." Had she been doing only analysis, she could have tasted to her heart's content. Nothing on Tosev 3 except ginger came close to contenting her heart.

Kazzop, now, Kazzop sounded happy and excited about what he was doing. Felless envied him his enthusiasm. They took seats side by side, then turned on the card readers in front of them. She set a sheet of paper by hers. When amber lights showed the machines were ready, Kazzop turned to the males at the door and said, "Let them in. Tell them they must stay in two neat lines or we cannot proceed."

"It shall be done, superior sir," one of the males answered, and swung the doors open. The Big Uglies outside roared. He and his comrades shouted in the local language. In came the Tosevites, more or less in two lines.

The first of them came up to thrust his card at Felless—she knew he was a male, for he let the hair on his upper lip grow. She took the card from him and stuck it into the reader. A number showed on the screen: a zero. She touched the message printed beside the zero on the sheet of paper she'd set next to the reader. In the local language, it read, *Sorry, you did not win anything today. Please try again.*

By the way the Big Ugly stared, she wondered for a moment if he could read at all. Then he let loose a torrent of what sounded like abuse. Felless was suddenly glad she knew no Français. The Tosevite stomped away, still loudly complaining.

Up came another Big Ugly, a female. Her card showed a one on the reader. Felless turned and grabbed a *skelkwank*-light disk player, which she handed to the Tosevite. She got a wave in return as the Big Ugly carried away her prize.

More Tosevites trooped up, one after another. Those who won nothing complained loudly about it, even though none of the cards had promised anyone a prize. Males and females of the Race would have done better at remembering that.

Most of the Big Uglies who did win got disk players. Some got portable computers. A few got good-sized cash awards— half a year's pay for the average Tosevite. Just as those who'd failed were more abusive than members of the Race would have been, so the winners were more excited. Hidden cameras recorded all their responses.

And then a female Big Ugly gave Felless her card. It showed a four, the only four among the cards the Race had given out. Felless turned to Kazzop. "Here is the biggest winner of them all," she said.

"Oh, good," he answered. "Now I get to play with my bells and whistles, as if I were a Tosevite advertiser." He turned on a raucous recording full of truly appalling noises. Felless winced. Kazzop laughed at her, remarking, "I have come to like the Big Uglies and the noises they enjoy."

"So I gather," Felless said coldly. "You have come to like them altogether too well, if you want my view of the matter."

"It could be, superior female; it could be." Kazzop sounded cheerful. "But look—all the Big Uglies in line and all the Big Uglies still waiting outside know she is the biggest winner. See how excited and envious they are?"

Felless still had trouble reading Tosevite expressions. She was willing to believe Kazzop, though. "Interpret for me, if you will," she said, and he made the affirmative gesture. "Tell the Tosevite congratulations, and ask her name."

Kazzop spoke in the language of the Français. The Big Ugly answered in what sounded like the same tongue. "She says thank you, and that her name is Monique," he told Felless.

"Just Monique?" Felless was puzzled. "Do they not usually have two names?"

After more conversation, Kazzop said, "She seems reluctant to give her family name. She also seems reluctant to give reasons for her reluctance. She is more curious about what she has won."

That, for once, was a reaction Felless completely understood. "Well, go ahead and tell her," Felless said. "Seeing how a couple of them have reacted to money, she will probably come to pieces when she learns she was won a home here with as many modern conveniences as we can include in it—something worth far more than our cash awards."

"Oh, without a doubt," Kazzop said. "The recording of her reaction should be both instructive and entertaining." He shifted from the language of the Race to that of the local Big Uglies.

Felless waited for the Tosevite to shriek and burst into hysterics. One of the males who'd won money had tried to caress her with his lips. She understood it was a gesture of affection among

Big Uglies, but the idea almost left her physically ill. She hoped this Tosevite would not try anything like that.

To her relief, the female Big Ugly didn't. Indeed, the Tosevite hardly showed any emotion at all for a moment. When she did speak, it was in quiet, measured tones. Kazzop was the one who jerked in astonishment. "What is going on?" Felless asked him.

"She—the female—says she cannot accept the prize." Kazzop sounded as if he couldn't believe the sounds impinging on his hearing diaphragms. "She asks if we can make a substitution for it."

"You had not planned to do anything of the sort," Felless said. "I realize that dealing with Big Uglies takes unusual flexibility, but still. . . . Find out why she does not want the prize as offered."

"Yes. That is worth knowing. It shall be done." Kazzop spoke in the local language. The Big Ugly's reply sounded hesitant. To Felless, Kazzop said, "She is not altogether forthcoming. I gather that such a prize might draw too much notice from the Deutsch authorities."

"Ah. If I were a local Big Ugly, I would not want the Deutsch authorities noticing me, either." Felless shuddered at some of the things the Deutsche had done. "Does she perhaps follow the—what is it called?—the Jewish superstition, that is it?"

"I will not even ask her that," Kazzop said. "If she follows it, she will lie. In any case, the Deutsche have exterminated most of their Jews by now. More likely she is a smuggler or other criminal—but she would be unlikely to admit anything of that sort, either."

"I wonder if she smuggles ginger." Felless spoke in musing tones, so musing that Kazzop sent her a sharp look. She wished she'd kept quiet. Sure enough, her reputation had preceded her to Marseille.

The Big Ugly female spoke again, this time without waiting for anyone to speak to her. "She is angry that we have something grand to give her that she cannot take," Kazzop said. "She wants to know if we can substitute the cash value for the house."

"This is your project," Felless said. "Were it mine, though, I would tell her no."

"I intend to," Kazzop said. "Doing anything else would exceed my budget." He paused, then stuck out his tongue to show he'd had an idea. "I will offer her a second prize instead." He spoke in the language of the Français. The Tosevite female replied with considerable warmth.

"What does she say?" Felless asked.

"That we are cheats, but that she has no choice but to let herself be cheated," Kazzop said. "She accepts with bitterness and anger."

Felless felt a certain sympathy toward the female. That was the way she'd gone to work in Nuremberg after disgracing herself. She handed the Big Ugly the sheaf of printed papers that passed for currency in the Greater German *Reich*. The Tosevite stuffed them into her carrying pouch and hurried away.

Kazzop sighed. "That was not what I expected, but the unexpected also offers valuable insights."

"Truth," Felless said.

A little scaly devil came up to Liu Han's hut in the prison camp and spoke to her in bad Chinese: "You come. Now."

For the most part, the little devils had ignored her since capturing her in the village not far from Peking. She wished they would have gone on ignoring her. Since they hadn't, she sighed and got to her feet. "It shall be done," she said.

"Where are you taking her?" Liu Mei asked from atop the *kang*, on which she huddled to get a little warmth.

"Not for you to know." The scaly devil spoke in Chinese, even though she'd used his language. He gestured with his rifle at Liu Han. "You come."

"I am coming," she said wearily. "Where are you taking me?"

"You come, you see." The scaly devil jerked the business end of his rifle again. Liu Han sighed and left the hut.

Even though she was wearing a quilted cotton jacket, the cold the *kang* held at bay smote with full force when she went outside. The little scaly devil let out an unhappy hiss; he liked the winter weather even less than she did. Old, dirty snow crunched under her feet—and under his. He plainly wanted to skitter ahead. To annoy him, Liu Han walked as slowly as he would let her. Maybe he would get frostbitten or catch chest fever. She didn't know if little scaly devils could catch chest fever, but she hoped so.

The camp was depressingly large. The scaly devils were doing their best to hold China down. Some of the people they'd scooped up were Communists like Liu Han, others Kuomintang reactionaries, still others men and women of no particular party whom they'd seized more or less at random. They didn't even try to keep the Communists and Kuomintang followers from one another's throats—their theory seemed to be that, if the humans quarreled among themselves, they wouldn't have to do so much work. Partly because of that, the Party and the Kuomintang did their best to keep a truce going.

"Here. This building." The scaly devil pointed again, this time not with his rifle but with his tongue. The building toward which he directed Liu Han stood near the prison camp's razor-wire perimeter. It was not the building where most interrogations were conducted; that one lay closer to the center of the camp. Some of the interrogators were the little devils' human running dogs; that building had an attached infirmary and a sinister reputation.

Liu Han had been there a couple of times. No one had done anything too dreadful to her, but she was relieved to be going somewhere else. Even though this building had machine guns mounted on it, she thought it was only an administrative center. She'd never heard of anyone being tortured there.

· When she went inside, she opened her jacket and then took it off; the place was heated to the scaly devils' standard of comfort, which meant she'd gone from winter to hottest summer in a couple of steps. The scaly devil who'd fetched her from her hut sighed with pleasure.

Another little devil took charge of her. "You are the Tosevite Liu Han?" he asked in his own language, knowing she could use it.

"Yes, superior sir," she answered.

"Good. You will come with me," he said. Liu Han did, to a chamber that contained nothing but a stool, a television camera, and a monitor; another scaly devil looked out of the monitor, presumably seeing her televised image. "You may sit on the stool," her guide told her. The little devil with the rifle positioned himself in the doorway to make sure she didn't do anything else. Her guide folded himself into the posture of respect before the little devil in the monitor, saying, "Here is the Tosevite female called Liu Han, Senior Researcher."

"Yes, I see her," that little devil replied. He raised his eye turrets, so that he seemed to look right at Liu Han. When he spoke again, it was in halting Chinese: "You remember me, Liu Han?"

"I'm sorry, but I don't," she replied in the same language. As far as she was concerned, one little scaly devil looked very much like another.

He shrugged just as if he were a person and returned to his own tongue: "I would not have recognized you, either, but we spent a lot of time making each other unhappy during the fighting. My name is Ttomalss."

"I greet you," she said, not wanting to acknowledge the pang of fear that ran through her. "The advantage is yours now. I did not kill you when I had the chance." That was as close as she would come to begging for mercy. She bit down on the inside of her lower lip. She hoped that was as close as she would come to begging for mercy. If Ttomalss wanted vengeance for being captured and imprisoned and threatened, what could she do to stop him?

At the moment, he seemed mild enough. He asked, "Is your hatchling—Liu Mei was the name you gave her, not so?—well?"

"Yes," Liu Han answered. Then she returned to Chinese for a sentence she couldn't say in the scaly devils' language: "She never did learn how to smile, though. You had her too long for that."

"I suppose I did," Ttomalss said. "I encountered this same problem with a Tosevite hatchling I succeeded in raising after you released me. I believe it lacks a solution, at least for Tosevites raised by the Race. Our faces are not mobile enough to give your hatchlings the cues they need to form expressions."

"So you did finally manage to steal another Tosevite hatchling?" Liu Han said. "Too bad. I had hoped I frightened you enough when I captured you to keep you from trying that again. Somewhere, a Tosevite female mourns, as I mourned when you took Liu Mei away from me."

"The Race needs to conduct this research," Ttomalss said. "We must learn how Tosevites and the Race can get along. We must learn what Tosevites raised as citizens of the Empire are like. I know you disapprove, but the work is important to us—and to everyone on Tosev 3."

"How would you like it if some of us stole your hatchlings from you and tried to raise them as Tosevites?" Liu Han asked. "That is what you have done to us."

"You could never do such a thing," Ttomalss told her. "You would never do such a thing. A project like the one I have undertaken requires far more patience than the usual Big Ugly has in him."

Liu Han wanted to set up a project to steal eggs from the little scaly devils and raise the chicks—or whatever one called newly hatched little devils—as if they were human beings. She had no idea how to go about it, and the little devils had learned a good deal about security since their early days in China, so she couldn't get in touch with anyone outside the prison camp anyhow. But the urge to take Ttomalss down a peg burned in her anyhow. As things were, she could only say, "I think you are mistaken."

"I do not," Ttomalss said calmly. Liu Han glared at him. Despite what she'd done to him years before, he had the little devils' arrogance in full measure.

Still, things could have been worse. As long as he was talking with her about hatchlings, he wasn't interrogating her about the Party. Of themselves, the scaly devils did not go in for painful questioning, but now they had Chinese stooges who did. If they gave her to them . . .

"When I first studied you, I did not think you would rise to become a power in the resistance against the Race hereabouts," Ttomalss said. "Your goals are not admirable, but you have shown great strength of character in trying to achieve them."

"I think freedom is admirable," Liu Han said. "If you do not, that is your misfortune, not mine."

"There is only one proper place for all the subregions of this planet: under the administration of the Race," Ttomalss said. "In the course of time, those subregions will take their proper place."

"Freedom is good for the Race, but not for the Big Uglies," Liu Han jeered. "That is what you are saying."

But Ttomalss made the negative hand gesture. "You misunderstand. You Tosevites always misunderstand. When the conquest is complete, Tosev 3 will be as free as Home, as free as Rabotev 2, as free as Halless 1. You will be contented subjects of the Emperor, as we are." He swung his eye turrets down toward the surface of the desk at which he sat, a gesture of respect for the ruler among the little scaly devils.

"I take it back," Liu Han said. "You do not think freedom is good for anyone, even your own kind."

"Too much freedom is not good for anyone," Ttomalss said. "Even your own faction would agree with that, seeing how it punishes Tosevites who disagree with it in any way."

"This is a revolutionary situation," Liu Han said. "The Communist Party is at war with you. Of course we have to weed out traitors."

Ttomalss let his mouth fall open: he was laughing at her. "I do not believe you. I do not even think you believe yourself. Your faction rules the not-empire called the SSSR, and kills off members regardless of whether they show allegiance to any other power or not."

"You do not understand," Liu Han said, but Ttomalss understood too well. He was, Liu Han recalled, a student of the human race in his own fashion. Liu Han had seen purges were sometimes necessary, not only to get rid of traitors but also to keep up the energy, enthusiasm, and alertness of people who didn't get purged.

"Do I not?" the little scaly devil said. "Perhaps you will enlighten me, then." In his own language, he had a fine, sarcastic turn of phrase.

Nettled, Liu Han started to answer him in great detail. But she bit down on the words before they passed her lips. She had seen many years before that Ttomalss was a clever little devil. He wasn't arguing abstracts with her here. He was trying to anger her, to make her say things before she thought about them. And he'd come within a hairsbreadth of succeeding.

What she did say after checking herself was, "I have nothing to tell you."

"No? Too bad," the little scaly devil said. "Shall we see whether you have anything to tell me after you watch your hatchling tormented in front of you? Your strong feelings for your blood kin can be a source of weakness for you, you see, as well as a source of strength. Or perhaps the hatchling should watch your interrogation. Which do you think would produce the better results?"

"I have nothing to tell you," Liu Han repeated, though she had to force the words out through lips numb with fear. One of the things the little scaly devils had learned from mankind was frightfulness. Just after coming to China, they would never have made such a threat.

"And yet," Ttomalss said in musing tones, "you did not physically torment me when I was in your power, though you could have done so. And, whether you believe me or not, I tried to do my best by your hatchling: the best I could do, at any rate, given my limitations. Because of that, ordering the two of you subjected to torment would be unpleasant."

A little scaly devil with a conscience? Liu Han would not have counted on finding such a bourgeois affectation among the scaly devils. But, having found it, she was more than willing to take advantage of it. "You are an honorable opponent," she said, though what was honor but another bourgeois affectation?

"I wish I could say the same of your faction," Ttomalss replied. "Since acquiring a hatchling to raise, I have not been involved with affairs in this subregion, you will understand, but I did review the record before making arrangements for this interview. Assassinations, sabotage . . ."

"They are the weapons of the weak against the strong," Liu Han said. "The Race is strong. If we had landcruisers and explosive-metal bombs, we would use them instead—believe me, we would."

"Oh, I do believe you," Ttomalss said. "You need have no doubt about that. The question now remaining is how to make sure you and your hatchling and your male companion can do the Race no further harm."

No matter how hot the chamber was, a chill ran through Liu Han. She knew what the Party would do under such circumstances. *Liquidation* was the word that sprang to mind. The little scaly devils had not been in the habit of executing their opponents, but they grew more ruthless as time went by. That was the dialectic in action, too, though not in a way that worked to Liu Han's advantage. She stood mute, waiting to hear her fate.

In the end, she didn't. Ttomalss said, "Those who administer the subregion will make the decision there. They can take their time; no point in haste as long as you are securely confined. If I am asked for my input, I will tell them that you could have done worse to me than you did."

"Thank you for that much," Liu Han said. Instead of answering, Ttomalss broke the connection; the screen Liu Han was facing went dark. Her hopes were dark, too. The guard gestured with his rifle. She pulled on her jacket once more as she followed him out of the building. It would be cold out there in the camp. She wondered if she would spend the rest of her life behind razor wire.

"Find Polaris," Sam Yeager muttered, peering into the northern sky. When he did find the North Star, he aimed the polar axis of the little refractor Barbara had bought him for

Christmas toward it. That would let the equatorial mount follow the stars with only one slow-motion control.

Loosening the tension screws on the right-ascension and declination axes, he swung the scope itself toward Jupiter, which glowed yellow-white in the southwestern sky. He sighted along the tube, then peered through the finder scope attached to it. When he spotted the planet in the finder's field, he grunted in satisfaction and, fumbling a little in the dark, tightened the screws so the gears in the slow-motion controls would mesh. The knob for the right-ascension control was by the telescope's focusing mechanism, that for the declination control on a flexible cable. Using them both, he brought Jupiter to the meeting point of the finder's crosshairs. That done, he peered into the eyepiece of the main telescope—and there was Jupiter, fifty times life size.

He fiddled with the focus. He could see three of the four Galilean satellites, and could also see the cloud bands girdling the planet. He thought about switching to an eyepiece with a shorter focal length for a closer look, but decided not to bother. With only a 2.4-inch objective lens, he wouldn't see that much more. He'd learned that light grasp was really more important than magnifying power.

Instead, he swung the scope toward Mars, a bloodred star in the east. When he found it, it looked like a tiny copper coin—only about a third as wide as Jupiter—in the low-power eyepiece. Now he did choose the 6mm orthoscopic instead of the 18mm Kellner—he wanted to see everything he possibly could. Mars got bigger and brighter day by day. It was nearing opposition, when it would be closest to Earth and best suited for observing.

Even at 150 power, he couldn't see much: the bright polar cap, and a dark patch on the red he thought was Syrtis Major. He couldn't see the craters that pocked the planet's surface. They weren't beyond just the reach of his little amateur's instrument; no Earth-based telescope could make them out.

He chuckled under his breath. "No canals, either. No thoats. No four-armed green men swinging swords. No nothing." The Lizards thought hysterically funny the Mars that people like Percival Lowell and Edgar Rice Burroughs had imagined. So did Yeager—now. When he was a kid, though, he'd devoured Burroughs' tales of Barsoom.

After he'd looked at Mars long enough to suit him, he turned on a flashlight whose plastic bulb cover he'd painted red with Barbara's nail polish—red light didn't hurt night vision. He chuckled again, thinking of all the things he'd learned in the couple of months since he'd got the scope for a present.

"Who would have thought I'd've found myself a hobby at my age?" he said. He'd bought himself a *Norton's Star Atlas* to find out what he could see now that he had the telescope. He ran his finger down the listing of double stars. "Gamma Leonis," he muttered, and then nodded. The star was bright enough to be easy to spot—not very far from Mars at the moment, in fact—and its components were far enough apart for his little refractor to be able to split them.

A couple of minutes later, he softly clapped his hands together. There they were, the brighter of the pair golden, the somewhat dimmer companion a dull red. *A handsome one,* he thought. Taking a pen from his breast pocket, he put a check by γ *Leonis* in the Norton's. Little by little, he was learning the Greek alphabet, one more thing he'd never thought he'd do.

That bright, moving light in the northern sky was a plane coming in for a landing at Los Angeles International Airport. Airplane lights coming straight at him had once tricked him into thinking he'd discovered a couple of supernovas. He knew better now.

He glanced toward the back of the house. The room Mickey and Donald used was quiet and dark; they'd gone to sleep. Jonathan was still up studying. He had had the courtesy to pull down the shade. That golden glow didn't bother Sam's night vision much, where raw light from the overhead lamp would have.

Yeager sighed. He'd hoped Jonathan might get interested in astronomy, too, but no such luck. Oh, the kid had come out and peered through the telescope a couple of times, but what he saw didn't excite him. Sam could tell. When Jonathan thought of heavenly bodies, he didn't think of Jupiter or Gamma Leonis—he thought of Karen, or possibly Kassquit.

I was like that myself once upon a time, Sam thought. He remembered some of the cheap sporting houses he'd visited in his minor-league days—cheap because a guy in the bush leagues couldn't afford any better and because a lot of the towns he went through didn't boast any better. If he ever found out Jonathan was doing anything along those lines, he'd tan the kid's hide for him. He recognized his own hypocrisy, and didn't feel like doing anything about it. *Do as I say, not as I do.*

He clicked on the red light again to check what other double stars he could look for as long as he was out here. N Hydrae—a pair of stars of just about sixth magnitude, separated by a bit more than nine seconds of arc—was easily within the capacity of his telescope. He swung it south from Leo.

Splitting N Hydrae wouldn't particularly challenge the scope. Finding it, though, would challenge him. Together, its stars added up to one fifth-magnitude object. In other words, it was invisible to the naked eye in the streetlight-saturated sky of Los Angeles. He would have to find a brighter nearby star he could see and then either starhop with the finder or use his setting circles to bring N Hydrae into view.

He decided to starhop; setting circles still seemed like black magic to him. Taking the telescope out to the middle of the back yard so he could see over the eucalyptus tree next door that helped spoil the view to the southeast, he realigned the polar axis on Polaris, then found the battered rectangle of stars that formed the main part of the constellation Corvus, and then went south and east from the Crow toward his target, checking his path with the star atlas each step of the way.

And there, by God, was the star that had to be N Hydrae. He turned off the flashlight and worked the slow-motion controls to center it on the finder's crosshairs. He'd just turned away from the finder and bent his head toward the main telescope's eyepiece when a noise from off to one side made him look up.

Someone was scrambling over the fence that separated Yeager's yard from the one behind it. Sam straightened. He wished he had his .45, but it was back in the house. The intruder—a man— dropped down into the yard and trotted toward the house.

He didn't see Sam, who was partly screened by a lemon tree he'd planted a few years before. And, plainly, the intruder wasn't looking for trouble. He came past the tree as if he had business to take care of and wanted to get it over with as fast as he could. Something that wasn't a gun glistened in his right hand.

"Hello, there," Yeager said. The other fellow stopped as dead as if he'd been turned to stone. Sam's dark-adapted eyes had no trouble seeing how astonished he looked. Yeager didn't waste more than an instant on his expression, though. He took advantage of the frozen surprise he'd created and jumped the intruder.

He got in a left to the face and a right to the belly that made the stranger double up. The other fellow tried to fight back after that, but never got the chance. One of the things the Army had taught Sam was that fighting fair wasted time and was liable to get you into trouble. As soon as he saw the opening, he kicked the intruder in the crotch.

The fellow let out a horrible shriek and dropped the thing he'd been holding. It was a bottle, and it smashed when it hit the grass. The stink of gasoline filled Yeager's nostrils. "Christ!" he burst out. "That's a fucking Molotov cocktail!"

Just winning the fight suddenly wasn't enough any more. The intruder was down on the grass, writhing and clutching at himself. Sam kicked him again, this time in the face. He groaned and went limp.

"Jonathan!" Yeager shouted. He stood there in the back yard, his heart pounding. *I'm too old for this,* he thought. Mutt Daniels had said that when they went into combat against the Lizards. Sam was as old now as Mutt had been then. He understood how his ex-manager had felt. "Jonathan!" he yelled again.

A moment later, the back door opened. The porch light came on. "What's up, Dad?" Jonathan asked.

Blinking against the glare, Sam pointed to the man he'd beaten. "This son of a bitch was going to try and burn our house down," he said. Barbara would have wanted him to say *try to burn*. Right this second, he didn't care what his wife would have wanted. "Don't just stand there, goddammit. Throw me some twine so I can tie him, and then call the cops."

"Right." The porch light gleamed off Jonathan's shaved scalp. He went back into the kitchen, found a ball of twine—good, solid stuff, not kite string—and threw it to Sam. Then he disappeared again. Yeager heard him talking on the phone and to Barbara. They both came out to see what was going on. By then, Sam had the intruder's hands tied behind him and his ankles bound together.

The man's eyes were open when the police got there. "Jesus Christ, Yeager," a cop said, looking at the fragments of glass and sniffing the gasoline. "Somebody out there doesn't like you much, does he?"

"Doesn't look that way," Sam answered. "Now that you've got this guy, maybe you can find out who."

"Hope so," the Gardena policeman said. "Let's get him into proper handcuffs—gotta look right when we take him to the station, you know."

"Okay by me," Yeager said. "Give me a call when you know something, will you? I want to get to the bottom of this." He shook his head. "I don't know why anybody'd have it in for me, but somebody sure does."

"Yeah." While his partner covered him, the cop cut the twine with which Sam had bound the intruder and handcuffed him instead. Then he hauled him to his feet. "Come on, pal. We've got some talking to do." He led him out to the squad car.

Yeager collapsed the legs to the telescope tripod and brought the instrument inside. "It's a good thing you were out there," Barbara said, shivering even though she was wearing a warm housecoat. "Otherwise . . ."

"Don't remind me." Sam stowed the scope on the service porch—the same spot Mickey and Donald's incubator had once occupied. Then he poured himself a stiff belt of bourbon. After he'd downed it, he poured another one. That let him get some sleep.

When the Gardena police didn't call him for two days, he called them. "Sorry, sir," said the lieutenant to whom his call was passed. "I can only tell you two things. That fellow didn't tell us anything much, but we didn't have him long. The FBI took charge of him yesterday morning."

"Did they?" Sam said. "Nobody tells me anything—they haven't called me for a statement yet, either. Give me their number, will you?"

"Yes, sir," the police lieutenant said. "It's KLondike 5-3971."

"Thanks." Yeager wrote it down, hung up, and dialed it. When he got the Los Angeles FBI headquarters, he explained who he was and what he wanted to know.

"I'm sorry, sir." The fellow on the other end of the line didn't sound sorry; he sounded bored. "I'm not allowed to release any information on the phone. I'm sure you understand why."

"Okay." Sam suppressed a sigh. *Bureaucrats,* he thought. He'd complained about them to Kassquit. "If I come down there and show you who I am, will somebody please tell me what the hell's going on?"

"I don't know anything about that, sir," the FBI man said, and hung up on him.

When Yeager drove downtown, he did it in full uniform, hoping to overawe the flunkies. That worked—to a point. He got kicked up to a senior inspector named O'Donohue. The Irishman looked him over, inspected his ID, and said, "All I can tell you, Lieutenant Colonel, is that we've flown this fellow to Little Rock for more questioning."

"Christ," Sam said. "Who the hell is he, anyway, and why won't anybody tell me anything?"

"We're still trying to find out, sir," O'Donohue answered. "When we do, I'm sure you'll be contacted."

"Are you? I wish I were." Yeager got to his feet. "All I see is that I'm getting the runaround, and I wish to hell I knew why."

O'Donohue just looked at him and didn't say a word. After perhaps half a minute, Yeager put on his hat and walked out. He wondered if anyone would call him. Nobody did.

"Would you believe," Ttomalss said, "there are actually times when I wish I were a Big Ugly?"

In the monitor on his desk, Felless' image drew back in surprise and alarm. "No, I would not believe that," she said, and used an emphatic cough to show how strongly she disbelieved it. "By the Emperor, why would you entertain such a mad desire?"

"Because our society has trained us for many thousands of years to treat vengeance as undesirable," he answered, "and because I wish I could enjoy taking my vengeance on the Tosevite female who kidnapped and imprisoned me during the fighting. Big Uglies still see nothing unfitting in revenge."

"Ah," Felless said. "That, at least, I can understand. What I would like is vengeance on the male from the conquest fleet who first discovered ginger."

"And I can understand that," Ttomalss said. "At least you finally managed to escape from Nuremberg."

"This Marseille place is not much of an improvement," Felless said with another emphatic cough. "And the Big Uglies here, I think, may be even more addled than those in Nuremberg. I even had one female refuse what would be a great reward for a Tosevite. Addled, I tell you."

"Most likely a criminal, or someone else with a good reason not to stick her snout in the air," Ttomalss said.

"It could be," Felless said. "I had wondered about that myself. Having someone of your experience confirm it is valuable."

"I thank you," Ttomalss said. But he didn't want to talk about things that concerned Felless; he wanted to go on with his own train of thought. "Revenge is not unknown among us, or else Shiplord Straha would not still be living the life of an exile in the not-empire called the United States. I doubt Fleetlord Atvar will ever forgive him."

"I have heard something of this scandal," Felless said. "Did Straha not try to raise a mutiny against the fleetlord?"

"Not exactly—he tried to relieve Atvar, but proved not to have quite enough support among the other fleetlords," Ttomalss answered. "But Atvar would have punished him as if it were a mutiny. I, though, cannot escape the belief that such efforts at vengeance are wrong."

"I have long been of the opinion that you males of the conquest fleet, from continual association with Big Uglies over so many years, have become more like them than is healthy," Felless said.

"It could be so," Ttomalss said. "The converse is that you of the colonization fleet sometimes seem to have no understanding whatever of the realities of life on Tosev 3 and the need for certain accommodations with the Tosevites."

"We understand more than you think," Felless replied. "But you of the conquest fleet do not seem to grasp the difference between understanding and approval. Approving of what goes on is in many cases impossible; we intend to change it."

"Good luck," Ttomalss said.

"And the continual sarcasm of the males of the conquest fleet is not appreciated, either," Felless snapped. "I bid you farewell." She broke the connection.

Ttomalss glared at the blank monitor screen. As far as he was concerned, Felless represented a good part of what had gone wrong with the colonization fleet. Finding he represented what she thought was wrong with the conquest fleet did nothing to increase his fondness for her.

He turned to more productive matters, calling up a recording of Kassquit's meeting with the two Big Uglies from the United

States. Neither the SSSR nor the *Reich* had requested similar meetings. *Of course not,* Ttomalss thought, annoyed at his own foolishness. *They do not realize we have a Tosevite here reared as if she were part of the Race.* Even the Big Ugly called Sam Yeager, who knew as much about the Race as any wild Tosevite, had discovered that only by listening to Kassquit's speech.

But Sam Yeager interested Ttomalss less than Jonathan Yeager did. The expert's hatchling might almost have come from the same egg as Kassquit. True, he wore Tosevite wrappings, but only of a minimal sort. He also wore body paint and removed most, though not all, of his unsightly hair. By the way he spoke, by the way he acted, he did not understand the Race quite so well as his father. But Jonathan Yeager was far more acculturated than Sam Yeager ever would be.

"And what will Jonathan Yeager's hatchlings be like?" Ttomalss said, trusting the computer to record and transcribe his words. "What will *their* hatchlings be like? Little by little, the Tosevites will come to accept our culture and to prefer it to their own. This is the slow route to conquest, but it also strikes me as offering far more certainty and security than force, given the force the Big Uglies can use in return. The key will be making sure they never wish to use that force, and using cultural dominance to gain political dominance."

He read the transcription of what he'd said, then made the affirmative gesture. Yes, that made excellent sense. He was proud of himself for thinking like a male of the Race, for remembering the importance of the long term.

And then, rereading his words, he was suddenly less pleased. The trouble was that, on Tosev 3, the short term had a way of making the long term obsolete. If the Big Uglies looked as if they were on the point of overtaking the Race technologically, the planet would go into the fire. It might go into the fire anyway, if the Deutsche or the other not-empires acted under the delusion they were stronger than they were. And the fire would swallow up the new, hopeful colonies, too. How to keep it from happening?

Slowing the Tosevites' acquisition of technology would do the job. The only problem with that was its impossibility. The Big Uglies either came up with new inventions of their own or started using ideas pirated from the Race almost every day. They were transforming their societies at a rate that struck Ttomalss as insanely rapid.

The only other choice he could see was making them not want to use whatever technology they ended up developing. That meant making them contented living side by side with the Race and, eventually, making them contented living under the rule of the Race. And that, he thought, meant encouraging them to produce more and more acculturated individuals like Jonathan Yeager.

Ttomalss didn't suppose Sam Yeager's hatchling gave reverence to the spirits of Emperors past. But maybe his hatchlings would, or their hatchlings. *We have to find ways to encourage that,* Ttomalss thought. The Race couldn't use economic incentives in the independent not-empires, as it could in the territory it presently ruled. Cultural incentives?

"Cultural incentives." Ttomalss spoke into the computer. "Up until now, we have observed young Tosevites imitating us. They have done this on their own, without encouragement from us. We might—we should—be able to encourage them. The more they are like us, the less interest they will have in assailing us."

He hoped that was true. It struck him as logical. It was the basis on which he'd urged the authorities to promote reverence to the spirits of Emperors past in those areas the Race did rule. That had drawn more resistance than he'd expected, but everything on Tosev 3 proved more difficult than the Race expected.

When the telephone hissed for attention, he hissed, too, in annoyance—the noise had frightened a thought out of his head. Kassquit's image appeared on the monitor. "I greet you, superior sir," she said.

"I greet you, Kassquit," he replied. "I hope you are well?"

"I am, thank you." Kassquit touched one of her arms. "I am certainly better now that I am not being immunized. That was a distinctly unpleasant process."

"Falling ill and possibly dying would have been even more unpleasant," Ttomalss pointed out. "You were vulnerable to illnesses the visiting Yeagers might have brought with them."

"I understand that. Understanding it and liking it are not the same." Kassquit had become a far more sardonic adult than Ttomalss would have expected. She went on, "And the Yeagers appear to have brought no illness with them, for I have not fallen sick since their visit."

"But you do not know whether you would have fallen sick had you not been immunized," Ttomalss said.

He gave Kassquit credit; after a moment's thought, his To-sevite ward used the affirmative gesture. She said, "No doubt you are right, superior sir. Still, now that I have proved I can safely meet them, would it be possible for them to come up here again?"

"Possible? Certainly, though we would have to make arrangements for their transport with the American Tosevites."

"I know that." Kassquit used the affirmative gesture again. "I hope you will begin making those arrangements, whatever they are."

"Very well," Ttomalss said, not without a certain pang. "May I ask why you are so eager for me to do this?" He tried not to show the worry he could hardly help feeling. Did blood call to blood more strongly than he had imagined possible? Did Kassquit wish she were an ordinary Big Ugly? On the face of it, the notion was absurd. But judging anything pertaining to Tosevites by first appearances could be deadly dangerous. The Race had learned that time and again.

Kassquit said, "Their visit will be something out of the ordinary. One day here is very much like another. This will give me something new to remember, something new to think about."

"I see," Ttomalss said, and Kassquit's explanation was sensible enough. It also relieved his mind. "All right, I will see what I can do. You understand, of course, that I cannot do this without approval from my superiors."

"Oh, yes, superior sir, that goes without saying," Kassquit agreed. "And perhaps, if this second meeting proves a success, I might eventually visit these Big Uglies down on the surface of Tosev 3. That would truly be an adventure for me."

"Would you like to do that?" Now Kassquit knew he sounded alarmed. He couldn't help himself. Day by day, Kassquit became a more autonomous individual. Ttomalss supposed that was inevitable; it happened with hatchlings of the Race, too. But watching it happen was acutely disconcerting.

"I would," Kassquit said with an emphatic cough. "I have been thinking about this. How can I be a bridge between the Empire and the independent Big Uglies if I do not reach to them as they reach to me?"

"Up until now, they have done the accommodating," Ttomalss

reminded her. "If you went down there, you would have to do some of your own. They would probably require you to wear cloth wrappings, for instance, to conform to their customs."

"That would also be something new for me," Kassquit said, sounding as enamored of novelty as any American Big Ugly. She added, "And wrappings would help keep me warm, would they not? The surface of Tosev 3 is supposed to be a chilly place."

"You have all the answers, I see," Ttomalss said wryly. "Let us discover how a second meeting goes before planning a third, if that suits you." To his relief, Kassquit didn't argue.

Nesseref was very pleased with how smoothly she'd brought her shuttlecraft out of its suborbital trajectory; it took much less atmospheric buffeting than usual on the way down toward the port outside Cairo. As the braking rockets ignited, she was thinking about how she could enjoy the layover at the Race's administrative center. From what she remembered of the transient barracks, she might have trouble enjoying it at all.

Her passenger, a regional subadministrator from China named Ppevel, was looking forward to the arrival. "By the spirits of Emperors past," he said, "it will be good to come to a place where the climate is close to decent. I have been cold for what seems like forever."

"So have I, superior sir," Nesseref replied. "Poland in winter reminds me of nothing so much as an enormous open-air freezer."

Ppevel started insisting China had to be colder. Before Nesseref could argue with him—and she intended to, because she had trouble imagining any place colder than Poland—a puff of black smoke and a loud bang outside the shuttlecraft distracted her. Another puff and bang, closer, were followed by metallic clatters as shell fragments struck the shuttlecraft. A warning light on the instrument panel came on.

"What is that noise?" Ppevel asked.

Ignoring him, Nesseref shouted into the radio microphone: "Cairo base! Cairo base! We are under attack, Cairo base!" She felt like a perfect target hanging up there, too; she couldn't interrupt the computer-controlled descent sequence, not unless she wanted to try to land manually, by eye turret and by guess. She wondered if she ought to. She might pilot the shuttlecraft right into the ground. But she might also make it harder to shoot down.

Before she could hit the override switch, a voice came out of the radio speaker: "Shuttlecraft Pilot, we have the Tosevite terrorists under assault. Maintain your present trajectory."

"It shall be done," Nesseref said as another shell burst all too close to the shuttlecraft. More fragments struck the machine. *Another hit like that and I disobey orders,* she thought.

But only one more antiaircraft shell exploded, this one farther away. The descent after that went as well as if no one had been shooting at her. She spied helicopters racing toward the spot from which, she presumed, the antiaircraft gun was firing.

Ppevel said, "I have also been under fire in China. The more often one endures it, the easier it is to bear."

"I have been under fire, too," Nesseref answered. "I do not think I will ever come to enjoy it."

She—and the computer—put the shuttlecraft down in the middle of the landing port. A vehicle hurried across the wide concrete expanse to meet the shuttlecraft. It was not the usual motorcar, but a mechanized combat vehicle. "The Big Uglies will have to work hard to destroy that machine," Ppevel observed.

"Truth," Nesseref said. But seeing the combat vehicle did not reassure her. If the Race sent it out to bring Ppevel—and, incidentally, herself—into Cairo, that meant there was some risk to them both.

"I thank you for a job well done," the regional subadministrator told her.

"You are welcome, superior sir." Nesseref didn't say the computer had done the work, with her along as little more than an organic emergency backup. She'd almost had to take over the controls of the shuttlecraft—this was as close as she'd ever come to doing just that. Had her luck been a little worse . . . but she didn't care to think about that. "If you like, I will go first, and attract whatever gunfire may be waiting for us."

"That will not be necessary, though I do appreciate the thought behind it," Ppevel said. He unstrapped himself and went down the ladder with easy haste that showed he'd flown in a good many shuttlecraft before. No one shot at him; the helicopters now buzzing around the port must have suppressed that Tosevite gun.

Nesseref followed him out of the shuttlecraft. A male in helmet and body armor said, "Into the vehicle! Do not waste time."

"I was not wasting time," Nesseref said indignantly. "Make

sure this shuttlecraft is well repaired. It took damage from the shells that exploded nearby. Had they cut a fuel or oxygen line, the craft—and my passenger, and I—would be scattered all over this port."

"It shall be done, superior female." The trooper lowered his voice as he went on, "Would you like a taste of ginger? That would make you feel better."

"No!" Nesseref used an emphatic cough. "If I had a taste of ginger, you would feel better, which is what you have in mind."

"Pheromones are in the air," the male admitted, "but I did not mean it like that."

"Of course you did," Nesseref told him. "If you do not mention the herb again, I will not have to learn your name and report you." She pushed past the male and into the mechanized combat vehicle. Glumly, he followed. She repeated her warning about the damage the shuttlecraft had taken to the driver, who relayed it by radio to the ground crew males and females at the shuttle-craft port. Nesseref relaxed a little after hearing him do that.

A couple of rocks and a glass bottle hit the combat vehicle as it rolled through the insanely crowded streets of Cairo. Ppevel took that in stride. "The same thing happens in China."

"Well, it does not happen in cities in Poland," Nesseref said. "The Big Uglies there are much better behaved. Why, I even invited one of them and his hatchling to supper at my apartment, and the evening proved quite pleasant."

"I have heard about Poland," Ppevel answered. "I must say I believe it to be a special case. The Big Uglies in that subregion find their Tosevite neighbors more unpleasant than they find us, and so look to us to protect them against those neighbors. That does not hold true either in China or here. I wish it did. It would make our rule much easier."

Remembering conversations with veteran administrators in Poland, Nesseref realized she had to yield the point, and did: "You are probably right, superior sir."

Right or wrong, Ppevel got better accommodations than she did. The mechanized combat vehicle took him to the Race's administrative center, which had been a luxurious Tosevite hotel before the conquest fleet arrived and had since been thoroughly modernized. After he went inside, the vehicle took Nesseref to the barracks for visiting males and females, some little distance away.

"You will be quartered in the hall to the left, the females' hall," the officer in charge of the barracks said, pointing with his tongue.

"Barracks separated by sex?" Nesseref exclaimed. "I never heard of such a thing."

"You will hear more of it in the future, superior female," the officer said. "Because of the Tosevite herb, we have had enough unfortunate incidents to reckon such segregation the wiser policy."

Nesseref thought about that. If a female who tasted ginger was liable to come into season at any time, and if a male inflamed by some other female's pheromones was liable to give a female ginger to provoke mating behavior in her . . . Nesseref made the affirmative gesture. "I see the need."

The barracks were as depressing as such places usually were. None of the females with whom she spoke knew anyone she knew. None of them was from the same region of Home as she was. Most of them appeared more interested in watching the video on a large wall monitor than in any sort of conversation.

One who did feel like talking had a definite goal in mind: "Do you have any ginger?" she asked Nesseref.

"I do not," Nesseref answered sharply. "I do not want any, either. Ginger is more trouble than it is worth."

"Nonsense," the other female said, and tacked on an emphatic cough. "Ginger is the only thing that makes this miserable, accursed planet worth inhabiting. Without it, I would just as soon have stayed in cold sleep."

"I think your wits did stay in cold sleep," Nesseref said. "How much trouble have you caused by broadcasting your pheromones far and wide? How many clutches of eggs have you laid because of the nasty herb?"

"Only one," the female said, sounding altogether unconcerned. "And I placed no burden whatever on the Race in doing so."

"Of course you did," Nesseref told her. "Someone is now raising the hatchlings who came from those eggs."

"No one from the Race." The other female remained blithe. "As soon as I laid my clutch, I sold the eggs to some Big Uglies who wanted them. Those hatchlings are their worry, not the Race's."

"You did what?" Nesseref could imagine depravity, but such utter indifference was beyond her comprehension. "By the Emperor, what would Tosevites do with hatchlings? What would they do *to* hatchlings?"

"I do not know, and I do not much care," the other female said. "I do know that I got enough ginger for the eggs to keep me happy for a long time. But now I have gone through it all, and I wish I had some more."

"Disgraceful," Nesseref said. "I ought to report you to the authorities."

"Go ahead," the female said. "Go right ahead. I will deny everything. How do you propose to prove any of this whatsoever?"

Nesseref had no good answer for that, however much she wanted one. She turned both eye turrets away from the other female, as if denying her the right to exist. The direct insult did what she wanted; the other female's toeclaws clicked on the hard floor as she went away. The almost equally hard cot on which Nesseref slept wasn't the only reason she passed a restless, uncomfortable night.

She had an uncomfortable flight back to Poland, too. She'd expected the local Big Uglies to stone the vehicle that took her to the airfield, and they did. Had that been all, she would have accepted it as an ordinary nuisance and thought little more about it. But it wasn't all—far from it.

As soon as her aircraft entered the *Reich*'s air space, a Deutsch killercraft met it and kept pace with it, so close that Nesseref could see the Big Ugly in the cockpit of the lean, deadly looking machine. Had he chosen to launch missiles or use his cannon, he could have shot down the aircraft in which she flew as easily as he pleased.

He didn't. When the aircraft left the *Reich* and flew into Polish air space, the Deutsch Tosevite peeled off and went back to one of his own air bases. But even the Deutsche had not offered such provocations for a long time. Nesseref was very happy indeed when her machine rolled to a stop outside of Warsaw and she got off.

Living in Lodz, not far from the eastern border of the Greater German *Reich*, meant Mordechai Anielewicz could receive German television programming. Speaking Yiddish, and having studied German in school, he understood the language well enough. That didn't mean he turned his receiver to the channels coming from the *Reich* very often. Football games were worth watching; the Germans and the nations subject to them fielded some fine clubs. But the interminable Nazi propaganda shows ranged from boring to savagely offensive.

Since Himmler's death, though, Mordechai had started paying more attention to German propaganda. He'd never imagined he would miss the SS chief and *Führer* who'd done the Jews so much harm. With something approaching horror, he realized he did. Himmler had been a known quantity—a known *mamzer* much of the time, certainly, but not someone who was likely to go off half-cocked. The Committee of Eight, on the other hand . . .

"Look at this!" Anielewicz exclaimed. His wife came over to the sofa in front of the television and dutifully looked. Mordechai pointed at the clumsy-looking panzers with crosses painted on them rolling across the screen. "Do you see what they're doing, Bertha?"

"Looks like another war film to me," she answered with a yawn. "May I go back and finish the dishes now?"

"Well, it is." Anielewicz clicked his tongue between his teeth. "But I don't like it when they start showing films about invading Poland. It's liable to mean they're gearing up to try it again."

"They wouldn't!" Bertha said. "They have to know they'll get smashed if they try."

"If they've got any sense, they have to know that," Mordechai answered. "But who says they've got any sense? When they start going on about provocations and insults, what are they doing but getting their people ready for trouble? That's what they did in 1939, after all."

On the screen, the German panzers mowed down charging Polish lancers wearing square hats. Bertha said, "It won't be that easy this time, if they're *meshuggeh* enough to try again."

"You know that. I know that. I think even Himmler knew that," Anielewicz said. "From what I've heard, the Lizards warned him off not so long ago, and he listened to them. But these fools?" He shook his head.

"What can we do?" Bertha asked.

That was more easily asked than answered. "I don't know," Mordechai said unhappily. "I know what I'd like to do—I'd like to put Jewish fighters on alert, and I'd like to get in touch with the Poles, too, so I know they'll be ready to move in case the Nazis really do intend to go after us here."

"Will the Poles listen to you?" his wife asked.

Anielewicz shrugged. "I don't know that, either. As far as they're concerned, what am I? Just a damned Jew, that's all. But they certainly won't listen to me if I don't get in touch with them." His smile looked cheerful, but wasn't. "*Gottenyu,* I don't even know if the Jews in Warsaw will pay any attention to me. As far as they're concerned, Poland *is* Warsaw, and the rest of the country can *geh in drerd*."

"But you came from Warsaw!" Bertha's voice quivered with indignation.

"I've been away a long time—plenty long enough for them to forget where I came from," Mordechai replied. His laugh didn't sound amused, either. "Of course, with some of those people you can walk around the corner for a loaf of bread and they'll forget about you by the time you get back."

"Ingrates, that's what they are." Bertha made a wife as loyal as any man could want. She was also a long way from a fool, asking, "Do you suppose they've forgotten about the explosive-metal bomb?"

"No, they'll remember that," Mordechai admitted. "I'm the one who wishes he could forget about it." He went into the kitchen and came back with a couple of glasses of slivovitz. Sipping from one, he handed Bertha the other. "I don't know if it will work, and God forbid I should ever have to find out."

"If you do, it won't be the only explosive-metal bomb going off, will it?" Bertha asked. When Anielewicz shook his head, she knocked back her plum brandy like a farm laborer. She said, "That won't be all that happens, either."

"Oh, no. Poison gas and panzers and who can say what all else?" Anielewicz poured down his brandy, too. "The other thing I'd better do is, I'd better talk with Bunim. I'm about as happy with that as I am with a trip to the dentist, and that Lizard loves me every bit as much as I love him. But if we're going to fight on the same side, we'd better have some notion of what we'll be trying to do."

"That makes good sense." His wife's mouth twisted. "Of course, if the whole world goes mad, whether or not anything makes sense stops mattering very much, doesn't it?"

Before Mordechai could answer her, the telephone rang. He walked over to the shabby end table on which it sat and picked it up. Everything in the flat was shabby: other people's hand-me-downs, charity after the arson fire that had forced the Anielewiczes from the building where they'd lived so long. "Hello?" he said, and then spent the next ten minutes in intense conversation, some in Yiddish, some in Polish.

When he hung up, his wife asked, "Was that Warsaw? Have they decided they need to worry about the *Reich* after all?"

He shook his head in some bemusement. "No. You would have thought so from the way I was talking, wouldn't you? That was the *Armia Krajowa*, the Polish Home Army. They want to cooperate with us, even if the learned fellows back in Warsaw haven't figured out there's anybody to cooperate against."

"The Poles want to cooperate with us?" Bertha sounded astonished. Mordechai didn't blame her; he was astonished himself. Her gaze sharpened. "You'd better go see Bunim—do it first thing tomorrow morning, too. If you don't get there ahead of the Home Army, who knows how much mischief the Poles may be able to stir up?"

"You're right," Mordechai said at once. "You always were the best politician we ever had in Lodz."

"Feh!" Bertha tossed her head, a most dismissive gesture. "You don't need to be a politician to see this. As long as you're not blind, it's there."

With tea warm inside him, with his greatcoat pulled tight around him, Anielewicz strode through snow-clogged streets to the Race's administrative offices overlooking the Bialut Market Square. As soon as the Lizards let him in, he shed the coat, folded it, and carried it over his arm: the Race kept their buildings heated not only to but past the point humans found pleasantly warm.

That Bunim was willing to see him with essentially no advance notice told him the Lizards were worried about the Greater German *Reich*, too. "I greet you, Regional Subadministrator," Mordechai said in the language of the Race.

"Good day," Bunim answered in fair Polish. The human language he spoke best was German. Neither he nor Anielewicz seemed to want to use it now. Having politely used a human language, the Lizard went back to his own: "And what is it you want to see me about?"

"What do you suppose?" Mordechai answered. "The increasing threat from the *Reich*, of course. Do you not agree that we will be better off if we prepare joint action well in advance of any certain need?"

More often than not, Bunim looked down his snout at the idea of cooperating with humans. Now, though, he said only, "Yes, that might be wise. What sort of notions do you have for unifying your forces, those of the *Armia Krajowa*, and our own to withstand whatever attacks may come from the west and south?"

Mordechai Anielewicz stared at him. "You *do* take these threats seriously," he blurted.

"Yes," Bunim said, and underscored that with an emphatic cough. "You know as well as I that the Deutsche can destroy this region. We cannot prevent it. We can only make it unpleasantly expensive."

"You are blunt about it," Mordechai said.

"Truth is what truth is," the regional subadministrator answered. "We do not change it by turning our eye turrets away from it. Tosevites sometimes seem to have trouble understanding this. The Deutsche, for example, see that they can overrun and wreck Poland. They refuse to see the price they will pay for doing so. If you have any suggestions for getting the point across to them, I would be grateful."

"I am the wrong Tosevite to ask, I fear," Anielewicz said. "As you know, the only thing that would delight the Deutsche is my death. I do not know how to dissuade them, or if anyone or anything can dissuade them. What I wanted to plan with you was how best to fight them."

"I understand," Bunim said. "Talks are also ongoing with your colleagues in Warsaw, and with the various Polish Tosevite factions. Had you not come to me, I would have called you in a few days."

"Would you?" That surprised Anielewicz, too. "After all the time you have spent saying that Big Uglies have no place in the defense of Poland?"

Bunim made the affirmative gesture. "You too are a leader, Mordechai Anielewicz. Have you never had to hold a position with which you did not personally agree? Have circumstances never forced you to change a position?"

"Many times," Mordechai admitted. "But I did not think it would also be so for the Race."

"Strange things hatch from strange eggs," Bunim said, which sounded as if it ought to be a proverb among the Race, something on the order of, *Politics make strange bedfellows.* The regional subadministrator went on, "If you can bring the forces under your control to full alert, I will be in touch with you on ways in which we can integrate them into the defense of this region. Is it agreed?"

"It is agreed," Anielewicz said, but then he held up a forefinger. "It is agreed, with the exception of our explosive-metal bomb. That stays under our control, no one else's."

"As you wish," Bunim said, which, more than anything else, told Mordechai how worried the Lizards were. "If you have this weapon, I trust you will use it against the Deutsche, who are your most important foes. I bid you good day."

"Good day," Mordechai said, accepting the dismissal more meekly than he'd dreamt he would. Still almost dazed, he went outside. A nondescript little man fell into step beside him. Somehow, that left him unsurprised, too. He nodded, almost as if to an old friend. "Hello, Nussboym. What brings you back to Lodz?"

"Trouble with the Nazis—what else?" David Nussboym answered, his Yiddish flavored these days by all the years he'd spent in the Soviet Union. He looked up at Mordechai, who was perhaps ten centimeters taller. "And I'm not so sorry as I was that we didn't quite manage to knock you off, either."

"That you—?" Anielewicz stopped in his tracks. "I ought to—"

"But you won't," Nussboym said. "You know damned well you won't. We've got the Germans to worry about first, right?" The worst of it was, Mordechai had to nod.

☆ 15 ☆

David Goldfarb had thought Ottawa's climate unfortunate. As a matter of fact, he hadn't just thought it—he'd been right. But compared to the weather Edmonton enjoyed—or rather, didn't enjoy—Ottawa might as well have been the earthly paradise. Blizzards came down off the Rockies one after another. Only some truly amazing machinery kept the city from coagulating for days at a time after a storm swept through.

But, of all the places in the Dominion of Canada, this was the one where electronics were booming. And so it was the place to which Goldfarb had moved his family, once he was finally able to move them anywhere. Escaping from the detention center near the Ministry of Defense felt so good, he was willing to overlook a few minor deficiencies in the weather.

As he crunched through snow on his way to work, he did wonder why Edmonton, of all places, had become Canada's electronic heartland. One answer readily springing to mind was that it was the most northerly big city Canada boasted, and so the one least likely to attract the Lizards' attention.

He almost got killed when he crossed 103rd Street while walking along Jasper Avenue. He was still in the habit of looking right first when crossing the street—but Canadians, like their American cousins to the south, drove on the right. They drove big American cars, too. The Chevrolet that came to a halt with blasting horn and a rattle of tire chains probably could have smashed the life out of Goldfarb without even getting dented.

He sprang back up onto the curb. "Sorry," he said with a weak smile. The fellow who'd almost run him down couldn't have heard him; the Chevy's windows were all up to give the heater a fighting chance. The car rolled on.

On his second try, Goldfarb got across 103rd Street without nearly committing suicide. He made a point of looking left first. When he made a point of it, he had no trouble. When he didn't, he acted from habit, and habit didn't work here.

The Saskatchewan River Widget Works, Ltd., operated out of a second-floor—Goldfarb would have called it a first-floor—suite of offices on Jasper near 102nd Street. The name of the firm had drawn him even before he had the faintest notion what a widget was. The short answer was that it was anything some ingenious engineer said it was.

He shed his overcoat with a sigh of relief. "Hello, Goldfarb," said Hal Walsh, the ingenious engineer who'd founded the firm. "Isn't it a lovely day out?"

"If you're a polar bear, possibly," Goldfarb said. "Otherwise, no."

Walsh and several other engineers, all of them Edmontonians, jeered at him. They took their beastly climate for granted. Goldfarb, used to something approaching moderation in his weather, didn't and couldn't. He jeered back.

One of the engineers, an alarmingly clever young fellow named Jack Devereaux, said, "It's bracing, that's what it is. Puts hair on your chest."

"Fur would do better," Goldfarb retorted. "And I'm sure the Eskimos up at the North Pole say the same thing, Jack. That's only a couple of miles outside of town, isn't it? We could go and check for ourselves."

The chaffing went on as he fixed himself a cup of tea and got to work. He'd thought that, coming out of the RAF, he would know more about electronics than these civilians did. It hadn't worked out like that. They took Lizard technology for granted in ways he didn't.

"But you'll learn," Walsh had told him, not unkindly, a few days after he was hired. "The difference is, the military—yours, mine, everybody's—has spent the past twenty years grafting the Lizards' technology onto our own to keep some sort of continuity with what we had before."

"Well, of course," said Goldfarb, who'd watched that happen—and who'd helped make it happen. "How else would you go about it?"

"Junk what we had before," his new boss had answered. "The more we steal from the Race, the more we develop what we've stolen from the Race, the better the widgets we come up with. That other stuff, that stuff we used to have, all belongs in the museum with buggy whips and gas lamps and whalebone corsets."

Goldfarb hadn't thought of it like that. He didn't care to think of it like that. But the Saskatchewan River Widget Works came up with gadgets he wouldn't have imagined possible in his long years with the RAF. The one that hooked up a little electronic gizmo—adapted from one the Lizards used—to a battery hardly bigger—stolen from a Lizard pattern—to make a children's book that included sound effects when the right buttons were pressed left him shaking his head. He wasn't surprised to find it had been Jack Devereaux's idea.

"Hardly seems right to use all that fancy technology for something to keep three-year-olds happy for a few hours," he remarked.

"Why not?" Devereaux asked around a big mouthful of lunchtime sandwich. "That's what this stuff is *for*, for heaven's sake. The military uses are all very well, but the Lizards live with these electronics every minute of the day and night. They make their lives better. They make them more interesting. They make them more fun, too. They can do the same for us."

He sounded very sure of himself, like a missionary spreading the word of God to the benighted heathen. And, the longer Goldfarb thought about it, the more convinced he was that the brash young engineer had a point. Britain had been a garrison state, arming itself to the teeth against the Lizards—and, incidentally, to make sure the *Reich* stayed friendly ally and mentor, not conqueror. Canada was different. Shielded by the USA from danger at the hands of the Race, Canadians could, as Devereaux said, have fun with the new technology. They could, and they did.

Sitting there at a drawing board with bins of electronic parts all around for him to play with, Goldfarb had to work at the notion that having fun was all right, that he wasn't betraying mankind by not working on some weapon that would make every Lizard on Earth shrivel up and turn purple. Designing a little plastic top that lit up and played music when you spun it struck him as absurdly frivolous.

When he said as much, Hal Walsh gave him an odd look and asked, "Are you sure you're not a Protestant?"

Goldfarb snorted. "I'm not sure of a great many things, but that's one of them."

"Well, okay." His boss laughed. "But look at it from a different angle. Suppose you took that top you're working on back to your radar station in 1940. Suppose you spun it on the floor there and it did what it's supposed to do. What would your chums have thought of it? What would *you* have thought of it back then?"

"Hmm." Goldfarb rubbed his chin. "The battery would have been impossible. The sound square would have been impossible. The light and the plastic would just have been improbable. Offhand, I'd say we'd have thought the Martians had landed."

"You wouldn't have been so far wrong, either, would you?" Walsh laughed some more. "Now suppose you gave it to your father when he was a little boy. What would his mother and father have thought?"

"Back in Warsaw before the turn of the century?" Goldfarb thought about that. "Jews don't burn people at the stake for witchcraft, but that's about the only thing that would have kept me in one piece." He got another chuckle from Walsh, but he hadn't been joking.

His boss was about to say something more when the telephone by Goldfarb's table rang. Walsh waved and went off. Goldfarb picked up the phone. Before he could even say hello, the fellow on the other end of the line announced, "It's not over yet. You may think it's over, but it's not."

"What?" Goldfarb said. "Who is this?"

"Who do you suppose?" the caller answered. "We don't forget. We do get even. You'll find out." The line went dead.

Goldfarb stared at the phone for a moment, then put the handset back in its cradle. "Who was that?" Walsh asked. "You look like you just saw a ghost."

"Maybe I did," Goldfarb said.

He waited for his boss to ask more questions, but Walsh surprised him by doing nothing of the kind, but turning away and going back to his own work. An Englishman might have done that, but Goldfarb hadn't expected it on this side of the Atlantic. From all the American films he'd seen, people over here were a lot more brash about sticking their noses into other people's business.

After a moment, he realized American films came out of the United States, not Canada. The Canadians who'd grilled him had done it out of duty, not because they were personally nosy. The reserve wasn't quite so strong as the notorious British stiff upper lip, but it was there.

He got back to work, waiting all the while for the phone to ring again. That was how these things worked, wasn't it? The bad eggs played on their victim's fear, and sometimes managed to drive him round the bend without even doing anything to him.

And, sure as the devil, the phone did ring again half an hour later. When Goldfarb picked it up, all he heard on the other end was silence. He listened for a little while, then hung up. Nobody'd drive him round the bend, by God, but someone had made a good start on getting his goat.

Somebody . . . He had no idea who, though whoever it was had to be a Canadian pal of Basil Roundbush's. Suddenly, he grinned and turned to Hal Walsh. "Mr. Widget, sir!"

Walsh grinned back. "At your service, Mr. Goldfarb. And what can I do for you today?"

"You're in the widget business," Goldfarb said. "Can you tell me if anyone's ever invented a widget that shows the number a telephone call is made from?"

"A fast and easy kind of tracer, you mean?" Walsh asked. "Something better than the police and the telephone company use?"

Goldfarb nodded. "That's what I'm talking about. Shouldn't be too hard, not if we put some of the Lizards' information-processing gadgets on the job. Suppose you could see at a glance it was your brother-in-law on the other end of the line, and you didn't want to talk to him because you owed him twenty quid— uh, fifty dollars. It'd be handy."

"You're right. It would." If Walsh was wondering why Goldfarb chose this exact moment to ask about that invention, he didn't let on. "And no, I don't think anything like that is on sale now, and yes, I can see how it might be popular." He looked past Goldfarb, or maybe through him. "I can see how you might do it, too."

"So can I," Goldfarb said, excitement kindling in him. Roundbush's nasty friends might have thought they were putting a scare in him, but, with a little luck, they'd just gone a long way toward making him a rich man. He started bouncing ideas off his boss, who also had some good ones of his own. Goldfarb was a tinkerer, and largely self-taught; Hal Walsh understood more about theory than he would if he lived to be ninety.

Both men started scribbling notes after the first couple of minutes. After half an hour, Goldfarb was hoping the nasty boys would call back again, and do it soon. Once he had their telephone number, he could pass it on to the police. Then they'd be out of his hair for good. From an office full of people who thought the same way he did, everything looked very simple.

When the telephone rang, Käthe Drucker answered it. After a moment, she turned and said, "It's for you, Hans."

"Who?" Johannes Drucker asked, setting down his newspaper and getting to his feet. His wife shrugged, as if to say it wasn't anybody she knew. Drucker tried to hide his worries as he walked to the phone. If that damned Gunther Grillparzer was raising more trouble . . . If Grillparzer was doing that, he'd just have to deal with it as best he could. He took the phone from Käthe. "Drucker here."

"Your leave is canceled," said a crisp voice on the other end of the line. "All leaves are canceled, by order of the Committee of Eight. Report to your duty station at Peenemünde immediately."

"Jawohl!" Drucker said, fighting the urge to come to attention. The line went dead. He hung up the telephone.

"What is it?" Käthe asked—she could see it was something. When he told her, her eyes went wide. "Does that mean what I'm afraid it means?"

"That the balloon's going up on account of Poland?" he asked, and she nodded. He answered the only way he could: with a shrug. "I don't know. No one tells me anything. I'll say this—I hope not. But whether it is or not, I have to report in." He raised his voice: "Heinrich!"

"What is it, Father?" His elder son's reply floated down from upstairs.

"Keep an eye on your brother and sister for a while. I have to report to the base, and your mother will come along so she can drive the car back here. Have you got that?"

"Yes, Father," Heinrich said, and then asked essentially the same question Käthe had: "Will it be war?" The difference was, he sounded excited, not afraid.

He's too young to know better, Drucker thought, remembering how enthusiastic a Hitler Youth he'd made at the same age. Not much later, he'd gone into the *Wehrmacht*, and he'd been there ever since. Did that mean he didn't know better, either? Maybe it did. He had no time to worry about it now.

Reliable no matter how ugly it was, the Volkswagen roared to life right away. Drucker didn't want to think about what he would have done if it hadn't started. Called for a taxi, he supposed—an order to report immediately meant that and nothing else. No one cared about excuses; the idea was that there shouldn't be any.

Drucker drove out of Greifswald and east across the flat, muddy ground toward Peenemünde. He cursed every car that got in his way. At the barbed-wire perimeter around the base, he showed the sentries his identification card. They shot out their arms in salute and let him by.

He stopped in front of the barracks where he spent almost as much time as he did with his family. When he jumped out of the Volkswagen, he started to take the keys with him. Käthe coughed reproachfully. Feeling foolish, Drucker left the keys alone. His wife got out, too, to come around to the driver's side. He took her in his arms and kissed her. He wasn't the only soldier doing such things; the road in front of the barracks was clogged with stopped cars and men saying goodbye to wives and sweethearts.

Käthe got back into the VW and drove away. Drucker hurried into the barracks and threw on the uniform that hung in the closet. "What's up?" he called to another space flier who was dressing with as much frantic haste as he.

"Damned if I know," his comrade answered. "Whatever it is, though, it can't be good. I'd bet on that."

"Not with me, you wouldn't, because I think you're right," Drucker told him.

They hurried toward the administrative center. Drucker looked at his wristwatch. Less than half an hour had gone by since the telephone rang. He couldn't get in trouble for being late, not when he'd had to come from Greifswald . . . could he? He resolved to raise a big stink if anyone complained.

No one did. He checked off his name on the duty roster and hurried into the auditorium to which soldiers in military-police metal- gorgets were directing people. The auditorium was already almost full; even though he'd done everything as fast as he could, he remained a latecomer. He slid into a chair near the back of the hall and shot disapproving glances at the men who came in after him.

General Dornberger stepped up onto the stage. Even from his distant seat, Drucker thought the commandant at Peenemünde looked worried. He couldn't have been the only man who thought so, either; the buzz in the hall rose abruptly, then died as Dornberger held up his hand for quiet.

"Soldiers of the *Reich*, our beloved fatherland is in danger," Dornberger said into that silence. "In their arrogance, the Lizards in Poland have attempted to impose limits on our sovereignty, the first step toward bringing the *Reich* under their rule. The Committee of Eight has warned them that their demands are intolerable to a free and independent people, but they have paid no attention to our just and proper protests."

He's building up toward a declaration of war, Drucker thought. Ice ran through him. He knew the *Reich* could hurt the Race. But, probably better than any man who'd never been into space, he also know what the Race could do to the *Reich*. He felt like a dead man walking. The only hope he had for his family's survival was the wind blowing the fallout from Peenemünde out to sea or toward Poland rather than onto Greifswald. *Ashes to ashes, dust to dust.*

"No state of war as yet exists between the Greater German *Reich* and the Race," Dornberger went on, "but we must show the Lizards that we are not to be intimidated by their threats and impositions. Accordingly, the *Reich* is now formally placed on a footing of *Kriegsgefahr*. Because of this war danger order, the armed forces are being brought to a maximum alert—which is why you are here."

It won't happen right this minute, then, Drucker thought. *Thank God for so much.* His wasn't the only soft sigh of relief in the auditorium.

"If the worst should befall, we shall not stand alone," General Dornberger said. "The governments of Hungary and Romania and Slovakia stand foursquare behind us, as loyal allies should. And we have also received an expression of support and best wishes from the British government."

That mixed good news and bad. Of course the allies stood by the *Reich*: if they didn't, they'd fall over, and in a hurry, too. If England really was supporting Germany, that was good news, very good indeed. The English were bastards, but they were tough bastards, no two ways about it.

But Dornberger hadn't said a word about Finland and Sweden. What were they doing? *Sitting on their hands,* Drucker thought. *Hoping that when the axe falls, it doesn't land on their necks.*

Sitting where they were, he might have done the same thing. That didn't mean he was happy they were staying quiet—far from it. But they had a better chance of coming through an all-out exchange between the Race and the *Reich* in one piece than a place like Greifswald did. *Damn them.*

"We are going to put as many men into space as fast as we can," the commandant said. "Once up there, they will await orders or await developments. If we down here fall, they shall avenge us. *Heil*—" He broke off, looking confused for a moment. He couldn't say "*Heil* Himmler!" any more, and "*Heil* the Committee of Eight!" sounded absurd. But he found a way around the difficulty: "*Heil* the *Reich*!"

"*Heil!*" Along with everyone else in the hall, Drucker gave back the acclamation. And, no doubt along with everyone else, he wondered what would happen next.

The enormous roar of an A-45 blasting off penetrated the auditorium's soundproofing. Sure enough, the *Reich* wasn't wasting any time getting its pieces on the board so it could play them. Those upper stages wouldn't do Germany any good if they got destroyed on the ground.

"Have we got a schedule yet for who's going into orbit when?" Drucker asked, hoping someone around him would know.

A couple of people said, "No." A couple of others laughed. Somebody remarked, "The way things are right now, we're damned lucky we know which side we're on." That brought a couple of more laughs, and told Drucker everything he needed to know. He wondered why everyone had been summoned so urgently if things were no better organized than this. *We might as well be Frenchmen,* he thought scornfully.

Major Neufeld pushed through the crowd toward him. General Dornberger's adjutant looked dyspeptic even when he was happy. When he wasn't, as now, he looked as if he belonged in the hospital. "Drucker!" he called urgently.

Drucker waved to show he'd heard. "What is it?" he asked. Whatever it was, he would have bet it wasn't anything good. Had it been good, Neufeld would have left him alone to do his job, just as the dour major was doing with everyone else.

Sure enough, Neufeld said, "The commandant wants to see you in his office right this minute."

"Jawohl!" Drucker obeyed without asking why. That was the Army way. Asking why wouldn't have done him any good, anyhow. He knew that only too well. Several people gave him curious looks as he left the auditorium. Hardly anyone knew why he'd had run-ins with higher-ups, but practically everyone knew that he'd had them.

"Reporting as ordered, sir," he said when he got to Dornberger's office.

"Come in, Drucker." Walter Dornberger took a puff on one of the fat cigars he favored, then set it in the ashtray. "Sit down, if you care to."

"Thank you, sir." As Drucker sat, he wondered if the commandant was going to offer him a blindfold and a cigarette next. Dornberger was usually brusque. Today he seemed almost courtly. Drucker asked, "What's up, sir?" He'd been asking that since he got to Peenemünde. If anyone knew, if anyone would tell him, the commandant was the man.

Dornberger picked up the cigar, looked at it, and set it down without putting it in his mouth. In conversational tones, he remarked, "I wish Field Marshal Manstein were as good a politician as he is a soldier."

"Do you?" Drucker asked, nothing at all in his voice. He didn't need a road map to see where that led. "The SS is in charge of the Committee of Eight?"

"And the Party, and Goebbels' lapdogs," General Dornberger answered. "Manstein knows better than to provoke the Lizards, or I assume he does. This—this is madness. We can defend ourselves against the Race, yes, certainly. But win an offensive struggle? Anyone who has dealt with them knows better."

"Yes, sir," Drucker said. Why was the commandant telling him this? Most likely because no one in authority trusted him, which, in an odd sort of way, made him safe. "Anyone who's been in space knows what they've got up there, that's for sure."

"Of course." Dornberger's nod was jerky. "Yes. Of course. And that brings me to the main reason I called you here, Lieutenant Colonel. Changes in the alignment of the Committee of Eight affect more than the broad foreign policy of the *Reich*. I must tell you that you will not be allowed into space during this crisis. I am sorry, but you are reckoned to be politically unreliable."

Drucker supposed he should have expected that, but it hit like a blow in the belly even so. Bitterly, he asked, "Why bother calling me here, then? I might as well have stayed at home with my family." *We could all die together then,* ran through his mind.

"Why? Because I am still working to get the restriction lifted. I know what a good man you are in space, regardless of your troubles on the ground," Dornberger answered. "Meanwhile . . . You may be lucky, you know."

"If we're all lucky, none of this will matter. We'd better be." Drucker got up and walked out without bothering to ask for permission. Normally, that was as close to lese majesty as made no difference. Today, General Dornberger said not a word.

"They are serious!" Vyacheslav Molotov sounded indignant. That, in its own way, was a prodigy. Andrei Gromyko knew as much. His shaggy eyebrows twitched in astonishment. Molotov was so agitated, he hardly noticed. "The Germans *are* serious, I tell you, Andrei Andreyevich."

"So it would seem," the foreign commissar answered. "You already told them we wanted no part of this madness. Past that, what can we do?"

"Prepare as best we can to have the western regions of the Soviet Union devastated by radioactive fallout," Molotov answered. "Past that, we can do nothing. We are one of the four greatest powers on the face of the Earth and above it, and we can do nothing. Against stupidity the very gods themselves contend in vain."

From a convinced Marxist-Leninist, that was almost blasphemy. It was also a telling measure of Molotov's agitation, perhaps even more telling than raising his voice. Gromyko understood as much.

Nodding, he commented, "And it was a German who said those words. He knew his people all too well."

"Was it?" Molotov had long since forgotten the source of the quotation. "Well, whoever it was, we are about to watch all of Europe west of our border go into the fire, and the only thing we can do is stand back and watch."

Gromyko lit a cigarette. After a couple of meditative drags, he said, "We could go in on the side of the *Reich*. That is the only action we have available to us. The Lizards will not want our assistance."

"No, we would only ruin ourselves by joining the Germans. I can see that," Molotov said. "But, damn it, we need the *Reich*. Can you imagine me saying such a thing? I can hardly imagine it, but it's true. We need every single counterbalance to the Lizards we can find. Without the Nazis, mankind is weaker." He grimaced, hating the words.

"I agree with you, Vyacheslav Mikhailovich," Gromyko said. "Unfortunately."

"Yes, unfortunately," Molotov said. "I have sent certain operatives into Poland, to give us contacts with the human groups there. I do not know how much good that will do, or whether it can do anything to minimize the destruction war will bring, but I am making the effort." He had control of himself again. He hated giving way to alarm, but there was so much about which to be alarmed here.

"Let us hope it will help." Gromyko didn't sound as if he thought it would. Molotov didn't really think it would, either, but David Nussboym had volunteered for the mission, and Molotov let him go. He owed Nussboym a debt; without the Jewish NKVD man, Beria would surely have liquidated him before Marshal Zhukov put paid to the spymaster's coup.

And, if the worst did happen in Poland, odds were that Nussboym wouldn't come back to claim any more payments on that debt. Molotov made such calculations almost without conscious thought.

Gromyko said, "The Americans are concerned about this crisis, too. Do you suppose President Warren can get the Germans to see reason? The Nazis do not automatically hate and disbelieve the United States, as they do with us."

"I have had consultations with the American ambassador, but

they were less satisfactory than I would have liked," Molotov answered. "I could be wrong, but I have the feeling the USA would not be sorry to see the *Reich* removed from the scene. The Americans, of course, would suffer far less incidental damage from a conflict over Poland than would we."

"They are shortsighted, though. Having the *Reich* on the board strengthens all of humanity, as you said, Comrade General Secretary." Gromyko was not going to contradict his boss. Molotov remembered trembling when he'd had to try to steer Stalin away from a course whose danger was obvious to everyone but the Great Leader. Molotov knew he wasn't so frightful as Stalin had been, but even so. . . . His foreign commissar sighed. "I don't suppose they would be Americans if they were not shortsighted."

"They also would not be Americans if they did not seek to profit from others' misfortunes," Molotov said. "Before the Lizards came, they were happy enough to send us aid against the Nazis, but how many soldiers in American uniform did you see? None. We did the dying for them." As Stalin had, he remembered that, remembered and resented it. Like Stalin, he'd been unable to avenge it.

Gromyko said, "If the Americans will not act, if the Nazis will not heed us, what about the Lizards themselves? Have they not warned the *Reich* of the dangers inherent in its provocative course?"

"I am given to understand that they have," Molotov said. "But telling a German something and getting him to listen are two quite different things." He drummed his fingers on the polished wood desktop in front of him. "Do you suppose we might be able to suggest ways in which the Race might gain the Nazis' attention?"

"I don't know," Gromyko answered. "But at this point, what have we got to lose?"

Molotov considered. "Nothing whatever. We might even worm our way into the good graces of the Race. A good suggestion, if I say so myself. I shall arrange a meeting with Queek."

The ease with which he arranged the meeting told him the Lizards were grasping at straws, too. And the Polish interpreter for the Race's ambassador to the Soviet Union showed none of his usual toploftiness. Plainly, he was worried about what might happen to his homeland.

Queek gave forth with a series of hisses and pops and coughs. The interpreter turned them into rhythmic, Polish-accented Russian: "The ambassador says he is grateful for your good offices, Comrade General Secretary, and welcomes any suggestions you have on how to keep this crisis from hatching into full-scale conflict."

"Tell him that the best way to make sure the Germans do not attack is to convince them they have no hope of winning," Molotov answered. "They do respect strength, if nothing else."

"That is not apparent in the present situation," Queek said. "We have repeatedly warned them what will happen if they attack Poland. They cannot help but know the strength at our command. And yet, to all appearances, they continue preparations to attack. I am baffled. The Race is baffled. If the *Reich* breaks the truce that has held so long, we shall not be gentle."

"I understand." Had Molotov been in Queek's position, he would have said the same thing. But he wasn't, and he didn't like the position he was in. He went on, "My own concern is not least related to the damage a conflict over Poland will cause to the peace-loving people of the Soviet Union, who do not deserve to be sacrificed because of the folly of others."

Queek shrugged as if he were a man. "I am not responsible for the geography of Tosev 3," he said. "If your not-empire does not provoke us, we shall do it no direct harm. What we need to do to defeat and punish the *Reich*, however, that, I assure you, we shall do."

Again, Molotov might have said the same thing in the same position. Again, he didn't like hearing it. He cast about for ways to head off the catastrophe he saw looming ahead. Here, he did not feel the dialectic was operating on his side. The dialectic . . . He didn't smile, but he felt like it. "Your ambassador in Nuremberg might tell the Germans that we hope they do attack Poland, because we expect to profit from their overthrow at your hands."

"Why do you say this?" Even in his own language, which Molotov couldn't understand, Queek sounded suspicious. The translation proved the Soviet leader had gauged the Lizard's tone aright. The ambassador went on, "I know that you and your not-empire love neither the Race nor the *Reich*."

"No, we do not," Molotov agreed, glad he didn't have to bother with hypocrisy here. "But a war would be almost as disastrous for us as for either side fighting, even if we are not directly involved. The Germans will not pay any attention to what we tell them, for they do not love us, either. But if they think we want them to do one thing, they might do the opposite to annoy us."

Before answering Molotov, Queek spoke back and forth with his interpreter in the language of the Race. Again, Molotov didn't understand, but he could guess what was going on: the ambassador wanted to know if the interpreter thought what he'd said was true. The Pole could damage the Soviet Union by saying no, but he would damage his own homeland worse.

Queek said, "Perhaps we shall try this. It cannot make things worse, and it may make them better. I thank you for the suggestion."

"I do it in my self-interest, not yours," Molotov said.

"I understand that," the Lizard replied. "Against the *Reich*, your self-interest and that of the Race coincide. You may rest assured, I also understand this is not the case in other areas where we impinge."

"I have no idea what you are talking about," Molotov said, lying through his teeth. "Our relations with the Race are correct in all regards."

Again, Queek and his interpreter conferred. " 'Correct,' I am given to understand, is a euphemism for 'chilly,' " the Lizard said at last. "This strikes me as an accurate summation. Before I go, I shall repay you for your assistance, however self-interested it may have been, by strongly suggesting that you should under no circumstances give the Chinese rebels an explosive-metal bomb. If they use one against us, you will be held responsible. Do you understand?"

"I do," Molotov said. "Since I had no intention of doing any such thing, the warning is pointless, but I accept it in the spirit in which it was offered." That sounded polite, and committed him to nothing.

After Queek and the interpreter left, Molotov stepped out of the office, too, by the side door that led to the changing room. There he took off his clothes and put on fresh ones brought in for the purpose. Only after he was sure he wasn't bringing along any electronic hangers-on did he return to the office where he handled everything except meetings with the Race.

He was about to call Marshal Zhukov when the telephone rang. He was something less than astonished when his secretary told him the marshal waited on the other end of the line. "Put him through, Pyotr Maksimovich," he said, and then, a moment later, "Good day, Comrade Marshal." Best to remind Zhukov he was still supposed to be subservient to the Party. Molotov wished theory and practice coincided more closely.

Sure enough, all Zhukov said was, "Well?"

Suppressing a sigh, Molotov summarized the conversation with Queek. He added, "This means, of course, that we cannot even think about Operation Proletarian Vengeance for some time. It would not be safe."

"No. It was always risky," Zhukov agreed. "We would have had to blame the bomb on the Nazis or the Americans, and we might well not have been believed. Now we can only hope the Germans don't give Mao a bomb and blame it on us." That was a horrifying thought. Before Molotov could do more than note it, Zhukov went on, "The west is more important. We are prepared for anything, Vyacheslav Mikhailovich, as best we can be."

"Good. Very good," Molotov said. "Now we hope the preparations are needless." He hung up. Zhukov let him get away with it. Why not? If things went wrong, who would get the blame? Molotov would, and he knew it.

Reuven Russie was examining the cyst on the back of a stocky old lady's calf when the air-raid sirens began to howl. *"Gevalt!"* the woman exclaimed, startled back into Yiddish from the Hebrew they'd been using. "Is it starting all over again, God forbid?"

"It's probably just a drill, Mrs. Zylbring," Reuven answered; the reassuring tones that came in so handy in medicine were useful in other ways, too. "We've been having a lot of them lately, you know, just in case."

"And would we have them if we didn't need them?" Mrs. Zylbring retorted, to which he lacked such a reassuring comeback.

Yetta the receptionist said, "No matter what it is, we'd better head for the basement." She'd stayed in the examining room to make sure Reuven didn't get fresh with Mrs. Zylbring. He couldn't imagine himself that desperate, but protocol was protocol. He also had no comeback for her.

His father and the fat, middle-aged man Moishe Russie'd been looking at came out of the other examination room. They too headed for the basement. As Reuven went down the steps, he wondered if hiding down there would save him from an explosive-metal bomb. He doubted it. He'd been a little boy on a freighter outside of Rome when the Germans smuggled in a bomb and blew the Eternal City's Lizard occupiers—and, incidentally, the papacy—to radioactive dust. That had been a horror from a lot of kilometers away. Close up? He didn't like to think about it.

He'd just gone into the shelter when the all-clear sounded. His father's patient said several pungent things in Arabic, from which the Jews of Palestine had borrowed most of their swear words: as a language used mostly in prayer for two thousand years, Hebrew had lost much of its own nastiness.

"It could be worse," Reuven told him. "It might have been the real thing."

"If they keep having alarms when no one's there, though, nobody will take shelter when it is the real thing," the man answered, which was also true.

He kept on grumbling as they all went back upstairs. Once they'd returned to the examination room, Mrs. Zylbring asked Reuven, "Well, what can you do about my leg?"

"You have two choices," he answered. "We can take out the cyst, which will hurt for a while, or we can leave it in there. It's not malignant; it won't get worse. It'll just stay the way it is."

"But it's an ugly lump!" Mrs. Zylbring said.

"Getting rid of it is a minor surgical procedure," Reuven said. "We'd do it under local anesthetic. It wouldn't hurt at all while it was happening."

"But it would hurt afterwards. You said so." Mrs. Zylbring made a sour face. "And it would be expensive, too."

Reuven nodded politely. The training he'd had at the Lizards' medical college hadn't prepared him for dealing with dilemmas like this. He suspected he was a good deal more highly trained than he needed to be to join his father's practice. No, he didn't suspect it: he knew it. But he was also trained in some of the wrong things.

The old lady waggled a finger at him. "If it were your leg, Doctor, what would you do?"

He almost burst out laughing. The Lizards had never asked him a question like that. But it wasn't a bad question, not really. Mrs. Zylbring assumed he had all the answers. That was what a doctor was for, wasn't it—having answers? Answering what kind of condition she had was easy. Knowing what to do about it was a different question, a different kind of question, one Shpaaka and the other physicians from the Race hadn't got him ready to handle.

He temporized: "If the fact that it doesn't disturb function satisfies you, leave it alone. If the way it looks bothers you, I can get rid of it inside half an hour."

"Of course the way it looks bothers me," she said. "If it weren't for that, I wouldn't have come here. But I don't like the idea of you cutting on me, and I don't have a whole lot of money, either. I don't know what to do."

In the hope Yetta would have a good idea, Reuven glanced over to her. She rolled her eyes in a way suggesting she'd seen patients like Mrs. Zylbring a million times before but didn't know what to do about them, either. In the end, the old woman went home with her cyst. Reuven wished he'd tried harder to talk her into getting rid of it; his urge was always to do something, to intervene. If he hadn't had that urge, he probably wouldn't have wanted to follow in his father's footsteps.

But when he said as much to his father, Moishe Russie shook his head. "If it's not really hurting the woman, it doesn't matter one way or another. She'd have been unhappy at the pain afterwards, too, mark my words. If she'd wanted you to do it, that would have been different."

"The pain would be the same either way," Reuven said.

"Yes—but at the same time no, too," his father said. "The difference is, she'd have accepted it better if she'd been the one urging you to have the thing out. She wouldn't blame you for it, if you know what I mean."

"I suppose so," Reuven said. "Things aren't so cut-and-dried here as they were back in the medical college. You were always supposed to come up with the one right answer there, and you got into trouble if you didn't."

His father's chuckle had a reminiscent feel to it. "Oh, yes. But the real world is more complicated than school, and you'd better believe it." He got up from behind his desk, came around it, and clapped Reuven on the shoulder. "Come on. Let's go home. You haven't got homework any more, anyhow."

"That's true." Reuven grinned. "I knew I must have had some good reason for getting out of there."

Moishe Russie laughed, but soon sobered. "You did have a good reason, a very good one. And I'm proud of you."

"Can't you get the fleetlord to do anything about that?" Reuven asked as they left the office—Moishe Russie locked up behind them—and started for home.

Late-afternoon sunlight gleamed off Moishe Russie's bald crown as he shook his head. "I've tried. He won't listen. He wants everybody to reverence the spirits of Emperors past"—he said the phrase in the Lizards' language—"so we'll get used to bowing down to the Race."

"He'd better not hold his breath, or he'll be the bluest Lizard ever hatched," Reuven said.

"I hope you're right. With all my heart, I hope you're right," his father said. "But the Race is stubborn, and the Race is very patient, too. That worries me."

"How much is patience worth if we all blow up tomorrow?" Reuven asked. "That's what worries me."

Moishe Russie started to step off the curb, then jumped back in a hurry to avoid an Arab hurtling past on a bicycle. "It worries me, too," he said quietly, and then switched to Yiddish to add, "God damn the stupid Nazis."

"Everyone's been saying that for the past thirty years," Reuven said. "If He's going to do it, He's taking His own sweet time about it."

"He works at His speed, not ours," Moishe Russie answered.

"If He's there at all," Reuven said. There were days— commonly days when people were more stupid or vicious than usual—when belief came hard.

His father sighed. "The night the Lizards came to Earth, I was—we all were—starving to death in the Warsaw ghetto. Your sister Sarah already had. I'd gone out to trade some of the family silver for a pork bone. I threw a candlestick over the wall around the ghetto, and the Pole threw me the bone. He could have just cheated me, but he didn't. As I was walking back to our flat, I prayed to God for a sign, and an explosive-metal bomb went off high in the sky. I thought I was a prophet, and other people did, too, for a while."

"Sarah . . ." Reuven felt a sudden rush of shame. He hadn't thought about his dead sister in years. "I hardly remember her." He couldn't have been more than three when she died. All he really had was a confused recollection of not being the only child in the family. Unlike his parents, he brought little in the way of memories with him from Poland.

"She was very sweet and very mischievous, and I think she would have been beautiful," Moishe Russie said, which was about as much as he'd ever talked about the girl who'd died before the Lizards came.

"She sounds like the twins," Reuven said. He walked on again.

"*Nu?* Why not?" his father said. "There's something to this genetics business, you know. But maybe God really was giving me a sign, there in Warsaw that night. If the Lizards hadn't come, we'd surely be dead now. So would all the Jews in Poland—all the Jews in Europe, come to that."

"Instead, it's only a big chunk that are, and the rest who are liable to be," Reuven said. "Maybe that's better, but it's a long way from good."

Moishe Russie raised an eyebrow. "So what you're accusing God of, then, is sloppy workmanship?"

Reuven thought about it. "Well, when you get right down to it, yes. If I do a sloppy job of something, I'm only human. I make mistakes. I know I'll make mistakes. But I expect better from God, somehow."

"Maybe He expects better from you, too." His father didn't sound reproachful. He just sounded thoughtful, thoughtful and a little sad.

"I don't like riddles." Reuven, now, Reuven sounded reproachful.

"No?" Moishe Russie's laugh came out sad, too. "What is life, then? You won't find the answer to that one till you can't tell anybody." He quoted from the Psalms: " 'What is man, that Thou art mindful of him?' God has riddles, too."

"Words," Reuven fleered, sounding even more secular than he felt. "Nothing but words. Where's the reality behind them?

When I work with patients, I know what is and what isn't." He scowled, remembering Mrs. Zylbring. Things weren't always simple with patients, either.

From the Bible, his father swung to Kipling, whom he quoted in Yiddish translation: " 'You're a better man than I am, Gunga Din.' " He laughed again. "Or more likely you're just a younger man. We're almost home. I wonder what your mother's making for supper." He set a hand on Reuven's shoulder, hurrying him along as if he were a little boy. Reuven started to shrug it off, but in the end let it stay.

When they got home, the odor of roasting lamb filled their nostrils. So did the excitement of the twins, who, like Jacob with the angel of the Lord, were wrestling with algebra. "It's fun," Judith said.

"It's fun after you figure out what's going on, anyhow," Esther amended.

"Till then, your head wants to fall off," Judith agreed. "But we've got it now."

"Good," Reuven said; he hadn't liked mathematics that much himself. "Will you still have it next week, when they show you something new?"

"Of course we will," Esther declared, and Judith nodded confidently. He started to laugh at them, then caught himself. All at once, he understood why his father had trouble taking his cocksure certainty seriously.

As Einstein had been, the Race was convinced nothing could travel faster than light. The crew of the *Lewis and Clark*, though, had discovered something that did: rumor. And so, having caught the news from someone who knew someone who knew a radio operator, Glen Johnson felt no hesitation in asking Mickey Flynn, "Do you think it's true?"

"Oh, probably," the number-two pilot answered. "But I'd have a better notion if I knew what we were talking about."

"That the Germans have sent *Hermann Göring* out this way," Johnson said.

"Last I heard, he was dead," Flynn remarked.

If he didn't have the deadest pan on the ship, Johnson was damned if he knew who did. He restrained himself from any of

COLONIZATION: DOWN TO EARTH

several obvious comments, and contented himself with saying, "No, the spaceship."

"Oh, the *spaceship*," Flynn said in artfully sudden enlightenment. "No, I hadn't heard that. I hadn't heard that it's not heading for this stretch of the asteroid belt, either, so you'd better tell me that, too."

Johnson snorted. That propelled him ever so slowly away from Flynn as they hung weightless just outside the control room. "I didn't think they could get it moving so soon," he said, reaching for a handhold.

"Life is full of surprises," Flynn said. "So is *Look*, but *Life* has more of them in color."

"You're impossible," Johnson said. Flynn regally inclined his head, acknowledging the compliment. Johnson went on, "What do you think it means that they pushed their schedule so hard? Do you think they think the hammer's going to drop back home, and they're sending the ship out so they don't have all their eggs in one basket?"

Maybe the number-two pilot considered launching another joke. Johnson couldn't tell, not with his poker face. If Flynn was considering it, he didn't do it. Some things were too big to joke about. After a few seconds, Flynn said, "If they do think that way, they're fools. The Lizards can go after them out here, too."

"Sure they can," Johnson agreed. "But we have defenses. The Nazis'll have 'em, too. They might even have better ones than ours—the bastards are awfully damn good with rockets."

Flynn nodded. "Okay, say they're twice as good as we are at knocking down whatever the Race sends after 'em. How often are you taking out the Lizards' missiles in our drills?"

"A little more than half the time."

"Sounds about right." Flynn nodded again. "Suppose they're getting eighty percent, then. I don't think they can do that well myself, but suppose. Now suppose the Lizards send ten pursuit missiles after them. How many are the Aryan supermen likely to stop?" He looked around, as if at an imaginary audience. "Come on, come on, don't everybody speak up at once. Did I make the statistics too hard?"

Fighting back laughter, Johnson said, "Odds are they'll knock down eight."

"That's true. Which leaves how many likely to get through?"

Mickey Flynn held up two fingers, giving a broad hint. Before Johnson could suggest what he might do with those fingers, he went on, "And how many of those missiles need to get through to give everybody an unhappy afternoon?" Johnson wondered if he'd fold down his index finger to give the answer, but he decorously lowered his middle finger instead, getting the message across by implication rather than overtly.

"And even if they knock down all ten—" Johnson began.

"Chances of that are a little better than ten percent, on the assumptions we're using," Flynn broke in.

"If you say so. Remind me not to shoot craps with you, if we ever get somewhere we can shoot craps." Johnson tried to remember where he'd been going. "Oh, yeah. Even if the Germans knock down all ten, the Lizards have a lot more than ten to send after 'em. And they only have to screw up once. They don't get a second chance."

"That's about the size of it, I'd say. The Germans can run, but it'll be a long time before they can hide." Flynn paused meditatively, then added, "And the Germans are liable to be looking over their shoulders all the way out here, anyhow. We took the Race by surprise. They had to be pretty sure of what the master race was up to."

"If the Lizards were human, I'd stand up and cheer if they whaled the stuffing out of the Nazis, you know what I mean?" Johnson said. "Even though they aren't, I don't think my heart would break."

Flynn pondered that. "The two questions are, how badly do we—people, I mean—get hurt if everything west of Poland goes up in smoke, and how badly can the Germans hurt the Lizards before they go down swinging?"

"Bombs in orbit." Johnson spoke with authority there; he'd kept an eye on the Nazis and Reds as well as the Lizards. Idly, he wondered how Hans Drucker was doing; he hadn't been a bad fellow, even if he did have a tendency to paw the air with his hooves and whinny whenever they played *Deutschland über Alles*. "Missiles inside the *Reich*. Submarines in the Mediterranean and prowling off Arabia and Australia, and every one of 'em loaded for bear. Not all the missiles would get through. . . ."

"No. The Race has better defenses, and more of 'em, than we

do," Flynn said. "But building missiles has been the German national sport for a long time."

"Heh," Johnson said, though it was anything but funny. "And the Nazis aren't the sort to stop shooting as long as they've got any bullets in the gun, either. They'd just as soon go out in a blaze of glory."

"I wish I could say I thought you were wrong," Flynn answered. "Actually, I can say it, but it would sully my reputation for truthfulness. And now, if you'll excuse me, I am going to earn my paycheck." He pushed off from his own handhold and glided into the control room.

Gloomily, Johnson went in the opposite direction, into the bowels of the *Lewis and Clark*. He hated war with the sincerity of a man who'd known it face-to-face. Even if it was a couple of hundred million miles away, even if it wouldn't directly involve the United States, he still hated it. And a war between the Lizards and the Germans would be big enough and nasty enough that the USA couldn't possibly be unaffected even if no American soldiers went into battle.

And, if the Lizards decided to get rid of the *Hermann Göring*, what would they do about the *Lewis and Clark*? Doing anything would get them into a war with the USA, but would they care if they were already fighting the *Reich*? In for a penny, in for a pound.

He wished the *Lewis and Clark* had a bar. He would have liked to go and sit and have a couple of drinks. Things would have looked better after that. So far as he knew, nobody had rigged up a still yet. It was probably only a matter of time. Brigadier General Healey would pitch a fit, but not even he could stop human nature.

"Human nature," Johnson muttered. If that wasn't what was pushing the Nazis into trouble, what was? Original sin? Was there any difference?

Human nature reared its head in a different way when Lucy Vegetti came swinging down an intersecting corridor. The *Lewis and Clark*'s traffic rules had grown up from those back in the USA. Little octagonal STOP signs were painted on the walls at every corner, to warn people to be alert when crossing. Johnson always paid attention to them; you got going fast enough to hurt somebody when you barreled along without a care in the world—and some people did just that.

Lucy stopped, too. She smiled at Johnson. "Hi, Glen. How are you?" Before he could answer, she took a second look at him and said, "You don't seem very happy."

He shrugged. "I've been better—sort of wondering whether things would blow up back home."

"Doesn't sound good, does it?" she said soberly. "Maybe we're lucky to be way out here—unless the Lizards decide to clean us up as long as they're busy back on Earth. Sooner or later, we'll spread out too much to make that easy, but—"

"But we haven't done it yet," Johnson broke in. "Yeah." His chuckle was flat and harsh. "Can't even go out and get drunk. Nothing to do but sit tight and wait and see."

"I know what you mean." Lucy hesitated, then said, "When I came up from Earth, I brought along a quart of scotch. If you promise not to be a pig, you can have a sip with me. Once it's gone, it's gone for good."

Solemnly, Johnson crossed his heart. "Hope to die," he said. He hadn't brought anything with him when he came up from Earth. Of course, he hadn't intended to stay aboard the *Lewis and Clark*, and she had.

"Come on, then." She swung off toward her tiny cubicle. Johnson followed. He knew the way, even though they still weren't anything more than friends. *But if she asks me in for a drink . . . I can hope, can't I?*

Lucy opened the door to the cubicle, then closed it after them. The place was crowded for two—hell, it was crowded for one. But closing the door didn't have to mean anything except that Lucy didn't want to advertise her whiskey. Johnson wouldn't have.

She took the bottle out of a duffel bag mostly full of clothes. Cutty Sark—not great scotch, but a hell of a lot better than no scotch. The bottle was almost full. She undid the screw top and replaced it with a perforated cork with a piece of glass tubing doing duty for a straw. "Go ahead," she said, and passed him the bottle.

"Thanks," he said from the bottom of his heart. He sucked up what he judged to be not quite a shot's worth of whiskey. It tasted so good, he wanted a lot more. Instead, he put his thumb over the top of the tubing and gave the bottle back to Lucy Vegetti. "Trust my germs?"

"If this stuff won't kill 'em, what will?" She drank about as much as he had, then yanked out the cork, put on the lid, and stowed away the scotch. An amber globule the size of a pea still floated in the air in the middle of the cubicle. Lucy and Johnson both moved toward it at the same time.

Johnson nodded to her. "Go ahead. It's yours."

"A gentleman." Lucy opened her mouth. The droplet of scotch disappeared. Then she leaned forward a couple of inches farther and kissed him.

Seemingly of themselves, his arms slipped around her. The kiss went on and on. "Jesus," he said when they finally broke apart. "I've wanted to do that for a long time."

"So have I," Lucy said. "Now I have a better notion that I can . . . I don't know, trust you isn't quite right, but it's close enough."

He wondered what she would have done—if she'd have done anything—had he been a pig with the bottle or stolen that floating drop of Cutty for himself. Then he stopped wondering, because she unzipped her coverall and wriggled out of it. She wore bra and panties underneath. A lot of women had stopped bothering with brassieres—what point to them in weightlessness?—but not her. Either she was too stubborn to care or she didn't want to put herself on display like that. Johnson was too busy getting out of his own clothes to worry about it.

They caressed each other and stroked each other and kissed each other all over. Floating free as they did, who was on top was a matter of opinion, unimportant opinion. Presently, a little awkwardly, he went into her. She wrapped her arms and legs around his back. He used one hand to snag a handhold and the other to keep on stroking her down where they were joined.

That brought her along about as quickly as he came himself: he'd gone without a long time. Then, before long, there were other little moist, sticky droplets floating in the air. They both hunted them down with rags. "Messy," he said with a grin, as happy and relaxed as he'd been for a long time.

"It always is," Lucy said. "Usually, though, men don't have to pay attention to it." He shrugged and snagged another drop before it hit a wall. The world was still every bit as liable to blow up as it had been half an hour before, but that didn't seem to matter nearly so much.

Kassquit read each day's news reports with mounting alarm. The Race had made it very plain to the Deutsche that any aggression the Big Uglies tried would be punished manyfold. The Deutsche had to understand that. But here they were, sounding fiercer and more determined every day.

"Are they addled?" she demanded of Ttomalss in the starship's refectory. "They must know what will happen to them if they go on. You were among them for a while. Why do they not believe us?"

"Tosevites have a greater capacity for self-delusion than do males and females of the Race," Ttomalss answered, and Kassquit knew no small pride that he spoke to her as if she were a female of the Race. He went on, "Past that, I will only say that fathoming their motivations remains difficult if not impossible."

"They cannot hope to defeat us," Kassquit exclaimed.

Ttomalss waved at the males and females (mostly males, for this ship had orbited Tosev 3 since the arrival of the conquest fleet, and still carried a large part of its old crew) of the Race in the refectory with them. "Our kind is relatively homogeneous," he said. "Big Uglies are more variable. We come from one culture; they still have many very different cultures. We are discovering that cultural differences can be almost as important as genetic variation. We had some evidence of this in the assimilation of the Hallessi, but it is much more striking here."

"I can see how it might be." Kassquit looked down at her soft, scaleless arms; at the preposterous organs on her chest that secreted, or could secrete, nutritive fluid; at the itchy stubble between her legs that reminded her she would soon need to shave it off again. "After all, what am I but a Big Ugly with cultural differences?"

"Exactly so," Ttomalss said, which was the last thing she wanted to hear. More often than not, Ttomalss hadn't the faintest idea he'd upset her; this time, for a wonder, he noticed, and amended his words: "You are a Tosevite citizen of the Empire, the first but surely not the last."

"There are times—there are many times—when I wish I could be altogether of the Race," Kassquit said wistfully.

"Culturally, you are," Ttomalss said, which she couldn't deny. He went on, "Physiologically, you are not, and you cannot be. But that has not stopped either the Rabotevs or the Hallessi from becoming full participants in imperial life."

That was also a truth. But it was only a partial truth. Kassquit said, "Both the Rabotevs and the Hallessi are more similar to the Race—physiologically and psychologically—than Big Uglies are."

"We have known from the beginning that assimilating this planet would be harder than incorporating Rabotev 2 or Halless 1," Ttomalss answered. "But we are willing—indeed, we have no choice but—to expend the time and effort necessary to do what must be done." He let his mouth fall open and waggled his lower jaw: wry laughter. "They are very perturbed back on Home. We have just received answers to some of our early communications after we discovered the true nature of this world. They are wondering if any of us still survive."

"Considering the attitude of the Deutsche, they have a right to be worried," Kassquit said. "If the *Reich* has a missile targeted on this ship, we could die in the next instant, probably before we even knew we were hit."

"If that happens—if anything like that happens—the *Reich* will cease to exist," Ttomalss said. "The Deutsche have to know as much. They have to." He sounded as if he was trying to reassure himself as well as Kassquit.

"But do they truly grasp it?" Kassquit persisted. "They have shown no sign of doing so. And even if they are smashed, can they weaken us enough to leave us vulnerable to uprisings from the areas we rule, or to attacks from the SSSR or the USA?"

"I am not the fleetlord; I do not know such things," Ttomalss said. "What I do know is that we will destroy all the Tosevites if we ever appear to be in danger of being conquered ourselves."

What felt like a lump of ice formed in Kassquit's belly. She tried to call up a word, and could not. "In ancient days, when incurable disease was spreading—"

"Quarantine," Ttomalss said, this time following her thought well. Kassquit made the affirmative gesture. The male who had reared her continued, "Yes, that is the planned strategy.

Tosevites here in this solar system can be managed, one way or another. Tosevites who might travel between the stars in their own ships . . . We cannot permit it. We shall not permit it."

That made sense. If it meant exterminating Kassquit's biological species . . . it still made sense. She could see as much. The idea of wild Big Uglies with starships—in essence, wild Big Uglies with a conquest fleet of their own—was truly horrifying. What might they do to Home or other planets of the Empire, all of which were essentially undefended? Far worse than the Race had done on Tosev 3: she was sure of that. They wouldn't want to colonize Home—they'd want to smash it.

Alternatives? Well, she herself was one of the alternatives. "We have to do everything we can to keep them from seeking such a thing, which means we have to do everything we can to assimilate them before they are technically able to do such a thing."

"Truth." Ttomalss added an emphatic cough.

"In aid of which," Kassquit said, "how are the arrangements going for another meeting between the American Tosevites and me?"

"Fairly well," her mentor answered. "For some reason, the Americans seem more hesitant now than they were before, but I still expect matters to be resolved before long."

"Who among the Americans is hesitant?" Kassquit asked in some surprise. "In my communications with Sam Yeager, he expresses eagerness, and says his hatchling feels the same way."

"In the hatchling's case, if not in that of the elder Yeager, such eagerness may in part be related to sexual desire," Ttomalss said dryly.

Not for the first time, Kassquit was glad her face didn't show what she felt. A pang of longing? It startled her. It embarrassed her. But it was there. She didn't want to think about it, and so, resolutely, she didn't. All she said was, "They showed no signs of it at the last meeting. And, if it is a factor, it is certainly not the only one involved."

"There I would agree with you," Ttomalss replied. "And, so long as you want them, I also want these meetings to go forward, as I have said. I shall do everything I can to resolve the difficulties, which appear to be bureaucratic in nature."

"I thank you, superior sir." Kassquit got to her feet, towering over the males and females in the refectory. She set her tray and bowl and utensils on the conveyor that took them off to be washed and reused, then went back to her cubicle. That little space gave her as much privacy as she could get aboard the starship. Somewhere, though, a tiny camera recorded everything she did. She was a Tosevite citizen of the Empire, true. But she was also a specimen for the Race to study.

She wished Ttomalss hadn't told her about the camera. Now, when she felt the overpowering need to stroke her private parts—as she sometimes did—she also felt even more constraint and guilt than she had before. It wasn't just that her biology made her different from the Race, not any more. It was also that Ttomalss—and other males and females—could watch her being different, and could scorn her for the differences.

As she checked for electronic messages, though, she let her mouth fall open in a laugh. The idea that struck her wasn't funny enough to make her laugh out loud—another difference rooted in Tosevite biology. But ginger had made the Race's reproductive behavior more like that prevailing down on Tosev 3. Ttomalss and other males and females—especially Felless, whom she intensely disliked—were no longer in such a good position to criticize what she did.

Sure enough, a couple of messages awaited her. One, assuming she truly did belong to the Race, tried to sell her a new, improved fingerclaw trimmer. She wondered how, after so many millennia of civilization, a fingerclaw trimmer could possibly be improved. Most likely, the merchant selling it had been on Tosev 3 so long, he'd acquired Tosevite notions of extravagant advertising. Kassquit deleted that one without a qualm.

The other message came from Sam Yeager. *Your people are being kind of picky about letting Jonathan and me come up for a second visit,* he wrote. *Seems they do not want an American spacecraft linking up with one of your starships. Hard to blame them, with the Deutsche making such nuisances of themselves, but we Americans are still mostly harmless.*

Kassquit pondered that. How was she supposed to take it? Tone was hard to gauge on electronic messages anyhow, and she had all the more trouble because Sam Yeager was a Big Ugly. She also noted that the story he told was different from the one she'd got from Ttomalss. She didn't suppose that should have surprised her; Tosevites were even more reluctant to admit they could be at fault than were males or females of the Race.

Would it be possible for you and your hatchling to fly here in one of our shuttlecraft? she asked.

No immediate answer came back, which didn't surprise her. Sam Yeager's message wasn't very recent, and he'd doubtless gone off to do other things instead of sitting at his computer waiting for her reply. She read for a while, then returned to the computer to check the news—the Deutsche still sounded as bellicose as ever—and then, in an act that brought her as much pleasure from defiance as from physical sensation, turned off the lights in the cubicle and caressed herself.

No doubt the camera monitored infrared. The watchers would know what she was doing even with the lights out. While she was doing it, she didn't care. That was a mixture of defiance and physical sensation, too. She'd seen videos of Big Uglies mating—more products of the Race's research on Tosevites. She wasn't usually in the habit of imagining herself in one of those videos, but today she did: another act of defiance. And she imagined the male with which she was doing the improbable deed had Jonathan Yeager's face.

After the pleasure faded, the shame for what she'd done seemed all the greater. As she turned the lights back on and washed her hands, she sighed. She wished her body wouldn't drive her to such extremes. But it did, and she had to come to terms with that.

A fair stretch of the day went by before Sam Yeager answered her. *I think you have a good idea there,* he wrote. *I will pass it on to my superiors. You do the same on your side of the fence, and we shall see what happens next.*

Good enough, Kassquit wrote back, adding, *I hope your own superiors will not prove difficult,* to see how he would respond.

Well, they may, he answered, this time promptly. *They do not trust me so far as I would like, it seems. But I am useful to them, and so they just have to put up with me.*

That sounds like my own position here, Kassquit wrote in some surprise. She wondered how Sam Yeager had fallen foul of his own kind. Not through looking the wrong way, anyhow: he looked like a typical Big Ugly. Maybe he would explain if he did come up to the starship again.

☆ 16 ☆

Nesseref let out a soft, astonished hiss as she guided the shuttle-craft down toward the Tosevite city called Los Angeles. She hadn't realized the Big Uglies built on such a scale. Few structures seemed very tall, but built-up areas stretched as far as her eye turrets could turn.

A Tosevite speaking the language of the Race said, "This is Los Angeles International Airport. Shuttlecraft, you are cleared for your final descent. All airplane traffic has been diverted from the area."

"I should hope so!" Nesseref exclaimed. That the Big Uglies didn't take the notion of clearing air traffic for granted, that they felt they had to mention it, chilled her. How many mishaps did their air travel system allow?

She didn't care to think about that. There was the concrete expanse of the airport. The radio beacon had guided the shuttle-craft well enough. Now she saw the visual beacons, too, the ones that would mark out her precise landing spot.

As she had while in Cairo, she let her fingerclaw hover above the switch that would fire the braking rockets if the shuttlecraft's electronics didn't do the job. But the braking rockets ignited when they should have. Deceleration pressed her into her seat. *Just routine,* she told herself. Landing at a port under the Big Uglies' control wasn't quite routine, but she'd done it before. Once more shouldn't be a problem.

Controlled by the computer, the braking rockets started burning just as the shuttlecraft's landing legs touched the concrete. "Very neat job there," the Big Ugly monitoring the descent said. "We will bring out more fuel and liquid oxygen for you, and also your passengers."

466

"I thank you," Nesseref answered, though she didn't feel particularly thankful. She just hoped the Tosevites knew what they were doing. Even the Race treated liquid hydrogen with a great deal of respect. If the Big Uglies didn't, they'd put her in danger.

But everything seemed to go as it should. The trucks the Big Uglies sent out had fittings that matched those of her oxygen and fuel tanks. She'd been told the fittings were supposed to be standardized, but was glad to find reality matching her suppositions. And the Tosevites handling the hoses exercised as much caution as they should have.

When the vehicles carrying the hydrogen and oxygen had withdrawn, a Tosevite motorcar approached the shuttlecraft. Two Big Uglies got out of it. One wore wrappings of a color not far removed from that of his own skin. The other . . . Nesseref stared at the image of the other in her monitor with more than a little bemusement. He wore minimal wrappings, shaved the hair on his head, and had body paint on his torso. She had heard some Big Uglies aped the styles of the Race, but had seldom seen it for herself—it was uncommon in Poland, and for all practical purposes nonexistent in Cairo.

She was supposed to fly two Tosevites up to a starship. She supposed these were the ones; after they got out, the motorcar had turned around and driven away. Making sure struck her as a good idea. She used the external speaker: "You are the American Tosevites Sam Yeager and Jonathan Yeager?" No doubt she was making a hash of the alien names, but she couldn't help that.

"We are, superior sir," answered the Big Ugly in the tan wrappings. "Mind if we join you?"

"Superior female, if you please," Nesseref said. "Yes, you have permission to come aboard. This shuttlecraft has been fitted with seats suitable to your species." She undogged the hatch and let in some of the local atmosphere, which was cool and moist and left the odor of partially burned hydrocarbons on her scent receptors.

"I am sorry," the same Tosevite said as he came through the hatch. "We cannot tell your gender by voice, as we can among our own kind." He spoke the language of the Race well, and seemed to have some feeling for proper behavior. As he lay down on one of the seats, he continued, "I am Sam Yeager, and this is my hatchling, whose familiar name is Jonathan."

"I greet you, superior female," said the Tosevite who wore the body paint of a psychologist's assistant.

"I greet you . . . Jonathan Yeager." Nesseref hoped she had that right. Neither Big Ugly corrected her, so she supposed she did. She went on, "We do not have long to wait before leaving for the rendezvous with the starship. Do you mind my asking the purpose of your visit?"

"By no means," said Sam Yeager, evidently the superior of the two. "We are going to meet one of our fellow Big Uglies." Nesseref wondered if he'd correctly understood the question. He proved he had by adding, "Yes, I mean exactly what I say there."

"Very well," Nesseref replied with a shrug. She had an eye turret on the chronometer, which showed the launch window rapidly approaching. When the proper moment came, she ignited the shuttlecraft's motors. Both Big Uglies grunted under acceleration, and both behaved well when it cut off and weightlessness began.

Docking was quick and routine. Nesseref could have gone aboard the starship while waiting for the proper time to descend from orbit and return to Poland, but she didn't bother. She just stayed where she was, enjoying a little weightlessness while knowing too much wasn't good for her.

When she did leave the docking station at the starship's central hub, she used her maneuvering jets to get clear of the great ship, then fired her braking rockets to fall out of orbit and down toward the surface of Tosev 3. She traveled, of course, from west to east, with the direction of the planet's rotation, which meant she had to pass above the territory of the Greater German *Reich* before reaching Poland.

"Do not deviate from your course," a Deutsch Big Ugly warned. "You and you alone will be responsible for the consequences if you do."

"I do not intend to deviate," Nesseref answered. "The *Reich* will be responsible for any aggression, as I am sure you know."

"Do not threaten me," the Tosevite said, and used an emphatic cough. "Do not threaten my not-empire, either. We are seeking our legitimate rights, nothing more, and we will have them. You cannot prevent it. You had better not try to prevent it."

Silence seemed the best response to that, and silence was what Nesseref gave it. Despite bluster, the Deutsch Big Uglies did not seek to attack the shuttlecraft. Nesseref let out a long sigh of relief as she landed at the port between Warsaw and Lodz whose construction she'd supervised.

"This is the first time in a while I have heard anyone be glad to return to Poland," a male in the control center said as she arranged ground transportation to her home. "Many males and females are looking for the chance to escape."

"If war comes, who knows which places will be safe?" Nesseref said. "Weapons can land anywhere."

"That is a truth, superior female," the males said. "Weapons *can* land anywhere. But if war comes, weapons *will* land on Poland."

And that was also a truth, even if one Nesseref didn't care to contemplate. She also didn't care to discover that no male or female of the Race was heading toward the new town in which she lived. The only driver available was a scrawny Big Ugly with an ancient, decrepit motorcar of Tosevite manufacture. Nesseref was anything but eager to entrust herself to it.

That must have shown, for the Big Ugly let loose one of the barking laughs of his kind and spoke in the language of the Race: "You flew between the stars. Are you afraid to drive to your apartment?"

"When I flew between the stars, I was in cold sleep," Nesseref replied with dignity. "I will be awake to experience this, worse luck."

The Tosevite laughed again. "That is funny. But come, get in. I have not killed anyone yet, even myself."

Nesseref found that a dubious recommendation, but did climb into the motorcar, which had the right-side front seat modified to fit a posterior of the sort the Race had. But the motorcar boasted no safety straps of any kind. And, she rapidly discovered, the Big Ugly drove as if he labored under the delusion of being a killer-craft pilot. Traveling a relatively short distance along a narrow, asphalt-topped road proved more terrifying than all the shuttlecraft flying Nesseref had ever done.

In the shuttlecraft, of course, she had radar and collision-avoidance alarms and radio to talk with the ground and with other pilots in the neighborhood. Here she and the driver had no aids whatever. All the other Big Uglies on the road drove with the same reckless disregard for life and limb as he displayed.

"Madness!" Nesseref exclaimed as he passed a lorry and then swung back into his lane so that another lorry, this one oncoming, missed him by a scale's thickness. She was too rattled even to bother appending an emphatic cough.

"You want to get home as soon as you can: is that not a truth?" the driver asked.

"I want to get there alive," Nesseref answered. This time, she did use an emphatic cough. It felt very emphatic, in fact.

"Is that really so important?" the Big Ugly said. "In the end, what difference will it make? When the war comes, you will be dead either way."

"Do you want to die sooner than you must?" Nesseref returned. She thought she would die in the next instant, when an animal-drawn wagon blithely started to cross the road on which she was traveling. But the Tosevite lunatic handling the motorcar had quick reflexes, even if he had no sense. Its suspension swaying, the motorcar dodged the wagon.

"That fellow is a fool," the driver said; Nesseref was convinced he said so because he had no trouble recognizing others of his own kind. After a moment, he went on, "I am a Jew. Do you know what the Deutsche did to Jews when they held Poland?" He didn't wait for her answer, but continued, "They could not kill me then. And I do not think they or anyone else will have an easy time killing me now."

If the way he drove hadn't killed him, Nesseref doubted explosive-metal bombs or poison gases could do the trick. But she asked, "If war does come, what will you do?"

He hesitated there no more than he did on the roadway: "Fight the Deutsche as long as I can. I have a rifle. I know what to do with it. If they want me, they will have to pay a high price for me."

With a squeal from his overworked, underpowered brakes, he pulled to a stop in front of Nesseref's building. She got out of his motorcar with so much relief, she almost forgot the bag in which she carried her personal belongings. The Big Ugly called her back to get it. He might be maniacal, but he wasn't larcenous.

When she got up to her apartment, Orbit greeted her with a yawn that displayed his mouthful of sharply pointed teeth. It was hard to impress a tsiongi. Had she bought a beffel, it would have danced around her and jumped up on her, squeaking wildly all the time. But a beffel would have wrecked the apartment while she was gone. Orbit didn't do things like that.

One of the pieces of mail she'd picked up was a flyer that began, IN CASE OF EMERGENCY. The emergency it was talking about was a Deutsch attack. Nesseref began to wonder if she should have been glad to come home.

Every step Sam Yeager took out from the hub of the starship made him feel heavier. Every step he took also made him hotter; the Race favored temperatures like those of a very hot day in Los Angeles. Turning to his son, he said, "You're dressed for the weather better than I am, that's for sure."

As at his previous meeting with Kassquit, Jonathan wore only a pair of shorts. He nodded and said, "You must be dying in that uniform."

"I'll get by." Sam chuckled. "Kassquit'll be better dressed for it than either one of us." Jonathan didn't answer that; Sam suspected he'd embarrassed his son by implying that he noticed what a woman was or wasn't wearing.

Somewhat to his surprise, the Lizard leading them to Kassquit turned out to speak English. He said, "The whole notion of wrappings, except to protect yourselves from the nasty cold on Tosev 3, is nothing but foolishness."

"No." Sam made the negative hand gesture. He thought about going into the language of the Race, but decided not to; English was better suited to the subject matter. "Clothes are also part of our sexual display. Sometimes they keep us from thinking about mating, but sometimes they make us think about it."

Had their guide been a human being, he would have sniffed. As things were, he waggled his eye turrets and spoke one dismissive word: "Foolishness."

"Do you think so?" Jonathan Yeager asked in the language of the Race. "Would you say the same thing after you smell the pheromones of a female who has just tasted ginger?" The Lizard didn't answer. In fact, he didn't say another word till he'd led Sam and Jonathan to the chamber in which Kassquit sat waiting for them.

"I greet you, superior female," Sam said in the language of the Race. His son echoed him. They both briefly assumed the posture of respect.

Kassquit got up from her seat and politely returned it. She was smoother at it than either of them, having no doubt had much more practice. "I greet you, Sam Yeager, Jonathan Yeager," she said, and sat down again.

"It is good to see you once more," Sam said. It was disconcerting to see so much of her; he had to work to keep his eyes on her face and not on her small, firm breasts or the slit between her legs, which looked all the more naked for being shaved. She made no move to conceal herself; she had no idea that she ought to conceal herself. *Jonathan's right,* Sam thought. *I'm not as used to skin as he is.*

"And it is good to see both of you," she answered seriously, innocent in her nakedness. "I shall remember your visits all the days of my life, for they are so different from anything I have known before."

"They are different for us, too," Jonathan said. "You live in space. To us, getting here is an adventure in itself."

"I did not think it would be so bad," Kassquit said in obvious dismay; *adventure* had connotations of hardship in the language of the Race that it lacked in English. "You came on one of our shuttlecraft, after all, and with us spaceflight is routine."

Sam did his best to spread oil on troubled waters: "One of these days, it would be nice if you could visit us down on the surface of Tosev 3."

"I have thought of this," Kassquit said. "I do not yet know whether it can be arranged, or whether it would prove expedient if it can."

Ever since he'd whiled away summer afternoons fishing for bluegill and crappie in the creek that ran through his parents' farm, Sam had known how to bait a hook. "Would you not be interested to learn what being among Tosevites is like?" he asked. "If you wore our style of wrappings and false hair, you would look just like everyone else."

If that wasn't bait, he didn't know what was. Poor Kassquit had to be the most isolated individual in the world. *Even Mickey and Donald don't have it so bad,* he thought uneasily. *They've got each other, and she's got nobody.* Tempting her hardly seemed fair, but he was a soldier on duty and a human being loyal to his species, while she wasn't human except by parentage, undoubtedly wished that parentage hadn't happened, and served the Race with all her heart.

He could tell the hook had gone home, all right. It might well tear out of her mouth, of course; people were a lot more complicated than bluegill. Her face didn't show much, but then, like Liu Mei's, her face never showed much. But she leaned forward in her seat and took a couple of deep breaths. If that wasn't intrigued interest, he had scales and eye turrets himself.

"To look like everyone else?" she said musingly. "I have never imagined such a thing—except in my wishes and dreams, where I look like a proper female of the Race." Nobody raised by humans would have told a near-stranger anything so intimate; Kassquit didn't understand the limits behind which people functioned. Then she said something that made Sam sit up and take notice: "If war comes, I may be safer in the not-empire called the United States than here aboard this starship."

"Do you really think there will be a war between the *Reich* and the Race?" Jonathan blurted. He hardly seemed better at concealing what he felt than Kassquit did, and what he felt was horrified dismay.

"Who can know?" Kassquit answered. "The Race does not want to fight the *Reich*, but the *Reich* has no business making demands on the Race."

"That is about what our government thinks, too, but we have little influence on what goes on in the *Reich*," Sam said.

"Too bad," Kassquit told him. "For Big Uglies, you seem sensible, you Americans, aside from your absurd custom of snoutcounting."

"We like it," Sam said. "It seems to suit us. We are not a people who care to be told what to do by anyone."

"But what if those who tell you what to do know more about a question than you do?" Kassquit asked. "Does a physician not know more about how to keep you healthy than you can know for yourself?"

"Judging who is an expert in public affairs is harder," Sam replied. "Many claim to be experts, but they all want to do different things. That makes choosing among them harder. So we let those who convince the largest number of us that they are wise and good govern our not-empire."

"What if they lie?" Kassquit asked bluntly.

"If we find out, we do not choose them again," Yeager said. "We choose them for terms of so many years, not for life, and we hope they cannot do too much damage while in office. What if the Race has a very bad Emperor? He is the Emperor for as long as he lives."

"His ministers will do what is right regardless," Kassquit said. "And even a bad Emperor's spirit will watch over the spirits of citizens of the Empire. What good is a bad Tosevite snout-counted official after he is dead? None whatever."

No sooner had Sam discarded one particular question as impolitic than Jonathan asked it: "How do you know spirits of Emperors past watch over other spirits? Is it not a superstition, the same as our Tosevite superstitions?"

"Of course it is not a superstition," Kassquit said indignantly. "It is a truth. The truth is not a superstition."

"How do you know?" Jonathan persisted. Sam made a small gesture, warning his son not to push it too hard.

He gave Kassquit credit. Instead of saying something like, *I just do,* she gave a serious answer: "All the males and females of three species on three worlds believe it. All the males and females of the Race have believed it for more than a hundred thousand years, since Home was unified. Could so many believe such a thing for so long if it were not true?"

"And you believe it?" Sam asked gently.

"I do." Kassquit made the affirmative gesture. "Spirits of Emperors past *will* cherish my spirit. And my spirit, when that time comes, will look no different from any other." She spoke with great confidence.

You poor kid, Yeager thought. He had to look away from her for a moment; tears were stinging his eyes, and he couldn't let her see that. *And the worst part of it is, you only know a fraction of what all the Lizards have done to you, because there's so much of it you can't see, any more than a fish sees water.* But then he shook his head. No, that wasn't the worst part of it after all. He could see just how warped the Race had made Kassquit, and he knew damn well he was going to go right on raising Mickey and Donald as if they were human beings. *What a son of a bitch I am. But it's my job, dammit.*

He supposed the SS men who put Jews and fairies and Gypsies into gas chambers said the same thing. How could they do anything else if they wanted to go home afterwards and kiss their wives and eat pig's knuckles and knock back a seidel or two of beer? If they really thought about what they were doing, wouldn't they go nuts?

It's not the same. He knew it wasn't, but had the uncomfortable feeling the difference was of degree, not of kind.

A silence had fallen in the chamber, as if nobody knew what to say next. Finally, Kassquit made a pointed return to a new take on an earlier subject: "Do you not think the present aggressive policy of the Deutsche makes it more likely that they were the Big Uglies who attacked the ships of the colonization fleet?"

"A good question," Sam said. Jonathan nodded, but then remembered to make the proper hand gesture, too. Sam went on, "I am not sure the one has anything to do with the other. It might, but I have no proof."

He would have been happy to incite the Race against the Nazis had he had proof. He didn't think that would make his superiors happy, though, and he more or less understood why: however thoroughgoing a lot of bastards the Germans were, they were also part of the balance of power. He sighed. Life never turned out to be as simple as you thought it would when you were Jonathan's age, or Kassquit's.

Kassquit said, "I can understand why you would not admit any such thing about your own not-empire, but are the Deutsche not your foes as well as the Race's?"

That was also balance-of-power politics. Speaking carefully, Sam answered, "It is a truth that the United States and the *Reich* were fighting a war when the Race came. But each decided the Race was a bigger danger than the other."

"I do not understand this," Kassquit said. "In the Empire, all Tosevites would be at peace. You would not fight the Race, and you would not fight among yourselves, either. Is this not good?"

"One of the parts of the United States—'provinces' is as close as I can come in your language, but that is not quite right—has a slogan," Sam said. "That slogan is, 'Live free or die.' Many, many Big Uglies feel that way."

"I do not understand," Kassquit repeated. "How are the Tosevites in the USA or the SSSR or the *Reich* freer than those the Empire rules?"

Sam wished she hadn't phrased the question like that. Millions of Frenchmen and Danes and Lithuanians and Ukrainians weren't free, or anything close to it. Neither were millions of Germans or Russians, for that matter. "Not all Tosevite not-empires are the same," he said at last.

"They look that way to us," Kassquit answered.

Whoever'd raised her had done a good job: she really did think of herself as a member of the Race. Sam made a small clucking noise. *I hope I can do that well with Mickey and Donald, no matter how unfair it is to them.*

Kassquit had trouble getting used to the way the wild Big Uglies looked at her. With a male or female of the Race, eye turrets said exactly where eyes pointed. The gaze of the Tosevites was shiftier, subtler. She thought their eyes kept drifting down her body, but they would return to her face whenever she was at the point of remarking on it.

Their words were also confusing and evasive. They steadfastly defended what was to her obvious nonsense. And they seemed sure they made perfect sense. *Alien,* she thought. *How can they be so strange, when they look so much like me?*

After a moment, she realized she was the strange one by Tosevite standards. That realization was something of an intellectual triumph, because she loathed the idea of judging herself by the standards of wild Big Uglies.

And the Tosevites insisted they didn't have one set of standards, but many—perhaps one for each of their not-empires. "You are all one species," she said. "How can you have more than one standard? The Empire has three species—four now, counting Tosevites—but only one standard. Having many on a single planet is absurd." Ttomalss had also said the Big Uglies varied by culture, but she wanted to hear how these wild ones explained it.

Jonathan Yeager said, "We do not always agree on what the right way to do things is."

Sam Yeager made the affirmative gesture. "Sometimes there is no right or wrong way to do something, only different ways. Being different is not always the same as being right or wrong. I think the Race has trouble seeing that."

"Back on Home, the Race has no trouble seeing right from

wrong," Kassquit said; that was what she'd been taught. "Contact with Tosevites has corrupted some of us."

To her surprise and annoyance, both wild Big Uglies burst into loud barking yips of laughter. "That is not a truth, superior female," Sam Yeager said, and used an emphatic cough. "I have met plenty of males—and some females now, too—who are as crooked as any Big Ugly ever hatched."

He sounded very sure of himself. In the face of direct experience, how much was teaching worth? Kassquit decided to change the subject again: "What do the two of you hope to learn by these visits with me?"

"How to meet the Race halfway," Jonathan Yeager answered.

Sam Yeager amended that: "To see whether we can meet the Race halfway. If we cannot, then perhaps war is the best hope we have after all."

Live free or die. It struck her as a slogan fit only for the hopelessly addled. Plainly, it meant something different to the wild Big Uglies. She did not want to explore that path again. Instead, she pointed with her tongue at Jonathan Yeager and said, "It seems to me that you are meeting the Race halfway."

"I enjoy your culture," he answered. "It interests me. I am learning your language, because I cannot deal with the Race without it. But under this"—he patted his shaven head and tapped the body paint on his chest—"under this, I am still a Tosevite with my own culture. Meeting you helped show me what a truth that is."

"Did it?" Kassquit felt a pang of disappointment. "Meeting you made me hope you were leading toward . . ." Her voice trailed away. She was not sure how to say what she wanted without giving offense.

Sam Yeager, who seemed not to take offense easily, spoke for her: "You thought Jonathan was leading toward the Race's quiet, bloodless conquest of Tosev 3."

"Well, yes." Kassquit made the affirmative gesture, even if she wouldn't have been so frank as the wild Tosevite.

Then the older Yeager surprised her again, saying, "You could be right. I do not know if you are. Frankly, I doubt that you are. But you could be."

"Why do you doubt it?" Kassquit asked.

"Because no matter how much of the Race's outward culture

we adopt—no matter whether we start using body paint instead of wrapping, no matter whether we reverence the spirits of Emperors past instead of keeping our own superstitions—we are still too different from you," Sam Yeager answered. "And we will stay different from you, because of our sexuality and the social patterns that come from it."

"Truth," Jonathan Yeager said. His agreement with his father hurt Kassquit more than the elder Yeager's words. And he went on, "In fact, is not ginger making males and females of the Race here on and around Tosev 3 more like us than like the Race as it is back on Home?"

Kassquit thought of Felless, who could not stop tasting ginger and who was going to lay her second clutch of eggs as a result. She thought of the mating she'd watched in a corridor of this very starship. That had shaken her faith in the Race's wisdom and rationality. She thought of the endless prohibitions against ginger, and of how widely they were flouted.

"I hope not," she said, and used an emphatic cough of her own.

"But you recognize the possibility?" Sam Yeager asked. "I do not suppose I have to tell you that officials of the Race recognize the possibility?"

"No, you do not have to tell me that," Kassquit admitted. "I am quite aware of it. I wish I were not, but such is life."

"Indeed," Sam Yeager said. "May I ask you another question?" He waited for her to use the affirmative gesture before going on, "You have talked about what you hope will happen with the Big Uglies, and you have talked about what you hope will happen with the Race. What do you hope will happen to you?"

Ttomalss would sometimes ask her what she thought would happen, or even what she wanted. But what she hoped? He didn't seem to think about that. Kassquit hadn't done a whole lot of thinking about it, either. After a long pause, she said, "I do not know. My position is too anomalous to give me the luxury of many hopes, would you not agree?"

"Yes, as a matter of fact, I would," he replied. "I wondered if you understood that. You might well be better off, or at least have more peace of mind, if you did not. Does that sound very callous?"

"It does indeed." Kassquit considered. "But then, the truth often sounds callous, does it not?"

"I fear it does," Sam Yeager said. "One more question, if you please." He asked it before she could tell him yes or no: "What would you wish for yourself? If you could have anything, what would it be?"

Kassquit had hardly dared ask that question of herself. Ttomalss hadn't thought to ask about her desires any more than he had about her hopes. To him, she remained part experimental animal, part hatchling. Over the past few years, he'd had to recognize that she had a will, a mind, of her own, but he was a long way from liking the idea. But she answered Sam Yeager without hesitation, saying, "If I could have anything I wanted, I would be rehatched as a female of the Race."

Sam Yeager and Jonathan Yeager both made the affirmative hand gesture. "Yes, I can see how you would want that," the older Big Ugly said. "Let me ask it a different way, then—if you could have anything you wanted that you might actually get, what would it be?"

That was harder. All of Kassquit's material needs were met; only in the social sphere did she have problems. "I do not know," she said at last. "I have plenty to eat; I have the Race's communication network; what more in that regard could I desire?" She met question with question: "What would *you* choose, Sam Yeager? See how you like answering."

The Big Ugly yipped Tosevite laughter. "The easy answer is, 'more money.' Ask any Tosevite, and he will say that, or something like it. He might ask for a bigger house, or a fancier motorcar, or other such things, but it all means the same in the end. Unlike you, we mostly do not have enough to keep us happy."

Kassquit turned her head toward Jonathan Yeager. "And what of you?"

"I do not know if this is possible or not," the younger Tosevite answered, "but I hope I live long enough to be able to travel to Home, either on a ship of the Race or on a Tosevite starship."

"A Tosevite starship?" The very idea was a nightmare to Kassquit, as it was to every male and female of the Race. She didn't know whether she ought to spell that out, so she contented herself with asking, "If that should prove impossible, what would you like?"

Jonathan Yeager hesitated. Sam Yeager said something in their own language. Jonathan Yeager's answer was short. Sam Yeager laughed again. He turned to Kassquit and returned to the language of the Race: "I told him that having a mate with whom he can be happy throughout his life is also important."

"You did not wish for that yourself," Kassquit pointed out.

"No, but then, I am lucky enough to have such a mate," Sam Yeager answered. "Jonathan has a female friend who may become such a mate, but it is difficult to be sure about such things ahead of time."

"What are the criteria for judging whether a mate is good or not?" Kassquit asked. If she was questioning the Big Uglies, they couldn't very well question her. She liked this better.

Jonathan Yeager's skin was more transparent than Kassquit's. She could watch blood rise to his face. She'd felt the same thing in herself in moments of embarrassment, so that was probably what he was feeling, too. If Sam Yeager also felt it, he showed no sign. He answered, "That varies from individual to individual. A mate who makes one male or female happy would addle another in short order."

"How does one judge the possibility that one of these lifelong matings"—the notion struck Kassquit as very strange—"will be successful?"

"Some of that involves the sexual desire each partner arouses in the other, and the sexual pleasure each gives the other," Sam Yeager answered. "Those are often enough reason for the partners to come together, but they do not mean that the mating will be a long-term success. The male and the female also have to be friends, to see things in similar ways, and to forgive each other's small failings. It is not easy to judge in advance whether this will happen."

She hadn't expected such a thoughtful answer. She had only the Race's view of Big Ugly sexuality—that it was constant and indiscriminate. It occurred to her that the Race might have as much trouble understanding Tosevites as the Big Uglies had understanding the Race. Though Ttomalss knew of her own sexual urges, she doubted he understood them. For that matter, she doubted she understood them herself, and wished she did.

"What makes one Tosevite sexually attractive to another?" she asked.

"Appearance," Jonathan Yeager answered at once.

"That is one thing, often the most important thing at first," Sam Yeager said, "but character is also important, and perhaps more important in the long run." He paused, then added, "I think character may be more important at first to females judging males than to males judging females."

"Why?" Kassquit asked. Both wild Big Uglies shrugged. They saw each other do it, and both laughed. Kassquit noted the byplay without having any notion what might have caused it. And then she found a question the Tosevites were uniquely suited to answer, one that would have been utterly meaningless if not repellent to Ttomalss: "By your standards, am I sexually attractive?"

Jonathan Yeager had never imagined being asked such a question by a naked woman who obviously didn't know the answer. He looked to his father for help, only to discover his father looking back at him. He needed a couple of seconds to understand why. Then he realized his dad was a married man, and probably thought he wasn't the one to be talking about whether a woman was sexy or not.

And so Jonathan had to figure out the answer for himself. After a moment, he realized only one answer was possible, regardless of what he really thought. "Yes," he said, and added an emphatic cough. Anything else would have been a diplomatic disaster. By the speed with which his father added the Lizards' affirmative hand gesture, he knew he'd done the right thing.

Better still, he hadn't been lying. He was used to girls who shaved their heads, even though his own girlfriend didn't. And living in Gardena, which a lot of Japanese-Americans called home, had accustomed him to Oriental standards of beauty. Kassquit had a pretty face—it would have been prettier still, of course, had it shown more expression—and he could be in no possible doubt that she had a nice figure to go with it.

To his astonishment, she folded herself into the posture of respect. "I thank you," she said with an emphatic cough of her own. "You will understand that this is not a question I could possibly ask Ttomalss or any other male or female of the Race." She corrected herself: "No, that is not true. I could ask, but without hope of obtaining a meaningful answer."

She certainly wouldn't have been attractive to the Lizards, not when their everyday name for *human being* was *Big Ugly*. Jonathan tried to imagine what living among aliens would be like after you discovered the truth about your body and the delights it could bring. He tried, yes, but felt himself failing. The one thought that stuck in his mind was that he was damn glad it hadn't happened to him.

His father said, "There are times, superior female, when you must have been—must be—very lonely."

"Truth," Kassquit said. What was she thinking? With her impassive features, Jonathan couldn't tell. She went on, "I do not know if I myself realized how lonely I was until I first began communicating with you wild Tosevites. Who can say with certainty where the intersection between biology and culture lies? Even among the Race, it remains a subject for debate."

"It is among us Tosevites, too," Jonathan said. Mickey and Donald, at least, wouldn't grow up worrying about whether they were sexually interesting. Unless they turned out to be females who went into their mating season or males who met a female in her season, they wouldn't worry about such things at all. Jonathan suspected being a Lizard was easier than being a human.

But what if one of them's a male and the other's a female? That hadn't occurred to him before. It would sure complicate things. Then he shrugged. Even if it was so, the Yeagers wouldn't have to worry about it for a good many years yet. How old were Lizards when they hit puberty? He couldn't remember. *Have to look it up,* he thought.

Kassquit said, "I do not find Tosevite scientific research likely to be of much value."

Before Jonathan could respond indignantly to that, his father shrugged and said, "Well, in that case I do not suppose you have any reason to want anything to do with us at all. Shall we go, Jonathan?"

Leaving was the last thing Jonathan wanted. But a glance at his father's face warned him he'd better play along. "All right," he said, and started to rise. He turned to Kassquit. "It was pleasant and interesting to talk with you again."

"No, do not go!" Kassquit's face still showed nothing—it could show nothing—but alarm and grief filled her voice.

"Please do not go. We had not yet come close to finishing this discussion."

Jonathan looked down at the metal floor of the chamber so Kassquit couldn't see him grin. Sure as hell, his old man knew how to bait a hook. And Kassquit had swallowed the bait, damned if she hadn't.

"Why should we stay, if you mock us?" Sam Yeager asked sternly. "You are proud, as the Race is proud, but it never occurs to the Race that we Big Uglies also have reason to be proud of what we have done."

"This is not something easy for a citizen of the Empire to grasp," Kassquit said. "I meant no offense." It wasn't quite an apology, but it came closer than Jonathan had expected.

He had to hide another smile. Kassquit wasn't apologizing because she hadn't intended to offend; she was apologizing because she wanted to go on talking with the only other human beings she'd ever met. Jonathan knew he wasn't the most socially conscious fellow around, but he had no trouble seeing that.

"Not long after the colonization fleet arrived," Kassquit said, "I was asked if I wanted a Tosevite male brought up from the surface of Tosev 3 as a means of obtaining sexual release. I said no at the time. The thought of a strange wild Big Ugly as a mate was too distressing to contemplate. But the two of you do not seem like such strangers to me now."

Jesus! Jonathan thought. *I've just been propositioned! How am I supposed to say no, when I just told her I thought she was attractive?*

Part of him—one particular part of him—didn't want to say no. If he said yes, of course, Karen would kill him. *But Karen's down there, and I'm up here in space. She wouldn't have to know. I wouldn't be unfaithful, not really. It's research, that's what it is.*

While those thoughts were going through his mind, his father said, "Superior female, you will have to forgive me. I do find you attractive, as I said, but I am not in a position to do anything about it. My permanent mate would be most unhappy if I were to mate with any female but her, and I do not wish to make her unhappy in any way."

Like any child, Jonathan had trouble imagining his parents making love with each other. When he tried to imagine his father making love with Kassquit, the picture in his mind did not want to form. And when he tried to imagine his father telling his mother he'd made love with Kassquit, that picture would not form at all. What he saw instead was the mushroom cloud from an explosive-metal bomb.

Kassquit said, "I do not understand why such a mating would make her unhappy."

"Because we try to concentrate all our affection on our principal mate, and an outside mating implies a loss of that affection," Jonathan's father answered. "We have a word in our language that means something like *affection*, but it is a stronger term. We say *love*." The last word, necessarily, was in English.

"Love," Kassquit echoed. To her, plainly, it was just a noise. Sure enough, she went on, "I do not understand. But I gather you are telling me this is a strong custom among American Tosevites." Jonathan's father made the affirmative hand gesture. Kassquit turned her attention back to Jonathan. "Do I gather that you, as yet, have no such permanent mating commitment?"

"Uh, that is, uh, correct," Jonathan said, and then wished he'd lied instead of telling the truth. A lie would have let him escape gracefully. The truth made things more complicated. He turned to his father and spoke in English: "What am I going to do, Dad?"

"Good question." His father sounded amused, which only made things worse. "If you want to be this particular kind of guinea pig, go ahead. If you don't, you'll figure out some way around it."

"What are the two of you talking about?" Kassquit asked sharply.

"We are trying to decide what is proper here," Jonathan answered, which was true enough. Picking his words with great care, he went on, "I do not have a permanent arrangement with a female, no, but I am seeing a female with whom I may have such an arrangement one day."

"What does this mean—you are seeing her?" Kassquit asked. "Is this a euphemism for mating with her?"

Jonathan's father had to translate *euphemism* for him. The question made Jonathan cough. It also made him wonder how to answer. He and Karen hadn't actually gone to bed with each other, but they'd sure done everything else. He was damned if he'd try to explain petting and oral sex to Kassquit with his father listening. Instead, keeping it simple, he just said, "Yes."

And that made his dad's eyebrows shoot up, too, as he'd known it would. Kassquit said, "If you do not have a permanent mating arrangement, you may mate with whomever you choose. Is this not a truth? Do you choose to mate with me, Jonathan Yeager?"

That wasn't a proposition; it was more like an ultimatum. Before Jonathan could answer, his father said, "Superior female, regardless of what my hatchling may decide, there should be no matings at this meeting."

"And why not?" Kassquit's face didn't show emotion, but her voice did. She sounded furious.

"Why not?" Jonathan's father echoed. "Because the purpose of mating—or a purpose of mating, anyhow—is reproduction. Do you want to take the chance of becoming gravid as a result of mating? How well equipped is the Race to handle that problem?"

"Oh." Kassquit bent into the posture of respect. "I had not thought of that."

"A lot of Tosevites do not think of it ahead of time," Sam Yeager answered dryly. "This ends up making their lives more difficult than they would be otherwise—or more interesting, anyhow." By his expression, he was looking a long way back into the past. Had they been somewhere else, Jonathan might have asked him about it. But not here, not now.

"What is the solution, then?" Kassquit asked. "It cannot be not mating. That, by what I am given to understand, is not the Tosevite way."

"The usual American solution is a thin rubber sheath worn on the male's reproductive organ," Sam Yeager said. Jonathan admired his dispassionate tone. It came easier in the language of the Race, but even so . . . His father went on, "This permits mating but keeps sperm and egg from meeting."

"Ingenious," Kassquit said. "Sanitary. Do you have any of these sheaths with you?"

"No," Jonathan said. "We did not expect the issue of mating to arise."

"Very well." Kassquit made the affirmative gesture. "Next time you visit, do bring some. Or I can arrange for a supply to be brought up from some of the territory the Race rules. Is it agreed?"

She sounded as brisk as if she were arranging a business deal. Maybe that was what she thought she was doing. She had no idea what being human meant—and she wanted to start learning in the most intimate way possible. That made sense of a sort, but only of a sort: Jonathan kept wondering if he wanted to be her teacher.

"Is it agreed?" she repeated.

Jonathan looked at Sam Yeager. His father's face said nothing at all. Jonathan knew it was up to him, no one else. Well, no one from the starship was likely to tell Karen, which was more than he could say about most Earthly situations. Ever so slightly, he nodded. "It is agreed," Sam Yeager said, and Jonathan couldn't tell for the life of him whether or not his dad thought he was doing the right thing.

"Tosevite sheaths for mating without the risk of reproduction," Ttomalss said bemusedly, one eye turret on the recording of the meeting between Kassquit and the two wild Big Uglies, the other on Kassquit herself.

"Yes, superior sir," Kassquit said. "I can certainly understand how becoming gravid as the result of a mating would be undesirable. These sheaths reduce the risk of such a mischance."

"Are you sure you are not being precipitate in this?" Ttomalss had trouble getting used to the idea of Kassquit grabbing at things with her own fingerclaws.

"Yes, superior sir. I am sure I would like to make the experiment, at any rate," Kassquit told him. "Remember, some time ago you offered me a wild Tosevite for such purposes. I declined then, but no longer wish to decline."

"I . . . see." What Ttomalss mostly saw was occasion to worry. He knew how strongly the mating urge and the urge to form families affected the Big Uglies. Would Kassquit become addicted to that gratification, as so many males and females of the Race had to ginger?

"Everything will be all right," Kassquit reassured him.

"How can you know that in advance of the event?" Ttomalss demanded. "The answer is, you cannot. You have committed yourself to this course of action without adequate forethought." And if that wasn't a Tosevite thing to do, what was? Ttomalss did not tax Kassquit with it, though, for fear of prompting an indignant denial—another typical Tosevite response.

"I have not," she said. "I have been considering this, pondering it, since you made your offer to me some time ago. Indeed, I have been pondering it longer than that—ever since I discovered some of the physiological responses of my own body. This is something evolution has adapted me to do."

She was likely to be right in that. She was almost certain to be right in that, in fact. Even so, Ttomalss said, "Suppose I forbid it? I have the authority to do so, as you must know."

"On what grounds would you do such a thing?" Kassquit demanded angrily. "And you do not have the authority."

"I most assuredly do." Ttomalss hadn't intended to get angry in return, but found he couldn't help himself. "And my authority is based on my continuing wardship of you."

"I see." Kassquit leaned forward and glared at him. "So all your talk about my being a citizen of the Empire was nothing but talk? Is that what you are telling me now, superior sir?" She made the title one of reproach. "So much for any hope of equality, I see."

"Calm yourself!" Ttomalss exclaimed, though he was feeling anything but calm himself. Dealing with Big Uglies had that effect on him, though he hadn't thought of Kassquit as a Big Ugly in such matters for quite a while. "I am trying to see what is best for you. This of course is for your own long-term good."

He wondered if mature Tosevites ever spoke to their hatchlings thus. He doubted it. How likely were any Big Uglies, young or old, to value the long-term at the expense of the immediate?

Kassquit certainly remained unconvinced. "Considering who I am and what I am, who are you to judge my long-term good? No one, either among the Race or among the Big Uglies, is so well suited to evaluate that as I am myself. I am, in this particular case, unique, and my judgment must stand."

"A moment ago, you were claiming you were not unique: you were claiming to be a citizen of the Empire," Ttomalss pointed out. "Which is it? It cannot be both at once, you know."

"You are being deliberately obstructive," Kassquit said. That was a truth, but not one Ttomalss intended to admit. Kassquit went on, "You realize you are trying to keep me from following a course you once urged on me? You cannot do both at once, either, superior sir."

"You do not seem to understand what a large step mating is for a Tosevite," Ttomalss said. "You are taking it too lightly."

"And *you* are equipped to understand this better? Forgive me, superior sir, but I doubt it." Yes, Kassquit could be devastating when she chose. And she chose now.

Ttomalss said, "I told you, I believe you were hasty in this. May I propose a compromise?"

"Go ahead, though I do not see where there is room for one," Kassquit said. "Either I shall mate with this wild Big Ugly or I shall not."

"We will obtain some of these sheaths." Ttomalss didn't think that would be difficult. "But I want you to consider whether they should be used, and I want there to be some little while before the wild Big Ugly comes up here. This may be wise in any case: in the event of war between the Race and the *Reich*, all space travel may well entail unacceptable risks."

Now Kassquit exclaimed in dismay, "Do you truly believe war is likely, superior sir?"

With a long, hissing sigh, Ttomalss answered, "I wish I did not, but I am afraid I do. Having visited the *Reich*, having sojourned there, I must say that the Deutsche are, of all the Tosevites I have seen and heard of, the least susceptible to reason. They are also among the most technically adept and the most arrogant. It strikes me as a combination bound to cause trouble and grief."

"It strikes me as a combination logically impossible," Kassquit replied.

"And that is also a truth," Ttomalss replied. "But logic, like reason, goes by the board far more often on Tosev 3 than it does here. And, because the Deutsche are so fond of reasoning from premises that strike even other Big Uglies as absurd, logic, however well applied, becomes less valuable: the most perfect logic cannot make truth hatch from false premises."

"What will we do if they attack this ship?" Kassquit asked.

"Logic should be able to tell you that," Ttomalss answered. "Unless we can deflect or prematurely detonate a missile with an explosive-metal warhead, it will destroy us. We have to hope we are not attacked."

He hoped Kassquit wouldn't ask him how likely it was that the Race could deflect or prematurely detonate Deutsch missiles. He knew too well what the answer was: *not very*. When the conquest fleet came to Tosev 3, no one had imagined the Big Uglies would ever be in a position to assail orbiting starships. The ships had had some antimissile launchers added in the years since the Tosevites taught the Race how inadequate its imagination was, but few males thought they could knock down everything.

Kassquit didn't choose the question Ttomalss dreaded, but did ask a couple related to it: "If the Deutsche do go to war with the Race, how much damage can they do to us and to our colonies? Can they cripple us to the point where we would be vulnerable to attacks from the other Tosevite not-empires?"

"I do not know the answers there," Ttomalss said slowly. "I would doubt that even the exalted fleetlord knows the answers there. My opinion—and it is only my opinion—is that they could hurt us badly, though I do not know just how badly, or whether they could, as you say, cripple us. But of this I am sure: if they undertake to attack us, we will smash them to the point where they will never be able to do so again." He used an emphatic cough to show how sure he was.

"Good," Kassquit said, with an emphatic cough of her own. "I thank you, superior sir. To some degree, that relieves my mind."

"I am glad to hear it," Ttomalss replied. That was a truth. The psychological researcher knew more than a little relief at having managed to distract his ward from thoughts of mating with the wild Big Ugly named Jonathan Yeager. Of course, the means of distracting her was contemplating great damage to the Race and the devastation of a good-sized stretch of Tosev 3. It occurred to him that such distractions might be more expensive than they were worth.

And this one didn't even prove completely successful. Kassquit said, "Very well, then, superior sir: after this discussion, I do understand the need for delay in carrying out these matings. But, once the crisis with the Deutsche is resolved, I want to go forward with them, assuming, of course, that part of the resolution does not involve the destruction of this ship."

"Yes—assuming." Ttomalss' tone was dry. "I assure you, Kassquit, you have made your views on that matter very plain, and I will do what I can, consistent with your safety and welfare, to obtain for you that which you desire." *That which you lust after,* he thought. Biologically, she was a Big Ugly, sure enough.

Pointing that out, though, would only inflame the situation further. Instead of doing anything so counterproductive, he asked, "Do we need to concern ourselves with other topics at this time?"

"No, superior sir," Kassquit answered. No matter what she was biologically, she did belong to the Race as far as culture went. Recognizing Ttomalss' question as a dismissal, she rose, briefly assumed the posture of respect, and left his office.

He sighed again once she was gone. He'd managed to slow her a bit, but she'd seized the initiative. She was going to do what she wanted to do, not what he and the rest of the Race wanted her to do. And if that didn't re-create in miniature the history of the relationship between the Race and the Big Uglies, he didn't know what did.

Hoping to distract himself from worries about Kassquit—and from larger worries about the Deutsche, a situation over which he had no control whatever—he turned to the latest news reports on the computer monitor. Deutsch bluster formed a part of those, too. If the Big Uglies were bluffing, they were doing a masterful job. He feared they weren't.

Video from elsewhere on Tosev 3 came up on the screen: rioting brown Big Uglies, most of whom wore only a strip of white cloth wrapped around their reproductive organs. The Race's commentator said, "Farmers in the subregion of the main continental mass known as India have resorted to violence to protest the appearance of hashett in their fields. The plant from Home is of course a prime feed source for our own domestic animals, but the Big Uglies are concerned because it is successfully competing against grains they use for food. No males or females of the Race were reported injured in this latest round of unrest, but property damage is widespread."

If hashett grew well on Tosev 3, other crops from Home would, too. They would help make this world a more Homelike place, as would the spread of the Race's domestic animals. If Tosev 3 did not go up in nuclear explosions, the Race might do very well for itself here. If . . .

Can we acculturate the Big Uglies before they go to war with us? That was the question, no doubt about it. Increasing the Tosevites' reverence for the spirits of Emperors past would help; Ttomalss was sure of that. But it would help only slowly. Danger was growing in a hurry. The Race was running up against a deadline, not a situation familiar to its males and females. *What can we do?* Ttomalss wondered. *Can we do anything?* He could hope. Past that, he had no answers, which worried him more than anything.

As Gorppet patrolled the streets of Cape Town, his eye turrets swiveled this way and that. He was, as always, alert for the possibility of trouble from the Big Uglies who crowded those streets. The dark-skinned Tosevites were supposed to be much more friendly to the Race than the pinkish beige ones, but he trusted none of them. To a male who'd served in the SSSR, in Basra, and in Baghdad, all Big Uglies were objects of suspicion till proved otherwise.

But Gorppet's eye turrets swiveled this way and that for other reasons, too. He kept waiting for a male with an investigator's commission to come up, tap him on the flank, and say, "Come along with me for interrogation."

It hadn't happened yet. He had trouble understanding why it hadn't. By the spirits of Emperors past, he and his pals had got into a firefight not only with the Big Uglies who'd wanted to hijack his gold without giving him any ginger but also with a patrol of his own kind! For all he knew, he might have shot another male of the Race. That wasn't mutiny, not quite, but it came too close for comfort. He knew the Race would be turning everything inside out to find out who had committed such a crime.

They haven't caught me yet, he thought. Maybe being officially a hero helped. He'd captured the infamous Khomeini, after all. Who could imagine that a male with such a glorious accomplishment on his record might also be a male interested in acquiring large amounts of ginger?

No one had imagined it yet. Gorppet counted himself very lucky that no one had. Any investigator with a nasty, suspicious mind would have noticed that his credit balance, which had swollen with the bonus he'd won for capturing the Tosevite fanatic, then proceeded to shrink not long after he came to Cape Town.

But it was growing again. By now, it was almost back to where it had been before he turned so much credit into gold. He'd sold a good deal of ginger. Even now, an investigator who looked only at his current balance and not at his transaction record would be unlikely to notice anything out of the ordinary.

Maybe I will get away with it, he thought. He wouldn't have bet a fingerclaw clipping on that when he'd returned to his barracks after the three-cornered gunfight. Had the investigators descended on him then, he would have confessed everything. Now . . . Now he intended to fight them as aggressively as if they were so many Big Ugly bandits.

He turned a corner and came onto a street where vehicle traffic had halted. Several hundred Tosevites on foot filled the street from curb to curb. Almost all of them were of the pinkish beige variety. They carried signs lettered in the angular local script, which Gorppet couldn't read. He couldn't understand their shouts, either, but those cries didn't sound friendly.

A handful of males of the Race were walking along with the Big Uglies, keeping an eye turret on what they were up to. There weren't nearly enough males, not in Gorppet's view. From his experience in Basra, a parade of this sort always led to fights, often to gunplay.

"Suppress them!" he called to one of the males.

But the male, to his surprise, made the negative hand gesture. "It is not necessary," he said, and then, noting Gorppet's body paint, "It is not necessary, superior sir. I do not expect any trouble to arise from this demonstration."

"Why not?" Gorppet exclaimed. "They will go from fighting to shooting any moment now. They always do."

"Do I gather, superior sir, that you are new to this subregion?" the other male asked. He sounded, of all things, amused.

"Well, what if I am?" Gorppet knew how he sounded: disbelieving. No male who wasn't addled would have sounded any other way.

"It is only that you do not know that peaceful protest was a tradition here, at least among these pale Big Uglies, before the Race conquered this area," the other male said. "If we let them yell and fuss and release energy in this fashion, we have less trouble here than we would otherwise. Think of it as a safety valve, venting pressure that might otherwise lead to an explosion."

In Gorppet's experience, parades didn't vent pressure—they manifested it. He asked, "What are they fussing and yelling about here?"

"A small increase in the tax on meat," the other male replied.

"That is *all*?" Gorppet had trouble believing it. "What do they do if they get worked up over something really important?"

"Then they start shooting at us from ambush, and we have to take steps against them," the other male replied. "But this is for show, nothing more. We may even end up reducing the tax increase somewhat, to give them the impression that we care about what they think even when we do not."

"I . . . see," Gorppet said slowly. "This has a kind of deviousness I find appealing. It is not like this, believe me, in the lands that cling to the Muslim superstition." He used an emphatic cough. "Marches there are not for show, no indeed."

"It is not usually like this with the dark-skinned Tosevites, either," said the male who was keeping an eye turret on the marching Big Uglies. "When they come out into the streets, trouble often follows. But these pale ones seem to take the parade for a real action. Strange, I know, but true."

"Very strange," Gorppet said. "It must make them easier to administer than they would be otherwise."

"Truth," the other male said. "When we ended the privileges their kind had enjoyed and we enforced equal treatment for all varieties of Tosevites within this subregion, they were outraged and rebellious. But once they saw we were not to be shifted from that course—and once we quashed their uprisings—they settled down, and now the biggest trouble we have with them is ginger trafficking."

"Ah," Gorppet said, and his guilty conscience twinged. "Is that a severe problem here?"

"Is it not a severe problem everywhere?" the other male answered. "When it was just a matter of you or me tasting, it was not such an important business, I agree. But with females involved, it became more important. Have you never had pheromones reach your scent receptors?"

"Every now and then," Gorppet admitted. "Sometimes more often than every now and then. It makes me feel as shameless as a Big Ugly."

"Well, there you are, superior sir," the other male said. "It is the same for everyone, which is why ginger is such a problem."

"Truth," Gorppet said, and went on his way. Ginger was not a problem for him. He'd been tasting ever since the Race first discovered what the herb could do. Oh, he'd let himself get a little addled every now and again, but most of the time he was pretty careful with his tastes. So were a large number of the males from the conquest fleet. They'd had plenty of practice with ginger. They knew what it could do for them, and they knew what it could do to them, too.

On the other fork of the tongue, the colonists were still learning—and females who had trouble learning addled the males around them, too. Most of the really large sales Gorppet had made were to colonists seeking excess. They were fools. Gorppet was convinced they would have got into trouble regardless of whether he was the one who sold them the herb.

He looked back with one eye turret. The protesting Big Uglies went round a corner, herded along by that handful of males from the Race. For all the noise the Tosevites made, they evidently weren't after trouble; they might as well have been a herd of azwaca driven to a fresh part of their feeding range.

Domesticated, Gorppet thought. They weren't completely domesticated, not the way azwaca were, but they were getting there. The Muslim Big Uglies farther north, by contrast, remained wild beasts. And what of the Tosevites in the independent not-empires? Gorppet hadn't had much to do with them since the fighting stopped, but they'd kept on being independent. That argued they were tough customers still, and a long way from domestication or assimilation or whatever the Race wanted to call it.

So did the pugnaciousness of the not-empire called the *Reich.* Gorppet had fought Deutsch soldiers as well as Russkis in the SSSR. He hadn't liked them then; he still didn't. And now they had more in the way of technology than they'd enjoyed then. That went a long way toward making them more dangerous.

But when Gorppet got back to his barracks, all thoughts of Big Uglies, even pugnacious ones, disappeared from his head. A couple of males whose body paint showed they were from the inspector general's office awaited him there. "You are Gorppet, recently promoted to the rank of small-unit group leader?" It was phrased as a question—it even came with an interrogative cough—but it was not a question.

"I am, superior sir," Gorppet answered, more calmly than he felt. "And who are you?" If they had him, they had him. If they didn't, he was cursed if he would make life easy for them.

"Who we are is of no consequence, nor is it any of your business," the other male said. "We ask the questions here." Sure enough, he had the arrogance that went with the office he served.

"Go ahead and ask, then. I have nothing to hide." Gorppet was

guilty of enough that one more lie wouldn't hurt him in the least—
if they had him. If they did, they'd have to show him they did.

The other inspector spoke up: "Are you now or have you ever
been acquainted with Tosevites named Rance Auerbach and
Penny Summers?"

If they knew enough to ask, they could tell whether he lied or
not on that one. "I have met them a few times," he answered.
"They are more interesting than most Big Uglies, because they
speak our language fairly well—the female better than the male.
I have not seen them for some little while, however. Why do you
wish to know?"

"We ask the questions here," the first male repeated. "Were
you aware that they were and are notorious ginger smugglers?"

"No, superior sir," Gorppet said. "Ginger-smuggling is illegal, and we never discussed anything illegal. Discussing illegal acts is illegal in itself, is it not?"

"It is indeed," both males from the inspectorate said together.
The second one went on, "Now—when was the last time you
saw these two Big Uglies?"

"I do not precisely remember," Gorppet answered. "As I say, it
was some time ago. Do you know what has become of them? I
rather miss their company." Was that too audacious? He'd find out.

Together, the two males made the negative gesture. "We were
hoping you would be able to tell us," the second one said.

Gorppet made the same gesture himself. "I am sorry, superior
sir, but I cannot do it. I hope nothing unfortunate has happened
to them." That was even true, especially when he thought of
Rance Auerbach. The Big Ugly had been through the worst the
fighting could do, just as Gorppet had himself.

"We do not know," the first inspector said. "We believe, however, that they were involved in the recent unfortunate incident.
You do know to which matter I refer?"

"I believe so, superior sir—gossip is everywhere," Gorppet
answered. "I hope not, for their sakes." *And you don't know
about me after all!* He felt like laughing in the inspectors' faces.

☆ **17** ☆

Mordechai Anielewicz had just sat down to supper when air-raid sirens began to wail in the streets of Lodz. Bertha exclaimed in dismay and set the roast chicken she was bringing in from the kitchen down on the table. Mordechai sprang to his feet. "Grab your masks, everyone!" he said. "Then down to the cellar as fast as we can go."

His own gas mask was right behind him. He pulled it on, wondering how much good it would do. He'd already made the acquaintance of German poison gas once. He'd been lucky then; Heinrich Jäger had had syringes of the antidote. Even so, he'd almost died. A second exposure . . . He didn't want to think about it.

Bertha had her mask on. So did Miriam and David. Heinrich . . . Where was Heinrich? Anielewicz shouted his younger son's name.

"I've got my mask, Father!" Heinrich Anielewicz shouted back from the bedroom. "But I can't find Pancer!"

"Leave the beffel!" Mordechai exclaimed. "We've got to get down to the cellar!"

"I can't leave him," Heinrich said. "Oh—here he is, under the bed. I've got him." He came out with the beffel in his arms. "All right—we can go now."

The sirens were shrieking like lost souls. Mordechai whacked Heinrich on the backside as his son hurried past him. "You put yourself in danger and your whole family with you, on account of your pet," he snapped.

"I'm sorry," Heinrich said. "But Pancer saved us once, you know, so I thought I ought to save him, too, if I could."

That wasn't the sort of response to which Anielewicz could find an easy comeback. Heinrich didn't see his life as more im-

portant than the beffel's. "Come on," Mordechai said. Bertha
carefully shut the door behind them as they hurried down the
hall, down the stairs, and into the cellar below the block of flats.
Everyone else in the building hurried with them, men, women,
and children all wearing masks that turned them from people
into pig-snouted aliens.

"There, you see!" From behind his mask, Heinrich's still-
piping voice rose in triumph. "They've got a dog, and *they've*
got a cat."

"I see," Anielewicz said. "The other thing I see is, they took
chances they shouldn't have, and so did you."

Heinrich's older brother had a more urgent, more important
question: "If an explosive-metal bomb goes off in Lodz, how
much good will hiding in the cellar do us?"

"It depends on just where the bomb goes off, David,"
Mordechai answered. "I don't know for sure how much good
it will do. I do know we've got a better chance in the cellar than
upstairs."

By the time he and his family got in, the cellar was already
packed. People talked in high, excited voices. Mordechai didn't
talk. He did worry. The cellar didn't hold enough food and water
to let people last very long before being forced to go out. He'd
complained to the manager, who'd nodded politely and not done
a thing. If the worst came . . .

It didn't, not this evening. Instead, the all-clear blew, a long,
steady blast of sound. "Thank God," Bertha said quietly.

"Just another drill," Mordechai agreed. "But with things
the way they are, we can't know ahead of time, so we have to
treat every one like the real thing. Let's go upstairs. Supper
won't even be cold." He took off his mask. Breathing unfiltered
air, even in the cramped quarters of the cellar, felt far better than
the seemingly lifeless stuff he got through the rubber and charcoal of the mask.

After supper, Bertha was washing dishes with Miriam helping her when the telephone rang. Mordechai picked it up.
"Hello?"

"Just another drill." David Nussboym sounded wryly amused
with the world.

"Yes, just another drill," Mordechai agreed. *"Nu?"* He didn't know how to respond to the man whose hirelings had come unpleasantly close to killing him a couple of times.

"When do you suppose the real thing will come along?" Nussboym asked. He didn't seem to feel the least bit guilty about what he'd done.

"What, Molotov didn't tell you before he sent you out here?" Anielewicz jeered.

"No, as a matter of fact, he didn't," replied the Jew from Lodz who'd become an NKVD man. "He told me I would be the best man on the spot because of my old connections here, but that was all."

Anielewicz wondered how to take that. "You know Molotov personally?" he said. "Sure you do, just like I know the Pope."

"Say hello to him for me next time you see him," Nussboym answered imperturbably. "Know Molotov personally? I don't think anyone does, except maybe his wife. But I deal with him, if that's what you mean. I'm the one who got him out of his cell in the middle of Beria's coup."

He spoke matter-of-factly enough. If he was lying, Anielewicz couldn't prove it by his tone. "If he sent you here thinking there'd be a war, he didn't do you any favors," he observed.

"This thought also occurred to me," Nussboym said. "But I serve the Soviet Union." He spoke without self-consciousness. He'd been a Red before Anielewicz and some of the other Jewish fighters in Lodz spirited him off to the USSR because he was also too friendly with the Lizards. They'd been playing a double game with the Race and the Germans. They'd got away with it, too, but Mordechai didn't ever want to have to take such chances again.

He said, "And what does serving the Soviet Union mean about your being here now?"

"I volunteered for this, because I know Lodz and because your interests and the Soviet Union's coincide for the time being," David Nussboym answered. "We both want to stop the war any way we can. This is what you get for going to bed with the fascists during the fighting." No, he hadn't forgotten what had happened all those years ago, either.

With a sigh, Anielewicz answered, "If the Race had beaten the Nazis then, odds are they'd have beaten the Russians, too. And what Soviet Union would you be serving these days if that had happened?"

"I don't deal in might-have-beens," Nussboym said, as if Mordechai had accused him of a particularly unsavory vice. "I deal in what's real."

"All right," Anielewicz said amiably. "What's real here? If the Germans come over the border, what do we do about it? Do we start yelling for Soviet soldiers to help drive them away?"

He chuckled under his breath, figuring that would get a rise out of his former colleague if anything could. And it did. "No!" Nussboym exclaimed. Had he been a Lizard, he would have used an emphatic cough. "Formally, the USSR is and will stay neutral in case of conflict."

"Molotov doesn't want the Germans *and* the Race landing on Russia with both feet, eh?" Behind that cynical tone, Mordechai felt a certain amount of sympathy for the Soviet leader's position.

"Would you?" Nussboym returned, which showed he was thinking along similar lines.

"Maybe yes, maybe no." Anielewicz was damned if he'd admit anything. "And that brings me back to what the devil you're doing here. If Russia's neutral, why aren't you back in Moscow twiddling your thumbs?"

"Formally, the Soviet Union is neutral," David Nussboym repeated. "Informally . . ."

"Informally, what?" Mordechai demanded. "Do you want to split Poland with the Germans again, the way you did in 1939?"

"That was proposed, I am given to understand," Nussboym answered. "General Secretary Molotov rejected the proposal out of hand."

"Was it? Did he?" Mordechai thought about what that was likely to mean. "He's more afraid of the Race than of the Nazis, then. Fair enough. If I were living in the Kremlin, I would be, too." He thought a little more. "If Russia gives informal help here, you might even end up on the Lizards' good side. Nobody ever said Molotov was a fool. Anybody who stayed alive all the way through Stalin's time couldn't be a fool."

"You don't know what you're talking about," Nussboym said softly. "You haven't the faintest idea what you're talking about. And if you still believe in God, you can thank Him you don't."

Mordechai's voice went harsh: "All right, then. *Tukhus afen tish,* Nussboym. What will you do? What won't you do? How much can we count on you?" Privately, he didn't intend to count on Nussboym at all. Counting on the USSR, though, was, or at least might be, something else again.

"We will not do anything that makes it look as though the Soviet Union is interfering in Poland," replied the NKVD man who'd grown up in Lodz. "Short of that . . . Well, there's always been a lot of smuggling along the border between White Russia and Poland. We can get you weapons. We can even get you a cadre of Polish-speaking soldiers to train new recruits."

"Oh, I'll bet you can," Anielewicz said. "And you'd train them to be just the finest little Marxist-Leninists anybody could want, wouldn't you?" He hadn't used the jargon much since the fighting stopped, but he still remembered it.

"One of these days, the revolution will come to Poland," Nussboym said. "One of these days, the revolution will come to Home." He might not believe in God any more, but he still had a strong and vibrant faith.

Arguing with him struck Anielewicz as more trouble than it was worth. Instead, he asked, "How much good is all this likely to do if the *Reich* hits us with explosive-metal bombs and poison gas?"

"They won't kill everyone." Nussboym spoke with a peculiar cold-blooded confidence. German generals doubtless sounded much the same way. "Soldiers will have to come into Poland and seize the land. When they do, the survivors from among your forces can make life difficult for them."

"You're leaving the Lizards out of your calculations," Anielewicz said. "Whatever else they do, they won't sit quietly."

"I know that," Nussboym said. "My assumption is that they will give the *Reich* exactly what it deserves. That ought to make the fight in Poland easier, don't you think? The Nazis won't be able to support their troops the way they could in 1939."

Again, cold calculation weighing the probable result of thousands—no, millions—of deaths. Again, that calculation, however horrific, struck Mordechai as reasonable. And wasn't making reasonable calculations about millions of deaths perhaps the most horrific thing of all?

"The next question, of course, is what happens after the Race finishes destroying the *Reich*," Mordechai said.

"Then the Soviet Union picks up the pieces—provided there are any pieces left to pick up," Nussboym answered. "The other half of the question is, how much damage can the Nazis do to the Lizards before going down?"

"However much it is, too much of it will be in Poland," Mordechai predicted gloomily. "So, from my point of view, that leads to a different question: can we do anything to keep the war from starting? You'd better think about that, too, Nussboym, as long as you're here."

"I have been thinking about it," David Nussboym answered. "What I haven't been able to do is come up with anything to stop the war. And neither, I gather, have you." He hung up before Mordechai could either curse him or tell him he was right.

Tahiti wasn't what Rance Auerbach had expected. Oh, the weather was gorgeous: always warm and mild and just a little muggy. And he could walk along the beach under the palm trees and watch the gentle surf roll in off the blue, blue Pacific. That was all terrific, even if he did get a hellacious sunburn the first time he tried it. He'd had to slather zinc-oxide ointment all over his poor medium-rare carcass. As far as setting went, he'd had everything straight.

Papeete, now, where he and Penny were renting an apartment even more crowded and cramped than the one they'd had in Cape Town, Papeete was something else. The town didn't quite know what to make of itself. Parts of it were still the sleepy, even languorous, backwater the place must have been back before the fighting started a generation earlier. The rest was what had come since: the place's role as the capital of Free France, such as Free France was.

The tricolor flew everywhere in Papeete, the same way the Stars and Stripes did back in the USA on the Fourth of July. But the Stars and Stripes flew out of honest pride and strength. Rance didn't think that was why the Free French draped their banner over everything that didn't move. Rather, they seemed to be saying, *Hey, look at us! We really are a country! Honest! No kidding! See? We've got a flag and everything!*

Stick tapping on the sidewalk, Auerbach made his way toward

his apartment building. Tahitian girls were all around, some walking like him, some on bicycles, some on the little motor-bikes that turned people into more or less guided missiles. A lot of them were very pretty. Even so, Rance's fantasy life wasn't what it had been before a series of battered freighters brought him and Penny here from South Africa. What he hadn't consid-ered was that a lot of those pretty Tahitian girls had hulking, bad-tempered Tahitian boyfriends, some of whom carried knives and some of whom were a lot more heavily armed than that.

One such massive Tahitian, wearing nothing but a pair of dun-garees and a gun belt with a pistol on his right hip, loomed up in front of Auerbach as he walked into his building. When the fellow grinned, he showed very white teeth—and a hole where one in front had been till he lost it in a brawl. "Allo, Rance. How you are today?" he asked in English flavored by both French and Tahitian.

"Not too bad, Jean-Claude," Auerbach answered—about as much as he'd ever say these days. "You take care of that leaky toilet in our bathroom yet?"

"I do it soon," the handyman promised. "Very, very soon." He'd been saying that ever since Rance and Penny moved in a couple of weeks before. Sometimes it was hard to tell tropical languor from being a lazy bum, but Rance didn't feel easy about leaning on a guy half his age who outweighed him almost two to one and packed a pistol to boot.

A fan buzzed inside the apartment. Penny Summers sat in a chair, letting the stream of moving air play on her face and neck. She turned her head when Rance came in. "We ever gonna get that toilet fixed?" she asked.

"Doesn't look likely," Rance said. "Maybe the son of a bitch'll do it if we pay him off. If we don't, you can forget about it."

"It'll just have to stay leaky, then," Penny said. She made a weary, unhappy gesture. "We took a hundred pounds of gold away from Cape Town, near enough. Who would've figured that wouldn't do the job?"

"Comes to something a little over forty thousand bucks," Rance said. "That's a pretty fair piece of change."

But Penny shook her head. A lock of blond hair escaped a hairpin and fell down in front of one eye. She brushed it back with an impatient gesture. "We had to spend like it was going out of style just to get here, and more to keep from getting handed over to the Lizards. And everything here costs more than anybody in his right mind'd believe."

"Of course it does," Auerbach said. "This is the boondocks, the ass end of nowhere. Nobody makes anything here; everything gets shipped in from places where they really do make stuff. No wonder we pay through the nose."

"Hey, they do make one thing here," Penny said.

Rance raised a dubious eyebrow. "Yeah? What's that, sweetheart?"

"Trouble," Penny answered with a grin. "And they make it in great big carload lots, too. Why else would we be here?"

"But we don't have enough money to make all the trouble we want," Auerbach said. "If we'd brought a hundred pounds of hundred-dollar bills—"

"Where was Gorppet going to get his hands on hundred-dollar bills in Cape Town?" Penny broke in. "Don't make me laugh. We've got a stake; we just can't afford to get fancy till we run it up some."

"I know, I know," Rance said.

"If we don't run it up, we're ruined when what we've got runs out," Penny said flatly. "If there's one thing this place runs on, it's cold, hard cash. They don't give a damn about whose cash it's supposed to be, either."

"I know that, too." Auerbach paused and lit a cigarette. He coughed as he sucked in smoke, which made his ruined chest hurt. And that wasn't the only ache the coffin nails gave him here. Holding up the pack, he said, "You know how much these goddamn things cost?"

"You bet I do," Penny answered. "Give me one, will you?" He took one out and handed it to her, then awkwardly bent forward, putting a lot of weight on his stick, so she could start it on his. Her cheeks hollowed as she inhaled. "Listen, I've got a line on a guy who'll sell us some ginger. Now all we need to do is get a Lizard to buy and we're in business for a while longer."

"Who's the guy?" Rance asked. "Somebody new, or do you know him from before?"

"From before—I dealt with him back when I was working with those people in Detroit," Penny said. "His name's Richard."

She pronounced it *Ree-shard*, which meant the fellow was a Frenchman.

"Is he pals with the guys you used to work for?" Rance asked. "If he is, he's liable to want you dead after the way you stiffed them."

"Nobody's really pals with anybody in the ginger racket," Penny said; from what Auerbach had seen of it, she wasn't far wrong. "I didn't stiff Richard, so him and me won't be anything but business."

"Here's hoping you're right." Auerbach limped into the kitchen, poured himself a drink of the nasty local brandy, and cut it with a little water; the stuff was too harsh and too potent for anybody in his right mind to want to drink it straight. He poured a knock for Penny, too.

She grinned and blew him a kiss when she saw the drinks in his hands. When he gave her one, she raised the glass and said, "Mud in your eye."

"Yeah." Rance sipped, wheezed, and, for a wonder, managed not to cough. "Jesus, that stuff kicks like a mule." As Penny also drank, he studied her. If he were this Richard, how far would he trust her? *About as far as I can throw her,* he decided. The fellow selling the ginger would have to be wondering where she'd got the cash this time, and whether she'd try to cheat him. He'd be a jerk if he didn't come loaded for bear.

For once, Penny didn't seem to know where his thoughts were going. She said, "We get ourselves a discount on the herb for paying in gold."

"Do we?" Auerbach thought about that, too. Not all his thoughts were pleasant. "We'd better talk with Jean-Claude, then, or with somebody. We'll want some firepower along so your pal doesn't try redistributing the wealth."

He watched Penny. She took a deep breath. He knew exactly what she was going to say: something along the lines of, *Oh, he wouldn't do anything like that.* Rance intended to land on her with both feet if she did. But she didn't; instead, she looked sheepish and answered, "Yeah, we'd better do something about that, hadn't we?"

He let out a rasping sigh of relief. "Oh, good. You remember Frederick after all."

"Yeah." Her mouth twisted. "That stupid, greedy son of a

bitch. You even told him there was plenty for everybody, and you were dead right, too. But would he listen? Hell, no. Of course, Frederick was an amateur, and Richard's a pro. He's been doing this for a long time."

"Anybody can get greedy." Rance spoke with great conviction. "Best way to make him think twice is to show he'd pay for it if he tried."

"Well, I won't try and tell you you're wrong, because I think you're right," Penny said. "You want to talk to Jean-Claude, or would you rather I did it?"

"Go ahead. Bat your baby blues. You'll get a better deal out of him than I could." Rance wasn't particularly worried about Penny fooling around with the Tahitian muscleman. For one thing, Jean-Claude was only in his mid-twenties, so he wasn't all that likely to find her appealing. And, for another, Jean-Claude had a girlfriend of formidable proportions and equally formidable temper. Auerbach wouldn't have wanted to cross her, and he didn't think Jean-Claude did, either.

Now Penny was following his thoughts, for she stuck out her tongue at him. He laughed and said, "You don't want to do that at a native; it's sort of like asking for a fight. Now, the next question is, once we've got the ginger, how much trouble will we have selling it to a Lizard?"

"We should manage," Penny said. "There's always plenty of 'em around. This place draws shady characters the way honey draws flies." She took another sip from her brandy. "We're here, aren't we?"

"Uh-huh. I wondered when you'd mention that," Rance said.

But she was right. The Free French ran a wide-open outfit. They stayed in business by skimming a little off the top of the deals that got made in their territory, by not asking a whole lot of inconvenient questions, and by keeping the Japanese, the Americans, and the Lizards all too busy eyeing one another for any of them to kill the goose that laid the golden eggs.

And so, even as Penny and he went to meet Richard along with Jean-Claude and several other large, beefy pieces of hired muscle, Auerbach saw half a dozen Lizards on the streets of Papeete, all of them in conversation with humans who looked shady. *Takes one to know one,* he thought.

Richard was small and lithe and surrounded by bodyguards

who looked a lot nastier than the ones Rance and Penny had along. He spoke English with an accent partly French, partly southwestern, as if he'd learned the language by watching a lot of horse operas. "You got the goods?" he asked—the subject under discussion might have been wagon wheels, not gold.

"Sure do," Penny answered. "Do you?"

"You bet," Richard said, and gestured to one of his henchmen. The burly Tahitian held up a parcel wrapped in twine. At Richard's gesture, he opened it. The spicy tang of ginger tickled Rance's nose. Richard gestured again, this time to Penny. "Check it—go right ahead. No false weight. No false measure. I'm a straight dealer."

Had he said he was a straight shooter, Auerbach would have believed that, too. Penny did check, tasting the herb and probing to make sure the package held nothing but ginger. When satisfied, she turned to Auerbach. "Pay him, Rance."

With a nod, he passed a little case—it didn't have to be a big one—holding ten pounds of gold to Richard. This was the nasty moment. As soon as the case was out of his hand, that hand slid down toward his own pistol. The temptation to keep the ginger and grab the gold had to be there—had to be there on both sides, in fact, for Richard and his bodyguards were awfully intent themselves.

But here, unlike the Cape Town park, everything went smoothly. The Frenchman examined the gold as carefully as Penny had checked the ginger. When he said, *"C'est bon,"* his bully boys visibly relaxed. Then he returned to English: "Good luck unloading that stuff. Enjoyed doing business with you." And off he went.

"We'd better unload it," Rance muttered. They'd just traded away a lot of what they were living on. They couldn't buy groceries with ginger, not directly. If things went wrong . . .

"Relax," Penny said. "We're in business again." She sounded confident. But then, she always sounded confident. Rance sighed. He had to hope she was right.

"Two, please," Reuven Russie said in Hebrew to the ticket-seller at the cinema. The man gave him a blank stare. He repeated the request in Arabic and handed the fellow a banknote. The ticket-seller's face lit up. He passed Reuven two tickets, then quickly and accurately made change. "Thanks," Reuven told him, again in Arabic. He switched to English: "Come on, Jane. Still should be plenty of good seats."

"Right," Jane Archibald said, also in English. She went on, "That bloke should know more Hebrew."

"He's probably just come from some little country village in the middle of nowhere," Reuven answered. "He'll learn, I expect."

He paused at the snack counter inside the building to buy a couple of rolled papers full of fried chickpeas and two glasses of Coca-Cola. Nibbling and drinking, he and Jane went through the curtains and into the theater itself. They did get good seats, but it was filling faster than Reuben had expected. The crowd was about two-thirds Jews, one-third Arabs. And . . .

"Will you look at that?" Reuven pointed to three or four Lizards who sat in the front row so they wouldn't have to peer over and around taller people in seats in front of them. "Why do you suppose they want to watch *The Battle of Chicago*? Their side lost, after all."

"Maybe they think it's funny. But them losing is good enough reason for me to want to see it." Jane's voice took on the grim edge it always held when she talked about the Lizards. She sighed. "I only wish they could make that kind of film about the fighting in Australia."

"I know." Reuven didn't have the same attitude about the coming of the Race. But then, the Lizards had conquered Jane's homeland, while they'd freed his people from almost certain death when they drove the Nazis out of Poland. He reached out and took her hand. She smiled at him and squeezed his. He went on, "What surprises me is that the Lizards are letting people here see the film."

Jane shrugged. "If the Americans ever conquer the world, it'll be on account of their cinema, not their guns."

Before Reuven could find a good answer for that, the house lights dimmed and the cartoon started. It too was American, with Donald Duck rampaging across the screen. He spoke—spluttered, rather—in English, with Hebrew and Arabic sub-titles. Children obviously too young to read, who obviously didn't speak English, giggled at his antics. So did Reuven. Anybody who couldn't laugh at Donald Duck had to have something wrong with him somewhere.

He also kept glancing over at Jane, her elegant profile illuminated by the flickering light from the screen. She was laughing, too. But after the cartoon ended and the main feature started, her features grew solemn, intent. As far as Reuven was concerned, *The Battle of Chicago* was just another shoot-'em-up, with tanks and airplanes instead of galloping horses and six-shooters. He paid more attention to the pretty blond French actress who played a nurse in an improbably tight, improbably skimpy uniform than he did to rattling machine guns and spectacular explosions.

Not so Jane. Whenever the Lizards looked as if they were on the point of breaking through, she squeezed his hand hard enough to hurt. And she whooped and cheered every time the Americans rallied. When the explosive-metal bomb went off and blew the Lizards' army to kingdom come, she leaned over and kissed him. For that, he would have put up with a much longer, much duller film.

"If only we could have done it to them in a lot more places," she said with another sigh as the credits rolled across the screen.

"Well, the Germans may try it again," Reuven answered. "Do you really like the notion of air-raid drills and more nuclear explosions and poison gas and who can guess what all else? I don't, not very much."

Jane thought for several seconds before saying, "If another war would get rid of the Lizards once and for all, I'd be for it no matter what else it might do. But I don't think that will happen, no matter how much I wish it would. And the bloody Nazis wouldn't be any better than the Race as top dogs, would they?"

"Worse, if you ask me," Reuven said. "Of course, they'd throw me in an oven first and ask questions later."

Jane got up and started for the exit. "Hard to believe they really did that to people—that it's not just Lizard propaganda, I mean."

"I wish it were," Reuven said. "But if you don't believe me, talk to my father. He saw a couple of their murder factories with his own eyes." This was, he knew, not the ideal sort of conversation when out for a good time with a very pretty girl. But *The*

Battle of Chicago and the present world situation had put such thoughts in both their minds. He went on, "If the Lizards hadn't come, there probably wouldn't be any Jews left in Poland." *I wouldn't be alive,* was what that meant, though he shied away from thinking of it in those terms. "If the Germans had won the war, there probably wouldn't be any Jews left anywhere."

They walked out into the night, past people coming in for the next show. Slowly, Jane said, "When I was a little girl, we used to think Jews were traitors because they got on so well with the Lizards. I never really understood why you did till I came here to Palestine to study at the medical college."

Reuven shrugged. "If the only choices you've got are the *Reich* and the Race, you're caught between—between . . ." He snapped his fingers in annoyance. "What are you caught between in English? I can't remember."

"The devil and the deep blue sea?" Jane suggested.

"That's it. Thanks," Reuven said. "What would you like to do now? Shall I walk you back to the dormitory?"

"No," Jane said, and used one of the Race's emphatic coughs. "Between the dorm and the college, I feel like I'm in gaol half the time. This is your city; you get to go out and about in it. I don't, not nearly enough."

"All right, then," Reuven said. "Let's go to Makarios' coffee-house. It's only a couple of blocks away." Jane nodded eagerly. Smiling, Reuven slid his arm around her waist. She snuggled against him. His smile got broader.

Run by a Greek from Cyprus, Makarios' was as close to neutral ground as Jerusalem had. Jews and Muslims and Christians all drank coffee—and sometimes stronger things—there, and ate stuffed grape leaves, and chatted and argued and dickered far into the night. Lizards showed up there, too, every now and again. Rumor was that Makarios sold ginger out the back door of the coffeehouse. Reuven didn't know if that was true, but it wouldn't have surprised him.

He and Jane found a quiet little table off in a corner. The coffee was Turkish style, thick and sweet and strong, served in small cups. Jane said, "Well, I won't have to worry about sleeping any more tonight." She opened her eyes very wide to show what she meant.

Reuven laughed. He drained his own demitasse and waved to the waiter for a refill. *"Evkharistô,"* he said when it arrived. He'd learned a few words of Greek from children he'd played with in London during the fighting. *Thank you* was one of the handful of clean phrases he remembered.

He and Jane didn't leave Makarios' till after midnight. The streets of Jerusalem were quiet, almost deserted; it wasn't a town that hummed around the clock. Reuven put his arm around Jane again. When she moved toward him instead of pulling back, he kissed her. Her arms went around him, too. She was as tall as he was and very nearly as strong—she all but squeezed the breath out of him.

His hands cupped her bottom, pulling her against him. She had to know what was going through his mind—and through his endocrine system. And she did. When at last the kiss broke, she murmured, "I wish there were somewhere we could go."

If they went back to the medical students' dormitory, they'd hatch gossip, maybe even scandal. Reuven didn't know which hotels turned a blind eye to couples who wanted to check in without baggage. He imagined making love to Jane in the parlor of his family's house and having the twins interrupt at the worst possible moment.

And then, instead of despair, inspiration struck. "There is!" he exclaimed, and kissed her again, as much from delight at his own cleverness as from desire—although desire was there, too: oh, indeed it was.

"Where?" Jane asked.

"You'll see," Reuven answered. "Come along with me."

He feared she'd said what she said because she thought they really didn't have anywhere to go, and that she would balk when she found they did. But she held his hand till he got out his keys and used one he'd certainly never thought he would need at this time of night. She gurgled laughter then. In a small, arch voice, she said, "I'm not your patient, Dr. Russie."

"And a good thing, too, Dr. Archibald," he answered, closing the outer door to the office behind them and locking it again. "If you were, this would be unethical."

It wasn't a perfect place; neither high, hard, narrow examining couches nor chairs made an adequate substitute for a bed. But it was quiet and private, and they managed well enough.

Better than well enough, Reuven thought dizzily as Jane crouched in front of him as he sat in one of the chairs, then rose from her knees, sat down on his lap, and impaled herself upon him.

It was as good as he'd thought it would be. Considering all his imaginings about Jane, that made it very fine indeed. He did his best to please her, too, letting his mouth glide from hers to the tips of her breasts and stroking between her legs as she rode him. She threw back her head and let out a couple of sharp, explosive gasps of pleasure. A moment later, he groaned as he too spent himself.

She leaned forward and kissed him on the end of the nose. With one arm round her back and his other hand resting on her smooth, bare thigh, he thought of something he realized should have crossed his mind sooner. "I should have worn a rubber," he blurted. He had stayed hard inside her; that was alarming enough to make him lose his ardor and slide out.

"Not too much to worry about," Jane said. "My period's due in a couple of days. I'd have fretted a good deal more a week or ten days ago."

"All right." Reuven ran a hand along the curves of her flank and hip. He didn't want to let go of her—but at the same time he began to wonder what would, or what ought to, happen next. "Not just friends any more," he said.

"No." Jane chuckled, then kissed him again. "Your family won't approve. Oh, your sisters might, but your mother and father won't. What are you going to do about that?"

It was a good question, and one Reuven heard with a certain amount of relief. She might have said, *Now are you going to ask me to marry you?* He was a long way from sure he wanted to marry Jane; that was a notion very different from wanting to lay her. And, even though she'd made love with him, he wasn't at all sure she wanted to marry him, either.

"Right now, I just don't know," he answered slowly. "We have to figure out what *we* want to do after this before we worry about my family, I think."

He hoped that wouldn't anger her. It didn't; she nodded and got off him. "Fair enough," she answered. "I didn't know if you wanted to play it by ear, but that suits me well enough for now. And," she added with brisk practicality, "we'd better make sure we don't leave any spots on the chair or the carpet, or else your father will know a lot sooner than we want him to."

Money of my own, Monique Dutourd thought. It was less money than it would have been had she been able to take the grand prize the Lizards tried to press on her. That still rankled. They should have been willing to give her the full cash value of the house she couldn't accept. Who would have thought there were cheapskates among the Race?

She had a fine mental picture of herself accepting the house and moving in. She might have stayed there by herself for five minutes before *Standartenführer* Dieter Kuhn started pounding on the door and demanding that she take him back to the bedroom. On the other hand, she might not have, too.

But twenty thousand Reichsmarks was a tidy little sum. And, best of all, Pierre didn't know she had the money—or she didn't think he did, anyhow. As far as she could tell, her brother didn't search her room. *I can do what I want with it,* she thought. *What I want, not what anybody else wants. If I can get a passport under a name that's not my own, I can even get out of the* Reich *altogether.*

From the bellicose rantings in the newspapers, that struck her as a better idea every day. The Germans seemed as intent on attacking Poland as they had when she was a girl. She thought they were insane, but she'd seen a lot of German insanity over the past generation. More wouldn't surprise her.

The only trouble was, if the Germans got into a war with the Lizards, the Lizards wouldn't care that Marseille was properly a part of France. To them, it would be just another city in the Greater German *Reich*—in other words, a target.

That cheerful thought made her more blunt with her brother than she might have been otherwise. Over breakfast one morning, she came right out and said, "I want an identity card with a false name on it."

Pierre Dutourd looked up from his croissant and *café au lait.* "And why do you want this?" he inquired, his tone one of mild curiosity.

"Because it's safer if I have one," Monique answered. She knew he'd be suspicious, not just curious, no matter how he sounded. He hadn't stayed in business all these years by virtue of a trusting disposition. She went on, "It's safer for me, and it's safer for you, too. In case I ever get picked up, the *Boches* won't have such an easy time learning who I am, and they won't squeeze me so hard."

Lucie took a drag on her cigarette, then stubbed it out. "Why do you think we can get you anything like that?" she asked.

Especially coming in the sexy-little-girl voice of Pierre's girl-friend, the question infuriated Monique. "Why? Because I'm not an idiot, that's why," she snapped. "How many false cards do the two of you have?"

"It could be that I have one or two," Pierre said mildly. "It could even be that Lucie has one or two. I do not say that it is, mind you, but it could be."

Acid still in her voice, Monique asked, "Well, could it be that I might have one? You would think I were asking for a diamond necklace."

"It would be less risky for me to get you a diamond necklace," her brother replied. "Let me think, and let me see what I can do." No matter how much she squawked, he would say no more than that.

She didn't know she'd won her point till she got summoned to a dingy photographic studio a couple of days later. Flashbulbs made her see glowing purple spots. "Those should do the job," the photographer told her. He didn't say what kind of job they were supposed to do, but she figured that out for herself.

A few days later, Pierre handed her a card that told the world, or at least the German and French officials therein, that she was Madeleine Didier. The photograph was one the fellow at the little hole-in-the-wall studio had taken. As for the rest of the document . . . She compared it to her old ID card, which she knew was genuine. "I can't see any difference."

Pierre looked smug. "There isn't any difference, not unless you chance to have a high-powered microscope. My friend the printer does these with great success."

"He'd better," Monique exclaimed. "No quicker way to commit suicide than an identification card that doesn't pass muster."

"I had not finished." Her brother looked annoyed at the inter-ruption; he liked to hear himself talk. "He has a Lizard machine that makes an image of whatever document he requires and stores it so he can alter it as he pleases on one of their computing devices. This, he assures me, is far easier and more convenient than working from photographs ever was."

"So the Lizards have brought us a golden age of forgery?" Monique said, amused. "And how long will it be before he finds it easier to print money in his shop than to earn it by honest work there?"

"For all I know, François may be doing just that," Pierre Dutourd replied. "You will understand, I do not ask him a great many questions about such things, just as he does not ask me a great many questions about my occupation."

"Yes, I can see that this might be so." Monique studied the new card. It really did seem perfect: not just the printing but also the rubber stamps and official signatures were exactly as they should have been. "Himmler himself would not suspect anything was wrong with it."

"Of course not." Pierre rolled his eyes. "He's dead, and good riddance, too." He paused, then after a moment shook his head. "No, it could be that I am wrong. We may be sorry he is gone, for these fools all trying to steal his seat may set the *Reich* on fire to show how manly they are." He made a sour face. "Some of my best customers are very worried about that."

"Some of the Lizards, you mean?" Monique asked.

"But of course," Pierre Dutourd replied. "And they do not care—they hardly even know, except as far as the language goes—we here are French, not Germans. As far as they are concerned, one part of the *Reich* is the same as another. To them, it is all *ein Volk, ein Reich, ein Führer.*" He looked disgusted now. *"Merde alors!"*

Monique almost laughed out loud. From everything she'd seen, her brother was far more mercenary than patriotic. She'd never heard him say much about the *Reich* till living under Nazi rule seemed likely to land him in trouble—he certainly hadn't cared a great deal when she got slapped around at the *Palais de Justice.* But hearing that he and the Race worried about war ahead did make her sit up and take notice. "Can we do anything?"

"Run for the hills," he suggested. "It could be I would not bring you back to the city, as I did before. It could be that I would also run. The best defense against an explosive-metal bomb is not to be there when it goes off. This is, I believe, an American saying. It is also, I believe, a true saying."

"Yes, I believe it could be," Monique said. She sat thoughtfully at the breakfast table. If she couldn't get a passport—if, even with a passport, she couldn't get out of Marseille—running into the hills didn't seem the worst idea in the world. "Will your friends among the Race know the war is on the point of breaking out before it does?"

"If anyone among the Race knows, they will know," Pierre answered. "But whether anyone will know, that I cannot say. All the Germans have to do is launch their rockets, and *voilà*—war!"

"No, it's not that simple," Monique said. "They have to move soldiers into position, and tanks, and airplanes. These things must be noticeable."

"Less than you'd think," her brother told her. "From what my friends say, the *Boches* move forces all the time, so it becomes difficult to be sure which movements are intended to confuse and which are intended to deploy. And the Germans are better at keeping things secret than they used to be, too."

That, unfortunately, seemed altogether too probable to Monique. Thanks to Dieter Kuhn, she knew the Nazis were getting better at unscrambling the Lizards' security devices. It seemed logical they should also be getting better with their own.

The conversation helped make up her mind for her. Leaving the Porte d'Aix made her nervous; she expected every SS man in France to descend on her with cocked submachine gun and possibly with unbuttoned fly. Only after she was already on the way to the *Préfecture* on Rue St. Ferréol did she pause to wonder whether Pierre's clever printer could forge passports as readily as ID cards. After pedaling on for another half a block, she shook her head. She didn't want Pierre to know she intended fleeing, because she wanted to flee from him, too. That meant she had to get the passport on her own, and *that* meant she had to get a real one; except through her brother, she had no illicit connections.

And so, the *Préfecture*. It was larger and more massive than the *Palais de Justice*, with a small square on the north side and a park over to the east. She set her bicycle in a rack in front of the building and chained it into place: even here, with gendarmes strolling about keeping an eye on things, thieves might thrive.

But at least the policemen were gendarmes and not the Germans who gave the *Palais de Justice* its sinister reputation: how well deserved that reputation was, she knew better than she'd ever wanted to.

Inside, languid ceiling fans did a halfhearted job of stirring the air. FILL OUT ALL FORMS BEFORE ENTERING LINE, a prominent sign warned. From everything Monique had heard, French bureaucracy had been bad before the *Reich* overran the country. From everything she'd seen, it was worse now, having added German thoroughness without the slightest trace of German efficiency.

As she'd expected, the forms for obtaining a passport were formidable. So were the fees required—officials wanted to know everything about anyone who might want to leave the *Reich*, and also wanted to soak would-be travelers for the privilege. Monique filled out page after page, much of the information being fictitious. If the bureaucrats did any careful checking, she was in trouble. But her assumption was that no one would have any reason to check on Madeleine Didier, who couldn't very well have fallen foul of the authorities because she'd existed for only a few days.

Do you really want to do this? she wondered. *If you're wrong, and if you get caught, you're back in Dieter Kuhn's hands—and probably back in his arms, too.* She didn't have to worry about that in Porte d'Aix, anyhow. But her brother wanted to use her, too, even if in a different way. If she could get away, she'd also be free of Pierre. She nodded briskly. The game was worth the candle.

The line moved forward a centimeter at a time. At last, though, she stood before a bored-looking functionary. He gave the forms a desultory glance, then said, "Your fee?" She pushed Reichsmarks across the counter. He riffled through them, nodded, and said, "Your identification card?" Heart thuttering, Monique passed that to him, too. He examined it more carefully than the forms, less carefully than the money, and pushed it back to her. "Very good. All appears to be in order. You may return in four weeks' time to pick up your passport. It must be done in person, you understand."

"Yes, of course," Monique answered. "Thank you." She turned away, thinking, *Either I get the passport—or the SS gets me*. She'd find out, if she still had the nerve . . . and if the world hadn't blown up in the meantime.

Atvar studied the latest reports from the subregion known as Poland, as well as those from the Race's spy satellites. He turned one eye turret from the monitor on which the reports were displayed to Kirel. "I begin to be optimistic," he told the second-highest-ranking male in the conquest fleet. "If the Deutsche had truly been on the point of launching an attack against us, I believe they would have done so by now. Every day they delay is another day in which they can have second thoughts."

"No doubt the Big Uglies are impetuous, Exalted Fleetlord," Kirel replied. "I agree, delay is likely to be advantageous to us. But they have not backed away from their preparations, either: see how many spacecraft they continue to keep in orbit around Tosev 3. If they truly intended relaxing into a peaceful posture, they would not be making such an effort—in my opinion, of course." Even the shiplord of the conquest fleet's bannership had to be careful when disagreeing with the fleetlord.

But Atvar did not have all his claws sunk deeply into his view of things here, as sometimes happened. "Indeed, that is a truth, Shiplord," he admitted. "But I wonder how much damage these crewed craft can do, as opposed to the many orbiting explosive-metal bombs and missiles that require only an electronic command for activation."

"I also wonder," Kirel said, "but I hope we do not have to find out. The Tosevites themselves have a nastier imagination than their mechanisms. Even with inferior means, they might find a way to do us more harm than we would expect."

"They have a knack for doing that, and I would be the last to deny it," Atvar said. "But they also must know what we would do to them. If they did not understand that, I believe they would already have gone to war."

"That is undoubtedly a truth," Kirel said. He swung one of his eye turrets toward the display. "Do we have any certain knowledge of where their submersible craft carrying missiles are presently located?"

"No." That didn't make Atvar happy, either. "And I must say I wish we did. But, on the other fork of the tongue, we rarely do. They and the Americans and the Russkis make a point of keeping the whereabouts of those vessels secret. In their position, I would do the same: we cannot target the submersibles, as we can their land-based missiles."

Pshing came into Atvar's office and waited to be noticed. When Atvar slid an eye turret toward him, he said, "Exalted Fleetlord, we have received replies from four Tosevite not-empires in regard to our request to open shrines dedicated to reverencing the spirits of Emperors past in their territories."

"Four at once?" Kirel said. "They must be acting in concert, then."

Atvar thought the same thing, but Pshing made the negative hand gesture. "No, Shiplord. Three of the replies are negative. The Nipponese say they strongly prefer to reverence their own emperors. The SSSR and the *Reich* simply refuse the request; the SSSR's rejection implies that we made it for purposes of espionage rather than reverence."

That was in some measure true. Atvar said, "And the fourth reply?"

"Exalted Fleetlord, it is from the United States, and gives us permission to do as we will there," Pshing replied. "The American Tosevites cite a doctrine of theirs called 'freedom of reverence' or something of the sort. I confess that I do not fully understand this doctrine."

"I often wonder if even the American Tosevites understand their own doctrines," Atvar replied. "This probably stems from their passion for snoutcounting. Most of their peculiar institutions do."

"Since they are not bellicose at the moment, I am inclined to forgive them their doctrines," Kirel said as Pshing left the office.

"No doubt some truth will hatch from that eggshell, Shiplord," Atvar said. "And we still await the reply from Britain. But the Americans do cause me some concern for the simple reason that they have prospered rather than falling to pieces in the interval since the fighting stopped. None of our analysts seems to understand why they have prospered, either. By all logic, government through snoutcounting should have failed almost immediately—should never have been attempted, in fact."

Kirel made the affirmative gesture. "I see what you are saying, Exalted Fleetlord. Nippon and Britain have systems similar to ours, though the British also use some of this snoutcounting silliness. And the *Reich* and the SSSR have rulers with the power of emperors, though they gain that power by murder or intrigue, not by inheritance. But the Americans truly are anomalous."

"And they are technically proficient," Atvar said discontentedly. "They are the ones with a spacecraft in the asteroid belt. They are the ones sending representatives to meet with the Big Ugly our researcher has raised as if she were a female of the Race."

"I have been keeping track of that, yes," Kirel said. "Truly a worthwhile project on the researcher's part. Do you think some of the wild Big Uglies are beginning to become acculturated? Video of one of the wild ones meeting with our specimen suggests he is one of that sort."

"The wild ones? My judgment is that acculturation is still superficial," Atvar said. "If they do begin to reverence the spirits of Emperors past, that would be a more significant turn toward the Empire's way of life than removing their hair and wearing body paint in place of their cloth wrappings."

"Indeed. I completely agree," Kirel said. "But the American Big Uglies, as you have pointed out, are not fools, even if they are barbarians. They too must realize the likely result of permitting such reverence, and yet they do so. Why?"

"Again, analysis is incomplete. We really do need to study the Americans more," Atvar said, and scribbled a note to that effect for himself. "Their ideology seems to be almost evolutionary in nature: they let individuals compete in snoutcounting contests, and they let ideas compete through 'freedom of reverence' and 'freedom of discussion.' Their assumption seems to be that the best will prevail as a result of this untrammeled competition."

"Now that is interesting, Exalted Fleetlord," Kirel said. "I had not seen their ideology expressed in quite those terms before." His mouth fell open in a laugh. "They certainly are optimists, are they not?"

"I think so. Every male of the Race I know thinks so. By all I can tell, most other Big Uglies think so, too," Atvar said. "And yet the Americans continue to do well. They continue to steal and adapt and build on our technology even more aggressively than the *Reich* or the SSSR. Puzzling, is it not?"

"Very much so," Kirel answered. "And their relations with us are less shrill and warlike than are those of the other two leading independent not-empires. They might almost be civilized."

"Almost," Atvar said. But then he realized the shiplord had a point. "We do seem to make more allowances for them than for the other not-empires, do we not? I wonder if the American Big Uglies are devious enough to take advantage of that."

"We have not suspected them of attacking the ships of the colonization fleet, at least not seriously suspected them," Kirel said. "Do you believe we should begin a more intensive investigation along those lines?"

After some thought, Atvar made the negative gesture. "We have no evidence that would lead us to suspect their guilt, and their behavior otherwise has been as near exemplary as Big Uglies come."

"We have no evidence to lead us to the *Reich* or to the SSSR, either, though each has tried to implicate the other," Kirel pointed out.

Before the fleetlord could respond to that, Pshing hurried into his office once more. Atvar saw his agitation even before he spoke: "Exalted Fleetlord!"

"By the Emperor, what now?" Atvar asked, casting down his eyes in respect for the sovereign so many light-years away.

"Exalted Fleetlord, I have just received a written communication from the ambassador of the Nipponese Empire."

"What now?" Atvar repeated in some irritation. Like Britain, Nippon had retained its independence when the fighting stopped. The Nipponese thought that entitled them to equality of status with the USA, the SSSR, and the *Reich*. The Race didn't, for the simple reason that Nippon, being without explosive-metal weapons, could not do them nearly so much harm as the three more prominent Tosevite powers.

Pshing said, "Exalted Fleetlord, the ambassador reports that Nippon has detonated an explosive-metal weapon of its own manufacture on an isolated island called"—he looked down at the paper he held—"'Bikini, that is the name."

Atvar let out a furious hiss and turned to the computer monitor. When he chose a reconnaissance and intelligence channel, he saw the explosion was just being reported. "The Nipponese must have timed the delivery of that note most precisely," he said, and then, dreading the answer, "Is there more?"

"There is, Exalted Fleetlord," Pshing said unhappily. "The note goes on to demand all privileges previously accorded only to Tosevite powers with explosive-metal weapons. It warns that Nippon has submersible craft of its own, and knows how to use them to its own best advantage."

"Even for Big Uglies, the Nipponese are arrogant," Kirel said.

"And now they have some good reason for arrogance." Atvar knew he sounded even more unhappy than his adjutant, but he had cause to sound that way. He turned an eye turret toward Pshing. "Do the Nipponese demand that we evacuate all territory that they occupied when the conquest fleet arrived?"

"Not in this note, no, Exalted Fleetlord," Pshing said. "What they may do in the future, however, is anyone's guess."

"That is a truth." Kirel's voice was mournful, too.

After calling up a map of Tosevite political conditions at the time of the conquest fleet's arrival, Atvar examined it. "There are occasions when I would be tempted to return to the Nipponese the subregion known as China. Considering the difficulties its inhabitants have given us, some other Big Uglies might as well have the dubious privilege of trying to rule them."

"You cannot mean that, Exalted Fleetlord!" Now Kirel sounded horrified.

And Atvar realized his chief subordinate was right. "No," he said with a sigh, "I suppose I cannot. All the Tosevite not-empires would take it for a sign of weakness, and they leap on weakness the way befflem leap on meat."

"What will you tell the Nipponese, then?" Pshing asked.

Atvar sighed once more. "Unfortunately, they have demonstrated strength. And they may be arrogant—or shortsighted—enough to use their new weapons without fear of punishment. Here, Pshing, tell them this: tell them we shall grant them all the diplomatic privileges they request. But tell them also that with privileges comes responsibility. Tell them we are now constrained to observe them more closely than ever before. Tell them we shall take a much more serious view of any potentially aggressive action they may prepare. Tell them they still are not powerful enough to seek any real test of strength against us, and that any attack on us will be crushed without mercy."

"Very good, Exalted Fleetlord!" his adjutant said, and used an emphatic cough. "It shall be done, in every particular."

"I thank you, Pshing. Oh—and one thing more," Atvar said. Pshing and Kirel both looked curious. The fleetlord explained: "Now we hope they listen."

As Liu Han paced through the prisoners' camp, she kept shaking her head. "No," she said. "I don't believe it: I don't want to believe it. It can't possibly be true."

Nieh Ho-T'ing gave her an amused look. "It can't possibly be true because you don't want to believe it? What kind of logic goes into a statement like that?"

"I don't know," she answered. "And I don't care, either. What do you think of that? Tell me where you heard that the eastern dwarfs used an explosive-metal bomb. Did the little scaly devils tell you? I doubt it." To show how much she doubted it, she used one of the little devils' emphatic coughs.

But Nieh said, "You do not want to believe it of the Japanese because you hate them even more than you hate the scaly devils."

"That . . ." Liu Han started to say that wasn't true, but discovered she couldn't. She did hate the Japanese, with a deep and abiding hatred. And why not, when they'd destroyed the village that had been her whole life and slaughtered the family she'd thought would be hers forever? She amended her words: "That doesn't matter. What matters is what's true and what isn't. And you didn't answer my question."

"Well, so I didn't," the People's Liberation Army officer admitted. He bowed to Liu Han, as if she were a noblewoman from the old days, the days of the Manchu Empire. "I will, then. No, the scaly devils didn't tell me. But I heard the guards talking among themselves. I don't think they knew I understood."

"Oh," Liu Han said unhappily. She knew the scaly devils often didn't pay any attention to what their human captives might hear. Why should they? Even if the humans understood, what could they do about it? Nothing, as Liu Han also knew all too well. She scowled and kicked at the dirt. "Will the Japanese start using their bombs against the little devils here in China, then?"

"Who knows what the Japanese will do?" Nieh Ho-T'ing answered. "I often wonder if even they know ahead of time. But whether they use bombs or not, they've gained a lot of face by having them."

"So they have." Now Liu Han's voice went savage. She kicked the dirt again, harder than before. "They learned imperialism from the round-eyed devils. All we ever learned was colonialist oppression. The little scaly devils threw them out of China, but they kept most of their empire and they kept their freedom. And what have we got from the little devils? More colonialist oppression. Where is the justice in that?"

Nieh shrugged. "Justice comes with power. The strong have it. And they give their version of it to the weak. We were unlucky, for we were found weak at the wrong time."

When Liu Han looked out to the horizon, she did so through strands of razor wire the little scaly devils had set up around the perimeter of the camp. If that didn't tell her everything she needed to know about strength and weakness, what would? She scowled. "How can we use the Japanese to our advantage?"

"Now that is a better thought." Nieh Ho-T'ing set a hand on her shoulder for a moment, as if to remind her they'd been lovers once. "The Russians have always refused to give us explosive-metal bombs of our own. So have the Americans. Maybe the Japanese will be more reasonable."

"Maybe they'll hope the Russians get the blame," Liu Han said, which made Nieh laugh and nod. "That might be a reasonable hope, too. I wonder if Mao has this news yet."

"Mao always knows the news." Nieh spoke with great assurance. "What he can do with it may be another question. I'm sure he'd be willing to deal with the Japanese to get an explosive-metal bomb. I'm not nearly so sure they'd be willing to deal with him."

"If I were one of the eastern dwarfs, I'd be afraid of dealing with anyone Chinese," Liu Han said. "They must know how much vengeance we owe them for what they did to us."

"That's true. No one would argue with it," Nieh said. "But how much do we owe the scaly devils? If that is more, then the Japanese wouldn't need to fear, for we would want to settle the bigger debt first."

Though Liu Han knew how to make such cold-blooded calculations, they didn't appeal to her. "I want to pay back the scaly devils, and I want to pay back the Japanese," she said. "How can we be free till we punish all our enemies?"

Nieh sighed. "I've been fighting for our freedom since I was a young man, and it seems further away than ever. The struggle ahead won't be any quicker or any easier than the one we've already made."

That made sense, too, but it wasn't what Liu Han wanted to hear. "I want Liu Mei to live in freedom," she said, and then her lips twisted into a bitter smile. "I want to live in freedom myself. I don't want either one of us to spend the rest of our days locked up in this prison camp."

"I don't want to spend the rest of my days here, either," Nieh Ho-T'ing said. "I am not a young man any more. I do not have so many days to spend anywhere, and this isn't the place I'd have chosen." His own smile showed wry amusement. "But the little devils gave us no choice. Your daughter helped make sure they would give us no choice."

Liu Han turned away. She didn't want to hear that, either, even though she knew it was true. She started to explain that she understood why Liu Mei had done as she did, but what difference did it make? None. She kept walking.

A man she didn't know came by her. He gave her a polite nod, so she returned one. *Probably with the Kuomintang,* she thought. Plenty of prisoners here were. The little devils didn't care if they and the Communists went right on with their civil war here inside this razor-wire perimeter. That just made life easier for them.

The first time she'd been taken to a camp, things had been a lot easier. The little devils were newer at the game then—and she'd been only an experimental animal to them, not a dangerous political prisoner. The Reds had helped spirit her out of the camp through a tunnel, and no one had been the wiser for a long time. Things weren't so simple here. No humans went into and out of this camp. People came in. They never went out.

Nothing seemed so tempting as giving way to despair. If she stopped caring about what happened to her, maybe she could accept the likelihood that she would never leave this place again. Then she could start shaping a life for herself within the razor-wire perimeter.

She shook her head. She wouldn't give up. She couldn't give

up. She hadn't given up after Ttomalss took her daughter away from her, and she'd got Liu Mei back. If she kept up the struggle, she might get her own life back one day, too. After all, who could guess what would happen? The Japanese might resume their war with the little scaly devils. Or the Germans might fight them. The Germans were strong, even if they were fascist reactionaries. If they caused the scaly devils enough trouble, maybe the little devils would have to loosen their grip on China. You never could tell.

She went back to the tent she shared with Liu Mei to tell her daughter the news she'd had from Nieh. But Liu Mei wasn't in the tent. Liu Han's carefully constructed bravado collapsed. If the little devils had taken her daughter off to do horrible things to her, what good was bravado?

A woman who lived in the tent next door said, "The scaly devils do not have her." She had a southwestern accent that hardly seemed Mandarin at all to Liu Han, who had trouble following her.

When at last she did, she asked, "Well, where is she, then?"

The other woman, who was not a Communist, smiled unpleasantly. "She went out walking with a young man."

"A young man!" Liu Han exclaimed. "Which young man?" The camp held a lot of them, far more than women.

"I have no idea." The other woman was full of sour virtue. "*My* children would never do such a thing without my knowing."

"You ugly old turtle, you must have had a blind husband if you have any children at all," Liu Han said. That produced a splendid fight. Each of the women called the other everything she could think of. The other woman took a step toward Liu Han, who only smiled. "Come ahead. I will snatch you even balder than you are already."

"Oh, shut up, you horrible, clapped-out whore!" the other woman screeched, but she backed away again.

Contemptuously, Liu Han turned her back. She listened for footsteps that would mean the other woman was rushing at her, but they didn't come. She wondered if she ought to wait in her tent for her daughter or to go after her.

She decided to wait. Liu Mei came back about an hour later, alone. "What have you been doing?" Liu Han asked.

"Walking with a friend," Liu Mei answered. Her face showed nothing, but then it never did—it never could.

"Who is this friend?" Liu Han persisted.

"Someone I met here," her daughter said.

"And what other sort of person is it likely to be?" Liu Han said, full of sarcasm. "Someone you met in Peking, maybe? Or in the United States? I am going to ask you again, and I want a straight answer this time: who is this friend?"

"Someone I met here," Liu Mei repeated.

"Is it a man or a woman? Is it a Communist or a Kuomintang reactionary?" Liu Han said. "Why do you beat around the bush?"

"Why do you hound me?" Liu Mei returned. If the nosy neighbor hadn't told Liu Han her daughter was walking with a man, that would have. "I can walk with whomever I like. It's not like there's anything else to do."

If she went walking with a man, they might soon find something else to do. Liu Han knew that perfectly well. If Liu Mei didn't, it wasn't because Liu Han hadn't told her. "Who is he?" Liu Han snapped.

Liu Mei's eyes blazed in her expressionless face. "Whoever he is, he's none of your business," she said. "Are you going to be a bourgeois mother worrying about a proper match? Or are you going to be an upper-class mother from the old days and bind up my feet till I walk like this?" She took several tiny, swaying, mocking steps. Her face might not show expression, but her body did.

"I am your mother, and I will thank you to remember it," Liu Han said.

"Treat me like a comrade, if you please, and not the way the keeper in a traveling beast show treats his animals," Liu Mei said.

"Is that what you think I do?" Liu Han demanded, and her daughter nodded. She threw her hands in the air. "All I want is for you to be happy and safe and sensible, and you always have—till now."

"All you want is to keep me in a cage!" Liu Han shouted, and tears streamed down her face. She stormed off. Liu Han stared after her, then started to cry herself. Everything she'd worked for lay in ruins around her.

☆ 18 ☆

Much as he would have liked to, Straha hadn't passed on to the
Race what he'd learned about the hatchlings Sam Yeager was
raising. In an odd sort of way, he was loyal to the United States.
After all, if this not-empire hadn't taken him in, Atvar would
have given him a very hard time. And Yeager was a friend, even if
he was a Big Ugly.

But those weren't the main reasons he'd kept quiet about that
business. His main concern was that he wouldn't get the reward
he most desired: a return to the society of the Race. After all, his
own kind had done the same sort of thing with a Tosevite hatchling. How could they condemn the Americans without con-
demning themselves at the same time?

His driver walked into the kitchen. "I greet you, Shiplord," he
said casually. "Looks as if the sun is finally coming out."

"You knew!" Straha said angrily. "You knew all along, and
you said not a thing—not a single, solitary thing."

Had the Big Ugly asked what he was talking about, Straha
thought he would have taken a bite out of him. But his driver
didn't bother affecting innocence. "I was following the orders of
my superiors, Shiplord. They wanted this secret kept, and so it
was. I am surprised Sam Yeager obtained permission to have you
visit his home, as a matter of fact."

"How do you know he even asked permission?" Straha asked.

"I do not know that he did," the driver answered. "I know that
he should have. If he did not, it will be one more black mark in
the book against him."

That was an English idiom, translated literally into the language of the Race. Straha had little trouble figuring out what it

527

meant. He said, "Yeager is a good officer. He should not have difficulties with his superiors."

"If he obeyed orders, if he did as he was told to do, he would not have difficulties with his superiors," the Big Ugly said. Then he let out a couple of grunts of Tosevite laughter. "Of course, if he acted in that fashion, he might not be such a good officer, either."

Straha would have reckoned a perfectly obedient officer a good officer. Or would he? He thought of himself as a good officer, and yet he was one of the most disobedient males in the history of the Race. *This planet corrupts everyone,* he thought.

His driver dropped into English. "You know what Yeager's problem is, Shiplord? Yeager's got too goddamn much initiative, that's what."

"Initiative is desirable, isn't it?" Straha switched to English, too.

"Yes and no," his driver replied. "Yes if you're going after what your superiors tell you to go after. No if you go off on your own. Especially no if you keep sticking your nose into places they told you to stay away from."

"Yeager does this?" Straha made a mental leap of his own. "Is that why he has had trouble with Tosevites trying to harm him and his family?"

"I really couldn't tell you anything about that," his driver said. "It might just be a run of bad luck, you know."

Like any male of the Race, Straha read Big Uglies imperfectly. But he'd been associating with this one for a long time. He had a fair notion when the Tosevite tried to lie by misdirection. This felt like one of those times.

He started to press his driver, to try to learn more from him: for he was sure the Big Ugly knew more. Instead, though, he left unuttered the questions he might have asked. He doubted the driver would have told him much; the Tosevite's first loyalty was to his American superiors, not to Straha. And if word got back to them that Straha had been asking such questions, Sam Yeager might land in more trouble still. The exiled shiplord didn't want that.

Maybe the Big Ugly had expected Straha to ask such questions. Eyeing him, the Tosevite asked, "Is there anything else,

Shiplord?" He returned to the language of the Race, and with it to formality.

"No, nothing else," Straha replied, also in his own language. "How you Big Uglies conduct your affairs is of no great consequence to me."

That made his driver relax. Males of the Race—and females, too, these days—had a reputation among the Big Uglies for being contemptuous of everything pertaining to Tosev 3. Straha was contemptuous of a great deal about the Tosevites, but not of everything, and not about all Big Uglies. But he used the reputation to his own advantage here, to conceal a genuine interest.

With a laugh, his driver said, "After all, it's not as if Yeager were a male of the Race."

"It certainly is not," Straha agreed. The driver nodded and went off making the small, somewhat musical noises the Big Uglies called *whistling*. That was a sign he was amused and unconcerned and happy.

Or maybe he wanted Straha to think it was a sign he was amused and unconcerned and happy. Big Uglies could be devious creatures. Straha knew from experience that his driver could be a devious creature. If he were to pick up the telephone now and call Sam Yeager, he had no doubt the driver would listen to every word he said. He wouldn't have been surprised if the Americans listened to every word he said whenever he picked up the telephone.

He waited till he was using the limited access to the Race's computer network a fellow male in exile had illicitly obtained for him before sending an electronic message to Maargyees, the false name Sam Yeager used on the network. *In case you did not know it, your own curiosity has aroused curiosity in others,* he wrote. Yeager was a clever male. He would have no trouble figuring out what that meant.

Having written the message, Straha erased it from his own computer. It would, of course, remain in the network's storage system, but the Americans didn't have access to that. He hoped with all his liver that the Americans didn't have access to it, anyhow. They'd known next to nothing about computers when the Race first came to Tosev 3. They knew a great deal more than that these days, worse luck.

The Race had phased in computers ever so gradually in the

couple of millennia following the unification of Home. Devices
with such important influence on society had to be phased in
gradually, to minimize disruption. That was the way the Race
looked at things, anyhow. The Big Uglies had other ideas.

Straha didn't suppose he should have been surprised. When
the Tosevites found a new technology, no matter what it was,
they always felt they had to do as much with it as they could as
soon as they could. Even if the troubles that would hatch as a result of rapid change were obvious, they went ahead all the same.
They'd done as much with computers in a generation as the Race
had in centuries.

Not all American Tosevites had the education they needed to
use computer systems to best advantage—or at all. That didn't
deter the Big Uglies. Those of them who could use the new technology did . . . and flourished. Those who didn't might as well
have stayed inside their eggshells. Their failure, their falling behind, bothered the others not at all.

And if upheaval followed because some Tosevites gained
more advantages than others—they didn't seem to care. That
struck Straha as madness, but it was as much dogma to the
Americans as reverencing the spirits of Emperors past was to
the Race. Straha knew an American saying: *look out for yourself
and let the devil take the hindmost.* To him, that was individu-
alism to the point of addlement, survival of the fittest made into
a law of society. To the Americans, it seemed common sense.
Those who succeeded in the United States succeeded spectacularly. Those who failed—and there were, by the nature of things,
many who did—failed the same way.

"And, all things considered, I am one of the ones who have
succeeded," Straha murmured. He had less than he would have
had back on Home, but he had everything with which the Big
Uglies could supply him.

The sliding glass door at the back of the house was open.
The spring air was chillier than he found ideal, but no worse than
a brisk winter's day back on Home. He didn't even bother
bundling up before he pushed open the sliding screen that kept
little flying and crawling pests out of the house and walked out
into the backyard.

He looked around with a certain amount of pride. Bare
ground and sand and succulents, some smooth, some spiky, put

him in mind of a landscape back on Home, though details differed. Here, even more than inside the house, he'd shaped things to suit himself. Inside, the place was built to suit Tosevites, and many of the devices he used every day—telephone, stove, refrigerator—were perforce of American manufacture, different from and usually inferior to their equivalents on his native world. They always reminded him what an alien he was.

Out here, though, he could look around and imagine himself somewhere on Home, somewhere a long way from his native city. Few Big Uglies cared for the effect, any more than he was enamored of the boring green lawns they so admired.

The dog next door started barking. It often did when he came outside; it probably disliked his odor. For that matter, he wasn't fond of the scent of its droppings, which the breeze sometimes wafted to his scent receptors. He didn't like the noise it made, either. Nothing on Home sounded remotely like a dog, and its yaps and growls spoiled the illusion the yard gave him.

A small bird with a bright green back and an even brighter red head buzzed among the flowers; red ones particularly attracted it. It too reminded him he wasn't on Home any more. Flying creatures there had bare, leathery wings, and none of them came close to matching the aerial gymnastics of a hummingbird. But, even though the flying creature was alien, it didn't irk him the way the dog did. It was small and quiet and attractive, not loud and annoying.

Suddenly the hummingbird, which had been swooping low, darted away as if something had startled it. Straha strode closer, and saw a scaly, four-legged creature a little longer than the distance between his wrist and the end of his middle fingerclaw. It was a brown not much different from the color of the dirt, with darker stripes to break up its outline. Like the succulents among which it crawled, it looked familiar without being identical to anything on Home.

It stuck out a short, dark tongue. Then, as if nervous about coming out into the open, it scuttled back under some of the plants and disappeared. Straha started to root around after it, but decided not to bother. It was living where it belonged and doing what it was supposed to do. He wished he could say the same.

Maybe he could return to the society of the Race . . . if he betrayed Sam Yeager. Maybe. His mouth fell open in a laugh that held little in the way of real mirth. He'd just warned his friend of danger from other Big Uglies, but he hadn't warned of danger from himself.

Of course, Yeager understood the Race about as well as any Tosevite could. He would have to understand that Straha might be able to buy his way back into Atvar's good graces by passing on the story of the hatchlings . . . wouldn't he?

From the exile that wasn't quite comfortable, from the garden that wasn't quite Home, Straha made the negative gesture. "If I have to buy my way back into Atvar's good graces, they are not worth having," the ex-shiplord said aloud. "Spirits of Emperors past turn their backs on him." He feared those spirits would reject him when he came before them, but he'd feared that ever since ordering his shuttlecraft pilot to take him down to the USA. Yet those spirits wouldn't approve of him if he betrayed a friend, either, not even if that friend was a Big Ugly. Now he made the affirmative gesture. He *would* stay quiet, and stay here.

"Okay, let's give it a try," Hal Walsh said. "David, would you like to do the honors?"

"As a matter of fact, no," David Goldfarb said. "I want to get the bloody call. I don't want to make it. I want to see the numbers light up on the gadget here. You don't know how much I want that."

His boss at the Saskatchewan River Widget Works eyed him. "Oh, maybe I do," he said. He dug in his pocket and tossed a dime to Jack Devereaux. "Go find a phone booth and call David."

"All right," Devereaux said. He put on his overcoat before leaving the office. The calendar said spring had come to Edmonton, but the weather paid no attention. "I'll even note the phone number, so we can see if it works the way it's supposed to."

"It had better." Walsh spoke as if a failed widget were a personal affront. That was how he thought, too, which probably went a long way toward making him such a good engineer.

Devereaux slammed the door behind him. David Goldfarb knew a phone booth—a far flimsier phone booth than the solid, red-painted British sort—stood around the corner. With this ghastly weather, he didn't understand why booths in Canada were so flimsy, but they were. It helped remind him he was in a foreign country. Waiting for Devereaux to call reminded him of the same thing. On the other side of the Atlantic, he'd be waiting for his colleague to ring.

The telephone rang. It did the same thing regardless of where it was. He picked it up. "Hullo—Goldfarb here." Numbers appeared on the screen of the widget hooked up to the phone, a widget that sent electronic tendrils through the telephone lines to the instrument the person on the other end of the connection was using.

"Yes, I'd like to order some pirogis to go." That was Devereaux's voice, even if he was trying to get Ukrainian dumplings.

"Bravo—you just wasted Hal's dime," Goldfarb said. Devereaux laughed and hung up on him.

Walsh came over and looked at the numbers, which remained on the screen. "I think we've got something here. Police, fire departments—this beats the hell out of having an operator try to trace a call."

"Businesses will use it, too," Goldfarb said. "If you have customers ringing you, you'll be able to ring back whenever you've got something on special." Walsh understood *ring*, just as Goldfarb understood *call*; he didn't bother using the North American term instead of the one he'd grown up with.

Jack Devereaux came back into the office. He was waving a scrap of paper. Goldfarb snatched it out of his hand. He compared it to the number he'd written down. They matched. Solemnly, Goldfarb, Walsh, and Devereaux shook hands. "We're in business," Hal Walsh said.

Devereaux said. "Not yet, we're not," he said. "We have a useful widget. Now we've got to convince people they really want to use it."

Walsh beamed at him. "You'd be handy to have around if you didn't know a slide rule from a *skelkwank* light," he said. "You've always got your eye on the main chance."

"I should hope so," Devereaux replied with dignity. "As for slide rules, another five years and they'll be nothing but antiques. Why get eyestrain trying to read a third significant figure when an electronic calculator will give you eight or ten just as fast?" He turned to Goldfarb. "Isn't that right, David?" he asked, as if Hal Walsh had challenged him.

"I expect it is," Goldfarb said in what he feared was a hollow voice. "I'll miss 'em, though." He felt very much an antique himself, remembering how proud he'd been when he learned to multiply and divide on a slide rule and how he'd been even prouder after he'd found a couple of tricks for keeping track of the decimal point—unlike a calculator, the slide rule wouldn't do it for him. He also knew he had no great head for business. That didn't make him a stereotypical Jew, but it did make him a man who'd spent his entire adult life in the RAF. He hadn't had to worry about what things cost, or about the best ways to sell them to a public that didn't know what it was missing by doing without them.

"So will I," Walsh said. "And you never have to worry about the batteries going dead with a slide rule, either. But if the calculator gives better results, you'd have to be a fool to want to use anything else, eh?"

Devereaux grinned a sassy grin. "David doesn't think like that. He's an Englishman, remember. They hang on to things because they're old, not because they're any good. Isn't that right?" he said again.

"Something to it, I shouldn't wonder," Goldfarb said. To the Canadians, he was an Englishman. To most of the Englishmen he'd known, he'd been nothing but a Jew. Perspective changed things, sure enough. Before he could say as much, the telephone rang. He picked it up. "Goldfarb here," he answered, as he had before.

"Hello, Goldfarb." That was his wife calling. "Can you pick up a loaf of bread on the way home tonight?"

"No, not a chance," he said, just to hear Naomi snort. "See you when I see you, sweetheart." He hung up. Even before he did that, he craned his neck to see the number displayed on the small screen of the Widget Works' latest widget.

His boss and Jack Devereaux were doing the same thing. "Is that your home number?" Hal Walsh asked, which somewhat surprised David—his working assumption was that, if it had to do with numbers in any way, Walsh already knew it without needing to check.

"Yes, that's it," Goldfarb agreed. "And I'd say we're really on to something here."

"I'd say you're right." Walsh looked as if he wanted to blow canary feathers off his chin. The Saskatchewan River Widget Works was his company; even though the phone-number-reading gadget hadn't been altogether his idea, the greater share of the profits from it would end up in his pocket. He might have picked that thought out of Goldfarb's mind, for he said, "Nobody will be poor on account of this, I promise you all. I think it'll be a big enough pie for everybody to have a big slice."

"Hal, you've played straight with us right from the start," Devereaux said. "I don't think anybody's worried you're going to pull a fast one this time."

"That's right," David Goldfarb said, though he hadn't been with the Widget Works right from the start. Walsh was the sort of boss who inspired confidence.

He laughed at his employees now. "In the old days, the days before the Race came, I could have turned everything into cash and headed down to Rio. Well, I still could, if I felt like living under the Lizards for the rest of my days. Since I don't, I suppose I'd have to go to Los Angeles instead."

"They'd ship you back from the USA," Devereaux pointed out.

"But at least you'd have decent weather while you were there," Goldfarb said with undisguised longing. By what he was used to, Los Angeles was liable to be beastly hot, but he preferred that to too bloody cold, which was how Canadian weather struck him.

Jack Devereaux said, "I wonder where the jet stream is this year, and where it'll take the fallout."

"Not that much from the Japanese test," Hal Walsh said. "Of course, they may set off some more."

"I wasn't thinking of that," Devereaux said. "I was thinking of the big dose, when the Nazis and the Race start going after each other."

"God forbid," Goldfarb said. "I've got family in Poland." The others wouldn't think of him as an Englishman any more, but too bad. He tried to look on the bright side of things: "Maybe the war won't happen after all. The Germans have been thumping their chests for a while now, but that's all they've been doing."

"There's a big part of me that would love to see Germany smashed to smithereens," Devereaux said, and Goldfarb could no more help nodding than he could help breathing. His colleague went on, "All the same, though, I hope you're right. There'd be too much damage to the rest of the world to make the war worthwhile."

"I think they're going to fight," Hal Walsh said. "I think they've done too much posturing to back down without looking yellow, and they don't dare do that. It'd be asking half the countries they're sitting on to rise up against 'em."

"That makes sense," Goldfarb said. "I wish it didn't." Before he could go on, his telephone rang yet again. He picked up the handset. "Hullo—Goldfarb here."

"You lousy, stinking kike," the voice on the other end of the line replied. "You think you're too goddamn good to play with us, do you? You'll pay for that, and so will your whole family. The Nazis have the right idea." *Slam!* The phone went dead.

"Who was that?" Walsh asked.

"Nobody I know," Goldfarb answered. "Nobody I want to know, either." He glanced over at the little screen attached to the telephone and jotted down the number it displayed. "But the police may be interested in doing something about it."

"Oh, really?" That was Jack Devereaux. "One of your charming friends?"

"As a matter of fact, yes." David Goldfarb held up the telephone number he'd just noted. "And I have an excellent notion of how to go about helping myself and getting some publicity for the Widget Works, both at the same time."

He called the Edmonton police and reported the threat he'd just received. "You got this by telephone, sir?" the policeman asked. "I'm afraid we can't do much about that—you do understand the difficulty."

"Not in this case, no," Goldfarb answered, and gave the number from which the threatening call had been placed.

After a long pause, the policeman asked, "How could you possibly know the call came from that number, sir?"

And Goldfarb spent the next ten minutes explaining who he was, for whom he worked, and exactly how he knew what he knew. He finished, "I assume you can find out which numbers go with which houses? If you can, you might find it worth your while to pay a visit to that particular one. Do be careful, though. These are not nice people."

"I make no promises," the policeman said, and hung up.

After David reported the other end of the conversation to his boss, Hal Walsh grinned from ear to ear. "If they go, and if they find things worth finding, we've just made our mark in big letters," he said, and held up an imaginary advertising signboard. " 'As endorsed by the Edmonton Police Department.' "

"Unless that number turns out to be another phone booth, of course," Goldfarb said. Walsh crossed his forefingers, as if to avert a vampire. David laughed. "That doesn't work. I'm Jewish, remember?"

Nobody at the Widget Works got much work done till Goldfarb's telephone rang again a couple of hours later. When he answered it, the Edmonton copper said, "Mr. Goldfarb, my hat's off to you. Thanks to your call and your device, we have four very nasty fellows in custody. We also have several illegal firearms, some illegal drugs, and a large quantity of ginger, which is, of course, not illegal—here. Now, if you would be so kind as to let me speak to Mr.—Welsh, was it?—about the possibility of acquiring this device for ourselves . . ."

"Walsh," Goldfarb corrected happily. "Hal Walsh." He gave his boss the phone. With his hand over the mouthpiece, he said, "We *are* in business."

Felless said, "I think it is extremely unfortunate that we should have to prepare to evacuate this area as a result of threats from these Tosevite savages."

Kazzop, the science officer at the Race's consulate in Marseille, waggled his eye turrets ever so slightly to show his bemusement. "Correct me if I am wrong, superior female," he said, "but is this evacuation not the only way in which you are likely to be able to return to territory ruled by the Race? Without it, would you not remain indefinitely in the Greater German *Reich*?"

"Well, yes, so I would," she admitted. "Ambassador Veffani holds a grudge against me." She preferred not to dwell on whether her disgrace had given the ambassador good reason to hold a grudge against her, but continued, "Still, I would sooner the Race were strong enough to make it safe for me to stay here than to have to go."

"We *are* strong. We are stronger than we were when the conquest fleet arrived," Kazzop said. As he was a male from that fleet, he knew whereof he spoke. He went on, "The trouble lies not in ourselves or in our strength, but in the Big Uglies. They are far stronger now than they were when we first came here, too, and infinitely stronger than we imagined they could be when we left Home."

"It is humiliating that the males of the conquest fleet cannot guarantee our safety here," Felless said. "Humiliating and disgraceful."

"Superior female, we are not being evacuated from Marseille because we are in any particular danger from the Deutsche," Kazzop said. "The Big Uglies will not harm us even in the event of war. They know we could retaliate against their males and females serving as diplomats or otherwise living in parts of Tosev 3 ruled by the Race. The Tosevites have developed elaborate and surprisingly sophisticated rules for exchanging individuals under these circumstances. Because of their own frequent conflicts, they have needed such rules."

"What then?" Felless said. "Perhaps you are correct. Perhaps I truly do not understand why we are being evacuated."

"I will make the eggshell clear, so you may see the hatching truth within." Kazzop sounded as if he was taking an almost Tosevite glee in explaining things to a superior as if she were a hatchling. "We are being evacuated because Marseille will make an important target for the Race if war breaks out. Explosive-metal bombs, unfortunately, are not very selective."

"Oh," Felless said in a small voice. "Please understand that I am new to the idea of war and to everything involved with it. I expected the conquest would have been completed before I woke from cold sleep."

"Life on Tosev 3 is full of surprises," the science officer said dryly.

"That is also a truth—and how I wish it weren't," Felless said. "Of course, Veffani also gets to leave the *Reich*. Since he has been stuck here much longer than I have, I am sure he will welcome the opportunity to escape."

But Kazzop made the negative gesture. "Veffani will not leave, any more than the Deutsche will call their ambassador back from Cairo. By Tosevite custom, ambassadors do not leave other lands until war breaks out."

Of all the things Felless had never imagined, a reason to feel sympathy toward Veffani certainly ranked high on the list. "Poor fellow," she said, and then, "But the only announcement of the war is liable to be the launch of missiles tipped with explosive-metal bombs. How can he be sure of safe evacuation?"

"He cannot," Kazzop answered, which surprised Felless all over again.

She said, "You males of the conquest fleet cannot always have had an easy time of it." She could hear the surprise in her own voice. She spent most of the time resenting the males of the conquest fleet because they hadn't given the colonization fleet so completely subdued a world as the newcomers had anticipated. Only rarely, as now, did she stop to think about the difficulties the males had faced and continued to face.

"Superior female, that is a great truth," Kazzop said. "It is also a truth few females or males of the colonization fleet ever realize. I am glad you have realized it, and I hope you will cling to the memory here."

"I shall not forget," Felless said. And then, as she sometimes did, she thought about the clutch of eggs she'd laid at Nuremberg. "I presume arrangements have been made to bring hatchlings out of the *Reich*."

"I believe so, yes," Kazzop said. "Some of us have to be responsible for them, or the species would perish, after all."

"I suppose that's true," Felless agreed. "I have never felt the urge to any great degree myself. Slomikk, the science officer at the embassy, did a far better job with the hatchlings than I could have. As far as I am concerned, he is welcome to it. Adults, now, adults are interesting. Hatchlings?" After the interrogative cough, she used the negative hand gesture.

"Slomikk is a very capable male in many ways. I have known him for a long time," Kazzop said. "I can see how he would be good with hatchlings. My own attitude, I confess, is more like yours. You do of course realize that the Tosevites are far more centered on their offspring than we are on ours."

"I have gathered that, yes." This time, Felless used the affirmative gesture. "I gather also that the reasons behind it are primarily biological. When the Big Uglies hatch, or rather, when they emerge from the bodies of the females who bear them" — Felless spoke with fastidious disgust— "they are much less developed, much less able to care for themselves, than are our hatchlings. If adult Big Uglies were not genetically programmed to care for them, they would perish in short order."

"Just so," Kazzop said. "These strong personal bonds permeate Tosevite society to a degree we can understand only intellectually, not emotionally. They are no small part of what makes the Big Uglies so vengeance-prone and so generally difficult to administer."

"I have also heard this from Senior Researcher Ttomalss," Felless said.

"Ah. Yes, I can see how you would have," Kazzop replied. "Ttomalss is very sound, very sound indeed, when it comes to Tosevite psychology. Why, he might almost be a Big Ugly himself, he understands Tosevites so well."

Having had her share of problems with Ttomalss, Felless did not care to hear him praised in such extravagant terms. "I have heard this about the Big Uglies," she repeated, "but I am not altogether convinced it is truth. It seems a very foolish principle on which to organize a society."

"But the Big Uglies use it constantly," Kazzop said. "Take the *Reich*, for example. You must know that its ruling ideology holds the Deutsche to be superior to other Tosevites by reason of their genetics."

"From every available bit of evidence, this is an ideology unsupported by truth," Felless pointed out.

"Oh, of course," the male from the conquest fleet said. "But the existence and popularity of an ideology are truths of their own, independent of the truth—if any—at the yolk of the ideology. And this one asserts that the Deutsche are part of a large family grouping descended from a common ancestor—derived, you see, from Tosevite family patterns."

"Well, perhaps," Felless admitted. "This is certainly not an organizing principle we would use for ourselves."

"No, among us it would be madness," Kazzop said. "Our matings are nonexclusive, after all. We could not tell family lines even if we wanted to, in most instances. But if you ignore the ways the Big Uglies differ from us, you will never come to a satisfactory understanding of them. That is where Ttomalss' insights have proved so useful, so valuable."

"Is it?" Felless said tonelessly.

Before she could add anything less complimentary to Ttomalss,

"They've sure got a wild hair up their ass about Poland, anyhow, if half of what we hear on the radio is true," Johnson said. "And I'll tell you something else: I wouldn't give you a plug nickel to be aboard the *Hermann Göring* right now, either."

Stone's chuckle was not a happy sound. "Me, neither. Can you say 'bull's-eye'? How many missiles do you suppose the Lizards have aimed at that baby?"

Remembering his conversation with Mickey Flynn, Johnson answered, "Enough to do the job—and probably about another ten more besides."

"That sounds about right," Stone agreed. "The Race doesn't like doing things by halves—which is one reason it's God's own miracle they didn't finish the fight back in the Forties."

"It was a question of who'd finish who," Johnson said. "They wanted the colonization fleet to have a planet worth landing on." His chuckle didn't show much in the way of good humor, either. "So now they can blow things up with the colonists here. Hot damn."

"Hot damn is right," Stone said. "Real hot."

"What worries me is, they might decide to go after us if they're going after the *Hermann Göring*," Johnson said. "In for a penny, in for a pound, you know what I mean? As long as they've got a war on their hands . . ."

"It'd be a lot bigger one if they're fighting us, too," Stone said.

"Yeah, but if you're a Lizard, the other question is, how big is too big if you're already fighting the Nazis?" Johnson said. "The only answer I can think of is, if it's big enough to blow up the planet, it's probably too big. Otherwise, who knows?"

Walter Stone looked at him. "You're in a nice, cheerful mood today, aren't you?"

"Wouldn't you be, the way things are now?" Glen Johnson returned. "Remember, you spent all the time before we left learning to fly the *Lewis and Clark*. I spend a lot of my duty time in orbit, watching the Race and the Nazis and the Russians. I know how fast things can go wrong. They almost did a few times."

"You tried to help make things go wrong, poking your nose in where it didn't belong," Stone said.

"And look what it got me," Johnson said. "I'm stuck for life with people like you." Before Stone could answer, a bell chimed the hour. Johnson sighed. "And I'm stuck on an exercise bicycle for the next hour."

"Have fun," Stone said. "I already did my bit today."

"Fun," Johnson said, as if it were a four-letter word. But he didn't have time to do any more complaining than that, not if he wanted to get to the gym on time. He didn't give two whoops in hell about getting to the gym on time, but he didn't want to listen to the lecture he'd get for missing some of his exercise period, either. And so he swung out of the control room and down the halls to the gymnasium. When he got there, he signed the sheet to log in, changed into sweat clothes in the little men's room off the gym, and then got onto a bike and got to work.

One of the main-engine technicians who'd started exercising before him grinned and said, "You sure you're really here, sir?"

"I think so, Bob," Johnson answered, grinning back. "I look like I'm here, don't I?"

"You never can tell," Bob said, and they both laughed. The joke was only funny if you looked at it the right way. Not very long before, the *Lewis and Clark* had gone through its first really juicy scandal. A good many people, including several of high rank, had got in the habit of signing their names on the sheet and then going off and doing something else instead of getting in their work. Brigadier General Healey had not been happy when word of what they were doing finally got to him. And when the commandant wasn't happy, nobody else was happy, either.

"One thing you've got to give Healey," Bob said: "he's fair. He came down on everybody, and who didn't matter."

"Yeah, that's true." Johnson's considered opinion was that the commandant hated everybody impartially, and that the crew of the *Lewis and Clark* returned the favor. He realized he wasn't objective, but he didn't much care. As far as he was concerned, Healey didn't rate objectivity.

Johnson's legs pumped hard as he did his best to keep calcium in his bones. He didn't want to think about gravity, not any more. The idea of having weight, of moving his muscles against resistance, seemed alien and repugnant. He pedaled on anyhow. When his body was working hard, he could stop thinking about the troubles back on Earth and, indeed, about everything else. Exercise wasn't as much fun as sex, but it did the job of distraction almost as well.

Thinking about sex made him think about Lucy Vegetti—and thinking about her was certainly more enjoyable than not thinking about anything at all. Trouble was, he couldn't do anything but think about Lucy right now. She was down on Ceres, helping to set up a habitat there. He missed her. He hoped she missed him. If she didn't, she could find plenty of guys to take his place.

He wondered if she'd taken her bottle of Cutty down to the surface of the asteroid. A jolt of scotch was almost enough to tempt him into some breaking and entering—almost, but not quite.

And then, before he let himself get more tempted than he should have, the intercom came to noisy life. "Lieutenant Colonel Johnson! Lieutenant Colonel Glen Johnson! Report to the commandant's office immediately! Lieutenant Colonel Glen Johnson! Report to the—"

"I'm coming," Johnson muttered. "Keep your shirt on." The intercom went right on bellowing.

"Lucky son of a gun," Bob said.

"Going to see the commandant?" Johnson shook his head. "I'd sooner keep exercising."

He unhooked the belt that tethered him to the bicycle and pushed off toward the nearest handhold. He didn't bother changing out of his exercise togs. If Healey wanted him immediately, that would be how the commandant got him. And if he was a little sweaty, a little smelly, what better proof he'd been doing his work like a good little boy?

He sailed right past Brigadier General Healey's adjutant and into the commandant's office, catching himself on a handhold there. "Reporting as ordered, sir," he said, saluting.

"Yes." Healey eyed him. "There are times when you find following orders to the letter more amusing than others, aren't there, Lieutenant Colonel?"

"I don't know what you're talking about, sir," Johnson said with the air of a maiden whose virtue had been questioned.

"Tell me another one," Healey said. "I shanghaied you, and you've been trying to make me sorry ever since. Sometimes you've even done it. But not today. This doesn't bother me, not a bit."

Johnson shrugged. "That's the way it goes, sir." If he was

disappointed—and he was, a little—he'd be damned if he'd admit it. "Did you want me for anything else besides seeing how fast I could get here?"

Brigadier General Healey, unlike Mickey Flynn, had the stereotypical Irishman's fair skin. When he got angry, he turned red. Johnson watched him flush now, and carefully pretended not to notice a thing. Biting off his words one at a time, the commandant said, "As a matter of fact, I did."

"All right, sir," Johnson said. "What is it?"

Healey leaned forward across his desk, for all the world as if he were back on Earth. Nobody else aboard the *Lewis and Clark* was so good at pretending weightlessness didn't exist. He said, "You're the one with the orbital patrol experience. If the Germans and the Lizards start slugging it out, which way do you think the Russians are likely to jump?"

That was a real question, all right. Johnson went from insolent to serious in the blink of an eye. "Sir, my best guess is, they sit on their hands. They hate the Nazis, and the Lizards scare the hell out of them. That'd be a war where they hope both sides lose, so they can pick up the pieces. If there are any pieces left to pick up, I mean."

Healey's jowls wobbled slightly as he nodded. "Okay. That makes pretty good sense. Matches up pretty well with what I've been hearing from back on Earth, too." As much to himself as to Johnson, he added, "You always like to get things from more than one source if you can."

You don't trust anybody, Johnson realized. *It's not just me. You don't trust the bigwigs who sent you out here, either.* "Besides, sir," he said, "the Russians fly tin cans. That's compared to what we've got and what the Germans have. Compared to what the Lizards have . . ." He shook his head.

To his surprise, Healey laughed. "What they fly doesn't matter much, not for this game. They've got their missiles aimed at the Lizards—and at the Nazis—and they've got their submarines. As long as those work, everything else is gravy."

Johnson didn't like to hear what he'd spent his career doing belittled. He could have argued about it; several relevant points occurred to him. Most times, he would have done it. At the moment, he had something more urgent on his mind. "Ask you a question, sir?" When Brigadier General Healey's bulldog head bobbed up and down, Johnson said, "If the Nazis and the Lizards go at it, sir, will we stay out of it?"

Healey's eyebrows sprang upward. "We'd damn well better, or this mission will fail. We still need resupply missions from home. We'll need more people, too, sooner or later."

"Yes, I understand all that." Johnson couldn't very well misunderstand it, not after so much time aboard the *Lewis and Clark*. "But *will* we stay out of it if it heats up?"

"I'm hoping it won't," the commandant said. "If the Germans were going to jump, they would have jumped by now—that's what the consensus back home is, anyhow." He paused and coughed, realizing he hadn't answered the question Johnson asked. With another cough, he did: "As far as I know, we aren't going to go to war unless we're attacked. Will that do?"

"Yes, sir," Johnson said. "It'll have to, won't it?" Brigadier General Healey nodded again.

Vyacheslav Molotov nodded to Paul Schmidt. "Good day," the Soviet leader said. "Be seated; take tea, if you care to." He gestured toward the samovar that stood on a table in a corner of his office.

"No thank you, Comrade General Secretary," the German ambassador said in his good Russian. "I suppose you are curious as to why I asked to see you on such short notice."

"Somewhat," Molotov said, and said no more. No matter how curious he was, he didn't intend to show Schmidt anything.

Rather to his annoyance (which he didn't show, either), the German ambassador smiled. Paul Schmidt had known him a long time—since before the Lizards came—and might well guess how much he was concealing. Schmidt said, "My government has charged me with announcing the dissolution of the Committee of Eight and the selection of a new *Führer* to guide the destiny of the Greater German *Reich*."

That was indeed news. It was news Molotov had awaited with a curious mixture of hope and dread. He concealed both of those, too, asking only, "And to whom are congratulations due?" *Who's come out on top in the intrigue and backstage bloodletting?*

"Why, to Dr. Ernst Kaltenbrunner, inheritor of the great mantle formerly worn by Hitler and Himmler," Schmidt replied.

"Please convey to him my heartiest and most sincere felicitations, and the hope that he will have a long, successful, and peaceful tenure at the head of the *Reich*," Molotov said.

Not even his legendary self-control could keep him from putting a little extra stress on the word *peaceful*. It did, however, keep his most sincere felicitations from sounding too dreadfully insincere. Kaltenbrunner was the man he had hoped would not rise to the top in Germany, and would surely have been Himmler's chosen successor had Himmler not dropped dead before choosing anyone. A big Austrian with cold eyes, Kaltenbrunner had stepped into Reinhard Heydrich's shoes after the British arranged Heydrich's untimely demise in Prague, and filled them all too well.

No one noticed him for a while, either, Molotov thought. Heydrich had been assassinated just as the Lizard invasion began, and the chaos that followed masked many things for a long time. But, when the dust settled, there was Kaltenbrunner, as much of a right-hand man as Himmler allowed himself.

Now Molotov asked the question he had to ask: "What will— Doctor, did you say?—yes, Dr. Kaltenbrunner's policies be?"

"I expect him to continue on the path laid down by his illustrious predecessor and continued by the Committee of Eight," the German ambassador said.

That was the answer Molotov had expected. It was also the answer he dreaded. Picking his words with some care, he said, "A change of leaders can sometimes lead to a change in policy with no disrespect for what has gone before." *I have not been nearly such a mad adventurist as Stalin, for instance.*

But Schmidt shook his head. "The new *Führer* is convinced his predecessor followed the proper course. Our neighbors ignore the legitimate claims of the *Reich* at their peril."

"At their peril, certainly," Molotov said. "But also at yours. I hope the new *Führer* bears that in mind as well."

Unlike the leaders he served, Schmidt was a man of culture. Molotov had thought so for many years. But the German did serve the ruffians who led the *Reich*, and served them loyally. He said, "The *Führer* does indeed have that in his mind. Because he does, he sent me to renew the offer his predecessor, *Reichs* Chancellor Himmler, extended to the Soviet Union in regard to the illegally occupied Polish regions."

"He wants us to join him in an attack on the Race, you are telling me," Molotov said.

"Yes." Schmidt nodded. "After all, part of the territory between our states was formerly occupied by the Soviet Union."

"So it was—till 22 June, 1941," Molotov said with a savage irony he did not try to hide. "I asked you once, and now I ask you again: if our borders marched with each other, how long would it be till the *Reich* was at the Soviet Union's throat again?"

"Perhaps longer than it would take for the Soviet Union to be at the *Reich*'s throat," Schmidt answered tartly. "Or perhaps—and it is certainly the new *Führer*'s earnest hope—we could live at peace with each other once the victory has been won."

"Living at peace with each other if our borders touched would take a small miracle," said Molotov, using the language of the religion in which he had not believed since youth. "Living in peace with the Race after attacking Poland, however, would take a large miracle."

"As *Reichs* Chancellor Himmler did not, Dr. Kaltenbrunner does not share this view," Schmidt said.

"As I told Himmler through you, so I tell Kaltenbrunner: if he wants to attack Poland on his own, that is his affair," Molotov said. "I do not think, however, he will be pleased with the result."

But did that matter to the Nazis? Molotov doubted it. Fascists wanted what they wanted because they imagined they were entitled to it. Whether their desires inconvenienced or infuriated anyone else mattered very little to them. What they wanted, after all, was legitimate. What anyone else wanted was nothing but the twisted desires of subhumans or, in the case of the Lizards, nonhumans.

They couldn't even see that. Not even the clever, able ones among them, of whom there were a depressing number, could see it. Paul Schmidt, for instance, only shrugged and said, "I obey the *Führer*."

"Take him my answer, then. It is the same one I gave to Himmler: no." Molotov spoke the word *nyet* with more than a little relish. "And now I will tell you something on a personal level—I think you are fortunate to be here in Moscow. If this war begins, you would not want to be in Germany."

"I am not worried," Schmidt said, and for once Molotov had met his match in obscurity. Did the ambassador mean he wasn't worried because he was in Moscow or because he did not fear what would happen to his homeland? Not even the Soviet leader quite had the crust to ask him.

What Molotov did ask was, "Have we any other issues to discuss?"

"No, Comrade General Secretary," Schmidt replied.

"Very well," Molotov said, in lieu of screaming, *You're mad! Your Führer is mad! Your whole country is mad! You are going to wreck yourselves, you won't beat the Lizards, and you'll hurt the USSR with the radioactive waste from the explosive-metal bombs you use and the ones the Race will use on you.*

Schmidt rose to his feet. He bowed to Molotov. "Good day, then. Be of good cheer. Everything will turn out for the best." Before Molotov could answer, the diplomat bowed again and left.

Molotov sat behind his desk for some time, silent and unmoving. His secretary looked in, saw him there, and silently withdrew. A few minutes later, though, the telephone jangled. Molotov picked it up. "Marshal Zhukov on the line," the secretary said.

"Put him through, Pyotr Maksimovich," Molotov said.

Without preamble, Zhukov demanded, "What did the German have to say?"

As bluntly, Molotov told him, "It's Kaltenbrunner."

"Is it?" After that, Zhukov said nothing for perhaps half a minute. As Molotov had been, he was adding up what that meant. When he did speak again, it was with one explosive word: "Shit."

"My thought exactly." Molotov's voice was dry. "As before, Schmidt felt me out for a joint attack on the Race in Poland."

"And what did you tell him?" Zhukov sounded worried.

"Georgi Konstantinovich, I am not suicidal," Molotov said. "You may rest assured that I declined the generous offer."

"I am ever so glad to hear it," the marshal replied. "The next question is, do you think that matters to the Germans, even in the slightest?"

"No," Molotov answered.

"Shit," Zhukov said again. "Comrade General Secretary, if they go at it, the western part of this country takes it on the chin."

"I am painfully aware of that," Molotov said. "If you have dis-

covered some secret weapon that will stop a fool from acting like
a fool, I suggest that you start using it. It may well be the most
powerful weapon in the world today, including explosive-metal
bombs."

"No such luck." Zhukov sounded like an angry peasant now, a
peasant watching his cattle die without being able to do anything
about it.

Molotov decided to match his tone: "Things could be worse,
you know: if we did go along with the Nazis, the whole country
would take it on the chin."

"Don't remind me," Marshal Zhukov said. His laugh was anything but pleasant. "I'm glad I didn't dispose of you when you
turned up alive while the Army was smashing Beria's men.
I thought about it, Vyacheslav Mikhailovich—believe me, I
thought about it."

"You would have been an idiot not to think about it. Whatever
else you are, you are no idiot." Molotov had discussed the liquidation of a great many other people—ever so coldly, ever so dispassionately. He knew a certain amount of pride in being able to
discuss his own the same way. "But why bring this up now?"

"Because, if I'd got rid of you, then I'd be the one left with
nothing to do but watch while the *Reich* and the Race throw
brickbats at each other," Zhukov answered. "This way, if anybody ends up needing to take the blame, you're the one."

"Yes, having a scapegoat around is always handy," Molotov
agreed. "Stalin was a master at it. The only trouble is, the *Reich*
and the Lizards have nastier things than brickbats to throw."

"That's the only trouble, is it?" Zhukov chuckled. "Have you
got any nerves at all, Vyacheslav Mikhailovich?"

"I try not to," Molotov said. "If you purge me, Marshal, you
purge me. I cannot do anything about it." *Not yet. I wish I could.
I'm working on it.* "I cannot do anything about the Nazis and the
Lizards, either. If I get excited about what I cannot help, that
doesn't change the situation, and it leaves me more liable to
make a mistake."

"You would not have made the worst soldier in the world,"
Zhukov remarked after a few seconds' thought.

He meant it as a compliment; of that Molotov was sure. And
so he said, *"Spasebo,"* though he was not at all sure he wanted
to thank Zhukov. To him, soldiers were crude and unsubtle men,

relying on force because they lacked the brains to do anything else. They were necessary, no doubt about it. But so were ditchdiggers and embalmers.

"You're welcome, Comrade General Secretary," the marshal answered. "Here, for the sake of the *rodina*, the motherland, we have to pull together."

When the Nazis invaded, Stalin had said the same thing. He'd practiced what he preached, too. He'd even cozied up to the Russian Orthodox Church after beating it about the head and shoulders for almost twenty years. In an emergency, he'd been willing to jettison a lot of ideology. And hadn't Lenin done the same when he'd instituted the New Economic Policy to keep the country from starving after the end of the civil war?

"Yes, we all have to pull together. We all have to do everything we can," Molotov agreed. And then, because he could speak as frankly to Zhukov as to anyone save possibly Gromyko, he added, "For the life of me, though, I don't know how much good it will do, or if it will do any good whatever." He hung up without waiting for a reply.

When Johannes Drucker strolled into the mess hall at Peenemünde, he discovered that the powers that be had wasted little time. Here it was, only two days after Ernst Kaltenbrunner had been named *Führer*, and a color photograph of him now occupied the frame that had held Heinrich Himmler's picture for years.

Drucker wasn't the only man studying it. From behind him, somebody said, "He looks like a tough son of a bitch. We need one of those right now."

That struck Drucker as a pretty fair assessment, though he was less sure about the need. Kaltenbrunner was in his vigorous early sixties, with a big head and heavy features. He was leaning forward, so that he seemed to stare out through the camera lens at whoever was looking at him. Even with the advantage of twenty years, Drucker wouldn't have cared to meet him in a dark alley.

Till Himmler's death and even afterwards, Drucker hadn't paid Kaltenbrunner much attention. Himmler kept his strength by not letting anyone around him be strong; the man who now led the Greater German *Reich* had been just another official in a fancy uniform standing at the old *Führer*'s back in Party rallies and state functions. Now the whole world would find out what sort of man had been inhabiting that uniform.

Grabbing a mess tray, Drucker got into line. Cooks' helpers spooned sauerkraut, boiled potatoes, and blood sausage onto the tray. Another helper gave him a small mug of beer. He carried the full tray to a table and sat down to eat.

Nobody sat near him. He'd got used to that. He knew he suffered from political unreliability, a disease always dangerous and often fatal—and highly contagious. He'd stayed away from men with such an illness in the days before the SS got curious about Käthe's racial purity, and before Gunther Grillparzer had tried blaming him for the murders during the fighting of which he was, unfortunately, guilty. No one had proved anything—he was still here, still breathing. Even so . . .

No sooner had that thought crossed his mind than the loud-speaker in the mess hall blared out his name: "Lieutenant Colonel Johannes Drucker! Lieutenant Colonel Johannes Drucker! Report to the base commandant's office! You are ordered to report to the base commandant's office!"

Drucker took a last bite of blood sausage. *It might really be the last bite I ever take,* he thought as he got to his feet. Most of the men in the hall looked down at their own mess trays. Sure enough, they thought political unreliability was contagious. A few stared avidly. They *wanted* him to get a noodle in the back of the neck.

He hurried to General Dornberger's office, wondering if a couple of hulking fellows in SS black would be waiting for him in the antechamber. If they were—well, he still had his service pistol on his hip. But what would they do to his family if he made them kill him fast instead of taking him away to do a lingering, nasty job?

With such thoughts going through his mind, he wondered why he kept heading toward the commandant's office instead of running. *Because you know damn well they'd catch you, that's why.* And maybe he wasn't in a whole lot of trouble. He laughed. Fat chance.

When he got to the antechamber, he saw no bully boys in black shirts, only Dornberger's dyspeptic adjutant. Shooting out his arm in salute, he said, "Reporting as ordered."

"Yes." Major Neufeld eyed him. "I rather wondered if you would. The general expected you, though. Go on in."

"Reporting as ordered," Drucker said again after he'd saluted General Dornberger.

Dornberger puffed on his cigar, then set it in the glass ashtray on his desk. He now had a photo of Dr. Kaltenbrunner in his office, too. "Drucker, you are a man who does his duty," he said.

"Yes, sir," Drucker said.

"In spite of everything," Dornberger went on, and then waved a hand to show Drucker didn't need to answer that. The base commandant drew on the cigar again. "I have an A-45 on the gantry, fueled and ready for launch. Are you prepared to go into space within the hour?"

"Jawohl!" Drucker saluted again. Then he went from military automaton to honestly confused human being. "Sir, am I allowed? Has my grounding been rescinded?"

Instead of answering, General Dornberger picked up a flimsy sheet of yellow paper. "I have here an order for your immediate arrest and incarceration. I got it half an hour ago. I have spent that half hour documenting how I ordered your launch last night because of shortages of pilots. I will finish the documentation in the time remaining until the rocket goes up. Then, of course, just too late, I will receive this telegram. How unfortunate that I could not obey the order, don't you agree?"

Try as he would, Drucker couldn't hold his stiff brace. His knees sagged. He stared at Walter Dornberger. "My God, sir," he breathed. "Won't they put your head on the block instead of mine?"

"Not a chance," Dornberger said calmly. "They haven't got anyone else who can run Peenemünde even a quarter as well, and they bloody well know it. They'll yell at me and tell me I was a naughty boy, and I'll go on about my business for as long as I can go on about it."

"For as long as you can go on about it," Drucker echoed. "What about me? What do I do if they order me to land?"

"Ignore them," General Dornberger told him. "You're carrying two missiles with explosive-metal bombs. They can't argue too hard—or they'd better not."

"But I can't stay up forever, even so," Drucker said. "What do I do when I run low on oxygen?"

"Maybe I can fix things by then," Dornberger replied. "If you hear the phrase 'served with honor' in any communication, you will know I have done it. If you do not hear that phrase, you would do better to land somewhere outside the Greater German *Reich*."

Drucker gulped. What would they do to his family if he did that?

Before he could speak, Dornberger held up a hand. "I do not expect any of this to matter, Lieutenant Colonel. When you go up there, I think you will have every opportunity to make yourself a hero for the *Vaterland*."

That could mean only one thing. In a small voice, Drucker said, "The balloon is going up?"

"With him at the helm?" Dornberger jerked a contemptuous thumb at the new color photograph on the wall behind him. "Yes, the balloon is going up. If he weren't the *Führer*, he'd make a good butcher's assistant. But he is, and we must obey." He might have been speaking more to himself than to Drucker. Then he grew brisk once more. "A motorcar will be waiting outside. It will take you to the gantry. And Drucker—"

"Yes, sir?"

"If we must go down, let the Lizards know they've been in a brawl."

"Yes, sir!" Drucker saluted, spun on his heel, and marched out of the office. He saluted Major Neufeld, too, even though he outranked the commandant's adjutant.

The Volkswagen was there. The driver said, "To the gantry, sir?" Drucker nodded, not trusting himself to speak. Air-cooled engine roaring flatulently, the VW sped off.

At the gantry the crew had Drucker's pressure suit, tailored to his measure, ready and waiting. The upper stage of the A-45 there wasn't *Käthe*; he could tell that at a glance. Someone else had his baby. This upper stage looked older, more battered, almost of an earlier generation. In the crisis, the *Reich* was using anything that could fly.

A couple of the technicians gave Drucker curious or hostile looks as they helped him into his pressure suit. His fellow pilots weren't the only ones who knew about his troubles with the higher-ups, of course. But then one of the techs said, "Good to see you cleared for launch again, sir."

"Thanks, Helmut," Drucker answered. "I've been away too long. Going back will feel good." *It will certainly feel a hell of a lot better than getting thrown in the guardhouse and handed over to the blackshirts for interrogation.*

But, as he rode the elevator to the upper stage of the A-45, he wondered about that. If the new *Führer* really was crazy enough to go to war with the Lizards over Poland, how long would the German spacecraft in Earth orbit last? For that matter, how much longer would the *Hermann Göring* last, out in the asteroid belt?

He shrugged. He couldn't do anything about that. And if the Race blew him out of orbit, odds were he'd be dead before he knew it. He wouldn't be able to say that if the SS got its hooks into him.

Hans-Ulrich's Bus. That was the name painted on the upper stage's flank. When Drucker climbed into the bus, he discovered it had seen better days. Everything looked worn, shabby; he half expected to find cigarette butts under the leather-covered acceleration couch. But, as he went through the checks, he found everything in working order. A good thing, too, because they were going to launch him any which way. A technician slammed the entry port shut. Drucker dogged it. Conversations with the launch crew were quicker, more perfunctory, than they had been before the crisis. They wanted to get him out there, and only some obviously looming disaster would keep them from doing it.

It would be a disaster for me if they aborted, all right, Drucker thought.

But they didn't. The last numbers of the countdown sounded in his earphones, and then the great thunder of the A-45's main engine sounded in every fiber of his body. Acceleration slammed him back into the seat. He wondered whether *Hans-Ulrich's Bus* had an old-model seat, or if it was simply that he hadn't gone up for a while. Whichever it was, the kick in the pants seemed harder than usual.

All the instruments read as they should have. As far as they could judge, the flight was perfect. When acceleration cut off, with the upper stage in its proper orbit, Drucker's stomach lurched a couple of times before settling down. *I've been away too long,* he thought with something approaching horror. He was normally one of the minority who enjoyed weightlessness.

And then, as he'd known it would, the radio squawked into life: "Lieutenant Colonel Drucker! Lieutenant Colonel Drucker! Do you read me, Lieutenant Colonel Drucker?"

"Not very well—your signal is breaking up," he lied.

It didn't matter. The radio operator on the other end of the circuit went right on talking: "You are to land your upper stage immediately, Lieutenant Colonel. Ground telemetry has discovered an oxygen-line leak. Your safety is endangered."

In normal times, that would have got him down in a hurry. Now he smiled and said, "My instruments say everything is normal. The *Reich* needs me here. I'll take the chance and stay."

"Your patriotism is appreciated"—*I'll bet,* Drucker thought—"but we cannot take the risk. You are ordered to return to Earth as soon as possible."

"For the sake of the *Vaterland*, I must disobey this order." Drucker's smile got bigger. Two hypocrites were trying to outlie each other.

The radioman cajoled. He talked about the blemish on Drucker's sterling service record. He talked about disciplinary action after Drucker did land. Before very long, he faded out of range. Another one would pick up the thread soon. Drucker was sure of it. But that didn't matter. They couldn't talk him down. He didn't think they'd have another flier in an upper stage try to shoot him down. His smile slipped then. No, they'd save that for the Lizards—and the Lizards were all too likely to be able to pull it off.

☆ **19** ☆

Jonathan Yeager's voice broke in exasperation, something that hadn't happened to him in a couple of years. "But, Mom!" he cried.

"No," his mother repeated. "N-O. No. You are not going up there while the Race and the Germans are liable to start throwing things at each other any minute now, and that's final."

"Your mother's right," his father said. "It's just too dangerous right now. Let's wait and see how things work out. Kassquit's not going anywhere."

"It's not just Kassquit," Jonathan said. "It's the chance to do all this stuff, to go up there, to talk with the Lizards." He felt his ears getting hot just the same. It wasn't just Kassquit, but a lot of it was.

His father shook his head. "Wait," he said. "After things settle down—if things settle down—the invitation will still be open."

"Dad . . ." Jonathan took a deep breath. "Dad, the invitation was for *me*, you know. If the Lizards want me up there, if they'll take me up there, I can go."

"You can," his mother said. "You can, but you may not. You do not have our permission."

Another deep breath—and then one more for luck. "I'd like your permission, sure, but I don't have to have it. I'm twenty-one now. If they'll take me, I'm going to go, and that's flat."

"You're doing no such thing," his mother said through clenched teeth.

"Barbara—" his father said in a tone of voice that made his mother look as if she'd been stabbed in the back. His father took a deep breath of his own, then went on, "I was eighteen when I left the farm, you know."

558

"You weren't heading off to places where the world could blow up any minute, though," Jonathan's mother said.

"No, but I might have if I'd been a little older," his father answered. "Plenty of boys Jonathan's age couldn't get off the farm fast enough to go fight in the trenches. And I tried to join the Army after Pearl Harbor, but they wouldn't have me." He opened his mouth and tapped one of the front teeth on his upper plate. "They took me after the Lizards landed, but they took anybody who was breathing then."

If they'd taken him earlier, I wouldn't be here, because he never would have met Mom, Jonathan thought. His mind shied away from things like that. Dealing with what was seemed hard enough; might-have-beens were a lot worse.

"Let him go, Barbara," his father said. "It's what he wants to do—and the Lizards have a lot of ships out there. Even if the worst happens, odds are he'll be fine."

"Odds!" His mother made it into the filthiest word in the language. She turned on her heel and walked back to the bedroom with long, furious strides. She slammed the door after her when she went in there. Jonathan couldn't remember her ever doing that before.

"Congratulations," his father said. "You've won. Go pack a bag. Your mom's right about this much: you may be up there longer than you expect."

"Okay. Jesus, Dad, thanks!" Jonathan bounced to his feet. He started to hurry off to his own room, then stopped and turned back. Hesitantly, he asked, "How much trouble will you get into for this?"

"As long as you come home safe, nothing that won't blow over." His father hesitated, too. "If anything happens to you, I'll be in too much trouble with myself to worry about what your mother does."

Jonathan didn't care to think about that, so he didn't. He hurried into his bedroom and packed shorts and underwear and socks, a toothbrush and toothpaste, and a razor and a pack of blades. He wasn't worried about food; if the Lizards had fed Kassquit all these years, they could take care of him, too. And he packed something he'd bought at a drugstore he didn't usually go to: a box of Trojans.

His father took care of the arrangements with the Race and

with his own superiors. At supper that evening—as brittle a meal as Jonathan had ever eaten—his dad said, "Launch from the Race's shuttlecraft is a little past four tomorrow afternoon. I'll drive you to the airport."

"Okay," Jonathan said. By his mother's closed expression, she didn't think it was anywhere close to okay. His dad didn't look convinced, either. Neither one of them contradicted him out loud, though.

He thought about calling Karen. In the end, he didn't. What could he say, considering why he was going into space? Either nothing or a pack of lies. Nothing seemed better.

He took care of Mickey and Donald the next day, knowing he wouldn't for a while. He waved to them. "I'm going away, but I'll come back pretty soon. Bye-bye." They waved back. Mickey made a noise that might have been bye-bye, but it might not have, too. He and Donald talked more than baby Lizards had any business doing, but less than baby people.

His father took him up to the airport. Cops—no, they were soldiers—escorted the car to the shuttlecraft's landing area. "Thanks, Dad," Jonathan said as he got out.

"I'm not so sure you're welcome," his father answered, but then he stuck out his hand. Jonathan leaned back in to shake it.

Down came the shuttlecraft, its braking rocket roaring louder than any jet engine Jonathan had ever heard. When the entry hatch opened, he climbed the ladder—awkwardly, with his bag—and got inside.

"Get in. Strap down. As soon as we are refueled, we shall depart," the shuttlecraft pilot said.

"It shall be done, superior sir." Jonathan hoped he'd guessed right. The pilot didn't contradict him, so he supposed he had.

Having gone into space twice before, Jonathan found the third launch routine, which was probably a testimony to the shuttlecraft pilot's skill. The male tended to the craft all the way through the flight, and said a lot less than the female named Nesseref had on his previous trip to the starship. Jonathan wondered what the male would have done if he'd been sick from weightlessness. He was glad he didn't have to find out.

As soon as he left the shuttlecraft and entered the starship, a Lizard seized his bag from him, declaring, "We shall search this." After he had searched it—he opened the toothpaste tube to see what was inside and asked what the razor was for—he gave it back. "Nothing useful in sabotaging the ship. Come along."

"It shall be done, superior sir," Jonathan said once more. Sabotaging the ship was the last thing he wanted to do. *The Race is worried*, he thought. *And I'm not even a German. I wonder if they really understand how different different countries are.*

As he had before, he got heavier the farther he went from the starship's hub. At last, when he was close to his proper weight, the Lizard escorting him said, "This is the chamber holding the female Kassquit."

Heart thumping, more sweat on his forehead than the heat could account for, Jonathan went inside. "I greet you, superior female," he said, and bent into the posture of respect.

"I greet you," Kassquit replied, and returned the gesture. To one side of the chamber stood something he hadn't expected to see in a starship: an army cot, from whose army he wasn't sure. The Lizards had done some research, then, and hadn't got everything wrong.

Jonathan was acutely conscious of being alone in a room with an attractive young woman not wearing any clothes. He was even more acutely conscious of Lizards walking along the corridor outside and every so often swiveling an eye turret toward the chamber to see what was going on. He said, "Can you shut that door?"

Kassquit made the affirmative gesture. She touched a button by the doorway. The door silently slid shut. "Is that better?" she asked. Now Jonathan used the gesture. Kassquit asked, "You prefer privacy, then? Among the Race, from what I have seen, it matters very little."

"It matters for Tosevites." Jonathan tacked on an emphatic cough.

"You may have less than you expect, but I suppose expectations count, too," Kassquit said. While Jonathan was still trying to untangle that, she added, "You understand, then, that you have come up here for the purpose of mating."

She didn't beat around the bush at all. Jonathan stopped worrying about the first part of what she'd said; the second demanded every bit of his attention. "Yes," he said carefully. "I understand that."

"Very well." Kassquit started to say something, then stopped.

When she spoke again, he would have bet it wasn't what she'd first intended to say. It was, instead, an almost plaintive question: "Are you nervous?"

"Yes," he repeated, and used another emphatic cough.

"Good," she said. "So am I. This is very strange for me. Being a Tosevite at all is strange for me. Being one in this way . . . it is something I have not done before, and had not imagined I would want to do before."

"I understand—I hope I understand," he said. He wondered if so much had ever ridden on a man and a woman's lying down together. He had his doubts. "I will do my best to please you."

"I thank you," Kassquit replied gravely. "I will do the same for you." Without missing a beat, she went on, "If we are to do this, should you not remove your wrappings?"

"I suppose so." Jonathan knew he sounded sheepish. He hadn't expected her to be quite so matter-of-fact. In one quick gesture, he pulled off his shorts and the jockeys he wore beneath them.

Kassquit studied him. *She's never seen a naked man before,* he realized. He knew a certain amount of pride in rising to the occasion. She came up to him and asked, "May I touch you?" He nodded, then remembered to use the gesture she understood. She wrapped her palm around him. Then, to his astonishment, she dropped to her knees and took him in her mouth.

"How . . . do you know to do that?" he spluttered.

"I watched videos," she answered seriously. "I wanted to be prepared. Am I doing it correctly?" She sounded anxious.

"Yes," he said with another emphatic cough, wondering where on Earth—or off it—she could have got stag movies. "Oh, yes." But as she bent toward him again, he said, "Wait." She looked up at him. Her face didn't, couldn't, show anything. Had it, he thought it would have shown puzzlement. He pointed toward the cot. "If you lie there, I will try to please you."

She got to her feet. As she walked to the cot, she remarked, "I do not think anyone has ever tried to please me." The resigned way she said it made tears come to Jonathan's eyes. It also made him all the more resolved to do everything he could for her.

She didn't get kissing. He found that out at once, when he knelt on the metal floor by the cot. But when his mouth went to her breasts instead of her lips, she let out a soft, surprised sigh. The one bit of advice he'd had from his father was, *Don't hurry.* He tried to

remember that now, when hurrying was what he most wanted to
do. He stroked her all over before he let his hand slip between her
legs. She was already wet. He moved his head down a little later.
He'd done that only a couple of times with Karen, and didn't know
how good he was. Kassquit's being shaved made things easier, or at
least less distracting. And the unrestrained noises Kassquit made
left him with no doubt he'd done well enough.

He went back to his bag and took out the box of Trojans.
Kassquit reached under the cot and held out an identical box.
They both laughed, Kassquit first in the Race's fashion and then
noisily, like a human.

Jonathan put on a rubber. He'd practiced at home; he hadn't
wanted to make a botch of it. He was about to get down on the
cot between Kassquit's legs when a horrible wordless hissing
broke out from a speaker overhead. Kassquit sprang up in alarm.
Words, words in the language of the Race, followed: "Emergency stations! We are under attack. Emergency stations at
once! We are under attack!"

Kassquit ran past the wild Big Ugly to the door. When she hit
the button, it slid open. "Come with me," she said to Jonathan
Yeager. "You have no proper emergency station, so come to my
compartment."

"It shall be done." He tossed the box of elastic sheaths into his
satchel, which he picked up. Then he realized he was still
wearing a sheath himself. He peeled it off and threw it on the
floor. Kassquit disapproved of such untidiness. As he followed
her out into the corridor, he asked, "Is it the Deutsche?"

"I do not know what else it could be," Kassquit answered.
"Hurry!" The emergency warning echoed through the ship.

Males and females of the Race rushed this way and that,
heading for their own emergency stations. Some few would defend the starship, the rest merely huddle in it. If an explosive-
metal bomb burst against its side, they would die where they
huddled, probably faster than they could realize they were dead.

Seeing Big Uglies inside the starship made some males and
females shout angrily. Kassquit shouted back. So did Jonathan
Yeager, not always quite grammatically. Then he asked the very
question she'd pondered a moment before: "What happens if we
are hit?"

She gave him the only answer she'd come up with: "We die." His face twisted. She knew little of the facial expressions wild Big Uglies used. From what she'd gathered, though, this one did not indicate pleasure.

Here was her home corridor. Here was her home doorway. She punched the keypad outside it. She had to try twice to get the combination right. When she did, the door opened. She went inside. Again, Jonathan Yeager followed. She closed the door behind them. Even through the metal, the clicks of toeclaws on metal and the cries of frightened males and females came clearly.

Kassquit was frightened, too. And so, no doubt, was Jonathan Yeager. She needed a little while to realize how frightened he must be. She, at least, was where she belonged, where she'd lived her whole life. He had to be as much adrift as she would have been had war broken out while she was on the surface of Tosev 3.

"What do we do now?" he asked. If there were any answers, he knew she had to be the one who had them.

He depends on me, she realized with a small shock. She'd never had anyone do that before. She'd always been the one who depended on Ttomalss. "Wait," she told him: the obvious. "Hope the all-clear sounds." Once past the obvious, she had to pause and think, but not for long. She wished she could form her face into the expression wild Big Uglies used to show amiability. "Also, we ought to go on with what we were doing before the alarm came."

Jonathan Yeager threw back his head and barked Tosevite laughter. "We have a saying: eat, drink, and be merry, for tomorrow we may die." The laughter stopped. "But it may not be tomorrow. It may be the next instant."

"That is a truth," Kassquit said. "Because it is a truth, should we not go on? Is there anything else you would rather do?"

"No," he said, and added an emphatic cough.

"Nor I." She lay down on her sleeping mat. It was less resilient than the cot brought up from Tosev 3—*it fits the Race's needs, not mine,* she thought—but it would have to do. "Let us continue, then."

She'd expected him to put on another sheath and continue from exactly the point where they were interrupted. Instead, to her surprise and delight, he knelt beside her and began stimulating her all over again.

She hadn't realized she could be stimulated on the web of

flesh between her thumb and forefinger or the crook of her elbow or her earlobes. She'd always hated her ears, which marred the smooth lines of her head, and wished she had hearing diaphragms instead, as the Race did. Here was a reason to change her mind she hadn't expected.

His mouth on her breasts gave her more pleasure than her own fingers had. She wasn't so sure that was true when his head went between her legs. She knew just what to do and when to do it there. He didn't; he was finding out by experiment. When she'd stroked herself, though, she'd always known what would happen next. With Jonathan Yeager's caresses, she didn't. Sometimes the surprises were disappointing. Sometimes they were altogether delightful. She gasped and shuddered, taken to her peak of pleasure almost by surprise.

After that, Jonathan Yeager did reach for the box of sheaths. "Would you not like me to stimulate you as well?" Kassquit asked.

The corners of his mouth turned up. "I *am* stimulated," he answered, and pointed to that part of himself which proved the truth of his words. "If you stimulate me much more, I will . . ." He paused, perhaps looking for a way to put what he wanted to say into the language of the Race. He found one: "I will spill my seed, and then you would have to wait a while before I could mate again."

That was the first Kassquit had heard of Tosevites having to wait between matings. "How long?" she asked. "A day? Ten days?"

He laughed again. "No, not so long as either of those. Maybe a tenth part of a day, maybe even less than that."

Kassquit considered. "You gave me pleasure—I would like to return it," she said at last. "It seems only fair, after all. If you spill your seed before we mate, then you do, that is all, and we will wait. If not, we will go on. Is that all right?"

The corners of his mouth turned up again. "Yes, indeed, superior female," he said, and lay back on the mat.

Partly remembering the videos of Big Uglies mating she'd watched, partly imitating what Jonathan Yeager had done with her, Kassquit worked her way down his body with her hands and mouth. By the small noises he made, she judged she was succeeding in giving him pleasure. As he had with her, she crouched between his legs and stimulated him with her mouth.

With a small whir, the door to her chamber slid open and

Ttomalss walked in. Jonathan Yeager's reaction astonished Kassquit—he made a noise that sounded something like *Eep!*, jerked away from her so quickly that she almost bit him, and held both hands in front of the organ she'd been stimulating.

Ttomalss said, "I greet you, Kassquit, and you, Jonathan Yeager. I wanted to make certain you were both safe. I am glad to see you are." He turned to go.

"I thank you, superior sir," Kassquit said as he left. Jonathan Yeager said *Eep!* again. Kassquit wondered what it meant in his language. She got up and closed the door once more then walked back to him. "Shall we go on?"

He said something else she didn't understand; it sounded like *Jesus!* Then he went back to the language of the Race: "After that, I hope I can."

Kassquit wondered what he meant. She found out: he had wilted. More stimulation seemed called for. She applied it. She wondered what was in his laugh as he rose again. She thought it sounded like relief, but had too little experience with Tosevites to be sure. "There," she said briskly after a little while. "Now— the sheath."

"It shall be done," he said, and did it.

In the videos, she'd seen several possible mating postures. Female astride male seemed as practical as male mounting female. She straddled Jonathan Yeager and joined their organs. As she lowered herself onto him, she stopped in sudden surprise and pain. "This is a mating!" she exclaimed. "It should not hurt!" The idea of mating that gave pain rather than pleasure struck her as addled even by the standards of Tosev 3.

But Jonathan Yeager said, "Female Tosevites have a . . . membrane that must be broken on the first mating. That can cause pain. After the membrane heals, this does not happen again."

"I see." Kassquit sighed. She hadn't known that. None of her research had shown it. She wondered if the Race even knew it. She shrugged. If she hadn't found out about it before, it couldn't matter much, even to wild Big Uglies.

She bore down. The membrane certainly was there. Jonathan Yeager had better information than she did. She bore down again, at the same time as he thrust up from beneath her. The membrane tore. She hissed. It did hurt, and she wasn't used to physical pain.

"Is it all right?" Jonathan Yeager asked.

"I—suppose so," Kassquit answered. "I have no standards of comparison."

He kept moving inside her. That went on hurting, but less than it had when he first pierced her. It brought a little pleasure with it, but not nearly so much as she got from a hand or from his tongue. She wondered if it would be different after she healed.

Beneath her, Jonathan Yeager's face went very red. He grunted, clutched her hindquarters almost painfully tight, and thrust himself into her to the hilt. Then he relaxed. His eyes, which had squeezed shut, opened again. The corners of his mouth turned upward.

Kassquit slid off him. Her blood streaked the sheath and her inner thighs. "Is it supposed to be like this?" she asked Jonathan Yeager.

"Yes, I think so," he answered. He took off the sheath, which was messy inside and out. "What do I do with this, superior female?"

She showed him. "Here—this is the trash chute. I do not think it would be wise to send it through the plumbing. It might cause a blockage in the pipes."

"That would not be good, not in a starship," he said.

"No, it would not," Kassquit agreed. "Tosevite wastes already give the plumbing difficulties it was not designed to handle." She went to the sink, wet a tissue, and wiped the blood from her legs and private parts. Then she sent the tissue down the trash chute, too.

Jonathan Yeager imitated everything she did as he washed himself. "You are going to have to show me things here," he told her. "I do not know how to live on this starship, any more than you would know how to live in my land on Tosev 3."

"It should not be too hard," she said.

He laughed. "Not for you—you have lived here all your life. For me, everything is strange. You have no idea how strange everything here is."

That was likely to be true. Kassquit said, "I only hope we can go on living here."

As if to underscore her words, the floor shuddered a little beneath her feet. "What was that?" Jonathan Yeager asked.

"I do not know, not for certain," she answered. "But I think it may have been missiles firing at a target."

"Oh," the wild Tosevite said, and then, "I hope they hit it."

"So do I," Kassquit answered. "If they do not hit it, it will hit us."

"I know that." Jonathan Yeager put his arm around her. No male or female of the Race would have made such a gesture. Physical contact mattered more among Big Uglies than it did to the Race. Having grown up among the Race, Kassquit had not thought it would matter to her. She was surprised to discover herself mistaken. Genetic programming mattered. The touch of another of her kind—and one with whom she'd known other physical intimacies—brought a certain reassurance.

Not that that will do us any good whatever if a missile does strike this starship, she thought, and then wished she hadn't.

For Mordechai Anielewicz, a quarter of a century might have fallen away in the course of bare days. Here again were the Nazis swarming over Poland's western border, panzer engines rumbling, attack aircraft diving on the forces defending the land where he'd lived all his life.

Coming out of Lodz, he was a lot closer to the border than he had been in 1939, when he'd lived in Warsaw. The Germans didn't have so far to come to get him this time. On the other hand, Poland was better able to fight back than she had been then.

A Lizard fired a missile at an oncoming German panzer. The panzer stopped coming on; it burst into flames. A hatch opened. German soldiers started bailing out.

Anielewicz squeezed the trigger on his automatic rifle. One of the Germans threw out his arms, spun, and fell facedown. A lot of bullets were flying; Mordechai didn't know whether he'd been the one who killed the Nazi. He hoped so, though.

The Lizards didn't have a lot of troops on the ground—most of their males were in landcruisers. By themselves, they'd had trouble with the *Wehrmacht* when the conquest fleet first landed. The Nazis were a lot better armed now than they had been in 1942. That was why Jewish fighters and Poles served as a lot of the infantry in the fight against the German invaders.

"Gas!" The cry rang out in Yiddish, in Polish, and in the language of the Race at almost the same instant. Mordechai Anielewicz yanked out his mask and put it on with almost desperate haste. It wasn't complete protection against nerve gas; he knew that all too well. And he'd already had one dose of what the Germans had used during the last round of fighting against the Race. He didn't know how much he could take now without quietly falling over dead.

Maybe you'll get to find out, he thought, breathing in air that tasted of rubber through an activated-charcoal canister that gave him a pig-snouted look. If he'd been a proper kind of fighting leader, he wouldn't have been at the front at all. He would have been back in a headquarters somewhere tens of kilometers to the rear, with aides to peel him grapes and with dancing girls to pinch whenever he felt he needed a break from commanding.

But headquarters weren't necessarily safe these days, either. He couldn't think of any place in Poland that was necessarily safe. As soon as talks between the Race and the Germans broke down, he'd got his wife and children (and Heinrich's beffel) out of Lodz and into a hamlet called Widawa, southwest of the city. Widawa wasn't safe, either, and the knowledge that it wasn't ate at him. It was closer to the German border than Lodz was. He didn't want to think about what would happen if the Nazis overran the little town.

Trouble was, he also didn't want to think about what would happen if the Nazis hit Lodz with an explosive-metal missile. If they did, the city would go—and, probably, the fallout from the blast would blow east. Looked at that way, Widawa made more sense than a lot of other refuges.

Machine-gun bullets stitched the ground in front of Anielewicz, kicking up dirt that bounced off the lenses of his gas mask. He blinked as if the dirt had gone in his eye. If he did get an eyelash in his eye or something like that, he would have to live with it. If he took off the mask to get it out, he would die on account of it.

Another German panzer started burning. They didn't go up like bombs the way they had before, though. Back in the last round of fighting, they'd used gasoline-fueled engines. Now they ran on diesel fuel, as Russian tanks had even then, or on hydrogen, as Lizard landcruisers did.

But the Germans had a lot of panzers. The flame that burst from a machine near the one that had taken a hit was muzzle flash, not damage. And a Lizard landcruiser off to Anielewicz's right caught fire itself. Males of the Race bailed out, as German soldiers had a moment before. Mordechai grunted, though he could hardly hear himself inside the mask. In the last round of fighting, the Germans had counted on losing five or six of their best panzers for every Lizard landcruiser they knocked out. The ratio would have been higher than that, but the Nazis were tactically better than the Race, as they had been tactically better than the Red Army.

And now they had panzers that could stand against the landcruisers the Lizards had brought from Home. That wasn't a pretty thought.

But before Mordechai could do more than form it, it vanished from his mind. The day was typical of Polish springtime, with clouds covering the sun more often than not. All of a sudden, though, a sharp, black shadow stretched out ahead of Anielewicz, toward the west.

He whirled. There, right about where Lodz was—would have been—had been—a great apricot-and-salmon-colored cloud, utterly unlike the gray ones spawned by nature, climbed into the sky. Crying inside the gas mask, Mordechai rapidly discovered, was almost as bad as getting something in his eye in there. He blinked and blinked, trying to clear his vision.

"Yisgadal v'yiskadash shmay rabo—" he began: the Kaddish, the prayer for the dead. Looking around, he saw Polish fighting men making the sign of the cross. The expression was different, but the sentiment was the same.

The repulsively beautiful cloud rose and rose. Mordechai wondered how many other explosive-metal bombs were going off in Poland. Then he wondered how many would go off above the Greater German *Reich*. And then, with horror that truly chilled him, he wondered how many people would survive between the Pyrenees and the Russian border.

He wondered if he would be one of them, too. But that thought came only later.

"We've got to fall back," somebody near him bawled. "The Germans are cutting us off!"

How many times had that frightened cry rung out on battlefields throughout Europe during the last round of fighting? This was how the *Wehrmacht* worked its brutal magic: pierce the enemy line with armor, then either surround his soldiers or make him retreat. It had worked in Poland, in France, in Russia. Why wouldn't it work again?

Anielewicz couldn't see any reason why it wouldn't work

again, not if the Nazis had broken through—and they had. "Form a rear guard!" he shouted. "We have to slow them down."

He fired at a German infantryman, who dove for cover. But more Germans kept coming, infantrymen following the panzers into the hole the armored machines had broken in the defenders' line. The Nazis had been doing that since 1939; they'd had more practice than any other human army in the world.

However much practice they had at it, though, not everything went their way. The Poles hated them as much as ever, and didn't like retreating. And the Jewish fighters whom Anielewicz led hated retreating and wouldn't be captured. They knew—those of his generation from the bitterest personal experience—the fate of Jews who fell into German hands.

German jets raced low over the battlefield, spraying it with rockets and rapid-firing cannon shells. They didn't have it all their own way, either; the Lizards' killercraft replied in kind, and were better in quality. But the Germans had been building like men obsessed—were men obsessed—and had more airplanes, as they had more panzers. Step by step, the defenders of Poland were forced back.

"What are we going to do?" one of Anielewicz's fighters asked him. Seen through the lenses of his gas mask, the man's eyes were wide with horror.

"Keep fighting," Mordechai answered. "I don't know what else we can do."

"What if the Poles give way?" the Jew demanded.

"They won't," Anielewicz said. "They've fought well. They'd better be fighting well. We have to have 'em—there are a lot more of them than there are of us." All the same, he worried, not so much that the Poles would throw in the towel as at the command structure, or lack of same, of the defenders. He commanded his Jews, the Poles led their own, and the Lizards, while theoretically in charge of everybody, were a lot more diffident than they might have been.

Whatever command problems the Germans might have had, diffidence wasn't one of them.

Battered by superior force, the defenders fell back toward Lodz—or rather, toward what had been Lodz. Before long, they began running into refugees streaming out from the city. Some of those plainly wouldn't last long: they were vomiting blood, and their hair fell out in clumps. They'd been far too close to the bomb; its radiation was killing them. Anielewicz had never seen burns like those in all his life. It was as if some of their faces had been melted to slag.

Some people were blind in one eye, some in both. That was a matter of luck, depending on the direction in which they'd happened to face when the bomb went off. Some were burned on one side but not the other, the shadow of their own bodies having protected them from the hideous flash of light.

And, bad off as they were, they told stories of worse horrors closer to the explosion. "Everything's melted down flat," an elderly Polish man said. "Just flat, with only little bits of things sticking out from what looks like glass. It's not glass, I don't guess. What it is is, it's what everything got melted down into, you know what I mean?"

A woman, a badly burned woman who probably wouldn't live, had her own tale: "I came out of what was left of my house, and there was my neighbor's wall next door. All the paint got burned off it—except where she'd been standing. I don't know what happened to her. I never saw her again. I think she burned up instead of that stretch of the wall, and all that was left of her was her silhouette."

"Here—drink," Mordechai said, and gave her water from his canteen. He thanked God his own family was in Widawa. Maybe they would live. If they'd stayed in Lodz, they would surely be dead.

Because the refugees filled the roads, they made fighting and moving harder. But then, to Anielewicz's delighted surprise, the German onslaught slowed. He and his comrades and the Lizards contained them well short of Lodz. Before long, he ran into someone with a radio who'd been listening to reports of how the wider war was going.

"Breslau," the fellow said. The Germans had set off an explosive-metal bomb east of it in the last round of fighting. It wasn't the Germans this time: it was the Race's turn. "Peenemünde. Leignitz. Frankfurt on the Oder." He tolled the roll of devastation. "Olmütz. Kreuzberg. Neustettin."

A light went on in Anielewicz's head. "No wonder the Germans have stalled. The Race is bombing all their cities near the border. They must be having the devil's time getting supplies through."

"That's not all the Race is bombing," the man with the radio answered. "The Lizards aren't playing the game halfway this time."

"Will there be anything left of the world when they're through?" Mordechai asked.

"I don't know about the world," the man answered. "But I'll tell you this: there won't be much left of the goddamn Greater German *Reich*."

Mordechai Anielewicz said, "Good."

So far, the Deutsche had aimed four missiles at Cairo. The Race had knocked down two. One warhead had failed to detonate. And even the explosive-metal bomb that had gone off exploded a good distance east of the city. All things considered, it could have been much worse, and Atvar knew it.

He swung an eye turret toward Kirel. "They thought we would be meek and mild and forbearing," he said. "Not this time. They miscalculated. In spite of all our warnings, they miscalculated. And now they are going to pay for it."

"Indeed, Exalted Fleetlord." Kirel pointed toward the map on the monitor in front of Atvar. "They have paid for it already."

"Not yet," Atvar said. "Not enough. This time, we are going to make a proper example of them."

"By the time we are through with the *Reich*, nothing will be left of it," Kirel said.

"Good," Atvar said coldly. "The Deutsche have troubled us altogether too much in the past. We—I—have been far too patient. The time for patience is past. In the future, the Deutsche shall not trouble us again."

Kirel ordered a different map up on the monitor. "They have also done us considerable damage in the present conflict."

Atvar sighed. "That, unfortunately, was to be expected. With their orbiting weapons and with those fired from their submersible boats, the time between launch and detonation is very short. Our colonies on the island continent and on the central peninsula of the main continental mass have suffered, as have those west of here."

"And our orbiting starships," Kirel said.

"And our orbiting starships," Atvar agreed. "And also Poland, very heavily, which is unfortunate."

"We might have done better not to settle so many colonists in

Poland," Atvar admitted. "The only reason we ended up administering the subregion was that none of the Tosevite factions involved in the area would admit that any of the others had the right to control it. To reduce the chances of an outbreak, we kept it—and see what our reward was for that."

" 'Reward' is hardly the term I would use, Exalted Fleetlord," Kirel said.

Pshing came into Atvar's office, which had become the command post for the Race's war against the *Reich*. "Exalted Fleetlord, our monitors have just picked up a new broadcast from the not-emperor of the Deutsche."

"Oh, a pestilence!" Atvar burst out. "We have expended several warheads on Nuremberg. I had hoped their command and control would be utterly disrupted by now. We shall just have to keep trying, that is all. Well, Pshing? What does the Big Ugly say?"

"His tone remains defiant, Exalted Fleetlord," his adjutant replied. "Translation indicates he still predicts ultimate victory for his side."

"He is as addled as an egg twenty days past hatching in the hot sun," Atvar said.

"Unfortunately, Exalted Fleetlord, he is not so addled as to have failed to take shelter against our attacks, at least not yet," Kirel said. "We kept getting reports that the Deutsche were constructing elaborate subterranean shelters. Those reports, if anything, appear to have been understatements."

"So they do," Atvar said. "And the Deutsche appear to have continued all the ruthlessness they displayed in the earlier fighting. You will recall that we hoped some of their subject allies would desert them?"

"Yes, Exalted Fleetlord," Kirel said. "And one of those not-empires—the one called Romania, wasn't it?—did attempt to do so."

"Yes, that not-empire attempted to do so," Atvar said, "whereupon the Deutsche detonated an explosive-metal bomb above its largest city. That not-empire, or what is left of it, now loudly proclaims its loyalty to the *Reich*, and the other subject allies are too terrified to do anything but obey."

"How much more harm can the Deutsche do us, Exalted Fleetlord?" Pshing asked.

"Their armies in Poland are already faltering for lack of supplies and reinforcements," Atvar replied. "Most of their facilities in space have been destroyed, as have as many of their ground-based launch sites as we could hunt down. Those submersible boats of theirs are our greatest problem now. Every so often, they will surface, throw more missiles, and then disappear again. And, once submerged, the miserable things are almost impossible to detect or destroy."

"In short," Kirel said, "they can go on hurting us for a while. They have no hope—none whatsoever—of defeating us."

Atvar made the affirmative gesture. "That is the truth at the yolk of the egg. Bit by bit, they are being smashed. They have harmed us, but they will be in no condition to keep on harming us much longer."

"And that is as it should be," Pshing said. An alert light appeared on the monitor. "I will answer your telephone in the antechamber," Pshing told the fleetlord, and hurried away. A moment later, he came back. "Exalted Fleetlord, it is the ambassador from the not-empire of the United States. He requests an immediate audience."

"Find out what he wants," Atvar said.

Pshing disappeared again. When he came back, he said, "He seeks terms for a cease-fire between the Race and the *Reich*."

"Is the *Reich* seeking to surrender and to yield itself to us?" Atvar asked. "Is he coming at the request of the Deutsch government?"

"I shall inquire." Pshing duly did so, then reported, "No, Exalted Fleetlord. His mover is his own not-emperor, seeking to end the war."

"Tell him I will not see him under those circumstances," Atvar replied. "If the Deutsche want to end the war, they can ask us for terms. No one else may do so. Tell him just that."

"It shall be done," Pshing said. When he came back this time, though, he sounded worried: "The ambassador says the American not-emperor will take a very dim view of our refusal to discuss terms with his representative."

"Does he?" Atvar let out an unhappy hiss. If the United States got angry enough to join the fighting, especially without much warning, victory looked much less secure, and the Race would suffer much more damage. The fleetlord changed his mind.

"Very well, then. He may come. Pick some reasonably short amount of time from now and tell him to arrive then."

"It shall be done," Pshing said, and made the arrangement.

Henry Cabot Lodge entered the fleetlord's office at precisely the appointed time. Even for a Tosevite, he was unusually tall and unusually erect. He spoke the language of the Race with a heavy accent, but was fluent enough. "I greet you, Exalted Fleetlord," he said, and bent into the posture of respect.

"I greet you, and I greet your not-emperor through you," Atvar replied. "What message does he wish to convey through you?"

"That you have punished the Deutsche enough," the American Big Ugly replied. "They cannot take Poland, their facilities in space are badly damaged, and their homeland is a shambles. President Warren strongly feels any more attacks against them would be superfluous."

"If your not-emperor sat in my chair, he would have a different opinion." Atvar stressed that with an emphatic cough, to show how sure he was. "He would aim to be certain the Deutsche could never menace him again, which is what we aim to do now."

"How was the *Hermann Göring* menacing you?" Henry Cabot Lodge asked. "In no way anyone could see, and yet you destroyed it."

"We do not know what the Deutsch spacecraft was doing or would be doing," Atvar replied. "We were not interested in taking a chance and finding out, either." He turned both eye turrets toward the Big Ugly. "We do not know what the *Lewis and Clark* is doing, either," he added pointedly.

"Whatever it is doing, it is none of the Race's concern," Lodge said, and used an emphatic cough of his own. "If you interfere with its operation in any way or attack it, the United States will reckon that an act of war, and we will answer with every means at our disposal. Do I make myself plain?"

"You do." Atvar seethed, but did his best not to show it. Before he'd gone into cold sleep, he'd never imagined he would have to submit to such insolence from a Tosevite. "But let me also make one thing clear to you. You are not a party to the dispute between the Race and the *Reich*. Because you are not a party, you would be well advised to remove your snout from the dispute, or it will be bitten. Do *I* make myself plain?"

"Events all over this planet are the concern of the United States."

"Oh?" Atvar spoke in a soft, menacing tone; he wondered if the Big Ugly could perceive that. "Do you consider yourself a party to this dispute, then? Is your not-empire declaring war on the Race? You had better make yourself very, very plain."

Lodge licked his fleshy lips, a sign of stress among the Tosevites. "No, we are not declaring war," he said at last. "We are trying to arrange a just and lasting peace."

"The Race will attend to that," Atvar answered. "Battering the Deutsche to the point where they are not dangerous to us is the best way I can think of to make certain the peace endures. And that peace will last, would you not agree?"

"Perhaps that peace will," Lodge said. "But you will also frighten the United States and the Soviet Union. Is that what you want? I know the Deutsche have hurt you. How much could we and the SSSR hurt you? Do you want to make us more likely to fight you? You may do that."

"How?" Atvar was genuinely curious. "Will you not think, *If we fight the Race, we will get what the* Reich *got?* Surely any sensible beings would think along those lines."

"Perhaps," Lodge said, "but perhaps not, too." His features were not so still as Molotov's or Gromyko's, but he revealed little. "We might think, *The Race will believe we have so much fear that it can make any demand at all upon us. We had better fight, to show that belief is mistaken.*"

Atvar didn't answer right away. Given what he knew of Tosevite psychology, the American ambassador's comment had an unpleasant ring of probability to it. But he could not admit as much without yielding more ground than he wanted. "We shall have to take that chance," he said. "Is there anything more?"

"No, Exalted Fleetlord," Lodge said. "I shall send your words back to President Warren. I fear he will be disappointed."

"I do not relish this war myself. It was forced on me," Atvar answered. "But now that I have it, I intend to win it. Is that clear?"

"Yes, that is clear." Lodge's sigh sounded much like that which might have come from a male of the Race. "But I will also say that your reply is a personal disappointment to me. I had hoped for better from the Race."

"And I had hoped for better from the Deutsche," Atvar said. "I warned them what would happen if they chose conflict. They did not care to believe me. Now they are paying for their error—and they deserve to pay for their error."

Before the American ambassador could reply, Pshing burst in and said, "Exalted Fleetlord, a Deutsch missile has just got through our defenses and wrecked Istanbul!"

"Oh, a plague!" Atvar cried. "That makes resupplying Poland all the more difficult." He turned both eye turrets back to Henry Cabot Lodge. "You see, Ambassador, that the Deutsche do not yet believe the war to be over. If they do not, I cannot, either. Goodbye." For a wonder, Lodge left without another word.

Not for the first time, Sam Yeager spoke reassuringly to his wife: "He's all right, hon. There's the message." He pointed to the computer monitor. "Read it yourself—he's fine. Nothing bad has happened to him." *As a matter of fact, he's probably screwing himself silly and having the time of his life.* He didn't say that to Barbara.

She wasn't reassured, either. "He shouldn't be up there in the first place," she said. "He ought to be down here in L.A., where it's safe."

Yeager sighed. Barbara was probably right. "I really didn't think the Germans would be dumb enough to start a war with the Lizards. Honest, I didn't."

"Well, you should have," Barbara said. "And you should have put your foot down and kept him from going, especially since you know the main thing he was going up there to do."

"It's one way to get to know somebody. Sometimes it's the fastest way to get to know somebody." Sam raised an eyebrow. "It worked like that for us, if you want to think back about it."

Barbara turned red. All she cared to remember these days was that she was respectably married, and had been for a long time. She didn't like remembering that she'd started sleeping with Sam during the fighting, when she'd thought her then-husband dead. She especially didn't like remembering that she'd married Sam not long before finding out her then-husband remained very much alive. Maybe the marriage wasn't so perfectly respectable after all.

If she hadn't got pregnant right away, she would have gone back to Jens Larssen in a red-hot minute, too, Sam thought. He'd heard Larssen had come to a hard, bad end later on. Sometimes he wondered what would have happened if Barbara had gone back to Jens. Would the physicist not have gone off the deep end? No way to tell. No way to know. Sam was pretty sure *he* would have been a lot less happy had she chosen the other way, though.

Barbara said, "What on earth are we going to tell Karen?"

"The only thing I'm going to tell her is that Jonathan's fine," Sam answered. "I've already told her that. I hope to heaven that's the only thing you're going to tell her, too. If Jonathan wants to tell her anything else, that's his business. Not yours. Not mine. His. His girlfriend is his problem. He's twenty-one."

"So he kept telling us." Barbara hardly bothered hiding her bitterness. "But he's living under our roof—"

"Not at the moment," Sam put in.

"And whose fault is that?" his wife demanded. "He couldn't have gone if you hadn't let him."

"It would have been harder," Yeager admitted. "But I think he would have managed it. And if we had put our feet down, he'd be mad at us for years. When would this chance have come along again?"

"This chance for what?" Barbara asked. "To go into space, or to go into . . . ?" She broke off, grimacing. "Now you've got me doing it."

"Sooner or later, the Nazis will run out of upper stages and or- biting bombs," Sam said. "Then it'll be safe for the Lizards to let Jonathan come home."

"In the meantime, I'll go out of my mind worrying," Barbara said.

"He's fine," Yeager said. "He'll be fine." He'd been saying that all along. Sometimes, on good days, he managed to convince himself for a little while. Most of the time, he was as nearly out of his mind with worry as his wife was. Long training in the minor leagues and in the Army had taught him not to show whether or not things were going his way at any given moment. That didn't mean he lacked feelings, only that he kept them in- side more than Barbara did.

"He never should have gone up there." Barbara glanced at the message—the very reassuring message—on the computer screen, shook her head, and strode out of the study.

Yeager left the connection to the Race's electronic network and went back to review messages he'd received in the past. The one he'd got from Straha a little before the Germans attacked Poland stuck in his mind. He examined it yet again, trying to extract fresh meaning from the shiplord's oracular phrases.

He had no great luck. He'd been wondering for some time whether his own superiors had it in for him. He had to wonder, since none of the people who'd tried to do bad things to his family and him suffered any great punishment. Some of those people hadn't suffered anything at all that he knew of—the fellow with the Molotov cocktail, for instance.

And how had Straha got wind of this? Probably from the hard-nosed fellow who did his errands for him. Sam wouldn't have wanted to wind up on that guy's bad side, not even a little he wouldn't.

The next interesting question was, how much did the Lizard's man Friday know about such things? Sam realized he might know a great deal. To work for Straha, he had to have a pretty high security clearance. He also had to know a good deal about the Race. Put those together, and the odds were that he knew quite a bit about Lieutenant Colonel Sam Yeager.

"How can I find out what he knows?" Yeager muttered. Inviting the fellow over and pumping him while they drank beer didn't strike him as the best idea he'd ever had. He didn't think it would do any good, and it would make the man suspicious. Of that Sam had no doubt whatever. Anybody who did what Straha's factotum did was bound to be suspicious for a living.

I'll have to operate through Straha, Yeager realized. He started to telephone the defector, but then checked himself. Straha hadn't phoned him, but had used the Race's electronic network to pass on the message. Did that mean Straha thought his own phone was tapped, or did he worry about Yeager's? Sam didn't know, and didn't care for either alternative.

He reconnected to the Lizards' network and asked, *Did you learn of my difficulties with my superiors from your driver?*

He stared at the screen, as if expecting the answer to appear immediately. As a matter of fact, he had expected the answer to appear immediately, and felt foolish because of it. Straha had a right to be doing something other than sitting around waiting for a message from a Big Ugly named Sam Yeager.

As long as Yeager was hooked up to the Race's electronic network, he checked the news feeds the Lizards were giving one another. By what they were saying, they'd squashed Germany flat, and everything was over but for the mopping up. *Scattered Deutsch units still refuse to acknowledge their inevitable defeat, but their resistance must soon come to an end.*

That wasn't the song the Nazis were singing. The Race hadn't been able to knock out all their radio transmitters. They claimed they were still advancing in Poland. They also claimed to have smashed the ground attacks the Lizards had made into southern France. Since the Lizards had stopped talking about those attacks a couple of days before, Yeager suspected German radio was telling the truth there.

It probably didn't matter, though. A map came up on the screen, showing where the Lizards had tossed explosive-metal bombs at the *Reich*. Showing where the Race hadn't sent them probably would have resulted in fewer marks on the display. Germany and its European puppets were going to glow in the dark for a long time to come. Before long, the Nazis would have to run out of men and equipment . . . wouldn't they?

The Race didn't show maps of where German explosive-metal bombs had hit. With his connections, Sam had seen some: rather more accurate versions than the papers were printing. Poland was wrecked, of course, but the Germans' submarines had managed surprisingly heavy blows against the new cities that had sprung up in Australia and the Arabian peninsula and North Africa—with the strong German presence in the Mediterranean, those last had been hit repeatedly. Without a doubt, the *Reich* had suffered and was suffering worse, but the Lizards had taken a pounding.

While that thought was still going through his mind, he got the warning hiss that told of an electronic message arriving. He checked to see who'd sent it: it could have been from Straha; from Kassquit, relaying news from Jonathan; or from Sorviss, the Lizard exile who'd first gained access to the network for him. He hadn't yet used what he'd got from Sorviss, so he couldn't very well give him any proper answer.

But the message turned out to be from Straha. *Yes, I received this information, this warning, from Gordon,* the ex-shiplord wrote. *I hope you will use it wisely.*

I thank you, Yeager wrote back. *I think I can do that.*

He chuckled under his breath. "What a liar I'm getting to be in my old age," he muttered. He knew what Straha meant by using the information wisely: staying out of things his own superiors thought were none of his business. He'd never been good at that, not when his itch to know wanted scratching. If things went wrong with what he was about to try, he'd land in even more hot water.

With a snort, he shook his head. People had already tried to kill him and burn down his house. How could he get into worse trouble than that?

After turning off the Lizard-made computer he used to join the Race's electronic network, he removed his artificial finger-claws and turned on the larger, clumsier American-built machine he used much less often. Its only advantage he could see was that it used a keyboard much like an ordinary typewriter's.

Even though it was made in the USA, it used a lot of technology adapted from what the Race also used. When he inserted the *skelkwank* disk he'd got from Sorviss, the computer accepted it without any fuss. The Lizard was convinced his coding would defeat any traps mere inexperienced humans could devise. Sam was interested in seeing if he was right.

Somewhere in the rudimentary American computer network lay an archive he'd tried to access a couple of times before, an archive of communications and radio intercepts covering the time just before and after the surprise attack that had done the colonization fleet so much harm. *Less harm than the Germans have done it now,* he thought, but that wasn't really what mattered, not any more. What mattered was that he'd tried repeatedly to access the archive and failed every time. And bad things had happened after every try, too.

By now, he wanted to know what was in there as much for his own sake as because he wanted to see whoever'd bombed the colonization fleet punished. *Curiosity killed the cat,* he thought. His own curiosity might well have come close to killing him. But the proverb had another line, too. *Satisfaction brought it back.*

There was the archive. He'd made it this far a couple of times—and the screen had gone blank as he'd been disconnected from the network. The first time, he'd thought that an accident. He didn't think so any more.

His computer started making small purring noises. He suspected he knew what that was: Sorviss' coding at war against the measures the government had set up to keep unwelcome visitors out of the archive. If humans had learned more about computers than Sorviss thought, Sam might be in live steam, not just hot water.

For a second, the screen started to go dark. He cursed—softly, so Barbara wouldn't notice. But then it cleared. ENTRY AUTHORIZED, it read. PROCEED. Proceed he did. As he read, his eyes got wider and wider. He finished, then left the archive at once. For good measure, he turned off the computer, too.

"Jesus!" he said, shaken as he hadn't been since watching a teammate get beaned. "What the hell do I do now?"

The first thing Nesseref did when she got up in the morning was check her computer monitor. That was the first thing she did any morning, of course, to see what the news was and what electronic messages had come in during the night. But she had a more urgent reason for checking it today: she wanted to find out what the fallout level was, to see if she could safely leave her block of flats.

She let out an unhappy hiss. It was very radioactive out there this morning. Were it not for the filters and scrubbers newly installed in the heating and air purification systems, it would have been very radioactive inside the apartment, too. The Deutsche were taking quite a pounding. In the abstract, Nesseref didn't mind that at all. But the prevailing winds on Tosev 3 blew from west to east. They brought the radioactive ashes from the *Reich*'s funeral pyre straight into Poland.

And the Deutsche had also managed to detonate several explosive-metal bombs of their own inside Poland. Those only made the fallout level worse. They'd also done a lot of damage to Tosevite centers and to those of the Race in this subregion.

Lodz had gone up in a hideous, beautiful cloud. Nesseref wondered if the Big Ugly called Mordechai Anielewicz remained among the living. She hoped so. She also wished his youngest hatchling well—she'd met young Heinrich, after all, and heard about his beffel. Her concern for the rest of Anielewicz's family was considerably more abstract. They mattered to her not for their own sakes but because her friend would be concerned if anything happened to them.

Orbit came up and turned an eye turret toward the screen, as if the tsiongi were examining the fallout levels, too. His other eye turret swung toward Nesseref. When she made no move to take him outside for a walk, he let out a dismayed hiss of his own. No matter how he looked at the monitor, he couldn't understand what the numbers displayed on it meant.

Unfortunately, Nesseref could. "We cannot go walking today," she said, and scratched him between the eye turrets. She'd said that so often lately, Orbit was starting to know what it meant. This time, the look he gave her was halfway between dismayed and speculative, as if he was wondering whether biting her on the tail-stump might get her to change her mind. She waggled a fore-finger at him. "Do not even think about it. I am the mistress. You are the pet. Remember your place in the hierarchy."

Orbit hissed again, as if to remind her that, while inferiors were bound to respect superiors, superiors had responsibilities to inferiors. One of her responsibilities was taking the tsiongi for a walk whenever she could. She'd never been home and still failed to take him out for such a long time. As far as he could see, she was falling down on the job.

The trouble was, Orbit couldn't see far enough. "Suppose I feed you?" Nesseref told him. "Will that make you happier?"

He wasn't smart enough to understand what she'd said, but he followed her out of the bedchamber and into the kitchen. When she pulled a tin of food from the shelf reserved for him, his tail lashed up and down, slapping the floor again and again. He knew what that meant.

She opened the tin. The food plopped into his dish. He started eating, then paused and turned an eye turret toward her. "I know," she said. "It is not just what you would get back on Home. It is made from the flesh of Tosevite animals, and it probably tastes funny to you. But it is what I have. You can eat it, or you can go hungry. Those are your only choices. I cannot give you what I do not have."

Orbit kept on giving her that reproachful stare, but he kept on eating, too: he kept on eating till the bowl was empty. Nesseref knew the food was nutritionally adequate for tsiongyu; the label on the tin assured her of that. But Orbit hadn't evolved eating the beasts from which the food was made. Animals were even more conservative than males and females of the Race. If something was unfamiliar to them, they were inclined to reject it.

Nesseref heated a slice of smoked and salted pork for herself. She found ham and bacon quite tasty, even if they weren't salty enough to suit her. After she'd eaten, she went back into the bedroom and ordered an exercise wheel for Orbit. It would take up a lot of space in the apartment, but it would also go a long way toward keeping the tsiongi healthy and happy.

When she entered her name and location, a signal flashed onto the screen. *Due to the present unfortunate emergency,* it read, *delivery of the ordered item is subject to indefinite delay.*

"Oh, go break an egg!" she snarled at the monitor. If only she could get out of her apartment, she could walk to the pet shop where she'd bought Orbit, buy an exercise wheel, and carry it back. But if she could walk to the pet shop, she could walk Orbit, too, and then she wouldn't need the wheel.

Your account will not be debited until the ordered item is delivered, the computer told her. *Thank you for your patience and cooperation during the present unfortunate emergency.*

"It is not an emergency," she said. "It is a war." She knew a war when she got stuck almost in the middle of one. She'd never expected to do that, not when she'd gone into cold sleep in orbit around Home. Everything about Tosev 3 had turned out to be different from what she'd expected.

She went over to the window and looked out to the streets that were so silently, so invisibly, dangerous. Far fewer motorcars and other vehicles moved in them than they usually held. The ones that did move had all their windows rolled up. Some of them, she knew, boasted air-filtration systems of their own. Even so, she was glad to be inside here.

At the moment, she couldn't launch out of the local shuttle-craft port even had she wanted to. Deutsch aircraft had pounded the site, doing their best to smash up all of the once-smooth landing surface. Repair efforts were supposed to be under way, but the radioactivity had inhibited them, and airfields had higher priority because more supplies and reinforcements went through them than through shuttlecraft ports, and there was generally too much to do and not enough with which to do it.

She was still peering out the window when a convoy of ambulances came racing into the new town from out of the west. Warning lights flickered atop them. Even through the double-paned insulated window, their alarm hisses hammered Nesseref's hearing diaphragms. They sped on toward the hospital a few blocks away.

She marveled that the hospital hadn't been overwhelmed; war produced injuries on a scale she'd never imagined till now.

Orbit came up and stood on his hind legs, leaning his forepaws on the glass so he could get his head up high enough to see out. Nesseref scratched him on the muzzle; he shot out his tongue and licked her hand. She wondered what he made of the view, and thought he'd come over mostly because he wanted companionship: like befflem, tsiongyu paid more attention to scent than to sight.

Other alarms began to hiss. A voice from the computer monitor shouted stridently: "Air raid! Take cover! Deutsch air raid! Take cover at once!"

Nesseref said, "Come on, Orbit!" She dove under the bed. The new town had been attacked before; she knew how terrifying that could be.

Antiaircraft missiles roared out of launchers around the town. Antiaircraft guns—some made by the Race, others of Tosevite manufacture but pressed into service all the same—began to bark and crash.

And then, above those barking crashes, she heard the screams from the jet engines of several Deutsch killercraft. That the Deutsche should have killercraft with jet engines still struck her as wrong, unnatural, even though she'd been on Tosev 3 for several years now. That she should be a target for those killercraft stuck her as a great deal worse. If one of the bombs they dropped struck her building, if one of the shells they fired struck her . . .

She didn't want to think about that. It was hard not to, though, when bombs burst in the town and when shells started slamming into the building. It shuddered, as if in an earthquake. Fortunately, it was harder to set on fire than a Tosevite structure. *But fallout is getting in,* Nesseref thought.

Even before the all-clear sounded, she left the shelter that probably wouldn't have done her much good and stuffed plastic sheeting under the door. She didn't know how much it would help; if polluted air was getting in through the ducts, it wouldn't do much of anything. But it couldn't hurt.

Orbit was intrigued. Nesseref had to speak sharply to keep the tsiongi from dragging away the plastic she'd used. The animal's answering stare was reproachful. She'd had the fun of putting the plastic down. Why wouldn't she let him have the fun of pulling it up again?

"Because it might not be healthy for either one of us if you did," Nesseref told her pet. That made no sense at all to Orbit. She'd known it wouldn't.

An ambulance hissed up in front of her building. Along with its flashing lights, she saw, it also had a red cross painted on top of it. That was no symbol the Race used; it belonged to the Big Uglies. It meant the vehicle was used only to aid the sick and injured, and so was not a proper military target.

Workers leaped out of the ambulance and ran skittering into the apartment building. When they came out again, they carried wounded males and females on stretchers or helped them get into the ambulance under their own power. The wounded left behind streaks and pools of blood Nesseref could see even from her upper-story flat. She turned away, more than a little sickened. She'd never imagined seeing so much blood, except perhaps at a rare traffic accident.

She swung an eye turret toward the monitor. *This building's filtration system is still functional,* she read. *Damaged windows are being resealed as rapidly as possible. Please remain calm.*

"Damaged windows!" Nesseref's mouth fell open in sardonic laughter. Did—could—anyone think the Deutsch cannon shells had penetrated only through window glass? They could have gone through the outer walls just as easily—and through several inner walls, too.

Anyone who thought would be able to see that in the flick of a nictitating membrane across an eyeball. *But how many males and females feel like thinking right now?* Nesseref wondered. *How many will just want to seize any reassurance they can find?*

Nesseref sighed. Colonists hadn't come to Tosev 3 expecting the conquest to be continuing here. They'd come to reconstruct lives as much like those back on Home as they could make them. She wondered how they would react to being plunged into the chaos of war. By all she'd seen, Big Uglies took it for granted. That wasn't so among her own kind—far from it.

The Deutsche will never have another chance to do this to us, she thought. But what of the other independent not-empires? If they didn't walk soft, they would be sorry. She was sure of that.

☆ **20** ☆

Back in South Africa, Gorppet had more ginger than he knew what to do with. When the Race uprooted him from the comfortable post he'd won as a reward for capturing the fanatic named Khomeini, he'd brought barely enough to Poland to keep himself happy for a little while. And most of what he had, he couldn't taste. He'd learned during the last round of fighting that a male who tasted too often thought he was braver and smarter and more nearly invulnerable than he really was. He usually found out his mistake by finding himself dead.

Gorppet had learned all sorts of things during the fighting. That, of course, was why the Race had summoned him back to combat. He could have done without the honor. He'd already given the Big Uglies too many chances to kill or maim him. That was his view of the matter, anyhow. As far as his superiors were concerned, he was just one more munition, to be expended as necessary.

At the moment, he waited in a barn that smelled powerfully of Tosevite animals. A regiment leader was briefing him and a good many other lower-ranking officers: "We can expect this latest Deutsch thrust to exhaust itself before long. The Big Uglies' ability to resupply is almost entirely destroyed."

"Superior sir!" Gorppet signaled for attention.

"Yes? What is it, Small-Unit Group Leader?" the officer asked.

"Superior sir, did you ever run up against the Deutsche during the last round of fighting?" Gorppet asked.

"No," the regimental leader admitted. "I served on the lesser continental mass then."

"Well, then, superior sir, all I can tell you is, don't count them

588

out of anything till you see them all dead. And be careful even then—they may be shamming," Gorppet said. "They are much tougher, male for male, than the Russkis or than any other kind of Big Ugly I can think of."

"I assure you, I have been thoroughly informed as to their proclivities," the regiment leader said. "I can also assure you that I know whereof I speak. We shall deal with them here in short order."

He spoke as if he knew everything there was to know. He probably thought he did. That meant he either hadn't seen hard fighting over on the lesser continental mass or had forgotten what it was like. Knowing he was wasting his time, Gorppet tried again: "The Deutsche, superior sir—"

"Are broken," the regiment leader said firmly. "Let us have no further doubts on that score. Do I make myself clear?"

"Yes, superior sir." Gorppet knew he sounded resigned and imperfectly subordinate, but had trouble caring. The regiment leader outranked him, but that didn't mean the fellow kept his brains anywhere but his cloaca.

And then, to Gorppet's astonishment, another male spoke up: "Superior sir, the small-unit group leader is right. As long as the Deutsche are in the field, they are dangerous. Underestimating them will do nothing but get good males killed to no purpose. I mean no disrespect when I say this, for it is a manifest truth."

In a deadly voice, the regiment leader said, "Give me your name, Mid-Group Leader. Your statement will go on the record."

"Very well, superior sir: I am Shazzer," the other male replied.

The regiment leader spoke into a computer hookup. There, all too probably, went Shazzer's reputation and hope for advancement. They would surely be gone if the regiment leader turned out to be right. They were also likely doomed even if the regiment leader turned out to be wrong. The Race did not like those who disagreed with duly constituted authority. The regiment leader's eye turrets swung toward Gorppet. "Give me your name, too, Small-Unit Group Leader."

"Superior sir, I am Gorppet," he answered. He'd never expected to become an officer. If he stopped being one, the eggshell of his world wouldn't shatter.

"Gorppet," the regiment leader repeated, this time into the computer hookup. Having finished that, he continued, "Now let us turn to the business at hand: wiping out the surviving remnants of the Deutsche."

"It shall be done, superior sir," the assembled officers chorused. Gorppet mouthed the words along with the rest, though they were bitter on his tongue. He longed for ginger to rid himself of their taste, but made himself hold back.

Out of the barn trooped the officers. Gorppet checked his radiation meter. This particular area wasn't doing too badly; he didn't need a breathing mask, let alone protective wrappings. The winds blowing the radioactive wreckage of the *Reich* to the east had been relatively kind here.

As the officers began to scatter and return to their units, Gorppet hurried over to Shazzer and said, "I thank you, superior sir, for what you tried to do in there. I fear you did not help yourself by doing it."

Shazzer shrugged. "You spoke plain truth, Gorppet. Any male who has ever fought the Deutsche knows you spoke plain truth. Only pity is, we could not make that male see it." He sounded not in the least concerned about what would happen to him.

Before Gorppet could say how much he admired that, aircraft streaked toward him out of the west. Concern about careers suddenly evaporated. "Those are Deutsch!" he shouted, and dove into a shell crater.

Shazzer dove in right behind him. Some of the other males were slower to take cover. Flames rippled under the wings of the enemy killercraft. "Rockets!" Shazzer screamed. He tried to scrabble deeper into the earth. Gorppet didn't blame him. He was trying to do the same thing.

The killercraft wailed past and were gone. Gorppet stuck up his head and looked around for the regiment leader who'd said the Deutsche were at the end of their tether. He didn't spot him. Maybe that meant the optimistic officer had found himself a hole in the ground, too. Maybe it meant he'd been blown to bits. Gorppet didn't much care, one way or the other.

He didn't keep his head up very long, either. Hisses in the air rose swiftly to shrieks. He shrieked, too: "Artillery!" He dove down into the crater once more.

He thought the shells that burst around him were of heavier caliber than most of the ones the Big Uglies had thrown during the last round of fighting. He cursed. The Race's artillery remained essentially the same as it had been when Home was unified a hundred thousand years before. Why change? It did the job well enough. The Big Uglies, unfortunately, didn't think that way.

Splinters whined overhead. The ground shook under Gorppet's prostrate body, reminding him of the earthquakes he'd known when stationed in Basra and Baghdad. Shazzer said, "I think these are all explosive shells. The ones with gas in them sound different when they burst."

"Praise the spirits of Emperors past for small favors," Gorppet said. "I truly hate the masks we have to wear to protect ourselves against the gas."

"And who does not?" the other veteran officer replied. "But I hate dying even more."

"Truth," Gorppet agreed.

If the Deutsche were short on ammunition, the bombardment they laid down gave no sign of it. Shells fell from the sky like rain. Shazzer said, "They are going to try to break through here. They would not be pounding us so hard if they were not."

"How can they do that?" Gorppet said mockingly. "We have smashed them. They are completely destroyed. The regiment leader has said so."

Shazzer laughed—it was either laugh or curse. "I do not think the regiment leader bothered informing the Deutsche of this fact—if it is a fact."

"I wish I could get back to my small group," Gorppet said. "They should have their commander with them."

"You would not last long if you climbed out of this hole," Shazzer said. "Have you never seen that, without its officers, a small group often fights about as well under the command of its underofficers? I would not say that to every male, but you do not strike me as the sort it would insult."

"No, superior sir, it does not insult me," Gorppet answered. "I have been an ordinary trooper and an underofficer myself. I never expected to be anything more. My opinion of officers is not far removed from yours."

"Then trust your soldiers," Shazzer said. "I think we may have to do some fighting of our own here."

Sure enough, Big Uglies started falling back past the barn

where the regiment leader had held his briefing. They were not Deutsche: they were the local Tosevites, as loyal to the Race as any Big Uglies were. But if they had to retreat, that meant the Deutsche were advancing. "I wish we had more landcruisers in the neighborhood," Gorppet said fretfully, "more landcruisers and more antilandcruiser rockets."

With a shrug, Shazzer answered, "The Deutsche previously concentrated their efforts farther south, in the direction of the city of Lodz—or what was the city of Lodz. Naturally, we concentrated our resources there, too."

"Naturally," Gorppet said bitterly. "And then the Big Uglies shifted their forces and did something we failed to anticipate. This has happened too many times."

Before Shazzer could reply, a clanking rumble announced that the Deutsche had landcruisers in these parts, even if the Race didn't. Gorppet stuck his head out of the hole again. The artillery barrage had moved on, and was now pounding positions farther east. Even if it hadn't been, he needed to see what was going on. The greater the distance at which he and his comrades engaged the landcruisers, the better.

"We have to fight as a small group ourselves now," he told Shazzer. The other male made the gesture of agreement.

And here came the landcruisers, three of them, much bigger and no doubt much more heavily armored than the ones the Big Uglies had used during the last round of fighting. A Tosevite stood up in the cupola of the closest one. Landcruiser commanders had a habit of doing that; it let them see much more than they could if they stayed buttoned up inside their machines and peered out through periscopes.

It also left them much more vulnerable. The Race had lost many fine landcruiser commanders—it was commonly the good ones who did stand up and look around—to Tosevite snipers. Now Gorppet did his best to redress the balance. He fired a quick burst from his rifle at the Big Ugly in the cupola. The Deutsch male toppled. "Got him!" Gorppet shouted.

But the rest of the landcruiser crew had spotted his muzzle flashes. The turret and the big gun it carried swung toward his hole. Before it could fire, though, a Tosevite leaped from cover, scrambled up onto the landcruiser, and threw something down through the open cupola into the turret. Flames and smoke rose.

Escape hatches popped open. Big Uglies bailed out. Gorppet gleefully shot them. A moment later, the landcruiser blew up.

"One of those nasty bottles of burning hydrocarbon distillate," Shazzer said. "Remember how they gave us fits?"

"I am not likely to forget," Gorppet answered. "And I am not sorry to see them used against the Deutsche by Tosevites on our side."

A second Deutsch landcruiser exploded, this one even more spectacularly—a hit from another landcruiser's big gun. Gorppet shouted in glee. Before his shout was through, the third Tosevite landcruiser went up in flames. One of the Race's machines rattled past the barn, heading west.

"Maybe the regiment leader was right after all," Gorppet said. He turned his eye turrets this way and that. "Maybe he is even still alive to find out he was right after all—but I do not see him." He shrugged. "I do not miss him very much, either. My guess is, we have a better chance against the Deutsche without him."

Ever since the fighting stopped—in fact, since before the fighting stopped—Ttomalss had devoted himself to the exhausting task of raising a Tosevite hatchling. From all he'd gathered, the task of raising a Tosevite hatchling was difficult and exhausting even for the Big Uglies themselves. It was doubly—odds were, a lot more than doubly—difficult and exhausting for him, since he was the first male of the Race to try it. He had neither instincts nor accumulated wisdom upon which to fall back.

Years of patient work had made Kassquit into a female very nearly independent of him. He was grateful for that; it let him analyze some of the work he'd done with her so that others who came after him could do it better, and it also let him do some work unrelated to her. After so long without it, he'd rediscovered the joys of having time to himself again.

And now the war had broken out once more, confining him to the starship for the time being. That would have been annoying enough by itself, but there was worse. Because he'd raised Kassquit, he was also expected to take charge of Jonathan Yeager, the wild Big Ugly who'd been brought up to the starship to mate with her.

"This is most unfair," he complained to the starship captain after receiving the order. "Most extremely unfair, superior sir.

Wild Tosevites are only a secondary interest of mine. My main concern his been civilizing Big Uglies unspoiled by their own cultures. In that I have succeeded beyond anyone's expectations. I cannot promise a result even remotely similar with this specimen."

"Senior Researcher, it is a Big Ugly," the captain said. "You have made a name for yourself as an expert on Big Uglies. If this one does not deal with you, with whom will it deal? With me? I thank you, but no. I have not the patience or the expertise to deal with it. The same holds true for my officers. You are the logical candidate for the job, and you will do it. That *is* an order, Senior Researcher. Do you understand me?"

"Only too well, superior sir," Ttomalss replied with a sigh. "Very well. It shall be done. To the best of my ability, it shall be done."

"It is not altogether wild," the captain reminded him, softening his manner now that he'd got his way. "It speaks our language fairly well for a Tosevite, and it has some knowledge of our culture."

"I placed greater hopes on such epiphenomena in former days than I do now," Ttomalss said. "They are the eggshell. The egg within, I fear, remains profoundly alien."

"You do not have to transform it into a female of the Race."

"Male," Ttomalss corrected.

With a shrug, the captain said, "Whichever. It could matter only to another Big Ugly. As I was trying to tell you, it does not have to become a male of the Race. All you have to do is keep it from getting under everyone else's scales and making males and females itch while it is up here. Eventually, it *will* return to its not-empire, after all. Go on. Tend to it."

"It shall be done," Ttomalss repeated miserably, and left the captain's office.

When he returned to his own chamber, he found Jonathan Yeager waiting in the hallway outside. The wild Big Ugly assumed the posture of respect and said, "I greet you, superior sir."

"I greet you, Jonathan Yeager," Ttomalss replied with no great warmth. "And what can I do for you today? Is it not something Kassquit could handle for you?" Several times, he had managed to use his Tosevite ward to keep this other Big Ugly from unduly bothering him.

But Jonathan Yeager shook his head in the Tosevite negative gesture, then remembered to shape his hand into the one the Race used. "No, superior sir, Kassquit cannot handle this. That is why I wanted to talk with you."

"Very well," Ttomalss said, as he had to the starship captain not long before. He opened the door. As it slid wide, he went on, "Come in and tell me what you require." The sooner he dealt with the Big Ugly, the sooner he could return to his own concerns once more.

"I thank you," Jonathan Yeager said. As he usually did, he wore wrappings around the area of his private parts. In a way, that marked him as a wild Big Ugly. In another way, though, it simplified his outline; his projecting reproductive organs were quite different from the unobtrusive ones Kassquit had. He sat down in the seat designed for Tosevite hindquarters that Ttomalss had installed in his office.

"What is it you want, then?" the psychological researcher asked. He was certain the Big Ugly wanted something.

And, sure enough, Jonathan Yeager said, "I would like to make an arrangement to get a gift for Kassquit, superior sir. I want it to be a surprise. That is why I cannot tell her, and why I had to come to you."

"A gift?" Ttomalss was floundering. "What sort of gift?"

"Something to show I care for her," the Tosevite replied. "I am not sure what sorts of things I can get for her here. That is another reason I came to you: to learn what is available in the way of such things."

"A gift to show you care for her," Ttomalss repeated. "Care for her in the alarmingly emotional way you Tosevites tend to care for your sexual partners? Is that what you mean?"

"Well . . . yes, superior sir," the wild Big Ugly said. "It is a custom among us, for those who are fond of each other."

Ttomalss remembered encountering the custom, now that the Big Ugly reminded him of it. He had never thought it would matter to him. More to the point, he had never thought it would matter to Kassquit. He asked, "If you were back in your own not-empire, what gift might you give a female for whom you had conceived such a foolish and violent fondness?"

"I might get her flowers, superior sir," Jonathan Yeager answered.

"Why?" Ttomalss demanded. "What possible good are flowers?"

"They are pretty," the Big Ugly replied. "And they smell sweet. Females like them."

"This liking is bound to be cultural," Ttomalss said. "Not having the proper conditioning, Kassquit is unlikely to share it. In any case, flowers are unlikely to be available. Are there other possibilities?"

"Yes," Jonathan Yeager said. "I might get her . . . I do not know the word in your language, superior sir, but it would be used to make her smell sweet."

"Perfume." Ttomalss supplied the term. Then he said, "No," and used an emphatic cough. "We are more sensitive to odors than you Big Uglies, and what you find pleasant is often unpleasant to us. Perfume would be altogether too public a gift. Try again, or else abandon this idea."

He hoped Jonathan Yeager would abandon it, but the wild Tosevite said, "I might also get her sweet things to eat. This is a common sort of gift between males and females in my not-empire."

"You should have mentioned it sooner," Ttomalss told him. "It is something we might possibly be able to supply. Return to the quarters you share with Kassquit. When I have the sweet foods, I will summon you."

"I thank you, superior sir," Jonathan Yeager said. "You do not have the custom of giving gifts, I gather?"

"To a much smaller degree than you Big Uglies, certainly," Ttomalss answered. "Among us, gifts are often slightly suspect. If someone gives me something, the first thing I wonder is what he wants in return."

"They can be among us, too," the Big Ugly said. "But they can also simply show affection, as I want to do here."

"Affection." Ttomalss spoke the word with amused contempt. All too often, Tosevites used it when they meant nothing but sexual attraction. "You are dismissed, Jonathan Yeager. I will try to get these sweets for you—and for Kassquit." He had a genuine disinterested affection for the hatchling he'd raised, since he could not possibly want to mate with her. Like any male of the Race, he viewed decisions influenced by sexuality with the greatest of suspicion.

He did sometimes wonder whether he or Veffani had fathered Felless' first brace of hatchlings when she'd come to them reeking of the pheromones ginger made females produce. He shrugged. If he had, he had. If not, not. Mating with Felless certainly made him feel no more affection for the difficult and cross-grained female.

But Big Uglies worked differently. He had seen that before, and saw it again with Kassquit and Jonathan Yeager. Their matings made them feel increased liking for each other; the video records made that quite plain. With the wild Big Ugly, such behavior might have been a cultural artifact. With Kassquit, it assuredly was not. But it was there nonetheless. Ttomalss sighed. He wished his ward's behavior in this matter were less like those of the Tosevites who'd grown up in independent squalor.

Sighing again, he made a few calls to learn when and from where shuttlecraft from the surface of Tosev 3 were scheduled to reach the starship— assuming they survived Deutsch attack on the way up. But the Deutsche, these days, had few spaceships left in orbit around Tosev 3; the Race had done a good job of getting rid of them. Supply missions were almost routine again.

Sure enough, a shuttlecraft brought what he'd asked for. He summoned Jonathan Yeager and said, "Here are the sweets you requested."

Instead of delight, the wild Big Ugly showed confusion. "I had expected what we call *choklit*," he said slowly. "These look like balls of *raiss*." A couple of words were in his own language. Ttomalss figured out what they were likely to mean.

He exhaled in some annoyance. "You asked for sweets. These are sweets. Moreover, they are sweets from the subregion of the main continental mass called China. This is the subregion from which Kassquit came."

"May I try one first?" Jonathan Yeager still sounded dubious. Ttomalss made the affirmative gesture. The Tosevite plucked one of the balls out of the syrup in which it came, put it in his mouth, and chewed thoughtfully. "It has *sesamisidz* inside," he said.

"Is this good or bad?" Ttomalss asked.

Jonathan Yeager shrugged. "I do not think it is as good as *choklit*. But it is a sweet, and I thank you for it. I hope Kassquit will like it. I think she will." He bent into the posture of respect—he did have manners, for a wild Tosevite—and took the container with the remaining sweets back to Kassquit's chamber.

Ttomalss eyed the video that came from the chamber. He listened to Kassquit exclaim in surprise and pleasure, and watched her try the sweets. She must have liked them; she ate several, one after another.

"No one has ever cared for me as you care for me," she told Jonathan Yeager. Before long, the two of them were mating again, though shielded from the possibility of reproduction.

Having seen that activity before, Ttomalss stopped watching the video feed. He hadn't imagined that Kassquit's words could hurt as much as they did. Who had fed her when she was helpless? Who had cleaned excrement from her skin? Who had taught her the language and the ways of the Race? Did a few sweets and pleasurable mating count for more than all that?

He let out a discontented hiss. He had not been the one to think of giving Kassquit an unexpected treat. Even so, it hardly seemed fair. He wondered if Tosevites ever so discounted the efforts of those of their own kind who raised them. It struck him as most unlikely. No, this case of ingratitude was surely unique.

I tried to get out, Monique Dutourd thought. *I did everything I could. Is it my fault that I didn't do it quite soon enough?*

Whose fault it was didn't matter. What mattered was that she remained stuck in Marseille. A passport, even a passport with a false name, did her no good whatever when she couldn't go anywhere with it. She had two choices now, as she saw things: run for the hills or wait for explosive-metal fire to burst over her city, as it had over so many cities of the Greater German *Reich.*

To her surprise, Pierre and Lucie were sitting tight. "How can you stay?" she asked them one morning over breakfast—croissants and *café au lait* as usual, war having affected the black market very little. "The radio said the Lizards blew up Lyon yesterday. How long can they keep from blowing us up, too?"

"Quite a while, I hope," Pierre answered placidly. "Pass the marmalade, if you would be so kind."

Monique didn't want to pass it; she wanted to throw it at him. "You are mad!" she cried. "We live on borrowed time, and you ask for marmalade?"

"Croissants are better with it," he said. She shook with fury. Her brother laughed. "I do not think we are all going to explode in the next few minutes. Will you calm yourself and let me explain why?"

"You had better, before I get on my bicycle and head for the hills," Monique said. "You were talking about doing that yourself, if you will remember."

"I know." Pierre nodded and paused to light a cigarette. He coughed a couple of times. "First one of the morning. Yes, I know I was talking about fleeing. You still may, if you feel you must. But I doubt it is necessary to flee from Marseille."

"Why do you doubt it?" Monique bit off the words one by one.

"Why?" Pierre grinned at her and said no more.

"Enough teasing, Pierre." Lucie could tell when Monique was on the ragged edge of cracking, where her own brother could not. Turning to Monique, she went on, "We have—which is to say, Marseille has—a good many friends in high places. From what we hear from them, the city is safe enough."

"Friends where? Among the Germans?" Monique demanded. "They can't keep any place in the whole blasted *Reich* safe."

Her brother and his lover both burst out laughing. "Among the Germans?" he said. "No, not at all. By no means. I would not trust what a German told me if Christ came down from Heaven with a choir of angels to assure me it was so. But we have plenty of friends in high places among the Race, of that you may be very certain. They do not want to see such a fine place of business wiped off the face of the Earth—and so it will not be."

Monique stared at him. "They will spare this city . . . for the sake of the ginger trade?" she said slowly. "I knew your connections with the Race were good. I never dreamt they were *that* good." She wondered if Pierre was fooling himself.

But Lucie said, "Here we are, an obvious target close to Spain, a target close to Africa, but have they attacked us? No, not at all. Are they likely to attack us? I do not think so."

"Well . . ." Monique hadn't thought of it in those terms. Marseille *was* an obvious target. The Nazis knew it as well as the Lizards did; they wouldn't have installed all those antiaircraft missiles in the hills outside the city if they hadn't known it. But not even an enemy airplane had appeared over Marseille, let alone an enemy missile. Grudgingly, Monique said, "It could be, I suppose."

"So far, it is," Pierre said. "I see no reason to believe the future will be very much different from the past."

That almost set Monique laughing, where nothing else had come close to doing the job. It was a very Roman attitude. It was, from everything she'd seen, also very much the attitude of the Race. But it wasn't the attitude of the *Reich*, and it didn't work so well for the Lizards here. That worried her.

Pierre wasn't worried. After stubbing out the cigarette, he said, "Go on, Monique. Go shopping. Spend my money on whatever you want. After the Lizards finish the Nazis, they will still need people to buy and sell for them. We will be waiting. And if the Germans come back in another twenty years"—he shrugged—"they will need people to buy and sell for them, too. And we will still be waiting."

That wasn't a classical Roman attitude, but she had no doubt the inhabitants of ancient Massilia had shared it. And they would have had reason to do so. But not even Caesar's sack of the ancient city would have wrecked it anywhere near so thoroughly as one explosive-metal bomb could. Monique wasn't sure how well Pierre understood that.

She found another question to ask her brother: "How long can you hold out if the Lizards don't come into Marseille to buy what you have to sell?"

He chuckled again. "Oh, twenty or thirty years, I would say. They make me extra money. I don't deny that. But I do most of my business with people, anyhow. I can go right on doing that. Whether there is a war or not, plenty of things come into the Old Port. There aren't enough Germans in the world to look through all the little boats that sail in from Spain and from Italy and from Greece and from Turkey."

"Ah, Turkey," Lucie said rapturously. "The business we do with Turkey, all by itself, could keep us afloat."

"Poppies, I suppose," Monique said, and her brother and his lover nodded. Monique had visions of opium dens and other sinister things. She didn't know any details. She didn't want to know any details. She shook her head. "Sordid."

"It could be." Pierre shrugged. "In fact, I suppose it is. You do not see Lucie or me using these things, do you? But there is a great deal of money to be had, from the Lizards and from the Nazis and from—" He broke off.

From the French, he'd been about to say. Monique knew it. Her brother wasn't too proud to take his profits wherever he could find them. And she'd been living off his largesse ever since escaping Dieter Kuhn. She hadn't thought till now about how filthy the bargain was. Maybe she hadn't let herself think about it.

She took a deep breath, getting ready to tell him in great detail what she thought of him for doing what he did. Before she could speak, though, sirens all through Marseille started to scream. She sprang to her feet. "That is the attack warning!"

"It can't be!" Pierre and Lucie said it together. But it was. The way they leaped up from their seats, the sudden horrid fear on their faces, said they knew it was, too.

Monique wasted no time arguing with them. "To the shelter, and pray God we aren't too late." With that, she was out the door and rushing down the stairs. Her brother and Lucie didn't argue with her, either. They followed.

"How soon?" Lucie moaned. Even terrified, she sounded sexy. Monique wondered if that was worth admiring. But she also wondered, much more, about the question. If the Lizards had launched a missile from Spain, it would be in before she got to the basement of the block of flats, and that would be that. If it came from farther away, she had more time—but not much.

Down, down, down. The sirens kept screaming. Monique felt like screaming, too. Farther behind her, people with slower reactions *were* screaming, screaming with the dreadful fear that they might be too late, too late. She knew that fear. She clamped down on it till she tasted blood and realized she was also clamping down on the inside of her lower lip.

And there was the door to the cellar. *"Merci, mon cher Dieu,"* she gasped as she rushed inside: the most sincere prayer she'd sent up in many years. Oh, she'd wished Dieter Kuhn dead, but wishing that turned out to be far more pallid than wishing that she herself should stay alive.

Pierre and Lucie came in right behind her. Pierre started to slam the door, but a big, burly man almost trampled him. Monique grabbed her brother. Cursing, he said, "You're going to kill us all."

She had no good answer to that, not after her prayer of a moment before. The discovery that there were circumstances under which she would rather not stay alive was as astonishing as the discovery of how much she wanted to live.

More people crowded into the shelter. And then came a roar like the end of the world—*just like the end of the world,* Monique thought—and the lights went out. The ground shook, as if in an earthquake. It knocked Monique off her feet. She thought she was dead then.

Someone—maybe the burly man—did slam the door. After that, the darkness should have been complete, absolute, stygian. But it wasn't, not quite. A light brighter than summer sunshine at its hottest showed all around the cracks between the door and its frame. Ever so slowly, it faded and reddened. Then it *was* black. Monique didn't think the light itself had vanished quite so abruptly. She judged it much more likely that the block of flats had fallen down and cut off the view.

People—men and women both—were screaming about being buried alive. In the pitch blackness, Monique understood the fear, not least because she felt it herself. And then her brother flicked a flame from a cigarette lighter. "Ahh," everyone in the shelter said together.

Pierre held up the lighter like a sacred talisman. "There will be candles," he said in a voice of great certainty. "Hurry and find them."

There were several boxes. They'd fallen off their shelf, but a woman brought one to him. He lit it and closed his lighter with a snap. The candle flame was pallid, but ever so much better than being stuck in the dark. Monique was still afraid, but much less than she had been.

Pierre went right on speaking with authority: "Now we wait. We wait as long as we have air and food and water—or, better, wine—and even this little light. The longer we wait, the safer it will be when we have to come out. I do not know if it will be safe—we will be taking a chance, of that there is no doubt—but it will be safer."

From everything Monique knew about explosive-metal weapons, he was speaking the gospel truth. Even now, radiation would be entering the shelter, but she didn't know what she could do about that. Or rather, she did know: nothing. She turned to—turned on—her brother and snarled, "No, they won't bomb Marseille. You have friends in high places. You know these things."

From the way the candlelight filled the lines of his face with shadow, he looked to have aged twenty years. He said, "I was wrong. Shall I tell you I was right? I have some hope. If we had been closer to where the bomb burst, we would already be dead."

Out of the darkness where the candlelight didn't reach, someone said, "Now we have to see whether radiation sickness kills us in the next day or two. If it doesn't kill us, we have to see how many years it takes off our lives."

"Shut up," Monique said fiercely. She didn't want to think about that; she wanted to remember she'd stayed alive so far. "We have to see how much there is to eat, and how much to drink, as my brother said. And we have to see how many buckets and pails we can find." Her nose wrinkled. The shelter would be a nasty place before long. Something else occurred to her. "And we'll need shovels and poles and picks, if there are any, to dig our way out when we can't stay here any more. If there aren't, we'll have to do it with our bare hands." *If we can.* She didn't want to think about that, about being entombed here forever. And she didn't want to think about what they would find when they did—if they did—dig themselves out. She stood there in the cellar, and stared and stared at the candle. With her classical training, the flickering flame put her in mind of her own life. But if the candle went out, they could light another. If she went out . . .

One more thing she didn't want to think about.

Johannes Drucker had done everything he could with *Hans-Ulrich's Bus*, but he wasn't going to be able to stay in space much longer. He'd managed to make the air purifier go a lot further than it was designed to, but he'd be eating his underwear before too long—though by now, after four mortal weeks, it was far too filthy to be appetizing.

He knew why he was still alive, when most if not all of his comrades up here had died: he'd never got orders to attack the Lizards. After a while, the *Reich* had stopped ordering him to land. But no one down on the ground had included him in the assault on the Race. Maybe the powers that be had thought him too unreliable to be trusted in the fight. Maybe, too, they'd just forgotten about him by now. He wasn't sure who, if anybody, was in charge down on the ground these days.

Maybe I should have done what I could to hurt the Lizards, even without orders, he thought, for about the five hundredth time. But the war was madness. As far as he was concerned, Poland wasn't worth having. He'd fought there, and did not hold the place in high esteem. But Himmler and then Kaltenbrunner had thought otherwise, and the new *Führer* threw the *Wehrmacht* over the border, as Hitler had in 1939.

"We did better then," Drucker muttered. The Poles hadn't been able to fight worth a damn, no matter how brave they were. The Race, on the other hand . . .

The Race, he realized, had decided to use the *Reich*'s attack as an excuse to smash Germany. The Lizards had warned they would do just that, but nobody in authority seemed to have listened to them. They hadn't been kidding.

"German upper stage!" The radio crackled to life—in English. "Anybody home in there, German upper stage? Over."

"Am I an idiot, that I'm going to answer you?" Drucker asked. He'd maintained radio silence ever since the slugging started. If he started transmitting, the Lizards would get a fix on him and blow him out of the sky. He'd known Americans were naive, but this struck him as excessive.

"German upper stage! German upper stage! If you're alive in there, you might as well give up," the American flier said. "What's the point to you ending up dead, and maybe more Lizards, too? You aren't going to win the war all by yourself." Silence for a few seconds, then, "Over and out."

Silence returned. Drucker grimaced. He scratched his chin. He'd grown quite a beard this past month. The American made good sense, in a way—but only in a way. As a soldier, he was supposed to strike at the enemy, wasn't he?

Then why haven't you? He pondered that, as he had so often before. He came up with the same answers he had before, too: "Nobody gave me any orders. And it's a goddamn stupid war, too."

He glanced down toward the Earth. He was approaching Europe, though clouds hid much of the continent. Even if they hadn't, he wouldn't have been able to see much. From 350 kilometers up, even massive devastation was invisible. But he'd seen bombs blazing like suns as they burst at night. And he knew there had been many more he hadn't seen.

Every time he passed above the wreckage of the *Reich*, he wondered if he would get orders at last, though by now he'd almost given up on it. If he did get them, this would be the place—the only place. The Lizards had knocked out all the German relay ships. It had taken them a while: longer than it should have, even if the delay worked to the *Reich*'s advantage. They never had paid as much attention to the seas as they should have. But they'd finally got round to it.

Did the *Reich* have any working radars these days? If not, his superiors wouldn't even know he was up here. Of course, all his superiors might well be dead. His family all too likely was. He'd cried himself sick about that the day the missiles started flying. He blamed Kaltenbrunner much more than the Lizards. The Race had been content with the status quo. The *Führer* hadn't.

"He should have been, damn him," Drucker said. He'd cursed himself sick that first day, too.

A burst of static came from the radio. "Spacecraft of the Greater German *Reich*! All spacecraft of the Greater German *Reich*! The fight for justice in Europe continues," a voice said in clear German. "Punish the Lizard aggressors however and wherever you may. Your sacrifice will not be in vain!"

When the message finished, it began repeating. As far as Drucker could tell, it was identical the second time around. A recording? He wouldn't have been surprised. Was anyone alive down there to give orders to the remaining German spacecraft? Could anybody down there be alive at all?

Millions, tens of millions, of people down there were surely dead. But what about the high command? He had to admit that he wasn't sure. Party and military leadership had known for a long time that a war with the Race might be coming. They would have done everything they could to make sure they could go on fighting it.

In the middle of the recorded message's third repetition, it suddenly broke off. A different voice came on the air, one that sounded both military and tired unto death: "Be it known that all charges against Lieutenant Colonel Johannes Drucker are rescinded and that he is raised in grade to colonel. By order of

Walter Dornberger, acting *Führer* of the Greater German *Reich*."

Drucker stared at the radio receiver. His boss at Peenemünde was running whatever was left of the *Reich*? How had that happened? When had it happened? Why hadn't Dornberger started broadcasting sooner?

And, even more to the point, if Dornberger *was* running the *Reich*, why in hell wasn't he surrendering just as fast as he could? He'd thought the idea of war against the Race utter madness, as Drucker had. It had proved to be utter madness, too. Why wasn't he giving up, then?

Did he think he could win? Had the Race refused to accept his surrender? Was he trying to prove he could still hurt the Lizards after they'd done their worst to Western and Central Europe?

Did any of that matter? Reluctantly, Drucker decided it didn't. An order that included all German spacecraft certainly included him. And, he had to admit, Dornberger was a *Führer* he could respect. If he was going to go out, he would go out in a blaze of glory.

For the first time in quite a while, he looked out through the canopy with a view to sizing up targets. The points of light that moved against the stars were in Earth orbit, as he was. Some of them, the bright ones, shone more brilliant than Venus. Those would be the starships of the conquest and colonization fleets, the ships the Lizards couldn't afford to lose.

He chose one by eye. They'd always orbited higher than upper stages usually did, and had moved higher still after the war with the *Reich* broke out. He could have fired up his radar to see exactly how far they'd moved, but he would have been shouting *Here I am!* if he did. Instead, he eyeballed a starship out ahead of him. If he could get close before turning on the radar and launching his missiles . . .

His calculations were automatic, instinctive, like a fighter pilot's. If it was at that altitude, it was moving about so fast, which meant he'd need a burn of about so long to take himself out of his present orbit and put him into firing position. If the Lizards were alert and blasted him into wreckage before he could launch, they'd win. If they weren't . . . He sighed. If they weren't, they'd blow him into wreckage after he launched.

Soldiers, unfortunately, found themselves in such positions

now and again. His finger poked the button that started his engine. The acceleration wasn't enormous, but he hadn't felt any acceleration at all for most of a month. Any at all made him seem to weigh five hundred kilos.

He used his fuel lavishly. It wasn't as if he'd be coming back. The starship he'd chosen as a target grew brighter and brighter, then started showing a visible disk. Drucker knew he'd be visible, too, on every Lizard radar screen in the neighborhood. That starship couldn't run away, not as massive as it was. They would need to interpose, or to come at him from some other direction, before he got close enough to do what he'd set out to do.

Now he did light up his radar. It showed the starship dead ahead, with just about the range and velocity he'd guessed. "I have good eyeballs," he said with a chuckle. If he was going to go out, he'd go out laughing—and as a colonel, no less.

And he thought he would take the starship with him. The Lizards never had been good at reacting to the unexpected. None of their missiles headed his way. None of their spacecraft designed to fight in orbit—nastier creatures than *Hans-Ulrich's Bus*—showed up on his screen. Somewhere on their starships, they were probably yelling back and forth at one another, trying to figure out what the devil to do. He didn't need to figure. He was already doing.

No, here came one of their spacecraft, under what looked like pretty good acceleration. But it was late, late. He used the attitude jets to align the nose of *Hans-Ulrich's Bus* on the starship. And then his thumb and forefinger found the red switch he'd never thought he would use. He pulled it out and activated it, then flipped it first to the left, then to the right.

His upper stage shuddered as the missiles left their tubes with puffs of compressed gas. When they were far enough from *Hans-Ulrich's Bus*, their motors came on. The radars they carried guided them straight toward the Lizards' starship, less than fifty kilometers away.

Drucker cursed horribly a moment later, for the Lizards aboard the starship weren't asleep after all. Countermissiles leaped away no more than a heartbeat after he launched his. One of his blew up almost at once. The other, though—the other bored in on its target. "Come on," Drucker whispered. "Come on!" The missiles had proximity fuses set to detonate them a hundred meters from a ship's skin. Would that one get through? All the countermissiles had missed it. If the Lizards didn't do something nasty . . .

They did. Something sparkled along the starship's center line: a close-in weapon system, nothing more dramatic than a computerized heavy machine-gun battery—and the missile exploded in a fireball made up not of bursting atoms but of bursting fuel tanks. Over. It was all over. Drucker swung *Hans-Ulrich's Bus* by the attitude jets so he could face the oncoming Lizard spacecraft. Without hope and without fear, he readied himself for his last fight.

"Deutsch upper stage!" That was a Lizard, speaking the language of the Race. "Surrender, Deutsch upper stage. You have no more missiles. You can do no more significant harm. Your not-empire is in ruins. What can you gain by further senseless sacrifice?"

That was a good question. The longer Drucker thought about it, the better it looked. He swung his thumb from the machine-gun trigger to the radio switch. "Male of the Race, I have no good answer for you," he said wearily. "You have me. I do not know what you will do with me. At the moment, I do not much care what you will do with me. Whatever it is, you have me. I surrender."

"What can I do for you today, Shiplord?" Straha's driver asked.

"I cannot think of anything," Straha answered. "If I need anything, you may be certain that I shall not be shy in letting you know."

His driver bent into the posture of respect. It was half true subordination, half mockery. The Tosevite had at least as much power in their relationship as did Straha himself. "I have no doubt that you will. In the meantime, if it suits you, I will do some work on your motorcar."

"Go ahead," Straha told him. "You could just as easily take it to someone specializing in repairs, you know. Funds would appear to be adequate for any necessary expenditures." Considering that the government of the not-empire of the United States paid for everything connected with Straha's upkeep, funds were bound to be adequate.

But the driver said, "I enjoy working on machinery. I would rather do it myself. That way, I am sure it is done right."

"Whatever pleases you," Straha replied. Now that he thought about it, he shouldn't even have tried to discourage the Big Ugly. With him out on the street tinkering with balky Tosevite machinery, Straha could come closer to living a normal, or at least an unspied-upon, life.

When Straha looked out the kitchen window a little later, he saw his driver bent over the engine compartment of the motorcar, happily repairing something or other. The ex-shiplord shrugged. He'd also known males and females of the Race who enjoyed messing about with machines. He had never understood the excitement himself—but then, most Big Uglies saw his gardening as a waste of time.

Straha hurried to his study and turned on the computer that connected him to the Race's computer network. Since his connection was highly unofficial—even more so than Sam Yeager's— he didn't get very many electronic messages, but a synthesized voice announced that he had one today. It was, he noted without surprise, from Yeager, under his pseudonym of Maargyees.

I greet you, Shiplord, the Tosevite had written. *I wonder if we could possibly meet without your driver's knowing about it.*

Perhaps, Straha replied. *It may not be easy. Are you sure it is necessary?* He wondered what the Tosevite had in mind. Something to do with one of the places into which Yeager had pushed his unwelcome snout, unless Straha missed his guess.

He also wondered if he would get an answer right away. The Tosevite had sent the message much earlier in the morning. But he stayed by the computer for a little while, on the off chance that Yeager was sitting in front of his, as he sometimes did.

And, sure enough, a reply came back quite quickly. *Yes, I am sure it is necessary,* Yeager wrote, and appended the conventional symbol for an emphatic cough. *I must trust someone. In that particular mess, I would sooner trust you than any of my Tosevite acquaintances.*

I am honored, Straha wrote back. *But are you sure you would not be better served by one of your fellow Big Uglies?*

I am sure of nothing, Yeager responded. *I have done a great deal of thinking, but my way is not plain any more. I do not think my way will ever be plain again.*

As you know, my driver clings to me as if he were a parasite under my scales, Straha wrote. *I do not know if I can arrange to have him disappear. I also do not know if I should.*

Well, you will do as you see fit, Yeager wrote back. *If you decide to make the arrangement, let me know. In all fairness, I should tell you that seeing me about this business may be risky for you.*

Are you yourself in danger now? Straha asked.

I have been in danger for some time, the Tosevite answered. *Had I not been careful—and lucky—I would be dead. That is why I want to see you: if I die suddenly and mysteriously, I want you to avenge me.*

That was stark enough. Many ancient classics from the Race's literature and videos revolved around such themes. Straha hadn't thought he would find himself caught in the middle of one, though. Something else occurred to him. He wrote, *This may involve me in no small amount of danger, then. Is that not a truth?*

Yes, Shiplord, I am afraid that is a truth, and I am sorry for it, Yeager answered. He was honest; Straha had seen as much many times. *If you do not wish to do it, I will understand, and I will look for someone else.*

Not necessary, Straha wrote at once. *Come here at midday tomorrow. If you see the motorcar in front of the house, I will not have succeeded in getting my driver to go elsewhere. If it is gone, you are welcome. Actually, you will be welcome in any case, but you might well make the driver suspicious.*

I understand. I thank you. It shall be done. Goodbye.

Goodbye, Straha wrote, but Yeager would probably get that message later. The ex-shiplord paused a while in thought. At last, he found an idea that satisfied him. In fact, he quite liked it. Had he been a Big Ugly, he would have used the curious grimace the Tosevites called smiling.

After a while, his driver came inside, greasy to the elbows and with a smile of his own on his face. He was indeed one of those individuals who enjoyed tinkering for the sake of tinkering. Straha asked, "Is everything now operating as it should?"

"Couldn't be better," the driver answered in English as he started cleaning himself off. His mind was plainly elsewhere, or he would have stuck to the language of the Race.

"Excellent." Straha did stay with his own tongue. "I would like you to drive down to the Race's consulate in the center of the city tomorrow for me, and to bring back a selection of new books and videos. The ones I have are growing stale."

As he'd expected, that made the driver's smile disappear. "Oh, very well," the Big Ugly said at last. "I do not suppose you can go to the consulate yourself, not when you would be seized and spirited away if you tried. But I must tell you that I will also use the visit as an opportunity to brief my own superiors, who are based not far away."

"If you must." Straha sounded sulky. The driver was punishing him. His report would take some time, which meant he would be later bringing back the things Straha wanted. But Straha also wanted other things, things the driver didn't know about. And to keep the Big Ugly from wondering if they might be there, the ex-shiplord had to act as if they weren't.

Rubbing in the punishment, his driver went on, "I will not want to start until late morning, to escape the worst of the traffic."

"Yes, think of your convenience first, and then of mine," Straha complained, though he was laughing inside.

In fact, the Big Ugly waited so long to leave the next day that Straha feared he would still be there when Sam Yeager arrived. Straha couldn't hurry him too much, either, not without rousing his suspicions. But he drove off not long before Yeager pulled up.

"I greet you," Straha said, opening the door for his friend.

"And I greet you, Shiplord," the Tosevite replied. "I also thank you from the bottom of my heart." That was an English idiom translated literally into the language of the Race. "You are a true friend."

"I feel the same about you," Straha said truthfully. "Now, tell me of this trouble, and of how I can help you with it." He led Yeager to the front room and got him comfortable on the sofa where his driver usually sat. "Can I bring you some alcohol? Some of that nasty bourbon you favor, perhaps?"

"That would be very good," Yeager said. "But can we talk in your garden out back?"

He didn't say why, but Straha had no trouble figuring out the answer: he feared things said inside the house might be recorded. Straha didn't know if they were or not, but recognized they might be. He said, "Of course. Go on out. I will follow with your drink, and with one for me."

His own drink was vodka without ice; like most members of the Race, he found whiskey of any sort vile. He carried the two glasses out to the backyard. For him, the weather was cool but not cold. Yeager, he judged, would find it ideal.

They sipped their glasses of alcohol, one flavored, one not. A hummingbird buzzed among the flowers, then flew off with startling speed. "Do you care to begin?" Straha asked.

"I wish I did not have to begin," the Big Ugly answered. Straha realized, slower than he should have, that Yeager wasn't wearing his usual uniform, but the wrappings a civilian would have chosen. What made the ex-shiplord notice was the Tosevite's pulling a sealed envelope from the inside pocket of his upper outer wrapping—a jacket, that was the English word. He handed Straha the envelope, saying, "Keep this for me. Hide it. You will know when to open it."

That Straha would; the envelope had TO BE OPENED IN THE EVENT OF MY DEATH written on it, in both English and the language of the Race. The ex-shiplord kept one eye turret on it and turned the other toward Sam Yeager. "And what do I do with this if I should have to open it?"

"When you see what is inside, you will know," Yeager said. "I trust you not to open it while I am still among those present." That was another English idiom. "If I ever ask on the telephone to have it back, do not give it to me unless I say 'it would help if you did.' Unless I use that exact phrase, I am asking under duress. Then tell me it was accidentally destroyed, or lost, or something of the sort."

"As you say, so shall it be. By the spirits of Emperors past, I swear it." Straha cast down his eyes. Sam Yeager's head bobbed up and down in the Tosevite gesture of agreement. Straha found another question: "What if I were to open it before anything happened to you?"

"One of the reasons I am giving it to you is that I trust you not to do that more than I trust any of my Big Ugly friends," Yeager answered. "Am I wrong?"

"No," Straha said firmly. He cast down his eyes again. "By the spirits of Emperors past, I swear that, too." He paused and slyly waggled an eye turret a little. "How much trouble would I cause if I did?"

Yeager laughed. He relied on Straha not to mean that. But his own voice was serious as he replied, "More than you can imagine, Shiplord. Even if you multiply that imagination by ten, more than you can imagine." He laughed again. "And that probably tempts you to open it more than anything else I have said."

"As a matter of fact, it does," Straha answered. What *did* Yeager have in the envelope he now held in his own scaly hand? Whatever it was, by the way he spoke it was even more important than his raising hatchlings of the Race as if they were Big Uglies. Straha wondered if it was some purely Tosevite affair or one also involving the Race. He could find out. He could . . .

"As I said, I trust you," Yeager told him.

"You may." Straha meant it. "I shall hide this envelope and keep it safe and not open it, as you require." He laughed. "But I shall go right on wondering what it holds."

Sam Yeager nodded. "Fair enough."

When the telephone rang, Vyacheslav Molotov feared it would be Marshal Zhukov. Ever since the Germans and the Lizards started fighting, Zhukov had called more often than Molotov really wanted to listen to him. The Soviet Union's leading soldier assumed that war close to the border brought him to the fore, and Molotov was in no position to contradict him.

But Molotov's secretary spoke in some excitement: "Comrade General Secretary, I have Paul Schmidt on the line."

"The German ambassador, Pyotr Maksimovich?" Molotov said. "Put him through, by all means." He waited, then spoke to Schmidt: "And what can I do for you today, your Excellency?"

"May I please see you as soon as I can reach the Kremlin?" Schmidt asked. "I would sooner not conduct my business over uncertainly secure wires."

"By all means, come. I will see you," Molotov replied. He wondered whether his wires were insecure, whether Zhukov was listening. Probably, he judged, but he called the marshal anyway as soon as he got off the phone with the German. Without preamble, he said, "Schmidt is on the way here."

"Did he say what for?"

"No. He said he would tell me when he got here."

"All right. Keep me apprised." Zhukov hung up.

Molotov had cakes and rolls stuffed with spiced meat set out beside the samovar in the corner of the office where he went to wait for Schmidt. He had never had any use for the man's Nazi bosses, but liked him as well as he liked anyone.

After the handshakes and polite greetings that followed the German ambassador's arrival, Schmidt took tea and did eat one of the rolls. Molotov waited patiently. Schmidt blotted his lips on a linen napkin, then, grimacing, said, "Comrade General Secretary, I would like you to use your good offices to help the Greater German *Reich* end its hostilities with the Race."

"Ah." Molotov had thought it might be so. He wasn't sure whether or not he'd hoped it might be so. He wouldn't have been altogether sorry to see the Germans and the Lizards pound on each other a while longer. Maybe the Nazis couldn't pound any more. Delicately, Molotov said, "You understand, this may involve negotiating a surrender."

Schmidt nodded. "Yes, I do understand that. General Dornberger, who has assumed the *Führer*'s office, understands it as well."

"I see." From the briefings Molotov had had from the GRU, Dornberger was indeed a capable, sensible man. But the briefings didn't explain everything. "How did General Dornberger survive the Race's attack on Peenemünde?"

"We knew the Race would attack there, and fortified our shelters to stand up to the worst we thought they could do," Schmidt replied. "There, our engineering proved adequate." He bowed his head. Molotov wondered if he should have offered vodka along with the tea. Gathering himself, Schmidt went on, "But we did not realize the Lizards would strike so many hard and violent blows against the *Reich*."

Molotov couldn't imagine why the Nazi leaders hadn't realized that. The Race had told them what would happen—told them in great detail. They'd chosen not to listen, and paid an enormous price for not listening. Now they had to settle accounts. Molotov didn't bring that up. All he said was, "If you would care to wait, I will withdraw and call Queek. I have another office where the two of you can confer, and I will be glad to assist in any way I can."

"Thank you," Schmidt said. "I would be grateful for your assistance."

As Molotov had expected, he had no trouble reaching Queek, or rather the Lizard's interpreter. After the interpreter spoke to his principal, he returned to Russian to tell Molotov, "We shall be there directly. This war has done too much damage to both sides for it to continue."

"I look forward to seeing the ambassador," Molotov replied. He went back to the office where Schmidt waited. "Queek and his interpreter are on their way. Come with me; I will take you to a room where you and he can discuss the matter."

"Why not this one?" the German ambassador asked.

"Security," Molotov answered, one word for which no counter-argument existed in the Soviet Union.

Servants—not that the dictator of the proletariat thought of them as such—hastily brought refreshments to the office where Molotov met with Queek. The ambassador from the Race and his interpreter arrived within fifteen minutes. After hypocritical expressions of personal esteem aimed at Paul Schmidt, Queek came to the point: "Is the *Reich* prepared to surrender without conditions?"

"Without conditions? No," Schmidt answered. "We still have resources we can use to hurt you, and we are prepared to go on doing that at need."

Queek rose from the chair that was suited to his posterior. "In that case, we have nothing to say to each other. Call me again when you come to your senses."

"Wait," Molotov said quickly. "You are here now. Why not listen to the conditions Schmidt proposes for surrender? They may be acceptable to you, or you may be able to negotiate with him until they become acceptable."

Molotov had seen how hard the concept of negotiating with humans was for the Race to grasp. The interpreter and Queek had to go back and forth several times before the Lizard grudgingly made the hand gesture his kind used for a nod. "Let it be as you request," he said. "I recognize that your government has broken no significant promises during this period of crisis." It was faint praise, but Molotov took it. Queek swung his eye turrets toward Schmidt and asked, "What conditions do you propose, then?"

"First, the *Reich* is to retain its political independence," Schmidt said.

"Why should we grant you that?" the Lizard demanded.

"You have devastated our land, but you do not occupy it," Schmidt replied. "In fighting on the ground, we have given at least as good as we've got."

"So what?" Queek said. "We have found other ways to win the war, found them and used them. If you do not think we have won, why did you ask for this meeting?"

"It is hard to imagine you could do more to wreck the *Reich* than you have already done," Schmidt said, fighting to salvage what he could with a skill Molotov had to admire. "But we still have land-based missiles unfired, and you have done next to nothing to our missile-carrying submarines. If you give us nothing, what have we got to lose by using all the explosive-metal bombs we have left against you?"

"This is a point worthy of consideration," Molotov said to Queek. The *Reich* wasn't going to be able to threaten his country for quite a while, and he didn't want the Lizards hitting it with any more explosive-metal bombs, not when the wind had already blown too much fallout into the USSR.

But Queek said, "If, on the other fork of the tongue, we rule the *Reich* from now on, we will have no fear of any such attacks in the future."

Molotov had to hide a grimace. Though it knew nothing of the dialectic, the Race did think in the long term. Before Molotov could say anything, Paul Schmidt did: "Do you have enough soldiers to garrison another land full of people who hate you? You have enough trouble holding down the mostly unindustrialized areas of the world that you rule. How hard would it be for you to occupy the *Reich*, too? How expensive would it be? And for how long would you have to do it?"

"Again, cogent points." Molotov didn't want to sound like Germany's advocate, but he didn't want the war to go on, either.

And Queek, this time, didn't reject out of hand. Instead, he said, "If you retain independence, it will necessarily be limited. We will restrict your military forces, and we will place inspectors in your not-empire to make sure you do not seek to exceed by stealth the restrictions we set."

"General Dornberger will accept such restrictions," Schmidt said at once. "Germany has known them in the past."

And Germany had got around them, too, Molotov knew. During the 1920s, there had been a good deal of clandestine co-operation between Germany and the Soviet Union, from which they'd both benefited. He wondered if the new *Führer* would try to make history repeat itself. That would be harder this time, he guessed. England and France hadn't had the will to make Germany live up to the restrictions of the Treaty of Versailles for very long. The Lizards had far more patience.

Then Queek proved the Race had been ready for this dicker after all, for he said, "If the *Reich* is to remain independent of the Race, then we shall also insist that the region of your not-empire known as France shall become independent—independent once more, I should say—of the *Reich*."

Schmidt looked as if he'd bitten into an apple and found half a worm. Molotov said, "Under the circumstances, this does not strike me as an unreasonable request."

"No, it wouldn't, would it?" Schmidt muttered. A resuscitated France weakened Germany against the USSR as well as against the Race.

"It is not a request," Queek said. "It is a demand. It is a minimum demand."

Scowling still, Paul Schmidt said, "I believe the new *Führer* will accept it."

"Further," Queek said, "the *Reich* will be prohibited from possessing explosive-metal weapons and missile delivery systems. The *Reich* will also be prohibited from flights into Earth orbit or to other regions of the solar system of Tosev 3."

"You leave us very little," Schmidt said bitterly.

"You deserve very little, after the damage you have done us," replied the Race's ambassador to the Soviet Union. "Many among us think we are overgenerous in allowing you anything at all. You may keep this reduced role, or you may fight on. After all of you are dead, occupying the *Reich* should not be difficult."

Molotov added, "I do not know if the new *Führer* of the *Reich* will listen to my views, but I think he would be wise to accept these terms. Do you believe he will get better ones if he goes on fighting?"

Schmidt could hardly have seemed more miserable. "If we do

accept them, we go from a first-rate power to one of the second or third class."

"And if you do not accept them, what will happen to you?" Queek retorted. "You will be altogether destroyed, and what sort of power will you retain after that? None. The *Reich* will become an empty eggshell, to be crushed underfoot."

"I shall have to consult with General Dornberger before finally accepting these terms," the German ambassador said.

"Consult quickly," Queek warned. "Every instant you delay will lead to more damage to your not-empire, and may result in harsher terms."

"May I use your facilities, Comrade General Secretary?" Schmidt asked.

"You may," Molotov answered. "I hope success attends your efforts." As Schmidt left, Molotov turned back to the Lizard and his interpreter. "Take more refreshments, if you care to." Queek used the negative hand gesture. The Pole who translated for him ate as if food and drink would be proscribed tomorrow. He was not sorry to see Germany discomfited—no, not even a little.

After less than half an hour, Schmidt returned. He bowed to Queek. "He agrees. He agrees to everything. You have won this war."

"We did not begin it," Queek said.

"Let us be glad it is over," Molotov put in. "Let us be glad it is over, and let us begin to rebuild." *And to plot against one another again*, he added, but only to himself.

Look for the first book in the series. . . .

COLONIZATION
SECOND CONTACT
by Harry Turtledove

It's twenty years since WWII became a war between worlds, and humans and their would-be alien conquerors must coexist peacefully on Earth. But when a new wave of invaders sparks a new war for domination of the planet, thus begins the stunning sequel series to the Worldwar saga.

Published by The Random House Publishing Group.
Available at bookstores near you.

And don't miss this classic
of Civil War alternate history. . . .

THE GUNS OF THE SOUTH
by
Harry Turtledove

The Confederacy is facing certain
defeat in its war against the Union—until
a mysterious stranger approaches
General Robert E. Lee with the
extraordinary offer of an incredibly
lethal weapon never before
seen: the AK-47 rifle.

"The most fascinating Civil War novel
I have ever read."

—JAMES M. MCPHERSON
author of *Battle Cry of Freedom*

Published by The Random House Publishing Group.
Available at your local bookstore.